"King has plenty of nightmares left. . . . *EVERYTHING'S EVENTUAL* makes a perfect showcase for all of King's strengths: his uncanny talent for creating vivid, fully realized characters in a few strokes, his ability to mine horror out of the mundane, and his knack for leavening even the most preposterous contraptions with genuine, universal emotions."

—*The Charlotte Observer*

"A roller-coaster ride through King's serpentine mind. . . . His characters are interesting, his prose engaging, his creativity formidable."

—*Windsor Star* (Canada)

"A milestone in compilations of King's shorter works."

—*Library Journal*

DREAMCATCHER

"Big, dynamic. . . . [A] craftily phantasmagoric story about dreams, telepathy, and extraterrestrials. . . . [*Dreamcatcher* is] a busy, vigorously told, increasingly trippy story . . . [with] some very neat tricks . . . [and written] with imaginative gusto. . . . King writes more fluently than ever . . . with simple, unexpected grace."

—*The New York Times*

"A tour de force. . . . [*Dreamcatcher*] has more passages of power and imagination than some writers produce in a lifetime . . . thrilling and spectacular. . . . [An] entertaining must-read."

—*Chicago Tribune*

"Don't start this one on a school night, kids. You'll be up till dawn."

—*People*

HEARTS IN ATLANTIS

STEPHEN KING

EVERYTHING'S EVENTUAL

14 DARK TALES

POCKET BOOKS

New York   London   Toronto   Sydney

POCKET BOOKS, a division of Simon & Schuster, Inc.
1230 Avenue of the Americas, New York, NY 10020

This book is a work of fiction. Names, characters, places, and incidents are products of the author's imagination or are used fictitiously. Any resemblance to actual events or locales or persons, living or dead, is entirely coincidental.

The following selections, some in different form, were previously published: "Autopsy Room Four" in Robert Bloch's *Psychos;* "The Man in the Black Suit" in *The New Yorker* and *Year's Best Fantasy & Horror 1995;* "All That You Love Will Be Carried Away" and "The Death of Jack Hamilton" in *The New Yorker;* "In the Deathroom" on *Blood and Smoke* (audio book); "The Little Sisters of Eluria" in *Legends;* "Everything's Eventual" in *Fantasy & Science Fiction* and on *F13* (CD-ROM); "L.T.'s Theory of Pets" in *The Best of the Best 1998;* "The Road Virus Heads North" in *999;* "Lunch at the Gotham Café" in *Dark Love, Year's Best Fantasy and Horror 1996* and on *Blood and Smoke* (audio book); "That Feeling, You Can Only Say What It Is in French" in *The New Yorker;* "1408" on *Blood and Smoke* (audio book); "Riding the Bullet" as a Scribner e-book; and "Luckey Quarter" in *USA Weekend.*

This Pocket Books paperback edition June 2007

POCKET and colophon are registered trademarks of Simon & Schuster, Inc.

Manufactured in the United States of America

10   9   8   7   6   5   4   3   2   1

ISBN-13: 978-1-4165-5213-0
ISBN-10:   1-4165-5213-8

For information regarding special discounts for bulk purchases, please contact Simon & Schuster Special Sales at 1-800-456-6798 or business@simonandschuster.com.

This is for Shane Leonard

Contents

What I did was take all the spades out of a deck of cards plus a joker. Ace to King = 1–13. Joker = 14. I shuffled the cards and dealt them. The order in which they came out of the deck became the order of the stories, based on their position in the list my publisher sent me. And it actually created a very nice balance between the literary stories and the all-out screamers. I also added an explanatory note before or after each story, depending on which seemed the more fitting position. Next collection: selected by Tarot.

Introduction:
Practicing the
(Almost) Lost Art

I've written more than once about the joy of writing and see no need to reheat that particular skillet of hash at this late date, but here's a confession: I also take an amateur's slightly crazed pleasure in the business side of what I do. I like to goof widdit, do a little media cross-pollination and envelope-pushing. I've tried doing visual novels (*Storm of the Century, Rose Red*), serial novels (*The Green Mile*), and serial novels on the Internet (*The Plant*). It's not about making more money or even precisely about creating new markets; it's about trying to see the act, art, and craft of writing in different ways, thereby refreshing the process and keeping the resulting artifacts—the stories, in other words—as bright as possible.

I started to write "keeping [the stories] new" in the line above, then deleted the phrase in the interest of honesty. I mean, come on here, ladies and gentlemen, whom can I possibly kid at this late date, except maybe myself? I sold my first story when I was twenty-one and a junior in college. I'm now fifty-four, and have run a lot of language through the 2.2-pound organic computer/word processor I hang my Red Sox cap on. The act of writing stories hasn't been new for me in a long time, but that doesn't mean it's lost its fascination. If I don't find ways of keeping it fresh and interesting, though, it'll get old and tired in a hurry. I don't want that to happen, because I don't want to cheat the people who read my stuff (that would be you, dear Constant Reader), and I don't want to cheat myself, either. We're in it together, after all. This is a date we're on. We should have fun. We should dance.

So, keeping that in mind, here's yet another story. My wife and I own these two radio stations, okay? WZON-AM, which is sports radio, and WKIT-FM, which is classic rock ("The Rock of Bangor," we say). Radio is a tough business these days, especially in a market like Bangor, where there are too many stations and not enough listeners. We've got contemporary country, *classic* country, oldies, *classic* oldies, Rush Limbaugh, Paul Harvey, and Casey Kasem. The Steve and Tabby King stations ran in the red for a lot of years—not deep in the red, but far enough to bug me. I like to be a winner, you see, and while we were winning in the Arbs (that would be the Arbitron ratings, which are to radio what the Nielsens are to TV), we kept coming up short on the bottom line at the end of the year. It was explained to me that there just wasn't enough ad revenue in the Bangor market, that the pie had been cut into too many slices.

So I had an idea. I'd write a radio play, I thought, sort of like the ones I used to listen to with my grandfather when I was growing up (and he was growing old) in Durham, Maine. A Halloween play, by God! I knew about Orson Welles's famous—or infamous—Halloween adaptation of *The War of the Worlds* on *The Mercury Theatre*, of course. It was Welles's conceit (his absolutely *brilliant* conceit) to do H. G. Wells's classic invasion story as a series of news bulletins and reports. It worked, too. It worked so well that it sparked a national panic and Welles (Orson, not H.G.) had to make a public apology on the following week's *Mercury Theatre*. (I bet he made it with a smile on his face—I know *I'd* be smiling, if I were ever to come up with a lie so powerful and persuasive.)

I thought what had worked for Orson Welles would work for me. Instead of starting with dance-band music, as the Welles adaptation did, mine would start with Ted Nugent wailing on "Cat Scratch Fever." Then an announcer breaks in, one of our actual WKIT air personalities (nobody calls em deejays anymore). "This is JJ West, WKIT news," he says. "I'm in downtown Bangor, where roughly a thousand people are jammed into Pickering Square, watching as a large, silvery disc-like object descends toward the ground . . . wait a minute, if I raise the mike, perhaps you can hear it."

And, just like that, we'd be off to the races. I could use our very own in-house production facilities to create the audio effects, local community-theater actors to do the roles, and the best part? The very best part of all? We could record the result and syndicate it to stations *all over the country!* The resulting income, I figured (and my accountant agreed), would be "radio station income" instead of "creative writing income." It was a way to get around the advertising revenue shortfall, and at the end of the year, the radio stations might actually be in the black!

The idea for the radio play was exciting, and the prospect of helping my stations into a profit position with my skills as a writer for hire was also exciting. So what happened? I couldn't do it, that's what happened. I tried and I tried, and everything I wrote came out sounding like narration. Not a play, the sort of thing that you see unspooling in your mind (those old enough to remember such radio programs as *Suspense* and *Gunsmoke* will know what I mean), but something more like a book on tape. I'm sure we still could have gone the syndication route and made some money, but I knew the play would not be a success. It was boring. It would cheat the listener. It was busted, and I didn't know how to fix it. Writing radio plays, it seems to me, is a lost art. We have lost the ability to see with our ears, although we had it once. I remember listening to some radio Foley guy tapping a hollow block of wood with his knuckles . . . and seeing Matt Dillon walking to the bar of the Long Branch Saloon in his dusty boots, clear as day. No more. Those days are gone.

Playwriting in the Shakespearean style—comedy and tragedy that works itself out in blank verse—is another lost art. Folks still go to see college productions of *Hamlet* and *King Lear*, but let's be honest with ourselves: how do you think one of those plays would do on TV against *Weakest Link* or *Survivor Five: Stranded on the Moon*, even if you could get Brad Pitt to play Hamlet and Jack Nicholson to do Polonius? And although folks still go to such Elizabethan extravaganzas as *King Lear* or *Macbeth*, the enjoyment of an art-form is light-years from the ability to create a new example of that art-form. Every now and then someone tries mounting a blank-verse production either on Broadway or off it. They inevitably fail.

Poetry is *not* a lost art. Poetry is better than ever. Of course you've got the usual gang of idiots (as the *Mad* magazine staff writers used to call themselves) hiding in the thickets, folks who have gotten pretension and genius all confused, but there are also many brilliant practitioners of the art out there. Check the literary magazines at your local bookstore, if you don't believe me. For every six crappy poems you read, you'll actually find one or two good ones. And that, believe me, is a very acceptable ratio of trash to treasure.

The short story is also not a lost art, but I would argue it is a good deal closer than poetry to the lip of the drop into extinction's pit. When I sold my first short story in the delightfully antique year of 1968, I was already bemoaning the steady attrition of markets: the pulps were gone, the digests were going, the weeklies (such as *The Saturday Evening Post*) were dying. In the years since, I have seen the markets for short stories continue to shrink. God bless the little magazines, where young writers can still publish their stories for contributors' copies, and God bless the editors who still read the contents of their slush piles (especially in the wake of 2001's anthrax scare), and God bless the publishers who still greenlight the occasional anthology of original stories, but God won't have to spend His whole day—or even His coffee break—blessing those people. Ten or fifteen minutes would do the trick. Their number is small, and every year there are one or two fewer. *Story* magazine, a lodestar for young writers (including myself, although I never actually published there), is now gone. *Amazing Stories* is gone, despite repeated efforts to revive it. Interesting science-fiction magazines such as *Vertex* are gone, and, of course, the horror mags like *Creepy* and *Eerie*. Those wonderful periodicals are *long* gone. Every now and then someone will try to revive one of these magazines; as I write this, *Weird Tales* is staggering through such a revival. Mostly, they fail. It's like those plays in blank verse, the ones that open and then close in what seems to be no more than the wink of an eye. When it's gone, you can't bring it back. What's lost has a way of staying lost.

I've continued to write short stories over the years, partly because the ideas still come from time to time—beautifully compressed ideas that cry out for three thousand words, maybe nine thousand, fifteen thousand at the very most—and partly because it's the way I affirm, at least to myself, the fact that I haven't sold out, no matter what the more unkind critics may think. Short stories are still piecework, the equivalent of those one-of-a-kind items you can buy in an artisan's shop. If, that is, you are willing to be patient and wait while it's made by hand in the back room.

But there's no reason for stories to be *marketed* by the same old just-like-Father-did-it methods, simply because the stories themselves are created that way, nor is there any reason to assume (as so many stodgies in the critical press seem to have done) that the way in which a piece of fiction is sold must in some way contaminate or cheapen the product itself.

I'm speaking here of "Riding the Bullet," which has surely been my oddest experience of selling my wares in the marketplace, and a story which illustrates the main points I'm trying to make: that what's lost cannot be easily retrieved, that once things go past a certain point, extinction is probably inevitable, but that a fresh perspective on one aspect of creative writing—the commercial aspect—can sometimes refresh the whole.

"Bullet" was composed after *On Writing,* and while I was still recuperating from an accident which left me in a state of nearly constant physical misery. Writing took me away from the worst of that pain; it was (and continues to be) the best pain-killer in my limited arsenal. The story I wanted to tell was simplicity itself; little more than a campfire ghost-story, really. It was The Hitchhiker Who Got Picked Up By A Dead Man.

While I was writing away at my story in the unreal world of my imagination, a dot-com bubble was growing in the equally unreal world of e-commerce. One aspect of this was the so-called electronic book, which, according to some, would spell the end of books as we'd always known them, objects of glue and binding, pages you turned by hand (and which sometimes fell out, if the glue was weak or the binding old). In early 2000, there was great interest in an essay by Arthur C. Clarke, which had been published only in cyberspace.

It was extremely short, though (like kissing your sister is what I thought when I first read it). My story, when it was done, was quite long. Susan Moldow, my editor at Scribner (as an *X-Files* fan, I call her *Agent* Moldow . . . *you* work it out), called one day prompted by Ralph Vicinanza and asked if I had anything I'd like to try in the electronic marketplace. I sent her "Bullet," and the three of us—Susan, Scribner, and I—made a little bit of publishing history. Several hundred thousand people downloaded the story, and I ended up making an embarrassing amount of money. (Except that's a fucking lie, I wasn't embarrassed a bit.) Even the audio rights went for over a hundred thousand dollars, a comically huge price.

Am I bragging here? Boasting my narrow white-boy ass off? In a way I am. But I'm also here to tell you that "Riding the Bullet" made me absolutely crazy. Usually, if I'm in one of those fancy-schamncy airport lounges, I'm ignored by the rest of the clientele; they're busy babbling into phones or making deals at the bar. Which is fine with me. Every now and then one of them will drop by and ask me to sign a cocktail napkin for the wife. The wife, these handsomely suited, briefcase-toting fellows usually want me to know, has read *all* my books. They, on the other hand, have read none. They want me to know that, too. Just too busy. Read *The Seven Habits of Highly Successful People*, read *Who Moved My Cheese?*, read *The Prayer of Jabez*, and that's pretty much it. Gotta hurry, gotta rush-rush, I got a heart attack due in about four years, and I want to be sure that I'm there to meet it with my 401(k) all in order when it shows up.

After "Bullet" was published as an e-book (cover, Scribner colophon, and all), that changed. I was *mobbed* in the airport lounges. I was even mobbed in the Boston Amtrak lounge. I was buttonholed on the street. For a little while there, I was turning down the chance to appear on a giddy three talk-shows a day (I was holding out for Springer, but Jerry never called). I even got on the cover of *Time*, and *The New York Times* pontificated at some length over the perceived success of "Riding the Bullet" and the perceived failure of its cyber-successor, *The Plant*. Dear God, I was on the front page of *The Wall Street Journal*. I had inadvertently become a mogul.

And what was driving me crazy? What made it all seem so pointless? Why, that nobody cared about the story. Hell, nobody even *asked* about the story, and do you know what? It's a pretty *good* story, if I do say so myself. Simple but fun. Gets the job done. If it got you to turn off the TV, as far as I'm concerned, it (or any of the stories in the collection which follows) is a total success.

But in the wake of "Bullet," all the guys in ties wanted to know was, "How's it doing? How's it selling?" How to tell them I didn't give a flying fuck how it was doing in the marketplace, that what I cared about was how it was doing in the reader's heart? Was it succeeding there? Failing? Getting through to the nerve-endings? Causing that little *frisson* which is the spooky story's *raison d'être?* I gradually realized that I was seeing another example of creative ebb, another step by another art on the road that may indeed end in extinction. There is something weirdly decadent about appearing on the cover of a major magazine simply because you used an alternate route into the marketplace. There is something weirder about realizing that all those readers might have been a lot more interested in the novelty of the electronic package than they were in what was inside the package. Do I want to know how many of the readers who downloaded "Riding the Bullet" actually *read* "Riding the Bullet"? I do not. I think I might be extremely disappointed.

E-publishing may or may not be the wave of the future; about that I care not a fiddler's fart, believe me. For me, going that route was simply another way of trying to keep myself fully involved in the process of writing stories. And then getting them to as many people as possible.

This book will probably end up on the best-seller lists for awhile; I've been very lucky that way. But if you see it there, you might ask yourself how many *other* books of short stories end up on the bestseller lists in the course of any given year, and how long publishers can be expected to publish books of a type that doesn't interest readers very much. Yet for me, there are few pleasures so excellent as sitting in my favorite chair on a cold night with a hot cup of tea, listening to the wind outside and reading a good story which I can complete in a single sitting.

Writing them is not so pleasurable. I can only think of two in the current collection—the title story and "L.T.'s Theory of Pets"—which were written without an amount of effort far greater than the relatively slight result. And yet I think I have succeeded in keeping my craft new, at least to myself, mostly because I refuse to let a year go by without writing at least one or two of them. Not for money, not even precisely for love, but as a kind of dues-paying. Because if you want to write short stories, you have to do more than *think* about writing short stories. It is *not* like riding a bicycle but more like working out in the gym: your choice is use it or lose it.

To see them collected here like this is a great pleasure for me. I hope it will be for you, as well. You can let me know at *www.stephenking.com,* and you can do something else for me (and yourself), as well: if these stories work for you, buy another collection. *Sam the Cat* by Matthew Klam, for instance, or *The Hotel Eden* by Ron Carlson. These are only two of the good writers doing good work out there, and although it's now officially the twenty-first century, they're doing it in the same old way, one word at a time. The format in which they eventually appear doesn't change that. If you care, support them. The best method of support really hasn't changed much: *read their stories*.

I'd like to thank a few of the people who've read mine: Bill Buford, at *The New Yorker;* Susan Moldow, at Scribner; Chuck Verrill, who has edited so much of my work across such a span of years; Ralph Vicinanza, Arthur Greene, Gordon Van Gelder, and Ed Ferman at *The Magazine of Fantasy and Science Fiction*; Nye Willden at

Cavalier; and the late Robert A. W. Lowndes, who bought that first short story back in '68. Also—most important—my wife, Tabitha, who remains my favorite Constant Reader. These are all people who have worked and are still working to keep the short story from becoming a lost art. So am I. And, by what you buy (and thus choose to subsidize) and by what you read, so are you. You most of all, Constant Reader. Always you.

Stephen King
Bangor, Maine
December 11, 2001

EVERYTHING'S EVENTUAL

Autopsy Room Four

It's so dark that for awhile—just how long I don't know—I think I'm still unconscious. Then, slowly, it comes to me that unconscious people don't have a sensation of movement through the dark, accompanied by a faint, rhythmic sound that can only be a squeaky wheel. And I can feel contact, from the top of my head to the balls of my heels. I can smell something that might be rubber or vinyl. This is not unconsciousness, and there is something too . . . too *what?* Too *rational* about these sensations for it to be a dream.

Then what is it?

Who am I?

And what's happening to me?

The squeaky wheel quits its stupid rhythm and I stop moving. There is a crackle around me from the rubber-smelling stuff.

A voice: "Which one did they say?"

A pause.

Second voice: "Four, I think. Yeah, four."

We start to move again, but more slowly. I can hear the faint scuff of feet now, probably in soft-soled shoes, maybe sneakers. The owners of the voices are the owners of the shoes. They stop me again. There's a thump followed by a faint whoosh. It is, I think, the sound of a door with a pneumatic hinge being opened.

What's going on here? I yell, but the yell is only in my head. My lips don't move. I can feel them—and my tongue, lying on the floor of my mouth like a stunned mole—but I can't move them.

The thing I'm on starts rolling again. A moving bed? Yes. A gurney, in other words. I've had some experience with them, a long time ago, in Lyndon Johnson's shitty little Asian adventure. It comes to me that I'm in a hospital, that something bad has happened to me, something like the explosion that almost neutered me twenty-three years before, and that I'm going to be operated on. There are a lot of answers in that idea, sensible ones, for the most part, but I don't hurt anywhere. Except for the minor matter of being scared out of my wits, I feel fine. And if these are orderlies wheeling me into an operating room, why can't I see? Why can't I *talk?*

A third voice: "Over here, boys."

My rolling bed is pushed in a new direction, and the question drumming in my head is *What kind of a mess have I gotten myself into?*

Doesn't that depend on who you are? I ask myself, but that's one thing, at least, I find I *do* know. I'm Howard Cottrell. I'm a stock broker known to some of my colleagues as Howard the Conqueror.

Second voice (from just above my head): "You're looking very pretty today, doc."

Fourth voice (female, and cool): "It's always nice to be validated by you, Rusty. Could you hurry up a little?

The babysitter expects me back by seven. She's committed to dinner with her parents."

Back by seven, back by seven. It's still the afternoon, maybe, or early evening, but black in here, black as your hat, black as a woodchuck's asshole, black as midnight in Persia, and *what's going on?* Where have I been? What have I been doing? Why haven't I been manning the phones?

Because it's Saturday, a voice from far down murmurs. *You were . . . were . . .*

A sound: *WHOCK!* A sound I love. A sound I more or less live for. The sound of . . . what? The head of a golf-club, of course. Hitting a ball off the tee. I stand, watching it fly off into the blue . . .

I'm grabbed, shoulders and calves, and lifted. It startles me terribly, and I try to scream. No sound comes out . . . or perhaps one does, a tiny squeak, much tinier than the one produced by the wheel below me. Probably not even that. Probably it's just my imagination.

I'm swung through the air in an envelope of blackness—*Hey, don't drop me, I've got a bad back!* I try to say, and again there's no movement of the lips or teeth; my tongue goes on lying on the floor of my mouth, the mole maybe not just stunned but dead, and now I have a terrible thought, one which spikes fright a degree closer to panic: what if they put me down the wrong way and my tongue slides backward and blocks my windpipe? I won't be able to breathe! That's what people mean when they say someone "swallowed his tongue," isn't it?

Second voice (Rusty): "You'll like this one, doc, he looks like Michael Bolton."

Female doc: "Who's that?"

Third voice—sounds like a young man, not much more than a teenager: "He's this white lounge-singer who wants to be black. I don't think this is him."

There's laughter at that, the female voice joining in (a little doubtfully), and as I am set down on what feels like a padded table, Rusty starts some new crack—he's got a whole standup routine, it seems. I lose this bit of hilarity in a burst of sudden horror. I won't be able to breathe if my tongue blocks my windpipe, that's the thought which has just gone through my mind, *but what if I'm not breathing now?*

What if I'm dead? What if this is what death is like?

It fits. It fits everything with a horrid prophylactic snugness. The dark. The rubbery smell. Nowadays I am Howard the Conqueror, stock broker *extraordinaire*, terror of Derry Municipal Country Club, frequent *habitué* of what is known at golf courses all over the world as The Nineteenth Hole, but in '71 I was part of a Medical Assistance Team in the Mekong Delta, a scared kid who sometimes woke up wet-eyed from dreams of the family dog, and all at once I know this feel, this smell.

Dear God, I'm in a bodybag.

First voice: "Want to sign this, doc? Remember to bear down hard—it's three copies."

Sound of a pen, scraping away on paper. I imagine the owner of the first voice holding out a clipboard to the woman doctor.

Oh dear Jesus let me not be dead! I try to scream, and nothing comes out.

I'm breathing though . . . aren't I? I mean, I can't feel

myself doing it, but my lungs seem okay, they're not throbbing or yelling for air the way they do when you've swum too far underwater, so I must be okay, right?

Except if you're dead, the deep voice murmurs, *they wouldn't be crying out for air, would they? No—because dead lungs don't need to breathe. Dead lungs can just kind of . . . take it easy.*

Rusty: "What are you doing next Saturday night, doc?"

But if I'm dead, how can I feel? How can I smell the bag I'm in? How can I hear these voices, the doc now saying that next Saturday night she's going to be shampooing her dog which is named Rusty, what a coincidence, and all of them laughing? If I'm dead, why aren't I either gone or in the white light they're always talking about on Oprah?

There's a harsh ripping sound and all at once I *am* in white light; it is blinding, like the sun breaking through a scrim of clouds on a winter day. I try to squint my eyes shut against it, but nothing happens. My eyelids are like blinds on broken rollers.

A face bends over me, blocking off part of the glare, which comes not from some dazzling astral plane but from a bank of overhead fluorescents. The face belongs to a young, conventionally handsome man of about twenty-five; he looks like one of those beach beefcakes on *Baywatch* or *Melrose Place*. Marginally smarter, though. He's got a lot of dark black hair under a carelessly worn surgical-greens cap. He's wearing the tunic, too. His eyes are cobalt blue, the sort of eyes girls reputedly die for. There are dusty arcs of freckles high up on his cheekbones.

"Hey, gosh," he says. It's the third voice. "This guy

does look like Michael Bolton! A little long in the old tootharoo; maybe . . ." He leans closer. One of the flat tie-ribbons at the neck of his greens tunic tickles against my forehead. ". . . but yeah. I see it. Hey, Michael, sing something."

Help me! is what I'm *trying* to sing, but I can only look up into his dark blue eyes with my frozen dead man's stare; I can only wonder if I *am* a dead man, if this is how it happens, if this is what *everyone* goes through after the pump quits. If I'm still alive, how come he hasn't seen my pupils contract when the light hit them? But I know the answer to that . . . or I think I do. They *didn't* contract. That's why the glare from the fluorescents is so painful.

The tie, tickling across my forehead like a feather.

Help me! I scream up at the *Baywatch* beefcake, who is probably an intern or maybe just a med-school brat. *Help me, please!*

My lips don't even quiver.

The face moves back, the tie stops tickling, and all that white light streams through my helpless-to-look-away eyes and into my brain. It's a hellish feeling, a kind of rape. I'll go blind if I have to stare into it for long, I think, and blindness will be a relief.

WHOCK! The sound of the driver hitting the ball, but a little flat this time, and the feeling in the hands is bad. The ball's up . . . but veering . . . veering off . . . veering toward . . .

Shit.

I'm in the rough.

Now another face bends into my field of vision. A white tunic instead of a green one below it, a great untidy mop of orange hair above it. Distress-sale IQ is my first impression. It can only be Rusty. He's wearing a big dumb grin that I think of as a high-school grin, the grin of a kid who should have a tattoo reading BORN TO SNAP BRA-STRAPS on one wasted bicep.

"Michael!" Rusty exclaims. "Jeez, ya lookin *gooood!* This'z an honor! *Sing* for us, big boy! Sing your dead ass off!"

From somewhere behind me comes the doc's voice, cool, no longer even pretending to be amused by these antics. "Quit it, Rusty." Then, in a slightly new direction: "What's the story, Mike?"

Mike's voice is the first voice—Rusty's partner. He sounds slightly embarrassed to be working with a guy who wants to be Andrew Dice Clay when he grows up. "Found him on the fourteenth hole at Derry Muni. Off the course, actually, in the rough. If he hadn't just played through the foursome behind him, and if they hadn't seen one of his legs stickin out of the pucker-brush, he'd be an ant-farm by now."

I hear that sound in my head again—*WHOCK!*—only this time it is followed by another, far less pleasant sound: the rustle of underbrush as I sweep it with the head of my driver. It *would* have to be fourteen, where there is reputedly poison ivy. Poison ivy and . . .

Rusty is still peering down at me, stupid and avid. It's not death that interests him; it's my resemblance to Michael Bolton. Oh yes, I know about it, have not been above using it with certain female clients. Otherwise, it gets old in a hurry. And in these circumstances . . . *God.*

"Attending physician?" the lady doc asks. "Was it Kazalian?"

"No," Mike says, and for just a moment he looks down at me. Older than Rusty by at least ten years. Black hair with flecks of gray in it. Spectacles. *How come none of these people can see that I am not dead?* "There was a doc in the foursome that found him, actually. That's his signature on page one . . . see?"

Riffle of paper, then: "Christ, Jennings. I know him. He gave Noah his physical after the ark grounded on Mount Ararat."

Rusty doesn't look as if he gets the joke, but he brays laughter into my face anyway. I can smell onions on his breath, a little leftover lunchstink, and if I can smell onions, I must be breathing. I *must* be, right? If only—

Before I can finish this thought, Rusty leans even closer and I feel a blast of hope. He's seen something! He's seen something and means to give me mouth-to-mouth. God bless you, Rusty! God bless you and your onion breath!

But the stupid grin doesn't change, and instead of putting his mouth on mine, his hand slips around my jaw. Now he's grasping one side with his thumb and the other side with his fingers.

"He's *alive!*" Rusty cries. "He's *alive,* and he's gonna sing for the Room Four Michael Bolton Fan Club!"

His fingers pinch tighter—it hurts in a distant coming-out-of the Novocain way—and begin to move my jaw up and down, clicking my teeth together. *"If she's ba-aaad, he can't see it,"* Rusty sings in a hideous, atonal voice that would probably make Percy Sledge's head explode. *"She can do no rrr-ongggg . . ."* My teeth open and close at the rough urging of his hand; my tongue rises and falls like a dead dog riding the surface of an uneasy waterbed.

"Stop it!" the lady doc snaps at him. She sounds genuinely shocked. Rusty, perhaps sensing this, does not stop but goes gleefully on. His fingers are pinching into my cheeks now. My frozen eyes stare blindly upward.

"Turn his back on his best friend if she put him d——"

Then she's there, a woman in a green gown with her cap tied around her throat and hanging down her back like the Cisco Kid's sombrero, short brown hair swept back from her brow, good-looking but severe—more handsome than pretty. She grabs Rusty with one short-nailed hand and pulls him back from me.

"Hey!" Rusty says, indignant. "Get your hands off me!"

"Then you keep your hands off *him*," she says, and there is no mistaking the anger in her voice. "I'm tired of your Sophomore Class wit, Rusty, and the next time you start in, I'm going to report you."

"Hey, let's all calm down," says the *Baywatch* hunk—doc's assistant. He sounds alarmed, as if he expects Rusty and his boss to start duking it out right here. "Let's just put a lid on it."

"Why's she bein such a bitch to me?" Rusty says. He's still trying to sound indignant, but he's actually whining now. Then, in a slightly different direction: "Why you being such a bitch? You on your period, is that it?"

Doc, sounding disgusted: "Get him out of here."

Mike: "Come on, Rusty. Let's go sign the log."

Rusty: "Yeah. And get some fresh air."

Me, listening to all this like it was on the radio.

Their feet, squeaking toward the door. Rusty now all huffy and offended, asking her why she doesn't just wear a mood-ring or something so people will *know*. Soft shoes squeaking on tile, and suddenly that sound is replaced by the sound of my driver, beating the bush for my goddam ball, where is it, it didn't go too far in, I'm sure of it, so where is it, Jesus, I *hate* fourteen, supposedly there's poison ivy, and with all this underbrush, there could easily be—

And then something bit me, didn't it? Yes, I'm almost sure it did. On the left calf, just above the top of my white athletic sock. A red-hot darning needle of pain, perfectly concentrated at first, then spreading . . .

. . . then darkness. Until the gurney, zipped up snug inside a bodybag and listening to Mike (*"Which one did they say?"*) and Rusty (*"Four, I think. Yeah, four"*).

I want to think it was some kind of snake, but maybe that's only because I was thinking about them while I hunted for my ball. It could have been an insect, I only recall the single line of pain, and after all, what does it matter? What matters here is that I'm alive and they don't know it. It's incredible, but they don't know it. Of course I had bad luck—I know Dr. Jennings, remember speaking to him as I played through his foursome on the eleventh hole. A nice enough guy, but vague, an antique. The antique had pronounced me dead. Then *Rusty,* with his dopey green eyes and his detention-hall grin, had pronounced me dead. The lady doc, Ms. Cisco Kid, hadn't even *looked* at me yet, not really. When she did, maybe—

"I *hate* that jerk," she says when the door is closed. Now it's just the three of us, only of course Ms. Cisco Kid thinks it's just the two of them. "Why do I always get the jerks, Peter?"

"I don't know," Mr. *Melrose Place* says, "but Rusty's a special case, even in the annals of famous jerks. Walking brain death."

She laughs, and something clanks. The clank is followed by a sound that scares me badly: steel instruments clicking together. They are off to the left of me, and although I can't see them, I know what they're getting ready to do: the autopsy. They are getting ready to cut into me. They intend to remove Howard Cottrell's heart and see if it blew a piston or threw a rod.

My leg! I scream inside my head. *Look at my* left leg! *That's the trouble, not my heart!*

Perhaps my eyes have adjusted a little, after all. Now I can see, at the very top of my vision, a stainless steel armature. It looks like a giant piece of dental equipment, except that thing at the end isn't a drill. It's a saw. From someplace deep inside, where the brain stores the sort of trivia you only need if you happen to be playing *Jeopardy!* on TV, I even come up with the name. It's a Gigli saw. They use it to cut off the top of your skull. This is after they've pulled your face off like a kid's Halloween mask, of course, hair and all.

Then they take out your brain.

Clink. Clink. Clunk. A pause. Then a *CLANK!* so loud I'd jump if I were capable of jumping.

"Do you want to do the pericardial cut?" she asks.

Pete, cautious: "Do you want me to?"

Dr. Cisco, sounding pleasant, sounding like someone who is conferring a favor and a responsibility: "Yes, I think so."

"All right," he says. "You'll assist?"

"Your trusty co-pilot," she says, and laughs. She punctuates her laughter with a *snick-snick* sound. It's the sound of scissors cutting the air.

Now panic beats and flutters inside my skull like a flock of starlings locked in an attic. The Nam was a long time ago, but I saw half a dozen field autopsies there—what the doctors used to call "tentshow post-mortems"—and I know what Cisco and Pancho mean to do. The scissors have long, sharp blades, *very* sharp blades, and fat finger-holes. Still, you have to be strong to use them. The lower blade slides into the gut like butter. Then, *snip,* up through the bundle of nerves at the solar plexus and into the beef-jerky weave of muscle and tendon above it. Then into the sternum. When the blades come together this time, they do so with a heavy crunch as the bone parts and the rib cage pops apart like a couple of barrels which have been lashed together with twine. Then on up with those scissors that look ike nothing so much as the poultry shears supermarket butchers use—*snip-CRUNCH, snip-CRUNCH, snip-CRUNCH,* splitting bone and shearing muscle, freeing the lungs, heading for the trachea, turning Howard the

Conqueror into a Thanksgiving dinner no one will eat.

A thin, nagging whine—this *does* sound like a dentist's drill.

Pete: "Can I—"

Dr. Cisco, actually sounding a bit maternal: "No. These." *Snick-snick.* Demonstrating for him.

They can't do this, I think. *They can't cut me up . . . I can FEEL!*

"Why?" he asks.

"Because that's the way I want it," she says, sounding a lot less maternal. "When you're on your own, Petie-boy, you can do what you want. But in Katie Arlen's autopsy room, you start off with the pericardial shears."

Autopsy room. There. It's out. I want to be all over goose-bumps, but of course, nothing happens; my flesh remains smooth.

"Remember," Dr. Arlen says (but now she's actually lecturing), "any fool can learn how to use a milking machine . . . but the hands-on procedure is always best." There is something vaguely suggestive in her tone. "Okay?"

"Okay," he says.

They're going to do it. I have to make some kind of noise or movement, or they're really doing to do it. If blood flows or jets up from the first punch of the scissors they'll know something's wrong, but by then it will be too late, very likely; that first *snip-CRUNCH* will have happened, and my ribs will be lying against my upper arms, my heart pulsing frantically away under the fluorescents in its blood-glossy sac—

I concentrate everything on my chest. I *push,* or try to . . . and something happens.

A sound!

I make a sound!

It's mostly inside my closed mouth, but I can also hear and feel it in my nose—a low hum.

Concentrating, summoning every bit of effort, I do it again, and this time the sound is a little stronger, leaking out of my nostrils like cigarette smoke: *Nnnnnnn—* It makes me think of an old Alfred Hitchcock TV program I saw a long, long time ago, where Joseph Cotten was paralyzed in a car crash and was finally able to let them know he was still alive by crying a single tear.

And if nothing else, that minuscule mosquito-whine of a sound has proved to *myself* that I'm alive, that I'm not just a spirit lingering inside the clay effigy of my own dead body.

Focusing all my concentration, I can feel breath slipping through my nose and down my throat, replacing the breath I have now expended, and then I send it out again, working harder than I ever worked summers for the Lane Construction Company when I was a teenager, working harder than I have ever worked in my *life,* because now I'm working *for* my life and they must hear me, dear Jesus, they must.

Nnnnnnnn—

"You want some music?" the woman doctor asks. "I've got Marty Stuart, Tony Bennett—"

He makes a despairing sound. I barely hear it, and take no immediate meaning from what she's saying . . . which is probably a mercy.

"All right," she says, laughing. "I've also got the Rolling Stones."

"*You?*"

"Me. I'm not quite as square as I look, Peter."

"I didn't mean . . ." He sounds flustered.

Listen to me! I scream inside my head as my frozen eyes stare up into the icy-white light. *Stop chattering like magpies and listen to me!*

I can feel more air trickling down my throat and the idea occurs that whatever has happened to me may be starting to wear off . . . but it's only a faint blip on the screen of my thoughts. Maybe it *is* wearing off, but very soon now recovery will cease to be an option for me. All my energy is bent toward making them hear me, and this time they *will* hear me, I know it.

"Stones, then," she says. "Unless you want me to run out and get a Michael Bolton CD in honor of your first pericardial."

"Please, no!" he cries, and they both laugh.

The sound starts to come out, and it *is* louder this time. Not as loud as I'd hoped, but loud enough. Surely loud enough. They'll hear, they *must.*

Then, just as I begin to force the sound out of my nose like some rapidly solidifying liquid, the room is filled with a blare of fuzztone guitar and Mick Jagger's voice bashing off the walls: *"Awww, no, it's only rock and roll, but I LIYYYYKE IT . . ."*

"Turn it down!" Dr. Cisco yells, comically overshouting, and amid these noises my own nasal sound, a desperate little humming through my nostrils, is no more audible than a whisper in a foundry.

Now her face bends over me again and I feel fresh horror as I see that she's wearing a Plexi eyeshield and a gauze mask over her mouth. She glances back over her shoulder.

"I'll strip him for you," she tells Pete, and bends toward me with a scalpel glittering in one gloved hand, bends toward me through the guitar-thunder of the Rolling Stones.

I hum desperately, but it's no good. I can't even hear myself.

The scalpel hovers, then cuts.

I shriek inside my own head, but there is no pain, only my polo shirt falling in two pieces at my sides. Sliding apart as my rib cage will after Pete unknowingly makes his first pericardial cut on a living patient.

I am lifted. My head lolls back and for a moment I see Pete upside down, donning his own Plexi eyeshield as he stands by a steel counter, inventorying a horrifying array of tools. Chief among them are the oversized scissors. I get just a glimpse of them, of blades glittering like merciless satin. Then I am laid flat again and my shirt is gone. I'm now naked to the waist. It's cold in the room.

Look at my chest! I scream at her. *You must see it rise and fall, no matter how shallow my respiration is! You're a goddam expert, for Christ's sake!*

Instead, she looks across the room, raising her voice to be heard above the music. (*I like it, like it, yes I do,* the Stones sing, and I think I will hear that nasal idiot chorus in the halls of hell through all eternity.) "What's your pick? Boxers or Jockeys?"

With a mixture of horror and rage, I realize what they're talking about.

"Boxers!" he calls back. "Of course! Just take a look at the guy!"

Asshole! I want to scream. *You probably think everyone over forty wears boxer shorts! You probably think when you get to be forty, you'll—*

She unsnaps my Bermudas and pulls down the zipper. Under other circumstances, having a woman as pretty as this (a little severe, yes, but still pretty) do that would make me extremely happy. Today, however—

"You lose, Petie-boy," she says. "Jockeys. Dollar in the kitty."

"On payday," he says, coming over. His face joins hers; they look down at me through their Plexi masks like a couple of space aliens looking down at an abductee. I try to make them see my eyes, to see me *looking at them,* but these two fools are looking at my undershorts.

"Ooooh, and *red,*" Pete says. "A sha-*vinguh!*"

"I call them more of a wash pink," she replies. "Hold him up for me, Peter, he weighs a ton. No wonder he had a heart attack. Let this be a lesson to you."

I'm in shape! I yell at her. *Probably in better shape than you, bitch!*

My hips are suddenly jerked upward by strong hands. My back cracks; the sound makes my heart leap.

"Sorry, guy," Pete says, and suddenly I'm colder than ever as my shorts and red underpants are pulled down.

"Upsa-daisy *once,*" she says, lifting one foot, "and

upsa-daisy *twice*," lifting the other foot, "off come the *mocs,* and off come the *socks*—"

She stops abruptly, and hope seizes me once more.

"Hey, Pete."

"Yeah?"

"Do guys ordinarily wear Bermuda shorts and moccasins to play golf in?"

Behind her (except that's only the source, actually it's all around us) the Rolling Stones have moved on to "Emotional Rescue." *I will be your knight in shining ahh-mah,* Mick Jagger sings, and I wonder how funky he'd dance with about three sticks of Hi-Core dynamite jammed up his skinny ass.

"If you ask me, this guy was just *asking* for trouble," she goes on. "I thought they had these special shoes, very ugly, very golf-specific, with little knobs on the soles—"

"Yeah, but wearing them's not the law," Pete says. He holds his gloved hands out over my upturned face, slides them together, and bends the fingers back. As the knuckles crack, talcum powder sprinkles down like fine snow. "At least not yet. Not like bowling shoes. They catch you bowling without a pair of bowling shoes, they can send you to state prison."

"Is that so?"

"Yes."

"Do you want to handle temp and gross examination?"

No! I shriek. *No, he's a kid, what are you DOING?*

He looks at her as if this same thought had crossed his own mind. "That's . . . um . . . not strictly legal, is it, Katie? I mean . . ."

She looks around as he speaks, giving the room a burlesque examination, and I'm starting to get a vibe that could be very bad news for me: severe or not, I think that Cisco—alias Dr. Katie Arlen—has got the hots for Petie with the dark blue eyes. Dear Christ, they have hauled me paralyzed off the golf course and into an episode of *General Hospital,* this week's subplot titled "Love Blooms in Autopsy Room Four."

"Gee," she says in a hoarse little stage-whisper. "I don't see anyone here but you and me."

"The tape—"

"Not rolling yet," she said. "And once it is, I'm right at your elbow every step of the way . . . as far as anyone will ever know, anyway. And mostly I will be. I just want to put away those charts and slides. And if you really feel uncomfortable—"

Yes! I scream up at him out of my unmoving face. *Feel uncomfortable! VERY uncomfortable! TOO uncomfortable!*

But he's twenty-four at most and what's he going to say to this pretty, severe woman who's standing inside his space, invading it in a way that can really only mean one thing? *No, Mommy, I'm scared?* Besides, he wants to. I can see the wanting through the Plexi eye-shield, bopping around in there like a bunch of overage punk rockers pogoing to the Stones.

"Hey, as long as you'll cover for me if—"

"Sure," she says. "Got to get your feet wet sometime, Peter. And if you really need me to, I'll roll back the tape."

He looks startled. "You can do that?"

She smiles. "Ve haff many see-grets in Autopsy Room Four, *mein Herr.*"

"I bet you do," he says, smiling back, then reaches past my frozen field of vision. When his hand comes back, it's wrapped around a microphone which hangs down from the ceiling on a black cord. The mike looks like a steel teardrop. Seeing it there makes this horror real in a way it wasn't before. Surely they won't really cut me up, will they? Pete is no veteran, but he *has* had training; surely he'll see the marks of whatever bit me while I was looking for my ball in the rough, and then they'll at least suspect. They'll *have* to suspect.

Yet I keep seeing the scissors with their heartless satin shine—jumped-up poultry shears—and I keep wondering if I will still be alive when he takes my heart out of my chest cavity and holds it up, dripping, in front of my locked gaze for a moment before turning to plop it into the weighing pan. I could be, it seems to me; I really could be. Don't they say the brain can remain conscious for up to three minutes after the heart stops?

"Ready, doctor," Pete says, and now he sounds almost formal. Somewhere, tape is rolling.

The autopsy procedure has begun.

"Let's flip this pancake," she says cheerfully, and I am turned over just that efficiently. My right arm goes flying out to one side and then falls back against the side of the table, banging down with the raised metal lip digging into the bicep. It hurts a lot, the pain is just short of excruciating, but I don't mind. I pray for the lip to bite through my skin, pray to *bleed,* something *bona fide* corpses don't do.

"Whoops-a-daisy," Dr. Arlen says. She lifts my arm up and plops it back down at my side.

Now it's my nose I'm most aware of. It's smashed against the table, and my lungs for the first time send out a distress message—a cottony, deprived feeling. My mouth is closed, my nose partially crushed shut (just how much I can't tell; I can't even feel myself breathing, not really). What if I suffocate like this?

Then something happens which takes my mind completely off my nose. A huge object—it feels like a glass baseball bat—is rammed rudely up my rectum. Once more I try to scream and can produce only the faint, wretched humming.

"Temp in," Peter says. "I've put on the timer."

"Good idea," she says, moving away. Giving him room. Letting him test-drive this baby. Letting him test-drive *me*. The music is turned down slightly.

"Subject is a white Caucasian, age forty-four," Pete says, speaking for the mike now, speaking for posterity. "His name is Howard Randolph Cottrell, residence is 1566 Laurel Crest Lane, here in Derry."

Dr. Arlen, at some distance: "Mary Mead."

A pause, then Pete again, sounding just a tiny bit flustered: "Dr. Arlen informs me that the subject actually lives in Mary Mead, which split off from Derry in—"

"Enough with the history lesson, Pete."

Dear God, what have they stuck up my ass? Some sort of cattle thermometer? If it was a little longer, I think, I could taste the bulb at the end. And they didn't exactly go crazy with the lubricant . . . but then, why would they? I'm dead, after all.

Dead.

"Sorry, doctor," Pete says. He fumbles mentally for

his place, and eventually finds it. "This information is from the ambulance form. Originally taken from a Maine state driver's license. Pronouncing doctor was, um, Frank Jennings. Subject was pronounced at the scene."

Now it's my nose that I'm hoping will bleed. *Please,* I tell it, *bleed. Only don't* just *bleed. GUSH.*

It doesn't.

"Cause of death may be a heart attack," Peter says. A light hand brushes down my naked back to the crack of my ass. I pray it will remove the thermometer, but it doesn't. "Spine appears to be intact, no attractable phenomena."

Attractable phenomena? *Attractable phenomena?* What the fuck do they think I am, a buglight?

He lifts my head, the pads of his fingers on my cheekbones, and I hum desperately—*Nnnnnnnnn*—knowing that he can't possibly hear me over Keith Richards's screaming guitar but hoping he may *feel* the sound vibrating in my nasal passages.

He doesn't. Instead he turns my head from side to side.

"No neck injury apparent, no rigor," he says, and I hope he will just let my head go, let my face smack down onto the table—*that'll* make my nose bleed, unless I really *am* dead—but he lowers it gently, considerately, mashing the tip again and once more making suffocation seem a distinct possibility.

"No wounds visible on the back or buttocks," he says, "although there's an old scar on the upper right thigh that looks like some sort of wound, shrapnel, perhaps. It's an ugly one."

It *was* ugly, and it *was* shrapnel. The end of my war. A mortar shell lobbed into a supply area, two men killed, one man—me—lucky. It's a lot uglier around front, and in a more sensitive spot, but all the equipment works . . . or did, up until today. A quarter of an inch to the left and they could have fixed me up with a hand-pump and a CO_2 cartridge for those intimate moments.

He finally plucked the thermometer out—oh dear God, the relief—and on the wall I could see his shadow holding it up.

"94.2," he said. "Gee, that ain't too shabby. This guy could almost be alive, Katie . . . Dr. Arlen."

"Remember where they found him," she said from across the room. The record they were listening to was between selections, and for a moment I could hear her lecturely tones clearly. "Golf course? Summer afternoon? If you'd gotten a reading of 98.6, I would not be surprised."

"Right, right," he said, sounding chastened. Then: "Is all this going to sound funny on the tape?" Translation: *Will I sound stupid on the tape?*

"It'll sound like a teaching situation," she said, "which is what it is."

"Okay, good. Great."

His rubber-tipped fingers spread my buttocks, then let them go and trail down the backs of my thighs. I would tense now, if I were capable of tensing.

Left leg, I send to him. *Left leg, Petie-boy, left calf, see it?*

He must see it, he *must,* because I can *feel* it, throbbing like a bee-sting or maybe a shot given by a clumsy nurse, one who infuses the injection into a muscle instead of hitting the vein.

"Subject is a really good example of what a really bad idea it is to play golf in shorts," he says, and I find myself wishing he had been born blind. Hell, maybe he *was* born blind, he's sure acting it. "I'm seeing all kinds of bug-bites, chigger-bites, scratches . . ."

"Mike said they found him in the rough," Arlen calls over. She's making one hell of a clatter; it sounds like she's doing dishes in a cafeteria kitchen instead of filing stuff. "At a guess, he had a heart attack while he was looking for his ball."

"Uh-huh . . ."

"Keep going, Peter, you're doing fine."

I find that an extremely debatable proposition.

"Okay."

More pokes and proddings. Gentle. Too gentle, maybe.

"There are mosquito-bites on the left calf that look infected," he says, and although his touch remains gentle, this time the pain is an enormous throb that would make me scream if I were capable of making any sound above the low-pitched hum. It occurs to me suddenly that my life may hang upon the length of the Rolling Stones tape they're listening to . . . always assuming it *is* a tape and not a CD that plays straight through. If it finishes before they cut into me . . . if I can hum loudly enough for them to hear before one of them turns it over to the other side . . .

"I may want to look at the bug-bites after the gross autopsy," she says, "although if we're right about his heart, there'll be no need. Or . . . do you want me to look now? They worrying you?"

"Nope, they're pretty clearly mosquito-bites," Gimpel the Fool says. "They grow em big over on the west side. He's got five . . . seven . . . eight . . . jeez, almost a dozen on his left leg alone."

"He forgot his Deep Woods Off."

"Never mind the Off, he forgot his digitalin," he says, and they have a nice little yock together, autopsy room humor.

This time he flips me by himself, probably happy to use those gym-grown Mr. Strongboy muscles of his, hiding the snake-bites and the mosquito-bites all around them, camouflaging them. I'm staring up into the bank of fluorescents again. Pete steps backward, out of my view. There's a humming noise. The table begins to slant, and I know why. When they cut me open, the fluids will run downhill to collection-points at its base. Plenty of samples for the state lab in Augusta, should there be any questions raised by the autopsy.

I focus all my will and effort on closing my eyes while he's looking down into my face, and cannot produce even a tic. All I wanted was eighteen holes of golf on Saturday afternoon, and instead I turned into Snow White with hair on my chest. And I can't stop wondering what it's going to feel like when those poultry shears go sliding into my midsection.

Pete has a clipboard in one hand. He consults it, sets it aside, then speaks into the mike. His voice is a lot less stilted now. He has just made the most hideous misdiagnosis of his life, but he doesn't know it, and so he's starting to warm up.

"I am commencing the autopsy at 5:49 P.M.," he says, "on Saturday, August 20th, 1994."

He lifts my lips, looks at my teeth like a man thinking about buying a horse, then pulls my jaw down. "Good color," he says, "and no petechiae on the cheeks." The current tune is fading out of the speakers and I hear a click as he steps on the footpedal which pauses the recording tape. "Man, this guy really *could* still be alive!"

I hum frantically, and at the same moment Dr. Arlen drops something that sounds like a bedpan. "Doesn't he *wish*," she says, laughing. He joins in and this time it's cancer I wish on them, some kind that is inoperable and lasts a long time.

He goes quickly down my body, feeling up my chest ("No bruising, swelling, or other exterior signs of cardiac arrest," he says, and what a big fucking surprise *that* is), then palpates my belly.

I burp.

He looks at me, eyes widening, mouth dropping open a little, and again I try desperately to hum, knowing he won't hear it over "Start Me Up" but thinking that maybe, along with the burp, he'll finally be ready to see what's right in front of him—

"Excuse yourself, Howie," Dr. Arlen, that bitch, says from behind me, and chuckles. "Better watch out, Pete—those postmortem belches are the worst."

He theatrically fans the air in front of his face, then goes back to what he's doing. He barely touches my groin, although he remarks that the scar on the back of my right leg continues around to the front.

Missed the big one, though, I think, *maybe because it's a little higher than you're looking. No big deal, my little*

Baywatch *buddy, but you also missed the fact that I'M STILL ALIVE, and that IS a big deal!*

He goes on chanting into the microphone, sounding more and more at ease (sounding, in fact, a little like Jack Klugman on *Quincy, M.E.*), and I know his partner over there behind me, the Pollyanna of the medical community, isn't thinking she'll have to roll the tape back over *this* part of the exam. Other than missing the fact that his first pericardial is still alive, the kid's doing a great job.

At last he says, "I think I'm ready to go on, doctor." He sounds tentative, though.

She comes over, looks briefly down at me, then squeezes Pete's shoulder. "Okay," she says. "On-na wid-da show!"

Now I'm trying to stick my tongue out. Just that simple kid's gesture of impudence, but it would be enough . . . and it seems to me I can feel a faint prickling sensation deep within my lips, the feeling you get when you're finally starting to come out of a heavy dose of Novocain. And I can feel a twitch? No, wishful thinking, just—

Yes! *Yes!* But a twitch is all, and the second time I try, nothing happens.

As Pete picks up the scissors, the Rolling Stones move on to "Hang Fire."

Hold a mirror in front of my nose! I scream at them. *Watch it fog up! Can't you at least do that?*

Snick, snick, snickety-snick.

Pete turns the scissors at an angle so the light runs down the blade, and for the first time I'm certain, really certain, that this mad charade is going to go all the way through to the end. The director isn't going to freeze the frame. The ref isn't going to stop the fight in the tenth round. We're not going to pause for a word from our sponsors. Petie-Boy's going to slide those scissors into my gut while I lie here helpless, and then he's going to open me up like a mail-order package from the Horchow Collection.

He looks hesitantly at Dr. Arlen.

No! I howl, my voice reverberating off the dark walls of my skull but emerging from my mouth not at all. *No, please no!*

She nods. "Go ahead. You'll be fine."

"Uh . . . you want to turn off the music?"

Yes! Yes, turn it off!

"Is it bothering you?"

Yes! It's bothering him! It's fucked him up so completely he thinks his patient is dead!

"Well . . ."

"Sure," she says, and disappears from my field of vision. A moment later Mick and Keith are finally gone. I try to make the humming noise and discover a horrible thing: now I can't even do that. I'm too scared. Fright has locked down my vocal cords. I can only stare up as she rejoins him, the two of them gazing down at me like pallbearers looking into an open grave.

"Thanks," he says. Then he takes a deep breath and lifts the scissors. "Commencing pericardial cut."

He slowly brings them down. I see them . . . see them . . . then they're gone from my field of vision. A long moment later, I feel cold steel nestle against my naked upper belly.

He looks doubtfully at the doctor.

"Are you sure you don't—"

"Do you want to make this your field or not, Peter?" she asks him with some asperity.

"You know I do, but—"

"Then cut."

He nods, lips firming. I would close my eyes if I could, but of course I cannot even do that; I can only steel myself against the pain that's only a second or two away now—steel myself for the steel.

"Cutting," he says, bending forward.

"Wait a sec!" she cries.

The dimple of pressure just below my solar plexus eases a little. He looks around at her, surprised, upset, maybe relieved that the crucial moment has been put off—

I feel her rubber-gloved hand slide around my penis as if she meant to give me some bizarre handjob, Safe Sex with the Dead, and then she says, "You missed this one, Pete."

He leans over, looking at what she's found—the scar in my groin, at the very top of my right thigh, a glassy, no-pore bowl in the flesh.

Her hand is still holding my cock, holding it out of the way, that's all she's doing; as far as she's concerned she might as well be holding up a sofa cushion so someone else can see the treasure she's found beneath it—coins, a lost wallet, maybe the catnip mouse you haven't been able to find—but something is happening.

Dear wheelchair Jesus on a chariot-driven crutch, *something is happening.*

"And look," she says. Her finger strokes a light, tickly line down the side of my right testicle. "Look at these hairline scars. His testes must have swollen up to damned near the size of grapefruits."

"Lucky he didn't lose one or both."

"You bet your . . . you bet your you-knows," she says, and laughs that mildly suggestive laugh again. Her gloved hand loosens, moves, then pushes down firmly, trying to clear the viewing area. She is doing by accident what you might pay twenty-five or thirty bucks to have done on purpose . . . under other circumstances, of course. "This is a war-wound, I think. Hand me that magnifier, Pete."

"But shouldn't I—"

"In a few seconds," she says. "*He's* not going anywhere." She's totally absorbed by what she's found. Her hand is still on me, still pressing down, and what was happening feels like it's *still* happening, but maybe I'm wrong. I *must* be wrong, or he would see it, she would *feel* it—

She bends down and now I can see only her green-clad back, with the ties from her cap trailing down it like odd pigtails. Now, oh my, I can feel her *breath* on me down there.

"Notice the outward radiation," she says. "It was a blast-wound of some sort, probably ten years ago at least, we could check his military rec—"

The door bursts open. Pete cries out in surprise. Dr. Arlen doesn't, but her hand tightens involuntarily, she's gripping me again and it's all at once like a hellish variation of the old Naughty Nurse fantasy.

"Don't cut im up!" someone screams, and his voice is

so high and wavery with fright that I barely recognize Rusty. *"Don't cut im up, there was a snake in his golf-bag and it bit Mike!"*

They turn to him, eyes wide, jaws dropped; her hand is still gripping me, but she's no more aware of that, at least for the time being, than Petie-Boy is aware that he's got one hand clutching the left breast of his scrub-gown. He looks like *he's* the one with the clapped-out fuel pump.

"What . . . what are you . . ." Pete begins.

"Knocked him flat!" Rusty was saying—babbling. "He's gonna be okay, I guess, but he can hardly talk! Little brown snake, I never saw one like it in my life, it went under the loadin bay, it's under there right now, but that's not the important part! I think it already bit that guy we brought in. I think . . . holy shit, doc, whatja tryin to do? Stroke im back to life?"

She looks around, dazed, at first not sure of what he's talking about . . . until she realizes that she's now holding a mostly erect penis. And as she screams— screams and snatches the shears out of Pete's limp gloved hand—I find myself thinking again of that old Alfred Hitchcock TV show.

Poor old Joseph Cotten, I think.

He only got to *cry.*

AFTERNOTE

It's been a year since my experience in Autopsy Room Four, and I have made a complete recovery, although the paralysis was both stubborn and scary; it was a full month before I began to get back the finer motions of my fingers and toes. I still can't play the piano, but then, of course, I never could. That is a joke, and I make no apologies for it. I think that in the first three months after my misadventure, my ability to joke provided a slim but vital margin between sanity and some sort of nervous breakdown. Unless you've actually felt the tip of a pair of post-mortem shears poking into your stomach, you don't know what I mean.

Two weeks or so after my close call, a woman on Dupont Street called the Derry Police to complain of a "foul stink" coming from the house next door. That house belonged to a bachelor bank clerk named Walter Kerr. Police found the house empty . . . of human life, that is. In the basement they found over sixty snakes of different varieties. About half of them were dead—starvation and dehydration—but many were extremely lively . . . and extremely dangerous. Several were very rare, and one was of a species believed to have been extinct since midcentury, according to consulting herpetologists.

Kerr failed to show up for work at Derry Community Bank on August 22nd, two days after I was bitten, one day after the story (PARALYZED MAN ESCAPES DEADLY AUTOPSY, the headline read; at one point I was quoted as saying I had been "scared stiff") broke in the press.

There was a snake for every cage in Kerr's basement menagerie, except for one. The empty cage was unmarked, and the snake that popped out of my golf-bag (the ambulance orderlies had packed it in with my "corpse" and had been practicing chip-shots out in the ambulance parking area) was never found. The toxin in my bloodstream—the same toxin found to a far lesser degree in orderly Mike Hopper's bloodstream—was documented but never identified. I have looked at a great many pictures of snakes in the last year, and have found at least one which has reportedly caused cases of full-body paralysis in humans. This is the Peruvian boomslang, a nasty viper which has supposedly been extinct since the 1920s. Dupont Street is less than half a mile from the Derry Municipal Golf Course. Most of the intervening land consists of scrub woods and vacant lots.

One final note. Katie Arlen and I dated for four months, November 1994 through February of 1995. We broke it off by mutual consent, due to sexual incompatibility.

I was impotent unless she was wearing rubber gloves.

At some point I think every writer of scary stories has to tackle the subject of premature burial, if only because it seems to be such a pervasive fear. When I was a kid of seven or so, the scariest TV program going was Alfred Hitchcock Presents, *and the scariest AHP—my friends and I were in total agreement on this—was the one starring Joseph Cotten as a man who has been injured in a car accident. Injured so badly, in fact, that the doctors think he's dead. They can't even find a heartbeat. They are on the verge of doing a postmortem on him—cutting him up while he's still alive and screaming inside, in other words—when he produces one single tear to let them know he's still alive. That was touching, but touching isn't in my usual repertoire. When my own thoughts turned to this subject, a more—shall we say* modern?—*method of communicating liveliness occurred to me, and this story was the result. One final note, regarding the snake: I doubt like hell if there's any such reptile as a Peruvian boomslang, but in one of her Miss Marple capers, Dame Agatha Christie* does *mention an* African *boomslang. I just liked the word so much (*boomslang, *not* African) *I had to put it in this story.*

The Man in the
Black Suit

I am now a very old man and this is something which
happened to me when I was very young—only nine
years old. It was 1914, the summer after my brother Dan
died in the west field and three years before America got
into World War I. I've never told anyone about what
happened at the fork in the stream that day, and I never
will . . . at least not with my mouth. I've decided to write
it down, though, in this book which I will leave on the
table beside my bed. I can't write long, because my
hands shake so these days and I have next to no strength,
but I don't think it will take long.

Later, someone may find what I have written. That
seems likely to me, as it is pretty much human nature to
look in a book marked DIARY after its owner has passed
along. So yes—my words will probably be read. A better
question is whether or not anyone will believe them.
Almost certainly not, but that doesn't matter. It's not
belief I'm interested in but freedom. Writing can give that,
I've found. For twenty years I wrote a column called
"Long Ago and Far Away" for the Castle Rock *Call,* and I
know that sometimes it works that way—what you write

down sometimes leaves you forever, like old photographs left in the bright sun, fading to nothing but white.

I pray for that sort of release.

A man in his nineties should be well past the terrors of childhood, but as my infirmities slowly creep up on me, like waves licking closer and closer to some indifferently built castle of sand, that terrible face grows clearer and clearer in my mind's eye. It glows like a dark star in the constellations of my childhood. What I might have done yesterday, who I might have seen here in my room at the nursing home, what I might have said to them or they to me . . . those things are gone, but the face of the man in the black suit grows ever clearer, ever closer, and I remember every word he said. I don't want to think of him but I can't help it, and sometimes at night my old heart beats so hard and so fast I think it will tear itself right clear of my chest. So I uncap my fountain pen and force my trembling old hand to write this pointless anecdote in the diary one of my great-grandchildren— I can't remember her name for sure, at least not right now, but I know it starts with an S—gave to me last Christmas, and which I have never written in until now. Now I will write in it. I will write the story of how I met the man in the black suit on the bank of Castle Stream one afternoon in the summer of 1914.

The town of Motton was a different world in those days—more different than I could ever tell you. That was a world without airplanes droning overhead, a world almost without cars and trucks, a world where the skies were not cut into lanes and slices by overhead power lines.

There was not a single paved road in the whole town, and the business district consisted of nothing but Corson's General Store, Thut's Livery & Hardware, the Methodist Church at Christ's Corner, the school, the town hall, and Harry's Restaurant half a mile down from there, which my mother called, with unfailing disdain, "the liquor house."

Mostly, though, the difference was in how people lived—how *apart* they were. I'm not sure people born after the middle of the twentieth century could quite credit that, although they might say they could, to be polite to old folks like me. There were no phones in western Maine back then, for one thing. The first one wouldn't be installed for another five years, and by the time there was one in our house, I was nineteen and going to college at the University of Maine in Orono.

But that is only the roof of the thing. There was no doctor closer than Casco, and no more than a dozen houses in what you would call town. There were no neighborhoods (I'm not even sure we knew the word, although we had a verb—*neighboring*—that described church functions and barn dances), and open fields were the exception rather than the rule. Out of town the houses were farms that stood far apart from each other, and from December until middle March we mostly hunkered down in the little pockets of stovewarmth we called families. We hunkered and listened to the wind in the chimney and hoped no one would get sick or break a leg or get a headful of bad ideas, like the farmer over in Castle Rock who had chopped up his wife and kids three winters before and then said in court that the ghosts made him do it. In those days before the Great

War, most of Motton was woods and bog, dark long places full of moose and mosquitoes, snakes and secrets. In those days there were ghosts everywhere.

This thing I'm telling about happened on a Saturday. My father gave me a whole list of chores to do, including some that would have been Dan's, if he'd still been alive. He was my only brother, and he'd died of being stung by a bee. A year had gone by, and still my mother wouldn't hear that. She said it was something else, *had* to have been, that no one ever died of being stung by a bee. When Mama Sweet, the oldest lady in the Methodist Ladies' Aid, tried to tell her—at the church supper the previous winter, this was—that the same thing had happened to her favorite uncle back in '73, my mother clapped her hands over her ears, got up, and walked out of the church basement. She'd never been back since, either, and nothing my father could say to her would change her mind. She claimed she was done with church, and that if she ever had to see Helen Robichaud again (that was Mama Sweet's real name), she would slap her eyes out. She wouldn't be able to help herself, she said.

That day, Dad wanted me to lug wood for the cook-stove, weed the beans and the cukes, pitch hay out of the loft, get two jugs of water to put in the cold pantry, and scrape as much old paint off the cellar bulkhead as I could. Then, he said, I could go fishing, if I didn't mind going by myself—he had to go over and see Bill Eversham about some cows. I said I sure didn't mind going by myself, and my Dad smiled like that didn't surprise him so very much. He'd given me a bamboo pole the week before—not because it was my birthday or anything, but just because he liked to give me things, sometimes—and I was wild to try it in Castle Stream, which was by far the troutiest brook I'd ever fished.

"But don't you go too far in the woods," he told me "Not beyond where it splits."

"No, sir."

"Promise me."

"Yessir, I promise."

"Now promise your mother."

We were standing on the back stoop; I had been bound for the springhouse with the waterjugs when my Dad stopped me. Now he turned me around to face my mother, who was standing at the marble counter in a flood of strong morning sunshine falling through the double windows over the sink. There was a curl of hair lying across the side of her forehead and touching her eyebrow—you see how well I remember it all? The bright light turned that little curl to filaments of gold and made me want to run to her and put my arms around her. In that instant I saw her as a woman, saw her as my father must have seen her. She was wearing a housedress with little red roses all over it, I remember, and she was kneading bread. Candy Bill, our little black Scottie dog, was standing alertly beside her feet, looking up, waiting for anything that might drop. My mother was looking at me.

"I promise," I said.

She smiled, but it was the worried kind of smile she always seemed to make since my father brought Dan back from the west field in his arms. My father had come sobbing and bare-chested. He had taken off his shirt and draped it over Dan's face, which had swelled and turned color. *My boy!* he had been crying. *Oh, look at my boy! Jesus, look at my boy!* I remember that as if it had been yesterday. It was the only time I ever heard my Dad take the Savior's name in vain.

"What do you promise, Gary?" she asked.

"Promise not to go no further than where it forks, ma'am."

"*Any* further."

"Any."

She gave me a patient look, saying nothing as her hands went on working in the dough, which now had a smooth, silky look.

"I promise not to go any further than where it forks, ma'am."

"Thank you, Gary," she said. "And try to remember that grammar is for the world as well as for school."

"Yes, ma'am."

Candy Bill followed me as I did my chores, and sat between my feet as I bolted my lunch, looking up at me with the same attentiveness he had shown my mother while she was kneading her bread, but when I got my new bamboo pole and my old, splintery creel and started out of the dooryard, he stopped and only stood in the dust by an old roll of snowfence, watching. I called him but he wouldn't come. He yapped a time or two, as if telling me to come back, but that was all.

"Stay, then," I said, trying to sound as if I didn't care. I did, though, at least a little. Candy Bill *always* went fishing with me.

My mother came to the door and looked out at me with her left hand held up to shade her eyes. I can see her that way still, and it's like looking at a photograph of someone who later became unhappy, or died suddenly. "You mind your Dad now, Gary!"

"Yes, ma'am, I will."

She waved. I waved, too. Then I turned my back on her and walked away.

The sun beat down on my neck, hard and hot, for the first quarter-mile or so, but then I entered the woods, where double shadow fell over the road and it was cool and fir-smelling and you could hear the wind hissing through the deep needled groves. I walked with my pole on my shoulder like boys did back then, holding my creel in my other hand like a valise or a salesman's sample-case. About two miles into the woods along a road which was really nothing but a double rut with a grassy strip growing up the center hump, I began to hear the hurried, eager gossip of Castle Stream. I thought of trout with bright speckled backs and pure white bellies, and my heart went up in my chest.

The stream flowed under a little wooden bridge, and the banks leading down to the water were steep and brushy. I worked my way down carefully, holding on where I could and digging my heels in. I went down out of summer and back into midspring, or so it felt. The cool rose gently off the water, and a green smell like moss. When I got to the edge of the water I only stood there for a little while, breathing deep of that mossy smell and watching the dragonflies circle and the skitterbugs skate. Then, farther down, I saw a trout leap at a butterfly—a good big brookie, maybe fourteen inches long—and remembered I hadn't come here just to sightsee.

I walked along the bank, following the current, and wet my line for the first time with the bridge still in sight upstream. Something jerked the tip of my pole down a time or two and ate half my worm, but he was too sly for my nine-year-old hands—or maybe just not hungry enough to be careless—so I went on.

I stopped at two or three other places before I got to the place where Castle Stream forks, going southwest into Castle Rock and southeast into Kashwakamak Township, and at one of them I caught the biggest trout I have ever caught in my life, a beauty that measured nineteen inches from tip to tail on the little ruler I kept in my creel. That was a monster of a brook trout, even for those days.

If I had accepted this as gift enough for one day and gone back, I would not be writing now (and this is going to turn out longer than I thought it would, I see that already), but I didn't. Instead I saw to my catch right then and there as my father had shown me— cleaning it, placing it on dry grass at the bottom of the creel, then laying damp grass on top of it—and went on. I did not, at age nine, think that catching a nineteen-inch brook trout was particularly remarkable, although I do remember being amazed that my line had not broken when I, netless as well as artless, had hauled it out and swung it toward me in a clumsy tail-flapping arc.

Ten minutes later, I came to the place where the stream split in those days (it is long gone now; there is a settlement of duplex homes where Castle Stream once went its course, and a district grammar school as well, and if there is a stream it goes in darkness), dividing around a huge gray rock nearly the size of our out-house. There was a pleasant flat space here, grassy and soft, overlooking what my Dad and I called South Branch. I squatted on my heels, dropped my line into the water, and almost immediately snagged a fine rainbow trout. He wasn't the size of my brookie—only a foot or so—but a good fish, just the same. I had it cleaned out before the gills had stopped flexing, stored it in my creel, and dropped my line back into the water.

This time there was no immediate bite so I leaned back, looking up at the blue stripe of sky I could see along the stream's course. Clouds floated by, west to east, and I tried to think what they looked like. I saw a unicorn, then a rooster, then a dog that looked a little like Candy Bill. I was looking for the next one when I drowsed off.

Or maybe slept. I don't know for sure. All I know is that a tug on my line so strong it almost pulled the bamboo pole out of my hand was what brought me back into the afternoon. I sat up, clutched the pole, and suddenly became aware that something was sitting on the tip of my nose. I crossed my eyes and saw a bee. My heart seemed to fall dead in my chest, and for a horrible second I was sure I was going to wet my pants.

The tug on my line came again, stronger this time, but although I maintained my grip on the end of the pole so it wouldn't be pulled into the stream and perhaps carried away (I think I even had the presence of mind to snub the line with my forefinger), I made no effort to pull in my catch. All of my horrified attention was fixed on the fat black-and-yellow thing that was using my nose as a rest-stop.

I slowly poked out my lower lip and blew upward.

The bee ruffled a little but kept its place. I blew again and it ruffled again . . . but this time it also seemed to shift impatiently, and I didn't dare blow anymore, for fear it would lose its temper completely and give me a shot. It was too close for me to focus on what it was doing, but it was easy to imagine it ramming its stinger into one of my nostrils and shooting its poison up toward my eyes. And my brain.

A terrible idea came to me: that this was the very bee which had killed my brother. I knew it wasn't true, and not only because honeybees probably didn't live longer than a single year (except maybe for the queens; about them I was not so sure). It couldn't be true because bees died when they stung, and even at nine I knew it. Their stingers were barbed, and when they tried to fly away after doing the deed, they tore themselves apart. Still, the idea stayed. This was a special bee, a devil-bee, and it had come back to finish the other of Albion and Loretta's two boys.

And here is something else: I had been stung by bees before, and although the stings had swelled more than is perhaps usual (I can't really say for sure), I had never died of them. That was only for my brother, a terrible trap which had been laid for him in his very making, a trap which I had somehow escaped. But as I crossed my eyes until they hurt in an effort to focus on the bee, logic did not exist. It was the *bee* that existed, only that, the bee that had killed my brother, killed him so bad that my father had slipped down the straps of his overalls so he could take off his shirt and cover Dan's swelled, engorged face. Even in the depths of his grief he had done that, because he didn't want his wife to see what had become of her firstborn. Now the bee had returned, and now it would kill me. It would kill me and I would die in convulsions on the bank, flopping just as a brookie flops after you take the hook out of its mouth.

As I sat there trembling on the edge of panic—of simply bolting to my feet and then bolting anywhere— there came a report from behind me. It was as sharp and peremptory as a pistol-shot, but I knew it wasn't a pistol-shot; it was someone clapping his hands. One single clap. At the moment it came, the bee tumbled off my nose and fell into my lap. It lay there on my pants with its legs sticking up and its stinger a threatless black thread against the old scuffed brown of the corduroy. It was dead as a doornail, I saw that at once. At the same moment, the pole gave another tug—the hardest yet—and I almost lost it again.

I grabbed it with both hands and gave it a big stupid yank that would have made my father clutch his head with both hands, if he had been there to see it. A rainbow trout, a good bit larger than the one I had already caught, rose out of the water in a wet, writhing flash, spraying fine drops of water from its filament of tail—it looked like one of those romanticized fishing pictures they used to put on the covers of men's magazines like *True* and *Man's Adventure* back in the forties and fifties. At that moment hauling in a big one was about the last thing on my mind, however, and when the line snapped and the fish fell back into the stream, I barely noticed. I looked over my shoulder to see who had clapped. A man was standing above me, at the edge of the trees. His face was very long and pale. His black hair was combed tight against his skull and parted with rigorous care on the left side of his narrow head. He was very tall. He was wearing a black three-piece suit, and I knew right away that he was not a human being, because his eyes were the orangey-red of flames in a woodstove. I don't just mean the irises, because he *had* no irises, and no pupils, and certainly no whites. His eyes were completely orange—an orange that shifted and flickered. And it's really too late not to say exactly what I mean, isn't it? He was on fire inside, and his eyes were like the little isinglass port-holes you sometimes see in stove doors.

My bladder let go, and the scuffed brown the dead bee was lying on went a darker brown. I was hardly aware of what had happened, and I couldn't take my eyes off the man standing on top of the bank and looking down at me, the man who had walked out of thirty miles of trackless western Maine woods in a fine black suit and narrow shoes of gleaming leather. I could see the watch-chain looped across his vest glittering in the summer sunshine. There was not so much as a single pine-needle on him. And he was smiling at me.

"Why, it's a fisherboy!" he cried in a mellow, pleasing voice. "Imagine that! Are we well-met, fisherboy?"

"Hello, sir," I said. The voice that came out of me did not tremble, but it didn't sound like my voice, either. It sounded older. Like Dan's voice, maybe. Or my father's, even. And all I could think was that maybe he would let me go if I pretended not to see what he was. If I pretended I didn't see there were flames glowing and dancing where his eyes should have been.

"I've saved you a nasty sting, perhaps," he said, and then, to my horror, he came down the bank to where I sat with a dead bee in my wet lap and a bamboo fishing pole in my nerveless hands. His slick-soled city shoes should have slipped on the low, grassy weeds which dressed the steep bank, but they didn't; nor did they leave tracks behind, I saw. Where his feet had touched—or seemed to touch—there was not a single broken twig, crushed leaf, or trampled shoe-shape.

Even before he reached me, I recognized the aroma baking up from the skin under the suit—the smell of burned matches. The smell of sulfur. The man in the black suit was the Devil. He had walked out of the deep woods between Motton and Kashwakamak, and now he was standing here beside me. From the corner of one eye I could see a hand as pale as the hand of a store window dummy. The fingers were hideously long.

He hunkered beside me on his hams, his knees popping just as the knees of any normal man might, but when he moved his hands so they dangled between his knees, I saw that each of those long fingers ended in what was not a fingernail but a long yellow claw.

"You didn't answer my question, fisherboy," he said in his mellow voice. It was, now that I think of it, like the voice of one of those radio announcers on the big-band shows years later, the ones that would sell Geritol and Serutan and Ovaltine and Dr. Grabow pipes. "Are we well-met?"

"Please don't hurt me," I whispered, in a voice so low I could barely hear it. I was more afraid than I could ever write down, more afraid than I want to remember . . . but I do. I do. It never even crossed my mind to hope I was having a dream, although I might have, I suppose, if I had been older. But I wasn't older; I was nine, and I knew the truth when it squatted down on its hunkers beside me. I knew a hawk from a handsaw, as my father would have said. The man who had come out of the woods on that Saturday afternoon in midsummer was the Devil, and inside the empty holes of his eyes, his brains were burning.

"Oh, do I smell something?" he asked, as if he hadn't heard me . . . although I knew he had. "Do I smell something . . . wet?"

He leaned forward toward me with his nose stuck out, like someone who means to smell a flower. And I noticed an awful thing; as the shadow of his head travelled over the bank, the grass beneath it turned yellow and died. He lowered his head toward my pants and sniffed. His glaring eyes half-closed, as if he had inhaled some sublime aroma and wanted to concentrate on nothing but that.

"Oh, bad!" he cried. "Lovely-bad!" And then he chanted: "Opal! Diamond! Sapphire! Jade! I smell Gary's lemonade!" Then he threw himself on his back in the little flat place and laughed wildly. It was the sound of a lunatic.

I thought about running, but my legs seemed two counties away from my brain. I wasn't crying, though; I had wet my pants like a baby, but I wasn't crying. I was too scared to cry. I suddenly knew that I was going to die, and probably painfully, but the worst of it was that that might not be the worst of it.

The worst of it might come later. *After* I was dead.

He sat up suddenly, the smell of burnt matches fluffing out from his suit and making me feel all gaggy in my throat. He looked at me solemnly from his narrow white face and burning eyes, but there was a sense of laughter about him, too. There was always that sense of laughter about him.

"Sad news, fisherboy," he said. "I've come with sad news."

I could only look at him—the black suit, the fine black shoes, the long white fingers that ended not in nails but in talons.

"Your mother is dead."

"No!" I cried. I thought of her making bread, of the curl lying across her forehead and just touching her eyebrow, standing there in the strong morning sunlight, and the terror swept over me again . . . but not for myself this time. Then I thought of how she'd looked when I set off with my fishing pole, standing in the kitchen doorway with her hand shading her eyes, and how she had looked to me in that moment like a photograph of someone you expected to see again but never did. "No, you lie!" I screamed.

He smiled—the sadly patient smile of a man who has often been accused falsely. "I'm afraid not," he said. "It was the same thing that happened to your brother, Gary. It was a bee."

"No, that's not true," I said, and now I *did* begin to cry. "She's old, she's thirty-five, if a bee-sting could kill her the way it did Danny she would have died a long time ago and you're a lying bastard!"

I had called the Devil a lying bastard. On some level I was aware of this, but the entire front of my mind was taken up by the enormity of what he'd said. My mother dead? He might as well have told me that there was a new ocean where the Rockies had been. But I believed him. On some level I believed him completely, as we always believe, on some level, the worst thing our hearts can imagine.

"I understand your grief, little fisherboy, but that particular argument just doesn't hold water, I'm afraid." He spoke in a tone of bogus comfort that was horrible, maddening, without remorse or pity. "A man can go his whole life without seeing a mockingbird, you know, but does that mean mockingbirds don't exist? Your mother—"

A fish jumped below us. The man in the black suit frowned, then pointed a finger at it. The trout convulsed in the air, its body bending so strenuously that for a split-second it appeared to be snapping at its own tail, and when it fell back into Castle Stream it was floating lifelessly, dead. It struck the big gray rock where the waters divided, spun around twice in the whirlpool eddy that formed there, and then floated off in the direction of Castle Rock. Meanwhile, the terrible stranger turned his burning eyes on me again, his thin lips pulled back from tiny rows of sharp teeth in a cannibal smile.

"Your mother simply went through her entire life without being stung by a bee," he said. "But then—less than an hour ago, actually—one flew in through the kitchen window while she was taking the bread out of the oven and putting it on the counter to cool."

"No, I won't hear this, I won't hear this, I *won't!*"

I raised my hands and clapped them over my ears. He pursed his lips as if to whistle and blew at me gently. It was only a little breath, but the stench was foul beyond belief—clogged sewers, outhouses that have never known a single sprinkle of lime, dead chickens after a flood.

My hands fell away from the sides of my face.

"Good," he said. "You need to hear this, Gary; you need to hear this, my little fisherboy. It was your mother who passed that fatal weakness on to your brother Dan; you got some of it, but you also got a protection from your father that poor Dan somehow missed." He pursed his lips again, only this time, he made a cruelly comic little *tsk-tsk* sound instead of blowing his nasty breath at me. "So, although I don't like to speak ill of the dead, it's almost a case of poetic justice, isn't it? After all, she killed your brother Dan as surely as if she had put a gun to his head and pulled the trigger."

"No," I whispered. "No, it isn't true."

"I assure you it is," he said. "The bee flew in the window and lit on her neck. She slapped at it before she even knew what she was doing—*you* were wiser than that, weren't you, Gary?—and the bee stung her. She felt her throat start to close up at once. That's what happens, you know, to people who are allergic to bee-venom. Their throats close and they drown in the open air. That's why Dan's face was so swollen and purple. That's why your father covered it with his shirt."

I stared at him, now incapable of speech. Tears streamed down my cheeks. I didn't want to believe him, and knew from my church schooling that the devil is the father of lies, but I *did* believe him, just the same. I believed he had been standing there in our dooryard, looking in the kitchen window, as my mother fell to her knees, clutching at her swollen throat while Candy Bill danced around her, barking shrilly.

"She made the most wonderfully awful noises," the man in the black suit said reflectively, "and she scratched her face quite badly, I'm afraid. Her eyes bulged out like a frog's eyes. She wept." He paused, then added: "She wept as she died, isn't that sweet? And here's the most beautiful thing of all. After she was dead . . . after she had been lying on the floor for fifteen minutes or so with no sound but the stove ticking and with that little stick of a bee-stinger still poking out of the side of her neck—so small, so small—do you know what Candy Bill did? That little rascal licked away her tears. First on one side . . . and then on the other."

He looked out at the stream for a moment, his face sad and thoughtful. Then he turned back to me and his expression of bereavement disappeared like a dream. His face was as slack and avid as the face of a corpse that has died hungry. His eyes blazed. I could see his sharp little teeth between his pale lips.

"I'm starving," he said abruptly. "I'm going to kill you and tear you open and eat your guts, little fisher-boy. What do you think about that?"

No, I tried to say, *please, no,* but no sound came out. He meant to do it, I saw. He really meant to do it.

"I'm just so *hungry*," he said, both petulant and teasing. "And you won't want to live without your precious mommy, anyhow, take my word for it. Because your father's the sort of man who'll have to have some warm hole to stick it in, believe me, and if you're the only one available, you're the one who'll have to serve. I'll save you all that discomfort and unpleasantness. Also, you'll go to Heaven, think of that. Murdered souls *always* go to Heaven. So we'll both be serving God this afternoon, Gary. Isn't that nice?"

He reached for me again with his long, pale hands, and without thinking what I was doing, I flipped open the top of my creel, pawed all the way down to the bottom, and brought out the monster brookie I'd caught earlier—the one I should have been satisfied with. I held it out to him blindly, my fingers in the red slit of its belly from which I had removed its insides as the man in the black suit had threatened to remove mine. The fish's glazed eye stared dreamily at me, the gold ring around the black center reminding me of my mother's wedding ring. And in that moment I saw her lying in her coffin with the sun shining off the wedding band and knew it was true—she had been stung by a bee, she had drowned in the warm, bread-smelling kitchen air, and Candy Bill had licked her dying tears from her swollen cheeks.

"Big fish!" the man in the black suit cried in a guttural, greedy voice. "Oh, *biiig fiiish!*"

He snatched it away from me and crammed it into a mouth that opened wider than any human mouth ever could. Many years later, when I was sixty-five (I know it was sixty-five because that was the summer I retired from teaching), I went to the New England Aquarium and finally saw a shark. The mouth of the man in the black suit was like that shark's mouth when it opened, only his gullet was blazing red, the same color as his awful eyes, and I felt heat bake out of it and into my face, the way you feel a sudden wave of heat come pushing out of a fireplace when a dry piece of wood catches alight. And I didn't imagine that heat, either, I know I didn't, because just before he slid the head of my nineteen-inch brook trout between his gaping jaws, I saw the scales along the sides of the fish rise up and begin to curl like bits of paper floating over an open incinerator.

He slid the fish in like a man in a travelling show swallowing a sword. He didn't chew, and his blazing eyes bulged out, as if in effort. The fish went in and went in, his throat bulged as it slid down his gullet, and now he began to cry tears of his own . . . except his tears were blood, scarlet and thick.

I think it was the sight of those bloody tears that gave me my body back. I don't know why that should have been, but I think it was. I bolted to my feet like a jack released from its box, turned with my bamboo pole still in one hand, and fled up the bank, bending over and tearing tough bunches of weeds out with my free hand in an effort to get up the slope more quickly.

He made a strangled, furious noise—the sound of any man with his mouth too full—and I looked back just as I got to the top. He was coming after me, the back of his suit-coat flapping and his thin gold watch-chain flashing and winking in the sun. The tail of the fish was still protruding from his mouth and I could smell the rest of it, roasting in the oven of his throat.

He reached for me, groping with his talons, and I fled along the top of the bank. After a hundred yards or so I found my voice and went to screaming— screaming in fear, of course, but also screaming in grief for my beautiful dead mother.

He was coming along after me. I could hear snapping branches and whipping bushes, but I didn't look back again. I lowered my head, slitted my eyes against the bushes and low-hanging branches along the stream's bank, and ran as fast as I could. And at every step I expected to feel his hands descending on my shoulders pulling me back into a final hot hug.

That didn't happen. Some unknown length of time later—it couldn't have been longer than five or ten minutes, I suppose, but it seemed like forever—I saw the bridge through layerings of leaves and firs. Still screaming, but breathlessly now, sounding like a teakettle which has almost boiled dry, I reached this second, steeper bank and charged up to it.

Halfway to the top I slipped to my knees, looked over my shoulder, and saw the man in the black suit almost at my heels, his white face pulled into a convulsion of fury and greed. His cheeks were splattered with his bloody tears and his shark's mouth hung open like a hinge.

"Fisherboy!" he snarled, and started up the bank after me, grasping at my foot with one long hand. I tore free, turned, and threw my fishing pole at him. He batted it down easily, but it tangled his feet up somehow and he went to his knees. I didn't wait to see anymore; I turned and bolted to the top of the slope. I almost slipped at the very top, but managed to grab one of the support struts running beneath the bridge and save myself.

"You can't get away, fisherboy!" he cried from behind me. He sounded furious, but he also sounded as if he were laughing. "It takes more than a mouthful of trout to fill *me* up!"

"Leave me alone!" I screamed back at him. I grabbed the bridge's railing and threw myself over it in a clumsy somersault, filling my hands with splinters and bumping my head so hard on the boards when I came down that I saw stars. I rolled over onto my belly and began crawling. I lurched to my feet just before I got to the end of the bridge, stumbled once, found my rhythm, and then began to run. I ran as only nine-year-old boys can run, which is like the wind. It felt as if my feet only touched the ground with every third or fourth stride, and for all I know, that may be true. I ran straight up the righthand wheelrut in the road, ran until my temples pounded and my eyes pulsed in their sockets, ran until I had a hot stitch in my left side from the bottom of my ribs to my armpit, ran until I could taste blood and something like metal-shavings in the back of my throat. When I couldn't run anymore I stumbled to a stop and looked back over my shoulder, puffing and blowing like a windbroke horse. I was convinced I would see him standing right there behind me in his natty black suit, the watch-chain a glittering loop across his vest and not a hair out of place.

But he was gone. The road stretching back toward Castle Stream between the darkly massed pines and spruces was empty. And yet I sensed him somewhere near in those woods, watching me with his grassfire eyes, smelling of burnt matches and roasted fish.

I turned and began walking as fast as I could, limping a little—I'd pulled muscles in both legs, and when I got out of bed the next morning I was so sore I could barely walk. I didn't notice those things then, though. I just kept looking over my shoulder, needing again and again to verify that the road behind me was still empty. It was, each time I looked, but those backward glances seemed to increase my fear rather than lessening it. The firs looked darker, massier, and I kept imagining what lay behind the trees which marched beside the road—long, tangled corridors of forest, leg-breaking deadfalls, ravines where anything might live. Until that Saturday in 1914, I had thought that

bears were the worst thing the forest could hold.
Now I knew better.

A mile or so further up the road, just beyond the place
where it came out of the woods and joined the Geegan
Flat Road, I saw my father walking toward me and
whistling "The Old Oaken Bucket." He was carrying
his own rod, the one with the fancy spinning reel from
Monkey Ward. In his other hand he had his creel, the
one with the ribbon my mother had woven through the
handle back when Dan was still alive. DEDICATED TO
JESUS, that ribbon said. I had been walking but when I
saw him I started to run again, screaming *Dad! Dad!
Dad!* at the top of my lungs and staggering from side to
side on my tired, sprung legs like a drunken sailor. The
expression of surprise on his face when he recognized me
might have been comical under other circumstances,
but not under these. He dropped his rod and creel into
the road without so much as a downward glance at
them and ran to me. It was the fastest I ever saw my
Dad run in his life; when we came together it was a
wonder the impact didn't knock us both senseless, and I
struck my face on his belt-buckle hard enough to start a
little nosebleed. I didn't notice that until later, though.
Right then I only reached out my arms and clutched
him as hard as I could. I held on and rubbed my hot face
back and forth against his belly, covering his old blue
workshirt with blood and tears and snot.

"Gary, what is it? What happened? Are you all right?"

"Ma's dead!" I sobbed. "I met a man in the woods
and he told me! Ma's dead! She got stung by a bee and
it swelled her all up just like what happened to Dan,

and she's dead! She's on the kitchen floor and Candy Bill . . . licked the t-t-tears . . . off her . . . off her . . ."

Face was the last word I had to say, but by then my chest was hitching so bad I couldn't get it out. My tears were flowing again, and my Dad's startled, frightened face had blurred into three overlapping images. I began to howl—not like a little kid who's skun his knee but like a dog that's seen something bad by moonlight— and my father pressed my head against his hard flat stomach again. I slipped out from under his hand, though, and looked back over my shoulder. I wanted to make sure the man in the black suit wasn't coming. There was no sign of him; the road winding back into the woods was completely empty. I promised myself I would never go back down that road again, not ever, no matter what, and I suppose now God's greatest blessing to His creatures below is that they can't see the future. It might have broken my mind if I had known I *would* be going back down that road, and not two hours later. For that moment, though, I was only relieved to see we were still alone. Then I thought of my mother—my beautiful dead mother—and laid my face back against my father's stomach and bawled some more.

"Gary, listen to me," he said a moment or two later. I went on bawling. He gave me a little longer to do that, then reached down and lifted my chin so he could look into my face and I could look into his. "Your Mom's fine," he said.

I could only look at him with tears streaming down my cheeks. I didn't believe him.

"I don't know who told you different, or what kind of dirty dog would want to put a scare like that into a little boy, but I swear to God your mother's fine."

"But . . . but he said . . ."

"I don't care *what* he said. I got back from Eversham's earlier than I expected—he doesn't want to sell any cows, it's all just talk—and decided I had time to catch up with you. I got my pole and my creel and your mother made us a couple of jelly fold-overs. Her new bread. Still warm. So she was fine half an hour ago, Gary, and there's nobody knows any different that's come from this direction, I guarantee you. Not in just half an hour's time." He looked over my shoulder. "Who was this man? And where was he? I'm going to find him and thrash him within an inch of his life."

I thought a thousand things in just two seconds—that's what it seemed like, anyway—but the last thing I thought was the most powerful: if my Dad met up with the man in the black suit, I didn't think my Dad would be the one to do the thrashing. Or the walking away.

I kept remembering those long white fingers, and the talons at the ends of them.

"Gary?"

"I don't know that I remember," I said.

"Were you where the stream splits? The big rock?"

I could never lie to my father when he asked a direct question—not to save his life or mine. "Yes, but don't go down there." I seized his arm with both hands and tugged it hard. "Please don't. He was a scary man." Inspiration struck like an illuminating lightning-bolt. "I think he had a gun."

He looked at me thoughtfully. "Maybe there wasn't a man," he said, lifting his voice a little on the last word and turning it into something that was almost but not quite a question. "Maybe you fell asleep while you were fishing, son, and had a bad dream. Like the ones you had about Danny last winter."

I *had* had a lot of bad dreams about Dan last winter, dreams where I would open the door to our closet or to the dark, fruity interior of the cider shed and see him standing there and looking at me out of his purple strangulated face; from many of these dreams I had awakened screaming, and awakened my parents, as well. I had fallen asleep on the bank of the stream for a little while, too—dozed off, anyway—but I hadn't dreamed and I was sure I had awakened just before the man in the black suit clapped the bee dead, sending it tumbling off my nose and into my lap. I hadn't dreamed him the way I had dreamed Dan, I was quite sure of that, although my meeting with him had already attained a dreamlike quality in my mind, as I suppose supernatural occurrences always must. But if my Dad thought that the man had only existed in my own head, that might be better. Better for him.

"It might have been, I guess," I said.

"Well, we ought to go back and find your rod and your creel."

He actually started in that direction, and I had to tug frantically at his arm to stop him again, and turn him back toward me.

"Later," I said. "Please, Dad? I want to see Mother. I've got to see her with my own eyes."

He thought that over, then nodded. "Yes, I suppose you do. We'll go home first, and get your rod and creel later."

So we walked back to the farm together, my father with his fishpole propped on his shoulder just like one of my friends, me carrying his creel, both of us eating folded-over slices of my mother's bread smeared with blackcurrant jam.

"Did you catch anything?" he asked as we came in sight of the barn.

"Yes, sir," I said. "A rainbow. Pretty good-sized." *And a brookie that was a lot bigger,* I thought but didn't say. *Biggest one I ever saw, to tell the truth, but I don't have that one to show you, Dad. I gave that one to the man in the black suit, so he wouldn't eat me. And it worked . . . but just barely.*

"That's all? Nothing else?"

"After I caught it I fell asleep." This was not really an answer, but not really a lie, either.

"Lucky you didn't lose your pole. You didn't, did you, Gary?"

"No, sir," I said, very reluctantly. Lying about that would do no good even if I'd been able to think up a whopper—not if he was set on going back to get my creel anyway, and I could see by his face that he was.

Up ahead, Candy Bill came racing out of the back door, barking his shrill bark and wagging his whole rear end back and forth the way Scotties do when they're excited. I couldn't wait any longer; hope and anxiety bubbled up in my throat like foam. I broke away from my father and ran to the house, still lugging his creel and still convinced, in my heart of hearts, that I was going to find my mother dead on the kitchen floor with her face swelled and purple like Dan's had been when my father carried him in from the west field, crying and calling the name of Jesus.

But she was standing at the counter, just as well and fine as when I had left her, humming a song as she shelled peas into a bowl. She looked around at me, first in surprise and then in fright as she took in my wide eyes and pale cheeks.

"Gary, what is it? What's the matter?"

I didn't answer, only ran to her and covered her with kisses. At some point my father came in and said, "Don't worry, Lo—he's all right. He just had one of his bad dreams, down there by the brook."

"Pray God it's the last of them," she said, and hugged me tighter while Candy Bill danced around our feet, barking his shrill bark.

"You don't have to come with me if you don't want to, Gary," my father said, although he had already made it clear that he thought I should—that I should go back, that I should face my fear, as I suppose folks would say nowadays. That's very well for fearful things that are make-believe, but two hours hadn't done much to change my conviction that the man in the black suit had been real. I wouldn't be able to convince my father of that, though. I don't think there was a nine-year-old that ever lived who would have been able to convince his father he'd seen the Devil come walking out of the woods in a black suit.

"I'll come," I said. I had walked out of the house to join him before he left, mustering all my courage in order to get my feet moving, and now we were standing by the chopping-block in the side yard, not far from the woodpile.

"What you got behind your back?" he asked.

I brought it out slowly. I would go with him, and I would hope the man in the black suit with the arrow-straight part down the left side of his head was gone . . . but if he wasn't, I wanted to be prepared. As prepared as I could be, anyway. I had the family Bible in the hand I had brought out from behind my back. I'd set out just to bring my New Testament, which I had won for memorizing the most psalms in the Thursday night Youth Fellowship competition (I managed eight, although most of them except the Twenty-third had floated out of my mind in a week's time), but the little red Testament didn't seem like enough when you were maybe going to face the Devil himself, not even when the words of Jesus were marked out in red ink.

My father looked at the old Bible, swelled with family documents and pictures, and I thought he'd tell me to put it back, but he didn't. A look of mixed grief and sympathy crossed his face, and he nodded. "All right," he said. "Does your mother know you took that?"

"No, sir."

He nodded again. "Then we'll hope she doesn't spot it gone before we get back. Come on. And don't drop it."

Half an hour or so later, the two of us stood on the bank looking down at the place where Castle Stream forked, and at the flat place where I'd had my encounter with the man with the red-orange eyes. I had my bamboo rod in my hand—I'd picked it up below the bridge—and my creel lay down below, on the flat place. Its wicker top was flipped back. We stood looking down, my father and I, for a long time, and neither of us said anything.

Opal! Diamond! Sapphire! Jade! I smell Gary's lemon-

ade! That had been his unpleasant little poem, and once he had recited it, he had thrown himself on his back, laughing like a child who has just discovered he has enough courage to say bathroom words like shit or piss. The flat place down there was as green and lush as any place in Maine that the sun can get to in early July . . . except where the stranger had lain. There the grass was dead and yellow in the shape of a man.

I looked down and saw I was holding our lumpy old family Bible straight out in front of me with both thumbs pressing so hard on the cover that they were white. It was the way Mama Sweet's husband Norville held a willow-fork when he was trying to dowse some- body a well.

"Stay here," my father said at last, and skidded side- ways down the bank, digging his shoes into the rich soft soil and holding his arms out for balance. I stood where I was, holding the Bible stiffly out at the ends of my arms like a willow-fork, my heart thumping wildly. I don't know if I had a sense of being watched that time or not; I was too scared to have a sense of any- thing, except for a sense of wanting to be far away from that place and those woods.

My Dad bent down, sniffed at where the grass was dead, and grimaced. I knew what he was smelling: something like burnt matches. Then he grabbed my creel and came on back up the bank, hurrying. He snagged one fast look over his shoulder to make sure nothing was coming along behind. Nothing was. When he handed me the creel, the lid was still hanging back on its cunning little leather hinges. I looked inside and saw nothing but two handfuls of grass.

"Thought you said you caught a rainbow," my father said, "but maybe you dreamed that, too."

Something in his voice stung me. "No, sir," I said. "I caught one."

"Well, it sure as hell didn't flop out, not if it was gutted and cleaned. And you wouldn't put a catch into your fisherbox without doing that, would you, Gary? I taught you better than that."

"Yes, sir, you did, but—"

"So if you didn't dream catching it and if it was dead in the box, something must have come along and eaten it," my father said, and then he grabbed another quick glance over his shoulder, eyes wide, as if he had heard something move in the woods. I wasn't exactly surprised to see drops of sweat standing out on his forehead like big clear jewels. "Come on," he said. "Let's get the hell out of here."

I was for that, and we went back along the bank to the bridge, walking quick without speaking. When we got there, my Dad dropped to one knee and examined the place where we'd found my rod. There was another patch of dead grass there, and the lady's slipper was all brown and curled in on itself, as if a blast of heat had charred it. While my father did this, I looked in my empty creel.

"He must have gone back and eaten my other fish, too," I said.

My father looked up at me. "*Other* fish!"

"Yes, sir. I didn't tell you, but I caught a brookie, too. A big one. He was awful hungry, that fella." I wanted to say more, and the words trembled just behind my lips, but in the end I didn't.

We climbed up to the bridge and helped one another over the railing. My father took my creel, looked into it, then went to the railing and threw it over. I came up beside him in time to see it splash down and float away like a boat, riding lower and lower in the stream as the water poured in between the wicker weavings.

"It smelled bad," my father said, but he didn't look at me when he said it, and his voice sounded oddly defensive. It was the only time I ever heard him speak just that way.

"Yes, sir."

"We'll tell your mother we couldn't find it. If she asks. If she doesn't ask, we won't tell her anything."

"No, sir, we won't."

And she didn't and we didn't and that's the way it was.

That day in the woods is eighty-one years gone, and for many of the years in between I have never even thought of it . . . not awake, at least. Like any other man or woman who ever lived, I can't say about my dreams, not for sure. But now I'm old, and I dream awake, it seems. My infirmities have crept up like waves which will soon take a child's abandoned sand castle, and my memories have also crept up, making me think of some old rhyme that went, in part, "Just leave them alone/And they'll come home/Wagging their tails behind them." I remember meals I ate, games I played, girls I kissed in the school cloakroom when we played Post Office, boys I chummed with, the first drink I ever took, the first cigarette I ever smoked (cornshuck behind Dicky Hammer's pig-shed, and I threw up). Yet of all the memories, the one of the man in the black suit is the strongest, and glows with its own spectral, haunted light. He was real, he was the Devil, and that day I was either his errand or his luck. I feel more and more strongly that escaping him was my luck—*just* luck, and not the intercession of the God I have worshipped and sung hymns to all my life.

As I lie here in my nursing-home room, and in the ruined sand castle that is my body, I tell myself that I need not fear the Devil—that I have lived a good, kindly life, and I need not fear the Devil. Sometimes I remind myself that it was I, not my father, who finally coaxed my mother back to church later on that summer. In the dark, however, these thoughts have no power to ease or comfort. In the dark comes a voice which whispers that the nine-year-old boy I was had done nothing for which he might legitimately fear the devil either . . . and yet the Devil came. And in the dark I sometimes hear that voice drop even lower, into ranges which are inhuman. *Big fish!* it whispers in tones of hushed greed, and all the truths of the moral world fall to ruin before its hunger. *Biiig fiiish!*

The Devil came to me once, long ago; suppose he were to come again now? I am too old to run now; I can't even get to the bathroom and back without my walker. I have no fine large brook trout with which to propitiate him, either, even for a moment or two; I am old and my creel is empty. Suppose he were to come back and find me so?

And suppose he is still hungry?

My favorite Nathaniel Hawthorne story is "Young Goodman Brown." I think it's one of the ten best stories ever written by an American. "The Man in the Black Suit" is my hommage *to it. As for the particulars, I was talking with a friend of mine one day, and he happened to mention that his Grandpa believed—truly* believed—*that he had seen the Devil in the woods, back around the turn of the twentieth century. Grandpa said the Devil came walking out of the woods and started talking to him just like a natural man. While Grandpa was chinning with him, he realized that the man from the woods had burning red eyes and smelled like sulfur. My friend's Grandpa became convinced that the Devil would kill him if he realized Grandpa had caught on, so he did his best to make normal conversation until he could eventually get away. My story grew from my friend's story. Writing it was no fun, but I went on with it, anyway. Sometimes stories cry out to be told in such loud voices that you write them just to shut them up. I thought the finished product a rather humdrum folktale told in pedestrian language, certainly miles from the Hawthorne story I liked so much. When* The New Yorker *asked to publish it, I was shocked. When it won first prize in the O. Henry Best Short Story competition for 1996, I was convinced someone had made a mistake (that did not keep me from accepting the award, however). Reader response was generally positive, too. This story is proof that writers are often the* worst *judges of what they have written.*

All That You Love
Will Be Carried Away

It was a Motel 6 on I-80 just west of Lincoln,
Nebraska. The snow that began at midafternoon had
faded the sign's virulent yellow to a kinder pastel shade
as the light ran out of the January dusk. The wind was
closing in on that quality of empty amplification one
encounters only in the country's flat midsection, usually in wintertime. That meant nothing but discomfort
now, but if big snow came tonight—the weather fore-
casters couldn't seem to make up their minds—then
the interstate would be shut down by morning. That
was nothing to Alfie Zimmer.

He got his key from a man in a red vest and drove
down to the end of the long cinder-block building. He
had been selling in the Midwest for twenty years, and
had formulated four basic rules about securing his
night's rest. First, always reserve ahead. Second,
reserve at a franchise motel if possible—your Holiday
Inn, your Ramada Inn, your Comfort Inn, your Motel
6. Third, always ask for a room on the end. That way,
the worst you could have was one set of noisy neighbors. Last, ask for a room that begins with a one. Alfie

was forty-four, too old to be fucking truck-stop whores, eating chicken-fried steak, or hauling his luggage upstairs. These days, the rooms on the first floor were usually reserved for non-smokers. Alfie rented them and smoked anyway.

Someone had taken the space in front of Room 190. All the spaces along the building were taken. Alfie wasn't surprised. You could make a reservation, guarantee it, but if you arrived late (late on a day like this was after 4 P.M.), you had to park and walk. The cars belonging to the early birds were nestled up to the gray cinder block and the bright-yellow doors in a long line, their windows already covered with a scrim of light snow.

Alfie drove around the corner and parked with the nose of his Chevrolet pointed at the white expanse of some farmer's field, swimming deep into the gray of day's end. At the farthest limit of vision he could see the spark lights of a farm. In there, they would be hunkered down. Out here, the wind blew hard enough to rock the car. Snow skated past, obliterating the farm lights for a few moments.

Alfie was a big man with a florid face and a smoker's noisy respiration. He was wearing a topcoat, because when you were selling that was what people liked to see. Not a jacket. Storekeepers sold to people wearing jackets and John Deere caps, they didn't buy from them. The room key lay on the seat beside him. It was attached to a diamond of green plastic. The key was a real key, not a MagCard. On the radio Clint Black was singing "Nothin' but the Tail Lights." It was a country song. Lincoln had an FM rocker now, but rock-and-roll music didn't seem right to Alfie. Not out here, where if you switched over to AM you could still hear angry old men calling down hellfire.

He shut off the engine, put the key to 190 in his pocket, and checked to make sure he still had his notebook in there, too. His old pal. "Save Russian Jews," he said, reminding himself. "Collect valuable prizes."

He got out of the car and a gust of wind hit him hard, rocking him back on his heels, flapping his pants around his legs, making him laugh a smoker's surprised rattlebox laugh.

His samples were in the trunk, but he wouldn't need them tonight. No, not tonight, not at all. He took his suitcase and his briefcase out of the backseat, shut the door, then pushed the black button on his key fob. That one locked all the doors. The red one set off an alarm, what you were supposed to use if you were going to get mugged. Alfie had never been mugged. He guessed that few salesmen of gourmet foods were, especially in this part of the country. There was a market for gourmet foods in Nebraska, Iowa, Oklahoma, and Kansas; even in the Dakotas, although many might not believe it. Alfie had done quite well, especially over the last two years as he got to know the market's deeper creases—but it was never going to equal the market for, let's say, fertilizer. Which he could smell even now on the winter wind that was freezing his cheeks and turning them an even darker shade of red.

He stood where he was a moment longer, waiting for the wind to drop. It did, and he could see the spark lights again. The farmhouse. And was it possible that behind those lights, some farmer's wife was even now heating up a pot of Cottager Split Pea Soup or perhaps microwaving a Cottager Shepherd's Pie or Chicken Français? It was. It was as possible as hell. While her husband watched the early news with his shoes off and his sock feet on a hassock, and overhead their son played a video game on his GameCube and their daughter sat in the tub, chin-deep in fragrant bubbles, her hair tied up with a ribbon, reading *The Golden Compass*, by Philip Pullman, or perhaps one of the Harry Potter books, which were favorites of Alfie's daughter, Carlene. All that going on behind the spark lights, some family's universal joint turning smoothly in its socket, but between them and the edge of this parking lot was a mile and a half of flat field, white in the running-away light of a low sky, comatose with the season. Alfie briefly imagined himself walking into that field in his city shoes, his briefcase in one hand and his suitcase in the other, working his way across the frozen furrows, finally arriving, knocking; the door would be opened and he would smell pea soup, that good hearty smell, and hear the KETV meteorologist in the other room saying, "But now look at this low-pressure system just coming over the Rockies."

And what would Alfie say to the farmer's wife? That he just dropped by for dinner? Would he advise her to save Russian Jews, collect valuable prizes? Would he begin by saying, "Ma'am, according to at least one source I've read recently, all that you love will be carried away"? That would be a good conversation opener, sure to interest the farmer's wife in the wayfaring stranger who had just walked across her husband's east field to knock on her door. And when she invited him to step in, to tell her more, he could open his brief-case and give her a couple of his sample books, tell her that once she discovered the Cottager brand of quick-serve gourmet delicacies she would almost certainly want to move on to the more sophisticated pleasures of Ma Mère. And, by the way, did she have a taste for caviar? Many did. Even in Nebraska.

Freezing. Standing here and freezing.

He turned from the field and the spark lights at the far end of it and walked to the motel, moving in care-ful duck steps so he wouldn't go ass over teakettle. He had done it before, God knew. Whoops-a-daisy in half a hundred motel parking lots. He had done most of it before, actually, and supposed that was at least part of the problem.

There was an overhang, so he was able to get out of the snow. There was a Coke machine with a sign say-ing, USE CORRECT CHANGE. There was an ice machine and a Snax machine with candy bars and various kinds of potato chips behind curls of metal like bedsprings. There was no USE CORRECT CHANGE sign on the Snax machine. From the room to the left of the one where he intended to kill himself, Alfie could hear the early news, but it would sound better in that farmhouse over yonder, he was sure of that. The wind boomed. Snow swirled around his city shoes, and then Alfie let himself into his room. The light switch was to the left. He turned it on and shut the door.

He knew the room; it was the room of his dreams. It was square. The walls were white. On one was a picture of a small boy in a straw hat, asleep with a fishing pole in his hand. There was a green rug on the floor, a quarter-inch of some nubbly synthetic stuff. It was cold in here right now, but when he pushed the Hi Heat button on the control panel of the Climatron beneath the window the place would warm up fast. Would probably become hot. A counter ran the length of one wall. There was a TV on it. On top of the TV was a piece of cardboard with ONE-TOUCH MOVIES! printed on it.

There were twin double beds, each covered with bright-gold spreads that had been tucked under the pillows and then pulled over them, so the pillows looked like the corpses of infants. There was a table between the beds with a Gideon Bible, a TV-channel guide, and a flesh-colored phone on it. Beyond the second bed was the door to the bathroom. When you turned on the light in there, the fan would go on, too. If you wanted the light, you got the fan, too. There was no way around it. The light itself would be fluorescent, with the ghosts of dead flies inside. On the counter beside the sink there would be a hot plate and a Proctor-Silex electric kettle and little packets of instant coffee. There was a smell in here, the mingling of some harsh cleaning fluid and mildew on the shower curtain. Alfie knew it all. He had dreamed it right down to the green rug, but that was no accomplishment, it was an easy dream. He thought about turning on the heater, but that would rattle, too, and, besides, what was the point?

Alfie unbuttoned his topcoat and put his suitcase on the floor at the foot of the bed closest to the bathroom. He put his briefcase on the gold coverlet. He sat down, the sides of his coat spreading out like the skirt of a dress. He opened his briefcase, thumbed through the various brochures, catalogues, and order forms; finally he found the gun. It was a Smith & Wesson revolver, .38 caliber. He put it on the pillows at the head of the bed.

He lit a cigarette, reached for the telephone, then remembered his notebook. He reached into his right coat pocket and pulled it out. It was an old Spiral, bought for a buck forty-nine in the stationery department of some forgotten five-and-dime in Omaha or Sioux City or maybe Jubilee, Kansas. The cover was creased and almost completely innocent of any printing it might once have borne. Some of the pages had pulled partially free of the metal coil that served as the notebook's binding, but all of them were still there. Alfie had been carrying this notebook for almost seven years, ever since his days selling Universal Product Code readers for Simonex.

There was an ashtray on the shelf under the phone. Out here, some of the motel rooms still came with ashtrays, even on the first floor. Alfie fished for it, put his cigarette on the groove, and opened his notebook. He flipped through pages written with a hundred different pens (and a few pencils), pausing to read a couple of entries. One read: "I suckt Jim Morrison's cock w/my poutie boy mouth (LAWRENCE KS)." Restrooms were filled with homosexual graffiti, most of it tiresome and repetitive, but "poutie boy mouth" was pretty good. Another was "Albert Gore is my favorite whore (MURDO S DAK)."

The last page, three-quarters of the way through the book, had just two entries. "Dont chew the Trojan Gum it taste's just like rubber (AVOCA IA)." And: "Poopie doopie you so loopy (PAPILLION NEB)." Alfie was crazy about that one. Something about the "-ie, -ie," and then, boom, you got "-y." It could have been no more than an illiterate's mistake (he was sure that would have been Maura's take on it) but why think like that? What fun was that? No, Alfie preferred (even now) to believe that "-ie, -ie," . . . wait for it . . . "-y" was an intended construction. Something sneaky but playful, with the feel of an e. e. cummings poem.

He rummaged through the stuff in his inside coat pocket, feeling papers, an old toll-ticket, a bottle of pills—stuff he had quit taking—and at last finding the pen that always hid in the litter. Time to record today's finds. Two good ones, both from the same rest area, one over the urinal he had used, the other written with a Sharpie on the map case beside the Hav-A-Bite machine. (Snax, which in Alfie's opinion vended a superior product line, had for some reason been disenfranchised in the I-80 rest areas about four years ago.) These days Alfie sometimes went two weeks and three thousand miles without seeing anything new, or even a viable variation on something old. Now, two in one day. Two on the *last* day. Like some sort of omen.

His pen had COTTAGER FOODS THE *GOOD* STUFF! written in gold along the barrel, next to the logo, a thatched hut with smoke coming out of the quaintly crooked chimney.

Sitting there on the bed, still in his topcoat, Alfie bent studiously over his old notebook so that his shadow fell on the page. Below "Dont chew the Trojan Gum" and "Poopie doopie you so loopy," Alfie added "Save Russian Jews, collect valuable prizes (WALTON NEB)" and "All that you love will be carried away (WALTON NEB)." He hesitated. He rarely added notes, liking his finds to stand alone. Explanation rendered the exotic mundane (or so he had come to believe; in the early years he had annotated much more freely), but from time to time a footnote still seemed to be more illuminating than demystifying.

He starred the second entry—"All that you love will be carried away (WALTON NEB)"—and drew a line two inches above the bottom of the page, and wrote.*

He put the pen back in his pocket, wondering why he or anyone would continue anything this close to ending everything. He couldn't think of a single answer. But of course you went on breathing, too. You couldn't stop it without rough surgery.

The wind gusted outside. Alfie looked briefly toward the window, where the curtain (also green, but a different shade from the rug) had been drawn. If he pulled it back, he would be able to see chains of light on Interstate 80, each bright bead marking sentient beings running on the rod of the highway. Then he looked back down at his book. He meant to do it, all right. This was just . . . well . . .

"Breathing," he said, and smiled. He picked his cigarette out of the ashtray, smoked, returned it to the groove, and thumbed back through the book again. The entries recalled thousands of truck stops and roadside chicken shacks and highway rest areas the way certain songs on the radio can bring back specific memories of a place, a time, the person you were with, what you were drinking, what you were thinking.

---

*To read this you must also look at the exit ramp from the Walton Rest Area back to highway, i.e. at departing transients."

"Here I sit, brokenhearted, tried to shit but only farted." Everyone knew that one, but here was an interesting variation from Double D Steaks in Hooker, Oklahoma: "Here I sit, I'm at a loss, trying to shit out taco sauce. I know I'm going to drop a load, only hope I don't explode." And from Casey, Iowa, where SR 25 crossed I-80: "My mother made me a whore." To which someone had added in very different penmanship: "If I supply the yarn will she make me one?"

He had started collecting when he was selling the UPCs, noting various bits of graffiti in the Spiral notebook without at first knowing why he was doing it. They were just amusing, or disconcerting, or both at the same time. Yet little by little he had become fascinated with these messages from the interstate, where the only other communications seemed to be dipped headlights when you passed in the rain, or maybe somebody in a bad mood flipping you the bird when you went by in the passing lane pulling a rooster-tail of snow behind you. He came gradually to see—or perhaps only to hope— that something was going on here. The e. e. cummings lilt of "Poopie doopie you so loopy," for instance, or the inarticulate rage of "1380 West Avenue kill my mother TAKE HER JEWELS."

Or take this oldie: "Here I sit, cheeks a-flexin', giving birth to another Texan." The meter, when you considered it, was odd. Not iambs but some odd triplet formula with the stress on the third: "Here I *sit,* cheeks a-*flex*in', giving *birth* to a*noth*er *Tex*an." Okay, it broke down a little at the end, but that somehow added to its memorability, gave it that final mnemonic twist of the tail. He had thought on many occasions that he could go back to school, take some courses, get all that feet-and-meter stuff down pat. Know what he was talking about instead of running on a tightrope of intuition. All he really remembered clearly from school was iambic pentameter: "To be or not to be, that is the question." He had seen that in a men's room on I-70, actually, to which someone had added, "The real question is who your father was, dipstick."

These triplets, now. What were *they* called? Was that trochaic? He didn't know. The fact that he could find out no longer seemed important, but he could find out, yes. It was something people taught; it was no big secret.

Or take this variation, which Alfie had also seen all over the country: "Here I sit, on the pooper, giving birth to a Maine state trooper." It was always Maine, no matter where you were it was always Maine State Trooper, and why? Because no other state would scan. Maine was the only one of the fifty whose name consisted of a single syllable. Yet again, it was in triplets: "Here I *sit,* on the *poop*er."

He had thought of writing a book. Just a little one. The first title to occur to him had been "Don't Look Up Here, You're Pissing on Your Shoes," but you couldn't call a book that. Not and reasonably hope someone would put it out for sale in a store, anyway. And, besides, that was light. Frothy. He had become convinced over the years that something was going on here, and it wasn't frothy. The title he had finally decided on was an adaptation of something he'd seen in a rest-area toilet stall outside Fort Scott, Kansas, on Highway 54. "I Killed Ted Bundy: The Secret Transit Code of America's Highways." By Alfred Zimmer. That sounded mysterious and ominous, almost scholarly. But he hadn't done it. And although he had seen "If I supply the yarn, will she make me one" added to "My mother made me a whore" all over the country, he had never expounded (at least in writing) on the startling lack of sympathy, the "just deal with it" sensibility, of the response. Or what about "Mammon is the King of New Jersey"? How did one explain why New Jersey made it funny and the name of some other state probably wouldn't? Even to try seemed almost arrogant. He was just a little man, after all, with a little man's job. He sold things. A line of frozen dinners, currently.

And now, of course . . . now . . .

Alfie took another deep drag on his cigarette, mashed it out, and called home. He didn't expect to get Maura and didn't. It was his own recorded voice that answered him, ending with the number of his cellphone. A lot of good that would do; the cell-phone was in the trunk of the Chevrolet, broken. He had never had good luck with gadgets.

After the beep he said, "Hi, it's me. I'm in Lincoln. It's snowing. Remember the casserole you were going to take over to my mother. She'll be expecting it. And she asked for the Red Ball coupons. I know you think she's crazy on that subject, but humor her, okay? She's old. Tell Carlene Daddy says hi." He paused, then for the first time in about five years added, "I love you."

He hung up, thought about another cigarette—no worries about lung cancer, not now—and decided against it. He put the notebook, open to the last page, beside the telephone. He picked up the gun and rolled out the cylinder. Fully loaded. He snapped the cylinder back in with a flick of his wrist, then slipped the short barrel into his mouth. It tasted of oil and metal. He thought, *Here I* SIT, *about to* COOL it, *my plan to* EAT a fuckin' BOOL-*it*. He grinned around the barrel. That was terrible. He never would have written that down in his book.

Then another thought occurred to him and he put the gun back in its trench on the pillow, drew the phone to him again, and once more dialed home. He waited for his voice to recite the useless cell-phone number, then said, "Me again. Don't forget Rambo's appointment at the vet day after tomorrow, okay? Also the sea-jerky strips at night. They really do help his hips. Bye."

He hung up and raised the gun again. Before he could put the barrel in his mouth, his eye fell on the notebook. He frowned and put the gun down. The book was open to the last four entries. The first thing anyone responding to the shot would see would be his dead body, sprawled across the bed closest to the bathroom, his head hanging down and bleeding on the nubbly green rug. The second thing, however, would be the Spiral notebook, open to the final written page.

Alfie imagined some cop, some Nebraska state trooper who would never be written about on any bathroom wall due to the disciplines of scansion, reading those final entries, perhaps turning the battered old notebook toward him with the tip of his own pen. He would read the first three entries—"Trojan Gum," "Poopie doopie," "Save Russian Jews"—and dismiss them as insanity. He would read the last line, "All that you love will be carried away," and decide that the dead guy had regained a little rationality at the end, just enough to write a halfway sensible suicide note.

Alfie didn't like the idea of people thinking he was crazy (further examination of the book, which contained such information as "Medger Evers is alive and well in Disneyland," would only confirm that impression). He was not crazy, and the things he had written here over the years weren't crazy, either. He was convinced of it. And if he was wrong, if these were the rantings of lunatics, they needed to be examined even more closely. That thing about don't look up here, you're pissing on your shoes, for instance, was that humor? Or a growl of rage?

He considered using the john to get rid of the notebook, then shook his head. He'd end up on his knees with his shirtsleeves rolled back, fishing around in there, trying to get the damn thing back out. While the fan rattled and the fluorescent buzzed. And although immersion might blur some of the ink, it wouldn't blur all of it. Not enough. Besides, the notebook had been with him so long, riding in his pocket across so many flat and empty Midwest miles. He hated the idea of just flushing it away.

The last page, then? Surely one page, balled up, would go down. But that would leave the rest for them (there was always a them) to discover, all that clear evidence of an unsound mind. They'd say, "Lucky he didn't decide to visit a schoolyard with an AK-47. Take a bunch of little kids with him." And it would follow Maura like a tin can tied to a dog's tail. "Did you hear about her husband?" they'd ask each other in the supermarket. "Killed himself in a motel. Left a book full of crazy stuff. Lucky he didn't kill *her*." Well, he could afford to be a little hard about that. Maura was an adult, after all. Carlene, on the other hand . . . Carlene was . . .

Alfie looked at his watch. At her j.v. basketball game, that's where Carlene was right now. Her teammates would say most of the same things the supermarket ladies would say, only within earshot and accompanied by those chilling seventh-grade giggles. Eyes full of glee and horror. Was that fair? No, of course not, but there was nothing fair about what had happened to him, either. Sometimes when you were cruising along the highway, you saw big curls of rubber that had unwound from the recap tires some of the independent truckers used. That was what he felt like now: thrown tread. The pills made it worse. They cleared your mind just enough for you to see what a colossal jam you were in.

"But I'm not crazy," he said. "That doesn't make me crazy." No. Crazy might actually be better.

Alfie picked up the notebook, flipped it closed much as he had flipped the cylinder back into the .38, and sat there tapping it against his leg. This was ludicrous.

Ludicrous or not, it nagged him. The way thinking a stove burner might still be on sometimes nagged him when he was home, nagged until he finally got up and checked and found it cold. Only this was worse. Because he loved the stuff in the notebook. Amassing graffiti—thinking about graffiti—had been his real work these last years, not selling price-code readers or frozen dinners that were really not much more than Swansons or Freezer Queens in fancy microwavable dishes. The daffy exuberance of "Helen Keller fucked her feller!" for instance. Yet the notebook might be a real embarrassment once he was dead. It would be like accidentally hanging yourself in the closet because you were experimenting with a new way of jacking off and got found that way with your shorts under your feet and shit on your ankles. Some of the stuff in his notebook might show up in the newspaper, along with his picture. Once upon a time he would have scoffed at the idea, but in these days, when even Bible Belt newspapers routinely speculated about a mole on the President's penis, the notion was hard to dismiss.

Burn it, then? No, he'd set off the goddamned smoke detector.

Put it behind the picture on the wall? The picture of the little boy with the fishing pole and the straw hat?

Alfie considered this, then nodded slowly. Not a bad idea at all. The Spiral notebook might stay there for years. Then, someday in the distant future, it would drop out. Someone—perhaps a lodger, more likely a maid—would pick it up, curious. Would flip through it. What would that person's reaction be? Shock? Amusement? Plain old head-scratching puzzlement? Alfie rather hoped for this last. Because things in the notebook were puzzling. "Elvis killed Big Pussy," someone in Hackberry, Texas, had written. "Serenity is being square," someone in Rapid City, South Dakota, had opined. And below that, someone had written, "No, stupid, serenity$=(va)^2+b$, if $v=$serenity, $a=$satisfaction, and $b=$sexual compatibility."

Behind the picture, then.

Alfie was halfway across the room when he remembered the pills in his coat pocket. And there were more in the glove compartment of the car, different kinds but for the same thing. They were prescription drugs, but not the sort the doctor gave you if you were feeling . . . well . . . sunny. So the cops would search this room thoroughly for other kinds of drugs and when they lifted the picture away from the wall the notebook would drop out onto the green rug. The things in it would look even worse, even crazier, because of the pains he had taken to hide it.

And they'd read the last thing as a suicide note, simply because it *was* the last thing. No matter where he left the book, that would happen. Sure as shit sticks to the ass of America, as some East Texas turnpike poet had once written.

"If they find it," he said, and just like that the answer came to him.

The snow had thickened, the wind had grown even stronger, and the spark lights across the field were gone. Alfie stood beside his snow-covered car at the edge of the parking lot with his coat billowing out in front of him. At the farm, they'd all be watching TV by now. The whole fam' damly. Assuming the satellite dish hadn't blown off the barn roof, that was. Back at his place, his wife and daughter would be arriving home from Carlene's basketball game. Maura and Carlene lived in a world that had little to do with the interstates, or fast-food boxes blowing down the breakdown lanes and the sound of semis passing you at seventy and eighty and even ninety miles an hour like a Doppler whine. He wasn't complaining about it (or hoped he wasn't); he was just pointing it out. "Nobody here even if there is," someone in Chalk Level, Missouri, had written on a shithouse wall, and sometimes in those rest-area bathrooms there was blood, mostly just a little, but once he had seen a grimy basin under a scratched steel mirror half filled with it. Did anyone notice? Did anyone report such things?

In some rest areas the weather report fell constantly from overhead speakers, and to Alfie the voice giving it sounded haunted, the voice of a ghost running through the vocal cords of a corpse. In Candy, Kansas, on Route 283, in Ness County, someone had written, "Behold, I stand at the door and knock," to which someone else had added, "If your not from Pudlishers Cleering House go away you Bad Boy."

Alfie stood at the edge of the pavement, gasping a little because the air was so cold and full of snow. In his left hand he held the Spiral notebook, bent almost double. There was no need to destroy it, after all. He would simply throw it into Farmer John's east field, here on the west side of Lincoln. The wind would help him. The notebook might carry twenty feet on the fly, and the wind could tumble it even farther before it finally fetched up against the side of the furrow and was covered. It would lie there buried all winter, long after his body had been shipped home. In the spring, Farmer John would come out this way on his tractor, the cab filled with the music of Patty Loveless or George Jones or maybe even Clint Black, and he would plow the Spiral notebook under without seeing it and it would disappear into the scheme of things. Always supposing there was one. "Relax, it's all just the rinse cycle," someone had written beside a pay phone on I-35 not far from Cameron, Missouri.

Alfie drew the book back to throw it, then lowered his arm. He hated to let it go, that was the truth of it. That was the bottom line everyone was always talking about. But things were bad, now. He raised his arm again and then lowered it again. In his distress and indecision he began to cry without being aware of it. The wind rushed around him, on its way to wherever. He couldn't go on living the way he had been living, he knew that much. Not one more day. And a shot in the mouth would be easier than any living change, he knew that, too. Far easier than struggling to write a book few people (if any at all) were likely to read. He raised his arm again, cocked the hand with the notebook in it back to his ear like a pitcher preparing to throw a fastball, then stood like that. An idea had occurred to him. He would count to sixty. If the spark lights of the farmhouse reappeared at any time during that count, he would try to write the book.

To write a book like that, he thought, you'd have to begin by talking about how it was to measure distance in green mile markers, and the very width of the land, and how the wind sounded when you got out of your car at one of those rest areas in Oklahoma or North Dakota. How it sounded almost like words. You'd have to explicate the silence, and how the bathrooms always smelled of piss and the great hollow farts of departed travellers, and how in that silence the voices on the walls began to speak. The voices of those who had written and then moved on. The telling would hurt, but if the wind dropped and the spark lights of the farm came back, he'd do it anyway.

If they didn't he'd throw the notebook into the field, go back into Room 190 (just hang a left at the Snax machine), and shoot himself, as planned.

Either way. Either way.

Alfie stood there counting to sixty inside his head, waiting to see if the wind would drop.

––––––––––

I like to drive, and I'm particularly addicted to those long interstate barrels where you see nothing but prairies to either side and a cinderblock rest area every forty miles or so. Rest-area bathrooms are always full of graffiti, some of it extremely weird. I started to collect these dispatches from nowhere, keeping them in a pocket notebook, got others off the Internet (there are two or three websites dedicated to them), and finally found the story in which they belonged. This is it. I don't know if it's good or not, but I cared very much for the lonely man at its center and really hope things turned out okay for him. In the first draft things did, but Bill Buford of The New Yorker *suggested a more ambiguous ending. He was probably right, but we could all say a prayer for the Alfie Zimmers of the world.*

The Death
of Jack Hamilton

Want you to get one thing straight from the start: wasn't nobody on earth didn't like my pal Johnnie Dillinger, except Melvin Purvis of the F.B.I. Purvis was J. Edgar Hoover's right-hand man, and he hated Johnnie like poison. Everyone else—well, Johnnie had a way of making folks like him, that's all. And he had a way of making people laugh. God makes it come right in the end, that's something he used to say. And how can you not like a guy with that kind of philosophy?

But people don't want to let a man like that die. You'd be surprised how many folks still say it wasn't Johnnie the Feds knocked down in Chicago beside the Biograph Theater on July 22, 1934. After all, it was Melvin Purvis who'd been in charge of hunting Johnnie down, and, besides being mean, Purvis was a goddam fool (the sort of man who'd try to piss out a window without remembering to open it first). You won't hear no better from me, either. Little fag of a dandy, how I hated him! How we all did!

We got away from Purvis and the Gees after the shootout at Little Bohemia, Wisconsin—all of us! The biggest mystery of the year was how that goddam pansy ever kept his job. Johnnie once said, "J. Edgar probably can't get that good a blow job from a dame." How we laughed! Sure, Purvis got Johnnie in the end, but only after setting an ambush outside the Biograph and shooting him in the back while he was running down an alley. He fell down in the muck and the cat shit and said, "How's this, then?" and died.

Still folks won't believe it. Johnnie was handsome, they say, looked almost like a movie star. The fella the Gees shot outside the Biograph had a fat face, all swollen up and bloated like a cooked sausage. Johnnie was barely thirty-one, they say, and the mug the cops shot that night looked forty, easy! Also (and here they drop their voices to a whisper), everyone knows John Dillinger had a pecker the size of a Louisville Slugger. That fella Purvis ambushed outside the Biograph didn't have nothing but the standard six inches. And then there's the matter of that scar on his upper lip. You can see it clear as day in the morgue photographs (like the one where some yo-yo is holding up my old pal's head and looking all solemn, as if to tell the world once and for all that Crime Does Not Pay). The scar cuts the side of Johnnie's mustache in two. Everyone knows John Dillinger never had a scar like that, people say; just look at any of the other pictures. God knows there's enough of them.

There's even a book that says Johnnie didn't die—that he lived on long after the rest of his running buddies, and finished up in Mexico, living in a haci and pleasing any number of *señoras* and *señoritas* with his oversized tool. The book claims that my old pal died

on November 20, 1963—two days before Kennedy—
at the ripe old age of sixty, and it wasn't no federal bullet that took him off but a plain old heart attack, that
John Dillinger died in bed.

It's a nice story, but it ain't true.

Johnnie's face looks big in those last photos because
he'd really packed on the pounds. He was the type who
eats when he's nervous, and after Jack Hamilton died,
in Aurora, Illinois, Johnnie felt he was next. Said as
much, in that gravel pit where we took poor old Jack.

As for his tool—well, I'd known Johnnie ever since
we met at Pendleton Reformatory in Indiana. I saw
him dressed and undressed, and Homer Van Meter is
here to tell you that he had a good one, but not an
especially great one. (I'll tell you who had a great one,
if you want to know: Dock Barker—the mama's boy!
Ha!)

Which brings me to the scar on Johnnie's upper lip,
the one you can see cutting through his mustache in
those pictures where he's lying on the cooling board.
The reason the scar doesn't show in any of Johnnie's
other pictures is that he got it near the end. It happened in Aurora, while Jack (Red) Hamilton, our old
pal, was on his deathbed. That's what I want to tell
you about: how Johnnie Dillinger got the scar on his
upper lip.

Me and Johnnie and Red Hamilton got away from the
Little Bohemia shootout through the kitchen windows
in back, making our way down the side of the lake
while Purvis and his idiots were still pouring lead into
the front of the lodge. Boy, I hope the kraut who

owned the place had insurance! The first car we found belonged to an elderly neighbor couple, and it wouldn't start. We had better luck with the second—a Ford coupe that belonged to a carpenter just up the road. Johnnie put him in the driver's seat, and he chauffeured us a good way back toward St. Paul. Then he was invited to step out—which he did quite willingly—and I took over.

We crossed the Mississippi about twenty miles downriver from St. Paul, and although the local cops were all on the lookout for what they called the Dillinger Gang, I think we would have been all right if Jack Hamilton hadn't lost his hat while we were making our escape. He was sweating like a pig—he always did when he was nervous—and when he found a rag on the backseat of the carpenter's car he whipped it into a kind of rope and tied it around his head, Injun style. That was what caught the eye of those cops parked on the Wisconsin side of the Spiral Bridge as we went past them, and they came after us for a closer look.

That might have been the end of us right there, but Johnnie always had the Devil's own luck—until the Biograph, anyway. He put a cattle truck right between us and them, and the cops couldn't get past.

"Step on it, Homer!" Johnnie shouts at me. He was in the backseat, and in rare good humor from the sound of him. "Make it walk!"

I did, too, and we left the cattle truck in the dust, with those cops stuck behind it. So long, Mother, I'll write when I get work. Ha!

Once it seemed we had them buried for good, Jack

says, "Slow down, you damned fool—no sense getting picked up for speeding."

So I slowed down to thirty-five and for a quarter of an hour everything was fine. We were talking about Little Bohemia, and whether or not Lester (the one they were always calling Baby Face) might have gotten away, when all at once there's the crackle of rifles and pistols, and the sound of bullets whining off the pavement. It was those hick cops from the bridge. They'd caught up, creeping easy the last ninety or a hundred yards, and were close enough now to be shooting for the tires—they probably weren't entirely sure, even then, that it was Dillinger.

They weren't in doubt for long. Johnnie broke out the back window of the Ford with the butt of his pistol and started shooting back. I mashed the gas pedal again and got that Ford all the way up to fifty, which was a tearing rush in those days. There wasn't much traffic, but what there was I passed any way I could— on the left, on the right, in the ditch. Twice I felt the driver's-side wheels go up, but we never tipped. Nothing like a Ford when it came to a getaway. Once Johnnie wrote to Henry Ford himself. "When I'm in a Ford, I can make any car take my dust," he told Mr. Ford, and we surely dusted them that day.

We paid a price, though. There were these *spink! spink! spink!* noises, and a crack ran up the windshield and a slug—I'm pretty sure it was a .45—fell dead on the dashboard. It looked like a big black elm beetle.

Jack Hamilton was in the passenger seat. He got his tommy gun off the floor and was checking the drum, ready to lean out the window, I imagine, when there came another of those *spink!* noises. Jack says, "Oh! Bastard! I'm hit!" That bullet had to have come in the busted back window and how it missed Johnnie to hit Jack I don't know.

"Are you all right?" I shouted. I was hung over the wheel like a monkey and driving like one, too, very likely. I passed a Coulee Dairy truck on the right, honking all the time, yelling for that white-coat-farmer-son-of-a-bitch to get out of my road. "Jack, are you all right?"

"I'm okay, I'm fine!" he says, and shoves himself and his sub gun out the window, almost to his waist. Only, at first the milk truck was in the way. I could see the driver in the mirror, gawking at us from under his little hat. And when I looked over at Jack as he leaned out I could see a hole, just as neat and round as something you'd draw with a pencil, in the middle of his overcoat. There was no blood, just that little black hole.

"Never mind Jack, just run the son of a bitch!" Johnnie shouted at me.

I ran it. We gained maybe half a mile on the milk truck, and the cops stuck behind it the whole while because there was a guardrail on one side and a line of slowpoke traffic coming the other way. We turned hard, around a sharp curve, and for a moment both the milk truck and the police car were out of sight. Suddenly, on the right, there was a gravel road all grown in with weeds.

"In there!" Jack gasps, falling back into the passenger seat, but I was already turning in.

It was an old driveway. I drove about seventy

yards, over a little rise and down the other side, ending at a farmhouse that looked long empty. I killed the engine, and we all got out and stood behind the car.

"If they come, we'll give em a show," Jack says. "I ain't going to no electric chair like Harry Pierpont."

But no one came, and after ten minutes or so we got back in the car and drove out to the main road, all slow and careful. And that's when I saw something I didn't like much. "Jack," I says, "you're bleeding out your mouth. Look out or it'll be on your shirt."

Jack wiped his mouth with the big finger of his right hand, looked at the blood on it, and then gave me a smile that I still see in my dreams: big and broad and scared to death. "I just bit the inside of my cheek," says he. "I'm all right."

"You sure?" Johnnie asks. "You sound kind of funny."

"I can't catch all my breath just yet," Jack says. He wiped his big finger across his mouth again and there was less blood, and that seemed to satisfy him. "Let's get the fuck out of here."

"Turn back toward the Spiral Bridge, Homer," Johnnie says, and I did like he told me. Not all the stories about Johnnie Dillinger are true, but he could always find his way home, even after he didn't have no home no more, and I always trusted him.

We were once again doing a perfectly legal parson-go-to-meeting thirty miles per, when Johnnie saw a Texaco station and told me to turn off to the right. We were soon on country gravel roads, Johnnie calling lefts and rights, even though all the roads looked the same to me: just wheel ruts running between clapped-out cornfields. The roads were muddy, and there were still scraps of snow in some of the fields. Every now and then there'd be some hick kid watching us go by. Jack was getting quieter and quieter. I asked him how he was doing and he said, "I'm all right."

"Yes, well, we ought to get you looked at when we cool off a little," Johnnie said. "And we have to get your coat mended, too. With that hole in it, it looks like somebody shot you!" He laughed, and so did I. Even Jack laughed. Johnnie could always cheer you up.

"I don't think it went deep," Jack said, just as we came out on Route 43. "I'm not bleeding out of my mouth anymore—look." He turned to show Johnnie his finger, which now just had a maroon smear on it. But when he twisted back into his seat blood poured out of his mouth and nose.

"I think it went deep enough," Johnnie said. "We'll take care of you—if you can still talk, you're likely fine."

"Sure," Jack said. "I'm fine." His voice was smaller than ever.

"Fine as a fiddler's fuck," I said.

"Aw, shut up, you dummocks," he said, and we all had a laugh. They laughed at me a lot. It was all in fun.

About five minutes after we got back on the main road, Jack passed out. He slumped against the window, and a thread of blood trickled from one corner of his mouth and smeared on the glass. It reminded me of swatting a mosquito that's had its dinner—the claret everywhere. Jack still had the rag on his head, but it had gone crooked. Johnny took it off and cleaned the blood from Jack's face with it. Jack muttered and raised his hands as if to push Johnnie away, but they dropped back into his lap.

"Those cops will have radioed ahead," Johnnie says. "If we go to St. Paul, we're finished. That's what I think. How about you, Homer?"

"The same," I says. "What does that leave? Chicago?"

"Yep," he says. "Only first we have to ditch this motor. They'll have the plates by now. Even if they didn't, it's bad luck. It's a damn hoodoo."

"What about Jack?" I says.

"Jack will be all right," he says, and I knew to say no more on the subject.

We stopped about a mile down the road, and Johnnie shot out the front tire of the hoodoo Ford while Jack leaned against the hood, looking pale and sick.

When we needed a car, it was always my job to flag one down. "People who wouldn't stop for any of the rest of us will stop for you," Johnnie said once. "Why is that, I wonder?"

Harry Pierpont answered him. This was back in the days when it was still the Pierpont Gang instead of the Dillinger Gang. "Because he looks like a Homer," he said. "Wasn't ever anyone looked so much like a Homer as Homer Van Meter does."

We all laughed at that, and now here I was again, and this time it was really important. You'd have to say life or death.

Three or four cars went by and I pretended to be fiddling with the tire. A farm truck was next, but it was too slow and waddly. Also, there were some fellas in the back. Driver slows down and says, "You need any help, amigo?"

"I'm fine," I says. "Workin' up a appetite for lunch. You go right on."

He gives me a laugh and on he went. The fellas in the back also waved.

Next up was another Ford, all by its lonesome. I waved my arms for them to stop, standing where they couldn't help but see that flat shoe. Also, I was giving them a grin. That big one that says I'm just a harmless Homer by the side of the road.

It worked. The Ford stopped. There was three folks inside, a man and a young woman and a fat baby. A family.

"Looks like you got a flat there, partner," the man says. He was wearing a suit and a topcoat, both clean but not what you'd call Grade A.

"Well, I don't know how bad it can be," I says, "when it's only flat on the bottom."

We was still laughing over that just like it was new when Johnnie and Jack come out of the trees with their guns drawn.

"Just hold still, sir," Jack says. "No one is going to get hurt."

The man looked at Jack, looked at Johnnie, looked at Jack again. Then his eyes went back to Johnnie and his mouth dropped open. I seen it a thousand times, but it always tickled me.

"You're Dillinger!" he gasps, and then shoots his hands up.

"Pleased to meet you, sir," Johnnie says, and grabs one of the man's hands out of the air. "Get those mitts down, would you?"

Just as he did, another two or three cars came

along—country-go-to-town types, sitting up straight as sticks in their old muddy sedans. We didn't look like nothing but a bunch of folks at the side of the road getting ready for a tire-changing party.

Jack, meanwhile, went to the driver's side of the new Ford, turned off the switch, and took the keys. The sky was white that day, as if with rain or snow, but Jack's face was whiter.

"What's your name, Ma'am?" Jack asks the woman. She was wearing a long gray coat and a cute sailor's cap.

"Deelie Francis," she says. Her eyes were as big and dark as plums. "That's Roy. He's my husband. Are you going to kill us?"

Johnnie give her a stern look and says, "We are the Dillinger Gang, Mrs. Francis, and we have never killed anyone." Johnnie always made this point. Harry Pierpont used to laugh at him and ask him why he wasted his breath, but I think Johnnie was right to do that. It's one of the reasons he'll be remembered long after the straw-hat-wearing little pansy is forgot.

"That's right," Jack says. "We just rob banks, and not half as many as they say. And who is this fine little man?" He chucked the kiddo under the chin. He was fat, all right; looked like W. C. Fields.

"That's Buster," Deelie Francis says.

"Well, he's a regular little bouncer, ain't he?" Jack smiled. There was blood on his teeth. "How old is he? Three or so?"

"Just barely two and a half," Mrs. Francis says proudly.

"Is that so?"

"Yes, but he's big for his age. Mister, are you all

right? You're awful pale. And there's blood on your—"

Johnnie speaks up then. "Jack, can you drive this one into the trees?" He pointed at the carpenter's old Ford.

"Sure," Jack says.

"Flat tire and all?"

"You just try me. It's just that . . . I'm awful thirsty. Ma'am—Missus Francis—do you have anything to drink?"

She turned around and bent over—not easy with that horse of a baby in her arms—and got a thermos from the back.

Another couple of cars went puttering by. The folks inside waved, and we waved back. I was still grinning fit to split, trying to look just as Homer as a Homer could be. I was worried about Jack and didn't know how he could stay on his feet, let alone tip up that thermos and swig what was inside. Iced tea, she told him, but he seemed not to hear. When he handed it back to her, there were tears rolling down his cheeks. He thanked her, and she asked him again if he was all right.

"I am now," Jack says. He got into the hoodoo Ford and drove it into the bushes, the car jouncing up and down on the tire Johnnie had shot out.

"Why couldn't you have shot out a back one, you goddam fool?" Jack sounded angry and out of breath. Then he wrestled the car into the trees and out of sight, and came back, walking slow and looking at his feet, like an old man on ice.

"All right," Johnnie says. He'd discovered a rabbit's foot on Mr. Francis's key ring, and was working it in a way that made me know that Mr. Francis wasn't ever going to see that Ford again. "Now, we're all friends here, and we're going to take a little ride."

Johnnie drove. Jack sat in the passenger seat. I squeezed in back with the Francises and tried to get the piglet to shoot me a grin.

"When we get to the next little town," Johnnie says to the Francis family in the backseat, "we're going to drop you off with enough for bus fare to get you where you were going. We'll take the car. We won't hurt it a bit, and if no one shoots any bullet holes in it you'll get it back good as new. One of us'll phone you where it is."

"We haven't got a phone yet," Deelie says. It was really a whine. She sounded like the kind of woman who needs a smack every second week or so to keep her tits up. "We're on the list, but those telephone people are slower than cold molasses."

"Well, then," Johnnie says, good-humored and not at all perplexed, "we'll give the cops a call, and they'll get in touch. But if you squawk, you won't ever get it back in running shape."

Mr. Francis nodded as if he believed every word. Probably he did. This was the Dillinger Gang, after all.

Johnnie pulled in at a Texaco, gassed up, and bought soda pops all around. Jack drank a bottle of grape like a man dying of thirst in the desert, but the woman wouldn't let Master Piglet have his. Not so much as a swallow. The kid was holding his hands out for it and bawling.

"He can't have pop before his lunch," she says to Johnnie, "what's wrong with you?"

Jack was leaning his head against the glass of the passenger window with his eyes shut. I thought he'd passed out again, but he says, "Shut that brat up, missus, or I will."

"I think you've forgotten whose car you're in," she says, all haughty.

"Give him his pop, you bitch," Johnnie says. He was still smiling, but now it was his other smile. She looked at him and the color in her cheeks disappeared. And that's how Master Piglet got his Nehi, lunch or no lunch. Twenty miles farther on, we dropped them off in some little town and went on our way toward Chicago.

"A man who marries a woman like that deserves all he gets," Johnnie remarked, "and he'll get plenty."

"She'll call the law," Jack says, still without opening his eyes.

"Never will," Johnnie says, as confident as ever. "Wouldn't spare the nickel." And he was right. We saw only two blue beetles before we got into Chi, both going the other way, and neither one of them so much as slowed down to look at us. It was Johnnie's luck. As for Jack, you had only to look at him to know that his supply of luck was running out fast. By the time we got to the Loop, he was delirious and talking to his mother.

"Homer!" Johnnie says, in that wide-eyed way that always used to tickle me. Like a girl doing a flirt.

"What!" I says, giving him the glad eye right back.

"We got no place to go. This is worse than St. Paul."

"Go to Murphy's," Jack says without opening his eyes. "I want a cold beer. I'm thirsty."

"Murphy's," Johnnie says. "You know, that's not a bad idea."

Murphy's was an Irish saloon on the South Side. Sawdust, a steam table, two bartenders, three bouncers, friendly girls at the bar, and a room upstairs where you could take them. More rooms in the back, where people sometimes met, or cooled off for a day or two. We knew four places like it in St. Paul, but only a couple in Chi. I parked the Francises' Ford up in the alley. Johnnie was in the backseat with our delirious friend—we weren't yet ready to call him our dying friend—and he was holding Jack's head against the shoulder of his coat.

"Go in and get Brian Mooney off the bar," Johnnie says.

"What if he isn't there?"

"Then I don't know," Johnnie says.

"Harry!" Jack shouts, presumably calling for Harry Pierpont. "That whore you set me up with has given me the goddam clap!"

"Go on," Johnnie says to me, soothing his hand through Jack's hair just like a mother.

Well, Brian Mooney was there—Johnnie's luck again—and we got a room for the night, although it cost two hundred dollars, which was pretty dear, considering the view was an alley and the toilet was at the far end of the hall.

"You boys are hotter than hell," Brian says. "Mickey McClure would have sent you right back into the street. There's nothing in the papers and on the radio but Little Bohemia."

Jack sat down on a cot in the corner, and got himself

a cigarette and a cold draft beer. The beer brought him back wonderful; he was almost himself again. "Did Lester get away?" he asked Mooney. I looked over at him when he spoke up and saw a terrible thing. When he took a drag off his Lucky and inhaled, a little puff come out of the hole in the back of his overcoat like a smoke signal.

"You mean Baby Face?" Mooney asked.

"You don't want to call him that where he can hear you," Johnnie said, grinning. He was happier now that Jack had come back around, but he hadn't seen that puff of smoke coming out of his back. I wished I hadn't, either.

"He shot a bunch of Gees and got away," Mooney said. "At least one of the Gees is dead, maybe two. Anyway, it just makes it that much worse. You can stay here tonight, but you have to be gone by tomorrow afternoon."

He went out. Johnnie waited a few seconds, then stuck his tongue out at the door like a little kid. I got laughing—Johnnie could always make me laugh. Jack tried to laugh, too, but quit. It hurt him too much.

"Time to get you out of that coat and see how bad it is, partner," Johnnie said.

It took us five minutes. By the time he was down to his undershirt, all three of us were soaked with sweat. Four or five times I had to put my hands over Jack's mouth to muffle him. I got blood all over my cuffs.

There was no more than a rose on the lining of his overcoat, but his white shirt had gone half red and his undershirt was soaked right through. Sticking up on the left side, just below his shoulder blade, was a lump with a hole in the middle of it, like a little volcano.

"No more," Jack says, crying. "Please, no more."

"That's all right," Johnnie says, running the palm of his hand through Jack's hair again. "We're all done. You can lie down now. Go to sleep. You need your rest."

"I can't," he says. "It hurts too much. Oh, God, if you only knew how it hurts! And I want another beer. I'm thirsty. Only don't put so much salt in it this time. Where's Harry, where's Charlie?"

Harry Pierpont and Charlie Makley, I guessed—Charlie was the Fagin who'd turned Harry and Jack out when they weren't no more than snotnoses.

"There he goes again," Johnnie says. "He needs a doc, Homer, and you're the boy who has to find one."

"Jesus, Johnnie, this ain't my town!"

"Doesn't matter," Johnnie says. "If I go out, you know what's going to happen. I'll write down some names and addresses."

It ended up being just one name and one address, and when I got there it was all for nothing. The doc (a pill-roller whose mission was giving abortions and acid melts to erase fingerprints) had happied himself to death on his own laudanum two months before.

We stayed in that cheesy room behind Murphy's for five days. Mickey McClure showed up and tried to turn us out, but Johnnie talked to him in the way that Johnnie had—when he turned on the charm, it was almost impossible to tell Johnnie no. And, besides, we paid. By the fifth night, the rent was four hundred, and we were forbidden to so much as show our faces in the taproom for fear someone would see us. No one did, and as far as I know the cops never found out where we were during those five days in late April. I wonder how much Mickey McClure made on the deal—it was more than a grand. We pulled bank jobs where we took less.

I ended up going around to half a dozen scrape artists and hairline-changers. There wasn't one of them who would come and look at Jack. Too hot, they said. It was the worst time of all, and even now I hate to think about it. Let's just say that me and Johnnie found out what Jesus felt like when Peter Pilot denied Him three times in the Garden of Gethsemane.

For a while, Jack was in and out of delirium, and then he was mostly in. He talked about his mother, and Harry Pierpont, and then about Boobie Clark, a famous fag from Michigan City we'd all known.

"Boobie tried to kiss me," Jack said one night, over and over, until I thought I'd go nuts. Johnnie never minded, though. He just sat there beside Jack on the cot, stroking his hair. He'd cut out a square of cloth in Jack's undershirt around the bullet hole, and kept painting it with Mercurochrome, but the skin had already turned gray-green, and a smell was coming out of the hole. Just a whiff of it was enough to make your eyes water.

"That's gangrene," Mickey McClure said on a trip to pick up the rent. "He's a goner."

"He's no goner," Johnnie said.

Mickey leaned forward with his fat hands on his fat

knees. He smelled Jack's breath like a cop with a drunk, then pulled back. "You better find a doc fast. Smell it in a wound, that's bad. Smell it on a man's breath . . ." Mickey shook his head and walked out.

"Fuck him," Johnnie said to Jack, still stroking his hair. "What does he know?"

Only, Jack didn't say nothing. He was asleep. A few hours later, after Johnnie and I had gone to sleep ourselves, Jack was on the edge of the bunk, raving about Henry Claudy, the warden at Michigan City. I-God Claudy, we used to call him, because it was always I-God I'll do this and I-God you'll do that. Jack was screaming that he'd kill Claudy if he didn't let us out. That got someone pounding on the wall and yelling for us to shut that man up.

Johnnie sat next to Jack and talked to him and got him soothed down again.

"Homer?" Jack says after a while.

"Yes, Jack," I says.

"Won't you do the trick with the flies?" he asks.

I was surprised he remembered it. "Well," I says, "I'd be happy to, but there ain't no flies in here. Around these parts, flies ain't in season just yet."

In a low, hoarse voice, Jack sang, "There may be flies on some of you guys but there ain't no flies on me. Right, Chummah?"

I had no idea who Chummah was, but I nodded and patted his shoulder. It was hot and sticky. "That's right, Jack."

There were big purple circles under his eyes and dried spit on his lips. He was already losing weight. I could smell him, too. The smell of piss, which wasn't so bad, and the smell of gangrene, which was. Johnnie, though, never gave no sign that he smelled anything bad at all.

"Walk on your hands for me, John," Jack said. "Like you used to."

"In a minute," Johnnie said. He poured Jack a glass of water. "Drink this first. Wet your whistle. Then I'll see if I can still get across the room upside down. Remember when I used to run on my hands in the shirt factory? After I ran all the way to the gate, they stuck me in the hole."

"I remember," Jack said.

Johnnie didn't do no walking on his hands that night. By the time he got the glass of water to Jack's lips, the poor bugger had gone back to sleep with his head on Johnnie's shoulder.

"He's gonna die," I said.

"He's not," Johnnie said.

The next morning, I asked Johnnie what we were going to do. What we could do.

"I got one more name out of McClure. Joe Moran. McClure says he was the go-between on the Bremer kidnapping. If he'll fix Jack up, it's worth a thousand to me."

"I got six hundred," I said. And I'd give it up, but not for Jack Hamilton. Jack had gone beyond needing a doctor; what Jack needed by then was a preacher. I did it for Johnnie Dillinger.

"Thanks, Homer," he said. "I'll be back in an hour. Meantime, you mind the baby." But Johnnie looked bleak. He knew that if Moran wouldn't help us we'd have to get out of town. It would mean taking Jack back to St. Paul and trying there. And we knew what going back in a stolen Ford would likely mean. It was the spring of 1934 and all three of us—me, Jack, and especially Johnnie—were on J. Edgar Hoover's list of "public enemies."

"Well, good luck," I says. "See you in the funny pages."

He went out. I mooned around. I was mighty sick of the room by then. It was like being back in Michigan City, only worse. Because when you were in stir they'd done the worst they could to you. Here, hiding out in the back of Murphy's, things could always get worse.

Jack muttered, then he dropped off again.

There was a chair at the foot of the cot, with a cushion. I took the cushion and sat down beside Jack. It wouldn't take long, I didn't think. And when Johnnie came back I'd only have to say that poor old Jack took one final breath and just copped out. The cushion would be back on the chair. Really, it would be doing Johnnie a favor. Jack, too.

"I see you, Chummah," Jack says suddenly. I tell you, it scared the living hell out of me.

"Jack!" I says, putting my elbows on that cushion. "How you doing?"

His eyes drifted closed. "Do the trick . . . with the flies," he says, and then he was asleep again. But he'd woken up at just the right time; if he hadn't, Johnnie would have found a dead man on that cot.

When Johnnie finally did come back, he practically busted down the door. I had my gun out. He saw it and laughed. "Put away the bean shooter, pal, and pack up your troubles in your old kit bag!"

"What's up?"

"We're getting out of here, that's what." He looked five years younger. "High time, wouldn't you say?"

"Yeah."

"He been all right while I was gone?"

"Yeah," I said. The cushion lying on the chair had SEE YOU IN CHICAGO written on it in needlework.

"No change?"

"No change. Where are we going?"

"Aurora," Johnnie said. "It's a little town upstate. We're going to move in with Volney Davis and his girlfriend." He leaned over the cot. Jack's red hair, thin to start with, had started falling out. It was on the pillow, and you could see the crown of his head, white as snow. "You hear that, Jack?" Johnnie shouts. "We're hot now, but we're going to cool off quick! You understand?"

"Walk on your hands like Johnnie Dillinger used to," Jack said, without opening his eyes.

Johnnie just kept smiling. He winked at me. "He understands," he said. "He's just not awake. You know?"

"Sure," I said.

On the ride up to Aurora, Jack sat against the window, his head flying up and then thumping against the glass every time we hit a pothole. He was holding long, muttery conversations with folks we couldn't see. Once we were out of town, me and Johnnie had to roll down our windows. The smell was just too bad otherwise. Jack was rotting from the inside out, but he wouldn't die. I've heard it said that life is fragile and fleeting, but I don't believe it. It would be better if it was.

"That Dr. Moran was a crybaby," Johnnie said. We were in the woods by then, the city behind us. "I decided I didn't want no crybaby like him working on my partner. But I wasn't going to leave without something." Johnnie always travelled with a .38 pistol tucked into his belt. Now he pulled it out and showed it to me, the way he must have shown it to Dr. Moran. "I says, 'If I can't take away nothing else, Doc, I'll just have to take your life.' He seen I meant business, and he called someone up there. Volney Davis."

I nodded as if that name meant something to me. I found out later that Volney was another member of Ma Barker's gang. He was a pretty nice fella. So was Dock Barker. And Volney's girlfriend, the one they called Rabbits. They called her Rabbits because she dug herself out of prison a few times. She was the best of the lot. Aces. Rabbits, at least, tried to help poor old troublesome Jack. None of the others would—not the pillrollers, the scrapers, the face artists, and certainly not Dr. Joseph (Crybaby) Moran.

The Barkers were on the run after a botched kidnapping; Dock's Ma had already left—gone all the way to Florida. The hideout in Aurora wasn't much—four rooms, no electricity, a privy out back—but it was better than Murphy's saloon. And, like I say, Volney's girlfriend at least tried to do something. That was on our second night there.

She set up kerosene lamps all around the bed, then

sterilized a paring knife in a pot of boiling water. "If you boys feel pukey," she said, "you just choke it back until I'm done."

"We'll be okay," Johnnie said. "Won't we, Homer?"

I nodded, but I was queasy even before she got going. Jack was laying on his stomach, head turned to the side, muttering. It seemed he never stopped. Whatever room he happened to be in was filled with people only he could see.

"I hope so," she says, "because once I start in, there's no going back." She looked up and seen Dock standing in the doorway. Volney Davis, too. "Go on, baldy," she says to Dock, "and take-um heap big chief with you." Volney Davis was no more a Indian than I was, but they used to rib him because he was born in the Cherokee Nation. Some judge had given him three years for stealing a pair of shoes, which was how he got into a life of crime.

Volney and Dock went out. When they were gone, Rabbits turned Jack over and then cut him open in a X, bearing down in a way I could barely stand to look at. I held Jack's feet. Johnnie sat beside his head, trying to soothe him, but it didn't do no good. When Jack started to scream, Johnnie put a dishtowel over his head and nodded for Rabbits to go on, all the time stroking Jack's head and telling him not to worry, everything would be just fine.

That Rabbits. They call them frails, but there was nothing frail about her. Her hands never even shook. Blood, some of it black and clotted, come pouring out of the sunken place when she cut it. She cut deeper and then out came the pus. Some was white, but there was big green chunks which looked like boogers. That was bad. But when she got to the lung the smell was a thousand times worse. It couldn't have been worse in France during the gas attacks.

Jack was gasping in these big whistling breaths. You could hear it in his throat, and from the hole in his back, too.

"You better hurry up," Johnnie says. "He's sprung a leak in his air hose."

"You're telling me," she says. "The bullet's in his lung. You just hold him down, handsome."

In fact, Jack wasn't thrashing much. He was too weak. The sound of the air shrieking in and out of him kept getting thinner and thinner. It was hotter than hell with those lamps set up all around the bed, and the stink of the hot oil was almost as strong as the gangrene. I wish we'd thought to open a window before we got started, but it was too late by then.

Rabbits had a set of tongs, but she couldn't get them in the hole. "Fuck this!" she cried, and tossed them to one side, and then stuck her fingers into the bloody hole, reached around until she found the slug that was in there, pulled it out, and threw it to the floor. Johnnie started to bend over for it and she said, "You can get your souvenir later, handsome. For now just hold him."

She went to work packing gauze into the mess she'd made.

Johnnie lifted up the dishtowel and peeked underneath it. "Not a minute too soon," he told her with a grin. "Old Red Hamilton has turned a wee bit blue."

Outside, a car pulled into the driveway. It could

have been the cops, for all we knew, but there wasn't nothing we could do about it then.

"Pinch this shut," she told me, and pointed at the hole with the gauze in it. "I ain't much of a seamstress, but I guess I can put in half a dozen."

I didn't want to get my hands anywhere near that hole, but I wasn't going to tell her no. I pinched it shut, and more watery pus ran out when I did. My midsection clenched up and I started making this *gurk-gurk* noise. I couldn't help it.

"Come on," she says, kind of smiling. "If you're man enough to pull the trigger, you're man enough to deal with a hole." Then she sewed him up with these big, looping overhand strokes—really punching the needle in. After the first two, I couldn't look.

"Thank you," Johnnie told her when it was done. "I want you to know I'm going to take care of you for this."

"Don't go getting your hopes up," she says. "I wouldn't give him one chance in twenty."

"He'll pull through now," Johnnie says.

Then Dock and Volney rushed back in. Behind them was another member of the gang—Buster Daggs or Draggs, I can't remember which. Anyway, he'd been down to the phone they used at the Cities Service station in town, and he said the Gees had been busy back in Chicago, arresting anyone and everyone they thought might be connected to the Bremer kidnapping, which had been the Barker Gang's last big job. One of the fellas they took was John J. (Boss) McLaughlin, a high mucky-muck in the Chicago political machine. Another was Dr. Joseph Moran, also known as the Crybaby.

"Moran'll give this place up, just as sure as shit sticks to a blanket," Volney says.

"Maybe it's not even true," Johnnie says. Jack was unconscious now. His red hair lay on the pillow like little pieces of wire. "Maybe it's just a rumor."

"You better not believe that," Buster says. "I got it from Timmy O'Shea."

"Who's Timmy O'Shea? The Pope's butt-wiper?" Johnnie says.

"He's Moran's nephew," Dock says, and that kind of sealed the deal.

"I know what you're thinking, handsome," Rabbits says to Johnnie, "and you can stop thinking it right now. You put this fella in a car and go bumping him over those back roads between here and St. Paul, he'll be dead by morning."

"You could leave him," Volney says. "The cops show up, they'll have to take care of him."

Johnnie sat there, sweat running down his face in streams. He looked tired, but he was smiling. Johnnie was always able to find a smile. "They'd take care of him, all right," he says, "but they wouldn't take him to any hospital. Stick a pillow over his face and sit down on it, most likely." Which gave me a start, as I'm sure you'll understand.

"Well, you better decide," Buster says, "because they'll have this joint surrounded by dawn. I'm getting the hell out."

"You all go," Johnnie says. "You, too, Homer. I'll stay here with Jack."

"Well, what the hell," Dock says. "I'll stay, too."

"Why not?" Volney Davis says.

Buster Daggs or Draggs looked at them like they was crazy, but you know what? I wasn't surprised a bit. That's just the effect Johnnie had on people.

"I'll stay, too," I says.

"Well, I'm getting out," Buster says.

"Fine," Dock says. "Take Rabbits with you."

"The hell you say," Rabbits pipes up. "I feel like cooking."

"Have you gone cuckoo?" Dock asks her. "It's one o'clock in the morning, and you're in blood right up to the elbows."

"I don't care what time it is, and blood washes off," she says. "I'm making you boys the biggest breakfast you ever ate—eggs, bacon, biscuits, gravy, hash browns."

"I love you, marry me," Johnnie says, and we all laughed.

"Oh, hell," Buster says. "If there's breakfast, I'll hang around."

Which is how we all wound up staying put in that Aurora farmhouse, ready to die for a man who was already—whether Johnnie liked it or not—on his way out. We barricaded the front door with a sofa and some chairs, and the back door with the gas stove, which didn't work anyway. Only the woodstove worked. Me and Johnnie got our tommy guns from the Ford, and Dock got some more from the attic. Also a crate of grenades, a mortar, and a crate of mortar shells. I bet the Army didn't have as much stuff in those parts as we did. Ha-ha!

"Well, I don't care how many of them we get, as long as that son of a bitch Melvin Purvis is one of them," Dock says. By the time Rabbits actually got the grub on the table, it was almost the time farmers eat. We took it in shifts, two men always watching the long driveway. Buster raised the alarm once and we all rushed to our places, but it was only a milk truck on the main road. The Gees never came. You could call that bad info; I called it more of John Dillinger's luck.

Jack, meanwhile, was on his not-so-merry way from bad to worse. By midafternoon of the next day, even Johnnie must have seen he couldn't go on much longer, although he wouldn't come right out and say so. It was the woman I felt bad for. Rabbits seen new pus oozing out between those big black stitches of hers, and she started crying. She just cried and cried. It was like she'd known Jack Hamilton her whole life.

"Never mind," Johnnie said. "Chin up, beautiful. You did the best you could. Besides, he might still come around."

"It's cause I took the bullet out with my fingers," she says. "I never should have done that. I knew better."

"No," I says, "it wasn't that. It was the gangrene. The gangrene was already in there."

"Bullshit," Johnnie said, and looked at me hard. "An infection, maybe, but no gangrene. There isn't any gangrene now."

You could smell it in the pus. There wasn't nothing to say.

Johnnie was still looking at me. "Remember what Harry used to call you when we were in Pendleton?"

I nodded. Harry Pierpont and Johnnie were always the best of friends, but Harry never liked me. If not for Johnnie, he never would've taken me into the gang, which was the Pierpont Gang to begin with, remember. Harry thought I was a fool. That was another thing Johnnie would never admit, or even talk about. Johnnie wanted everyone to be friends.

"I want you to go out and wrangle up some big uns," Johnnie says, "just like you used to when you was on the Pendleton mat. Some big old buzzers." When he asked for that, I knew he finally understood Jack was finished.

Fly-Boy was what Harry Pierpont used to call me at Pendleton Reformatory, when we were all just kids and I used to cry myself to sleep with my head under my pillow so the screws wouldn't hear. Well, Harry went on and rode the lightning in Ohio State, so maybe I wasn't the only fool.

Rabbits was in the kitchen, cutting up vegetables for supper. Something was simmering on the stove. I asked her if she had thread, and she said I knew goddam well she did, hadn't I been right beside her when she sewed up my friend? You bet, I said, but that was black and I wanted white. Half a dozen pieces, about so long. And I held out my index fingers maybe eight inches apart. She wanted to know what I was going to do. I told her that if she was that curious she could watch right out the window over the sink.

"Ain't nothing out there but the privy," she says. "I got no interest in watching you do your personal business, Mr. Van Meter."

She had a bag hanging on the pantry door, and she rummaged through it and came out with a spool of white thread and cut me off six pieces. I thanked her kindly and then asked if she had a Band-Aid. She took some out of the drawer right beside the sink—because, she said, she was always cutting her fingers. I took one, then went to the door.

I got in Pendleton for robbing wallets off the New York Central line with that same Charlie Makley— small world, ain't it? Ha! Anyhow, when it come to ways of keeping the bad boys busy, the reformatory at Pendleton, Indiana, was loaded. They had a laundry, a carpentry shop, and a clothes factory where the dubs made shirts and pants, mostly for the guards in the Indiana penal system. Some called it the shirt shop; some called it the shit shop. That's what I drew—and met both Johnnie and Harry Pierpont. Johnnie and Harry never had any problem "making the day," but I was always coming up ten shirts short, or five pairs of trousers short, and being made to stand on the mat. The screws thought it was because I was always clowning around. Harry thought the same thing. The truth was that I was slow, and clumsy—which Johnnie seemed to understand. *That* was why I played around.

If you didn't make your day, you had to spend the next day in the guardhouse, where there was a rush mat, about two feet square. You had to take off everything but your socks and then stand there all day. If you stepped off the mat once, you got your ass paddled. If you stepped off twice, a screw held you while another worked you over. Step off a third time and it was a week in solitary. You were allowed all the water you wanted to drink, but that was a trick, because you were allowed only one toilet break in the course of the day. If you were caught standing there with piss running down your leg, you got a beating and a trip to the hole.

It was boring. Boring at Pendleton, boring at Michigan City, I-God's prison for big boys. Some fellows told themselves stories. Some fellows sang. Some made lists of all the women they were going to screw when they got out.

Me, I taught myself to rope flies.

A privy's a damned fine place for fly-roping. I took up my station outside the door, then proceeded to make loops in the pieces of thread Rabbits had given me. After that, there was nothing to it except not moving much. Those were the skills I'd learned on the mat. You don't forget them.

It didn't take long. Flies are out in early May, but they're slow flies. And anyone who thinks it's impossible to lasso a horsefly . . . well, all I can say is, if you want a challenge, try mosquitoes.

I took three casts and got my first one. That was nothing; there were times on the mat when I'd spend half the morning before I got my first. Right after I snagged him, Rabbits cried out, "What in God's name are you doing? Is it magic?"

From a distance, it *did* look like magic. You have to imagine how it appeared to her, twenty yards away: man standing by a privy throws out a little piece of thread—at nothing, so far as you can see—but, instead of drifting to the ground, the thread hangs in midair! It was attached to a good-sized horsefly. Johnnie would have seen it, but Rabbits didn't have Johnnie's eyes.

I got the end of the thread and taped it to the handle

of the privy door with the Band-Aid. Then I went after the next one. And the next. Rabbits came out to get a closer look, and I told her that she could stay if she was quiet, and she tried, but she wasn't good at being quiet and finally I had to tell her she was scaring off the game and send her back inside.

I worked the privy for an hour and a half—long enough that I couldn't smell it anymore. Then it started getting cold, and my flies were sluggish. I'd got five. By Pendleton standards, that was quite a herd, although not that many for a man standing next to a shithouse. Anyway, I had to get inside before it got too cold for them to stay airborne.

When I came walking slowly through the kitchen, Dock, Volney, and Rabbits were all laughing and clapping. Jack's bedroom was on the other side of the house, and it was shadowy and dim. That was why I'd asked for white thread instead of black. I looked like a man with a handful of strings leading up to invisible balloons. Except that you could hear the flies buzzing—all mad and bewildered, like anything else that's been caught it don't know how.

"I be dog," Dock Barker says. "I mean it, Homer. Double dog. Where'd you learn to do that?"

"Pendleton Reformatory," I says.

"Who showed you?"

"Nobody," I said. "I just did it one day."

"Why don't they tangle the strings?" Volney asked. His eyes were as big as grapes. It tickled me, I tell you that.

"Dunno," I says. "They always fly in their own space and don't hardly ever cross. It's a mystery."

"Homer!" Johnnie yells from the other room. "If you got em, this'd be a good time to get in here with em!"

I started across the kitchen, tugging the flies along by their halters like a good fly cowboy, and Rabbits touched my arm. "Be careful," she says. "Your pal is going, and it's made your other pal crazy. He'll be better—after—but right now he's not safe."

I knew it better than she did. When Johnnie set his heart on a thing, he almost always got it. Not this time, though.

Jack was propped up on the pillows with his head in the corner, and although his face was white as paper, he was in his right mind again. He'd come around at the end, like folks sometimes do.

"Homer!" he says, just as bright as you could want. Then he sees the strings and laughs. It was a shrill, whistley laughter, not a bit right, and immediately he starts to cough. Coughing and laughing, all mixed together. Blood comes out of his mouth—some splattered on my strings. "Just like Michigan City!" he says, and pounds his leg. More blood now, running down his chin and dripping onto his undershirt. "Just like old times!" He coughed again.

Johnnie's face looked terrible. I could see he wanted me to get out of the bedroom before Jack tore himself apart; at the same time, he knew it didn't matter a fiddler's fuck, and if this was a way Jack could die happy, looking at a handful of roped shithouse flies, then so be it.

"Jack," I says, "you got to be quiet."

"Naw, I'm all right now," he says, grinning and wheezing. "Bring em over here! Bring em over where I can see!" But before he could say any more he was coughing again, all bent over with his knees up, and the sheet, spattered with a spray of blood, like a trough between them.

I looked at Johnnie and he nodded. He'd passed beyond something in his mind. He beckoned me over. I went slowly, the strings in my hand, floating up, just white lines in the gloom. And Jack too tickled to know he was coughing his last.

"Let em go," he says, in a wet and husky voice I could hardly understand. "I remember . . ."

And so I did. I let the strings go. For a second or two, they stayed clumped together at the bottom— stuck together on the sweat from my palm—and then they drifted apart, hanging straight and upright in the air. I suddenly thought of Jack standing in the street after the Mason City bank job. He was firing his tommy gun and was covering me and Johnnie and Lester as we herded the hostages to the getaway car. Bullets flew all around him, and although he took a flesh wound, he looked like he'd live forever. Now he lay with his knees sticking up in a sheet filled with blood.

"Golly, look at em," he says as the white strings rose up, all on their own.

"That ain't all, either," Johnnie says. "Watch this." He then walked one step to the kitchen door, turned, and took a bow. He was grinning, but it was the saddest grin I ever saw in my life. All we did was the best we could; we couldn't very well give him a last meal, could we? "Remember how I used to walk on my hands in the shirt shop?"

"Yeah! Don't forget the spiel!" Jack says.

"Ladies and gentlemen!" Johnnie says. "Now in the center ring for your delight and amazement, John Herbert Dillinger!" He said the "G" hard, the way his old man said it, the way he had said it himself before he got so famous. Then he clapped once and dived forward onto his hands. Buster Crabbe couldn't have done it better. His pants slid up to his knees, showing the tops of his stockings and his shins. His change come out of his pockets and rattled away across the boards. He started walking across the floor that way, limber as ever, singing "Tra-ra-ra-boom-de-ay!" at the top of his voice. The keys from the stolen Ford fell out of his pocket, too. Jack was laughing in these big hoarse gusts—like he had the flu—and Dock Barker and Rabbits and Volney, all crowded in the doorway, were also laughing. Fit to split. Rabbits clapped her hands and called "Bravo! Encore!" Above my head the white threads were still floating on, only drifting apart a little at a time. I was laughing along with the rest, and then I saw what was going to happen and I stopped.

"Johnnie!" I shouted. "Johnnie, look out for your gun! Look out for your gun!"

It was that goddam .38 he kept tucked into the top of his pants. It was working free of his belt.

"Huh?" he said, and then it dropped onto the floor on top of the keys and went off. A .38 isn't the world's loudest gun, but it was loud enough in that back bedroom. And the flash was plenty bright. Dock yelled and Rabbits screamed. Johnnie didn't say nothing, just did a complete somersault and fell flat on his face. His feet came down with a crash, almost hitting the foot of the bed Jack Hamilton was dying in. Then he just lay there. I ran to him, brushing the white threads aside.

At first I thought he was dead, because when I turned him over there was blood all over his mouth and his cheek. Then he sat up. He wiped his face, looked at the blood, then looked at me.

"Holy shit, Homer, did I just shoot myself?" Johnnie says.

"I think you did," I says.

"How bad is it?"

Before I could tell him I didn't know, Rabbits pushed me to the side and wiped away the blood with her apron. She looked at him hard for a second or two, and then she says, "You're all right. It's just a scrape." Only we seen later, when she dabbled him up with the iodine, that it was actually two scrapes. The bullet cut through the skin over his lip on the right side, flew through maybe two inches of air, then it cut him again on the cheekbone, right beside his eye. After that it went into the ceiling, but before it did it plugged one of my flies. I know that's hard to believe, but it's true, I swear. The fly lay there on the floor in a little heap of white thread, nothing left of it but a couple of legs.

"Johnnie?" Dock says. "I think I got some bad news for you, partner." He didn't have to tell us what it was. Jack was still sitting up, but now his head was bowed over so far that his hair was touching the sheet between his knees. While we were checking to see how bad Johnnie was hurt, Jack had died.

*   *   *

Dock told us to take the body to a gravel pit about two miles farther down the road, just past the Aurora town line. There was a bottle of lye under the sink, and Rabbits gave it to us. "You know what to do with this, don't you?" she asks.

"Sure," Johnnie says. He had one of her Band-Aids stuck on his upper lip, over that place where his mustache never grew in later on. He sounded listless and he wouldn't meet her eye.

"Make him do it, Homer," she says, then jerked her thumb toward the bedroom, where Jack was laying wrapped up in the bloodstained sheet. "If they find that one and identify him before you get clear, it'll make things just so much worse for you. Us, too, maybe."

"You took us in when nobody else would," Johnnie says, "and you won't live to regret it."

She gave him a smile. Women almost always fell for Johnnie. I'd thought this one was an exception because she was so businesslike, but now I seen she wasn't. She'd just kept it all business because she knew she wasn't much in the looks department. Also, when a bunch of men with guns are cooped up like we were, a woman in her right mind doesn't want to make trouble among them.

"We'll be gone when you get back," Volney says. "Ma keeps talking about Florida, she got her eye on a place in Lake Weir—"

"Shut up, Vol," Dock says, and gives him a hard poke in the shoulder.

"Anyway, we're gettin' out of here," he says, rubbing the sore place. "You ought to get out, too. Take your luggage. Don't even pull in on your way back. Things can change in a hurry."

"Okay," Johnnie says.

"At least he died happy," Volney says. "Died laughin'."

I didn't say nothing. It was coming home to me that Red Hamilton—my old running buddy—was really dead. It made me awful sad. I turned my mind to how the bullet had just grazed Johnnie (and then gone on to kill a fly instead), thinking that would cheer me up. But it didn't. It only made me feel worse.

Dock shook my hand, then Johnnie's. He looked pale and glum. "I don't know how we ended up like this, and that's the truth," he says. "When I was a boy, the only goddam thing I wanted was to be a railroad engineer."

"Well, I'll tell you something," Johnnie says. "We don't have to worry. God makes it all come right in the end."

We took Jack on his last ride, wrapped up in a blood-stained sheet and pushed into the back of that stolen Ford. Johnnie drove us to the far side of the pit, all bump and jounce (when it comes to rough riding, I'll take a Terraplane over a Ford any day). Then he killed the engine and touched the Band-Aid riding his upper lip. He says, "I used up the last of my luck today, Homer. They'll get me now."

"Don't talk like that," I says.

"Why not? It's true." The sky above us was white and full of rain. I reckoned we'd have a muddy splash of it between Aurora and Chicago (Johnnie had decided we should go back there because the Feds would be expecting us in St. Paul). Somewhere crows was calling. The only other sound was the ticktock of the cooling engine. I kept looking into the mirror at the wrapped-up body in the backseat. I could see the bumps of elbows and knees, the fine red spatters where he'd bent over, coughing and laughing, at the end.

"Look at this, Homer," Johnnie says, and points to the .38, which was tucked back in his belt. Then he twiddled Mr. Francis's key ring with the tips of his fingers, where the prints were growing back in spite of all his trouble. There were four or five keys on the ring besides the one to the Ford. And that lucky rabbit's foot. "Butt of the gun hit this when it come down," he says. He nodded his head. "Hit my very own lucky piece. And now my luck's gone. Help me with him."

We lugged Jack to the gravel slope. Then Johnnie got the bottle of lye. It had a big brown skull and crossbones on the label.

Johnnie knelt down and pulled the sheet back. "Get his rings," he says, and I pulled them off. Johnnie put them in his pocket. We ended up getting forty-five dollars for them in Calumet City, although Johnnie swore up and down that the little one had a real diamond in it.

"Now hold out his hands."

I did, and Johnnie poured a cap of lye over the tip of each finger. That was one set of prints wasn't ever going to come back. Then he leaned over Jack's face and kissed him on the forehead. "I hate to do this, Red, but I know you'd do the same to me if it'd gone the other way."

He then poured the lye over Jack's cheeks and mouth and brow. It hissed and bubbled and turned white. When it started to eat through his closed eyelids, I turned away. And of course none of it done no good; the body was found by a farmer after a load of gravel. A pack of dogs had knocked away most of the stones we covered him with and were eating what was left of his hands and face. As for the rest of him, there were enough scars for the cops to I.D. him as Jack Hamilton.

It was the end of Johnnie's luck, all right. Every move he made after that—right up to the night Purvis and his badge-carrying gunsels got him at the Biograph—was a bad one. Could he have just thrown up his hands that night and surrendered? I'd have to say no. Purvis meant to have him dead one way or the other. That's why the Gees never told the Chicago cops Johnnie was in town.

I'll never forget the way Jack laughed when I brought them flies in on their strings. He was a good fellow. They all were, mostly—good fellows who got into the wrong line of work. And Johnnie was the best of the bunch. No man ever had a truer friend. We robbed one more bank together, the Merchants National in South Bend, Indiana. Lester Nelson joined us on that caper. Getting out of town, it seemed like every hick in Indiana was throwing lead at us, and we still got away. But for what? We'd been expecting more than a hundred grand, enough to move to Mexico and live like kings. We ended up with a lousy twenty thousand, most of it in dimes and dirty dollar bills.

God makes it all come right in the end, that's what Johnnie told Dock Barker just before we parted company. I was raised a Christian—I admit I fell away a bit along my journey—and I believe that: we're stuck with what we have, but that's all right; in God's eyes, none of us are really much more than flies on strings and all that matters is how much sunshine you can spread along the way. The last time I seen Johnnie Dillinger was in Chicago, and he was laughing at something I said. That's good enough for me.

———

As a kid, I was fascinated by tales of the Depression-era outlaws, an interest that probably peaked with Arthur Penn's remarkable Bonnie and Clyde. *In the spring of 2000, I re-read John Toland's history of that era,* The Dillinger Days, *and was particularly taken by his story about how Dillinger's sidekick, Homer Van Meter, taught himself how to rope flies in Pendleton Reformatory. Jack "Red" Hamilton's lingering death is a documented fact; my story of what happened in Dock Barker's hideout is, of course, pure imagination . . . or myth, if you like that word better; I do.*

In the Deathroom

It was a deathroom. Fletcher knew it for what it was as
soon as the door opened. The floor was gray industrial
tile. The walls were discolored white stone, marked
here and there with darker patches that might have
been blood—certainly blood had been spilled in this
room. The overhead lights were cupped in wire cages.
Halfway across the room stood a long wooden table
with three people seated behind it. Before the table
was an empty chair, waiting for Fletcher. Beside the
chair stood a small wheeled trolley. The object on it
had been draped with a piece of cloth, as a sculptor
might cover his work-in-progress between sessions.

Fletcher was half-led, half-dragged toward the chair
which had been placed for him. He reeled in the
guard's grip and let himself reel. If he looked more
dazed than he really was, more shocked and unthink-
ing, that was fine. He thought his chances of ever leaving this basement room in the Ministry of Information
were perhaps one or two in thirty, and perhaps that
was optimistic. Whatever they were, he had no intention of thinning them further by looking even halfway
alert. His swelled eye, puffy nose, and broken lower lip
might help in this regard; so might the crust of blood,

like a dark red goatee, around his mouth. One thing Fletcher knew for sure: if he *did* leave, the others—the guard and the three sitting in tribunal behind the table—would be dead. He was a newspaper reporter and had never killed anything much larger than a hornet, but if he had to kill to escape this room, he would. He thought of his sister, on her retreat. He thought of his sister swimming in a river with a Spanish name. He thought of the light on the water at noon, moving river light too bright to look at. They reached the chair in front of the table. The guard pushed him into it so hard that Fletcher almost tipped himself over.

"Careful now, that's not the way, no accidents," said one of the men behind the table. It was Escobar. He spoke to the guard in Spanish. To Escobar's left sat the other man. To Escobar's right sat a woman of about sixty. The woman and the other man were thin. Escobar was fat and as greasy as a cheap candle. He looked like a movie Mexican. You expected him to say, "Batches? *Batches?* We don't need no steenkin batches." Yet this was the Chief Minister of Information. Sometimes he gave the English-language portion of the weather on the city television station. When he did this he invariably got fan mail. In a suit he didn't look greasy, just roly-poly. Fletcher knew all this. He had done three or four stories on Escobar. He was colorful. He was also, according to rumor, an enthusiastic torturer. *A Central American Himmler,* Fletcher thought, and was amazed to discover that one's sense of humor—rudimentary, granted—could function this far into a state of terror.

"Handcuffs?" the guard asked, also in Spanish, and held up a pair of the plastic kind. Fletcher tried to keep his look of dazed incomprehension. If they cuffed him, it was over. He could forget about one chance in thirty, or one in three hundred.

Escobar turned briefly to the woman on his right. Her face was very dark, her hair black with startling white streaks. It flowed back and up from her forehead as if blown by a gale-force wind. The look of her hair reminded Fletcher of Elsa Lanchester in *Bride of Frankenstein*. He gripped this similarity with a fierceness that was close to panic, the way he gripped the thought of bright light on the river, or his sister laughing with her friends as they walked to the water. He wanted images, not ideas. Images were luxury items now. And ideas were no good in a place like this. In a place like this all you got were the wrong ideas.

The woman gave Escobar a small nod. Fletcher had seen her around the building, always garbed in shapeless dresses like the one she wore now. She had been with Escobar often enough for Fletcher to assume she was his secretary, personal assistant, perhaps even his biographer—Christ knew that men like Escobar had egos large enough to warrant such accessories. Now Fletcher wondered if he'd had it backward all along, if she was *his* boss.

In any case, the nod seemed to satisfy Escobar. When he turned back to Fletcher, Escobar was smiling. And when he spoke, it was in English. "Don't be silly, put them away. Mr. Fletcher is only here to help us in a few matters. He will soon be returning to his own country"—Escobar sighed deeply to show how deeply he regretted this. ". . . but in the meantime he is an honored guest."

We don't need no steenkin handcuffs, Fletcher thought.

The woman who looked like the Bride of Frankenstein with a very deep tan leaned toward Escobar and whispered briefly behind her hand. Escobar nodded, smiling.

"Of course, Ramón, if our guest should try anything foolish or make any aggressive moves, you would have to shoot him a little." He roared laughter—roly-poly TV laughter—and then repeated what he had said in Spanish, so that Ramón would understand as well as Fletcher. Ramón nodded seriously, replaced his handcuffs on his belt, and stepped back to the periphery of Fletcher's vision.

Escobar returned his attention to Fletcher. From one pocket of his parrot-and-foliage-studded guayabera he removed a red-and-white package: Marlboros, the preferred cigarette of third-world peoples everywhere. "Smoke, Mr. Fletcher?"

Fletcher reached toward the pack, which Escobar had placed on the edge of the table, then withdrew his hand. He had quit smoking three years ago, and supposed he might take the habit up again if he actually did get out of this—drinking high-tension liquor as well, quite likely—but at this moment he had no craving or need for a cigarette. He had wanted them to see his fingers shaking, that was all.

"Perhaps later. Right now a cigarette might—"

Might what? It didn't matter to Escobar; he just nodded understandingly and left the red-and-white pack where it was, on the edge of the table. Fletcher had a sudden, agonizing vision in which he saw himself stopping at a newsstand on Forty-third Street and buying a pack of Marlboros. A free man buying the happy poison on a New York street. He told himself that if he got out of this, he would do that. He would do it as some people went on pilgrimages to Rome or Jerusalem after their cancer was cured or their sight was restored.

"The men who did that to you"—Escobar indicated Fletcher's face with a wave of one not-particularly-clean hand—"have been disciplined. Yet not too harshly, and I myself stop short of apology, you will notice. Those men are patriots, as are we here. As you are yourself, Mr. Fletcher, yes?"

"I suppose." It was his job to appear ingratiating and frightened, a man who would say anything in order to get out of here. It was Escobar's job to be soothing, to convince the man in the chair that his swelled eye, split lip, and loosened teeth meant nothing; all that was just a misunderstanding which would soon be straightened out, and when it was he would be free to go. They were still busy trying to deceive each other, even here in the deathroom.

Escobar switched his attention to Ramón the guard and spoke in rapid Spanish. Fletcher's Spanish wasn't good enough to pick up everything, but you couldn't spend almost five years in this shithole capital city without picking up a fair vocabulary; Spanish wasn't the world's most difficult language, as both Escobar and his friend the Bride of Frankenstein undoubtedly knew.

Escobar asked if Fletcher's things had been packed and if he had been checked out of the Hotel Magnificent: *Sí.* Escobar wanted to know if there was a car waiting outside the Ministry of Information to take Mr. Fletcher to the airport when the interrogation was done. *Sí,* around the corner on the Street Fifth of May.

Escobar turned back and said, "Do you understand what I ask him?" From Escobar, *understand* came out *unnerstand,* and Fletcher thought again of Escobar's TV appearances. *Low bressure? What low bressure? We don't need no steenkin low bressure.*

"I ask have you been checked out of your room—although after all this time it probably seems more like an apartment to you, yes?—and if there's a car to take you to the airport when we finish our conversation." Except conversation hadn't been the word he used.

"Ye-es?" Sounding as if he could not believe his own good fortune. Or so Fletcher hoped.

"You'll be on the first Delta flight back to Miami," the Bride of Frankenstein said. She spoke without a trace of Spanish accent. "Your passport will be given back to you once the plane has touched down on American soil. You will not be harmed or held here, Mr. Fletcher—not if you cooperate with our inquiries—but you are being deported, let's be clear on that. Kicked out. Given what you Americans call the bum's rush."

She was much smoother than Escobar. Fletcher found it amusing that he had thought her Escobar's assistant. *And you call yourself a reporter,* he thought. Of course if he was just a reporter, the *Times's* man in Central America, he would not be here in the basement of the Ministry of Information, where the stains on the wall looked suspiciously like blood. He had ceased being a reporter some sixteen months ago, around the time he'd first met Núñez.

"I understand," Fletcher said.

Escobar had taken a cigarette. He lighted it with a gold-plated Zippo. There was a fake ruby in the side of the Zippo. He said, "Are you prepared to help us in our inquiries, Mr. Fletcher?"

"Do I have any choice?"

"You always have a choice," Escobar said, "but I think you have worn out your carpet in our country, yes? Is that what you say, worn out your carpet?"

"Close enough," Fletcher said. He thought: *What you must guard against is your desire to believe them. It is natural to want to believe, and probably natural to want to tell the truth—especially after you've been grabbed outside your favorite café and briskly beaten by men who smell of refried beans—but giving them what they want won't help you. That's the thing to hold onto, the only idea that's any good in a room like this. What they say means nothing. What matters is the thing on that trolley, the thing under that piece of cloth. What matters is the guy who hasn't said anything yet. And the stains on the walls, of course.*

Escobar leaned forward, looking serious.

"Do you deny that for the last fourteen months you have given certain information to a man named Tomás Herrera, who has in turn funneled it to a certain Communist insurgent named Pedro Núñez?"

"No," Fletcher said. "I don't deny it." To adequately keep up his side of this charade—the charade summarized by the difference between the words *conversation* and *interrogation*—he should now justify, attempt to explain. As if anyone in the history of the world had

ever won a political argument in a room like this. But
he didn't have it in him to do so. "Although it was a little longer than that. Almost a year and a half in all, I
think."

"Have a cigarette, Mr. Fletcher." Escobar opened a
drawer and took out a thin folder.

"Not just yet. Thank you."

"Okay." From Escobar it of course came out *ho-kay*.
When he did the TV weather, the boys in the control
room would sometimes superimpose a photograph of a
woman in a bikini on the weather map. When he saw
this, Escobar would laugh and wave his hands and pat
his chest. People liked it. It was comical. It was like the
sound of *ho-kay*. It was like the sound of *steenkin batches*.

Escobar opened the folder with his own cigarette
planted squarely in the middle of his mouth with the
smoke running up into his eyes. It was the way you
saw the old men smoking on the street corners down
here, the ones who still wore straw hats, sandals, and
baggy white pants. Now Escobar was smiling, keeping
his lips shut so his Marlboro wouldn't fall out of his
mouth and onto the table but smiling just the same.
He took a glossy black-and-white photograph out of
the thin folder and slid it across to Fletcher. "Here is
your friend Tomás. Not too pretty, is he?"

It was a high-contrast full-face shot. It made
Fletcher think of photographs by that semi-famous
news photographer of the forties and fifties, the one
who called himself Weegee. It was a portrait of a dead
man. The eyes were open. The flashbulb had reflected
in them, giving them a kind of life. There was no
blood, only one mark and no blood, but still one knew

at once that the man was dead. His hair was combed, one could still see the toothmarks the comb had left, and there were those little lights in his eyes, but they were reflected lights. One knew at once the man was dead.

The mark was on the left temple, a comet shape that looked like a powder burn, but there was no bullet hole, no blood, and the skull wasn't pushed out of shape. Even a low-caliber pistol like a .22, fired close enough to the skin to leave a powder burn, would have pushed the skull out of shape.

Escobar took the picture back, put it in the folder, closed the folder, and shrugged as if to say *You see? You see what happens?* When he shrugged, the ash fell off his cigarette onto the table. He brushed it off onto the gray lino floor with the side of one fat hand.

"We dint actually want to bother you," Escobar said. "Why would we? This a small country. We are small people in a small country. *The New York Times* a big paper in a big country. We have our pride, of course, but we also have our . . ." Escobar tapped his temple with one finger. "You see?"

Fletcher nodded. He kept seeing Tomás. Even with the picture back in the folder he could see Tomás, the marks the comb had left in Tomás's dark hair. He had eaten food Tomás's wife had cooked, had sat on the floor and watched cartoons with Tomás's youngest child, a little girl of perhaps five. Tom and Jerry cartoons, with what little dialogue there was in Spanish.

"We don't want to bother you," Escobar was saying as the cigarette smoke rose and broke apart on his face and curled around his ears, "but for a long time we was watching. You dint see us—maybe because you are so big and we are just little—but we was watching. We know that you know what Tomás knows, and so we go to him. We try to get him to tell what he knows so we don't have to bother you, but he won't. Finally we ask Heinz here to try and make him tell. Heinz, show Mr. Fletcher how you try to make Tomás tell, when Tomás was sitting right where Mr. Fletcher was sitting now."

"I can do that," said Heinz. He spoke English in a nasal New York accent. He was bald, except for a fringe of hair around his ears. He wore little glasses. Escobar looked like a movie Mexican, the woman looked like Elsa Lanchester in *Bride of Frankenstein*, Heinz looked like an actor in a TV commercial, the one who explained why Excedrin was best for your headache. He walked around the table to the trolley, gave Fletcher a look both roguish and conspiratorial, and flicked away the cloth over the top.

There was a machine underneath, something with dials and lights that were now all dark. Fletcher at first thought it was a lie detector—that made a certain amount of sense—but in front of the rudimentary control panel, connected to the side of the machine by a fat black cord, was an object with a rubber grip. It looked like a stylus or some sort of fountain pen. There was no nib, though. The thing just tapered to a blunt steel point.

Below the machine was a shelf. On the shelf was a car battery marked DELCO. There were rubber cups over the battery terminals. Wires rose from the rubber cups to the back of the machine. No, not a lie detector. Except maybe to these people it was.

Heinz spoke briskly, with the pleasure of a man who likes to explain what he does. "It's quite simple, really, a modification of the device neurologists use to administer electric shocks to people suffering unipolar neurosis. Only this administers a far more powerful jolt. The pain is really secondary, I find. Most people don't even remember the pain. What makes them so eager to talk is an aversion to the process. This might almost be called an atavism. Someday I hope to write a paper."

Heinz picked up the stylus by its insulated rubber grip and held it in front of his eyes.

"This can be touched to the extremities . . . the torso . . . the genitals, of course . . . but it can also be inserted in places where—forgive the crudity—the sun never shines. A man whose shit has been electrified never forgets it, Mr. Fletcher."

"Did you do that to Tomás?"

"No," Heinz said, and replaced the stylus carefully in front of the shock-generator. "He got a jolt at half-power on the hand, just to acquaint him with what he was up against, and when he still declined to discuss El Cóndor—"

"Never mind that," the Bride of Frankenstein said.

"Beg pardon. When he still wouldn't tell us what we wanted to know, I applied the wand to his temple and administered another measured jolt. Carefully measured, I assure you, half-power, not a bit more. He had a seizure and died. I believe it may have been epilepsy. Did he have a history of epilepsy, do you know, Mr. Fletcher?"

Fletcher shook his head.

"Nevertheless, I believe that's what it was. The autopsy revealed nothing wrong with his heart." Heinz folded his long-fingered hands in front of him and looked at Escobar.

Escobar removed his cigarette from the center of his mouth, looked at it, dropped it to the gray tile floor, stepped on it. Then he looked at Fletcher and smiled. "Very sad, of course. Now I ask you some questions, Mr. Fletcher. Many of them—I tell you this frankly—are the questions Tomás Herrera refused to answer. I hope you will not refuse, Mr. Fletcher. I like you. You sit there in dignity, do not cry or beg or urinate the pants. I like you. I know you only do what you believe. It is patriotism. So I tell you, my friend, it's good if you answer my questions quickly and truthfully. You don't want Heinz to use his machine."

"I've said I'd help you," Fletcher said. Death was closer than the overhead lights in their cunning wire cages. Pain, unfortunately, was closer yet. And how close was Núñez, El Cóndor? Closer than these three guessed, but not close enough to help him. If Escobar and the Bride of Frankenstein had waited another two days, perhaps even another twenty-four hours . . . but they had not, and he was here in the deathroom. Now he would see what he was made of.

"You said it and you had better mean it," the woman said, speaking very clearly. "We're not fucking around, *gringo*."

"I know you're not," Fletcher said in a sighing, trembling voice.

"You want that cigarette now, I think," said Escobar,

and when Fletcher shook his head, Escobar took one himself, lit it, then seemed to meditate. At last he looked up. This cigarette was planted in the middle of his face like the last one. "Núñez comes soon?" he asked. "Like Zorro in that movie?"

Fletcher nodded.

"How soon?"

"I don't know." Fletcher was very aware of Heinz standing next to his infernal machine with his long-fingered hands folded in front of him, looking ready to talk about pain-relievers at the drop of a cue. He was equally aware of Ramón standing to his right, at the edge of his peripheral vision. He could not see, but guessed that Ramón's hand would be on the butt of his pistol. And here came the next question.

"When he comes, will he strike at the garrison in the hills of El Cándido, the garrison at St. Thérese, or will he come right into the city?"

"The garrison at St. Thérese," Fletcher said.

He will come to the city, Tomás had said while his wife and daughter now watched cartoons, sitting on the floor side by side and eating popcorn from a white bowl with a blue stripe around the rim. Fletcher remembered the blue stripe. He could see it clearly. Fletcher remembered everything. *He will come at the heart. No fucking around. He will strike for the heart, like a man who would kill a vampire.*

"He will not want the TV station?" Escobar asked. "Or the government radio station?"

First the radio station on Civil Hill, Tomás had said while the cartoons played. By then it was the Road Runner, always gone in a puff of dust just ahead of whatever Acme Road Runner–catching device the Coyote was using, just beep-beep and gone.

"No," Fletcher said. "I've been told El Cóndor says 'Let them babble.'"

"Does he have rockets? Air-to-ground rockets? Copter-killers?"

"Yes." It was true.

"Many?"

"Not many." This was not true. Núñez had better than sixty. There were only a dozen helicopters in the country's whole shitpot air force——bad Russian helicopters that never flew for long.

The Bride of Frankenstein tapped Escobar on the shoulder. Escobar leaned toward her. She whispered without covering her mouth. She had no need to cover her mouth because her lips barely moved. This was a skill Fletcher associated with prisons. He had never been to prison but he had seen movies. When Escobar whispered back, he raised a fat hand to cover his own mouth.

Fletcher watched them and waited, knowing that the woman was telling Escobar he was lying. Soon Heinz would have more data for his paper, *Certain Preliminary Observations on the Administration and Consequences of Electrifying the Shit of Reluctant Interrogation Subjects.* Fletcher discovered that terror had created two new people inside him, at least two, sub-Fletchers with their own useless but quite powerful views on how this was going to go. One was sadly hopeful, the other just sad. The sadly hopeful one was Mr. Maybe They Will, as in maybe they really will let me go, maybe there really is a car parked on the Street

Fifth of May, just around the corner, maybe they really mean to kick me out of the country, maybe I really will be landing in Miami tomorrow morning, scared but alive, with this already beginning to seem like a bad dream.

The other one, the one who was merely sad, was Mr. Even If I Do. Fletcher might be able to surprise them by making a sudden move—he had been beaten and they were arrogant, so yes, he might be able to surprise them.

But Ramón will shoot me even if I do.

And if he went for Ramón? Managed to get his gun? Unlikely but not impossible; the man was fat, fatter than Escobar by at least thirty pounds, and he wheezed when he breathed.

Escobar and Heinz will be all over me before I can shoot even if I do.

The woman too, maybe; she talked without moving her lips; she might know judo or karate or tae kwon do, as well. And if he shot them all and managed to escape this room?

There'll be more guards everywhere even if I do—they'll hear the shots and come running.

Of course rooms like this tended to be sound-proofed, for obvious reasons, but even if he got up the stairs and out the door and onto the street, that was only the beginning. And Mr. Even If I Do would be running with him the whole way, for however long his run lasted.

The thing was, neither Mr. Maybe They Will or Mr. Even If I Do could help him; they were only distractions, lies his increasingly frantic mind tried to tell itself. Men like him did not talk themselves out of rooms like this. He might as well try inventing a third sub-Fletcher, Mr. Maybe I Can, and go for it. He had nothing to lose. He only had to make sure they didn't know he knew that.

Escobar and the Bride of Frankenstein drew apart. Escobar put his cigarette back in his mouth and smiled sadly at Fletcher. "*Amigo*, you are lying."

"No," he said. "Why would I lie? Don't you think I want to get out of here?"

"We have no *idea* why you would lie," said the woman with the narrow blade of a face. "We have no idea why you would choose to aid Núñez in the first place. Some have suggested American naiveté, and I have no doubt that played its part, but that cannot be all. It doesn't matter. I believe a demonstration is in order. Heinz?"

Smiling, Heinz turned to his machine and flicked a switch. There was a hum, the kind that comes from an old-fashioned radio when it's warming up, and three green lights came on.

"No," Fletcher said, trying to get to his feet, thinking that he did panic very well, and why not? He *was* panicked, or almost panicked. Certainly the idea of Heinz touching him anywhere with that stainless steel dildo for pygmies was terrifying. But there was another part of him, very cold and calculating, that knew he would have to take at least one shock. He wasn't aware of anything so coherent as a plan, but he had to take at least one shock. Mr. Maybe I Can insisted that this was so.

Escobar nodded to Ramón.

"You can't do this, I'm an American citizen and I work for *The New York Times,* people know where I am."

A heavy hand pressed down on his left shoulder, pushing him back into the chair. At the same moment, the barrel of a pistol went deep into his right ear. The pain was so sudden that bright dots appeared before Fletcher's eyes, dancing frantically. He screamed, and the sound seemed muffled. Because one ear was plugged, of course—one ear was plugged.

"Hold out your hand, Mr. Fletcher," Escobar said, and he was smiling around his cigarette again.

"Right hand," Heinz said. He held the stylus by its black rubber grip like a pencil, and his machine was humming.

Fletcher gripped the arm of the chair with his right hand. He was no longer sure if he was acting or not—the line between acting and panic was gone.

"Do it," the woman said. Her hands were folded on the table; she leaned forward over them. There was a point of light in each of her pupils, turning her dark eyes into nailheads. "Do it or I can't account for the consequences."

Fletcher began to loosen his fingers on the chair arm, but before he could get the hand up, Heinz darted forward and poked the tip of the blunt stylus against the back of Fletcher's left hand. That had probably been his target all along—certainly it was closer to where Heinz stood.

There was a snapping sound, very thin, like a twig, and Fletcher's left hand closed into a fist so tight his nails cut into his palm. A kind of dancing sickness raced up from his wrist to his forearm to his flopping elbow and finally to his shoulder, the side of his neck, and to his gums. He could even feel the shock in his teeth on that side, or in the fillings. A grunt escaped him. He bit his tongue and shot sideways in the chair. The gun was gone from his ear and Ramón caught him. If he hadn't, Fletcher would have fallen on the gray tile floor.

The stylus was withdrawn. Where it had touched, between the second and third knuckles of the third finger of his left hand, there was a small hot spot. It was the only real pain, although his arm still tingled and the muscles still jumped. Yet it was horrible, being shocked like that. Fletcher felt he would seriously consider shooting his own mother to avoid another touch of the little steel dildo. An atavism, Heinz had called it. Someday he hoped to write a paper.

Heinz's face loomed down, lips pulled back and teeth revealed in an idiotic grin, eyes alight. "How do you describe it?" he cried. "Now, while the experience is still fresh, how do you describe it?"

"Like dying," Fletcher said in a voice that didn't sound like his own.

Heinz looked transported. "Yes! And you see, he has wet himself! Not much, just a little, but yes . . . and Mr. Fletcher—"

"Stand aside," the Bride of Frankenstein said. "Don't be an ass. Let us take care of our business."

"And that was only *one-quarter power*," Heinz said in a tone of awed confidentiality, and then he stood aside and refolded his hands in front of him.

"Mr. Fletcher, you been bad," Escobar said reproachfully. He took the stub of his cigarette from his mouth, examined it, threw it on the floor.

The cigarette, Fletcher thought. *The cigarette, yes.* The shock had seriously insulted his arm—the muscles were still twitching and he could see blood in his cupped palm—but it seemed to have revitalized his brain, refreshed it. Of course that was what shock treatments were supposed to do.

"No . . . I want to help . . ."

But Escobar was shaking his head. "We know Núñez will come to the city. We know on the way he will take the radio station if he can . . . and he probably can."

"For awhile," said the Bride of Frankenstein. "Only for awhile."

Escobar was nodding. "Only for awhile. A matter of days, perhaps hours. Is of no concern. What matters is we give you a bit of rope, see if you make a noose . . . and you do."

Fletcher sat up straight in the chair again. Ramón had retreated a step or two. Fletcher looked at the back of his left hand and saw a small smudge there, like the one on the side of Tomás's dead face in the photograph. And there was Heinz who had killed Fletcher's friend, standing beside his machine with his hands folded in front of him, smiling and perhaps thinking about the paper he would write, words and graphs and little pictures labeled Fig. 1 and Fig. 2 and, for all Fletcher knew, Fig. 994.

"Mr. Fletcher?"

Fletcher looked at Escobar and straightened the fingers of his left hand. The muscles of that arm were still twitching, but the twitch was subsiding. He thought that when the time came, he would be able to use the arm. And if Ramón shot him, so what? Let Heinz see if his machine could raise the dead.

"Do we have your attention, Mr. Fletcher?"

Fletcher nodded.

"Why do you want to protect this man Núñez?" Escobar asked. "Why do you want to suffer to protect this man? He takes the cocaine. If he wins his revolution he will proclaim himself President for Life and sell the cocaine to your country. He will go to mass on Sunday and fuck his coke-whores the rest of the week. In the end who wins? Maybe the Communists. Maybe United Fruit. Not the people." Escobar spoke low. His eyes were soft. "Help us, Mr. Fletcher. Of your own free will. Don't make us make you help us. Don't make us pull on your string." He looked up at Fletcher from beneath his single bushy eyebrow. He looked up with his soft cocker spaniel eyes. "You can still be on that plane to Miami. On the way you like a drink, yes?"

"Yes," Fletcher said. "I'll help you."

"Ah, good." Escobar smiled, then looked at the woman.

"Does he have rockets?" she asked.

"Yes."

"Many?"

"At least sixty."

"Russian?"

"Some are. Others came in crates with Israeli markings, but the writing on the missiles themselves looks Japanese."

She nodded, seeming satisfied. Escobar beamed.

"Where are they?"

"Everywhere. You can't just swoop down and grab them. There might still be a dozen at Ortiz." Fletcher knew that wasn't so.

"And Núñez?" she asked. "Is El Cóndor at Ortiz?"

She knew better. "He's in the jungle. Last I knew, he was in Belén Province." This was a lie. Núñez had been in Cristóbal, a suburb of the capital city, when Fletcher last saw him. He was probably still there. But if Escobar and the woman had known that, there would have been no need of this interrogation. And why would they believe Núñez would trust Fletcher with his whereabouts, anyway? In a country like this, where Escobar and Heinz and the Bride of Frankenstein were only three of your enemies, why would you trust a Yankee newspaper reporter with your address? *Loco!* Why was the Yankee newspaperman involved at all? But they had stopped wondering about that, at least for now.

"Who does he talk to in the city?" the woman asked. "Not who he fucks, who he talks to."

This was the point where he had to move, if he was going to. The truth was no longer safe and they might know a lie.

"There's a man . . ." he started, then paused. "Could I have that cigarette now?"

"Mr. Fletcher! But of course!" Escobar was for a moment the concerned dinner-party host. Fletcher did not think this was play-acting. Escobar picked up the red-and-white pack—the kind of pack any free man or woman could buy at any newsstand like the one

Fletcher remembered on Forty-third Street—and shook out a cigarette. Fletcher took it, knowing he might be dead before it burned all the way down to the filter, no longer a part of this earth. He felt nothing, only the fading twitch of the muscles in his left arm and a funny baked taste in his fillings on that side of his mouth.

He put the cigarette between his lips. Escobar leaned further forward and snapped back the cover of his gold-plated lighter. He flicked the wheel. The lighter produced a flame. Fletcher was aware of Heinz's infernal machine humming like an old radio, the kind with tubes in the back. He was aware of the woman he had come to think of, without a trace of humor, as the Bride of Frankenstein, looking at him the way the Coyote in the cartoons looked at the Road Runner. He was aware of his heart beating, of the remembered circular feel of the cigarette in his mouth—"a tube of singular delight," some playwright or other had called it—and of the beat of his heart, incredibly slow. Last month he'd been called upon to make an after-luncheon speech at the Club Internacional, where all the foreign press geeks hung out, and his heart had beat faster then.

Here it was, and so what? Even the blind found their way through this; even his sister had, there by the river.

Fletcher bent to the flame. The end of the Marlboro caught fire and glowed red. Fletcher drew deep, and it was easy to start coughing; after three years without a cigarette, it would have been harder not to cough. He sat back in the chair and added a harsh, gagging growl to the cough. He began to shake all over, throwing his elbows out, jerking his head to the left, drumming his feet. Best of all, he recalled an old childhood talent and rolled his eyes up to the whites. During none of this did he let go of the cigarette.

Fletcher had never seen an actual epileptic fit, although he vaguely remembered Patty Duke throwing one in *The Miracle Worker*. He had no way of knowing if he was doing what epileptics actually did, but he hoped that the unexpected death of Tomás Herrera would help them to overlook any false notes in his own act.

"Shit, not *again!*" Heinz cried in a shrill near-scream; in a movie it might have been funny.

"Grab him, Ramón!" Escobar yelled in Spanish. He tried to stand up and struck the table so hard with his meaty thighs that it rose up and thumped back down. The woman didn't move, and Fletcher thought: *She suspects. I don't think she even knows it yet, but she's smarter than Escobar, smarter by a mile, and she suspects.*

Was this true? With his eyes rolled up he could see only a ghost of her, not enough to really know if it was or not . . . but he knew. What did it matter? Things had been set in motion, and now they would play out. They would play out very fast.

"*Ramón!*" Escobar shouted. "Don't let him fall on the floor, you idiot! Don't let him swallow his t—"

Ramón bent over and grabbed Fletcher's shaking shoulders, perhaps wanting to get Fletcher's head back, perhaps wanting to make sure Fletcher's tongue was still safely unswallowed (a person *couldn't* swallow his own tongue, not unless it was cut off; Ramón clearly did not watch *ER*). Whatever he wanted didn't matter. When his face was where Fletcher could get at it, Fletcher struck the burning end of the Marlboro in Ramón's eye.

Ramón shrieked and jerked backward. His right hand rose toward his face, where the still-burning cigarette hung askew in the socket of his eye, but his left hand remained on Fletcher's shoulder. It was now tightened down to a clamp, and when he stepped back, Ramón pulled Fletcher's chair over. Fletcher spilled out of it, rolled over, and got to his feet.

Heinz was screaming something, words, maybe, but to Fletcher he sounded like a girl of about ten screaming at the sight of a singing idol—one of the Hansons, perhaps. Escobar wasn't making any noise at all and that was bad.

Fletcher didn't look back at the table. He didn't have to look to know that Escobar was coming for him. Instead he shot both hands forward, grabbed the butt of Ramón's revolver, and pulled it from its holster. Fletcher didn't think Ramón ever knew it was gone. He was screaming a flood of Spanish and pawing at his face. He struck the cigarette but instead of coming free it broke off, the burning end still stuck in his eye.

Fletcher turned. Escobar was there, already around the end of the long table, coming for him with his fat hands out. Escobar no longer looked like a fellow who sometimes did the TV weather and talked about high bressure.

"Get that Yankee son of a bitch!" the woman spat.

Fletcher kicked the overturned chair into Escobar's path and Escobar tripped on it. As he went down,

Fletcher stuck the gun out, still held in both hands, and shot it into the top of Escobar's head. Escobar's hair jumped. Gouts of blood burst from his nose and mouth and from the underside of his chin, where the bullet came out. Escobar fell flat on his bleeding face. His feet drummed on the gray tile floor. The smell of shit rose from his dying body.

The woman was no longer in her chair, but she had no intention of approaching Fletcher. She ran for the door, fleet as a deer in her dark shapeless dress. Ramón, still bellowing, was between Fletcher and the woman. And he was reaching for Fletcher, wanting to grab him by the neck, throttle him.

Fletcher shot him twice, once in the chest and once in the face. The face-shot tore off most of Ramón's nose and right cheek, but the big man in the brown uniform came on just the same, roaring, the cigarette still dangling from his eye, his big sausage fingers, a silver ring on one of them, opening and closing.

Ramón stumbled over Escobar just as Escobar had stumbled over the chair. Fletcher had a moment to think of a famous cartoon that shows fish in a line, each with his mouth open to eat the next one down in size. *The Food Chain,* that drawing was called.

Ramón, facedown and with two bullets in him, reached out and clamped a hand on Fletcher's ankle. Fletcher tore free, staggered, and fired a fourth shot into the ceiling when he did. Dust sifted down. There was a strong smell of gunsmoke in the room now. Fletcher looked at the door. The woman was still there, yanking at the doorknob with one hand and fumbling at the turn-lock with the other hand, but she couldn't open the door. If she'd been able to, she'd have already done it. She'd be all the way down the hall by now, and screaming bloody murder up the stairs.

"Hey," Fletcher said. He felt like an ordinary guy who goes to his Thursday-night bowling league and rolls a 300 game. "Hey, you bitch, look at me."

She turned and put her palms flat against the door, as if she were holding it up. There was still a little nail-head of light in each of her eyes. She began to tell him he mustn't hurt her. She started in Spanish, hesitated, then began to say the same thing in English. "You mustn't hurt me in any way, Mr. Fletcher, I am the only one who can guarantee your safe conduct from here, and I swear I will on my solemn oath, but you must not hurt me."

From behind them, Heinz was keening like a child in love or terror. Now that Fletcher was close to the woman—the woman standing against the door of the deathroom with her hands pressed flat against its metal surface—he could smell some bittersweet perfume. Her eyes were shaped like almonds. Her hair streamed back above the top of her head. *We're not just fucking around,* she had told him, and Fletcher thought: *Neither am I.*

The woman saw the news of her death in his eyes and began to talk faster, pressing her butt and back and palms harder and harder against the metal door as she talked. It was as if she believed she could somehow melt herself through the door and come out whole on the other side if she just pushed hard enough. She had papers, she said, papers in his name, and she would give him these papers. She also had money, a great deal of money, also gold; there was a Swiss bank account which he could access by computer from her home. It occurred to Fletcher that in the end there might only be one way to tell the thugs from the patriots: when they saw their own death rising in your eyes like water, patriots made speeches. The thugs, on the other hand, gave you the number of their Swiss bank account and offered to put you on-line.

"Shut up," Fletcher said. Unless this room was very well insulated indeed, a dozen ordinary troops from upstairs were probably on their way now. He had no means of standing them off, but this one was not going to get away.

She shut up, still standing against the door, pressing it with her palms. Still with the nailheads in her eyes. How old was she? Fletcher wondered. Sixty-five? And how many had she killed in this room, or rooms like it? How many had she ordered killed?

"Listen to me," Fletcher said. "Are you listening?"

What she was undoubtedly listening for were the sounds of approaching rescue. *In your dreams,* Fletcher thought.

"The weatherman there said that El Cóndor uses cocaine, that he's a Communist butt-boy, a whore for United Fruit, who knows what else. Maybe he's some of those things, maybe none. I don't know or care. What I know about, what I care about, was he was never in charge of the ordinaries patrolling the Caya River in the summer of 1994. Núñez was in New York then. At NYU. So he wasn't part of the bunch that found the nuns on retreat from La Caya. They put three of the nuns' heads up on sticks, there by the water's edge. The one in the middle was my sister."

Fletcher shot her twice and then Ramón's gun clicked empty. Two was enough. The woman went sliding down the door, her bright eyes never leaving Fletcher's. *You were the one who was supposed to die,* those eyes said. *I don't understand this, you were the one who was supposed to die.* Her hand clawed at her throat once, twice, then was still. Her eyes remained on his a moment longer, the bright eyes of an ancient mariner with a whale of a tale to tell, and then her head fell forward.

Fletcher turned around and began walking toward Heinz with Ramón's gun held out. As he walked he realized that his right shoe was gone. He looked at Ramón, who was still lying facedown in a spreading pool of blood. Ramón still had hold of Fletcher's loafer. He was like a dying weasel that refuses to let go of a chicken. Fletcher stopped long enough to put it on.

Heinz turned as if to run, and Fletcher waggled the gun at him. The gun was empty but Heinz didn't seem to know that. And maybe he remembered there was nowhere to run anyway, not here in the deathroom. He stopped moving and only stared at the oncoming gun and the oncoming man behind it. Heinz was crying. "One step back," Fletcher said, and, still crying, Heinz took one step back.

Fletcher stopped in front of Heinz's machine. What was the word Heinz had used? Atavism, wasn't it?

The machine on the trolley looked much too simple for a man of Heinz's intelligence—three dials, one switch marked ON and OFF (now in the OFF position), and a rheostat which had been turned so the white line on it pointed to roughly eleven o'clock. The needles on the dials all lay flat on their zeroes.

Fletcher picked up the stylus and held it out to Heinz. Heinz made a wet sound, shook his head, and took another step backward. His face would lift and pull together in a kind of grief-struck sneer, then loosen again. His forehead was wet with sweat, his cheeks with tears. This second backward step took him almost beneath one of the caged lights, and his shadow puddled around his feet.

"Take it or I'll kill you," Fletcher said. "And if you take another step backward I'll kill you." He had no time for this and it felt wrong in any case, but Fletcher could not stop himself. He kept seeing that picture of Tomás, the open eyes, the little scorched mark like a powder burn.

Sobbing, Heinz took the blunt fountain-pen-shaped object, careful to hold it only by the rubber insulated sleeve.

"Put it in your mouth," Fletcher said. "Suck on it like it was a lollipop."

"*No!*" Heinz cried in a weepy voice. He shook his head and water flew off his face. His face was still going through its contortions: cramp and release, cramp and release. There was a green bubble of snot at the entrance to one of his nostrils; it expanded and contracted with Heinz's rapid breathing but didn't break. Fletcher had never seen anything quite like it. "*No, you can't make me!*"

But Heinz knew Fletcher could. The Bride of Frankenstein might not have believed it, and Escobar likely hadn't had time to believe it, but Heinz knew he had no more right of refusal. He was in Tomás Herrera's position, in Fletcher's position. In one way that was revenge enough, but in another way it wasn't. Knowing was an idea. Ideas were no good in here. In here seeing was believing.

"Put it in your mouth or I'll shoot you in the head," Fletcher said, and shoved the empty gun at Heinz's face. Heinz recoiled with a wail of terror. And now Fletcher heard his own voice drop, become confidential, become sincere. In a way it reminded him of Escobar's voice. *We are havin an area of low bressure,* he thought. *We are havin the steenkin rain-showers.* "I'm not going to shock you if you just do it and hurry up. But I need you to know what it feels like."

Heinz stared at Fletcher. His eyes were blue and red-rimmed, swimming with tears. He didn't believe Fletcher, of course, what Fletcher was saying made no sense, but Heinz very clearly wanted to believe it anyway, because, sense or nonsense, Fletcher was holding out the possibility of life. He just needed to be pushed a single step further.

Fletcher smiled. "Do it for your *research.*"

Heinz was convinced—not completely, but enough to believe Fletcher could be Mr. Maybe He Will after all. He put the steel rod into his mouth. His bulging eyes stared at Fletcher. Below them and above the jutting stylus—which looked not like a lollipop but an old-fashioned fever thermometer—that green bubble of snot swelled and retreated, swelled and retreated. Still pointing the gun at Heinz, Fletcher flicked the switch on the control panel from OFF to ON and gave the rheostat a hard turn. The white line on the knob went from eleven in the morning to five in the afternoon.

Heinz might have had time to spit the stylus out, but shock caused him to clamp his lips down on the stainless steel barrel instead. The snapping sound was louder this time, like a small branch instead of a twig. Heinz's lips pressed down even tighter. The green mucus bubble in his nostril popped. So did one of his eyes. Heinz's entire body seemed to vibrate inside his clothes. His hands were bent at the wrists, the long fingers splayed. His cheeks went from white to pale gray to a darkish purple. Smoke began to pour out of his nose. His other eye popped out on his cheek. Above the dislocated eyes there were now two raw sockets that stared at Fletcher with surprise. One of Heinz's cheeks either tore open or melted. A quantity of smoke and a strong odor of burned meat came out through the hole, and Fletcher observed small flames, orange and blue. Heinz's mouth was on fire. His tongue was burning like a rug.

Fletcher's fingers were still on the rheostat. He turned it all the way back to the left, then flicked the switch to OFF. The needles, which had swung all the way to the +50 marks on their little dials, immediately fell dead again. The moment the electricity left him, Heinz crashed to the gray tile floor, trailing smoke from his mouth as he went. The stylus fell free, and Fletcher saw there were little pieces of Heinz's lips on it. Fletcher's gorge gave a salty, burping lurch, and he closed his throat against it. He didn't have time to vomit over what he had done to Heinz; he might consider vomiting at a later time. Still, he lingered a moment longer, leaning over to look at Heinz's smoking mouth and dislocated eyes. "How do you describe it?" he asked the corpse. "Now, while the experience is still fresh? What, nothing to say?"

Fletcher turned and hurried across the room, detouring around Ramón, who was still alive and moaning. He sounded like a man having a bad dream.

He remembered that the door was locked. Ramón had locked it; the key would be on the ring hanging at Ramón's belt. Fletcher went back to the guard, knelt beside him, and tore the ring off his belt. When he did, Ramón groped out and seized Fletcher by the ankle again. Fletcher was still holding the gun. He rapped the butt down on the top of Ramón's head. For a moment the hand on his ankle gripped even tighter, and then it let go.

Fletcher started to get up and then thought, *Bullets. He must have more. The gun's empty.* His next thought was that he didn't need no steenkin bullets, Ramón's gun had done all that it could for him. Shooting outside this room would bring the ordinaries like flies.

Even so, Fletcher felt along Ramón's belt, opening the little leather snap pouches until he found a speed-loader. He used it to fill up the gun. He didn't know if he could actually bring himself to shoot ordinaries who were only men like Tomás, men with families to feed, but he could shoot officers and he could save at least one bullet for himself. He would very likely not be able to get out of the building—that would be like rolling a second 300 game in a row—but he would never be brought back to this room again, and set in the chair next to Heinz's machine.

He pushed the Bride of Frankenstein away from the door with his foot. Her eyes glared dully at the ceiling. Fletcher was coming more and more to understand that he had survived and these others had not. They were cooling off. On their skin, galaxies of bacteria had already begun to die. These were bad thoughts to be having in the basement of the Ministry of Information, bad thoughts to be in the head of a man who had become—perhaps only for a little while, more likely forever—a *desaparecido*. Still, he couldn't help having them.

The third key opened the door. Fletcher stuck his head out into the hall—cinder-block walls, green on the bottom half and a dirty cream-white on the top half, like the walls of an old school corridor. Faded red lino on the floor. No one was in the hall. About thirty feet down to the left, a small brown dog lay asleep against the wall. His feet were twitching. Fletcher didn't know if the dog was dreaming about chasing or being chased, but he didn't think he would be asleep at all if the gunshots—or Heinz's screaming—had been very loud out here. *If I ever get back,* he thought, *I'll write that soundproofing is the great triumph of dictatorship. I'll tell the world. Of course I probably won't get back, those stairs down to the right are probably as close to Forty-third Street as I'm ever going to get, but—*

But there was Mr. Maybe I Can.

Fletcher stepped into the hall and pulled the door of the deathroom shut behind him. The little brown dog lifted its head, looked at Fletcher, puffed its lips out in a *woof* that was mostly a whisper, then lowered its head again and appeared to go back to sleep.

Fletcher dropped to his knees, put his hands (one

still holding Ramón's gun) on the floor, bent, and kissed the lino. As he did it he thought of his sister— how she had looked going off to college eight years before her death by the river. She had been wearing a tartan skirt on the day she'd gone off to college, and the red in it hadn't been the exact same red of the faded lino, but it was close. Close enough for government work, as they said.

Fletcher got up. He started down the hall toward the stairs, the first-floor hallway, the street, the city, Highway 4, the patrols, the roadblocks, the border, the checkpoints, the water. The Chinese said a journey of a thousand miles started with a single step.

I'll see how far I get, Fletcher thought as he reached the foot of the stairs. *I might just surprise myself.* But he was already surprised, just to be alive. Smiling a little, holding Ramón's gun out before him, Fletcher started up the stairs.

A month later, a man walked up to Carlo Arcuzzi's newsstand kiosk on Forty-third Street. Carlo had a nasty moment when he was almost sure the man meant to stick a gun in his face and rob him. It was only eight o'clock and still light, lots of people about, but did any of those things stop a man who was *pazzo?* And this man looked plenty *pazzo*—so thin his white shirt and gray pants seemed to float on him, and his eyes lay at the bottom of great round sockets. He looked like a man who had just been released from a concentration camp or (by some huge mistake) a loony bin. When his hand went into his pants pocket, Carlo Arcuzzi thought, *Now comes the gun.*

But instead of a gun came a battered old Lord Buxton, and from the wallet came a ten-dollar bill. Then, in a perfectly sane tone of voice, the man in the white shirt and gray pants asked for a pack of Marlboros. Carlo got them, put a package of matches on top of them, and pushed them across the counter of his kiosk. While the man opened the Marlboros, Carlo made change.

"No," the man said when he saw the change. He had put one of the cigarettes in his mouth.

"No? What you mean no?"

"I mean keep the change," the man said. He offered the pack to Carlo. "Do you smoke? Have one of these, if you like."

Carlo looked mistrustfully at the man in the white shirt and gray pants. "I don't smoke. It's a bad habit."

"Very bad," the man agreed, then lit his cigarette and inhaled with apparent pleasure. He stood smoking and watching the people on the other side of the street. There were girls on the other side of the street. Men would look at girls in their summer clothes, that was human nature. Carlo didn't think this customer was crazy anymore, although he had left the change of a ten-dollar bill sitting on the narrow counter of the kiosk.

The thin man smoked the cigarette all the way down to the filter. He turned toward Carlo, staggering a little, as if he was not used to smoking and the cigarette had made him dizzy.

"A nice night," the man said.

Carlo nodded. It was. It was a nice night. "We're lucky to be alive," Carlo said.

The man nodded. "All of us. All of the time."

He walked to the curb, where there was a litter basket. He dropped the pack of cigarettes, full save one, into the litter basket. "All of us," he said. "All of the time." He walked away. Carlo watched him go and thought that maybe he was *pazzo* after all. Or maybe not. Crazy was a hard state to define.

――――――

This is a slightly Kafka-esque story about an interrogation room in the South American version of Hell. In such stories, the fellow being interrogated usually ends up spilling everything and then being killed (or losing his mind). I wanted to write one with a happier ending, however unreal that might be. And here it is.

The Little Sisters
of Eluria

*If there's a magnum opus in my life, it's probably the yet
unfinished seven-volume series about Roland Deschain
of Gilead and his search for the Dark Tower which
serves as the hub of existence. In 1996 or 1997, Ralph
Vicinanza (my sometime agent and foreign rights man
of business) asked me if I'd like to contribute a story
about Roland's younger years for a whopper fantasy
anthology Robert Silverberg was putting together. I tentatively agreed. Nothing came, though, and nothing
came. I was about to give up when I woke one morning
thinking about* The Talisman, *and the great pavilion
where Jack Sawyer first glimpses the Queen of the
Territories. In the shower (where I invariably do my
best imagining—I think it's a womb thing), I started
to visualize that tent in ruins . . . but still filled with
whispering women. Ghosts. Maybe vampires. Little
Sisters. Nurses of death instead of life. Composing a
story from that central image was amazingly difficult. I
had lots of space to move around in—Silverberg wanted
short novels, not short stories—but it was still hard.
These days, everything about Roland and his friends*

wants to be not just long but sort of epic. *One thing this story has going for it is that you don't need to have read the Dark Tower novels to enjoy it. And by the way, for you Tower junkies, DT 5 is now finished, all nine hundred pages of it. It's called* Wolves of the Calla.

[Author's Note: The Dark Tower books begin with Roland of Gilead, the last gunslinger in an exhausted world that has "moved on," pursuing a magician in a black robe. Roland has been chasing Walter for a very long time. In the first book of the cycle, he finally catches up. This story, however, takes place while Roland is still casting about for Walter's trail. S. K.]

I. FULL EARTH. THE EMPTY TOWN. THE BELLS. THE DEAD BOY. THE OVERTURNED WAGON. THE GREEN FOLK.

On a day in Full Earth so hot that it seemed to suck the breath from his chest before his body could use it, Roland of Gilead came to the gates of a village in the Desatoya Mountains. He was travelling alone by then, and would soon be travelling afoot, as well. This whole last week he had been hoping for a horse doctor, but guessed such a fellow would do him no good now, even if this town had one. His mount, a two-year-old roan, was pretty well done for.

The town gates, still decorated with flowers from some festival or other, stood open and welcoming, but the silence beyond them was all wrong. The gunslinger heard no clip-clop of horses, no rumble of wagon wheels, no merchants' huckstering cries from the marketplace.

The only sounds were the low hum of crickets (some sort of bug, at any rate; they were a bit more tuneful than crickets, at that), a queer wooden knocking sound, and the faint, dreamy tinkle of small bells.

Also, the flowers twined through the wrought-iron staves of the ornamental gate were long dead.

Between his knees, Topsy gave two great, hollow sneezes—*K'chow! K'chow!*—and staggered sideways. Roland dismounted, partly out of respect for the horse, partly out of respect for himself—he didn't want to break a leg under Topsy if Topsy chose this moment to give up and canter into the clearing at the end of his path.

The gunslinger stood in his dusty boots and faded jeans under the beating sun, stroking the roan's matted neck, pausing every now and then to yank his fingers through the tangles of Topsy's mane, and stopping once to shoo off the tiny flies clustering at the corners of Topsy's eyes. Let them lay their eggs and hatch their maggots there after Topsy was dead, but not before.

Roland thus honored his horse as best he could, listening to those distant, dreamy bells and the strange wooden tocking sound as he did. After awhile he ceased his absent grooming and looked thoughtfully at the open gate.

The cross above its center was a bit unusual, but otherwise the gate was a typical example of its type, a western commonplace which was not useful but traditional—all the little towns he had come to in the last tenmonth seemed to have one such where you came in (grand) and one more such where you went out (not so grand). None had been built to exclude visitors, certainly not this one. It stood between two walls of pink adobe that ran into the scree for a distance of about twenty feet on either side of the road and then simply stopped. Close the gate, lock it with many locks, and all that meant was a short walk around one bit of adobe wall or the other.

Beyond the gate, Roland could see what looked in most respects like a perfectly ordinary High Street—an inn, two saloons (one of which was called The Bustling Pig; the sign over the other was too faded to read), a mercantile, a smithy, a Gathering Hall. There was also a small but rather lovely wooden building with a modest bell tower on top, a sturdy fieldstone foundation on the bottom, and a gold-painted cross on its double doors. The cross, like the one over the gate, marked this as a worshipping place for those who held to the Jesus Man. This wasn't a common religion in Mid-World, but far from unknown; that same thing could have been said about most forms of worship in those days, including the worship of Baal, Asmodeus, and a hundred others. Faith, like everything else in the world these days, had moved on. As far as Roland was concerned, God o' the Cross was just another religion which taught that love and murder were inextricably bound together—that in the end, God always drank blood.

Meanwhile, there was the singing hum of insects that sounded *almost* like crickets. The dreamlike tinkle of the bells. And that queer wooden thumping, like a fist on a door. Or on a coffintop.

Something here's a long way from right, the gunslinger

thought. *'Ware, Roland; this place has a reddish odor.*

He led Topsy through the gate with its adornments of dead flowers and down the High Street. On the porch of the mercantile, where the old men should have congregated to discuss crops, politics, and the follies of the younger generation, there stood only a line of empty rockers. Lying beneath one, as if dropped from a careless (and long-departed) hand, was a charred corncob pipe. The hitching rack in front of The Bustling Pig stood empty; the windows of the saloon itself were dark. One of the batwing doors had been yanked off and stood propped against the side of the building; the other hung ajar, its faded green slats spattered with maroon stuff that might have been paint but probably wasn't.

The shopfront of the livery stable stood intact, like the face of a ruined woman who has access to good cosmetics, but the double barn behind it was a charred skeleton. That fire must have happened on a rainy day, the gunslinger thought, or whole damned town would have gone up in flames; a jolly spin and raree-show for anyone around to see it.

To his right now, halfway up to where the street opened into the town square, was the church. There were grassy borders on both sides, one separating the church from the town's Gathering Hall, the other from the little house set aside for the preacher and his family (if this was one of the Jesus-sects which allowed its shamans to have wives and families, that was; some of them, clearly administered by lunatics, demanded at least the appearance of celibacy). There were flowers in these grassy strips, and while they looked parched, most were still alive. So whatever had happened here to empty the place out had not happened long ago. A week, perhaps. Two at the outside, given the heat.

Topsy sneezed again—*K'chow!*—and lowered his head wearily.

The gunslinger saw the source of the tinkling. Above the cross on the church doors, a cord had been strung in a long, shallow arc. Hung from it were perhaps two dozen tiny silver bells. There was hardly any breeze today, but enough so these smalls were never quite still . . . and if a real wind should rise, Roland thought, the sound made by the tintinnabulation of the bells would probably be a good deal less pleasant; more like the strident parlay of gossips' tongues.

"Hello!" Roland called, looking across the street at what a large false-fronted sign proclaimed to be the Good Beds Hotel. "Hello, the town!"

No answer but the bells, the tunesome insects, and that odd wooden clunking. No answer, no movement . . . but there were folk here. Folk or *something*. He was being watched. The tiny hairs on the nape of his neck had stiffened.

Roland stepped onward, leading Topsy toward the center of town, puffing up the unlaid High Street dust with each step. Forty paces farther along, he stopped in front of a low building marked with a single curt word: LAW. The Sheriff's office (if they had such this far from the Inners) looked remarkably similar to the church— wooden boards stained a rather forbidding shade of dark brown above a stone foundation.

The bells behind him rustled and whispered.

He left the roan standing in the middle of the street

and mounted the steps to the LAW office. He was very aware of the bells, of the sun beating against his neck, and of the sweat trickling down his sides. The door was shut but unlocked. He opened it, then winced back, half-raising a hand as the heat trapped inside rushed out in a soundless gasp. If all the closed buildings were this hot inside, he mused, the livery barns would soon not be the only burnt-out hulks. And with no rain to stop the flames (and certainly no volunteer fire department, not anymore), the town would not be long for the face of the earth.

He stepped inside, trying to sip at the stifling air rather than taking deep breaths. He immediately heard the low drone of flies.

There was a single cell, commodious and empty, its barred door standing open. Filthy skin-shoes, one of the pair coming unsewn, lay beneath a bunk sodden with the same dried maroon stuff that had marked The Bustling Pig. Here was where the flies were, crawling over the stain, feeding from it.

On the desk was a ledger. Roland turned it toward him and read what was embossed upon its red cover:

REGISTRY OF MISDEEDS & REDRESS
IN THE YEARS OF OUR LORD
ELURIA

So now he knew the name of the town, at least— Eluria. Pretty, yet somehow ominous, as well. But any name would have seemed ominous, Roland supposed, given these circumstances. He turned to leave, and saw a closed door secured by a wooden bolt.

He went to it, stood before it for a moment, then drew one of the big revolvers he carried low on his hips. He stood a moment longer, head down, thinking (Cuthbert, his old friend, liked to say that the wheels inside Roland's head ground slow but exceedingly fine), and then retracted the bolt. He opened the door and immediately stood back, leveling his gun, expecting a body (Eluria's Sheriff, mayhap) to come tumbling into the room with his throat cut and his eyes gouged out, victim of a MISDEED in need of REDRESS—

Nothing.

Well, half a dozen stained jumpers which longer-term prisoners were probably required to wear, two bows, a quiver of arrows, an old, dusty motor, a rifle that had probably last been fired a hundred years ago, and a mop . . . but in the gunslinger's mind, all that came down to nothing. Just a storage closet.

He went back to the desk, opened the register, and leafed through it. Even the pages were warm, as if the book had been baked. In a way, he supposed it had been. If the High Street layout had been different, he might have expected a large number of religious offenses to be recorded, but he wasn't surprised to find none here—if the Jesus-Man church had coexisted with a couple of saloons, the churchfolk must have been fairly reasonable.

What Roland found was the usual petty offenses, and a few not so petty—a murder, a horse-thieving, the Distressal of a Lady (which probably meant rape). The murderer had been removed to a place called Lexingworth to be hanged. Roland had never heard of it. One note toward the end read *Green folk sent hence*. It meant nothing to Roland. The most recent entry was this:

12/Fe/99. Chas. Freeborn, cattle-theef to be tryed.

Roland wasn't familiar with the notation *12/Fe/99,* but as this was a long stretch from February, he supposed *Fe* might stand for Full Earth. In any case, the ink looked about as fresh as the blood on the bunk in the cell, and the gunslinger had a good idea that Chas. Freeborn, cattle-theef, had reached the clearing at the end of his path.

He went out into the heat and the lacy sound of bells. Topsy looked at Roland dully, then lowered his head again, as if there were something in the dust of the High Street which could be cropped. As if he would ever want to crop again, for that matter.

The gunslinger gathered up the reins, slapped the dust off them against the faded no-color of his jeans, and continued on up the street. The wooden knocking sound grew steadily louder as he walked (he had not holstered his gun when leaving LAW, nor cared to holster it now), and as he neared the town square, which must have housed the Eluria market in more normal times, Roland at last saw movement.

On the far side of the square was a long watering trough, made of ironwood from the look (what some called "seequoiah" out here), apparently fed in happier times from a rusty steel pipe which now jutted waterless above the trough's south end. Lolling over one side of this municipal oasis, about halfway down its length, was a leg clad in faded gray pants and terminating in a well-chewed cowboy boot.

The chewer was a large dog, perhaps two shades grayer than the corduroy pants. Under other circumstances, Roland supposed, the mutt would have had the boot off long since, but perhaps the foot and lower calf inside it had swelled. In any case, the dog was well on its way to simply chewing the obstacle away. It would seize the boot and shake it back and forth. Every now and then the boot's heel would collide with the wooden side of the trough, producing another hollow knock. The gunslinger hadn't been so wrong to think of coffintops after all, it seemed.

Why doesn't it just back off a few steps, jump into the trough, and have at him? Roland wondered. *No water coming out of the pipe, so it can't be afraid of drowning.*

Topsy uttered another of his hollow, tired sneezes, and when the dog lurched around in response, Roland understood why it was doing things the hard way. One of its front legs had been badly broken and crookedly mended. Walking would be a chore for it, jumping out of the question. On its chest was a patch of dirty white fur. Growing out of this patch was black fur in a roughly cruciform shape. A Jesus-dog, mayhap, hoping for a spot of afternoon communion.

There was nothing very religious about the snarl which began to wind out of its chest, however, or the roll of its rheumy eyes. It lifted its upper lip in a trembling sneer, revealing a goodish set of teeth.

"Light out," Roland said. "While you can."

The dog backed up until its hindquarters were pressed against the chewed boot. It regarded the oncoming man fearfully, but clearly meant to stand its ground. The revolver in Roland's hand held no significance for it. The gunslinger wasn't surprised—he guessed the dog had never seen one, had no idea it was anything other than a club of some kind, which could only be thrown once.

"Hie on with you, now," Roland said, but still the dog wouldn't move.

He should have shot it—it was no good to itself, and a dog that had acquired a taste for human flesh could be no good to anyone else—but he somehow didn't like to. Killing the only thing still living in this town (other than the singing bugs, that was) seemed like an invitation to bad luck.

He fired into the dust near the dog's good forepaw, the sound crashing into the hot day and temporarily silencing the insects. The dog *could* run, it seemed, although at a lurching trot that hurt Roland's eyes . . . and his heart, a little, too. It stopped at the far side of the square, by an overturned flatbed wagon (there looked to be more dried blood splashed on the freighter's side), and glanced back. It uttered a forlorn howl that raised the hairs on the nape of Roland's neck even further. Then it turned, skirted the wrecked wagon, and limped down a lane which opened between two of the stalls. This way toward Eluria's back gate, Roland guessed.

Still leading his dying horse, the gunslinger crossed the square to the ironwood trough and looked in.

The owner of the chewed boot wasn't a man but a boy who had just been beginning to get his man's growth—and that would have been quite a large

growth, indeed, Roland judged, even setting aside the
bloating effects which had resulted from being
immersed for some unknown length of time in nine
inches of water simmering under a summer sun.

The boy's eyes, now just milky balls, stared blindly
up at the gunslinger like the eyes of a statue. His hair
appeared to be the white of old age, although that was
the effect of the water; he had likely been a towhead.
His clothes were those of a cowboy, although he couldn't
have been much more than fourteen or sixteen. Around
his neck, gleaming blearily in water that was slowly
turning into a skin stew under the summer sun, was a
gold medallion.

Roland reached into the water, not liking to but feeling a certain obligation. He wrapped his fingers around
the medallion and pulled. The chain parted, and he
lifted the thing, dripping, into the air.

He rather expected a Jesus-Man *sigul*—what was
called the crucifix or the rood—but a small rectangle
hung from the chain, instead. The object looked like
pure gold. Engraved into it was this legend:

James
Loved of family. Loved of GOD

Roland, who had been almost too revolted to reach
into the polluted water (as a younger man, he could
never have brought himself to that), was now glad he'd
done it. He might never run into any of those who had
loved this boy, but he knew enough of *ka* to think it
might be so. In any case, it was the right thing. So was
giving the kid a decent burial . . . assuming, that was,

he could get the body out of the trough without having it break apart inside the clothes.

Roland was considering this, trying to balance what might be his duty in this circumstance against his growing desire to get out of this town, when Topsy finally fell dead.

The roan went over with a creak of gear and a last whuffling groan as it hit the ground. Roland turned and saw eight people in the street, walking toward him in a line, like beaters who hope to flush out birds or drive small game. Their skin was waxy green. Folk wearing such skin would likely glow in the dark like ghosts. It was hard to tell their sex, and what could it matter—to them or anyone else? They were slow mutants, walking with the hunched deliberation of corpses reanimated by some arcane magic.

The dust had muffled their feet like carpet. With the dog banished, they might well have gotten within attacking distance if Topsy hadn't done Roland the favor of dying at such an opportune moment. No guns that Roland could see; they were armed with clubs. These were chair legs and table legs, for the most part, but Roland saw one that looked made rather than seized—it had a bristle of rusty nails sticking out of it, and he suspected it had once been the property of a saloon bouncer, possibly the one who kept school in The Bustling Pig.

Roland raised his pistol, aiming at the fellow in the center of the line. Now he could hear the shuffle of their feet, and the wet snuffle of their breathing. As if they all had bad chest colds.

Came out of the mines, most likely, Roland thought.

There are radium mines somewhere about. That would account for the skin. I wonder that the sun doesn't kill them.

Then, as he watched, the one on the end—a creature with a face like melted candle wax—*did* die . . . or collapsed, at any rate. He (Roland was quite sure it was a male) went to his knees with a low, gobbling cry, groping for the hand of the thing walking next to it—something with a lumpy bald head and red sores sizzling on its neck. This creature took no notice of its fallen companion, but kept its dim eyes on Roland, lurching along in rough step with its remaining companions.

"Stop where you are!" Roland said. " 'Ware me, if you'd live to see day's end! 'Ware me very well!"

He spoke mostly to the one in the center, who wore ancient red suspenders over rags of shirt, and a filthy bowler hat. This gent had only one good eye, and it peered at the gunslinger with a greed as horrible as it was unmistakable. The one beside Bowler Hat (Roland believed this one might be a woman, with the dangling vestiges of breasts beneath the vest it wore) threw the chair leg it held. The arc was true, but the missile fell ten yards short.

Roland thumbed back the trigger of his revolver and fired again. This time the dirt displaced by the slug kicked up on the tattered remains of Bowler Hat's shoe instead of on a lame dog's paw.

The green folk didn't run as the dog had, but they stopped, staring at him with their dull greed. Had the missing folk of Eluria finished up in these creatures' stomachs? Roland couldn't believe it . . . although he knew perfectly well that such as these held no scruple against cannibalism. (And perhaps it wasn't cannibalism, not really; how could such things as these be considered human, whatever they might once have been?) They were too slow, too stupid. If they had dared come back into town after the Sheriff had run them out, they would have been burned or stoned to death.

Without thinking about what he was doing, wanting only to free his other hand to draw his second gun if the apparitions didn't see reason, Roland stuffed the medallion that he had taken from the dead boy into the pocket of his jeans, pushing the broken fine-link chain in after.

They stood staring at him, their strangely twisted shadows drawn out behind them. What next? Tell them to go back where they'd come from? Roland didn't know if they'd do it, and in any case had decided he liked them best where he could see them. And at least there was no question now about staying to bury the boy named James; that conundrum had been solved.

"Stand steady," he said in the low speech, beginning to retreat. "First fellow that moves——"

Before he could finish, one of them—a thick-chested troll with a pouty toad's mouth and what looked like gills on the sides of his wattled neck—lunged forward, gibbering in a high-pitched and peculiarly flabby voice. It might have been a species of laughter. He was waving what looked like a piano leg.

Roland fired. Mr. Toad's chest caved in like a bad piece of roofing. He ran backward several steps, trying to catch his balance and clawing at his chest with the hand not holding the piano leg. His feet, clad in dirty red velvet slippers with curled-up toes, tangled in each other and he fell over, making a queer and somehow lonely gargling sound. He let go of his club, rolled over on one side, tried to rise, and then fell back into the dust. The brutal sun glared into his open eyes, and as Roland watched, white tendrils of steam began to rise from his skin, which was rapidly losing its green undertint. There was also a hissing sound, like a gob of spit on top of a hot stove.

Saves explaining, at least, Roland thought, and swept his eyes over the others. "All right; he was the first one to move. Who wants to be the second?"

None did, it seemed. They only stood there, watching him, not coming at him . . . but not retreating, either. He thought (as he had about the cross-dog) that he should kill them as they stood there, just draw his other gun and mow them down. It would be the work of seconds only, and child's play to his gifted hands, even if some ran. But he couldn't. Not just cold, like that. He wasn't that kind of killer . . . at least, not yet.

Very slowly, he began to step backward, first bending his course around the watering trough, then putting it between him and them. When Bowler Hat took a step forward, Roland didn't give the others in the line a chance to copy him; he put a bullet into the dust of the High Street an inch in advance of Bowler Hat's foot.

"That's your last warning," he said, still using the low speech. He had no idea if they understood it, didn't really care. He guessed they caught this tune's music well enough. "Next bullet I fire eats up someone's heart. The way it works is, you stay and I go. You get this one chance. Follow me, and you all die. It's too hot to play games and I've lost my—"

"Booh!" cried a rough, liquidy voice from behind him. There was unmistakable glee in it. Roland saw a shadow grow from the shadow of the overturned freight wagon, which he had now almost reached, and had just time to understand that another of the green folk had been hiding beneath it.

As he began to turn, a club crashed down on Roland's shoulder, numbing his right arm all the way to the wrist. He held onto the gun and fired once, but the bullet went into one of the wagon wheels, smashing a wooden spoke and turning the wheel on its hub with a high screeing sound. Behind him, he heard the green folk in the street uttering hoarse, yapping cries as they charged forward.

The thing which had been hiding beneath the overturned wagon was a monster with two heads growing out of his neck, one with the vestigial, slack face of a corpse. The other, although just as green, was more lively. Broad lips spread in a cheerful grin as he raised his club to strike again.

Roland drew with his left hand—the one that wasn't numbed and distant. He had time to put one bullet through the bushwhacker's grin, flinging him backward in a spray of blood and teeth, the bludgeon flying out of his relaxing fingers. Then the others were on him, clubbing and drubbing.

The gunslinger was able to slip the first couple of blows, and there was one moment when he thought he might be able to spin around to the rear of the overturned wagon, spin and turn and go to work with his guns. Surely he would be able to do that. Surely his quest for the Dark Tower wasn't supposed to end on the sun-blasted street of a little far western town called Eluria, at the hands of half a dozen green-skinned slow mutants. Surely *ka* could not be so cruel.

But Bowler Hat caught him with a vicious sidehand blow, and Roland crashed into the wagon's slowly spinning rear wheel instead of skirting around it. As he went to his hands and knees, still scrambling and trying to turn, trying to evade the blows which rained down on him, he saw there were now many more than half a dozen. Coming up the street toward the town square were at least thirty green men and women. This wasn't a clan but a damned *tribe* of them. And in broad, hot daylight! Slow mutants were, in his experience, creatures that loved the dark, almost like toadstools with brains, and he had never seen any such as these before. They—

The one in the red vest was female. Her bare breasts swinging beneath the dirty red vest were the last things he saw clearly as they gathered around and above him, bashing away with their clubs. The one with the nails studded in it came down on his lower right calf, sinking its stupid rusty fangs in deep. He tried again to raise one of the big guns (his vision was fading, now, but that wouldn't help them if he got to shooting; he had always been the most hellishly talented of them, Jamie DeCurry had once proclaimed that Roland could shoot blindfolded, because he had eyes in his fingers), and it was kicked out of his hand and into the dust. Although he could still feel the smooth sandalwood grip of the other, he thought it was nevertheless already gone.

He could smell them—the rich, rotted smell of decaying meat. Or was that only his hands, as he raised them in a feeble and useless effort to protect his head? His hands, which had been in the polluted water where flecks and strips of the dead boy's skin floated?

The clubs slamming down on him, slamming down all over him, as if the green folk wanted not just to beat him to death but to tenderize him as they did so. And as he went down into the darkness of what he most certainly believed would be his death, he heard the bugs singing, the dog he had spared barking, and the bells hung on the church door ringing. These sounds merged together into strangely sweet music. Then that was gone, too; the darkness ate it all.

II. RISING. HANGING SUSPENDED. WHITE BEAUTY. TWO OTHERS. THE MEDALLION.

The gunslinger's return to the world wasn't like coming back to consciousness after a blow, which he'd done several times before, and it wasn't like waking from sleep, either. It was like rising.

I'm dead, he thought at some point during this process . . . when the power to think had been at least partially restored to him. *Dead and rising into whatever afterlife there is. That's what it must be. The singing I hear is the singing of dead souls.*

Total blackness gave way to the dark gray of rainclouds, then to the lighter gray of fog. This brightened to the uniform clarity of a heavy mist moments before the sun breaks through. And through it all was that sense of *rising,* as if he had been caught in some mild but powerful updraft.

As the sense of rising began to diminish and the brightness behind his eyelids grew, Roland at last began to believe he was still alive. It was the singing that convinced him. Not dead souls, not the heavenly host of angels sometimes described by the Jesus-Man preachers, but only those bugs. A little like crickets, but sweeter-voiced. The ones he had heard in Eluria.

On this thought, he opened his eyes.

His belief that he was still alive was severely tried, for Roland found himself hanging suspended in a world of white beauty—his first bewildered thought was that he was in the sky, floating within a fair-weather cloud. All around him was the reedy singing of the bugs. Now he could hear the tinkling of bells, too.

He tried to turn his head and swayed in some sort of harness. He could hear it creaking. The soft singing of the bugs, like crickets in the grass at the end of day back home in Gilead, hesitated and broke rhythm. When it did, what felt like a tree of pain grew up Roland's back. He had no idea what its burning branches might be, but the trunk was surely his spine. A far deadlier pain sank into one of his lower legs—in his confusion, the gunslinger could not tell which one. *That's where the club with the nails in it got me,* he thought. And more pain in his head. His skull felt like a badly cracked egg. He cried out, and could hardly believe that the harsh crow's caw he heard came from his own throat. He thought he could also hear, very faintly, the barking of the cross-dog, but surely that was his imagination.

Am I dying? Have I awakened once more at the very end?

A hand stroked his brow. He could feel it but not see it—fingers trailing across his skin, pausing here and there to massage a knot or a line. Delicious, like a drink of cool water on a hot day. He began to close his eyes, and then a horrible idea came to him: suppose that hand were green, its owner wearing a tattered red vest over her hanging dugs?

What if it is? What could you do?

"Hush, man," a young woman's voice said . . . or perhaps it was the voice of a girl. Certainly the first person Roland thought of was Susan, the girl from Mejis, she who had spoken to him as *thee*.

"Where . . . where . . ."

"Hush, stir not. 'Tis far too soon."

The pain in his back was subsiding now, but the image of the pain as a tree remained, for his very skin seemed to be moving like leaves in a light breeze. How could that be?

He let the question go—let all questions go—and concentrated on the small, cool hand stroking his brow.

"Hush, pretty man, God's love be upon ye. Yet it's sore hurt ye are. Be still. Heal."

The dog had hushed its barking (if it had ever been there in the first place), and Roland became aware of that low creaking sound again. It reminded him of horse tethers, or something

(hangropes)

he didn't like to think of. Now he believed he could feel pressure beneath his thighs, his buttocks, and per-haps . . . yes . . . his shoulders.

I'm not in a bed at all. I think I'm above a bed. Can that be?

He supposed he could be in a sling. He seemed to remember once, as a boy, that some fellow had been sus-pended that way in the horse doctor's room behind the Great Hall. A stablehand who had been burned too badly by kerosene to be laid in a bed. The man had died, but not soon enough; for two nights, his shrieks had filled the sweet summer air of the Gathering Fields.

Am I burned, then, nothing but a cinder with legs, hanging in a sling?

The fingers touched the center of his brow, rubbing away the frown forming there. And it was as if the voice which went with the hand had read his thoughts, picking them up with the tips of her clever, soothing fingers.

"Ye'll be fine if God wills, sai," the voice which went with the hand said. "But time belongs to God, not to you."

No, he would have said, if he had been able. *Time belongs to the Tower.*

Then he slipped down again, descending as smoothly as he had risen, going away from the hand and the dreamlike sounds of the singing insects and chiming bells. There was an interval that might have been sleep, or perhaps unconsciousness, but he never went all the way back down.

At one point he thought he heard the girl's voice, although he couldn't be sure, because this time it was raised in fury, or fear, or both. "No!" she cried. "Ye can't have it off him and ye know it! Go your course and stop talking of it, do!"

When he rose back to consciousness the second time, he was no stronger in body, but a little more himself in mind. What he saw when he opened his eyes wasn't the inside of a cloud, but at first that same phrase—*white beauty*—recurred to him. It was in some ways the most beautiful place Roland had ever been in his life . . . partially because he still *had* a life, of course, but mostly because it was so fey and peaceful.

It was a huge room, high and long. When Roland at last turned his head—cautiously, so cautiously—to take its measure as well as he could, he thought it must run at least two hundred yards from end to end. It was built narrow, but its height gave the place a feeling of tremendous airiness.

There were no walls or ceilings such as those he was familiar with, although it was a little like being in a vast tent. Above him, the sun struck and diffused its light across billowy panels of thin white silk, turning them into the bright swags that he had first mistaken for clouds. Beneath this silk canopy, the room was as gray as twilight. The walls, also silk, rippled like sails in a faint breeze. Hanging from each wall panel was a curved rope bearing small bells. These lay against the fabric and rang in low and charming unison, like wind chimes, when the walls rippled.

An aisle ran down the center of the long room; on either side of it were scores of beds, each made up with clean white sheets and headed with crisp white pillows. There were perhaps forty on the far side of the aisle, all empty, and another forty on Roland's side. There were two other occupied beds here, one next to Roland on his right. This fellow—

It's the boy. The one who was in the trough.

The idea ran goose-bumps up Roland's arms and gave him a nasty, superstitious start. He peered more closely at the sleeping boy.

Can't be. You're just dazed, that's all; it can't be.

Yet closer scrutiny refused to dispel the idea. It certainly *seemed* to be the boy from the trough, probably ill (why else would he be in a place like this?) but far from dead; Roland could see the slow rise and fall of his chest, and the occasional twitch of the fingers that dangled over the side of the bed.

You didn't get a good enough look at him to be sure of anything, and after a few days in that trough, his own mother couldn't have said for sure who it was.

But Roland, who'd had a mother, knew better than that. He also knew that he'd seen the gold medallion around the boy's neck. Just before the attack of the green folk, he had taken it from this lad's corpse and put it in his pocket. Now someone—the proprietors of this place, most likely, those who had sorcerously restored the lad named James to his interrupted life—had taken it back from Roland and put it around the boy's neck again.

Had the girl with the wonderfully cool hand done that? Did she in consequence think Roland a ghoul who would steal from the dead? He didn't like to think so. In fact, the notion made him more uncomfortable than the idea that the young cowboy's bloated body had been somehow returned to its normal size and then reanimated.

Farther down the aisle on this side, perhaps a dozen empty beds away from the boy and Roland Deschain, the gunslinger saw a third inmate of this queer infirmary. This fellow looked at least four times the age of the lad, twice the age of the gunslinger. He had a long beard, more gray than black, that hung to his upper chest in two straggly forks. The face above it was sun-darkened, heavily lined, and pouched beneath the eyes. Running from his left cheek and across the bridge of his nose was a thick dark mark which Roland took to be a scar. The bearded man was either asleep or unconscious—Roland could hear him snoring—and was suspended three feet above his bed, held up by a complex series of white belts that glimmered in the dim air. These crisscrossed each other, making a series of figure eights all the way around the man's body. He looked like a bug in some exotic spider's web. He wore a gauzy white bed-dress. One of the belts ran beneath his buttocks, elevating his crotch in a way that seemed to offer the bulge of his privates to the gray and dreaming air. Farther down his body, Roland could see the dark shadow-shapes of his legs. They appeared to be twisted like ancient dead trees. Roland didn't like to think in how many places they must have been broken to look like that. And yet they appeared to be *moving*. How could they be, if the bearded man was unconscious? It was a trick of the light, perhaps, or of the shadows . . . perhaps the gauzy singlet the man was wearing was stirring in a light breeze, or . . .

Roland looked away, up at the billowy silk panels high above, trying to control the accelerating beat of his heart. What he saw hadn't been caused by the wind, or a shadow, or anything else. The man's legs were somehow moving without moving . . . as Roland had seemed to feel his own back moving without moving. He didn't know what could cause such a phenomenon, and didn't want to know, at least not yet.

"I'm not ready," he whispered. His lips felt very dry. He closed his eyes again, wanting to sleep, wanting not to think about what the bearded man's twisted legs might indicate about his own condition. But—

But you'd better get *ready.*

That was the voice that always seemed to come when he tried to slack off, to scamp a job or take the easy way around an obstacle. It was the voice of Cort, his old teacher. The man whose stick they had all feared, as boys. They hadn't feared his stick as much as his mouth, however. His jeers when they were weak, his contempt when they complained or tried whining about their lot.

Are you a gunslinger, Roland? If you are, you better get ready.

Roland opened his eyes again and turned his head to the left again. As he did, he felt something shift against his chest.

Moving very slowly, he raised his right hand out of the sling that held it. The pain in his back stirred and muttered. He stopped moving until he decided the pain was going to get no worse (if he was careful, at least), then lifted the hand the rest of the way to his chest. It encountered finely woven cloth. Cotton. He moved his chin to his breastbone and saw that he was wearing a bed-dress like the one draped on the body of the bearded man.

Roland reached beneath the neck of the gown and felt a fine chain. A little farther down, his fingers encountered a rectangular metal shape. He thought he knew what it was, but had to be sure. He pulled it out, still moving with great care, trying not to engage any of the muscles in his back. A gold medallion. He dared the pain, lifting it until he could read what was engraved upon it:

James
Loved of family. Loved of GOD

He tucked it into the top of the bed-dress again and looked back at the sleeping boy in the next bed—*in* it, not suspended over it. The sheet was only pulled up to the boy's rib cage, and the medallion lay on the pristine white breast of his bed-dress. The same medallion Roland now wore. Except . . .

Roland thought he understood, and understanding was a relief.

He looked back at the bearded man, and saw an exceedingly strange thing: the thick black line of scar across the bearded man's cheek and nose was gone. Where it had been was the pinkish-red mark of a healing wound . . . a cut, or perhaps a slash.

I imagined it.

No, gunslinger, Cort's voice returned. *Such as you was not made to imagine. As you well know.*

The little bit of movement had tired him out again . . . or perhaps it was the thinking which had really tired him out. The singing bugs and chiming bells combined had made something too much like a lullaby to resist. This time when Roland closed his eyes, he slept.

III. FIVE SISTERS. JENNA. THE DOCTORS OF ELURIA. THE MEDALLION. A PROMISE OF SILENCE.

When Roland awoke again, he was at first sure that he was still sleeping. Dreaming. Having a nightmare.

Once, at the time he had met and fallen in love with Susan Delgado, he had known a witch named Rhea— the first real witch of Mid-World he had ever met. It was she who had caused Susan's death, although Roland had played his own part. Now, opening his eyes and seeing Rhea not just once but five times over, he thought: *This is what comes of remembering those old times. By conjuring Susan, I've conjured Rhea of the Cöos, as well. Rhea and her sisters.*

The five were dressed in billowing habits as white as the walls and the panels of the ceiling. Their antique crones' faces were framed in wimples just as white, their skin as gray and runneled as droughted earth by comparison. Hanging like phylacteries from the bands of silk imprisoning their hair (if they indeed had hair) were lines of tiny bells which chimed as they moved or spoke. Upon the snowy breasts of their habits was embroidered a blood-red rose . . . the *sigul* of the Dark Tower. Seeing this, Roland thought: *I am not dreaming. These harridans are real.*

"He wakes!" one of them cried in a gruesomely coquettish voice.

"Oooo!"

"Ooooh!"

"Ah!"

They fluttered like birds. The one in the center stepped forward, and as she did, their faces seemed to shimmer like the silk walls of the ward. They weren't old after all, he saw—middle-aged, perhaps, but not old.

Yes. They are *old. They* changed.

The one who now took charge was taller than the others, and with a broad, slightly bulging brow. She bent toward Roland, and the bells that fringed her forehead tinkled. The sound made him feel sick, somehow, and weaker than he had felt a moment before. Her hazel eyes were intent. Greedy, mayhap. She touched his cheek for a moment, and a numbness seemed to spread there. Then she glanced down, and a look which could have been disquiet cramped her face. She took her hand back.

"Ye wake, pretty man. So ye do. 'Tis well."

"Who are you? Where am I?"

"We are the Little Sisters of Eluria," she said. "I am Sister Mary. Here is Sister Louise, and Sister Michela, and Sister Coquina——"

"And Sister Tamra," said the last. "A lovely lass of one-and-twenty." She giggled. Her face shimmered, and for a moment she was again as old as the world. Hooked of nose, gray of skin. Roland thought once more of Rhea.

They moved closer, encircling the complication of harness in which he lay suspended, and when Roland shrank back, the pain roared up his back and injured leg again. He groaned. The straps holding him creaked.

"Ooooo!"

"It hurts!"

"Hurts him!"

"Hurts so fierce!"

They pressed even closer, as if his pain fascinated them. And now he could smell them, a dry and earthy smell. The one named Sister Michela reached out——

"Go away! Leave him! Have I not told ye before?"

They jumped back from this voice, startled. Sister Mary looked particularly annoyed. But she stepped back, with one final glare (Roland would have sworn it) at the medallion lying on his chest. He had tucked it back under the bed-dress at his last waking, but it was out again now.

A sixth sister appeared, pushing rudely in between Mary and Tamra. This one perhaps *was* only one-and-twenty, with flushed cheeks, smooth skin, and dark eyes. Her white habit billowed like a dream. The red rose over her breast stood out like a curse.

"Go! Leave him!"

"Oooo, my *dear!*" cried Sister Louise in a voice both laughing and angry. "Here's Jenna, the baby, and has she fallen in love with him?"

"She has!" Tamra said, laughing. "Baby's heart is his for the purchase!"

"Oh, so it *is!*" agreed Sister Coquina.

Mary turned to the newcomer, lips pursed into a tight line. "Ye have no business here, saucy girl."

"I do if I say I do," Sister Jenna replied. She seemed more in charge of herself now. A curl of black hair had escaped her wimple and lay across her forehead in a comma. "Now go. He's not up to your jokes and laughter."

"Order us not," Sister Mary said, "for we never joke. So you know, Sister Jenna."

The girl's face softened a little, and Roland saw she was afraid. It made him afraid for her. For himself, as well. "Go," she repeated. "'Tis not the time. Are there not others to tend?"

Sister Mary seemed to consider. The others watched her. At last she nodded, and smiled down at Roland. Again her face seemed to shimmer, like something seen through a heat-haze. What he saw (or thought he saw) beneath was horrible and watchful. "Bide well, pretty man," she said to Roland. "Bide with us a bit, and we'll heal ye."

What choice have I? Roland thought.

The others laughed, birdlike titters which rose into the dimness like ribbons. Sister Michela actually blew him a kiss.

"Come, ladies!" Sister Mary cried. "We'll leave Jenna with him a bit in memory of her mother, whom we loved well!" And with that, she led the others away, five white birds flying off down the center aisle, their skirts nodding this way and that.

"Thank you," Roland said, looking up at the owner of the cool hand . . . for he knew it was she who had soothed him.

She took up his fingers as if to prove this, and caressed them. "They mean ye no harm," she said . . . yet Roland saw she believed not a word of it, nor did he. He was in trouble here, very bad trouble.

"What is this place?"

"Our place," she said simply. "The home of the Little Sisters of Eluria. Our convent, if'ee like."

"This is no convent," Roland said, looking past her at the empty beds. "It's an infirmary. Isn't it?"

"A hospital," she said, still stroking his fingers. "We serve the doctors . . . and they serve us." He was fascinated by the black curl lying on the cream of her brow—would have stroked it, if he had dared reach up. Just to tell its texture. He found it beautiful because it was the only dark thing in all this white. The white had lost its charm for him. "We are hospitalers . . . or were, before the world moved on."

"Are you for the Jesus Man?"

She looked surprised for a moment, almost shocked, and then laughed merrily. "No, not us!"

"If you are hospitalers . . . nurses . . . where are the doctors?"

She looked at him, biting at her lip, as if trying to decide something. Roland found her doubt utterly charming, and he realized that, sick or not, he was looking at a woman *as* a woman for the first time since Susan Delgado had died, and that had been long ago. The whole world had changed since then, and not for the better.

"Would you really know?"

"Yes, of course," he said, a little surprised. A little disquieted, too. He kept waiting for her face to shimmer and change, as the faces of the others had done. It didn't. There was none of that unpleasant dead-earth smell about her, either.

Wait, he cautioned himself. *Believe nothing here, least of all your senses. Not yet.*

"I suppose you must," she said with a sigh. It tinkled the bells at her forehead, which were darker in color than those the others wore—not black like her hair but charry, somehow, as if they had been hung in the smoke of a campfire. Their sound, however, was brightest silver. "Promise me you'll not scream and wake the pube in yonder bed."

"Pube?"

"The boy. Do ye promise?"

"Aye," he said, falling into the half-forgotten patois of the Outer Arc without even being aware of it. Susan's dialect. "It's been long since I screamed, pretty."

She colored more definitely at that, roses more natural and lively than the one on her breast mounting in her cheeks.

"Don't call pretty what ye can't properly see," she said.

"Then push back the wimple you wear."

Her face he could see perfectly well, but he badly wanted to see her hair—hungered for it, almost. A full flood of black in all this dreaming white. Of course it might be cropped, those of her order might wear it that way, but he somehow didn't think so.

"No, 'tis not allowed."

"By whom?"

"Big Sister."

"She who calls herself Mary?"

"Aye, her." She started away, then paused and looked back over her shoulder. In another girl her age, one as pretty as this, that look back would have been flirtatious. This girl's was only grave.

"Remember your promise."

"Aye, no screams."

She went to the bearded man, skirt swinging. In the dimness, she cast only a blur of shadow on the empty beds she passed. When she reached the man (this one was unconscious, Roland thought, not just sleeping), she looked back at Roland once more. He nodded.

Sister Jenna stepped close to the suspended man, on the far side of his bed, so that Roland saw her through the twists and loops of woven white silk. She placed her hands lightly on the left side of his chest, bent over him . . . and shook her head from side to side, like one expressing a brisk negative. The bells she wore on her forehead rang sharply, and Roland once more felt that weird stirring up his back, accompanied by a low ripple of pain. It was as if he had shuddered without actually shuddering, or shuddered in a dream.

What happened next almost *did* jerk a scream from him; he had to bite his lips against it. Once more the unconscious man's legs seemed to move without moving . . . because it was what was *on* them that moved. The man's hairy shins, ankles, and feet were exposed below the hem of his bed-dress. Now a black wave of bugs moved down them. They were singing fiercely, like an army column that sings as it marches.

Roland remembered the black scar across the man's cheek and nose—the scar that had disappeared. More such as these, of course. And they were on *him,* as well. That was how he could shiver without shivering. They were all over his back. *Battening* on him.

No, keeping back a scream wasn't as easy as he had expected it to be.

The bugs ran down to the tips of the suspended man's toes, then leaped off them in waves, like creatures springing off an embankment and into a swimming hole. They organized themselves quickly and easily on the bright white sheet below, and began to march down to the floor in a battalion about a foot wide. Roland couldn't get a good look at them, the distance was too far and the light too dim, but he thought they were perhaps twice the size of ants, and a little smaller than the fat honeybees which had swarmed the flower beds back home.

They sang as they went.

The bearded man didn't sing. As the swarms of bugs that had coated his twisted legs began to diminish, he shuddered and groaned. The young woman put her hand on his brow and soothed him, making Roland a little jealous even in his revulsion at what he was seeing.

And was what he was seeing really so awful? In Gilead, leeches had been used for certain ailments—swellings of the brain, the armpits, and the groin, primarily. When it came to the brain, the leeches, ugly as they were, were certainly preferable to the next step, which was trepanning.

Yet there *was* something loathsome about them, perhaps only because he couldn't see them well, and something awful about trying to imagine them all over his back as he hung here, helpless. Not singing, though. Why? Because they were feeding? Sleeping? Both at once?

The bearded man's groans subsided. The bugs marched away across the floor, toward one of the mildly rippling silken walls. Roland lost sight of them in the shadows.

Jenna came back to him, her eyes anxious. "Ye did well. Yet I see how ye feel; it's on your face."

"The doctors," he said.

"Yes. Their power is very great, but . . ." She dropped her voice. "I believe that drover is beyond their help. His legs are a little better, and the wounds on his face are all but healed, but he has injuries where the doctors cannot reach." She traced a hand across her midsection, suggesting the location of these injuries, if not their nature.

"And me?" Roland asked.

"Ye were ta'en by the green folk," she said. "Ye must have angered them powerfully, for them not to kill ye outright. They roped ye and dragged ye, instead. Tamra, Michela, and Louise were out gathering herbs. They saw the green folk at play with ye, and bade them stop, but—"

"Do the muties always obey you, Sister Jenna?"

She smiled, perhaps pleased he remembered her name. "Not always, but mostly. This time they did, or ye'd have now found the clearing in the trees."

"I suppose so."

"The skin was stripped almost clean off your back— red ye were from nape to waist. Ye'll always bear the scars, but the doctors have gone far toward healing ye. And their singing is passing fair, is it not?"

"Yes," Roland said, but the thought of those black things all over his back, roosting in his raw flesh, still revolted him. "I owe you thanks, and give it freely. Anything I can do for you—"

"Tell me your name, then. Do that."

"I'm Roland of Gilead. A gunslinger. I had revolvers, Sister Jenna. Have you seen them?"

"I've seen no shooters," she said, but cast her eyes aside. The roses bloomed in her cheeks again. She might be a good nurse, and fair, but Roland thought her a poor liar. He was glad. Good liars were common. Honesty, on the other hand, came dear.

Let the untruth pass for now, he told himself. *She speaks it out of fear, I think.*

"Jenna!" The cry came from the deeper shadows at the far end of the infirmary—today it seemed longer than ever to the gunslinger—and Sister Jenna jumped guiltily. "Come away! Ye've passed words enough to entertain twenty men! Let him sleep!"

"Aye!" she called, then turned back to Roland. "Don't let on that I showed you the doctors."

"Mum is the word, Jenna."

She paused, biting her lip again, then suddenly swept back her wimple. It fell against the nape of her neck in a soft chiming of bells. Freed from its confinement, her hair swept against her cheeks like shadows.

"*Am* I pretty? *Am* I? Tell me the truth, Roland of Gilead—no flattery. For flattery's kind only a candle's length."

"Pretty as a summer night."

What she saw in his face seemed to please her more than his words, because she smiled radiantly. She pulled the wimple up again, tucking her hair back in with quick little finger-pokes. "Am I decent?"

"Decent as fair," he said, then cautiously lifted an arm and pointed at her brow. "One curl's out . . . just there."

"Aye, always that one to devil me." With a comical little grimace, she tucked it back. Roland thought how much he would like to kiss her rosy cheeks . . . and perhaps her rosy mouth for good measure.

"All's well," he said.

"*Jenna!*" The cry was more impatient than ever. "Meditations!"

"I'm coming just now!" she called, and gathered her voluminous skirts to go. Yet she turned back once more, her face now very grave and very serious. "One more thing," she said in a voice only a step above a whisper. She snatched a quick look around. "The gold medallion ye wear—ye wear it because it's yours. Do'ee understand . . . James?"

"Yes." He turned his head a bit to look at the sleeping boy. "This is my brother."

"If they ask, yes. To say different would be to get Jenna in serious trouble."

How serious he did not ask, and she was gone in any case, seeming to flow along the aisle between all the empty beds, her skirt caught up in one hand. The roses had fled from her face, leaving her cheeks and brow ashy. He remembered the greedy look on the faces of the others, how they had gathered around him in a tightening knot . . . and the way their faces had shimmered.

Six women, five old and one young.

Doctors that sang and then crawled away across the floor when dismissed by jingling bells.

And an improbable hospital ward of perhaps a hundred beds, a ward with a silk roof and silk walls . . .

. . . and all the beds empty save three.

Roland didn't understand why Jenna had taken the dead boy's medallion from his pants pocket and put it around his neck, but he had an idea that if they found out she had done so, the Little Sisters of Eluria might kill her.

Roland closed his eyes, and the soft singing of the doctor-insects once again floated him off into sleep.

IV. A BOWL OF SOUP. THE BOY IN THE NEXT BED. THE NIGHT-NURSES.

Roland dreamed that a very large bug (a doctor-bug, mayhap) was flying around his head and banging repeatedly into his nose—collisions which were annoying rather than painful. He swiped at the bug repeatedly, and although his hands were eerily fast under ordinary circumstances, he kept missing it. And each time he missed, the bug giggled.

I'm slow because I've been sick, he thought.

No, ambushed. Dragged across the ground by slow mutants, saved by the Little Sisters of Eluria.

Roland had a sudden, vivid image of a man's shadow growing from the shadow of an overturned freight wagon; heard a rough, gleeful voice cry "Booh!"

He jerked awake hard enough to set his body rocking in its complication of slings, and the woman who had been standing beside his head, giggling as she tapped his nose lightly with a wooden spoon, stepped back so quickly that the bowl in her other hand slipped from her fingers.

Roland's hands shot out, and they were as quick as ever—his frustrated failure to catch the bug had been only part of his dream. He caught the bowl before more than a few drops could spill. The woman—Sister Coquina—looked at him with round eyes.

There was pain all up and down his back from the sudden movement, but it was nowhere near as sharp as it had been before, and there was no sensation of movement on his skin. Perhaps the "doctors" were only sleeping, but he had an idea they were gone.

He held out his hand for the spoon Coquina had been teasing him with (he found he wasn't surprised at all that one of these would tease a sick and sleeping man in such a way; it would have surprised him only if it had been Jenna), and she handed it to him, her eyes still big.

"How speedy ye are!" she said. "'Twas like a magic trick, and you still rising from sleep!"

"Remember it, sai," he said, and tried the soup. There

were tiny bits of chicken floating in it. He probably would have considered it bland under other circumstances, but under these, it seemed ambrosial. He began to eat greedily.

"What do'ee mean by that?" she asked. The light was very dim now, the wall panels across the way a pinkish orange that suggested sunset. In this light, Coquina looked quite young and pretty . . . but it was a glamour, Roland was sure; a sorcerous kind of makeup.

"I mean nothing in particular." Roland dismissed the spoon as too slow, preferring to tilt the bowl itself to his lips. In this way he disposed of the soup in four large gulps. "You have been kind to me—"

"Aye, so we *have!*" she said, rather indignantly.

"—and I hope your kindness has no hidden motive. If it does, Sister, remember that I'm quick. And, as for myself, I have not always been kind."

She made no reply, only took the bowl when Roland handed it back. She did this delicately, perhaps not wanting to touch his fingers. Her eyes dropped to where the medallion lay, once more hidden beneath the breast of his bed-dress. He said no more, not wanting to weaken the implied threat by reminding her that the man who made it was unarmed, next to naked, and hung in the air because his back couldn't yet bear the weight of his body.

"Where's Sister Jenna?" he asked.

"Oooo," Sister Coquina said, raising her eyebrows. "We like her, do we? She makes our heart go . . ." She put her hand against the rose on her breast and fluttered it rapidly.

"Not at all, not at all," Roland said, "but she was

kind. I doubt she would have teased me with a spoon, as some would."

Sister Coquina's smile faded. She looked both angry and worried. "Say nothing of that to Mary, if she comes by later. Ye might get me in trouble."

"Should I care?"

"I might get back at one who caused me trouble by causing little Jenna trouble," Sister Coquina said. "She's in Big Sister's black books, just now, anyway. Sister Mary doesn't care for the way Jenna spoke to her about ye . . . nor does she like it that Jenna came back to us wearing the Dark Bells."

This was scarcely out of her mouth before Sister Coquina put her hand over that frequently imprudent organ, as if realizing she had said too much.

Roland, intrigued by what she'd said but not liking to show it just now, only replied, "I'll keep my mouth shut about you, if you keep your mouth shut to Sister Mary about Jenna."

Coquina looked relieved. "Aye, that's a bargain." She leaned forward confidingly. "She's in Thoughtful House. That's the little cave in the hillside where we have to go and meditate when Big Sister decides we've been bad. She'll have to stay and consider her impudence until Mary lets her out." She paused, then said abruptly, "Who's this beside ye? Do ye know?"

Roland turned his head and saw that the young man was awake, and had been listening. His eyes were as dark as Jenna's.

"Know him?" Roland asked, with what he hoped was the right touch of scorn. "Should I not know my own brother?"

"Is he, now, and him so young and you so old?" Another of the sisters materialized out of the darkness: Sister Tamra, who had called herself one-and-twenty. In the moment before she reached Roland's bed, her face was that of a hag who will never see eighty again . . . or ninety. Then it shimmered and was once more the plump, healthy countenance of a thirty-year-old matron. Except for the eyes. They remained yellowish in the corneas, gummy in the corners, and watchful.

"He's the youngest, I the eldest," Roland said. "Betwixt us are seven others, and twenty years of our parents' lives."

"How sweet! And if he's yer brother, then ye'll know his name, won't ye? Know it very well."

Before the gunslinger could flounder, the young man said, "They think you've forgotten such a simple hook as John Norman. What culleens they be, eh, Jimmy?"

Coquina and Tamra looked at the pale boy in the bed next to Roland's, clearly angry . . . and clearly trumped. For the time being, at least.

"You've fed him your muck," the boy (whose medallion undoubtedly proclaimed him *John, Loved of family. Loved of GOD*) said. "Why don't you go, and let us have a natter?"

"Well!" Sister Coquina huffed. "I like the gratitude around here, so I do!"

"I'm grateful for what's given me," Norman responded, looking at her steadily, "but not for what folk would take away."

Tamra snorted through her nose, turned violently enough for her swirling dress to push a draught of air into Roland's face, and then took her leave. Coquina stayed a moment.

"Be discreet, and mayhap someone ye like better than ye like me will get out of hack in the morning, instead of a week from tonight."

Without waiting for a reply, she turned and followed Sister Tamra.

Roland and John Norman waited until they were both gone, and then Norman turned to Roland and spoke in a low voice. "My brother. Dead?"

Roland nodded. "The medallion I took in case I should meet with any of his people. It rightly belongs to you. I'm sorry for your loss."

"Thankee-sai." John Norman's lower lip trembled, then firmed. "I knew the green men did for him, although these old biddies wouldn't tell me for sure. They did for plenty, and scotched the rest."

"Perhaps the Sisters didn't know for sure."

"They knew. Don't you doubt it. They don't say much, but they know *plenty*. The only one any different is Jenna. That's who the old battle-axe meant when she said 'your friend.' Aye?"

Roland nodded. "And she said something about the Dark Bells. I'd know more of that, if would were could."

"She's something special, Jenna is. More like a princess—someone whose place is made by bloodline and can't be refused—than like the other Sisters. I lie here and look like I'm asleep—it's safer, I think—but I've heard em talking. Jenna's just come back among em recently, and those Dark Bells mean something special . . . but Mary's still the one who swings the weight. I think the Dark Bells are only ceremonial, like the rings the old Barons used to hand down from father to son. Was it she who put Jimmy's medal around your neck?"

"Yes."

"Don't take it off, whatever you do." His face was strained, grim. "I don't know if it's the gold or the God, but they don't like to get too close. I think that's the only reason I'm still here." Now his voice dropped all the way to a whisper. "They ain't human."

"Well, perhaps a bit fey and magical, but . . ."

"No!" With what was clearly an effort, the boy got up on one elbow. He looked at Roland earnestly. "You're thinking about hubberwomen, or witches. These ain't hubbers, nor witches, either. *They ain't human!*"

"Then what are they?"

"Don't know."

"How came you here, John?"

Speaking in a low voice, John Norman told Roland what he knew of what had happened to him. He, his brother, and four other young men who were quick and owned good horses had been hired as scouts, riding drogue-and-forward, protecting a long-haul caravan of seven freight wagons taking goods—seeds, food, tools, mail, and four ordered brides—to an unincorporated township called Tejuas some two hundred miles farther west of Eluria. The scouts rode fore and aft of the goods-train in turn-and-turn-about fashion; one brother rode with each party because, Norman explained, when they were together they fought like . . . well . . .

"Like brothers," Roland suggested.

John Norman managed a brief, pained smile. "Aye," he said.

The trio of which John was a part had been riding drogue, about two miles behind the freight wagons, when the green mutants had sprung an ambush in Eluria.

"How many wagons did you see when you got there?" he asked Roland.

"Only one. Overturned."

"How many bodies?"

"Only your brother's."

John Norman nodded grimly. "They wouldn't take him because of the medallion, I think."

"The muties?"

"The Sisters. The muties care nothing for gold or God. These bitches, though . . ." He looked into the dark, which was now almost complete. Roland felt lethargy creeping over him again, but it wasn't until later that he realized the soup had been drugged.

"The other wagons?" Roland asked. "The ones not overturned?"

"The muties would have taken them, and the goods, as well," Norman said. "They don't care for gold or God; the Sisters don't care for goods. Like as not they have their own foodstuffs, something I'd as soon not think of. Nasty stuff . . . like those bugs."

He and the other drogue riders galloped into Eluria, but the fight was over by the time they got there. Men had been lying about, some dead but many more still alive. At least two of the ordered brides had still been alive, as well. Survivors able to walk were being herded together by the green folk—John Norman remembered the one in the bowler hat very well, and the woman in the ragged red vest.

Norman and the other two had tried to fight. He had seen one of his pards gutshot by an arrow, and then he saw no more—someone had cracked him over the head from behind, and the lights had gone out.

Roland wondered if the ambusher had cried "Booh!" before he had struck, but didn't ask.

"When I woke up again, I was here," Norman said. "I saw that some of the others—*most* of them—had those cursed bugs on them."

"Others?" Roland looked at the empty beds. In the growing darkness, they glimmered like white islands. "How many were brought here?"

"At least twenty. They healed . . . the bugs healed em . . . and then, one by one, they disappeared. You'd go to sleep, and when you woke up there'd be one more empty bed. One by one they went, until only me and that one down yonder was left."

He looked at Roland solemnly.

"And now you."

"Norman," Roland's head was swimming. "I—"

"I reckon I know what's wrong with you," Norman said. He seemed to speak from far away . . . perhaps from all the way around the curve of the earth. "It's the soup. But a man has to eat. A woman, too. If she's a natural woman, anyway. These ones ain't natural. Even Sister Jenna's not natural. Nice don't mean natural." Farther and farther away. "And she'll be like them in the end. Mark me well."

"Can't move." Saying even that required a huge effort. It was like moving boulders.

"No." Norman suddenly laughed. It was a shocking

sound, and echoed in the growing blackness which filled Roland's head. "It ain't just sleep medicine they put in their soup; it's can't-move medicine, too. There's nothing much wrong with me, brother . . . so why do you think I'm still here?"

Norman was now speaking not from around the curve of the earth but perhaps from the moon. He said: "I don't think either of us is ever going to see the sun shining on a flat piece of ground again."

You're wrong about that, Roland tried to reply, and more in that vein, as well, but nothing came out. He sailed around to the black side of the moon, losing all his words in the void he found there.

Yet he never quite lost awareness of himself. Perhaps the dose of "medicine" in Sister Coquina's soup had been badly calculated, or perhaps it was just that they had never had a gunslinger to work their mischief on, and did not know they had one now.

Except, of course, for Sister Jenna—*she* knew.

At some point in the night, whispering, giggling voices and lightly chiming bells brought him back from the darkness where he had been biding, not quite asleep or unconscious. Around him, so constant he now barely heard it, were the singing "doctors."

Roland opened his eyes. He saw pale and chancy light dancing in the black air. The giggles and whispers were closer. Roland tried to turn his head and at first couldn't. He rested, gathered his will into a hard blue ball, and tried again. This time his head *did* turn. Only a little, but a little was enough.

It was five of the Little Sisters—Mary, Louise, Tamra, Coquina, Michela. They came up the long aisle of the black infirmary, laughing together like children out on a prank, carrying long tapers in silver holders, the bells lining the forehead-bands of their wimples chiming little silver runs of sound. They gathered about the bed of the bearded man. From within their circle, candleglow rose in a shimmery column that died before it got halfway to the silken ceiling.

Sister Mary spoke briefly. Roland recognized her voice, but not the words—it was neither low speech nor the High, but some other language entirely. One phrase stood out—*can de lach, mi him en tow*—and he had no idea what it might mean.

He realized that now he could hear only the tinkle of bells—the doctor-bugs had stilled.

"Ras me! On! On!" Sister Mary cried in a harsh, powerful voice. The candles went out. The light that had shone through the wings of their wimples as they gathered around the bearded man's bed vanished, and all was darkness once more.

Roland waited for what might happen next, his skin cold. He tried to flex his hands or feet, and could not. He had been able to move his head perhaps fifteen degrees; otherwise he was as paralyzed as a fly neatly wrapped up and hung in a spider's web.

The low jingling of bells in the black . . . and then sucking sounds. As soon as he heard them, Roland knew he'd been waiting for them. Some part of him had known what the Little Sisters of Eluria were, all along.

If Roland could have raised his hands, he would have put them to his ears to block those sounds out. As it was, he could only lie still, listening and waiting for them to stop.

For a long time—forever, it seemed—they did not. The women slurped and grunted like pigs snuffling half-liquefied feed up out of a trough. There was even one resounding belch, followed by more whispered giggles (these ended when Sister Mary uttered a single curt word—*"Hais!"*). And once there was a low, moaning cry—from the bearded man, Roland was quite sure. If so, it was his last on this side of the clearing.

In time, the sounds of their feeding began to taper off. As it did, the bugs began to sing again—first hesitantly, then with more confidence. The whispering and giggling recommenced. The candles were relit. Roland was by now lying with his head turned in the other direction. He didn't want them to know what he'd seen, but that wasn't all; he had no urge to see more on any account. He had seen and heard enough.

But the giggles and whispers now came his way. Roland closed his eyes, concentrating on the medallion that lay against his chest. *I don't know if it's the gold or the God, but they don't like to get too close,* John Norman had said. It was good to have such a thing to remember as the Little Sisters drew nigh, gossiping and whispering in their strange other tongue, but the medallion seemed a thin protection in the dark.

Faintly, at a great distance, Roland heard the cross-dog barking.

As the Sisters circled him, the gunslinger realized he could smell them. It was a low, unpleasant odor, like spoiled meat. And what else *would* they smell of, such as these?

"Such a pretty man it is." Sister Mary. She spoke in a low, meditative tone.

"But such an ugly *sigul* it wears." Sister Tamra.

"We'll have it off him!" Sister Louise.

"And then we shall have kisses!" Sister Coquina.

"Kisses for all!" exclaimed Sister Michela, with such fervent enthusiasm that they all laughed.

Roland discovered that not *all* of him was paralyzed, after all. Part of him had, in fact, arisen from its sleep at the sound of their voices and now stood tall. A hand reached beneath the bed-dress he wore, touched that stiffened member, encircled it, caressed it. He lay in silent horror, feigning sleep, as wet warmth almost immediately spilled from him. The hand remained where it was for a moment, the thumb rubbing up and down the wilting shaft. Then it let him go and rose a little higher. Found the wetness pooled on his lower belly.

Giggles, soft as wind.

Chiming bells.

Roland opened his eyes the tiniest crack and looked up at the ancient faces laughing down at him in the light of their candles—glittering eyes, yellow cheeks, hanging teeth that jutted over lower lips. Sister Michela and Sister Louise appeared to have grown goatees, but of course that wasn't the darkness of hair but of the bearded man's blood.

Mary's hand was cupped. She passed it from Sister to Sister; each licked from her palm in the candlelight.

Roland closed his eyes all the way and waited for them to be gone. Eventually they were.

I'll never sleep again, he thought, and was five minutes later lost to himself and the world.

V. Sister Mary. A Message. A Visit from Ralph.
Norman's Fate. Sister Mary Again.

When Roland awoke, it was full daylight, the silk roof overhead a bright white and billowing in a mild breeze. The doctor-bugs were singing contentedly. Beside him on his left, Norman was heavily asleep with his head turned so far to one side that his stubbly cheek rested on his shoulder.

Roland and John Norman were the only ones here. Farther down on their side of the infirmary, the bed where the bearded man had been was empty, its top sheet pulled up and neatly tucked in, the pillow neatly nestled in a crisp white case. The complication of slings in which his body had rested was gone.

Roland remembered the candles—the way their glow had combined and streamed up in a column, illuminating the Sisters as they gathered around the bearded man. Giggling. Their damned bells jingling.

Now, as if summoned by his thoughts, came Sister Mary, gliding along rapidly with Sister Louise in her wake. Louise bore a tray, and looked nervous. Mary was frowning, obviously not in good temper.

To be grumpy after you've fed so well? Roland thought. *Fie, Sister.*

She reached the gunslinger's bed and looked down at him. "I have little to thank ye for, sai," she said with no preamble.

"Have I asked for your thanks?" he responded in a voice that sounded as dusty and little-used as the pages of an old book.

She took no notice. "Ye've made one who was only

impudent and restless with her place outright rebellious. Well, her mother was the same way, and died of it not long after returning Jenna to her proper place. Raise your hand, thankless man."

"I can't. I can't move at all."

"Oh, cully! Haven't you heard it said 'fool not your mother 'less she's out of face'? I know pretty well what ye can and can't do. Now raise your hand."

Roland raised his right hand, trying to suggest more effort than it actually took. He thought that this morning he might be strong enough to slip free of the slings . . . but what then? Any real walking would be beyond him for hours yet, even without another dose of "medicine" . . . and behind Sister Mary, Sister Louise was taking the cover from a fresh bowl of soup. As Roland looked at it, his stomach rumbled.

Big Sister heard and smiled a bit. "Even lying in bed builds an appetite in a strong man, if it's done long enough. Wouldn't you say so, Jason, brother of John?"

"My name is James. As you well know, Sister."

"Do I?" She laughed angrily. "Oh, la! And if I whipped your little sweetheart hard enough and long enough—until the blood jumped out her back like drops of sweat, let us say—should I not whip a different name out of her? Or didn't ye trust her with it, during your little talk?"

"Touch her and I'll kill you."

She laughed again. Her face shimmered; her firm mouth turned into something that looked like a dying jellyfish. "Speak not of killing to us, cully; lest we speak of it to you."

"Sister, if you and Jenna don't see eye to eye, why not

release her from her vows and let her go her course?"

"Such as us can never be released from our vows, nor be let go. Her mother tried and then came back, her dying and the girl sick. Why, it was we nursed Jenna back to health after her mother was nothing but dirt in the breeze that blows out toward End-World, and how little she thanks us! Besides, she bears the Dark Bells, the *sigul* of our sisterhood. Of our *ka-tet*. Now eat—yer belly says ye're hungry!"

Sister Louise offered the bowl, but her eyes kept drifting to the shape the medallion made under the breast of his bed-dress. *Don't like it, do you?* Roland thought, and then remembered Louise by candlelight, the freighter's blood on her chin, her ancient eyes eager as she leaned forward to lick his spend from Sister Mary's hand.

He turned his head aside. "I want nothing."

"But ye're hungry!" Louise protested. "If'ee don't eat, James, how will'ee get'ee strength back?"

"Send Jenna. I'll eat what she brings."

Sister Mary's frown was black. "Ye'll see her no more. She's been released from Thoughtful House only on her solemn promise to double her time of meditation . . . and to stay out of infirmary. Now eat, James, or whoever ye are. Take what's in the soup, or we'll cut ye with knives and rub it in with flannel poultices. Either way, makes no difference to us. Does it, Louise?"

"Nar," Louise said. She still held out the bowl. Steam rose from it, and the good smell of chicken.

"But it might make a difference to you." Sister Mary grinned humorlessly, baring her unnaturally large teeth. "Flowing blood's risky around here. The doctors don't like it. It stirs them up."

It wasn't just the bugs that were stirred up at the sight of blood, and Roland knew it. He also knew he had no choice in the matter of the soup. He took the bowl from Louise and ate slowly. He would have given much to wipe out the look of satisfaction he saw on Sister Mary's face.

"Good," she said after he had handed the bowl back and she had peered inside to make sure it was completely empty. His hand thumped back into the sling which had been rigged for it, already too heavy to hold up. He could feel the world drawing away again.

Sister Mary leaned forward, the billowing top of her habit touching the skin of his left shoulder. He could smell her, an aroma both ripe and dry, and would have gagged if he'd had the strength.

"Have that foul gold thing off ye when yer strength comes back a little—put it in the pissoir under the bed. Where it belongs. For to be even this close to where it lies hurts my head and makes my throat close."

Speaking with enormous effort, Roland said, "If you want it, take it. How can I stop you, you bitch?"

Once more her frown turned her face into something like a thunderhead. He thought she would have slapped him, if she had dared touch him so close to where the medallion lay. Her ability to touch seemed to end above his waist, however.

"I think you had better consider the matter a little more fully," she said. "I can still have Jenna whipped, if I like. She bears the Dark Bells, but I am the Big Sister. Consider that very well."

She left. Sister Louise followed, casting one look—a strange combination of fright and lust—back over her shoulder.

Roland thought, *I must get out of here—I must.*

Instead, he drifted back to that dark place which wasn't quite sleep. Or perhaps he did sleep, at least for awhile; perhaps he dreamed. Fingers once more caressed his fingers, and lips first kissed his ear and then whispered into it: "Look beneath your pillow, Roland . . . but let no one know I was here."

At some point after this, Roland opened his eyes again, half-expecting to see Sister Jenna's pretty young face hovering above him. And that comma of dark hair once more poking out from beneath her wimple. There was no one. The swags of silk overhead were at their brightest, and although it was impossible to tell the hours in here with any real accuracy, Roland guessed it to be around noon. Perhaps three hours since his second bowl of the Sisters' soup.

Beside him, John Norman still slept, his breath whistling out in faint, nasal snores.

Roland tried to raise his hand and slide it under his pillow. The hand wouldn't move. He could wiggle the tips of his fingers, but that was all. He waited, calming his mind as well as he could, gathering his patience. Patience wasn't easy to come by. He kept thinking about what Norman had said—that there had been twenty survivors of the ambush . . . at least to start with. *One by one they went, until only me and that one down yonder was left. And now you.*

The girl wasn't here. His mind spoke in the soft, regretful tone of Alain, one of his old friends, dead these many years now. *She wouldn't dare, not with the others watching. That was only a dream you had.*

But Roland thought perhaps it had been more than a dream.

Some length of time later—the slowly shifting brightness overhead made him believe it had been about an hour—Roland tried his hand again. This time he was able to get it beneath his pillow. This was puffy and soft, tucked snugly into the wide sling that supported the gunslinger's neck. At first he found nothing, but as his fingers worked their slow way deeper, they touched what felt like a stiffish bundle of thin rods.

He paused, gathering a little more strength (every movement was like swimming in glue), and then burrowed deeper. It felt like a dead bouquet. Wrapped around it was what felt like a ribbon.

Roland looked around to make sure the ward was still empty and Norman still asleep, then drew out what was under the pillow. It was six brittle stems of fading green with brownish reed heads at the tops. They gave off a strange, yeasty aroma that made Roland think of early-morning begging expeditions to the Great House kitchens as a child—forays he had usually made with Cuthbert. The reeds were tied with a wide white silk ribbon, and smelled like burnt toast. Beneath the ribbon was a fold of cloth. Like everything else in this cursed place, it seemed, the cloth was of silk.

Roland was breathing hard and could feel drops of sweat on his brow. Still alone, though—good. He took the scrap of cloth and unfolded it. Printed painstakingly in blurred charcoal letters was this message:

NIBBLE HEDS. ONCE EACH HOUR. TOO
MUCH, CRAMPS OR DETH.
TOMORROW NITE. CAN'T BE SOONER.
BE CAREFUL!

No explanation, but Roland supposed none was needed. Nor did he have any option; if he remained here, he would die. All they had to do was have the medallion off him, and he felt sure Sister Mary was smart enough to figure a way to do that.

He nibbled at one of the dry reed heads. The taste was nothing like the toast they had begged from the kitchen as boys; it was bitter in his throat and hot in his stomach. Less than a minute after his nibble, his heart rate had doubled. His muscles awakened, but not in a pleasant way, as after good sleep; they felt first trembly and then hard, as if they were gathered into knots. This feeling passed rapidly, and his heartbeat was back to normal before Norman stirred awake an hour or so later, but he understood why Jenna's note had warned him not to take more than a nibble at a time—this was very powerful stuff.

He slipped the bouquet of reeds back under the pillow, being careful to brush away the few crumbles of vegetable matter which had dropped to the sheet. Then he used the ball of his thumb to blur the painstaking charcoaled words on the bit of silk. When he was finished, there was nothing on the square but meaningless smudges. The square he also tucked back under his pillow.

When Norman awoke, he and the gunslinger spoke briefly of the young scout's home—Delain, it was, sometimes known jestingly as Dragon's Lair, or Liar's Heaven. All tall tales were said to originate in Delain. The boy asked Roland to take his medallion and that of his brother home to their parents, if Roland was able, and explain as well as he could what had happened to James and John, sons of Jesse.

"You'll do all that yourself," Roland said.

"No." Norman tried to raise his hand, perhaps to scratch his nose, and was unable to do even that. The hand rose perhaps six inches, then fell back to the counterpane with a small thump. "I think not. It's a pity for us to have run up against each other this way, you know—I like you."

"And I you, John Norman. Would that we were better met."

"Aye. When not in the company of such fascinating ladies."

He dropped off to sleep again soon after. Roland never spoke with him again . . . although he certainly heard from him. Yes. Roland was lying above his bed, shamming sleep, as John Norman screamed his last.

Sister Michela came with his evening soup just as Roland was getting past the shivery muscles and galloping heartbeat that resulted from his second nibble of brown reed. Michela looked at his flushed face with some concern, but had to accept his assurances that he did not feel feverish; she couldn't bring herself to touch him and judge the heat of his skin for herself—the medallion held her away.

With the soup was a popkin. The bread was leathery and the meat inside it tough, but Roland demolished it greedily, just the same. Michela watched with a complacent smile, hands folded in front of her, nodding from time to time. When he had finished the soup, she took the bowl back from him carefully, making sure their fingers did not touch.

"Ye're healing," she said. "Soon you'll be on yer way, and we'll have just yer memory to keep, Jim."

"Is that true?" he asked quietly.

She only looked at him, touched her tongue against her upper lip, giggled, and departed. Roland closed his eyes and lay back against his pillow, feeling lethargy steal over him again. Her speculative eyes . . . her peeping tongue. He had seen women look at roast chickens and joints of mutton that same way, calculating when they might be done.

His body badly wanted to sleep, but Roland held onto wakefulness for what he judged was an hour, then worked one of the reeds out from under the pillow. With a fresh infusion of their "can't-move medicine" in his system, this took an enormous effort, and he wasn't sure he could have done it at all, had he not separated this one reed from the ribbon holding the others. Tomorrow night, Jenna's note had said. If that meant escape, the idea seemed preposterous. The way he felt now, he might be lying in this bed until the end of the age.

He nibbled. Energy washed into his system, clenching his muscles and racing his heart, but the burst of vitality was gone almost as soon as it came, buried beneath the Sisters' stronger drug. He could only hope . . . and sleep.

When he woke it was full dark, and he found he could move his arms and legs in their network of slings almost naturally. He slipped one of the reeds out from beneath his pillow and nibbled cautiously. She had left half a dozen, and the first two were now almost entirely consumed.

The gunslinger put the stem back under the pillow, then began to shiver like a wet dog in a downpour. *I took too much,* he thought. *I'll be lucky not to convulse—*

His heart, racing like a runaway engine. And then, to make matters worse, he saw candlelight at the far end of the aisle. A moment later he heard the rustle of their gowns and the whisk of their slippers.

Gods, why now? They'll see me shaking, they'll know—

Calling on every bit of his willpower and control, Roland closed his eyes and concentrated on stilling his jerking limbs. If only he had been in bed instead of in these cursed slings, which seemed to tremble as if with their own ague at every movement!

The Little Sisters drew closer. The light of their candles bloomed red within his closed eyelids. Tonight they were not giggling, nor whispering among themselves. It was not until they were almost on top of him that Roland became aware of the stranger in their midst—a creature that breathed through its nose in great, slobbery gasps of mixed air and snot.

The gunslinger lay with his eyes closed, the gross twitches and jumps of his arms and legs under control, but with his muscles still knotted and crampy, thrumming beneath the skin. Anyone who looked at him closely would see at once that something was wrong with him. His heart was larruping away like a horse under the whip, surely they must see—

But it wasn't him they were looking at—not yet, at least.

"Have it off him," Mary said. She spoke in a bas-
tardized version of the low speech Roland could barely
understand. "Then t'other 'un. Go on, Ralph."

"U'se has whik-sky?" the slobberer asked, his dialect
even heavier than Mary's. "U'se has 'backky?"

"Yes, yes, plenty whiskey and plenty smoke, but not
until you have these wretched things off!" Impatient. Perhaps afraid, as well.

Roland cautiously rolled his head to the left and
cracked his eyelids open.

Five of the six Little Sisters of Eluria were clustered
around the far side of the sleeping John Norman's bed,
their candles raised to cast their light upon him. It also
cast light upon their own faces, faces which would have
given the strongest man nightmares. Now, in the ditch
of the night, their glamours were set aside, and they
were but ancient corpses in voluminous habits.

Sister Mary had one of Roland's guns in her hand.
Looking at her holding it, Roland felt a bright flash of
hate for her, and promised himself she would pay for her
temerity.

The thing standing at the foot of the bed, strange as
it was, looked almost normal in comparison with the Sisters. It was one of the green folk. Roland recognized
Ralph at once. He would be a long time forgetting that
bowler hat.

Now Ralph walked slowly around to the side of Norman's bed closest to Roland, momentarily blocking the
gunslinger's view of the Sisters. The mutie went all the
way to Norman's head, however, clearing the hags to
Roland's slitted view once more.

Norman's medallion lay exposed—the boy had perhaps wakened enough to take it out of his bed-dress, hoping it would protect him better so. Ralph picked it up in his melted-tallow hand. The Sisters watched eagerly in the glow of their candles as the green man stretched it to the end of its chain . . . and then put it down again. Their faces drooped in disappointment.

"Don't care for such as that," Ralph said in his clotted voice. "Want whik-sky! Want 'backky!"

"You shall have it," Sister Mary said. "Enough for you and all your verminous clan. But first, you must have that horrid thing off him! Off both of them! Do you understand? And you shan't tease us."

"Or what?" Ralph asked. He laughed. It was a choked and gargly sound, the laughter of a man dying from some evil sickness of the throat and lungs, but Roland still liked it better than the giggles of the Sisters. "Or what, Sisser Mary, you'll drink my bluid? My bluid'd drop'ee dead where'ee stand, and glowing in the dark!"

Mary raised the gunslinger's revolver and pointed it at Ralph. "Take that wretched thing, or you die where *you* stand."

"And die after I've done what you want, likely."

Sister Mary said nothing to that. The others peered at him with their black eyes.

Ralph lowered his head, appearing to think. Roland suspected his friend Bowler Hat *could* think, too. Sister Mary and her cohorts might not believe that, but Ralph *had* to be trig to have survived as long as he had. But of course when he came here, he hadn't considered Roland's guns.

"Smasher was wrong to give them shooters to you,"

he said at last. "Give em and not tell me. Did u'se give him whik-sky? Give him 'backky?"

"That's none o' yours," Sister Mary replied. "You have that gold-piece off the boy's neck right now, or I'll put one of yonder man's bullets in what's left of yer brain."

"All right," Ralph said. "Just as you wish, sai."

Once more he reached down and took the gold medallion in his melted fist. That he did slow; what happened after, happened fast. He snatched it away, breaking the chain and flinging the gold heedlessly into the dark. With his other hand he reached down, sank his long and ragged nails into John Norman's neck, and tore it open.

Blood flew from the hapless boy's throat in a jetting, heart-driven gush more black than red in the candlelight, and he made a single bubbly cry. The women screamed—but not in horror. They screamed as women do in a frenzy of excitement. The green man was forgotten; Roland was forgotten; all was forgotten save the life's blood pouring out of John Norman's throat.

They dropped their candles. Mary dropped Roland's revolver in the same hapless, careless fashion. The last the gunslinger saw as Ralph darted away into the shadows (whiskey and tobacco another time, wily Ralph must have thought; tonight he had best concentrate on saving his own life) was the Sisters bending forward to catch as much of the flow as they could before it dried up.

Roland lay in the dark, muscles shivering, heart pounding, listening to the harpies as they fed on the boy lying in the bed next to his own. It seemed to go on forever, but at last they had done with him. The Sisters relit their candles and left, murmuring.

When the drug in the soup once more got the better of the drug in the reeds, Roland was grateful . . . yet for the first time since he'd come here, his sleep was haunted.

In his dream he stood looking down at the bloated body in the town trough, thinking of a line in the book marked REGISTRY OF MISDEEDS AND REDRESS. *Green folk sent hence,* it had read, and perhaps the green folk *had* been sent hence, but then a worse tribe had come. The Little Sisters of Eluria, they called themselves. And a year hence, they might be the Little Sisters of Tejuas, or of Kambero, or some other far western village. They came with their bells and their bugs . . . from where? Who knew? Did it matter?

A shadow fell beside his on the scummy water of the trough. Roland tried to turn and face it. He couldn't; he was frozen in place. Then a green hand grasped his shoulder and whirled him about. It was Ralph. His bowler hat was cocked back on his head; John Norman's medallion, now red with blood, hung around his neck.

"Booh!" cried Ralph, his lips stretching in a toothless grin. He raised a big revolver with worn sandalwood grips. He thumbed the hammer back—

—and Roland jerked awake, shivering all over, dressed in skin both wet and icy cold. He looked at the bed on his left. It was empty, the sheet pulled up and tucked about neatly, the pillow resting above it in its snowy sleeve. Of John Norman there was no sign. It might have been empty for years, that bed.

Roland was alone now. Gods help him, he was the last patient of the Little Sisters of Eluria, those sweet and patient hospitalers. The last human being still alive in this terrible place, the last with warm blood flowing in his veins.

Roland, lying suspended, gripped the gold medallion in his fist and looked across the aisle at the long row of empty beds. After a little while, he brought one of the reeds out from beneath his pillow and nibbled at it.

When Mary came fifteen minutes later, the gunslinger took the bowl she brought with a show of weakness he didn't really feel. Porridge instead of soup this time . . . but he had no doubt the basic ingredient was still the same.

"How well ye look this morning, sai," Big Sister said. She looked well herself—there were no shimmers to give away the ancient *wampir* hiding inside her. She had supped well, and her meal had firmed her up. Roland's stomach rolled over at the thought. "Ye'll be on yer pins in no time, I'll warrant."

"That's shit," Roland said, speaking in an ill-natured growl. "Put me on my pins and you'd be picking me up off the floor directly after. I've started to wonder if you're not putting something in the food."

She laughed merrily at that. "La, you lads! Always eager to blame yer weakness on a scheming woman! How scared of us ye are—aye, way down in yer little boys' hearts, how scared ye are!"

"Where's my brother? I dreamed there was a commotion about him in the night, and now I see his bed's empty."

Her smile narrowed. Her eyes glittered. "He came over fevery and pitched a fit. We've taken him to

Thoughtful House, which has been home to contagion more than once in its time."

To the grave is where you've taken him, Roland thought. *Mayhap that is a Thoughtful House, but little would you know it, sai, one way or another.*

"I know ye're no brother to that boy," Mary said, watching him eat. Already Roland could feel the stuff hidden in the porridge draining his strength once more. "*Sigul* or no *sigul,* I know ye're no brother to him. Why do you lie? 'Tis a sin against God."

"What gives you such an idea, sai?" Roland asked, curious to see if she would mention the guns.

"Big Sister knows what she knows. Why not 'fess up, Jimmy? Confession's good for the soul, they say."

"Send me Jenna to pass the time, and perhaps I'd tell you much," Roland said.

The narrow bone of smile on Sister Mary's face disappeared like chalk-writing in a rainstorm. "Why would ye talk to such as her?"

"She's passing fair," Roland said. "Unlike some."

Her lips pulled back from her overlarge teeth. "Ye'll see her no more, cully. Ye've stirred her up, so you have, and I won't have that."

She turned to go. Still trying to appear weak and hoping he would not overdo it (acting was never his forte), Roland held out the empty porridge bowl. "Do you not want to take this?"

"Put it on your head and wear it as a nightcap, for all of me. Or stick it in your ass. You'll talk before I'm done with ye, cully—talk till I bid you shut up and then beg to talk some more!"

On this note she swept regally away, hands lifting the

front of her skirt off the floor. Roland had heard that such as she couldn't go about in daylight, and that part of the old tales was surely a lie. Yet another part was almost true, it seemed: a fuzzy, amorphous shape kept pace with her, running along the row of empty beds to her right, but she cast no real shadow at all.

VI. JENNA. SISTER COQUINA. TAMRA, MICHELA, LOUISE. THE CROSS-DOG. WHAT HAPPENED IN THE SAGE.

That was one of the longest days of Roland's life. He dozed, but never deeply; the reeds were doing their work, and he had begun to believe that he might, with Jenna's help, actually get out of here. And there was the matter of his guns, as well—perhaps she might be able to help there, too.

He passed the slow hours thinking of old times—of Gilead and his friends, of the riddling he had almost won at one Wide Earth Fair. In the end another had taken the goose, but he'd had his chance, aye. He thought of his mother and father; he thought of Abel Vannay, who had limped his way through a life of gentle goodness, and Eldred Jonas, who had limped his way through a life of evil . . . until Roland had blown him loose of his saddle, one fine desert day.

He thought, as always, of Susan.

If you love me, then love me, she'd said . . . and so he had.

So he had.

In this way the time passed. At rough hourly intervals, he took one of the reeds from beneath his pillow and nibbled it. Now his muscles didn't tremble so badly as the stuff passed into his system, nor his heart pound so fiercely. The medicine in the reeds no longer had to battle the Sisters' medicine so fiercely, Roland thought; the reeds were winning.

The diffused brightness of the sun moved across the white silk ceiling of the ward, and at last the dimness which always seemed to hover at bed-level began to rise. The long room's western wall bloomed with the rose-melting-to-orange shades of sunset.

It was Sister Tamra who brought him his dinner that night—soup and another popkin. She also laid a desert lily beside his hand. She smiled as she did it. Her cheeks were bright with color. All of them were bright with color today, like leeches that had gorged until they were full almost to bursting.

"From your admirer, Jimmy," she said. "She's so sweet on ye! The lily means 'Do not forget my promise.' What has she promised ye, Jimmy, brother of Johnny?"

"That she'd see me again, and we'd talk."

Tamra laughed so hard that the bells lining her forehead jingled. She clasped her hands together in a perfect ecstasy of glee. "Sweet as honey! Oh, yes!" She bent her smiling gaze on Roland. "It's sad such a promise can never be kept. Ye'll never see her again, pretty man." She took the bowl. "Big Sister has decided." She stood up, still smiling. "Why not take that ugly gold *sigul* off?"

"I think not."

"Yer brother took his off—look!" She pointed, and Roland spied the gold medallion lying far down the aisle, where it had landed when Ralph threw it.

Sister Tamra looked at him, still smiling.

"He decided it was part of what was making him sick, and cast it away. Ye'd do the same, were ye wise."

Roland repeated, "I think not."

"So," she said dismissively, and left him alone with the empty beds glimmering in the thickening shadows.

Roland hung on, in spite of growing sleepiness, until the hot colors bleeding across the infirmary's western wall had cooled to ashes. Then he nibbled one of the reeds and felt strength—real strength, not a jittery, heart-thudding substitute—bloom in his body. He looked toward where the castaway medallion gleamed in the last light and made a silent promise to John Norman: he would take it with the other one to Norman's kin, if *ka* chanced that he should encounter them in his travels.

Feeling completely easy in his mind for the first time that day, the gunslinger dozed. When he awoke it was full dark. The doctor-bugs were singing with extraordinary shrillness. He had taken one of the reeds out from under the pillow and had begun to nibble on it when a cold voice said, "So—Big Sister was right. Ye've been keeping secrets."

Roland's heart seemed to stop dead in his chest. He looked around and saw Sister Coquina getting to her feet. She had crept in while he was dozing and hidden under the bed on his right side to watch him.

"Where did ye get that?" she asked. "Was it—"

"He got it from me."

Coquina whirled about. Jenna was walking down the aisle toward them. Her habit was gone. She still wore her wimple with its forehead-fringe of bells, but its hem rested on the shoulders of a simple checkered shirt.

Below this she wore jeans and scuffed desert boots. She had something in her hands. It was too dark for Roland to be sure, but he thought—

"*You,*" Sister Coquina whispered with infinite hate. "When I tell Big Sister—"

"You'll tell no one anything," Roland said.

If he had planned his escape from the slings that entangled him, he no doubt would have made a bad business of it, but, as always, the gunslinger did best when he thought least. His arms were free in a moment; so was his left leg. His right caught at the ankle, however, twisting, hanging him up with his shoulders on the bed and his leg in the air.

Coquina turned on him, hissing like a cat. Her lips pulled back from teeth that were needle-sharp. She rushed at him, her fingers splayed. The nails at the ends of them looked sharp and ragged.

Roland clasped the medallion and shoved it out toward her. She recoiled from it, still hissing, and whirled back to Sister Jenna in a flare of white skirt. "I'll do for ye, ye interfering trull!" she cried in a low, harsh voice.

Roland struggled to free his leg and couldn't. It was firmly caught, the shitting sling actually wrapped around the ankle somehow, like a noose.

Jenna raised her hands, and he saw he had been right: it was his revolvers she had brought, holstered and hanging from the two old gunbelts he had worn out of Gilead after the last burning.

"Shoot her, Jenna! Shoot her!"

Instead, still holding the holstered guns up, Jenna shook her head as she had on the day when Roland had persuaded her to push back her wimple so he could see her hair. The bells rang with a sharpness that seemed to go into the gunslinger's head like a spike.

The Dark Bells. The sigul *of their* ka-tet. *What—*

The sound of the doctor-bugs rose to a shrill, reedy scream that was eerily like the sound of the bells Jenna wore. Nothing sweet about them now. Sister Coquina's hands faltered on their way to Jenna's throat; Jenna herself had not so much as flinched or blinked her eyes.

"No," Coquina whispered. "You *can't!*"

"I *have,*" Jenna said, and Roland saw the bugs. Descending from the legs of the bearded man, he'd observed a battalion. What he saw coming from the shadows now was an army to end all armies; had they been men instead of insects, there might have been more than all the men who had ever carried arms in the long and bloody history of Mid-World.

Yet the sight of them advancing down the boards of the aisle was not what Roland would always remember, nor what would haunt his dreams for a year or more; it was the way they coated the *beds.* These were turning black two by two on both sides of the aisle, like pairs of dim rectangular lights going out.

Coquina shrieked and began to shake her own head, to ring her own bells. The sound they made was thin and pointless compared with the sharp ringing of the Dark Bells.

Still the bugs marched on, darkening the floor, blacking out the beds.

Jenna darted past the shrieking Sister Coquina, dropped Roland's guns beside him, then yanked the twisted sling straight with one hard pull. Roland slid his leg free.

"Come," she said. "I've started them, but staying them could be a different thing."

Now Sister Coquina's shrieks were not of horror but of pain. The bugs had found her.

"Don't look," Jenna said, helping Roland to his feet. He thought that never in his life had he been so glad to be upon them. "Come. We must be quick— she'll rouse the others. I've put your boots and clothes aside up the path that leads away from here— I carried as much as I could. How are ye? Are ye strong?"

"Thanks to you." How long he would stay strong Roland didn't know . . . and right now it wasn't a question that mattered. He saw Jenna snatch up two of the reeds—in his struggle to escape the slings, they had scattered all over the head of the bed—and then they were hurrying up the aisle, away from the bugs and from Sister Coquina, whose cries were now failing.

Roland buckled on his guns and tied them down without breaking stride.

They passed only three beds on each side before reaching the flap of the tent . . . and it *was* a tent, he saw, not a vast pavilion. The silk walls and ceiling were fraying canvas, thin enough to let in the light of a three-quarters Kissing Moon. And the beds weren't beds at all, but only a double row of shabby cots.

He turned and saw a black, writhing hump on the floor where Sister Coquina had been. At the sight of her, Roland was struck by an unpleasant thought.

"I forgot John Norman's medallion!" A keen sense of regret—almost of mourning—went through him like wind.

Jenna reached into the pocket of her jeans and brought it out. It glimmered in the moonlight.

"I picked it up off the floor."

He didn't know which made him gladder—the sight of the medallion or the sight of it in her hand. It meant she wasn't like the others.

Then, as if to dispel that notion before it got too firm a hold on him, she said, "Take it, Roland—I can hold it no more." And, as he took it, he saw unmistakable marks of charring on her fingers.

He took her hand and kissed each burn.

"Thankee-sai," she said, and he saw she was crying. "Thankee, dear. To be kissed so is lovely, worth every pain. Now . . ."

Roland saw her eyes shift, and followed them. Here were bobbing lights descending a rocky path. Beyond them he saw the building where the Little Sisters had been living—not a convent but a ruined *hacienda* that looked a thousand years old. There were three candles; as they drew closer, Roland saw that there were only three sisters. Mary wasn't among them.

He drew his guns.

"Oooo, it's a gunslinger-man he is!" Louise.

"A *scary* man!" Michela.

"And he's found his ladylove as well as his shooters!" Tamra.

"His slut-whore!" Louise.

Laughing angrily. Not afraid . . . at least, not of *his* weapons.

"Put them away," Jenna told him, and when she looked, saw that he already had.

The others, meanwhile, had drawn closer.

"Ooo, see, she cries!" Tamra.

"Doffed her habit, she has!" Michela. "Perhaps it's her broken vows she cries for."

"Why such tears, pretty?" Louise.

"Because he kissed my fingers where they were burned," Jenna said. "I've never been kissed before. It made me cry."

"Ooooo!"

"*Luv*-ly!"

"Next he'll stick his thing in her! Even *luv*-lier!"

Jenna bore their japes with no sign of anger. When they were done, she said, "I'm going with him. Stand aside."

They gaped at her, counterfeit laughter disappearing in shock.

"No!" Louise whispered. "Are ye mad? Ye know what'll happen!"

"No, and neither do you," Jenna said. "Besides, I care not." She half-turned and held her hand out to the mouth of the ancient hospital tent. It was a faded olive-drab in the moonlight, with an old red cross drawn on its roof. Roland wondered how many towns the Sisters had been to with this tent, which was so small and plain on the outside, so huge and gloriously dim on the inside. How many towns and over how many years.

Now, cramming the mouth of it in a black, shiny tongue, were the doctor-bugs. They had stopped their singing. Their silence was terrible.

"Stand aside or I'll have them on ye," Jenna said.

"Ye never would!" Sister Michela cried in a low, horrified voice.

"Aye. I've already set them on Sister Coquina. She's a part of their medicine, now."

Their gasp was like cold wind passing through dead trees. Nor was all of that dismay directed toward their own precious hides. What Jenna had done was clearly far outside their reckoning.

"Then you're damned," Sister Tamra said.

"Such ones to speak of damnation! Stand aside."

They did. Roland walked past them and they shrank away from him . . . but they shrank from her more.

"Damned?" he asked after they had skirted the *hacienda* and reached the path beyond it. The Kissing Moon glimmered above a tumbled scree of rocks. In its light Roland could see a small black opening low on the scarp. He guessed it was the cave the Sisters called Thoughtful House. "What did they mean, damned?"

"Never mind. All we have to worry about now is Sister Mary. I like it not that we haven't seen her."

She tried to walk faster, but he grasped her arm and turned her about. He could still hear the singing of the bugs, but faintly; they were leaving the place of the Sisters behind. Eluria, too, if the compass in his head was still working; he thought the town was in the other direction. The husk of the town, he amended.

"Tell me what they meant."

"Perhaps nothing. Ask me not, Roland—what good is it? 'Tis done, the bridge burned. I can't go back. Nor would if I could." She looked down, biting her lip, and when she looked up again, Roland saw fresh tears falling on her cheeks. "I have supped with them. There were times when I couldn't help it, no more than you could help drinking their wretched soup, no matter if you knew what was in it."

Roland remembered John Norman saying *A man has to eat . . . a woman, too.* He nodded.

"I'd go no farther down that road. If there's to be damnation, let it be of my choosing, not theirs. My mother meant well by bringing me back to them, but she was wrong." She looked at him shyly and fearfully . . . but met his eyes. "I'd go beside ye on yer road, Roland of Gilead. For as long as I may, or as long as ye'd have me."

"You're welcome to your share of my way," he said. "And I am—"

Blessed by your company, he would have finished, but before he could, a voice spoke from the tangle of moon-shadow ahead of them, where the path at last climbed out of the rocky, sterile valley in which the Little Sisters had practiced their glamours.

"It's a sad duty to stop such a pretty elopement, but stop it I must."

Sister Mary came from the shadows. Her fine white habit with its bright red rose had reverted to what it really was: the shroud of a corpse. Caught, hooded in its grimy folds, was a wrinkled, sagging face from which two black eyes stared. They looked like rotted dates. Below them, exposed by the thing's smile, four great incisors gleamed.

Upon the stretched skin of Sister Mary's forehead, bells tinkled . . . but not the Dark Bells, Roland thought. There was that.

"Stand clear," Jenna said. "Or I'll bring the *can tam* on ye."

"No," Sister Mary said, stepping closer, "ye won't. They'll not stray so far from the others. Shake your head and ring those damned bells until the clappers fall out, and still they'll never come."

Jenna did as bid, shaking her head furiously from side to side. The Dark Bells rang piercingly, but without that extra, almost psychic tone-quality that had gone through Roland's head like a spike. And the doctor-bugs—what Jenna had called the *can tam*—did not come.

Smiling ever more broadly (Roland had an idea Mary herself hadn't been completely sure they wouldn't come until the experiment was made), the corpse-woman closed in on them, seeming to float above the ground. Her eyes flicked toward him. "And put that away," she said.

Roland looked down and saw that one of his guns was in his hand. He had no memory of drawing it.

"Unless 'tis been blessed or dipped in some sect's holy wet—blood, water, semen—it can't harm such as me, gunslinger. For I am more shade than substance . . . yet still the equal to such as yerself, for all that."

She thought he would try shooting her, anyway; he saw it in her eyes. *Those shooters are all ye have,* her eyes said. *Without em, you might as well be back in the tent we dreamed around ye, caught up in our slings and awaiting our pleasure.*

Instead of shooting, he dropped the revolver back into its holster and launched himself at her with his hands out. Sister Mary uttered a scream that was mostly surprise, but it was not a long one; Roland's fingers clamped down on her throat and choked the sound off before it was fairly started.

The touch of her flesh was obscene—it seemed not just alive but *various* beneath his hands, as if it was trying to crawl away from him. He could feel it running like liquid, *flowing,* and the sensation was horrible beyond description. Yet he clamped down harder, determined to choke the life out of her.

Then there came a blue flash (not in the air, he would think later; that flash happened inside his head, a single stroke of lightning as she touched off some brief but powerful brainstorm), and his hands flew away from her neck. For one moment his dazzled eyes saw great wet gouges in her gray flesh—gouges in the shapes of his hands. Then he was flung backward, hitting the scree on his back and sliding, hitting his head on a jutting rock hard enough to provoke a second, lesser, flash of light.

"Nay, my pretty man," she said, grimacing at him, laughing with those terrible dull eyes of hers. "Ye don't choke such as me, and I'll take ye slow for'ee impertinence—cut ye shallow in a hundred places to refresh my thirst! First, though, I'll have this vowless girl . . . and I'll have those damned bells off her, in the bargain."

"Come and see if you can!" Jenna cried in a trembling voice, and shook her head from side to side. The Dark Bells rang mockingly, provokingly.

Mary's grimace of a smile fell away. "Oh, I can," she breathed. Her mouth yawned. In the moonlight, her fangs gleamed in her gums like bone needles poked through a red pillow. "I can and I—"

There was a growl from above them. It rose, then

splintered into a volley of snarling barks. Mary turned to her left, and in the moment before the snarling thing left the rock on which it was standing, Roland could clearly read the startled bewilderment on Big Sister's face.

It launched itself at her, only a dark shape against the stars, legs outstretched so it looked like some sort of weird bat, but even before it crashed into the woman, striking her in the chest above her half-raised arms and fastening its own teeth on her throat, Roland knew exactly what it was.

As the shape bore her over onto her back, Sister Mary uttered a gibbering shriek that went through Roland's head like the Dark Bells themselves. He scrambled to his feet, gasping. The shadowy thing tore at her, forepaws on either side of her head, rear paws planted on the grave-shroud above her chest, where the rose had been.

Roland grabbed Jenna, who was looking down at the fallen Sister with a kind of frozen fascination.

"Come on!" he shouted. "Before it decides it wants a bite of you, too!"

The dog took no notice of them as Roland pulled Jenna past. It had torn Sister Mary's head mostly off.

Her flesh seemed to be changing, somehow—decomposing, very likely—but whatever was happening, Roland did not want to see it. He didn't want Jenna to see it, either.

They half-walked, half-ran to the top of the ridge, and when they got there paused for breath in the moonlight, heads down, hands linked, both of them gasping harshly.

The growling and snarling below them had faded, but was still faintly audible when Sister Jenna raised her head and asked him, "What was it? You know—I saw it in your face. And how could it attack her? We all have power over animals, but she has—had—the most."

"Not over that one." Roland found himself recalling the unfortunate boy in the next bed. Norman hadn't known why the medallions kept the Sisters at arm's length—whether it was the gold or the God. Now Roland knew the answer. "It was a dog. Just a town-dog. I saw it in the square, before the green folk knocked me out and took me to the Sisters. I suppose the other animals that could run away *did* run away, but not that one. It had nothing to fear from the Little Sisters of Eluria, and somehow it knew it didn't. It bears the sign of the Jesus Man on its chest. Black fur on white. Just an accident of its birth, I imagine. In any case, it's done for her now. I knew it was lurking around. I heard it barking two or three times."

"Why?" Jenna whispered. "Why would it come? Why would it stay? And why would it take on her as it did?"

Roland of Gilead responded as he ever had and ever would when such useless, mystifying questions were raised: "*Ka*. Come on. Let's get as far as we can from this place before we hide up for the day."

As far as they could turned out to be eight miles at most . . . and probably, Roland thought as the two of them sank down in a patch of sweet-smelling sage beneath an overhang of rock, a good deal less. Five, perhaps. It was him slowing them down; or rather, it was the residue of the poison in the soup. When it was clear to him that he could not go farther without help, he asked her for one of the reeds. She refused, saying that the stuff in it might combine with the unaccustomed exercise to burst his heart.

"Besides," she said as they lay back against the embankment of the little nook they had found, "they'll not follow. Those that are left—Michela, Louise, Tamra—will be packing up to move on. They know to leave when the time comes; that's why the Sisters have survived as long as they have. As *we* have. We're strong in some ways, but weak in many more. Sister Mary forgot that. It was her arrogance that did for her as much as the cross-dog, I think."

She had cached not just his boots and clothes beyond the top of the ridge, but the smaller of his two purses, as well. When she began to apologize for not bringing his bedroll and the larger purse (she'd tried, she said, but they were simply too heavy), Roland hushed her with a finger to her lips. He thought it a miracle to have as much as he did. And besides (this he did not say, but perhaps she knew it, anyway), the guns were the only things that really mattered. The guns of his father, and his father before him, all the way back to the days of Arthur Eld, when dreams and dragons had still walked the earth.

"Will you be all right?" he asked her as they settled down. The moon had set, but dawn was still at least three hours away. They were surrounded by the sweet smell of the sage. A purple smell, he thought it then . . . and ever after. Already he could feel it forming a kind of magic carpet under him, which would soon float him away to sleep. He thought he had never been so tired.

"Roland, I know not." But even then, he thought she had known. Her mother had brought her back once; no mother would bring her back again. And she had eaten with the others, had taken the communion of the Sisters. *Ka* was a wheel; it was also a net from which none ever escaped.

But then he was too tired to think much of such things . . . and what good would thinking have done, in any case? As she had said, the bridge was burned. Roland guessed that even if they were to return to the valley, they would find nothing but the cave the Sisters had called Thoughtful House. The surviving Sisters would have packed their tent of bad dreams and moved on, just a sound of bells and singing insects moving down the late night breeze.

He looked at her, raised a hand (it felt heavy), and touched the curl which once more lay across her forehead.

Jenna laughed, embarrassed. "That one always escapes. It's wayward. Like its mistress."

She raised her hand to poke it back in, but Roland took her fingers before she could. "It's beautiful," he said. "Black as night and as beautiful as forever."

He sat up—it took an effort; weariness dragged at his body like soft hands. He kissed the curl. She closed her eyes and sighed. He felt her trembling beneath his lips. The skin of her brow was very cool; the dark curve of the wayward curl like silk.

"Push back your wimple, as you did before," he said.

She did it without speaking. For a moment he only looked at her. Jenna looked back gravely, her eyes never leaving his. He ran his hands through her hair, feeling its smooth weight (like rain, he thought, rain with weight), then took her shoulders and kissed each of her cheeks. He drew back for a moment.

"Would ye kiss me as a man does a woman, Roland? On my mouth?"

"Aye."

And, as he had thought of doing as he lay caught in the silken infirmary tent, he kissed her lips. She kissed back with the clumsy sweetness of one who has never kissed before, except perhaps in dreams. Roland thought to make love to her then—it had been long and long, and she was beautiful—but he fell asleep instead, still kissing her.

He dreamed of the cross-dog, barking its way across a great open landscape. He followed, wanting to see the source of its agitation, and soon he did. At the far edge of that plain stood the Dark Tower, its smoky stone outlined by the dull orange ball of a setting sun, its fearful windows rising in a spiral. The dog stopped at the sight of it and began to howl.

Bells—peculiarly shrill and as terrible as doom— began to ring. Dark Bells, he knew, but their tone was as bright as silver. At their sound, the dark windows of the Tower glowed with a deadly red light—the red of poisoned roses. A scream of unbearable pain rose in the night.

The dream blew away in an instant, but the scream remained, now unraveling to a moan. That part was real—as real as the Tower, brooding in its place at the very end of End-World. Roland came back to the brightness of dawn and the soft purple smell of desert sage. He had drawn both his guns, and was on his feet before he had fully realized he was awake.

Jenna was gone. Her boots lay empty beside his purse. A little distance from them, her jeans lay as flat as discarded snakeskins. Above them was her shirt. It was, Roland observed with wonder, still tucked into the pants. Beyond them was her empty wimple, with its fringe of bells lying on the powdery ground. He thought for a moment that they were ringing, mistaking the sound he heard at first.

Not bells but bugs. The doctor-bugs. They sang in the sage, sounding a bit like crickets, but far sweeter.

"Jenna?"

No answer . . . unless the bugs answered. For their singing suddenly stopped.

"Jenna?"

Nothing. Only the wind and the smell of the sage.

Without thinking about what he was doing (like playacting, reasoned thought was not his strong suit), he bent, picked up the wimple, and shook it. The Dark Bells rang.

For a moment there was nothing. Then a thousand small dark creatures came scurrying out of the sage, gathering on the broken earth. Roland thought of the battalion marching down the side of the freighter's bed and took a step back. Then he held his position. As, he saw, the bugs were holding theirs.

He believed he understood. Some of this understanding came from his memory of how Sister Mary's flesh had felt under his hands . . . how it had felt *various*, not one thing but many. Part of it was what she had said: *I have supped with them.* Such as them might never die . . . but they might *change*.

The insects trembled, a dark cloud of them blotting out the white, powdery earth.

Roland shook the bells again.

A shiver ran through them in a subtle wave, and then they began to form a shape. They hesitated as if unsure of how to go on, regrouped, began again. What they eventually made on the whiteness of the sand there between the blowing fluffs of lilac-colored sage was one of the Great Letters: the letter C.

Except it wasn't really a letter, the gunslinger saw; it was a curl.

They began to sing, and to Roland it sounded as if they were singing his name.

The bells fell from his unnerved hand, and when they struck the ground and chimed there, the mass of bugs broke apart, running in every direction. He thought of calling them back—ringing the bells again might do that—but to what purpose? To what end?

Ask me not, Roland. 'Tis done, the bridge burned.

Yet she had come to him one last time, imposing her will over a thousand various parts that should have lost the ability to think when the whole lost its cohesion . . . and yet she *had* thought, somehow—enough to make that shape. How much effort might that have taken?

They fanned wider and wider, some disappearing into the sage, some trundling up the sides of a rock overhang, pouring into the cracks where they would, mayhap, wait out the heat of the day.

They were gone. *She* was gone.

Roland sat down on the ground and put his hands over his face. He thought he might weep, but in time the urge passed; when he raised his head again, his eyes were as dry as the desert he would eventually come to, still following the trail of Walter, the man in black.

If there's to be damnation, she had said, *let it be of my choosing, not theirs.*

He knew a little about damnation himself . . . and he had an idea that the lessons, far from being done, were just beginning.

She had brought him the purse with his tobacco in it. He rolled a cigarette and smoked it hunkered over his knees. He smoked it down to a glowing roach, looking at her empty clothes the while, remembering the steady gaze of her dark eyes. Remembering the scorch-marks on her fingers from the chain of the medallion. Yet she had picked it up, because she had known he would want it; had dared that pain, and Roland now wore both around his neck.

When the sun was fully up, the gunslinger moved on west. He would find another horse eventually, or a mule, but for now he was content to walk. All that day he was haunted by a ringing, singing sound in his ears, a sound like bells. Several times he stopped and looked around, sure he would see a dark following shape flowing over the ground, chasing after as the shadows of our best and worst memories chase after, but no shape was ever there. He was alone in the low hill country west of Eluria.

Quite alone.

Everything's Eventual

One day, out of nowhere, I had a clear image of a young man pouring change into a sewer grating outside of the small suburban house in which he lived. I had nothing else, but the image was so clear—and so disturbingly odd—that I had to write a story about it. It came out smoothly and without a single hesitation, supporting my idea that stories are artifacts: not really made things which we create (and can take credit for), but preexisting objects which we dig up.

I

I've got a good job now, and no reason to feel glum. No more hanging out with the gumbyheads at the Supr Savr, policing up the Kart Korral and getting bothered by assholes like Skipper. Skipper's munching the old dirt sandwich these days, but one thing I have learned in my nineteen years on this Planet Earth is don't relax, there are Skippers everywhere.

Ditto no more pulling pizza patrol on rainy nights, driving my old Ford with the bad muffler, freezing my ass off with the driver's-side window down and a little Italian flag sticking out on a wire. Like somebody in Harkerville was going to salute. Pizza Roma. Quarter tips from people who don't even see you, because most of their mind's still on the TV football game. Driving for Pizza Roma was the lowest point, I think. Since then I've even had a ride in a private jet, so how could things be bad?

"This is what comes of leaving school without a diploma," Ma would say during my Delivery Dan stint. And, "You've got this to look forward to *for the rest of your life.*" Good old Ma. On and on, until I actually thought about writing her one of those special letters. As I say, that was the low point. You know what Mr. Sharpton told me that night in his car? "It's not just a job, Dink, it's a goddam adventure." And he was right. Whatever he might have been wrong about, he was right about that.

I suppose you're wondering about the salary of this famous job. Well, I got to tell you, there's not much money in it. Might as well get that right up front. But a job isn't just about money, or getting ahead. That's what Mr. Sharpton told me. Mr. Sharpton said that a real job is about the fringe benefits. He said that's where the power is.

Mr. Sharpton. I only saw him that once, sitting behind the wheel of his big old Mercedes-Benz, but sometimes once is enough.

Take that any way you want. Any old way at all.

II

I've got a house, okay? My very own house. That's fringe benefit number one. I call Ma sometimes, ask how her bad leg is, shoot the shit, but I've never invited her over here, although Harkerville is only seventy or so miles away and I know she's practically busting a gut with curiosity. I don't even have to go see her unless I want to. Mostly I don't want to. If you knew my mother, you wouldn't want to, either. Sit there in that living room with her while she talks about all her relatives and whines about her puffy leg. Also I never noticed how much the house smelled of catshit until I got out of it. I'm never going to have a pet. Pets bite the big one.

Mostly I just stay here. It's only got one bedroom, but it's still an excellent house. *Eventual,* as Pug used to say. He was the one guy at the Supr Savr I liked. When he wanted to say something was really good, Pug'd never say it was awesome, like most people do; he'd say it was eventual. How funny is that? The old Pugmeister. I wonder how he's doing. Okay, I suppose. But I can't call him and make sure. I can call my Ma, and I have an emergency number if anything ever goes wrong or if I think somebody's getting nosy about what's not their business, but I can't buzz any of my old friends (as if any of them besides Pug gave Shit One about Dinky Earnshaw). Mr. Sharpton's rules.

But never mind that. Let's go back to my house here in Columbia City. How many nineteen-year-old high-school dropouts do *you* know who have their own houses? Plus a new car? Only a Honda, true, but the first three numbers on the odometer are still zeroes, and that's the important part. It has a CD/tape-player, and I don't slide in behind the wheel wondering if the goddam thing'll start, like I always did with the Ford, which Skipper used to make fun of. The Assholemobile, he called it. Why are there so many Skippers in the world? That's what I really wonder about.

I do get *some* money, by the way. More than enough to meet my needs. Check this out. I watch *As the World Turns* every day while I'm eating my lunch, and on Thursdays, about halfway through the show, I hear the clack of the mail-slot. I don't do anything then, I'm not supposed to. Like Mr. Sharpton said, "Them's the rules, Dink."

I just watch the rest of my show. The exciting stuff on the soaps always happens around the weekends—murders on Fridays, fucking on Mondays—but I watch right to the end every day, just the same. I'm especially careful to stay in the living room until the end on Thursdays. On Thursdays I don't even go out to the kitchen for another glass of milk. When *World* is over, I turn off the TV for awhile—Oprah Winfrey comes on next, I hate her show, all that sitting-around-talking shit is for the Mas of the world—and go out to the front hall.

Lying on the floor under the mail-slot, there's always a plain white envelope, sealed. Nothing written on the front. Inside there'll be either fourteen five-dollar bills or seven ten-dollar bills. That's my money for the week. Here's what I do with it. I go to the movies twice, always in the afternoon, when it's just $4.50. That's $9. On Saturday I fill up my Honda with gas, and that's usually about $7. I don't drive much. I'm not invested in it, as Pug would say. So now we're up to $16. I'll eat out maybe four times at Mickey D's, either at breakfast (Egg McMuffin, coffee, two hash browns) or at dinner (Quarter Pounder with Cheese, never plant, or wherever it goes. By then I'll be gone. I'm *not* going to spend my life in Columbia City, I can tell you that. I'm leaving, and soon. One way or the other.

The currency is easier. I just poke it down the garbage disposal in the kitchen. Another magic trick, presto-change-o, money into lettuce. You probably think that's very weird, running money through the sink-pig. I did, too, at first. But you get used to just about anything after you do it awhile, and besides, there's always another seventy falling through the letter-slot. The rule is simple: no squirrelling it away. End the week broke. Besides, it's not millions we're talking about, only eight or ten bucks a week. Chump-change, really.

III

DINKY'S DAYBOARD. That's another fringe benefit. I write down whatever I want during the week, and I get everything I ask for (except sex-mags, as I told you). Maybe I'll get bored with that eventually, but right now it's like having Santa Claus all year round. Mostly what I write down is groceries, like anyone does on their kitchen chalkboard, but by no means is groceries all.

I might, for instance, write down "New Bruce Willis Video" or "New Weezer CD" or something like that. A funny thing about that Weezer CD, since we're on the subject. I happened to go into Toones Xpress one Friday after my movie was over (I always go to the show on Friday afternoons, even if there's nothing I really want to see, because that's when the cleaners come), just killing time inside because it was rainy and

that squashed going to the park, and while I was looking at the new releases, this kid asks a clerk about the
new Weezer CD. The clerk tells him it won't be in for
another ten days or so, but I'd had it since the Friday
before.

Fringe benefits, like I say.

If I write down "sport shirt" on the DAYBOARD, there
it is when I get back to the house on Friday night,
always in one of the nice earth-tone colors I like. If I
write down "new jeans" or "chinos," I get those. All stuff
from The Gap, which is where I'd go myself, if I had to
do stuff like that. If I want a certain kind of after-shave
lotion or cologne, I write the name on DINKY'S DAY-
BOARD and it's on the bathroom counter when I get
home. I don't date, but I'm a fool for cologne. Go figure.

Here's something you'll laugh at, I bet. Once I
wrote down "Rembrandt Painting" on the DAYBOARD.
Then I spent the afternoon at the movies and walking
in the park, watching people making out and dogs
catching Frisbees, thinking how eventual it would be if
the cleaners actually brought me my own fucking
Rembrandt. Think of it, a genuine Old Master on the
wall of a house in the Sunset Knoll section of Columbia
City. How eventual would *that* be?

And it happened, in a manner of speaking. My
Rembrandt was hung on the living room wall when I
got home, over the sofa where the velvet clowns used
to be. My heart was beating about two hundred a
minute as I walked across the room toward it. When I
got closer, I saw it was just a copy . . . you know, a
reproduction. I was disappointed, but not very. I mean,
it *was* a Rembrandt. Just not an *original* Rembrandt.

Another time, I wrote "Autographed Photo of Nicole Kidman" on the DAYBOARD. I think she's the best-looking actress alive, she just gets me on so much. And when I got home that day, there was a publicity still of her on the fridge, held there by a couple of those little vegetable magnets. She was on her *Moulin Rouge* swing. And that time it was the real deal. I know because of the way it was signed: "To Dinky Earnshaw, with love & kisses from Nicole."

Oh, baby. Oh, honey.

Tell you something, my friend—if I worked hard and really wanted it, there might be a *real* Rembrandt on my wall someday. Sure. In a job like this, there is nowhere to go but up. In a way, that's the scary part.

IV

I never have to make grocery lists. The cleaners know what I like—Stouffer's frozen dinners, especially that boil-in-the-bag stuff they call creamed chipped beef and Ma had always called shit on a shingle, frozen strawberries, whole milk, pre-formed hamburger patties that you just have to slap in a hot frying pan (I hate playing with raw meat), Dole puddings, the ones that come in plastic cups (bad for my complexion but I love em), ordinary food like that. If I want something special, I write it down on DINKY'S DAYBOARD.

Once I asked for a homemade apple pie, specifically *not* from the supermarket, and when I came back that night around the time it was getting dark, my pie was in the fridge with the rest of the week's groceries. Only it wasn't wrapped up, it was just sitting there on a blue plate. That's how I knew it was homemade. I was a little hesitant about eating it at first, not knowing where it came from and all, and then I decided I was being stupid. A person doesn't really know where *supermarket* food comes from, not really. I mean, we assume it's okay because it's wrapped up or in a can or "double-sealed for your protection," but anyone could have been handling it with dirty fingers *before* it was double-sealed, or sneezing great big whoops of booger-breath on it, or even wiping their asses with it. I don't mean to gross you out, but it's true, isn't it? The world is full of strangers, and a lot of them are "up to no good." I have had personal experience of this, believe me.

Anyway, I tried the pie and it was delicious. I ate half of it Friday night and the rest on Saturday morning, while I was running the numbers in Cheyenne, Wyoming. Most of Saturday night I spent on the toilet, shitting my guts out from all those apples, I guess, but I didn't care. The pie was worth it. "Like mother used to make" is what people say, but it can't be my mother they say it about. My Ma couldn't fry Spam.

V

I never have to write down underwear on the DAY-BOARD. Every five weeks or so the old drawers disappear and there are brand-new Hanes Jockey-shorts in my bureau, four three-packs still in their plastic bags. Double-sealed for my protection, ha-ha. Toilet-paper, laundry soap, dishwasher soap, I never have to write any of that shit down. It just appears.

Very eventual, don't you think?

VI

I have never seen the cleaners, any more than I have ever seen the guy (or maybe it's a gal) who delivers my seventy bucks every Thursday during *As the World Turns.* I never *want* to see them, either. I don't need to, for one thing. For another, yes, okay, I'm afraid of them. Just like I was afraid of Mr. Sharpton in his big gray Mercedes on the night I went out to meet him. So sue me.

I don't eat lunch in my house on Fridays. I watch *As the World Turns,* then jump in my car and drive into town. I get a burger at Mickey D's, then go to a movie, then to the park if the weather is good. I like the park. It's a good place to think, and these days I've got an awful lot to think about.

If the weather is bad, I go to the mall. Now that the days are beginning to shorten, I'm thinking about taking up bowling again. It'd be something to do on Friday afternoons, at least. I used to go now and then with Pug.

I sort of miss Pug. I wish I could call him, just shoot the shit, tell him some of the stuff that's been going on. Like about that guy Neff, for instance.

Oh, well, spit in the ocean and see if it comes back.

While I'm away, the cleaners are doing my house from wall to wall and top to bottom—wash the dishes (although I'm pretty good about that myself), wash the floors, wash the dirty clothes, change the sheets, put out fresh towels, restock the fridge, get any of the incidentals that are written on the DAYBOARD. It's like living in a hotel with the world's most efficient (not to mention eventual) maid service.

The one place they don't mess around with much is the study off the dining room. I keep that room fairly dark, the shades always pulled, and they have never raised them to let in so much as a crack of daylight, like they do in the rest of the house. It never smells of Lemon Pledge in there, either, although every other room just about reeks of it on Friday nights. Sometimes it's so bad I have these sneezing fits. It's not an allergy; more like a nasal protest-demonstration.

Someone vacuums the floor in there, and they empty the wastepaper basket, but no one has ever moved any of the papers that I keep on the desk, no matter how cluttered-up and junky-looking they are. Once I put a little piece of tape over where the drawer above the kneehole opens, but it was still there, unbroken, when I got back home that night. I don't keep anything top secret in that drawer, you understand; I just wanted to know.

Also, if the computer and modem are on when I leave, they're still on when I come back, the VDT showing one of the screen-saver programs (usually the one of the people doing stuff behind their blinds in this high-rise building, because that's my favorite). If my stuff was off when I left, it's off when I come back. They don't mess around in Dinky's study.

Maybe the cleaners are a little afraid of me, too.

VII

I got the call that changed my life just when I thought the combination of Ma and delivering for Pizza Roma was going to drive me crazy. I know how melodramatic that sounds, but in this case, it's true. The call came on my night off. Ma was out with her girlfriends, playing Bingo at the Reservation, all of them smoking up a storm and no doubt laughing every time the caller pulled B-12 out of the hopper and said, "All right, ladies, it's time to take your vitamins." Me, I was watching a Clint Eastwood movie on TNT and wishing I was anywhere else on Planet Earth. Saskatchewan, even.

The phone rings, and I think, oh good, it's Pug, gotta be, and so when I pick it up I say in my smoothest voice, "You have reached the Church of Any Eventuality, Harkerville branch, Reverend Dink speaking."

"Hello, Mr. Earnshaw," a voice says back. It was one I'd never heard before, but it didn't seem the least put-out or puzzled by my bullshit. I was mortified enough for both of us, though. Have you ever noticed that when you do something like that on the phone—try to be cool right from the pickup—it's never the person you expected on the other end? Once I heard about this girl who picked up the phone and said "Hi, it's Helen, and I want you to fuck me raw" because she was sure it was her boyfriend, only it turned out to be her father. That story is probably made up, like the one about the alligators in the New York sewers (or the letters in *Penthouse*), but you get the point.

"Oh, I'm sorry," I say, too flustered to wonder how the owner of this strange voice knows that Reverend

Dink is also Mr. Earnshaw, actual name Richard Ellery Earnshaw. "I thought you were someone else."

"I *am* someone else," the voice says, and although I didn't laugh then, I did later on. Mr. Sharpton was someone else, all right. Seriously, eventually someone else.

"Can I help you?" I asked. "If you wanted my mother, I'll have to take a message, because she's—"

"—out playing Bingo, I know. In any case, I want you, Mr. Earnshaw. I want to offer you a job."

For a moment I was too surprised to say anything. Then it hit me—some sort of phone-scam. "I got a job," I go. "Sorry."

"Delivering pizza?" he says, sounding amused. "Well, I suppose. If you call that a job."

"Who are you, mister?" I ask.

"My name is Sharpton. And now let me 'cut through the bullshit,' as you might say, Mr. Earnshaw. Dink? May I call you Dink?"

"Sure," I said. "Can I call you Sharpie?"

"Call me whatever you want, just listen."

"I'm listening." I was, too. Why not? The movie on the tube was *Coogan's Bluff,* not one of Clint's better efforts.

"I want to make you the best job-offer you've ever had, and the best one you probably ever will have. It's not just a job, Dink, it's an adventure."

"Gee, where have I heard that before?" I had a bowl of popcorn in my lap, and I tossed a handful into my mouth. This was turning into fun, sort of.

"Others promise; I deliver. But this is a discussion we must have face-to-face. Will you meet me?"

"Are you a queer?" I asked.

"No." There was a touch of amusement in his voice. Just enough so that it was hard to disbelieve. And I was already in the hole, so to speak, from the smartass way I'd answered the phone. "My sexual orientation doesn't come into this."

"Why're you yanking my chain, then? I don't know *anybody* who'd call me at nine-thirty in the fucking night and offer me a job."

"Do me a favor. Put the phone down and go look in your front hall."

Crazier and crazier. But what did I have to lose? I did what he said, and found an envelope lying there. Someone had poked it through the mail-slot while I was watching Clint Eastwood chase Don Stroud through Central Park. The first envelope of many, although of course I didn't know that then. I tore it open, and seven ten-dollar bills fell out into my hand. Also a note.

This can be the beginning of a great career!

I went back into the living room, still looking at the money. Know how weirded-out I was? I almost sat on my bowl of popcorn. I saw it at the last second, set it aside, and plopped back on the couch. I picked up the phone, really sort of expecting Sharpton to be gone, but when I said hello, he answered.

"What's this all about?" I asked him. "What's the seventy bucks for? I'm keeping it, but not because I think I owe you anything. I didn't fucking *ask* for anything."

"The money is absolutely yours," Sharpton says, "with not a string in the world attached. But I'll let you in on a secret, Dink—a job isn't just about money. A real job is about the fringe benefits. That's where the power is."

"If you say so."

"I absolutely do. And all I ask is that you meet me and hear a little more. I'll make you an offer that will change your life, if you take it. That will open the door to a *new* life, in fact. Once I've made that offer, you can ask all the questions you like. Although I must be honest and say you probably won't get all the *answers* you'd like."

"And if I just decide to walk away?"

"I'll shake your hand, clap you on the back, and wish you good luck."

"When did you want to meet?" Part of me—most of me—still thought all this was a joke, but there was a minority opinion forming by then. There was the money, for one thing; two weeks' worth of tips driving for Pizza Roma, and that's if business was good. But mostly it was the way Sharpton talked. He sounded like he'd been to school . . . and I don't mean at Sheep's Rectum State College over in Van Drusen, either. And really, what harm could there be? Since Skipper's accident, there was no one on Planet Earth who wanted to take after me in a way that was dangerous or painful. Well, Ma, I suppose, but her only weapon was her mouth . . . and she wasn't into elaborate practical jokes. Also, I couldn't see her parting with seventy dollars. Not when there was still a Bingo game in the vicinity.

"Tonight," he said. "Right now, in fact."

"All right, why not? Come on over. I guess if you can

we go through most of our lives only getting TV-scared. Like when we're waiting for our blood-tests to come back from the doctor or when we're walking home from the library in the dark and thinking about bad guys in the bushes. We don't get real-scared about shit like that, because we know in our heart of hearts that the blood-tests will come back clean and there won't be any bad guys in the bushes. Why? Because stuff like that only happens to the people on TV.

When I saw that big gray Mercedes, the only car in about an acre of empty parking lot, I got real-scared for the first time since the thing in the box-room with Skipper Brannigan. That time was the closest we ever came to really getting into it.

Mr. Sharpton's ride was sitting under the light of the lot's yellow mercury-vapor lamps, a big old Krautmobile, at least a 450 and probably a 500, the kind of car that costs a hundred and twenty grand these days. Sitting there next to the Kart Korral (now almost empty for the night, all the carts except for one poor old three-wheeled cripple safely locked up inside) with its parking lights on and white exhaust drifting up into the air. Engine rumbling like a sleepy cat.

I drove toward it, my heart pumping slow but hard and a taste like pennies in my throat. I wanted to just mat the accelerator of my Ford (which in those days always smelled like a pepperoni pizza) and get the hell out of there, but I couldn't get rid of the idea that the guy knew about Skipper. I could tell myself there was nothing to know, that Charles "Skipper" Brannigan had either had an accident or committed suicide, the cops weren't sure which (they couldn't have known him very well; if they had, they would have thrown the idea of suicide right out the window—guys like Skipper don't off themselves, not at the age of twenty-three they don't), but that didn't stop the voice from yammering away that I was in trouble, someone had figured it out, someone had gotten hold of the letter and figured it out.

That voice didn't have logic on its side, but it didn't need to. It had good lungs and just outscreamed logic. I parked beside the idling Mercedes and rolled my window down. At the same time, the driver's-side window of the Mercedes rolled down. We looked at each other, me and Mr. Sharpton, like a couple of old friends meeting at the Hi-Hat Drive-In.

I don't remember much about him now. That's weird, considering all the time I've spent thinking about him since, but it's the truth. Only that he was thin, and that he was wearing a suit. A good one, I think, although judging stuff like that's not my strong point. Still, the suit eased me a little. I guess that, unconsciously, I had this idea that a suit means business, and jeans and a tee-shirt means fuckery.

"Hello, Dink," he says. "I'm Mr. Sharpton. Come on in here and sit down."

"Why don't we just stay the way we are?" I asked. "We can talk to each other through these windows. People do it all the time."

He only looked at me and said nothing. After a few seconds of that, I turned off the Ford and got out. I don't know exactly why, but I did. I was more scared than ever, I can tell you that. Real-scared. Real as real as real. Maybe that was why he could get me to do what he wanted.

I stood between Mr. Sharpton's car and mine for a minute, looking at the Kart Korral and thinking about Skipper. He was tall, with this wavy blond hair he combed straight back from his forehead. He had pimples, and these red lips, like a girl wearing lipstick. "Hey Dinky, let's see your dinky," he'd say. Or "Hey Dinky, you want to suck my dinky?" You know, witty shit like that. Sometimes, when we were rounding up the carts, he'd chase me with one, nipping at my heels with it and going "Rmmmm! Rmmmmm! Rmmmmm!" like a fucking race-car. A couple of times he knocked me over. At dinner-break, if I had my food on my lap, he'd bump into me good and hard, see if he could knock something onto the floor. You know the kind of stuff I'm talking about, I'm sure. It was like he'd never gotten over those ideas of what's funny to bored kids sitting in the back row of study hall.

I had a ponytail at work, you had to wear your hair in a ponytail if you had it long, supermarket rules, and sometimes Skipper would come up behind me, grab the rubber band I used, and yank it out. Sometimes it would snarl in my hair and pull it. Sometimes it would break and snap against my neck. It got so I'd stick two or three extra rubber bands in my pants pocket before I left for work. I'd try not to think about why I was doing it, what I was putting up with. If I did, I'd probably start hating myself.

Once I turned around on my heels when he did that, and he must have seen something on my face, because his teasing smile went away and another one came up where it had been. The teasing smile didn't show his teeth, but the new one did. Out in the box-room, this was, where the north wall is always cold because it backs up against the meat-locker. He raised his hands and made them into fists. The other guys sat around with their lunches, looking at us, and I knew none of them would help. Not even Pug, who stands about five-feet-four anyway and weighs about a hundred and ten pounds. Skipper would have eaten him like candy, and Pug knew it.

"Come on, assface," Skipper said, smiling that smile. The broken rubber band he'd stripped out of my hair was dangling between two of his knuckles, hanging down like a little red lizard's tongue. "Come on, you want to fight me? Come on, sure. I'll fight you."

What I wanted was to ask why it had to be me he settled on, why it was me who somehow rubbed his fur wrong, why it had to be *any* guy. But he wouldn't have had an answer. Guys like Skipper never do. They just want to knock your teeth out. So instead, I just sat back down and picked up my sandwich again. If I tried to fight Skipper, he'd likely put me in the hospital. I started to eat, although I wasn't hungry anymore. He looked at me a second or two longer, and I thought he might go after me, anyway, but then he unrolled his fists. The broken rubber band dropped onto the floor beside a smashed lettuce-crate. "You waste," Skipper said. "You fucking longhair hippie waste." Then he walked away. It was only a few days later that he mashed my fingers between two of the carts in the Korral, and a few days after that Skipper was lying on satin in the Methodist Church with the organ playing. He brought it on himself, though. At least that's what I thought then.

"A little trip down Memory Lane?" Mr. Sharpton asked, and that jerked me back to the present. I was standing between his car and mine, standing by the Kart Korral where Skipper would never mash anyone else's fingers.

"I don't know what you're talking about."

"And it doesn't matter. Hop in here, Dink, and let's have a little talk."

I opened the door of the Mercedes and got in. Man, that smell. It's leather, but not just leather. You know how, in Monopoly, there's a Get-Out-of-Jail-Free card? When you're rich enough to afford a car that smells like Mr. Sharpton's gray Mercedes, you must have a Get-Out-of-Everything-Free card.

I took a deep breath, held it, then let it out and said, "This is eventual."

Mr. Sharpton laughed, his clean-shaven cheeks gleaming in the dashboard lights. He didn't ask what I meant; he knew. "Everything's eventual, Dink," he said. "Or can be, for the right person."

"You think so?"

"*Know* so." Not a shred of doubt in his voice.

"I like your tie," I said. I said it just to be saying something, but it was true, too. The tie wasn't what I'd call eventual, but it was good. You know those ties that are printed all over with skulls or dinosaurs or little golf-clubs, stuff like that? Mr. Sharpton's was printed all over with swords, a firm hand holding each one up.

He laughed and ran a hand down it, kind of stroking it. "It's my lucky tie," he said. "When I put it on, I feel like King Arthur." The smile died off his face, little by little, and I realized he wasn't joking. "King

Arthur, out gathering the best men there ever were. Knights to sit with him at the Round Table and remake the world."

That gave me a chill, but I tried not to show it. "What do you want with me, Art? Help you hunt for the Holy Grail, or whatever they call it?"

"A tie doesn't make a man a king," he said. "I know that, in case you were wondering."

I shifted, feeling a little uncomfortable. "Hey, I wasn't trying to put you down—"

"It doesn't matter, Dink. Really. The answer to your question is I'm two parts headhunter, two parts talent scout, and four parts walking, talking destiny. Cigarette?"

"I don't smoke."

"That's good, you'll live longer. Cigarettes are killers. Why else would people call them coffin-nails?"

"You got me," I said.

"I hope so," Mr. Sharpton said, lighting up. "I most sincerely hope so. You're top-shelf goods, Dink. I doubt if you believe that, but it's true."

"What's this offer you were talking about?"

"Tell me what happened to Skipper Brannigan."

Kabam, my worst fear come true. He couldn't know, *nobody* could, but somehow he did. I only sat there feeling numb, my head pounding, my tongue stuck to the roof of my mouth like it was glued there.

"Come on, tell me." His voice seemed to be coming in from far away, like on a shortwave radio late at night.

I got my tongue back where it belonged. It took an effort, but I managed. "I didn't do anything." My own voice seemed to be coming through on that same shitty shortwave band. "Skipper had an accident, that's all. He was driving home and he went off the road. His car rolled over and went into Lockerby Stream. They found water in his lungs, so I guess he drowned, at least technically, but it was in the paper that he probably would have died, anyway. Most of his head got torn off in the rollover, or that's what people say. And some people say it wasn't an accident, that he killed himself, but I don't buy that. Skipper was . . . he was getting too much fun out of life to kill himself."

"Yes. You were part of his fun, weren't you?"

I didn't say anything, but my lips were trembling and there were tears in my eyes.

Mr. Sharpton reached over and put his hand on my arm. It was the kind of thing you'd expect to get from an old guy like him, sitting with him in his big German car in a deserted parking lot, but I knew when he touched me that it wasn't like that, he wasn't hitting on me. It was good to be touched the way he touched me. Until then, I didn't know how sad I was. Sometimes you don't, because it's just, I don't know, all around. I put my head down. I didn't start bawling or anything, but the tears went running down my cheeks. The swords on his tie doubled, then tripled—three for one, such a deal.

"If you're worried that I'm a cop, you can quit. And I gave you money—that screws up any sort of prosecution that might come out of this. But even if that wasn't the case, no one would believe what really happened to young Mr. Brannigan, anyway. Not even if you confessed on nationwide TV. Would they?"

"No," I whispered. Then, louder: "I put up with a

lot. Finally I couldn't put up with any more. He made me, he brought it on himself."

"'Tell me what happened," Mr. Sharpton said.

"I wrote him a letter," I said. "A special letter."

"Yes, very special indeed. And what did you put in it so it could only work on him?"

I knew what he meant, but there was more to it than that. When you personalized the letters, you increased their power. You made them lethal, not just dangerous.

"His sister's name," I said. I think that was when I gave up completely. "His sister, Debbie."

IX

I've always had something, some kind of deal, and I sort of knew it, but not how to use it or what its name was or what it meant. And I sort of knew I had to keep quiet about it, because other people didn't have it. I thought they might put me in the circus if they found out. Or in jail.

I remember once—vaguely, I might have been three or four, it's one of my first memories—standing by this dirty window and looking out at the yard. There was a wood-chopping block and a mailbox with a red flag, so it must have been while we were at Aunt Mabel's, out in the country. That was where we lived after my father ran off. Ma got a job in the Harkerville Fancy Bakery and we moved back to town later on, when I was five or so. We were living in town when I started school, I know that. Because of Mrs. Bukowski's dog, having to walk past that fucking canine cannibal five days a week. I'll never forget that dog. It was a boxer with a white ear. Talk about Memory Lane.

Anyway, I was looking out and there were these flies buzzing around at the top of the window, you know how they do. I didn't like the sound, but I couldn't reach high enough, even with a rolled-up magazine, to swat them or make them go away. So instead of that, I made these two triangles on the windowpane, drawing in the dirt with the tip of my finger, and I made this other shape, a special circle-shape, to hold the triangles together. And as soon as I did that, as soon as I closed the circle, the flies—there were four or five of them—dropped dead on the windowsill. Big as jellybeans, they were—the black jellybeans that taste like licorice. I picked one up and looked at it, but it wasn't very interesting, so I dropped it on the floor and went on looking out the window.

Stuff like that would happen from time to time, but never on purpose, never because I made it happen. The first time I remember doing something absolutely on purpose—before Skipper, I mean—was when I used my whatever-it-was on Mrs. Bukowski's dog. Mrs. Bukowski lived on the corner of our street, when we rented on Dugway Avenue. Her dog was mean and dangerous, every kid on the West Side was afraid of that white-eared fuck. She kept it tied in her side yard—hell, *staked out* in her side yard is more like it— and it barked at everyone who went by. Not harmless yapping, like some dogs do, but the kind that says *If I could get you in here with me or get out there with you, I'd tear your balls off, Brewster.* Once the dog *did* get loose, and it bit the paperboy. Anyone else's dog probably would have sniffed gas for that, but Mrs. Bukowski's son was the police chief, and he fixed it up, somehow.

I hated that dog the way I hated Skipper. In a way, I suppose, it *was* Skipper. I had to go by Mrs. Bukowski's on my way to school unless I wanted to detour all the way around the block and get called a sissy-boy, and I was terrified of the way that mutt would run to the end of its rope, barking so hard that foam would fly off its teeth and muzzle. Sometimes it hit the end of the rope so hard it'd go right off its feet, *boi-yoi-yoinng,* which might have looked funny to some people but never looked funny to me; I was just scared the rope (not a chain, but a plain old piece of rope) would break one day, and the dog would jump over the low picket fence between Mrs. Bukowski's yard and Dugway Avenue, and it would rip my throat out.

Then one day I woke up with an idea. I mean it was right there. I woke up with it the way some days I'd wake up with a great big throbbing boner. It was a Saturday, bright and early, and I didn't have to go anywhere near Mrs. Bukowski's if I didn't want to, but that day I *did* want to. I got out of bed and threw on my clothes just as fast as I could. I did everything fast because I didn't want to lose that idea. I would, too— I'd lose it the way you eventually lose the dreams you wake up with (or the boners you wake up with, if you want to be crude)—but right then I had the whole thing in my mind just as clear as a bell: words with triangles around them and curlicues over them, special circles to hold the whole shebang together . . . two or three of those, overlapping for extra strength.

I just about flew through the living room (Ma was still sleeping, I could hear her snoring, and her pink bakery uniform was hung over the shower rod in the bathroom) and went into the kitchen. Ma had a little blackboard by the phone for numbers and reminders to herself—MA'S DAYBOARD instead of DINKY'S DAY-BOARD, I guess you'd say—and I stopped just long enough to gleep the piece of pink chalk hanging on a string beside it. I put it in my pocket and went out the door. I remember what a beautiful morning that was, cool but not cold, the sky so blue it looked like some-one had run it through the Happy Wheels Carwash, no one moving around much yet, most folks sleeping in a little, like everyone likes to do on Saturdays, if they can.

Mrs. Bukowski's dog wasn't sleeping in. Fuck, no. That dog was a firm believer in rooty-tooty, do your duty. It saw me coming through the picket-fence and went charging to the end of its rope as hard as ever, maybe even harder, as if some part of its dim little doggy brain knew it was Saturday and I had no busi-ness being there. It hit the end of the rope, *boi-yoi-yoinng,* and went right over backward. It was up again in a second, though, standing at the end of its rope and barking in its choky I'm-strangling-but-I-don't-care way. I suppose Mrs. Bukowski was used to that sound, maybe even *liked* it, but I've wondered since how the neighbors stood it.

I paid no attention that day. I was too excited to be scared. I fished the chalk out of my pocket and dropped down on one knee. For one second I thought the whole works had gone out of my head, and that was bad. I felt despair and sadness trying to fill me up and I thought, No, don't let it, don't let it, Dinky, fight it. Write anything, even if it's only FUCK MRS. BUKOWSKI'S DOG.

But I didn't write that. I drew this shape, I think it was a sankofite, instead. Some weird shape, but the *right* shape, because it unlocked everything else. My head flooded with stuff. It was wonderful, but at the same time it was really scary because there was so fucking much of it. For the next five minutes or so I knelt there on the sidewalk, sweating like a pig and writing like a mad fiend. I wrote words I'd never heard and drew shapes I'd never seen—shapes *nobody* had ever seen: not just sankofites but japps and fouders and mirks. I wrote and drew until I was pink dust halfway to my right elbow and Ma's piece of chalk was nothing but a little pebble between my thumb and finger. Mrs. Bukowski's dog didn't die like the flies, it barked at me the whole time, and it probably drew back and ran out the length of its rope leash another time or two, but I didn't notice. I was in this total frenzy. I could never describe it to you in a million years, but I bet it's how great musicians like Mozart and Eric Clapton feel when they're writing their music, or how painters feel when they're getting their best work on canvas. If someone had come along, I would have ignored him. Shit, if Mrs. Bukowski's dog had finally broken its rope, jumped the fence, and clamped down on my ass, I probably would have ignored *that*.

It was eventual, man. It was so fucking eventual I can't even tell you.

No one *did* come, although a few cars went by and maybe the people in them wondered what that kid was doing, what he was drawing on the sidewalk, and Mrs. Bukowski's dog went on barking. At the end, I realized I had to make it stronger, and the way to do that was to make it just for the dog. I didn't know its name, so I printed BOXER with the last of the chalk, drew a circle around it, then made an arrow at the bottom of the circle, pointing to the rest. I felt dizzy and my head was throbbing, the way it does when you've just finished taking a super-hard test, or if you spend too long watching TV. I felt like I was going to be sick . . . but I still also felt totally eventual.

I looked at the dog—it was still just as lively as ever, barking and kind of prancing on its back legs when it ran out of slack—but that didn't bother me. I went back home feeling easy in my mind. I knew Mrs. Bukowski's dog was toast. The same way, I bet, that a good painter knows when he's painted a good picture, or a good writer knows when he's written a good story. When it's right, I think you just know. It sits there in your head and hums.

Three days later the dog was eating the old dirt sandwich. I got the story from the best possible source when it comes to mean asshole dogs: the neighborhood mailman. Mr. Shermerhorn, his name was. Mr. Shermerhorn said Mrs. Bukowski's boxer for some reason started running around the tree he was tied to, and when he got to the end of his rope (ha-ha, end of his rope), he couldn't get back. Mrs. Bukowski was out shopping somewhere, so she was no help. When she got home, she found her dog lying at the base of the tree in her side yard, choked to death.

The writing on the sidewalk stayed there for about a week; then it rained hard and afterward there was just a pink blur. But until it rained, it stayed pretty sharp. And while it was sharp, no one walked on it. I saw this for myself. People—kids walking to school, ladies walking downtown, Mr. Shermerhorn, the mailman— would just kind of veer around it. They didn't even seem to know they were doing it. And nobody ever talked about it, either, like "What's up with this weird shit on the sidewalk?" or "What do you suppose you call something that looks like that?" (A fouder, dim-bulb.) It was as if they didn't even see it was there. Except part of them must have. Why else would they have walked around it?

X

I didn't tell Mr. Sharpton all that, but I told him what he wanted to know about Skipper. I had decided I could trust him. Maybe that secret part of me knew I could trust him, but I don't think so. I think it was just the way he put his hand on my arm, like your Dad would. Not that I have a Dad, but I can imagine.

Plus, it was like he said—even if he was a cop and arrested me, what judge and jury would believe Skipper Brannigan had driven his car off the road because of a letter I sent him? Especially one full of nonsense words and symbols made up by a pizza delivery-boy who had flunked high school geometry. *Twice.*

When I was done, there was silence between us for a long time. At last Mr. Sharpton said, "He deserved it. You know that, don't you?"

And for some reason that did it. The dam burst and I cried like a baby. I must have cried for fifteen minutes or more. Mr. Sharpton put his arm around me and pulled me against his chest and I watered the lapel of his suit. If someone had driven by and seen us that way, they would have thought we were a couple of queers for sure, but nobody did. There was just him and me under the yellow mercury-vapor lamps, there by the Kart Korral. Yippy-ti-yi-yo, get along little shopping cart, Pug used to sing, for yew know Supr Savr will be yer new home. We'd laugh till we cried.

At last I was able to turn off the waterworks. Mr. Sharpton handed me a hanky and I wiped my eyes with it. "How did you know?" I asked. My voice sounded all deep and weird, like a foghorn.

"Once you were spotted, all it took was a little rudimentary detective work."

"Yeah, but how was I spotted?"

"We have certain people—a dozen or so in all—who look for fellows and gals like you," he said. "They can actually *see* fellows and gals like you, Dink, the way certain satellites in space can see nuclear piles and power-plants. You folks show up yellow. Like match-flames is how this one spotter described it to me." He shook his head and gave a wry little smile. "I'd like to see something like that just once in my life. Or be able to do what you do. Of course, I'd also like to be given a day—just one would be fine—when I could paint like Picasso or write like Faulkner."

I gaped at him. "Is that true? There are people who can *see*—"

"Yes. They're our bloodhounds. They crisscross the country—and all the other countries—looking for that bright yellow glow. Looking for matchheads in the darkness. This particular young woman was on Route 90, actually headed for Pittsburgh to catch a plane home—to grab a little R-and-R—when she saw you. Or sensed you. Or whatever it is they do. The finders don't really know themselves, any more than you really know what you did to Skipper. Do you?"

"What—"

He raised a hand. "I told you that you wouldn't get all the answers you'd like—this is something you'll have to decide on the basis of what you feel, not on what you know—but I can tell you a couple of things. To begin with, Dink, I work for an outfit called the Trans Corporation. Our job is getting rid of the world's Skipper Brannigans—the big ones, the ones who do it on a grand scale. We have company headquarters in Chicago and a training center in Peoria . . . where you'll spend a week, if you agree to my proposal."

I didn't say anything then, but I knew already I was going to say yes to his proposal. Whatever it was, I was going to say yes.

"You're a tranny, my young friend. Better get used to the idea."

"What is it?"

"A trait. There are folks in our organization who think of what you have . . . what you can do . . . as a talent or an ability or even a kind of glitch, but they're wrong. Talent and ability are born of trait. Trait is general, talent and ability are specific."

"You'll have to simplify that. I'm a high-school dropout, remember."

"I know," he said. "I also know that you didn't drop out because you were stupid; you dropped out because you didn't fit. In that way, you are like every other tranny I've ever met." He laughed in the sharp way people do when they're not really amused. "All twenty-one of them. Now listen to me, and don't play dumb. Creativity is like a hand at the end of your arm. But a hand has many fingers, doesn't it?"

"Well, at least five."

"Think of those fingers as abilities. A creative person may write, paint, sculpt, or think up math formulae; he or she might dance or sing or play a musical instrument. Those are the fingers, but creativity is the hand that gives them life. And just as all hands are basically the same—form follows function—all creative people are the same once you get down to the place where the fingers join.

"Trans is also like a hand. Sometimes its fingers are called precognition, the ability to see the future. Sometimes they're postcognition, the ability to see the past—we have a guy who knows who killed John F. Kennedy, and it wasn't Lee Harvey Oswald; it was, in fact, a woman. There's telepathy, pyrokinesis, telempathy, and who knows how many others. We don't know, certainly; this is a new world, and we've barely begun to explore its first continent. But trans is different from creativity in one vital way: it's much rarer. One person in eight hundred is what occupational psychologists call 'gifted.' We believe that there may only be one tranny in each eight *million* people."

That took my breath away—the idea that you might be one in eight million would take *anybody's* breath away, right?

"That's about a hundred and twenty for every *billion* ordinary folks," he said. "We think there may be no more than three thousand so-called trannies in the whole world. We're finding them, one by one. It's slow work. The sensing ability is fairly low-level, but we still only have a dozen or so finders, and each one takes a lot of training. This is a hard calling . . . but it's also fabulously rewarding. We're finding trannies and we're putting them to work. That's what we want to do with you, Dink: put you to work. We want to help you focus your talent, sharpen it, and use it for the betterment of all mankind. You won't be able to see any of your old friends again—there's no security risk on earth like an old friend, we've found—and there's not a whole lot of cash in it, at least to begin with, but there's a lot of satisfaction, and what I'm going to offer you is only the bottom rung of what may turn out to be a very high ladder."

"Don't forget those fringe benefits," I said, kind of raising my voice on the last word, turning it into a question, if he wanted to take it that way.

He grinned and clapped me on the shoulder. "That's right," he said. "Those famous fringe benefits."

By then I was starting to get excited. My doubts weren't gone, but they were melting away. "So tell me about it," I said. My heart was beating hard, but it wasn't fear. Not anymore. "Make me an offer I can't refuse."

And that's just what he did.

XI

Three weeks later I'm on an airplane for the first time in my life—and what a way to lose your cherry! The only passenger in a Lear 35, listening to Counting Crows pouring out of quad speakers with a Coke in one hand, watching as the altimeter climbs all the way to forty-two thousand feet. That's over a mile higher than most commercial jetliners fly, the pilot told me. And a ride as smooth as the seat of a girl's underpants.

I spent a week in Peoria, and I was homesick. *Really* homesick. Surprised the shit out of me. There were a couple of nights when I even cried myself to sleep. I'm ashamed to say that, but I've been truthful so far, and don't want to start lying or leaving things out now.

Ma was the least of what I missed. You'd think we would have been close, as it was "us against the world," in a manner of speaking, but my mother was never much for loving and comforting. She didn't whip on my head or put out her cigarettes in my armpits or anything like that, but so what? I mean, big whoop. I've never had any kids, so I guess I can't say for sure, but I somehow don't think being a great parent is about the stuff you *didn't* do to your rug monkeys. Ma was always more into her friends than me, and her weekly trip to the beauty shop, and Friday nights out at the Reservation. Her big ambition in life was to win a twenty-number Bingo and drive home in a brand-new Monte Carlo. I'm not sitting on the pity-pot, either. I'm just telling you how it was.

Mr. Sharpton called Ma and told her that I'd been chosen to intern in the Trans Corporation's advanced computer training and placement project, a special deal for non-diploma kids with potential. The story was actually pretty believable. I was a shitty math student and froze up almost completely in classes like English, where you were supposed to talk, but I was always on good terms with the school computers. In fact, although I don't like to brag (and I never let any of the faculty in on this little secret), I could program rings around Mr. Jacubois and Mrs. Wilcoxen. I never cared much about computer games—they're strictly for dickbrains, in my humble opinion—but I could keyjack like a mad motherfucker. Pug used to drop by and watch me, sometimes.

"I can't believe you," he said once. "Man, you got that thing smokin and tokin."

I shrugged. "Any fool can peel the Apple," I said. "It takes a real man to eat the core."

So Ma believed it (she might have had a few more questions if she knew the Trans Corporation was flying me out to Illinois in a private jet, but she didn't), and I didn't miss her all that much. But I missed Pug, and John Cassiday, who was our other friend from our Supr Savr days. John plays bass in a punk band, wears a gold ring in his left eyebrow, and has just about every Subpop record ever made. He cried when Kurt Cobain ate the dirt sandwich. Didn't try to hide it or blame it on allergies, either. Just said, "I'm sad because Kurt died." John's eventual.

And I missed Harkerville. Perverse but true. Being at the training center in Peoria was like being born again, somehow, and I guess being born always hurts.

I thought I might meet some other people like me—if this was a book or a movie (or maybe just an episode of *The X-Files*), I would meet a cute chick with nifty little tits and the ability to shut doors from across the room—but that didn't happen. I'm pretty sure there were other trannies at Peoria when I was there, but Dr. Wentworth and the other folks running the place were careful to keep us separated. I once asked why, and got a runaround. That's when I started to realize that not everybody who had TRANSCORP printed on their shirts or walked around with TransCorp clipboards was my pal, or wanted to be my long-lost Dad.

And it was about killing people; that's what I was training for. The folks in Peoria didn't talk about that all the time, but no one tried to sugarcoat it, either. I just had to remember the targets were bad guys, dictators and spies and serial killers, and as Mr. Sharpton said, people did it in wars all the time. Plus, it wasn't personal. No guns, no knives, no garrotes. I'd never get blood splashed on me.

Like I told you, I never saw Mr. Sharpton again—at least not yet, I haven't—but I talked to him every day of the week I was in Peoria, and that eased the pain and strangeness considerably. Talking to him was like having someone put a cool cloth on your brow. He gave me his number the night we talked in his Mercedes, and told me to call him anytime. Even at three in the morning, if I was feeling upset. Once I did just that. I almost hung up on the second ring, because people may *say* call them anytime, even at three in the morning, but they don't really expect you to do it. But I hung in there. I was homesick, yeah, but it was more than that. The place wasn't what I had expected, exactly, and I wanted to tell Mr. Sharpton so. See how he took it, kind of.

He answered on the third ring, and although he sounded sleepy (big surprise there, huh?), he didn't sound at all pissed. I told him that some of the stuff they were doing was quite weird. The test with all the flashing lights, for example. They said it was a test for epilepsy, but—

"I went to sleep right in the middle of it," I said. "And when I woke up, I had a headache and it was hard to think. You know what I felt like? A file-cabinet after someone's been rummaging through it."

"What's your point, Dink?" Mr. Sharpton asked.

"I think they hypnotized me," I said.

A brief pause. Then: "Maybe they did. *Probably* they did."

"But why? Why would they? I'm doing everything they ask, so why would they want to hypnotize me?"

"I don't know all their routines and protocols, but I suspect they're programming you. Putting a lot of housekeeping stuff on the lower levels of your mind so they won't have to junk up the conscious part . . . and maybe screw up your special ability, while they're at it. Really no different than programming a computer's hard disk, and no more sinister."

"But you don't know for sure?"

"No—as I say, training and testing are not my purview. But I'll make some calls, and Dr. Wentworth will talk to you. It may even be that an apology is due. If that's the case, Dink, you may be sure that it will be tendered. Our trannies are too rare and too valuable to be upset needlessly. Now, is there anything else?"

I thought about it, then said no. I thanked him and hung up. It had been on the tip of my tongue to tell him I thought I'd been drugged, as well . . . given some sort of mood-elevator to help me through the worst of my homesickness, but in the end I decided not to bother him. It was three in the morning, after all, and if they had been giving me anything, it was probably for my own good.

XII

Dr. Wentworth came to see me the next day—he was the Big Kahuna—and he *did* apologize. He was perfectly nice about it, but he had a look, I don't know, like maybe Mr. Sharpton had called him about two minutes after I hung up and gave him a hot reaming.

Dr. Wentworth took me for a walk on the back lawn—green and rolling and damned near perfect there at the end of spring—and said he was sorry for not keeping me "up to speed." The epilepsy test really *was* an epilepsy test, he said (and a CAT-scan, too), but since it induced a hypnotic state in most subjects, they usually took advantage of it to give certain "baseline instructions." In my case, they were instructions about the computer programs I'd be using in Columbia City.

Dr. Wentworth asked me if I had any other questions. I lied and said no.

You probably think that's weird, but it's not. I mean, I had a long and sucky school career which ended three months short of graduation. I had teachers I liked as well as teachers I hated, but never one I entirely trusted. I was the kind of kid who always sat in the back of the room if the teacher's seating-chart wasn't alphabetical, and never took part in class discussions. I mostly said "Huh?" when I was called on, and wild horses wouldn't have dragged a question out of me. Mr. Sharpton was the only guy I ever met who was able to get into where I lived, and ole Doc Wentworth with his bald head and sharp eyes behind his little rimless glasses was no Mr. Sharpton. I could imagine pigs flying south for the winter before I could imagine opening up to that dude, let alone crying on his shoulder.

And fuck, I didn't know what else to ask, anyway. A lot of the time I liked it in Peoria, and I was excited by the prospects ahead—new job, new house, new town. People were great to me in Peoria. Even the food was great—meatloaf, fried chicken, milkshakes, everything I liked. Okay, I didn't like the diagnostic tests, those boogersnots you have to do with an IBM pencil, and sometimes I'd feel dopey, as if someone had put something in my mashed potatoes (or hyper, sometimes I'd feel that way, too), and there were other times—at least two—when I was pretty sure I'd been hypnotized again. But so what? I mean, was any of it a big deal after you'd been chased around a supermarket parking lot by a maniac who was laughing and making race-car noises and trying to run you over with a shopping cart?

XIII

I had one more talk on the phone with Mr. Sharpton that I suppose I should mention. That was just a day before my second airplane ride, the one that took me to Columbia City, where a guy was waiting with the keys to my new house. By then I knew about the cleaners, and the basic money-rule—start every week broke, end every week broke—and I knew who to call locally if I had a problem. (Any big problem and I call Mr. Sharpton, who is technically my "control.") I had maps, a list of restaurants, directions to the cinema complex and the mall. I had a line on everything but the most important thing of all.

"Mr. Sharpton, I don't know what to *do*," I said. I was talking to him on the phone just outside the caff. There was a phone in my room, but by then I was too nervous to sit down, let alone lie on my bed. If they were still putting shit in my food, it sure wasn't working that day.

"I can't help you there, Dink," he said, calm as ever. "So solly, Cholly."

"What do you mean? You've *got* to help me! You *recruited* me, for jeepers' sake!"

"Let me give you a hypothetical case. Suppose I'm the President of a well-endowed college. Do you know what *well-endowed* means?"

"Lots of bucks. I'm not stupid, I told you that."

"So you did—I apologize. Anyhow, let's say that I, President Sharpton, use some of my school's plentiful bucks to hire a great novelist as the writer-in-residence, or a great pianist to teach music. Would that entitle me to tell the novelist what to write, or the pianist what to compose?"

"Probably not."

"*Absolutely* not. But let's say it did. If I told the novelist, 'Write a comedy about Betsy Ross screwing around with George Washington in Gay Paree,' do you think he could do it?"

I got laughing. I couldn't help it. Mr. Sharpton's just got a vibe about him, somehow.

"Maybe," I said. "Especially if you whipped a bonus on the guy."

"Okay, but even if he held his nose and cranked it out, it would likely be a very bad novel. Because creative people aren't always in charge. And when they do their best work, they're hardly *ever* in charge. They're just sort of rolling along with their eyes shut, yelling *Wheeeee.*"

"What's all that got to do with me? Listen, Mr. Sharpton—when I try to imagine what I'm going to do in Columbia City, all I see is a great big blank. Help people, you said. Make the world a better place. Get rid of the Skippers. All that sounds great, except *I don't know how to do it!*"

"You will," he said. "When the time comes, you will."

"You said Wentworth and his guys would focus my talent. Sharpen it. Mostly what they did was give me a bunch of stupid tests and make me feel like I was back in school. Is it *all* in my subconscious? Is it *all* on the hard disk?"

"Trust me, Dink," he said. "Trust me, and trust yourself."

So I did. I have. But just lately, things haven't been so good. Not so good at all.

That goddam Neff—all the bad stuff started with him. I wish I'd never seen his picture. And if I *had* to see a picture, I wish I'd seen one where he wasn't smiling.

XIV

My first week in Columbia City, I did nothing. I mean absolutely zilch. I didn't even go to the movies. When the cleaners came, I just went to the park and sat on a bench and felt like the whole world was watching me. When it came time to get rid of my extra money on Thursday, I ended up shredding better than fifty dollars in the garbage disposal. And doing that was new to me then, remember. Talk about feeling *weird*—man, you don't have a clue. While I was standing there, listening to the motor under the sink grinding away, I kept thinking about Ma. If Ma had been there to see what I was doing, she would have probably run me through with a butcher-knife to make me stop. That was a dozen twenty-number Bingo games (or two dozen cover-alls) going straight down the kitchen pig.

I slept like shit that week. Every now and then I'd go to the little study—I didn't want to, but my feet would drag me there. Like they say murderers always return to the scenes of their crimes, I guess. Anyway, I'd stand there in the doorway and look at the dark computer screen, at the Global Village modem, and I'd just sweat with guilt and embarrassment and fear. Even the way the desk was so neat and clean, without a single paper or note on it, made me sweat. I could just about hear the walls muttering stuff like "Nah, nothing going on in here" and "Who's *this* turkey, the cable-installer?"

I had nightmares. In one of them, the doorbell rings and when I open it, Mr. Sharpton's there. He's got a pair of handcuffs. "Put out your wrists, Dink," he says. "We thought you were a tranny, but obviously we were wrong. Sometimes it happens."

"No, I *am*," I say. "I *am* a tranny, I just need a little more time to get acclimated. I've never been away from home before, remember."

"You've had five years," he goes.

I'm stunned. I can't believe it. But part of me knows it's true. It *feels* like days, but it's really been *five fucking years,* and I haven't turned on the computer in the little study a single time. If not for the cleaners, the desk it sits on would be six inches deep in dust.

"Hold out your hands, Dink. Stop making this hard on both of us."

"I won't," I say, "and you can't make me."

He looks behind him then, and who should come up the steps but Skipper Brannigan. He is wearing his red nylon tunic, only now TRANSCORP is sewn on it instead of SUPR SAVR. He looks pale but otherwise okay. Not dead is what I mean. "You thought you did something to me, but you didn't," Skipper says. "You couldn't do anything to anyone. You're just a hippie waste."

"I'm going to put these cuffs on him," Mr. Sharpton says to Skipper. "If he gives me any trouble, run him over with a shopping cart."

"Totally eventual," Skipper says, and I wake up half out of my bed and on the floor, screaming.

XV

Then, about ten days after I moved in, I had another kind of dream. I don't remember what it was, but it must have been a good one, because when I woke up, I was smiling. I could feel it on my face, a big, happy smile. It was like when I woke up with the idea about Mrs. Bukowski's dog. Almost exactly like that.

I pulled on a pair of jeans and went into the study. I turned on the computer and opened the window marked TOOLS. There was a program in there called DINKY'S NOTEBOOK. I went right to it, and all my symbols were there—circles, triangles, japps, mirks, rhomboids, bews, smims, fouders, hundreds more. *Thousands* more. Maybe *millions* more. It's sort of like Mr. Sharpton said: a new world, and I'm on the coastline of the first continent.

All I know is that all at once it was *there* for me, I had a great big Macintosh computer to work with instead of a little piece of pink chalk, and all I had to do was type the words for the symbols and the symbols would appear. I was jacked to the max. I mean my God. It was like a river of fire burning in the middle of my head. I wrote, I called up symbols, I used the mouse to drag everything where it was supposed to be. And when it was done, I had a letter. One of the special letters.

But a letter to who?

A letter to where?

Then I realized it didn't matter. Make a few minor customizing touches, and there were many people the letter could go to . . . although this one had been written for a man rather than a woman. I don't know how I knew that; I just did. I decided to start with Cincinnati, only because Cincinnati was the first city to come into my mind. It could as easily have been Zurich, Switzerland, or Waterville, Maine.

I tried to open a TOOLS program titled DINKYMAIL. Before the computer would let me in there, it prompted me to wake up my modem. Once the modem was running, the computer wanted a 312 area code. 312's Chicago, and I imagine that, as far as the phone company is concerned, my compu-calls all come from TransCorp's headquarters. I didn't care one way or another; that was their business. I had found my business and was taking care of it.

With the modem awake and linked to Chicago, the computer flashed

DINKYMAIL READY.

I clicked on LOCALE. I'd been in the study almost three hours by then, with only one break to take a quick piss, and I could smell myself, sweating and stinking like a monkey in a greenhouse. I didn't mind. I liked the smell. I was having the time of my life. I was fucking delirious.

I typed CINCINNATI and hit EXECUTE.

NO LISTINGS CINCINNATI

the computer said. Okay, not a problem. Try Columbus—closer to home, anyway. And yes, folks! We have a Bingo.

TWO LISTINGS COLUMBUS

There were two telephone numbers. I clicked on the top one, curious and a little afraid of what might pop out. But it wasn't a dossier, a profile, or—God forbid—a photograph. There was one single word:

MUFFIN.

Say *what?*

But then I knew. Muffin was Mr. Columbus's pet. Very likely a cat. I called up my special letter again, transposed two symbols and deleted a third. Then I added MUFFIN to the top, with an arrow pointing down. There. Perfect.

Did I wonder who Muffin's owner was, or what he had done to warrant TransCorp's attention, or exactly what was going to happen to him? I did not. The idea that my conditioning at Peoria might have been partially responsible for this disinterest never crossed my mind, either. I was doing my thing, that was all. Just doing my thing, and as happy as a clam at high tide.

I called the number on the screen. I had the computer's speaker on, but there was no hello, only the screechy mating-call of another computer. Just as well, really. Life's easier when you subtract the human element. Then it's like that movie, *Twelve O'Clock High,* cruising over Berlin in your trusty B-25, looking through your trusty Norden bombsight and waiting for just the right moment to push your trusty button. You might see smokestacks, or factory roofs, but no people. The guys who dropped the bombs from their

B-25s didn't have to hear the screams of mothers whose children had just been reduced to guts, and I didn't even have to hear anyone say hello. A very good deal.

After a little bit, I turned off the speaker anyway. I found it distracting.

MODEM FOUND,

the computer flashed, and then

SEARCH FOR E-MAIL ADDRESS Y/N.

I typed Y and waited. This time the wait was longer. I think the computer was going back to Chicago again, and getting what it needed to unlock the e-mail address of Mr. Columbus. Still, it was less than thirty seconds before the computer was right back at me with

E-MAIL ADDRESS FOUND
SEND DINKYMAIL Y/N.

I typed Y with absolutely no hesitation. The computer flashed

SENDING DINKYMAIL

and then

DINKYMAIL SENT.

That was all. No fireworks.

I wonder what happened to Muffin, though. You know. After.

XVI

That night I called Mr. Sharpton and said, "I'm working."

"That's good, Dink. Great news. Feel better?" Calm as ever. Mr. Sharpton is like the weather in Tahiti.

"Yeah," I said. The fact was, I felt blissful. It was the best day of my life. Doubts or no doubts, worries or no worries, I still say that. The most eventual day of my life. It was like a river of fire in my head, *a fucking river of fire,* can you get that? "Do *you* feel better, Mr. Sharpton? Relieved?"

"I'm happy for you, but I can't say I'm relieved, because—"

"—you were never worried in the first place."

"Got it in one," he said.

"Everything's eventual, in other words."

He laughed at that. He always laughs when I say that. "That's right, Dink. Everything's eventual."

"Mr. Sharpton?"

"Yes?"

"E-mail's not exactly private, you know. Anybody who's really dedicated can hack into it."

"Part of what you send is a suggestion that the recipient delete the message from all files, is it not?"

"Yes, but I can't absolutely guarantee that he'll do it. Or she."

"Even if they don't, nothing can happen to someone

else who chances on such a message, am I correct? Because it's . . . personalized."

"Well, it might give someone a headache, but that would be about all."

"And the communication itself would look like so much gibberish."

"Or a code."

He laughed heartily at that. "Let them try to break it, Dinky, eh? Just let them try!"

I sighed. "I suppose."

"Let's discuss something more important, Dink . . . how did it *feel?*"

"Fucking *wonderful.*"

"Good. Don't question wonder, Dink. Don't ever question wonder."

And he hung up.

XVII

Sometimes I have to send actual letters—print out the stuff I whomp up in DINKY'S NOTEBOOK, stick it in an envelope, lick stamps, and mail it off to somebody somewhere. Professor Ann Tevitch, University of New Mexico at Las Cruces. Mr. Andrew Neff, c/o The New York *Post,* New York, New York. Billy Unger, General Delivery, Stovington, Vermont. Only names, but they were still more upsetting than the phone numbers. More *personal* than the phone numbers. It was like seeing faces swim up at you for a second inside your Norden bombsight. I mean, what a freak-out, right? You're up there at twenty-five thousand feet, no faces allowed up there, but sometimes one shows up for a second or two, just the same.

I wondered how a University Professor could get along without a modem (or a guy whose address was a fucking New York newspaper, for that matter), but I never wondered too much. I didn't have to. We live in a modern world, but letters don't *have* to be sent by computer, after all. There's still snail-mail. And the stuff I really needed was always in the database. The fact that Unger had a 1957 Thunderbird, for instance. Or that Ann Tevitch had a loved one—perhaps her husband, perhaps her son, perhaps her father—named Simon.

And people like Tevitch and Unger were exceptions. Most of the folks I reach out and touch are like that first one in Columbus—fully equipped for the twenty-first century. SENDING DINKYMAIL, DINKY-MAIL SENT, velly good, so long, Cholly.

I could have gone on like that for a long time, maybe forever—browsing the database (there's no schedule to follow, no list of primary cities and targets; I'm completely on my own . . . unless all that shit is *also* in my subconscious, down there on the hard disk), going to afternoon movies, enjoying the Ma-less silence of my little house, and dreaming of my next step up the ladder, except I woke up feeling horny one day. I worked for an hour or so, browsing around in Australia, but it was no good—my dick kept trespassing on my brain, so to speak. I shut off the computer and went down to News Plus to see if I could find a magazine featuring pretty ladies in frothy lingerie.

As I got there, a guy was coming out, reading the

Columbus *Dispatch*. I never read the paper myself. Why bother? It's the same old shit day in and day out, dictators beating the ching-chong out of people weaker than they are, men in uniforms beating the ching-chong out of soccer balls or footballs, politicians kissing babies and kissing ass. Mostly stories about the Skipper Brannigans of the world, in other words. And I wouldn't have seen this story even if I'd happened to look at the newspaper display rack once I got inside, because it was on the bottom half of the front page, below the fold. But this fucking dimbulb comes out with the paper hanging open and his face buried inside it.

In the lower right corner was a picture of a white-haired guy smoking a pipe and smiling. He looked like a good-humored fuck, probably Irish, eyes all crinkled up and these white bushy eyebrows. And the headline over the photo—not a big one, but you could read it—said NEFF SUICIDE STILL PUZZLES, GRIEVES COLLEAGUES.

For a second or two I thought I'd just skip News Plus that day, I didn't feel like ladies in lingerie after all, maybe I'd just go home and take a nap. If I went in, I'd probably pick up a copy of the *Dispatch*, wouldn't be able to help myself, and I wasn't sure I wanted to know any more about that Irish-looking guy than I already did . . . which was nothing at all, as you can fucking believe I hastened to tell myself. Neff couldn't be that weird a name anyway, only four letters, not like Shittendookus or Horecake, there must be thousands of Neffs, if you're talking coast to coast. This one didn't have to be the Neff I knew about, the one who loved Frank Sinatra records.

It would be better, in any case, to just leave and

come back tomorrow. Tomorrow the picture of that guy with the pipe would be gone. Tomorrow somebody else's picture would be there, on the lower right corner of page one. People always dying, right? People who aren't superstars or anything, just famous enough to get their pictures down there in the lower right corner of page one. And sometimes people were puzzled about it, the way folks back home in Harkerville had been puzzled about Skipper's death—no alcohol in his blood, clear night, dry road, not the suicidal type.

The world is full of mysteries like that, though, and sometimes it's best not to solve them. Sometimes the solutions aren't, you know, too eventual.

But willpower has never been my strong point. I can't always keep away from the chocolate, even though I know my skin doesn't like it, and I couldn't keep away from the Columbus *Dispatch* that day. I went on inside and bought one.

I started home, then had a funny thought. The funny thought was that I didn't want a newspaper with Andrew Neff's picture on the front page going out with my trash. The trash pick-up guys came in a city truck, surely they didn't—*couldn't*—have anything to do with TransCorp, but . . .

There was this show me and Pug used to watch one summer back when we were little kids. *Golden Years*, it was called. You probably don't remember it. Anyway, there was a guy on that show who used to say "Perfect paranoia is perfect awareness." It was like his motto. And I sort of believe that.

Anyway, I went to the park instead of back home. I sat on a bench and read the story, and when I was done, I stuck the paper in a park trashbarrel. I didn't even like doing that, but hey—if Mr. Sharpton has got a guy following me around and checking on every little thing I throw away, I'm fucked up the wazoo no matter what.

There was no doubt that Andrew Neff, age sixty-two, a columnist for the *Post* since 1970, had committed suicide. He took a bunch of pills that probably would have done the trick, then climbed into his bathtub, put a plastic bag over his head, and rounded the evening off by slitting his wrists. There was a man totally dedicated to avoiding counselling.

He left no note, though, and the autopsy showed no signs of disease. His colleagues scoffed at the idea of Alzheimer's, or even early senility. "He was the sharpest guy I've ever known, right up to the day he died," a guy named Pete Hamill said. "He could have gone on *Challenge Jeopardy!* and run both boards. I have no idea why Andy did such a thing." Hamill went on to say that one of Neff's "charming oddities" was his complete refusal to participate in the computer revolution. No modems for him, no laptop word processor, no hand-held spell-checker from Franklin Electronic Publishers. He didn't even have a CD player in his apartment, Hamill said; Neff claimed, perhaps only half-joking, that compact discs were the Devil's work. He loved the Chairman of the Board, but only on vinyl.

This guy Hamill and several others said Neff was unfailingly cheerful, right up to the afternoon he filed his last column, went home, drank a glass of wine, and then demo'd himself. One of the *Post*'s chatter columnists, Liz Smith, said she'd shared a piece of pie with him just before he left on that last day, and Neff had seemed "a trifle distracted, but otherwise fine."

Distracted, sure. With a headful of fouders, bews, and smims, you'd be distracted, too.

Neff, the piece went on, had been something of an anomaly on the *Post,* which sticks up for the more conservative view of life—I guess they don't come right out and recommend electrocuting welfare recipients after three years and still no job, but they *do* hint that it's always an option. I guess Neff was the house liberal. He wrote a column called "Eneff Is Eneff," and in it he talked about changing the way New York treated single teen mothers, suggested that maybe abortion wasn't always murder, argued that the low-income housing in the outer boroughs was a self-perpetuating hate machine. Near the end of his life, he'd been writing columns about the size of the military, and asking why we as a country felt we had to keep pouring on the bucks when there was, essentially, no one left to fight except for the terrorists. He said we'd do better to spend that money creating jobs. And *Post* readers, who would have crucified anyone else saying stuff like that, pretty much loved it when Neff laid it down. Because he was funny. Because he was charming. Maybe because he was Irish and had kissed the Blarney Stone.

That was about all. I started home. Somewhere along the way I took a detour, though, and ended up walking all over downtown. I zigged and zagged, walking down boulevards and cutting through parking lots, all the time thinking about Andrew Neff climbing into his bathtub and putting a Baggie over his head. A big one, a gallon-size, keeps all your leftovers supermarket-fresh.

He was funny. He was charming. And I had killed him. Neff had opened my letter and it had gotten into his head, somehow. Judging by what I'd read in the paper, the special words and symbols took maybe three days to fuck him up enough to swallow the pills and climb into the tub.

He deserved it.

That's what Mr. Sharpton said about Skipper, and maybe he was right . . . that time. But did Neff deserve it? Was there shit about him I didn't know, did he maybe like little girls in the wrong way or push dope or go after people too weak to fight back, like Skipper had gone after me with the shopping cart?

We want to help you use your talent for the betterment of all mankind, Mr. Sharpton said, and surely that didn't mean making a guy off himself because he thought the Defense Department was spending too much money on smart-bombs. Paranoid shit like that is strictly for movies starring Steven Seagal and Jean-Claude Van Damme.

Then I had a bad idea—a scary idea.

Maybe TransCorp didn't want him dead because he wrote that stuff.

Maybe they wanted him dead because people—the wrong people—were starting to *think* about what he wrote.

"That's crazy," I said, right out loud, and a woman looking into the window of Columbia City-Oh So Pretty turned around and gave me the old fish-eye.

I ended up at the public library around two o'clock,

with my legs aching and my head throbbing. I kept seeing that guy in the bathtub, with his wrinkled old man's tits and white chest-hair, his nice smile gone, replaced by this vague Planet X look. I kept seeing him putting a Baggie over his head, humming a Sinatra tune ("My Way," maybe) as he snugged it down tight, then peered through it the way you'd peer through a cloudy window, so he could see to slit the veins in his wrists. I didn't want to see that stuff, but I couldn't stop. My bombsight had turned into a telescope.

They had a computer room in the library, and you could get on the Internet at a very reasonable cost. I had to get a library card, too, but that was okay. A library card is good to have, you can never have too much ID.

It took me only three bucks' worth of time to find Ann Tevitch and call up the report of her death. The story started, I saw with a sinking sensation, in the bottom righthand corner of page one, The Official Dead Folks' Nook, and then jumped to the obituary page. Professor Tevitch had been a pretty lady, blond, thirty-seven. In the photo she was holding her glasses in her hand, as if she wanted people to know she wore them . . . but as if she'd wanted people to see what pretty eyes she had, too. That made me feel sad and guilty.

Her death was startlingly like Skipper's—coming home from her office at UNM just after dark, maybe hurrying a little because it was her turn to make supper, but what the hell, good driving conditions and great visibility. Her car—vanity license plate DNA FAN, I happened to know—had veered off the road, overturned, and landed in a drywash. She was still alive when someone spotted the headlights and found her, but there had never been any real hope; her injuries were too grave.

There was no alcohol in her system and her marriage was in good shape (no kids, at least, thank God for small favors), so the idea of suicide was farfetched. She had been looking forward to the future, had even talked about getting a computer to celebrate a new research grant. She'd refused to own a PC since 1988 or so; had lost some valuable data in one when it locked up, and had distrusted them ever since. She would use her department's equipment when she absolutely had to, but that was all.

The coroner's verdict had been accidental death.

Professor Ann Tevitch, a clinical biologist, had been in the forefront of West Coast AIDS research. Another scientist, this one in California, said that her death might set back the search for a cure five years. "She was a key player," he said. "Smart, yes, but more—I once heard someone refer to her as 'a natural-born facilitator,' and that's as good a description as any. Ann was the kind of person who holds other people together. Her death is a great loss to the dozens of people who knew and loved her, but it's an even greater loss to this cause."

Billy Unger was also easy enough to find. His picture topped page one of the Stovington *Weekly Courant* instead of getting stuck down there in The Dead Folks' Nook, but that might have been because there weren't many famous people in Stovington. Unger had been General William "Roll Em" Unger, winner of the Silver Star and Bronze Star in Korea. During the Kennedy administration he was an Undersecretary of Defense

(Acquisition Reform), and one of the really big warhawks of that time. Kill the Russkies, drink their blood, keep America safe for the Macy's Thanksgiving Day Parade, that sort of thing.

Then, around the time Lyndon Johnson was escalating the war in Vietnam, Billy Unger had a change of mind and heart. He began writing letters to newspapers. He started his op-ed page career by saying that we were handling the war wrong. He progressed to the idea that we were wrong to be in Vietnam at all. Then, around 1975 or so, he got to the point of saying *all* wars were wrong. That was okay with most Vermonters.

He served seven terms in the state legislature, starting in 1978. When a group of Progressive Democrats asked him to run for the U.S. Senate in 1996, he said he wanted to "do some reading and consider his options." The implication was that he would be ready for a national career in politics by 2000, 2002 at the latest. He was getting old, but Vermonters like old guys, I guess. 1996 went past without Unger declaring himself a candidate for anything (possibly because his wife died of cancer), and before 2002 came around, he bought himself a big old dirt sandwich and ate every bite.

There was a small but loyal contingent in Stovington which claimed Roll Em's death was an accident, that Silver Star winners don't jump off their roofs even if they *have* lost a wife to cancer in the last year or so, but the rest pointed out that the guy probably hadn't been repairing the shingles—not in his nightshirt, not at two o'clock in the morning.

Suicide was the verdict.

Yeah. Right. Kiss my ass and go to Heaven.

XVIII

I left the library and thought I'd head home. Instead, I went back to the same park bench again. I sat there until the sun was low and the place had pretty much emptied out of kids and Frisbee-catching dogs. And although I'd been in Columbia City for three months by then, it was the latest I'd ever been out. That's sad, I guess. I thought I was living a life here, finally getting away from Ma and living a life, but all I've been doing is throwing a shadow.

If people, certain people, were checking up on me, they might wonder why the change in routine. So I got up, went on home, boiled up a bag of that shit-on-a-shingle stuff, and turned on my TV. I've got cable, the full package including premium movie channels, and I've never seen a single bill. How's that for an eventual deal? I turned on Cinemax. Rutger Hauer was playing a blind karate-fighter. I sat down on the couch beneath my fake Rembrandt and watched the show. I didn't see it, but I ate my chow and looked at it.

I thought about stuff. About a newspaper columnist who had liberal ideas and a conservative readership. About an AIDS researcher who served an important linking function with other AIDS researchers. About an old general who changed his mind. I thought about the fact that I only knew these three by name because they didn't have modems and e-mail capability.

There was other stuff to think about, too. Like how you could hypnotize a talented guy, or drug him, or maybe even expose him to other talented guys in order to keep him from asking any of the wrong questions or doing any of the wrong things. Like how you could make sure such a talented guy couldn't run away even if he happened to wake up to the truth. You'd do that by setting him up in what was, essentially, a cashless existence . . . a life where rule number one was no ratholing any extra dough, not even pocket-change. What sort of talented guy would fall for something like that? A naive one, with few friends and next to no self-image. A guy who would sell you his talented soul for a few groceries and seventy bucks a week, because he believes that's about what it's worth.

I didn't want to think about any of that. I tried to concentrate on Rutger Hauer, doing all that amusing blind karate shit (Pug would have laughed his ass off if he'd been there, believe me), so I wouldn't *have* to think about any of that.

Two hundred, for instance. There was a number I didn't want to think about. 200. 10 x 20, 40 x 5. CC, to the old Romans. At least two hundred times I'd pushed the button that brought the message DINKY-MAIL SENT up on my screen.

It occurred to me—for the first time, as if I was finally waking up—that I was a murderer. A *mass* murderer.

Yes indeed. That's what it comes down to.

Good of mankind? Bad of mankind? Indifferent of mankind? Who makes those judgements? Mr. Sharpton? His bosses? *Their* bosses? And does it matter?

I decided it didn't matter a fuck in a rabbit-hutch. I further decided I really couldn't spend too much time moaning (even to myself) how I had been drugged, hypnotized, or exposed to some kind of mind-control. The truth was, I'd been doing what I was doing because I loved the feeling I got when I was composing the special letters, the feeling that there was a river of fire running through the center of my head.

Mostly, I'd been doing it because I could.

"That's not true," I said . . . but not real loud. I whispered it under my breath. They probably don't have any bugs planted here, I'm sure they don't, but it's best to be safe.

I started writing this . . . what is it? A report, maybe. I started writing this report later that night . . . as soon as the Rutger Hauer movie was over, in fact. I write in a notebook, though, not on my computer, and I write in plain old English. No sankofites, no bews, no smims. There's a loose floor-tile under the Ping-Pong table down in the basement. That's where I keep my report. I just now looked back at how I started. *I've got a good job now*, I wrote, *and no reason to feel glum.* Idiotic. But of course, any fool who can pucker is apt to whistle past the graveyard.

When I went to bed that night, I dreamed I was in the parking lot of the Supr Savr. Pug was there, wearing his red duster and a hat on his head like the one Mickey Mouse wore in *Fantasia*—that's the movie where Mickey played the Sorcerer's Apprentice. Halfway across the parking lot, shopping carts were lined up in a row. Pug would raise his hand, then lower it. Each time he did this, a cart would start rolling by itself, gathering speed, rushing across the lot until it crashed into the brick side of the supermarket. They were piling up there, a glittering junkheap of metal and wheels. For once in his life, Pug wasn't smiling. I wanted to ask him what he was doing and what it meant, but of course I knew.

"He's been good to me," I told Pug in this dream. It was Mr. Sharpton I meant, of course. "He's been really, really eventual."

Pug turned fully to me then, and I saw it wasn't Pug at all. It was Skipper, and his head had been smashed in all the way down to the eyebrows. Shattered hunks of skull stuck up in a circle, making him look like he was wearing a bone crown.

"You're not looking through a bombsight," Skipper said, and grinned. "You *are* the bombsight. How do you like that, Dinkster?"

I woke up in the dark of my room, sweating, with my hands over my mouth to hold in a scream, so I guess I didn't like it very much.

XIX

Writing this has been a sad education, let me tell you. It's like hey, Dink, welcome to the real world. Mostly it's the image of grinding up dollar bills in the kitchen pig that comes to me when I think about what has happened to me, but I know that's only because it's easier to think of grinding up money (or chucking it into the storm-drain) than it is to think about grinding up people. Sometimes I hate myself, sometimes I'm scared for my immortal soul (if I have one), and sometimes I'm just embarrassed. Trust me, Mr. Sharpton said, and I did. I mean, duh, how dumb can you get? I tell myself I'm just a kid, the same age as the kids who crewed those B-25s I some-times think about, that kids are allowed to be dumb.

But I wonder if that's true when lives are at stake.

And, of course, I'm still doing it.

Yes.

I thought at first that I wouldn't be able to, no more than the kids in *Mary Poppins* could keep floating around the house when they lost their happy thoughts . . . but I could. And once I sat down in front of the computer screen and that river of fire started to flow, I was lost. You see (at least I *think* you do), this is what I was put on Planet Earth for. Can I be blamed for doing the thing that finishes me off, that completes me?

Answer: yes. Absolutely.

But I can't stop. Sometimes I tell myself that I've gone on because if I do stop—maybe even for a day— they'll know I've caught on, and the cleaners will make an unscheduled stop. Except what they'll clean up this time will be *me*. But that's not why. I do it because I'm just another addict, same as a guy smoking crack in an alley or some chick taking a spike in her arm. I do it because of the hateful fucking rush, I do it because when I'm working in DINKY'S NOTEBOOK, everything's eventual. It's like being caught in a candy trap. And it's all the fault of that dork who came out of News Plus with his fucking *Dispatch* open. If not for him, I'd still see nothing but cloud-hazy buildings in the crosshairs. No people, just targets.

You are *the bombsight,* Skipper said in my dream. *You* are *the bombsight, Dinkster.*

That's true. I know it is. Horrible but true. I'm just another tool, just the lens the *real* bombardier looks through. Just the button he pushes.

What bombardier, you ask?

Oh come on, get real.

I thought of calling him, how's that for crazy? Or maybe it's not. "Call me anytime, Dink, even three in the morning." That's what the man said, and I'm pretty sure that's what the man meant—about that, at least, Mr. Sharpton wasn't lying.

I thought of calling him and saying, "You want to know what hurts the most, Mr. Sharpton? That thing you said about how I could make the world a better place by getting rid of people like Skipper. The truth is, *you're* the guys like Skipper."

Sure. And I'm the shopping cart they chase people with, laughing and barking and making race-car sounds. I work cheap, too . . . at bargain-basement rates. So far I've killed over two hundred people, and what did it cost TransCorp? A little house in a third-rate Ohio town, seventy bucks a week, and a Honda automobile. Plus cable TV. Don't want to forget that.

I stood there for awhile, looking at the telephone, then put it down again. Couldn't say any of that. It would be the same as putting a Baggie over my head and then slitting my wrists.

So what am I going to do?

Oh God, what am I going to do?

XX

It's been two weeks since I last took this notebook out from under the basement tile and wrote in it. Twice I've heard the mail-slot clack on Thursdays, during *As the World Turns,* and gone out into the hall to get my money. I've gone to four movies, all in the afternoon. Twice I've ground up money in the kitchen pig, and thrown my loose change down the storm-drain, hiding what I was doing behind the blue plastic recycling basket when I put it down on the curb. One day I went down to News Plus, thinking I'd get a copy of *Variations* or *Forum,* but there was a headline on the front of the *Dispatch* that once again took away any sexy feelings I might have had. POPE DIES OF HEART ATTACK ON PEACE MISSION, it said.

Did I do it? Nah, the story said he died in Asia, and I've been sticking to the American Northwest these last few weeks. But I could have been the one. If I'd been nosing around in Pakistan last week, I very likely *would* have been the one.

Two weeks of living in a nightmare.

Then, this morning, there was something in the mail. Not a letter, I've only gotten three or four of those (all from Pug, and now he's stopped writing, and I miss him so much), but a Kmart advertising circular. It flopped open just as I was putting it into the trash, and something fluttered out. A note, printed in block letters. DO YOU WANT OUT? it read. IF YES, SEND MESSAGE *"DON'T STAND SO CLOSE TO ME"* IS BEST POLICE SONG.

My heart was beating hard and fast, the way it did on the day I came into my house and saw the Rembrandt print over the sofa where the velvet clowns had been.

Below the message, someone had drawn a fouder. It was harmless just sitting there all by itself, but looking at it still made all the spit in my mouth dry up. It was a real message, the fouder proved it, but who had it again that night. 'Ye know not the day or the hour,' the Bible says. I believe that particular verse is about dying, but it fits everything else, boys. Everything else in this world. You just never know when you're going to bust a fiddle-string.

"When I turn into the driveway I see the garage door's open and the little Subaru she brought to the marriage is gone, but that doesn't strike me as immediately peculiar. She was always driving off someplace—to a yard sale or someplace—and leaving the goddam garage door open. I'd tell her, 'Lulu, if you keep doing that long enough, someone'll eventually take advantage of it. Come in and take a rake or a bag of peat moss or maybe even the power mower. Hell, even a Seventh-Day Adventist fresh out of college and doing his merit badge rounds will steal if you put enough temptation in his way, and that's the worst kind of person to tempt, because they feel it more than the rest of us.' Anyway, she'd always say, 'I'll do better, L.T., try, anyway, I really will, honey.' And she *did* do better, just backslid from time to time like any ordinary sinner.

"I park off to the side so she'll be able to get her car in when she comes back from wherever, but I close the garage door. Then I go in by way of the kitchen. I check the mailbox, but it's empty, the mail inside on the counter, so she must have left after eleven, because he don't come until at least then. The mailman, I mean.

"Well, Lucy's right there by the door, crying in that way Siamese have—I like that cry, think it's sort of cute, but Lulu always hated it, maybe because it sounds like a baby's cry and she didn't want anything to do with babies. 'What would I want with a rug-monkey?' she'd say.

"Lucy being at the door wasn't anything out of the ordinary, either. That cat loved my ass. Still does. She's two years old now. We got her at the start of the last year we were married. Right around. Seems impossible to believe Lulu's been gone a year, and we were only together three to start with. But Lulubelle was the type to make an impression on you. Lulubelle had what I have to call star quality. You know who she always reminded me of? Lucille Ball. Now that I think of it, I guess that's why I named the cat Lucy, although I don't remember thinking it at the time. It might have been what you'd call a subconscious association. She'd come into a room—Lulubelle, I mean, not the cat—and just light it up somehow. A person like that, when they're gone you can hardly believe it, and you keep expecting them to come back.

"Meanwhile, there's the cat. Her name was Lucy to start with, but Lulubelle hated the way she acted so much that she started calling her Screwlucy, and it kind of stuck. Lucy wasn't nuts, though, she only wanted to be loved. Wanted to be loved more than any other pet I ever had in my life, and I've had quite a few.

"Anyway, I come in the house and pick up the cat and pet her a little and she climbs up onto my shoulder and sits there, purring and talking her Siamese talk. I check the mail on the counter, put the bills in the basket, then go over to the fridge to get Lucy something to eat. I always keep a working can of cat food in there, with a piece of tinfoil over the top. Saves having Lucy get excited and digging her claws into my shoulder when she hears the can opener. Cats are smart, you know. Much smarter than dogs. They're different in other ways, too. It might be that the biggest division in the world isn't men and women but folks who like cats and folks who like dogs. Did any of you pork-packers ever think of that?

"Lulu bitched like hell about having an open can of cat food in the fridge, even one with a piece of foil over the top, said it made everything in there taste like old tuna, but I wouldn't give in on that one. On most stuff I did it her way, but that cat food business was one of the few places where I really stood up for my rights. It didn't have anything to do with the cat food, anyway. It had to do with the *cat*. She just didn't like Lucy, that was all. Lucy was her cat, but she didn't like it.

"Anyway, I go over to the fridge, and I see there's a note on it, stuck there with one of the vegetable magnets. It's from Lulubelle. Best as I can remember, it goes like this:

"'Dear L.T.—I am leaving you, honey. Unless you come home early, I will be long gone by the time you get this note. I don't think you will get home early, you have never got home early in all the time we have been married, but at least I know you'll get this almost as soon as you get in the door, because the first thing you always do when you get home isn't to come see me and say "Hi sweet girl I'm home" and give me a kiss but go to the fridge and get whatever's left of the last nasty can of Calo you put in there and feed Screwlucy. So at least I know you won't just go upstairs and get shocked when you see my Elvis Last Supper picture is gone and my half of the closet is mostly empty and think we had a burglar who likes ladies' dresses (unlike some who only care about what is under them).

"'I get irritated with you sometimes, honey, but I still think you're sweet and kind and nice, you will always be my little maple duff and sugar dumpling, no matter where our paths may lead. It's just that I have decided I was never cut out to be a Spam-packer's wife. I don't mean that in any conceited way, either. I even called the Psychic Hotline last week as I struggled with this decision, lying awake night after night (and listening to you snore, boy, I don't mean to hurt your feelings but have you ever got a snore on *you*), and I was given this message: "A broken spoon may become a fork." I didn't understand that at first, but I didn't give up on it. I am not smart like some people (or like some people *think* they are smart), but I *work* at things. The best mill grinds slow but exceedingly fine, my mother used to say, and I ground away at this like a pepper mill in a Chinese restaurant, thinking late at night while you snored and no doubt dreamed of how many pork-snouts you could get in a can of Spam. And it came to me that saying about how a broken spoon can become a fork is a beautiful thing to behold. Because a fork has tines. And those tines may have to separate, like you and me must now have to separate, but still they have the same handle. So do we. We are both human beings, L.T., capable of loving and respecting one another. Look at all the fights we had about Frank and Screwlucy and still we mostly managed to get along. Yet the time has now come for me to seek my fortune along different lines from yours, and to poke into the great roast of life with a different point from yours. Besides, I miss my mother.' "

(I can't say for sure if all this stuff was really in the note L.T. found on his fridge; it doesn't seem entirely likely, I must admit, but the men listening to his story would be rolling in the aisles by this point—or around on the loading dock, at least—and it did *sound* like Lulubelle, that I can testify to.)

" 'Please do not try to follow me, L.T., and although I'll be at my mother's and I know you have that number, I would appreciate you not calling but waiting for me to call you. In time I will, but in the meanwhile I have a lot of thinking to do, and although I have gotten on a fair way with it, I'm not "out of the fog" yet. I suppose I will be asking you for a divorce eventually, and think it is only fair to tell you so. I have never been one to hold out false hope, believing it better to "tell the truth and smoke out the Devil." Please remember that what I do I do in love, not in hatred and resentment. And please remember what was told to me and what I now tell to you: a broken spoon may be a fork in disguise. All my love, Lulubelle Simms.' "

L.T. would pause there, letting them digest the fact that she had gone back to her maiden name, and giving his eyes a few of those patented L. T. DeWitt rolls. Then he'd tell them the P.S. she'd tacked on the note.

" 'I have taken Frank with me and left Screwlucy for you. I thought this would probably be the way you'd want it. Love, Lulu.' "

If the DeWitt family was a fork, Screwlucy and Frank were the other two tines on it. If there wasn't a fork (and speaking for myself, I've always felt marriage was more like a knife—the dangerous kind with two sharp edges), Screwlucy and Frank could still be said to sum up everything that went wrong in the marriage of L.T. and Lulubelle. Because, think of it—although Lulubelle bought Frank for L.T. (first wedding anniversary) and L.T. bought Lucy, soon to be Screwlucy, for Lulubelle (second wedding anniversary), they each wound up with the other one's pets when Lulu walked out on the marriage.

"She got me that dog because I liked the one on *Frasier*," L.T. would say. "That kind of dog's a terrier, but I don't remember now what they call that kind. A Jack something. Jack Sprat? Jack Robinson? Jack Shit? You know how a thing like that gets on the tip of your tongue?"

Somebody would tell him that the dog on *Frasier* was a Jack Russell terrier and L.T. would nod emphatically.

"That's right!" he'd exclaim. "Sure! Exactly! That's what Frank was, all right, a Jack Russell terrier. But you want to know the cold hard truth? An hour from now, that will have slipped away from me again—it'll be there in my brain, but like something behind a rock. An hour from now, I'll be going to myself, '*What* did that guy say Frank was? A Jack Handle terrier? A Jack Rabbit terrier? That's close, I know that's close . . .' And so on. Why? I think because I just hated that little fuck so much. That barking rat. That fur-covered shit machine. I hated it from the first time I laid eyes on it. There. It's out and I'm glad. And do you know what? Frank felt the same about me. It was hate at first sight.

"You know how some men train their dog to bring them their slippers? Frank wouldn't bring me my slippers, but he'd *puke* in them. Yes. The first time he did it, I stuck my right foot right into it. It was like sticking your foot into warm tapioca with extra-big lumps in it. Although I didn't see him, my theory is that he waited outside the bedroom door until he saw me coming—fucking *lurked* outside the bedroom door—then went in, unloaded in my right slipper, then hid under the bed to watch the fun. I deduce that on the basis of how it was still warm. Fucking dog. Man's best friend my ass. I wanted to take it to the pound after that, had the leash out and everything, but Lulu threw an absolute shit fit. You would have thought she'd come into the kitchen and caught me trying to give the dog a drain-cleaner enema.

"'If you take Frank to the pound, you might as well take me to the pound,' she says, starting to cry. 'That's all you think of him, and that's all you think of me. Honey, all we are to you is nuisances you'd like to be rid of. That's the cold hard truth.' I mean, oh my bleeding piles, on and on.

"'He puked in my slipper,' I says.

"'The dog puked in his slipper so off with his head,' she says. 'Oh sugarpie, if only you could *hear* yourself!'

"'Hey,' I say, 'you try sticking *your* bare foot into a slipper filled with dog-puke and see how *you* like it.' Getting mad by then, you know.

"Except getting mad at Lulu never did any good. Most times, if you had the king, she had the ace. If you had the ace, she had a trump. Also, the woman would fucking *escalate.* If something happened and I got irritated, she'd get pissed. If I got pissed, she'd get mad. If I got mad, she'd go fucking Red Alert Defcon I and empty the missile silos. I'm talking scorched fucking earth. Mostly it wasn't worth it. Except almost every time we'd get into a fight, I'd forget that.

"She goes, 'Oh dear. Maple duff stuck his wittle footie in a wittle spit-up.' I tried to get in there, tell her that wasn't right, spit-up is like drool, spit-up doesn't have these big fucking *chunks* in it, but she won't let me get a word out. By then she's over in the passing lane and cruising, all pumped up and ready to teach school.

"'Let me tell you something, honey,' she goes, 'a little drool in your slipper is very minor stuff. You men slay me. Try being a woman sometimes, okay? Try always being the one that ends up laying with the small of your back in that come-spot, or the one that goes to the toilet in the middle of the night and the guy's left the goddam ring up and you splash your can right down into this cold water. Little midnight skindiving. The toilet probably hasn't been flushed, either, men think the Urine Fairy comes by around two A.M. and takes care of that, and there you are, sitting crack-deep in piss, and all at once you realize your *feet're* in it, too, you're paddling around in Lemon Squirt because, although guys think they're dead-eye Dick with that thing, most can't shoot for shit; drunk or sober they gotta wash the goddam floor all around the toilet before they can even start the main event. All my life I've been living with this, honey—a father, four brothers, one ex-husband, plus a few roommates that are none of your business at this late date—and you're ready to send poor Frank off to the gas factory because just one time he happened to reflux a little drool into your slipper.'

" 'My *fur-lined* slipper,' I tell her, but it's just a little shot back over my shoulder. One thing about living with Lulu, and maybe to my credit, I always knew when I was beat. When I lost, it was fucking decisive. One thing I certainly wasn't going to tell her even though I knew it for a fact was that the dog puked in my slipper on purpose, the same way that he peed on my underwear on purpose if I forgot to put it in the hamper before I went off to work. She could leave her bras and pants scattered around from hell to Harvard—and did—but if I left so much as a pair of athletic socks in the corner, I'd come home and find that fucking Jack Shit terrier had given it a lemonade shower. But tell her that? She would have been booking me time with a psychiatrist. She would have been doing that *even though she knew it was true.* Because then she might have had to take the stuff I was saying seriously, and she didn't want to. She loved Frank, you see, and Frank loved her. They were like Romeo and Juliet or Rocky and Adrian.

"Frank would come to her chair while we were watching TV, lie down on the floor beside her, and put his muzzle on her shoe. Just lie there like that all night, looking up at her, all soulful and loving, and with his butt pointed in my direction so if he should have to blow a little gas, I'd get the full benefit of it. He loved her and she loved him. Why? Christ knows. Love's a mystery to everyone except the poets, I guess, and nobody sane can understand a thing they write about it. I don't think most of them can understand it themselves on the rare occasions when they wake up and smell the coffee.

"But Lulubelle never gave me that dog so she could have it, let's get that one thing straight. I know that some people do stuff like that—a guy'll give his wife a trip to Miami because he wants to go there, or a wife'll give her husband a NordicTrack because she thinks he ought to do something about his gut—but this wasn't that kind of deal. We were crazy in love with each other at the beginning; I know I was with her, and I'd stake my life she was with me. No, she bought that dog for me because I always laughed so hard at the one on *Frasier.* She wanted to make me happy, that's all. She didn't know Frank was going to take a shine to her, or her to him, no more than she knew the dog was going to dislike me so much that throwing up in one of my slippers or chewing the bottoms of the curtains on my side of the bed would be the high point of his day."

L.T. would look around at the grinning men, not grinning himself, but he'd give his eyes that knowing, long-suffering roll, and they'd laugh again, in anticipation. Me too, likely as not, in spite of what I knew about the Axe Man.

"I haven't ever been hated before," he'd say, "not by man or beast, and it unsettled me a lot. It unsettled me *bigtime.* I tried to make friends with Frank—first for my sake, then for the sake of her that gave him to me—but it didn't work. For all I know, he might've tried to make friends with me . . . with a dog, who can tell? If he did, it didn't work for him, either. Since then I've read—in "Dear Abby," I think it was—that a pet is just about the worst present you can give a person, and I agree. I mean, even if you like the animal and the animal likes you, think about what that kind of gift says. 'Say, darling, I'm giving you this wonderful present, it's a machine that eats at one end and shits out the other, it's going to run for fifteen years, give or take, merry fucking Christmas.' But that's the kind of thing you only think about *after,* more often than not. You know what I mean?

"I think we did try to do our best, Frank and I. After all, even though we hated each other's guts, we both loved Lulubelle. That's why, I think, that although he'd sometimes growl at me if I sat down next to her on the couch during *Murphy Brown* or a movie or something, he never actually bit. Still, it used to drive me crazy. Just the fucking *nerve* of it, that little bag of hair and eyes daring to growl at me.

" 'Listen to him,' I'd say, 'he's growling at me.'

"She'd stroke his head the way she hardly ever stroked mine, unless she'd had a few, and say it was really just a dog's version of purring. That he was just happy to be with us, having a quiet evening at home. I'll tell you something, though, I never tried patting him when she wasn't around. I'd feed him sometimes, and I never gave him a kick (although I was tempted a few times, I'd be a liar if I said different), but I never tried patting him. I think he would have snapped at me, and then we would have gotten into it. Like two guys living with the same pretty girl, almost. *Ménage à trois* is what they call it in the *Penthouse* 'Forum.' Both of us love her and she loves both of us, but as time goes by, I start realizing that the scales are tipping and she's starting to love Frank a little more than me. Maybe because Frank never talks back and never pukes in *her* slippers, and with Frank the goddam toilet ring is never an issue, because he goes outside. Unless, that is, I forget and leave a pair of my shorts in the corner or under the bed."

At this point L.T. would likely finish off the iced coffee in his Thermos, crack his knuckles, or both. It was his way of saying the first act was over and Act Two was about to commence.

"So then one day, a Saturday, Lulu and I are out to the mall. Just walking around, like people do. You know. And we go by Pet Notions, up by J.C. Penney, and there's a whole crowd of people in front of the display window. 'Oh, let's see,' Lulu says, so we go over and work our way to the front.

"It's a fake tree with bare branches and fake grass— AstroTurf—all around it. And there are these Siamese kittens, half a dozen of them chasing each other around, climbing the tree, batting each other's ears.

"'Oh ain' day jus' da key-youtest *ones!*' Lulu says. 'Oh ain't dey jus' the key-youtest wittle *babies!* Look, honey, look!'

"'I'm lookin,' I says, and what I'm thinking is that I just found what I wanted to get Lulu for our anniversary. And that was a relief. I wanted it to be something extra-special, something that would really bowl her over, because things had been quite a bit short of great between us during the last year. I thought about Frank, but I wasn't too worried about him; cats and dogs always fight in the cartoons, but in real life they usually get along, that's been my experience. They usually get along better than people do. Especially when it's cold outside.

"To make a long story just a little bit shorter, I bought one of them and gave it to her on our anniversary. Got it a velvet collar, and tucked a little card under it. 'HELLO, I am LUCY!' the card said. 'I come with love from L.T.! Happy second anniversary!'

"You probably know what I'm going to tell you now, don't you? Sure. It was just like goddam Frank the terrier all over again, only in reverse. At first I was as happy as a pig in shit with Frank, and Lulubelle was as happy as a pig in shit with Lucy at first. Held her up over her head, talking that baby-talk to her, 'Oh yookit *you,* oh yookit my wittle pwecious, she so *key-yout,*' and so on and so on . . . until Lucy let out a yowl and batted at the end of Lulubelle's nose. With her claws out, too. Then she ran away and hid under the kitchen table. Lulu laughed it off, like it was the funniest thing she'd ever had happen to her, and as key-yout as anything else a little kitten might do, but I could see she was miffed.

"Right then Frank came in. He'd been sleeping up in our room—at the foot of her side of the bed—but Lulu'd let out a little shriek when the kitten batted her nose, so he came down to see what the fuss was about.

"He spotted Lucy under the table right away and walked toward her, sniffing the linoleum where she'd been.

" 'Stop them, honey, stop them, L.T., they're going to get into it,' Lulubelle says. 'Frank'll kill her.'

" 'Just let them alone a minute,' I says. 'See what happens.'

"Lucy humped up her back the way cats do, but stood her ground and watched him come. Lulu started forward, wanting to get in between them in spite of what I'd said (listening up wasn't exactly one of Lulu's strong points), but I took her wrist and held her back. It's best to let them work it out between them, if you can. Always best. It's quicker.

"Well, Frank got to the edge of the table, poked his nose under, and started this low rumbling way back in his throat. 'Let me go, L.T. I got to get her,' Lulubelle says, 'Frank's growling at her.'

" 'No, he's not,' I say, 'he's just purring. I recognize it from all the times he's purred at me.'

"She gave me a look that would just about have boiled water, but didn't say anything. The only times in the three years we were married that I got the last word, it was always about Frank and Screwlucy. Strange but true. Any other subject, Lulu could talk rings around me. But when it came to the pets, it seemed she was always fresh out of comebacks. Used to drive her crazy.

"Frank poked his head under the table a little farther, and Lucy batted at his nose the way she'd batted at Lulubelle's—only when she batted at Frank, she did it without popping her claws. I had an idea Frank would go for her, but he didn't. He just kind of whoofed and turned away. Not scared, more like he's thinking, 'Oh, okay, so that's what *that's* about.' Went back into the living room and laid down in front of the TV.

"And that was all the confrontation there ever was between them. They divvied up the territory pretty much the way that Lulu and I divvied it up that last year we spent together, when things were getting bad; the bedroom belonged to Frank and Lulu, the kitchen belonged to me and Lucy—only by Christmas, Lulubelle was calling her Screwlucy—and the living room was neutral territory. The four of us spent a lot of evenings there that last year, Screwlucy on my lap, Frank with his muzzle on Lulu's shoe, us humans on the couch, Lulubelle reading a book and me watching *Wheel of Fortune* or *Lifestyles of the Rich and Famous,* which Lulubelle always called *Lifestyles of the Rich and Topless.*

"The cat wouldn't have a thing to do with her, not from day one. Frank, every now and then you could get the idea Frank was at least *trying* to get along with me. His nature would always get the better of him in the end and he'd chew up one of my sneakers or take another leak on my underwear, but every now and then it did seem like he was putting forth an effort. Lap my hand, maybe give me a grin. Usually if I had a plate of something he wanted a bite of, though.

"Cats are different, though. A cat won't curry favor even if it's in their best interests to do so. A cat can't be a hypocrite. If more preachers were like cats, this would be a religious country again. If a cat likes you, you know. If she doesn't, you know that, too. Screwlucy never liked Lulu, not one whit, and she made it clear from the start. If I was getting ready to feed her, Lucy'd rub around my legs, purring, while I spooned it up and dumped it in her dish. If Lulu fed her, Lucy'd sit all the way across the kitchen, in front of the fridge, watching her. And wouldn't go to the dish until Lulu had cleared off. It drove Lulu crazy. 'That cat thinks she's the Queen of Sheba,' she'd say. By then she'd given up the baby-talk. Given up picking Lucy up, too. If she did, she'd get her wrist scratched, more often than not.

"Now, I tried to pretend I liked Frank and Lulu tried to pretend she liked Lucy, but Lulu gave up pretending a lot sooner than I did. I guess maybe neither one of them, the cat or the woman, could stand being a hypocrite. I don't think Lucy was the only reason Lulu left—hell, I know it wasn't—but I'm sure Lucy helped Lulubelle make her final decision. Pets can live a long time, you know. So the present I got her for our second was really the straw that broke the camel's back. Tell *that* to "Dear Abby"!

"The cat's talking was maybe the worst, as far as Lulu was concerned. She couldn't stand it. One night Lulubelle says to me, 'If that cat doesn't stop yowling, L.T., I think I'm going to hit it with an encyclopedia.'

" 'That's not yowling,' I said, 'that's chatting.'

" 'Well,' Lulu says, 'I wish it would stop chatting.'

"And right about then, Lucy jumped up into my lap and she did shut up. She always did, except for a little low purring, way back in her throat. Purring that really *was* purring. I scratched her between her ears like she likes, and I happened to look up. Lulu turned her eyes back down on her book, but before she did, what I saw was real hate. Not for me. For Screwlucy. Throw an encyclopedia at it? She looked like she'd like to stick the cat between *two* encyclopedias and just kind of clap it to death.

"Sometimes Lulu would come into the kitchen and

catch the cat up on the table and swat it off. I asked her once if she'd ever seen me swat Frank off the bed that way—he'd get up on it, you know, always on her side, and leave these nasty tangles of white hair. When I said that, Lulu gave me a kind of grin. Her teeth were showing, anyway. 'If you ever tried, you'd find yourself a finger or three shy, most likely,' she says.

"Sometimes Lucy really *was* Screwlucy. Cats are moody, and sometimes they get manic; anyone who's ever had one will tell you that. Their eyes get big and kind of glarey, their tails bush out, they go racing around the house; sometimes they'll rear right up on their back legs and prance, boxing at the air, like they're fighting with something they can see but human beings can't. Lucy got into a mood like that one night when she was about a year old—couldn't have been more than three weeks before the day when I come home and found Lulubelle gone.

"Anyway, Lucy came racing in from the kitchen, did a kind of racing slide on the wood floor, jumped over Frank, and went skittering up the living room drapes, paw over paw. Left some pretty good holes in them, with threads hanging down. Then she just perched at the top of the rod, staring around the room with her blue eyes all big and wild and the tip of her tail snapping back and forth.

"Frank only jumped a little and then put his muzzle back on Lulubelle's shoe, but the cat scared the hell out of Lulubelle, who was deep in her book, and when she looked up at the cat, I could see that outright hate in her eyes again.

"'All right,' she said, 'that's enough. Everybody out

of the goddam pool. We're going to find a good home for that little blue-eyed bitch, and if we're not smart enough to find a home for a purebred Siamese, we're going to take her to the animal shelter. I've had enough.'

" 'What do you mean?' I ask her.

" 'Are you blind?' she asks. 'Look what she did to my *drapes!* They're full of holes!'

" 'You want to see drapes with holes in them,' I say, 'why don't you go upstairs and look at the ones on my side of the bed. The bottoms are all ragged. Because *he* chews them.'

" 'That's different,' she says, glaring at me. 'That's different and you know it.'

"Well, I wasn't going to let that lie. No way was I going to let that one lie. 'The only reason you think it's different is because you like the dog you gave me and you don't like the cat I gave you,' I says. 'But I'll tell you one thing, Mrs. DeWitt: you take the cat to the animal shelter for clawing the living room drapes on Tuesday, I guarantee you I'll take the dog to the animal shelter for chewing the bedroom drapes on Wednesday. You got that?'

"She looked at me and started to cry. She threw her book at me and called me a bastard. A *mean* bastard. I tried to grab hold of her, make her stay long enough for me to at least *try* to make up—if there was a way to make up without backing down, which I didn't mean to do that time—but she pulled her arm out of my hand and ran out of the room. Frank ran out after her. They went upstairs and the bedroom door slammed.

"I gave her half an hour or so to cool off; then I went upstairs myself. The bedroom door was still shut, and

L.T.'s Theory of Pets

I guess if I have a favorite in this collection of stories, "L.T." would be it. The origin of the story, so far as I can remember, was a "Dear Abby" column where Abby opined that a pet is just about the worst sort of present one can give anyone. It makes the assumption that the pet and the recipient will hit it off, for one thing; it assumes that feeding an animal twice a day and cleaning up its messes (both indoors and out) was the very thing you had been pining to do. So far as I can remember, she called the giving of pets "an exercise in arrogance." I think that's laying it on a bit thick. My wife gave me a dog for my fortieth birthday, and Marlowe—a Corgi who's now fourteen and has only one eye—has been an honored part of the family ever since. During five of those years we also had a rather crazed Siamese cat named Pearl. It was while watching Marlowe and Pearl interact—which they did with a kind of cautious respect—that I first started thinking about a story where the pets in a marriage would imprint not upon the nominal owner of each, but on the other. I had a marvelous time working on it, and whenever I'm called upon to read a story out loud, this is the one I choose, always assuming I have the required fifty minutes it takes. It makes people laugh, and I like that. What I like even more is the unexpected shift in tone, away from humor and toward sadness and horror, which occurs near the end. When it comes, the reader's defenses are down and the story's emotional payoff is a little higher. For me, that emotional payoff is what it's all about. I want to make you laugh or cry when you read a story . . . or do both at the same time. I want your heart, in other words. If you want to learn something, go to school.

My friend L.T. hardly ever talks about how his wife disappeared, or how she's probably dead, just another victim of the Axe Man, but he likes to tell the story of how she walked out on him. He does it with just the right roll of the eyes, as if to say, "She fooled me, boys—right, good, and proper!" He'll sometimes tell the story to a bunch of men sitting on one of the loading docks behind the plant and eating their lunches, him eating his lunch, too, the one he fixed for himself—no Lulubelle back at home to do it for him these days. They usually laugh when he tells the story, which always ends with L.T.'s Theory of Pets. Hell, *I* usually laugh. It's a funny story, even if you *do* know how it turned out. Not that any of us do, not completely.

"I punched out at four, just like usual," L.T. will say, "then went down to Deb's Den for a couple of beers, just like most days. Had a game of pinball, then went home. That was where things stopped being just like usual. When a person gets up in the morning, he doesn't have the slightest idea how much may have changed in his life by the time he lays his head down when I started to open it, I was pushing against Frank. I could move him, but it was slow work with him sliding across the floor, and also noisy work. He was growling. And I mean *growling,* my friends; that was no fucking *purr.* If I'd gone in there, I believe he would have tried his solemn best to bite my manhood off. I slept on the couch that night. First time.

"A month later, give or take, she was gone."

If L.T. had timed his story right (most times he did; practice makes perfect), the bell signalling back to work at the W. S. Hepperton Processed Meats Plant of Ames, Iowa, would ring just about then, sparing him any questions from the new men (the old hands knew . . . and knew better than to ask) about whether or not L.T. and Lulubelle had reconciled, or if he knew where she was today, or—the all-time sixty-four-thousand-dollar question—if she and Frank were still together. There's nothing like the back-to-work bell to close off life's more embarrassing questions.

"Well," L.T. would say, putting away his Thermos and then standing up and giving a stretch. "It has all led me to create what I call L. T. DeWitt's Theory of Pets."

They'd look at him expectantly, just as I had the first time I heard him use that grand phrase, but they would always end up feeling let down, just as I always had; a story that good deserved a better punchline, but L.T.'s never changed.

"If your dog and cat are getting along better than you and your wife," he'd say, "you better expect to come home some night and find a Dear John note on your refrigerator door."

* * *

He told that story a lot, as I've said, and one night when he came to my house for dinner, he told it for my wife and my wife's sister. My wife had invited Holly, who had been divorced almost two years, so the boys and the girls would balance up. I'm sure that's all it was, because Roslyn never liked L. T. DeWitt. Most people do, most people take to him like hands take to warm water, but Roslyn has never been most people. She didn't like the story of the note on the fridge and the pets, either—I could tell she didn't, although she chuckled in the right places. Holly . . . shit, I don't know. I've never been able to tell what that girl's thinking. Mostly just sits there with her hands in her lap, smiling like Mona Lisa. It was my fault that time, though, and I admit it. L.T. didn't want to tell it, but I kind of egged him on because it was so quiet around the dinner table, just the click of silverware and the clink of glasses, and I could almost feel my wife disliking L.T. It seemed to be coming off her in waves. And if L.T. had been able to feel that little Jack Russell terrier disliking him, he would probably be able to feel my wife doing the same. That's what I figured, anyhow.

So he told it, mostly to please me, I suppose, and he rolled his eyeballs in all the right places, as if saying, "Gosh, she fooled me right and proper, didn't she?" and my wife chuckled here and there—those chuckles sounded as phony to me as Monopoly money looks— and Holly smiled her little Mona Lisa smile with her eyes downcast. Otherwise the dinner went off all right, and when it was over L.T. told Roslyn that he thanked her for "a sportin-fine meal" (whatever that is) and she told him to come anytime, she and I liked to see his

face in the place. That was a lie on her part, but I doubt there was ever a dinner-party in the history of the world where a few lies weren't told. So it went off all right, at least until I was driving him home. L.T. started to talk about how it would be a year Lulubelle had been gone in just another week or so, their fourth anniversary, which is flowers if you're old-fashioned and electrical appliances if you're newfangled. Then he said as how Lulubelle's mother—at whose house Lulubelle had never shown up—was going to put up a marker with Lulubelle's name on it at the local cemetery. "Mrs. Simms says we have to consider her as one dead," L.T. said, and then he began to bawl. I was so shocked I nearly ran off the goddam road.

He cried so hard that when I was done being shocked I began to be afraid all that pent-up grief might kill him with a stroke or a burst blood-vessel or something. He rocked back and forth in the seat and slammed his open hands down on the dashboard. It was like there was a twister loose inside him. Finally I pulled over to the side of the road and began patting his shoulder. I could feel the heat of his skin right through his shirt, so hot it was baking.

"Come on, L.T.," I said. "That's enough."

"I just miss her," he said in a voice so thick with tears I could barely understand what he was saying. "Just so goddam *much*. I come home and there's no one but the cat, crying and crying, and pretty soon I'm crying, too, both of us crying while I fill up her dish with that goddam muck she eats."

He turned his flushed, streaming face full on me. Looking back into it was almost more than I could

take, but I *did* take it; felt I *had* to take it. Who had gotten him telling the story about Lucy and Frank and the note on the refrigerator that night, after all? It hadn't been Mike Wallace or Dan Rather, that was for sure. So I looked back at him. I didn't quite dare hug him, in case that twister should somehow jump from him to me, but I kept patting his arm.

"I think she's alive somewhere, that's what I think," he said. His voice was still thick and wavery, but there was a kind of pitiful weak defiance in it, as well. He wasn't telling me what he believed, but what he wished he could believe. I'm pretty sure of that.

"Well," I said, "you can believe that. No law against it, is there? And it isn't as if they found her *body,* or anything."

"I like to think of her out there in Nevada singing in some little casino hotel," he said. "Not in Vegas or Reno, she couldn't make it in one of the big towns, but in Winnemucca or Ely I'm pretty sure she could get by. Some place like that. She just saw a SINGER WANTED sign and gave up her idea of going home to her mother. Hell, the two of them never got on worth a shit anyway, that's what Lu used to say. And she *could* sing, you know. I don't know if you ever heard her, but she could. I don't guess she was great, but she was good. The first time I saw her, she was singing in the lounge of the Marriott Hotel. In Columbus, Ohio, that was. Or, another possibility . . ."

He hesitated, then went on in a lower voice.

"Prostitution is legal out there in Nevada, you know. Not in all the counties, but in most of them. She could be working one of them Green Lantern trailers

or the Mustang Ranch. Lots of women have got a streak of whore in them. Lu had one. I don't mean she stepped around on me, or *slept* around on me, so I can't say how I know, but I do. She . . . yes, she could be in one of those places."

He stopped, eyes distant, maybe imagining Lulubelle on a bed in the back room of a Nevada trailer whorehouse, Lulubelle wearing nothing but stockings, washing off some unknown cowboy's stiff cock while from the other room came the sound of Steve Earle and the Dukes singing "Six Days on the Road" or a TV playing *Hollywood Squares*. Lulubelle whoring but not dead, the car by the side of the road—the little Subaru she had brought to the marriage—meaning nothing. The way an animal's look, so seemingly attentive, usually means nothing.

"I can believe that if I want," he said, swiping at his swollen eyes with the insides of his wrists.

"Sure," I said, "you bet, L.T.," wondering what the grinning men who listened to his story while they ate their lunches would make of this L.T., this shaking man with his pale cheeks and red eyes and hot skin.

"Hell," he said, "I *do* believe that." He hesitated, then said it again: "I *do* believe that."

When I got back, Roslyn was in bed with a book in her hand and the covers pulled up to her breasts. Holly had gone home while I was driving L.T. back to his house. Roslyn was in a bad mood, and I found out why soon enough. The woman behind the Mona Lisa smile had been quite taken with my friend. Smitten by him, maybe. And my wife most definitely did not approve.

"How did he lose his license?" she asked, and before I could answer: "Drinking, wasn't it?"

"Drinking, yes. OUI." I sat down on my side of the bed and slipped off my shoes. "But that was nearly six months ago, and if he keeps his nose clean another two months, he gets it back. I think he will. He goes to AA, you know."

My wife grunted, clearly not impressed. I took off my shirt, sniffed the armpits, hung it back in the closet. I'd only worn it an hour or two, just for dinner.

"You know," my wife said, "I think it's a wonder the police didn't look a little more closely at *him* after his wife disappeared."

"They asked him some questions," I said, "but only to get as much information as they could. There was never any question of him doing it, Ros. They were never suspicious of him."

"Oh, you're so sure."

"As a matter of fact, I am. I know some stuff. Lulubelle called her mother from a hotel in eastern Colorado the day she left, and called her again from Salt Lake City the next day. She was fine then. Those were both weekdays, and L.T. was at the plant. He was at the plant the day they found her car parked off that ranch road near Caliente, as well. Unless he can magically transport himself from place to place in the blink of an eye, he didn't kill her. Besides, he wouldn't. He loved her."

She grunted. It's this hateful sound of skepticism she makes sometimes. After almost thirty years of marriage, that sound still makes me want to turn on her and yell at her to stop it, to shit or get off the pot, either say what she means or keep quiet. This time I thought about telling her how L.T. had cried; how it had been like there was a cyclone inside of him, tearing loose everything that wasn't nailed down. I thought about it, but I didn't. Women don't trust tears from men. They may say different, but down deep they don't trust tears from men.

"Maybe you ought to call the police yourself," I said. "Offer them a little of your expert help. Point out the stuff they missed, just like Angela Lansbury on *Murder, She Wrote*."

I swung my legs into bed. She turned off the light. We lay there in darkness. When she spoke again, her tone was gentler.

"I don't like him. That's all. I don't, and I never have."

"Yeah," I said. "I guess that's clear."

"And I didn't like the way he looked at Holly."

Which meant, as I found out eventually, that she hadn't liked the way Holly looked at *him*. When she wasn't looking down at her plate, that is.

"I'd prefer you didn't ask him back to dinner," she said.

I kept quiet. It was late. I was tired. It had been a hard day, a harder evening, and I was tired. The last thing I wanted was to have an argument with my wife when I was tired and she was worried. That's the sort of argument where one of you ends up spending the night on the couch. And the only way to stop an argument like that is to be quiet. In a marriage, words are like rain. And the land of a marriage is filled with dry washes and arroyos that can become raging rivers in almost the wink of an eye. The therapists believe in talk, but most of them are either divorced or queer. It's silence that is a marriage's best friend.

Silence.

After awhile, my best friend rolled over on her side, away from me and into the place where she goes when she finally gives up the day. I lay awake a little while longer, thinking of a dusty little car, perhaps once white, parked nose-down in the ditch beside a ranch road out in the Nevada desert not too far from Caliente. The driver's-side door standing open, the rearview mirror torn off its post and lying on the floor, the front seat sodden with blood and tracked over by the animals that had come in to investigate, perhaps to sample.

There was a man—they assumed he was a man, it almost always is—who had butchered five women out in that part of the world, five in three years, mostly during the time L.T. had been living with Lulubelle. Four of the women were transients. He would get them to stop, somehow, then pull them out of their cars, rape them, dismember them with an axe, leave them a rise or two away for the buzzards and crows and weasels. The fifth one was an elderly rancher's wife. The police call this killer the Axe Man. As I write this, the Axe Man has not been captured. Nor has he killed again; if Cynthia Lulubelle Simms DeWitt was the Axe Man's sixth victim, she was also his last, at least so far. There is still some question, however, as to whether or not she *was* his sixth victim. If not in most minds, that question exists in the part of L.T.'s mind which is still allowed to hope.

The blood on the seat wasn't human blood, you see; it didn't take the Nevada State Forensics Unit five hours to determine that. The ranch hand who found Lulubelle's Subaru saw a cloud of circling birds half a mile away, and when he reached them, he found not a dismembered woman but a dismembered dog. Little was left but bones and teeth; the predators and scavengers had had their day, and there's not much meat on a Jack Russell terrier to begin with. The Axe Man most definitely got Frank; Lulubelle's fate is probable, but far from certain.

Perhaps, I thought, she *is* alive. Singing "Tie a Yellow Ribbon" at The Jailhouse in Ely or "Take a Message to Michael" at The Rose of Santa Fe in Hawthorne. Backed up by a three-piece combo. Old men trying to look young in red vests and black string ties. Or maybe she's blowing GM cowboys in Austin or Wendover—bending forward until her breasts press flat on her thighs beneath a calendar showing tulips in Holland; gripping set after set of flabby buttocks in her hands and thinking about what to watch on TV that night, when her shift is done. Perhaps she just pulled over to the side of the road and walked away. People do that. I know it, and probably you do, too. Sometimes people just say fuck it and walk away. Maybe she left Frank behind, thinking someone would come along and give him a good home, only it was the Axe Man who came along, and . . .

But no. I met Lulubelle, and for the life of me I can't see her leaving a dog to most likely roast to death or starve to death in the barrens. Especially not a dog she loved the way she loved Frank. No, L.T. hadn't been exaggerating about that; I saw them together, and I know.

She could still be alive somewhere. Technically speaking, at least, L.T.'s right about that. Just because I can't think of a scenario that would lead from that car with the door hanging open and the rearview mirror lying on the floor and the dog lying dead and crowpicked two rises away, just because I can't think of a scenario that would lead from that place near Caliente to some other place where Lulubelle Simms sings or sews or blows truckers, safe and unknown, well, that doesn't mean that no such scenario exists. As I told L.T., it isn't as if they found her *body;* they just found her *car,* and the remains of the dog a little way from the car. Lulubelle herself could be anywhere. You can see that.

I couldn't sleep and I felt thirsty. I got out of bed, went into the bathroom, and took the toothbrushes out of the glass we keep by the sink. I filled the glass with water. Then I sat down on the closed lid of the toilet and drank the water and thought about the sound that Siamese cats make, that weird crying, how it must sound good if you love them, how it must sound like coming home.

The Road Virus Heads North

I actually have the picture described in this story, how weird is that? My wife saw it and thought I'd like it (or at least react to it), so she gave it to me as a . . . birthday present? Christmas present? I can't remember. What I can remember is that none of my three kids liked it. I hung it in my office, and they claimed the driver's eyes followed them as they crossed the room (as a very small boy, my son Owen was similarly freaked by a picture of Jim Morrison). I like stories about pictures that change, and finally I wrote this one about my picture. The only other time I can remember being inspired to write a story based on an actual picture was "The House on Maple Street," based on a black-and-white drawing by Chris Van Allsburg. That story is in Nightmares and Dreamscapes. I also wrote a novel about a picture that changes. It's called Rose Madder, and is probably the least read of my novels (no movie, either). In that story, the Road Virus is named Norman.

————

Richard Kinnell wasn't frightened when he first saw the picture at the yard sale in Rosewood.

He was fascinated by it, and he felt he'd had the good luck to find something which might be very special, but fright? No. It didn't occur to him until later ("not until it was too late," as he might have written in one of his own numbingly successful novels) that he had felt much the same way about certain illegal drugs as a young man.

He had gone down to Boston to participate in a PEN/New England conference titled "The Threat of Popularity." You could count on PEN to come up with such subjects, Kinnell had found; it was actually sort of comforting. He drove the two hundred and sixty miles from Derry rather than flying because he'd come to a plot impasse on his latest book and wanted some quiet time to try to work it out.

At the conference, he sat on a panel where people who should have known better asked him where he got his ideas and if he ever scared himself. He left the city by way of the Tobin Bridge, then got on Route 1. He never took the turnpike when he was trying to work out problems; the turnpike lulled him into a state that was like dreamless, waking sleep. It was restful, but not very creative. The stop-and-go traffic on the coast road, however, acted like grit inside an oyster—it created a fair amount of mental activity . . . and sometimes even a pearl.

Not, he supposed, that his critics would use that word. In an issue of *Esquire* last year, Bradley Simons had begun his review of *Nightmare City* this way: "Richard Kinnell, who writes like Jeffrey Dahmer cooks, has suffered a fresh bout of projectile vomiting. He has titled this most recent mass of ejecta *Nightmare City*."

Route 1 took him through Revere, Malden, Everett, and up the coast to Newburyport. Beyond Newburyport and just south of the Massachusetts–New Hampshire border was the tidy little town of Rosewood. A mile or so beyond the town center, he saw an array of cheap-looking goods spread out on the lawn of a two-story Cape. Propped against an avocado-colored electric stove was a sign reading YARD SALE. Cars were parked on both sides of the road, creating one of those bottlenecks which travellers unaffected by the yard sale mystique curse their way through. Kinnell liked yard sales, particularly the boxes of old books you sometimes found at them. He drove through the bottleneck, parked his Audi at the head of the line of cars pointed toward Maine and New Hampshire, then walked back.

A dozen or so people were circulating on the littered front lawn of the blue-and-gray Cape Cod. A large television stood to the left of the cement walk, its feet planted on four paper ashtrays that were doing absolutely nothing to protect the lawn. On top was a sign reading MAKE AN OFFER——YOU MIGHT BE SUR-PRISED. An electrical cord, augmented by an extension, trailed back from the TV and through the open front door. A fat woman sat in a lawn chair before it, shaded by an umbrella with CINZANO printed on the colorful scalloped flaps. There was a card table beside her with a cigar box, a pad of paper, and another hand-lettered sign on it. This sign read ALL SALES CASH, ALL SALES

FINAL. The TV was on, tuned to an afternoon soap opera where two beautiful young people looked on the verge of having deeply unsafe sex. The fat woman glanced at Kinnell, then back at the TV. She looked at it for a moment, then looked back at him again. This time her mouth was slightly sprung.

Ah, Kinnell thought, looking around for the liquor box filled with paperbacks that was sure to be here someplace, *a fan.*

He didn't see any paperbacks, but he saw the picture, leaning against an ironing board and held in place by a couple of plastic laundry baskets, and his breath stopped in his throat. He wanted it at once.

He walked over with a casualness that felt exaggerated and dropped to one knee in front of it. The painting was a watercolor, and technically very good. Kinnell didn't care about that; technique didn't interest him (a fact the critics of his own work had duly noted). What he liked in works of art was *content,* and the more unsettling the better. This picture scored high in that department. He knelt between the two laundry baskets, which had been filled with a jumble of small appliances, and let his fingers slip over the glass facing of the picture. He glanced around briefly, looking for others like it, and saw none—only the usual yard sale art collection of Little Bo Peeps, praying hands, and gambling dogs.

He looked back at the framed watercolor, and in his mind he was already moving his suitcase into the back-seat of the Audi so he could slip the picture comfortably into the trunk.

It showed a young man behind the wheel of a muscle car—maybe a Grand Am, maybe a GTX, something with a T-top, anyway—crossing the Tobin Bridge at sunset. The T-top was off, turning the black car into a half-assed convertible. The young man's left arm was cocked on the door; his right wrist was draped casually over the wheel. Behind him, the sky was a bruise-colored mass of yellows and grays, streaked with veins of pink. The young man had lank blond hair that spilled over his low forehead. He was grinning, and his parted lips revealed teeth which were not teeth at all but fangs.

Or maybe they're filed to points, Kinnell thought. *Maybe he's supposed to be a cannibal.*

He liked that; liked the idea of a cannibal crossing the Tobin Bridge at sunset. In a Grand Am. He knew what most of the audience at the PEN panel discussion would have thought—*Oh, yes, great picture for Rich Kinnell; he probably wants it for inspiration, a feather to tickle his tired old gorge into one more fit of projectile vomiting*—but most of those folks were ignoramuses, at least as far as his work went, and what was more, they treasured their ignorance, cossetted it the way some people inexplicably treasured and cossetted those stupid, mean-spirited little dogs that yapped at visitors and sometimes bit the paperboy's ankles. He hadn't been attracted to this painting because he wrote horror stories; he wrote horror stories because he was attracted to things like this painting. His fans sent him stuff—pictures, mostly—and he threw most of them away, not because they were bad art but because they were tiresome and predictable. One fan from Omaha had sent him a little ceramic sculpture of a screaming, horrified monkey's head poking out of a refrigerator door, how-ever, and that one he had kept. It was unskillfully exe-cuted, but there was an unexpected juxtaposition there that lit up his dials. This painting had some of the same quality, but it was even better. *Much* better.

As he was reaching for it, wanting to pick it up right now, this second, wanting to tuck it under his arm and proclaim his intentions, a voice spoke up behind him: "Aren't you Richard Kinnell?"

He jumped, then turned. The fat woman was stand-ing directly behind him, blotting out most of the immediate landscape. She had put on fresh lipstick before approaching, and now her mouth had been transformed into a bleeding grin.

"Yes, I am," he said, smiling back.

Her eyes dropped to the picture. "I should have known you'd go right to that," she said, simpering. "It's so *you*."

"It is, isn't it?" he said, and smiled his best celebrity smile. "How much would you need for it?"

"Forty-five dollars," she said. "I'll be honest with you, I started it at seventy, but nobody likes it, so now it's marked down. If you come back tomorrow, you can probably have it for thirty." The simper had grown to frightening proportions. Kinnell could see little gray spit-buds in the dimples at the corners of her stretched mouth.

"I don't think I want to take that chance," he said. "I'll write you a check right now."

The simper continued to stretch; the woman now looked like some grotesque John Waters parody. Divine does Shirley Temple. "I'm really not supposed to take checks, but *all right,*" she said, her tone that of a teenage girl finally consenting to have sex with her boyfriend. "Only while you have your pen out, could you write an autograph for my daughter? Her name is Robin?"

"What a nice name," Kinnell said automatically. He took the picture and followed the fat woman back to the card table. On the TV next to it, the lustful young people had been temporarily displaced by an elderly woman gobbling bran flakes.

"Robin reads all your books," the fat woman said. "Where in the world do you get all those crazy ideas?"

"I don't know," Kinnell said, smiling more widely than ever. "They just come to me. Isn't that amazing?"

The yard sale minder's name was Judy Diment, and she lived in the house next door. When Kinnell asked her if she knew who the artist happened to be, she said she certainly did; Bobby Hastings had done it, and Bobby Hastings was the reason she was selling off the Hastingses' things. "That's the only painting he didn't burn," she said. "Poor Iris! She's the one I really feel sorry for. I don't think George cared much, really. And I *know* he didn't understand why she wants to sell the house." She rolled her eyes in her large, sweaty face— the old can-you-imagine-that look. She took Kinnell's check when he tore it off, then gave him the pad where she had written down all the items she'd sold and the prices she'd obtained for them. "Just make it out to Robin," she said. "Pretty please with sugar on it?" The simper reappeared, like an old acquaintance you'd hoped was dead.

"Uh-huh," Kinnell said, and wrote his standard thanks-for-being-a-fan message. He didn't have to watch his hands or even think about it anymore, not after twenty-five years of writing autographs. "Tell me about the picture, and the Hastingses."

Judy Diment folded her pudgy hands in the manner of a woman about to recite a favorite story.

"Bobby was just twenty-three when he killed himself this spring. Can you believe that? He was the tortured-genius type, you know, but still living at home." Her eyes rolled, again asking Kinnell if he could imagine it. "He must have had seventy, eighty paintings, plus all his sketchbooks. Down in the basement, they were." She pointed her chin at the Cape Cod, then looked at the picture of the fiendish young man driving across the Tobin Bridge at sunset. "Iris—that's Bobby's mother—said most of them were real bad, lots worse'n this. Stuff that'd curl your hair." She lowered her voice to a whisper, glancing at a woman who was looking at the Hastingses' mismatched silverware and a pretty good collection of old McDonald's plastic glasses in a *Honey, I Shrunk the Kids* motif. "Most of them had sex stuff in them."

"Oh no," Kinnell said.

"He did the worst ones after he got on drugs," Judy Diment continued. "After he was dead—he hung himself down in the basement, where he used to paint—they found over a hundred of those little bottles they sell crack cocaine in. Aren't drugs awful, Mr. Kinnell?"

"They sure are."

"Anyway, I guess he finally just got to the end of his rope, no pun intended. He took all of his sketches and paintings out into the backyard—except for that one, I guess—and burned them. Then he hung himself down in the basement. He pinned a note to his shirt. It said, 'I can't stand what's happening to me.' Isn't that awful, Mr. Kinnell? Isn't that just the horriblest thing you ever heard?"

"Yes," Kinnell said, sincerely enough. "It just about is."

"Like I say, I think George would go right on living in the house if he had his druthers," Judy Diment said. She took the sheet of paper with Robin's autograph on it, held it up next to Kinnell's check, and shook her head, as if the similarity of the signatures amazed her. "But men are different."

"Are they?"

"Oh, yes, much less sensitive. By the end of his life, Bobby Hastings was just skin and bone, dirty all the time—you could smell him—and he wore the same Tee-shirt, day in and day out. It had a picture of the Led Zeppelins on it. His eyes were red, he had a scraggle on his cheeks that you couldn't quite call a beard, and his pimples were coming back, like he was a teenager again. But she loved him, because a mother's love sees past all those things."

The woman who had been looking at the silverware and the glasses came over with a set of Star Wars placemats. Mrs. Diment took five dollars for them, wrote the sale carefully down on her pad below "ONE DOZ. ASSORTED POTHOLDERS & HOTPADS," then turned back to Kinnell.

"They went out to Arizona," she said, "to stay with Iris's folks. I know George is looking for work out there in Flagstaff—he's a draftsman—but I don't know if he's found any yet. If he has, I suppose we might not ever see them again here in Rosewood. She marked out all the stuff she wanted me to sell—Iris did—and told me I could keep twenty per cent for my trouble. I'll send a check for the rest. There won't be much." She sighed.

"The picture is great," Kinnell said.

"Yeah, too bad he burned the rest, because most of this other stuff is your standard yard sale crap, pardon my French. What's that?"

Kinnell had turned the picture around. There was a length of Dymotape pasted to the back.

"A title, I think."

"What does it say?"

He grabbed the picture by the sides and held it up so she could read it for herself. This put the picture at eye-level to him, and he studied it eagerly, once again taken by the simpleminded weirdness of the subject: kid behind the wheel of a muscle car, a kid with a nasty, knowing grin that revealed the filed points of an even nastier set of teeth.

It fits, he thought. *If ever a title fitted a painting, this one does.*

"*The Road Virus Heads North,*" she read. "I never noticed that when my boys were lugging stuff out. *Is* it the title, do you think?"

"Must be." Kinnell couldn't take his eyes off the blond kid's grin. *I know something,* the grin said. *I know something you never will.*

"Well, I guess you'd have to believe the fella who did this was high on drugs," she said, sounding upset—authentically upset, Kinnell thought. "No wonder he could kill himself and break his mamma's heart."

"I've got to be heading north myself," Kinnell said, tucking the picture under his arm. "Thanks for—"

"Mr. Kinnell?"

"Yes?"

"Can I see your driver's license?" She apparently found nothing ironic or even amusing in this request. "I ought to write the number on the back of your check."

Kinnell put the picture down so he could dig for his wallet. "Sure. You bet."

The woman who'd bought the Star Wars placemats had paused on her way back to her car to watch some of the soap opera playing on the lawn TV. Now she glanced at the picture, which Kinnell had propped against his shins.

"Ag," she said. "Who'd want an ugly old thing like that? I'd think about it every time I turned the lights out."

"What's wrong with that?" Kinnell asked.

Kinnell's Aunt Trudy lived in Wells, which is about six miles north of the Maine–New Hampshire border. Kinnell pulled off at the exit which circled the bright green Wells water tower, the one with the comic sign on it (KEEP MAINE GREEN, BRING MONEY in letters four feet high), and five minutes later he was turning into the driveway of her neat little saltbox house. No TV sinking into the lawn on paper ashtrays here, only Aunt Trudy's amiable masses of flowers. Kinnell needed to pee and hadn't wanted to take care of that in a roadside rest-stop when he could come here, but he also wanted an update on all the family gossip. Aunt Trudy retailed the best; she was to gossip what Zabar's is to deli. Also, of course, he wanted to show her his new acquisition.

She came out to meet him, gave him a hug, and covered his face with her patented little birdy-kisses, the ones that had made him shiver all over as a kid.

"Want to see something?" he asked her. "It'll blow your panty-hose off."

"What a charming thought," Aunt Trudy said, clasping her elbows in her palms and looking at him with amusement.

He opened the trunk and took out his new picture. It affected her, all right, but not in the way he had expected. The color fell out of her face in a sheet—he had never seen anything quite like it in his entire life. "It's horrible," she said in a tight, controlled voice. "I hate it. I suppose I can see what attracted you to it, Richie, but what you play at, it does for real. Put it back in your trunk, like a good boy. And when you get to the Saco River, why don't you pull over into the breakdown lane and throw it in?"

He gaped at her. Aunt Trudy's lips were pressed tightly together to stop them trembling, and now her long, thin hands were not just clasping her elbows but clutching them, as if to keep her from flying away. At that moment she looked not sixty-one but ninety-one.

"Auntie?" Kinnell spoke tentatively, not sure what was going on here. "Auntie, what's wrong?"

"That," she said, unlocking her right hand and pointing at the picture. "I'm surprised you don't feel it more strongly yourself, an imaginative guy like you."

Well, he felt *something,* obviously he had, or he never would have unlimbered his checkbook in the first place. Aunt Trudy was feeling something else, though . . . or something *more.* He turned the picture around so he could see it (he had been holding it out for her, so the side with the Dymotaped title faced him), and looked at it again. What he saw hit him in the chest and belly like a one-two punch.

The picture had *changed,* that was punch number one. Not much, but it had clearly changed. The young blond man's smile was wider, revealing more of those filed cannibal-teeth. His eyes were squinted down more, too, giving his face a look which was more knowing and nastier than ever.

The degree of a smile . . . the vista of sharpened teeth widening slightly . . . the tilt and squint of the eyes . . . all pretty subjective stuff. A person could be mistaken about things like that, and of course he hadn't really *studied* the painting before buying it. Also, there had been the distraction of Mrs. Diment, who could probably talk the cock off a brass monkey.

But there was also punch number two, and that *wasn't* subjective. In the darkness of the Audi's trunk, the blond young man had turned his left arm, the one cocked on the door, so that Kinnell could now see a tattoo which had been hidden before. It was a vine-wrapped dagger with a bloody tip. Below it were words. Kinnell could make out DEATH BEFORE, and he supposed you didn't have to be a big best-selling novelist to figure out the word that was still hidden. DEATH BEFORE DISHONOR was, after all, just the sort of a thing a hoodoo travelling man like this was apt to have on his arm. *And an ace of spades on the other one,* Kinnell thought.

"You hate it, don't you, Auntie?" he asked.

"Yes," she said, and now he saw an even more amazing thing: she had turned away from him, pretending to look out at the street (which was dozing and deserted in the hot afternoon sunlight) so she wouldn't have to look at the picture. "In fact, Auntie *loathes* it. Now put it away and come on into the house. I'll bet you need to use the bathroom."

Aunt Trudy recovered her *savoir-faire* almost as soon as the watercolor was back in the trunk. They talked about Kinnell's mother (Pasadena), his sister (Baton Rouge), and his ex-wife, Sally (Nashua). Sally was a space-case who ran an animal shelter out of a double-wide trailer and published two newsletters each month. *Survivors* was filled with astral info and supposedly true tales of the spirit world; *Visitors* contained the reports of people who'd had close encounters with space aliens. Kinnell no longer went to fan conventions which specialized in fantasy and horror. One Sally in a lifetime, he thought, was enough.

When Aunt Trudy walked him back out to the car, it was four-thirty and he'd turned down the obligatory dinner invitation. "I can get most of the way back to Derry in daylight, if I leave now."

"Okay," she said. "And I'm sorry I was so mean about your picture. Of *course* you like it, you've always liked your . . . your oddities. It just hit me the wrong way. That awful *face*." She shuddered. "As if we were looking at him . . . and he was looking right back."

Kinnell grinned and kissed the tip of her nose. "You've got quite an imagination yourself, sweetheart."

"Of course, it runs in the family. Are you sure you don't want to use the facility again before you go?"

He shook his head. "That's not why I stop, anyway, not really."

"Oh? Why do you?"

He grinned. "Because you know who's being naughty and who's being nice. And you're not afraid to share what you know."

"Go on, get going," she said, pushing at his shoulder but clearly pleased. "If I were you, I'd want to get home quick. I wouldn't want that nasty guy riding along behind *me* in the dark, even in the trunk. I mean, did you see his teeth? *Ag!*"

He got on the turnpike, trading scenery for speed, and made it as far as the Gray service area before deciding to have another look at the picture. Some of his aunt's unease had transmitted itself to him like a germ, but he didn't think that was really the problem. The problem was his perception that the picture had changed.

The service area featured the usual gourmet chow—burgers by Roy Rogers, cones by TCBY—and had a small, littered picnic and dog-walking area at the rear. Kinnell parked next to a van with Missouri plates, drew in a deep breath, let it out. He'd driven to Boston in order to kill some plot gremlins in the new book, which was pretty ironic. He'd spent the ride down working out what he'd say on the panel if certain tough questions were tossed at him, but none had been—once they'd found out he didn't *know* where he got his ideas, and yes, he *did* sometimes scare himself, they'd only wanted to know how you got an agent.

And now, heading back, he couldn't think of anything but the damned picture.

Had it changed? If it had, if the blond kid's arm had moved enough so he, Kinnell, could read a tattoo which had been partly hidden before, then he could write a column for one of Sally's magazines. Hell, a four-part series. If, on the other hand, it *wasn't* changing, then . . . what? He was suffering a hallucination? Having a breakdown? That was crap. His life was pretty much in order, and he felt good. *Had,* anyway, until his fascination with the picture had begun to waver into something else, something darker.

"Ah, fuck, you just saw it wrong the first time," he said out loud as he got out of the car. Well, maybe. Maybe. It wouldn't be the first time his head had screwed with his perceptions. That was also a part of what he did. Sometimes his imagination got a little . . . well . . .

"Feisty," Kinnell said, and opened the trunk. He took the picture out of the trunk and looked at it, and it was during the space of the ten seconds when he looked at it without remembering to breathe that he became authentically afraid of the thing, afraid the way you were afraid of a sudden dry rattle in the bushes, afraid the way you were when you saw an insect that would probably sting if you provoked it.

The blond driver was grinning insanely at him now—yes, at *him,* Kinnell was sure of it—with those filed cannibal-teeth exposed all the way to the gum-lines. His eyes simultaneously glared and laughed. And the Tobin Bridge was gone. So was the Boston skyline. So was the sunset. It was almost dark in the painting now, the car and its wild rider illuminated by a single streetlamp that ran a buttery glow across the road and the car's chrome. It looked to Kinnell as if the car (he was pretty sure it was a Grand Am) was on the edge of a small town on Route 1, and he was pretty sure he knew what town it was—he had driven through it himself only a few hours ago.

"Rosewood," he muttered. "That's Rosewood. I'm pretty sure."

The Road Virus was heading north, all right, coming up Route 1 just as he had. The blond's left arm was still cocked out the window, but it had rotated enough back toward its original position so that Kinnell could no longer see the tattoo. But he knew it was there, didn't he? Yes, you bet.

The blond kid looked like a Metallica fan who had escaped from a mental asylum for the criminally insane.

"Jesus," Kinnell whispered, and the word seemed to come from someplace else, not from him. The strength suddenly ran out of his body, ran out like water from a bucket with a hole in the bottom, and he sat down heavily on the curb separating the parking lot from the dog-walking zone. He suddenly understood that this was the truth he'd missed in all his fiction, this was how people really reacted when they came face-to-face with something which made no rational sense. You felt as if you were bleeding to death, only inside your head.

"No wonder the guy who painted it killed himself," he croaked, still staring at the picture, at the ferocious grin, at the eyes that were both shrewd and stupid.

There was a note pinned to his shirt, Mrs. Diment had said. *"I can't stand what's happening to me." Isn't that awful, Mr. Kinnell?*

Yes, it was awful, all right.

Really awful.

He got up, gripping the picture by its top, and strode across the dog-walking area. He kept his eyes trained strictly in front of him, looking for canine land mines. He did not look down at the picture. His legs felt trembly and untrustworthy, but they seemed to support him all right. Just ahead, close to the belt of trees at the rear of the service area, was a pretty young thing in white shorts and a red halter. She was walking a cocker spaniel. She began to smile at Kinnell, then saw something in his face that straightened her lips out in a hurry. She headed left, and fast. The cocker didn't want to go that fast, so she dragged it, coughing, in her wake.

The scrubby pines behind the service area sloped down to a boggy acre that stank of plant and animal decomposition. The carpet of pine-needles was a road-litter fallout zone: burger wrappers, paper soft-drink cups, TCBY napkins, beer cans, empty wine-cooler bottles, cigarette butts. He saw a used condom lying like a dead snail next to a torn pair of panties with the word TUESDAY stitched on them in cursive girly-girl script.

Now that he was here, he chanced another look down at the picture. He steeled himself for further changes—even for the possibility that the painting would be in motion, like a movie in a frame—but there was none. There didn't have to be, Kinnell realized; the blond kid's face was enough. That stone-crazy grin. Those pointed teeth. The face said, *Hey, old man, guess what? I'm done fucking with civilization. I'm a representative of the real generation X, the next millennium is right here behind the wheel of this fine, high-steppin' mosheen.*

Aunt Trudy's initial reaction to the painting had been to advise Kinnell that he should throw it into the Saco River. Auntie had been right. The Saco was now almost twenty miles behind him, but . . .

"This'll do," he said. "I think this'll do just fine."

He raised the picture over his head like a guy holding up some kind of sports trophy for the postgame photographers and then heaved it down the slope. It flipped over twice, the frame catching winks of hazy late-day sun, then struck a tree. The glass facing shattered. The picture fell to the ground and then slid down the dry, needle-carpeted slope, as if down a chute. It landed in the bog, one corner of the frame protruding from a thick stand of reeds. Otherwise, there was nothing visible but the strew of broken glass, and Kinnell thought that went very well with the rest of the litter.

He turned and went back to his car, already picking up his mental trowel. He would wall this incident off in its own special niche, he thought . . . and it occurred to him that that was probably what *most* people did when they ran into stuff like this. Liars and wannabees (or maybe in this case they were wanna*sees*) wrote up their fantasies for publications like *Survivors* and called them truth; those who blundered into authentic occult phenomena kept their mouths shut and used those trowels. Because when cracks like this appeared in your life, you had to do something about them; if you didn't, they were apt to widen and sooner or later everything would fall in.

Kinnell glanced up and saw the pretty young thing watching him apprehensively from what she probably hoped was a safe distance. When she saw him looking at her, she turned around and started toward the restaurant building, once more dragging her cocker spaniel behind her and trying to keep as much sway out of her hips as possible.

You think I'm crazy, don't you, pretty girl? Kinnell thought. He saw he had left his trunk lid up. It gaped like a mouth. He slammed it shut. *But I'm not crazy. Absolutely not. I just made a little mistake, that's all. Stopped at a yard sale I should have passed up. Anyone could have done it.* You *could have done it. And that picture—*

"*What* picture?" Rich Kinnell asked the hot summer evening, and tried on a smile. "*I* don't see any picture."

He slid behind the wheel of his Audi and started the engine. He looked at the fuel gauge and saw it had dropped under a half. He was going to need gas before he got home, but he thought he'd fill the tank a little farther up the line. Right now all he wanted to do was to put a belt of miles—as thick a one as possible—between him and the discarded painting.

* * *

Once outside the city limits of Derry, Kansas Street becomes Kansas Road. As it approaches the incorporated town limits (an area that is actually open countryside), it becomes Kansas Lane. Not long after, Kansas Lane passes between two fieldstone posts. Tar gives way to gravel. What is one of Derry's busiest downtown streets eight miles east of here has become a driveway leading up a shallow hill, and on moonlit summer nights it glimmers like something out of an Alfred Noyes poem. At the top of the hill stands an angular, handsome barnboard structure with reflectorized windows, a stable that is actually a garage, and a satellite dish tilted at the stars. A waggish reporter from the Derry *News* once called it the House that Gore Built . . . *not* meaning the vice president of the United States. Richard Kinnell simply called it home, and he parked in front of it that night with a sense of weary satisfaction. He felt as if he had lived through a week's worth of time since getting up in the Boston Harbor hotel that morning at nine o'clock.

No more yard sales, he thought, looking up at the moon. *No more yard sales ever.*

"Amen," he said, and started toward the house. He probably should stick the car in the garage, but the hell with it. What he wanted right now was a drink, a light meal—something microwaveable—and then sleep. Preferably the kind without dreams. He couldn't wait to put this day behind him.

He stuck his key in the lock, turned it, and punched 3817 to silence the warning bleep from the burglar-alarm panel. He turned on the front-hall light, stepped through the door, pushed it shut behind him, began to turn, saw what was on the wall where his collection of framed book covers had been just two days ago, and screamed. In his *head* he screamed. Nothing actually came out of his mouth but a harsh exhalation of air. He heard a thump and a tuneless little jingle as his keys fell out of his relaxing hand and dropped to the carpet between his feet.

The Road Virus Heads North was no longer in the puckerbrush behind the Gray turnpike service area.

It was mounted on his entry wall.

It had changed yet again. The car was now parked in the driveway of the yard sale yard. The goods were still spread out everywhere—glassware and furniture and ceramic knickknacks (Scottie dogs smoking pipes, bare-assed toddlers, winking fish), but now they gleamed beneath the light of the same skullface moon that rode in the sky above Kinnell's house. The TV was still there, too, and it was still on, casting its own pallid radiance onto the grass, and what lay in front of it, next to an overturned lawn chair. Judy Diment was on her back, and she was no longer all there. After a moment, Kinnell saw the rest. It was on the ironing board, dead eyes glowing like fifty-cent pieces in the moonlight.

The Grand Am's taillights were a blur of red-pink watercolor paint. It was Kinnell's first look at the car's back deck. Written across it in Old English letters were three words: THE ROAD VIRUS.

Makes perfect sense, Kinnell thought numbly. *Not him, his car. Except for a guy like this, there's probably not much difference.*

"This isn't happening," he whispered, except it was.

ING A YARD SALE. NO SCREAMS WERE HEARD AND MRS. DIMENT WAS NOT FOUND UNTIL EIGHT O'CLOCK, WHEN A NEIGHBOR ACROSS THE STREET CAME OVER TO COMPLAIN ABOUT LOUD TELEVISION NOISE. THE NEIGHBOR, MATTHEW GRAVES, SAID THAT MRS. DIMENT HAD BEEN DECAPITATED. "HER HEAD WAS ON THE IRONING BOARD," HE SAID. "IT WAS THE MOST AWFUL THING I'VE EVER SEEN IN MY LIFE." GRAVES SAID HE HEARD NO SIGNS OF A STRUGGLE, ONLY THE TV AND, SHORTLY BEFORE FINDING THE BODY, A LOUD CAR, POSSIBLY EQUIPPED WITH A GLASSPACK MUFFLER, ACCELERATING AWAY FROM THE VICINITY ALONG ROUTE ONE. SPECULATION THAT THIS VEHICLE MAY HAVE BELONGED TO THE KILLER—

Except that wasn't speculation; that was a simple fact.

Breathing hard, not quite panting, Kinnell hurried back into the entryway. The picture was still there, but it had changed once more. Now it showed two glaring white circles—headlights—with the dark shape of the car hulking behind them.

He's on the move again, Kinnell thought, and Aunt Trudy *was* on top of his mind now—sweet Aunt Trudy, who always knew who had been naughty and who had been nice. Aunt Trudy, who lived in Wells, no more than forty miles from Rosewood.

"God, please God, please send him by the coast road," Kinnell said, reaching for the picture. Was it his imagination or were the headlights farther apart now, as if the car were actually moving before his eyes . . . but stealthily, the way the minute hand moved on a pocket watch? "Send him by the coast road, please."

He tore the picture off the wall and ran back into the living room with it. The screen was in place before the fireplace, of course; it would be at least two months before a fire was wanted in here. Kinnell batted it aside and threw the painting in, breaking the glass fronting—which he had already broken once, at the Gray service area—against the firedogs. Then he pelted for the kitchen, wondering what he would do if this didn't work either.

It has to, he thought. *It will because it has to, and that's all there is to it.*

He opened the kitchen cabinets and pawed through them, spilling the oatmeal, spilling a canister of salt, spilling the vinegar. The bottle broke open on the counter and assaulted his nose and eyes with the high stink.

Not there. What he wanted wasn't there.

He raced into the pantry, looked behind the door—nothing but a plastic bucket and an O Cedar—and then on the shelf by the dryer. There it was, next to the briquets.

Lighter fluid.

He grabbed it and ran back, glancing at the telephone on the kitchen wall as he hurried by. He wanted to stop, wanted to call Aunt Trudy. Credibility wasn't an issue with her; if her favorite nephew called and told her to get out of the house, to get out *right now,* she would do it . . . but what if the blond kid followed her? Chased her?

And he would. Kinnell *knew* he would.

He hurried across the living room and stopped in front of the fireplace.

"Jesus," he whispered. "Jesus, no."

The picture beneath the splintered glass no longer showed oncoming headlights. Now it showed the Grand Am on a sharply curving piece of road that could only be an exit ramp. Moonlight shone like liquid satin on the car's dark flank. In the background was a water tower, and the words on it were easily readable in the moonlight. KEEP MAINE GREEN, they said. BRING MONEY.

Kinnell didn't hit the picture with the first squeeze of lighter fluid; his hands were shaking badly and the aromatic liquid simply ran down the unbroken part of the glass, blurring the Road Virus's back deck. He took a deep breath, aimed, then squeezed again. This time the lighter fluid squirted in through the jagged hole made by one of the firedogs and ran down the picture, cutting through the paint, making it run, turning a Goodyear Wide Oval into a sooty teardrop.

Kinnell took one of the ornamental matches from the jar on the mantel, struck it on the hearth, and poked it in through the hole in the glass. The painting caught at once, fire billowing up and down across the Grand Am and the water tower. The remaining glass in the frame turned black, then broke outward in a shower of flaming pieces. Kinnell crunched them under his sneakers, putting them out before they could set the rug on fire.

He went to the phone and punched in Aunt Trudy's number, unaware that he was crying. On the third ring, his aunt's answering machine picked up. "Hello," Aunt Trudy said, "I know it encourages the burglars to say things like this, but I've gone up to Kennebunk to watch the new Harrison Ford movie. If you intend to break in, please don't take my china pigs. If you want to leave a message, do so at the beep."

Kinnell waited, then, keeping his voice as steady as possible, he said: "It's Richie, Aunt Trudy. Call me when you get back, okay? No matter how late."

He hung up, looked at the TV, then dialed Newswire again, this time punching in the Maine area code. While the computers on the other end processed his order, he went back and used a poker to jab at the blackened, twisted thing in the fireplace. The stench was ghastly—it made the spilled vinegar smell like a flowerpatch in comparison—but Kinnell found he didn't mind. The picture was entirely gone, reduced to ash, and that made it worthwhile.

What if it comes back again?

"It won't," he said, putting the poker back and returning to the TV. "I'm sure it won't."

But every time the news scroll started to recycle, he got up to check. The picture was just ashes on the hearth . . . and there was no word of elderly women being murdered in the Wells-Saco-Kennebunk area of the state. Kinnell kept watching, almost expecting to see A GRAND AM MOVING AT HIGH SPEED CRASHED INTO A KENNEBUNK MOVIE THEATER TONIGHT, KILLING AT LEAST TEN, but nothing of the sort showed up.

At a quarter of eleven the telephone rang. Kinnell snatched it up. "Hello?"

"It's Trudy, dear. Are you all right?"

"Yes, fine."

"You don't *sound* fine," she said. "Your voice sounds

trembly and . . . funny. What's wrong? What is it?" And then, chilling him but not really surprising him: "It's that picture you were so pleased with, isn't it? That goddamned picture!"

It calmed him somehow, that she should guess so much . . . and, of course, there was the relief of knowing she was safe.

"Well, maybe," he said. "I had the heebie-jeebies all the way back here, so I burned it. In the fireplace."

She's going to find out about Judy Diment, you know, a voice inside warned. *She doesn't have a twenty-thousand-dollar satellite hookup, but she does subscribe to the* Union Leader *and this'll be on the front page. She'll put two and two together. She's far from stupid.*

Yes, that was undoubtedly true, but further explanations could wait until the morning, when he might be a little less freaked . . . when he might've found a way to think about the Road Virus without losing his mind . . . and when he'd begun to be sure it was really over.

"Good!" she said emphatically. "You ought to scatter the ashes, too!" She paused, and when she spoke again, her voice was lower. "You were worried about me, weren't you? Because you showed it to me."

"A little, yes."

"But you feel better now?"

He leaned back and closed his eyes. It was true, he did. "Uh-huh. How was the movie?"

"Good. Harrison Ford looks wonderful in a uniform. Now, if he'd just get rid of that little bump on his chin . . ."

"Good night, Aunt Trudy. We'll talk tomorrow."

"Will we?"

"Yes," he said. "I think so."

He hung up, went over to the fireplace again, and stirred the ashes with the poker. He could see a scrap of fender and a ragged little flap of road, but that was it. Fire was what it had needed all along, apparently. Wasn't that how you usually killed supernatural emissaries of evil? Of course it was. He'd used it a few times himself, most notably in *The Departing*, his haunted train station novel.

"Yes, indeed," he said. "Burn, baby, burn."

He thought about getting the drink he'd promised himself, then remembered the spilled bottle of vinegar (which by now would probably be soaking into the spilled oatmeal—what a thought). He decided he would simply go on upstairs instead. In a book—one by Richard Kinnell, for instance—sleep would be out of the question after the sort of thing which had just happened to him.

In real life, he thought he might sleep just fine.

He actually dozed off in the shower, leaning against the back wall with his hair full of shampoo and the water beating on his chest. He was at the yard sale again, and the TV standing on the paper ashtrays was broadcasting Judy Diment. Her head was back on, but Kinnell could see the medical examiner's primitive industrial stitchwork; it circled her throat like a grisly necklace. "Now this New England Newswire update," she said, and Kinnell, who had always been a vivid dreamer, could actually see the stitches on her neck stretch and relax as she spoke. "Bobby Hastings took *all* his paintings and burned them, including yours, Mr. Kinnell . . . and it *is* yours, as I'm sure you know. All sales are final, you saw the sign. Why, you just ought to be glad I took your check."

Burned all his paintings, yes, of course he did, Kinnell thought in his watery dream. *He couldn't stand what was happening to him, that's what the note said, and when you get to that point in the festivities, you don't pause to see if you want to except one special piece of work from the bonfire. It's just that you got something special into* The Road Virus Heads North, *didn't you, Bobby? And probably completely by accident. You were talented, I could see that right away, but talent has nothing to do with what's going on in* that *picture.*

"Some things are just good at survival," Judy Diment said on the TV. "They keep coming back no matter *how* hard you try to get rid of them. They keep coming back like viruses."

Kinnell reached out and changed the channel, but apparently there was nothing on all the way around the dial except for *The Judy Diment Show.*

"You might say he opened a hole into the basement of the universe," she was saying now. "Bobby Hastings, I mean. And this is what drove out. Nice, isn't it?"

Kinnell's feet slid then, not enough to go out from under him completely, but enough to snap him to.

He opened his eyes, winced at the immediate sting of the soap (Prell had run down his face in thick white rivulets while he had been dozing), and cupped his hands under the shower-spray to splash it away. He did this once and was reaching out to do it again when he heard something. A ragged rumbling sound.

Don't be stupid, he told himself. *All you hear is the*

shower. The rest is only imagination. Your stupid, overtrained imagination.

Except it wasn't.

Kinnell reached out and turned off the water.

The rumbling sound continued. Low and powerful. Coming from outside.

He got out of the shower and walked, dripping, across his bedroom on the second floor. There was still enough shampoo in his hair to make him look as if it had turned white while he was dozing—as if his dream of Judy Diment had turned it white.

Why did I ever stop at that yard sale? he asked himself, but for this he had no answer. He supposed no one ever did.

The rumbling sound grew louder as he approached the window overlooking the driveway—the driveway that glimmered in the summer moonlight like something out of an Alfred Noyes poem.

As he brushed aside the curtain and looked out, he found himself thinking of his ex-wife, Sally, whom he had met at the World Fantasy Convention in 1978. Sally, who now published two newsletters out of her trailer home, one called *Survivors,* one called *Visitors.* Looking down at the driveway, these two titles came together in Kinnell's mind like a double image in a stereopticon.

He had a visitor who was definitely a survivor.

The Grand Am idled in front of the house, the white haze from its twin chromed tailpipes rising in the still night air. The Old English letters on the back deck were perfectly readable. The driver's-side door stood open, and that wasn't all; the light spilling down the porch steps suggested that Kinnell's front door was also open.

Forgot to lock it, Kinnell thought, wiping soap off his forehead with a hand he could no longer feel. *Forgot to reset the burglar alarm, too . . . not that it would have made much difference to this guy.*

Well, he might have caused it to detour around Aunt Trudy, and that was something, but just now the thought brought him no comfort.

Survivors.

The soft rumble of the big engine, probably at least a 442 with a four-barrel carb, reground valves, fuel injection.

He turned slowly on legs that had lost all feeling, a naked man with a headful of soap, and saw the picture over his bed, just as he'd known he would. In it, the Grand Am stood in his driveway with the driver's door open and two plumes of exhaust rising from the chromed tailpipes. From this angle he could also see his own front door, standing open, and a long man-shaped shadow stretching down the hall.

Survivors.

Survivors and *visitors.*

Now he could hear feet ascending the stairs. It was a heavy tread, and he knew without having to see that the blond kid was wearing motorcycle boots. People with DEATH BEFORE DISHONOR tattooed on their arms always wore motorcycle boots, just as they always smoked unfiltered Camels. These things were like a national law.

And the knife. He would be carrying a long, sharp knife—more of a machete, actually, the sort of knife that could strike off a person's head in a single stroke.

And he would be grinning, showing those filed cannibal teeth.

Kinnell *knew* these things. He was an imaginative guy, after all.

He didn't need anyone to draw him a picture.

"No," he whispered, suddenly conscious of his global nakedness, suddenly freezing all the way around his skin. "No, please, go away." But the footfalls kept coming, of course they did. You couldn't tell a guy like this to go away. It didn't work; it wasn't the way the story was supposed to end.

Kinnell could hear him nearing the top of the stairs. Outside, the Grand Am went on rumbling in the moonlight.

The feet coming down the hall now, worn bootheels rapping on polished hardwood.

A terrible paralysis had gripped Kinnell. He threw it off with an effort and bolted toward the bedroom door, wanting to lock it before the thing could get in here, but he slipped in a puddle of soapy water and this time he *did* go down, flat on his back on the oak planks, and what he saw as the door clicked open and the motorcycle boots crossed the room toward where he lay, naked and with his hair full of Prell, was the picture hanging on the wall over his bed, the picture of the Road Virus idling in front of his house with the driver's-side door open.

The driver's-side bucket seat, he saw, was full of blood. *I'm going outside, I think,* Kinnell thought, and closed his eyes.

Lunch at
the Gotham Café

One day when I was in New York, I walked past a very nice-looking restaurant. Inside, the maître d' was showing a couple to their table. The couple was arguing. The maître d' caught my eye and tipped me what may have been the most cynical wink in the universe. I went back to my hotel and wrote this story. For the three days it was in work, I was totally possessed by it. For me what makes it go isn't the crazy maître d' but the spooky relationship between the divorcing couple. In their own way, they're crazier than he is. By far.

One day I came home from the brokerage house where I worked and found a letter—more of a note, actually—from my wife on the dining room table. It said she was leaving me, that she was pursuing a divorce, that I would hear from her lawyer. I sat on the chair at the kitchen end of the table, reading this communication over and over again, not able to believe it. After awhile I got up, went into the bedroom, and looked in the closet. All her clothes were gone except for one pair of sweatpants and a joke sweatshirt someone had given her, with the words RICH BLONDE printed on the front in spangly stuff.

I went back to the dining room table (which was actually at one end of the living room; it was only a four-room apartment) and read the six sentences over again. It was the same, but looking into the half-empty bedroom closet had started me on the way to believing what it said. It was a chilly piece of work, that note. There was no "Love" or "Good luck" or even "Best" at the bottom of it. "Take care of yourself" was as warm as it got. Just below that she had scratched her name, Diane.

I walked into the kitchen, poured myself a glass of orange juice, then knocked it onto the floor when I tried to pick it up. The juice sprayed onto the lower cabinets and the glass broke. I knew I would cut myself if I tried to pick up the glass—my hands were shaking—but I picked it up anyway, and I cut myself. Two places, neither deep. I kept thinking that it was a joke, then realizing it wasn't. Diane wasn't much of a joker. But the thing was, I didn't see it coming. I didn't have a clue. I didn't know if that made me stupid or insensitive. As the days passed and I thought about the last six or eight months of our two-year marriage, I realized I had been both.

That night I called her folks in Pound Ridge and asked if Diane was there. "She is, and she doesn't want to talk to you," her mother said. "Don't call back." The phone went dead in my ear.

Two days later I got a call at work from Diane's lawyer, who introduced himself as William Humboldt, and, after ascertaining that he was indeed speaking to Steven Davis, began calling me Steve. I suppose that's a little hard to believe, but it's what happened. Lawyers are so bizarre.

Humboldt told me I would be receiving "preliminary paperwork" early the following week, and suggested I prepare "an account overview prefatory to dissolving your domestic corporation." He also advised me not to make any "sudden fiduciary movements" and suggested that I keep all receipts for items purchased, even the smallest, during this "financially difficult passage." Last of all, he suggested that I find myself a lawyer.

"Listen a minute, would you?" I asked. I was sitting at my desk with my head down and my left hand curled around my forehead. My eyes were shut so I wouldn't have to look into the bright gray socket of my computer screen. I'd been crying a lot, and my eyes felt like they were full of sand.

"Of course," he said. "Happy to listen, Steve."

"I've got two things for you. First, you mean 'preparatory to ending your marriage,' not 'prefatory to dissolving your domestic corporation' . . . and if Diane thinks I'm going to try and cheat her out of what's hers, she's wrong."

"Yes," Humboldt said, not indicating agreement but that he understood my point.

"Second, you're *her* lawyer, not mine. I find you calling me by my first name patronizing and insensitive. Do it again on the phone and I'll hang up on you. Do it to my face and I'll probably try to punch your lights out."

"Steve . . . Mr. Davis . . . I hardly think—"

I hung up on him. It was the first thing I'd done that gave me any pleasure since finding that note on the dining room table, with her three apartment keys on top of it to hold it down.

That afternoon I talked to a friend in the legal department, and he recommended a friend of his who did divorce work. The divorce lawyer was John Ring, and I made an appointment with him for the following day. I went home from the office as late as I could, walked back and forth through the apartment for awhile, decided to go out to a movie, couldn't find anything I wanted to see, tried the television, couldn't find anything there to look at, either, and did some more walking. And at some point I found myself in the bedroom, standing in front of an open window fourteen floors above the street, and chucking out all my cigarettes, even the stale old pack of Viceroys from the very back of my top desk drawer, a pack that had probably been there for ten years or more—since before I had any idea there was such a creature as Diane Coslaw in the world, in other words.

Although I'd been smoking between twenty and forty cigarettes a day for twenty years, I don't remember any sudden decision to quit, nor any dissenting interior opinions—not even a mental suggestion that maybe two days after your wife walks out is not the optimum time to quit smoking. I just stuffed the full carton, the half carton, and the two or three half-used packs I found lying around out the window and into the dark. Then I shut the window (it never once occurred to me that it might have been more efficient to throw the user out instead of the product; it was never *that* kind of situation), lay down on my bed, and closed my eyes. As I drifted off, it occurred to me that tomorrow was probably going to be one of the worst days of my life. It further occurred to me that I would probably be smoking again by noon. I was right about the first thing, wrong about the second.

The next ten days—the time during which I was going through the worst of the physical withdrawal from nicotine—were difficult and often unpleasant, but perhaps not as bad as I had thought they would be. And although I was on the verge of smoking dozens—no, hundreds—of times, I never did. There were moments when I thought I would go insane if I didn't have a cigarette, and when I passed people on the street who were smoking I felt like screaming *Give that to me, motherfucker, that's mine!* at them, but I didn't.

For me, the worst times were late at night. I think (but I'm not sure; all my thought processes from around the time Diane left are very blurry in my mind) I had an idea that I would sleep better if I quit, but I didn't. I lay awake some mornings until three, hands laced together under my pillow, looking up at the ceiling, listening to sirens and to the rumble of trucks headed downtown. At those times I would think about the twenty-four-hour Korean market almost directly across the street from my building. I would think about the white fluorescent light inside, so bright it was almost like a Kübler-Ross near-death experience, and how it spilled out onto the sidewalk between the displays which, in another hour, two young Korean men in white paper hats would begin to fill with fruit. I would think about the older man behind the counter, also Korean, also in a paper hat, and the formidable racks of cigarettes behind him, as big as the stone tablets Charlton Heston brought down from Mount Sinai in *The Ten Commandments*. I would think about getting up, dressing, going over there, getting a pack of cigarettes (or maybe nine or ten of them), and sitting by the window, smoking one Marlboro after another as the sky lightened to the east and the sun came up. I never did, but on many early mornings I went to sleep counting cigarette brands instead of sheep: Winston . . . Winston 100s . . . Virginia Slims . . . Doral . . . Merit . . . Merit 100s . . . Camels . . . Camel Filters . . . Camel Lights.

Later—around the time I was starting to see the last three or four months of our marriage in a clearer light, as a matter of fact—I began to understand that my decision to quit smoking when I did was perhaps not so unconsidered as it at first seemed, and a very long way from ill-considered. I'm not a brilliant man, not a brave one, either, but that decision might have been both. It's certainly possible; sometimes we rise above ourselves. In any case, it gave my mind something concrete to pitch upon in the days after Diane left; it gave my misery a vocabulary it would not otherwise have had.

Of course I have speculated that quitting when I did may have played a part in what happened at the Gotham Café that day, and I'm sure there's some truth to that. But who can foresee such things? None of us can predict the final outcomes of our actions, and few of us even try; most of us just do what we do to prolong a moment's pleasure or to stop the pain. And even when we act for the noblest reasons, the last link of the chain all too often drips with someone's blood.

Humboldt called me again two weeks after the evening when I'd bombed West Eighty-third Street with my cigarettes, and this time he stuck with Mr. Davis as a form of address. He thanked me for the copies of various documents forwarded him through Mr. Ring and said that the time had come for "all four of us" to sit down to lunch. *All four of us* meant Diane. I hadn't seen her since the morning of the day she'd left, and even then I hadn't really seen her; she'd been sleeping with her face buried in her pillow. I hadn't even talked to her. My heart speeded up in my chest, and I could feel a pulse tapping away in the wrist of the hand holding the telephone.

"There are a number of details to be worked out, and a number of pertinent arrangements to be discussed, and this seems to be the time to put that process in work," Humboldt said. He chuckled fatly in my ear, like a repulsive adult giving a child some minor treat. "It's always best to let some time pass before bringing the principals together, a little cooling-off period, but in my judgement a face-to-face meeting at this time would facilitate—"

"Let me get this straight," I said. "You're talking about—"

"Lunch," he said. "The day after tomorrow? Can you clear that on your schedule?" *Of course you can,* his voice said. *Just to see her again . . . to experience the slightest touch of her hand. Eh, Steve?*

"I don't have anything on for lunch Thursday anyhow, so that's not a problem. And I should bring my lawyer?"

The fat chuckle came again, shivering in my ear like something just turned out of a Jell-O mold. "I imagine Mr. Ring would like to be included, yes."

"Did you have a place in mind?" I wondered for a moment who would be paying for this lunch, and then had to smile at my own naiveté. I reached into my pocket for a cigarette and poked the tip of a toothpick under my thumbnail instead. I winced, brought the pick out, checked the tip for blood, saw none, and stuck it in my mouth.

Humboldt had said something, but I had missed it. The sight of the toothpick had reminded me all over again that I was floating smokeless on the waves of the world.

"Pardon me?"

"I asked if you know the Gotham Café on Fifty-third Street," he said, sounding a touch impatient now. "Between Madison and Park."

"No, but I'm sure I can find it."

"Noon?"

"Noon's fine," I said, and thought of telling him to tell Diane to wear the green dress with the little black speckles and the slit up the side. "I'll just check with my lawyer." It occurred to me that that was a pompous, hateful little phrase, one I couldn't wait to stop using.

"Do that, and call me back if there's a problem."

I called John Ring, who hemmed and hawed enough to justify his retainer (not outrageous, but considerable) and then said he supposed a meeting was in order "at this time."

I hung up, settled back in front of my computer terminal, and wondered how I was possibly going to be able to meet Diane again without at least one cigarette beforehand.

On the morning of our scheduled lunch, John Ring called and told me he couldn't make it, and that I would have to cancel. "It's my mother," he said, sounding harried. "She fell down the damned stairs and broke her hip. Out in Babylon. I'm leaving now for Penn Station. I'll have to take the train." He spoke in the tone of a man saying he'll have to go by camel across the Gobi.

I thought for a second, jiggling a fresh toothpick between my fingers. Two used ones lay beside my computer terminal, the ends frayed. I was going to have to watch that; it was all too easy to imagine my stomach filling up with sharp little splinterettes. The replacement of one bad habit with another seems almost inevitable, I've noticed.

"Steven? Are you there?"

"Yes," I said. "I'm sorry about your mother, but I'm going to keep the lunch-date."

He sighed, and when he spoke he sounded sympathetic as well as harried. "I understand that you want to see her, and that's the reason why you have to be very careful, and make no mistakes. You're not Donald Trump and she's not Ivana, but this isn't a no-faulter

we got here, either, where you get your decree by registered mail. You've done very well for yourself, Steven,
especially in the last five years."

"I know, but—"

"And for thuh-*ree* of those years," Ring overrode
me, now putting on his courtroom voice like an overcoat, "Diane Davis was not your wife, not your live-in
companion, and not by any stretch of the imagination
your helpmate. She was just Diane Coslaw from
Pound Ridge, and she did not go before you tossing
flower-petals or blowing a cornet."

"No, but I want to see her." And what I was
thinking would have driven him mad: I wanted to
see if she was wearing the green dress with the black
speckles, because she knew damned well it was my
favorite.

He sighed again. "I can't have this discussion, or I'm
going to miss my train. There isn't another one until
one-oh-one."

"Go and catch your train."

"I will, but first I'm going to make one more effort
to get through to you. A meeting like this is like a
joust. The lawyers are the knights; the clients are
reduced, for the time being, to no more than squires
with Sir Barrister's lance in one hand and the reins of
his horse in the other." His tone suggested that this
was an old image, and well-loved. "What you're telling
me is that, since I can't be there, you're going to hop
on my nag and go galloping at the other guy with no
lance, no armor, no faceplate, probably not even a
jockstrap."

"I want to see her," I said. "I want to see how she is.

How she looks. Hey, without you there, maybe Humboldt won't even want to talk."

"Oh, wouldn't that be nice," he said, and came out with a small, cynical laugh. "I'm not going to talk you out of it, am I?"

"No."

"All right, then I want you to follow certain instructions. If I find out you haven't, and that you've gummed up the works, I may decide it would be simpler to just resign the case. Are you hearing me?"

"I'm hearing you."

"Good. Don't yell at her, Steven. That's big number one. Are you hearing *that*?"

"Yes." I wasn't going to yell at her. If I could quit smoking two days after she had walked out—and stick to it—I thought I could get through a hundred minutes and three courses without calling her a bitch.

"Don't yell at him, that's number two."

"Okay."

"Don't just say okay. I know you don't like him, and he doesn't like you much, either."

"He's never even met me. How can he have an opinion about me one way or another?"

"Don't be dense," he said. "He's being *paid* to have an opinion, that's how. So say okay like you mean it."

"Okay like I mean it."

"Better." But *he* didn't say it like he really meant it; he said it like a man who is checking his watch.

"Don't get into substantive matters," he said. "Don't discuss financial-settlement issues, not even on a 'What would you think if I suggested this' basis. If he gets pissed off and asks why you kept the lunch-date if you weren't going to discuss nuts and bolts, tell him just what you told me, that you wanted to see your wife again."

"Okay."

"And if they leave at that point, can you live with it?"

"Yes." I didn't know if I could or not, but I thought I could, and I knew that Ring wanted to catch his train.

"As a lawyer—*your* lawyer—I'm telling you that this is a bullshit move, and that if it backfires in court, I'll call a recess just so I can pull you out into the hall and say I told you so. Now have you got that?"

"Yes. Say hello to your mother."

"Maybe tonight," Ring said, and now he sounded as if he were rolling his eyes. "I won't get a word in until then. I have to run, Steven."

"Okay."

"I hope she stands you up."

"I know you do."

He hung up and went to see his mother, out in Babylon. When I saw him next, a few days later, there was something between us that didn't quite bear discussion, although I think we would have talked about it if we had known each other even a little bit better. I saw it in his eyes and I suppose he saw it in mine, as well—the knowledge that if his mother hadn't fallen down the stairs and broken her hip, he might have wound up as dead as William Humboldt.

I walked from my office to the Gotham Café, leaving at eleven-fifteen and arriving across from the restaurant at eleven-forty-five. I got there early for my own peace of mind—to make sure the place was where Humboldt had said it was, in other words. That's the way I am, and pretty much the way I've always been. Diane used to call it my "obsessive streak" when we were first married, but I think that by the end she knew better. I don't trust the competence of others very easily, that's all. I realize it's a pain-in-the-ass characteristic, and I know it drove her crazy, but what she never seemed to realize was that I didn't exactly love it in myself, either. Some things take longer to change than others, though. And some things you can never change, no matter how hard you try.

The restaurant was right where Humboldt had said it would be, the location marked by a green awning with the words GOTHAM CAFÉ on it. A white city sky-line was traced across the plate-glass windows. It looked New York–trendy. It also looked pretty una-mazing, just one of the eight hundred or so pricey restaurants crammed together in midtown.

With the meeting-place located and my mind tem-porarily set at rest (about that, anyway; I was tense as hell about seeing Diane again and craving a cigarette like mad), I walked up to Madison and browsed in a luggage store for fifteen minutes. Mere window-shopping was no good; if Diane and Humboldt came from uptown, they might see me. Diane was liable to recognize me by the set of my shoulders and the hang of my topcoat even from behind, and I didn't want that. I didn't want them to know I'd arrived early. I thought it might look needy. So I went inside.

I bought an umbrella I didn't need and left the shop

at straight up noon by my watch, knowing I could step through the door of the Gotham Café at twelve-oh-five. My father's dictum: If you need to be there, show up five minutes early. If they need *you* to be there, show up five minutes late. I had reached a point where I didn't know who needed what or why or for how long, but my father's dictum seemed like the safest course. If it had been just Diane alone, I think I would have arrived dead on time.

No, that's probably a lie. I suppose if it had just been Diane, I would have gone in at eleven-forty-five, when I first arrived, and waited for her.

I stood under the awning for a moment, looking in. The place was bright, and I marked that down in its favor. I have an intense dislike for dark restaurants where you can't see what you're eating or drinking. The walls were white and hung with vibrant Impressionist drawings. You couldn't tell what they were, but that didn't matter; with their primary colors and broad, exuberant strokes, they hit your eyes like visual caffeine. I looked for Diane and saw a woman that might be her, seated about halfway down the long room and by the wall. It was hard to say, because her back was turned and I don't have her knack of recognition under difficult circumstances. But the heavyset, balding man she was sitting with certainly looked like a Humboldt. I took a deep breath, opened the restaurant door, and went in.

There are two phases of withdrawal from tobacco, and I'm convinced that it's the second that causes most cases of recidivism. The physical withdrawal lasts ten days to two weeks, and then most of the symptoms—sweats, headaches, muscle twitches, pounding eyes, insomnia, irritability—disappear. What follows is a much longer period of mental withdrawal. These symptoms may include mild to moderate depression, mourning, some degree of anhedonia (emotional flat-line, in other words), forgetfulness, even a species of transient dyslexia. I know all this stuff because I read up on it. Following what happened at the Gotham Café, it seemed very important that I do that. I suppose you'd have to say that my interest in the subject fell somewhere between the Land of Hobbies and the Kingdom of Obsession.

The most common symptom of phase-two withdrawal is a feeling of mild unreality. Nicotine improves synaptic transferral and improves concentration—widens the brain's information highway, in other words. It's not a big boost, and not really necessary to successful thinking (although most confirmed cigarette junkies believe differently), but when you take it away, you're left with a feeling—a *pervasive* feeling, in my case—that the world has taken on a decidedly dreamy cast. There were many times when it seemed to me that people and cars and the little sidewalk vignettes I observed were actually passing by me on a moving screen, a thing controlled by hidden stagehands turning enormous cranks and revolving enormous drums. It was also a little like being mildly stoned all the time, because the feeling was accompanied by a sense of helplessness and moral exhaustion, a feeling that things had to simply go on the way they were going, for good or for ill, because you (except of course it's me

I'm talking about) were just too damned busy *not-smoking* to do much of anything else.

I'm not sure how much all this bears on what happened, but I know it has *some* bearing, because I was pretty sure something was wrong with the maître d' almost as soon as I saw him, and as soon as he spoke to me, I knew.

He was tall, maybe forty-five, slim (in his tux, at least; in ordinary clothes he probably would have looked skinny), mustached. He had a leather-bound menu in one hand. He looked like battalions of maître d's in battalions of fancy New York restaurants, in other words. Except for his bow-tie, which was askew, and something on his shirt that was a splotch just above the place where his jacket buttoned. It looked like either gravy or a glob of some dark jelly. Also, several strands of his hair stuck up defiantly in back, making me think of Alfalfa in the old *Little Rascals* one-reelers. That almost made me burst out laughing—I was very nervous, remember—and I had to bite my lips to keep it in.

"Yes, sir?" he asked as I approached the desk. It came out sounding like *Yais sair?* All maître d's in New York City have accents, but it is never one you can positively identify. A girl I dated in the mid-eighties, one who *did* have a sense of humor (along with a fairly large drug habit, unfortunately), told me once that they all grew up on the same little island and hence all spoke the same language.

"What language is it?" I asked her.

"Snooti," she said, and I cracked up.

This thought came back to me as I looked past the

desk to the woman I'd seen while outside—I was now almost positive it was Diane—and I had to bite the insides of my lips again. As a result, Humboldt's name came out of me sounding like a half-smothered sneeze.

The maître d's high, pale brow contracted in a frown. His eyes bored into mine. I had taken them for brown as I approached the desk, but now they looked black.

"Pardon, sir?" he asked. It came out sounding like *Pahdun, sair* and looking like *Fuck you, Jack.* His long fingers, as pale as his brow—concert pianist's fingers, they looked like—tapped nervously on the cover of the menu. The tassel sticking out of it like some sort of half-assed bookmark swung back and forth.

"Humboldt," I said. "Party of three." I found I couldn't take my eyes off his bow-tie, so crooked that the left side of it was almost brushing the shelf under his chin, and that blob on his snowy-white dress shirt. Now that I was closer, it didn't look like either gravy or jelly; it looked like partially dried blood.

He was looking down at his reservations book, the rogue tuft at the back of his head waving back and forth over the rest of his slicked-down hair. I could see his scalp through the grooves his comb had laid down, and a speckle of dandruff on the shoulders of his tux. It occurred to me that a good headwaiter might have fired an underling put together in such sloppy fashion.

"Ah, yes, *monsieur.*" (*Ah yais, messoo.*) He had found the name. "Your party is—" He was starting to look up. He stopped abruptly, and his eyes sharpened even more, if that was possible, as he looked past me and down. "You cannot bring that dog in here," he said sharply. "How many times have I told you you can't bring that *dog* in here!"

He didn't quite shout, but spoke so loudly that several of the diners closest to his pulpit-like desk stopped eating and looked around curiously.

I looked around myself. He had been so emphatic I expected to see *somebody's* dog, but there was no one behind me and most certainly no dog. It occurred to me then, I don't know why, that he was talking about my umbrella, that perhaps on the Island of the Maître D's, *dog* was a slang term for umbrella, especially when carried by a patron on a day when rain did not seem likely.

I looked back at the maître d' and saw that he had already started away from his desk, holding my menu in his hands. He must have sensed that I wasn't following, because he looked back over his shoulder, eyebrows slightly raised. There was nothing on his face now but polite enquiry—*Are you coming, messoo?*—and I came. I knew something was wrong with him, but I came. I could not take the time or effort to try to decide what might be wrong with the maître d' of a restaurant where I had never been before today and where I would probably never be again; I had Humboldt and Diane to deal with, I had to do it without smoking, and the maître d' of the Gotham Café would have to take care of his own problems, dog included.

Diane turned around and at first I saw nothing in her face and in her eyes but a kind of frozen politeness. Then, just below it, I saw anger, or thought I did. We'd done a lot of arguing during our last three or four months together, but I couldn't recall ever seeing the sort of concealed anger I sensed in her now, anger that was meant to be hidden by the makeup and the new dress (blue, no speckles, no slit up the side) and the new hairdo. The heavyset man she was with was saying something, and she reached out and touched his arm. As he turned toward me, beginning to get to his feet, I saw something else in her face. She was afraid of me as well as angry with me. And although she hadn't said a single word, I was already furious at her. Everything on her face and in her eyes was negative; she might as well have been wearing a CLOSED UNTIL FURTHER NOTICE sign on her forehead. I thought I deserved better.

"Monsieur," the maître d' said, pulling out the chair to Diane's left. I barely heard him, and certainly any thought of his eccentric behavior and crooked bow-tie had left my head. I think that even the subject of tobacco had briefly vacated my head for the first time since I'd quit smoking. I could only consider the careful composure of her face and marvel at how I could be angry with her and still want her so much it made me ache to look at her. Absence may or may not make the heart grow fonder, but it certainly freshens the eye.

I also found time to wonder if I had really seen all I'd surmised. Anger? Yes, that was possible, even likely. If she hadn't been angry with me to at least some degree, she never would have left in the first place, I supposed. But afraid? Why in God's name would Diane be afraid of me? I'd never laid a single finger on her. Yes, I suppose I had raised my voice during some of our arguments, but so had she.

"Enjoy your lunch, monsieur," the maître d' said from some other universe—the one where service people usually stay, only poking their heads into ours when we call them, either because we need something or to complain.

"Mr. Davis, I'm Bill Humboldt," Diane's companion said. He held out a large hand that looked reddish and chapped. I shook it briefly. The rest of him was as big as his hand, and his broad face wore the sort of flush habitual drinkers often get after the first one of the day. I put him in his mid-forties, about ten years away from the time when his sagging cheeks would turn into jowls.

"Pleasure," I said, not thinking about what I was saying any more than I was thinking about the maître d' with the blob on his shirt, only wanting to get the hand-shaking part over so I could turn back to the pretty blonde with the rose-and-cream complexion, the pale pink lips, and the trim, slim figure. The woman who had, not so long ago, liked to whisper "Do me do me do me" in my ear while she held onto my ass like a saddle with two pommels.

"Where is Mr. Ring?" Humboldt asked, looking around (a bit theatrically, I thought).

"Mr. Ring is on his way to Long Island. His mother fell downstairs and broke her hip."

"Oh, wonderful," Humboldt said. He picked up the half-finished martini in front of him on the table and drained it until the olive with the toothpick in it rested against his lips. He spat it back, then set the glass down and looked at me. "And I bet I can guess what he told you."

I heard this but paid no attention. For the time being, Humboldt was no more important than minor static on a radio program you really want to hear. I looked at Diane instead. It was marvellous, really, how she looked smarter and prettier than previous. As if she had learned things—yes, even after only two weeks of separation, and while living with Ernie and Dee Dee Coslaw in Pound Ridge—that I could never know.

"How are you, Steve?" she asked.

"Fine," I said. Then, "Not so fine, actually. I've missed you."

Only watchful silence from the lady greeted this. Those big blue-green eyes looking at me, no more. Certainly no return serve, no *I've missed you, too*.

"And I quit smoking. That's also played hell with my peace of mind."

"Did you, finally? Good for you."

I felt another flash of anger, this time a really ugly one, at her politely dismissive tone. As if I might not be telling the truth, but it didn't really matter if I was. She'd carped at me about the cigarettes every day for two years, it seemed—how they were going to give me cancer, how they were going to give *her* cancer, how she wouldn't even consider getting pregnant until I stopped, so I could just save any breath I might have been planning to waste on *that* subject—and now all at once it didn't matter anymore, because I didn't matter anymore.

"We have a little business to transact," Humboldt said. "If you don't mind, that is."

There was one of those big, boxy lawyer suitcases on the floor beside him. He picked it up with a grunt and set it on the chair where my lawyer would have been if his mother hadn't broken her hip. Humboldt began unsnapping the clasps, but I quit paying attention at that point. The fact was, I *did* mind. It wasn't a matter of caution, either; it was a matter of priorities. I felt an instant's gratitude that Ring had been called away. It had certainly clarified the issues.

I looked at Diane and said, "I want to try again. Can we reconcile? Is there any chance of that?"

The look of absolute horror on her face crashed hopes I hadn't even known I'd been holding onto. Instead of answering, she looked past me at Humboldt.

"You said we didn't have to talk about this!" Her voice was trembling, accusatory. "You said you wouldn't even let it come up!"

Humboldt looked a little flustered. He shrugged and glanced briefly down at his empty martini glass before looking back up at Diane. I think he was wishing he'd ordered a double. "I didn't know Mr. Davis would be attending this meeting without his lawyer. You should have called me, Mr. Davis. Since you did not, I feel it necessary to inform you that Diane did not greenlight this meeting with any thoughts of reconciliation in mind. Her decision to seek a divorce is final."

He glanced at her briefly, seeking confirmation, and got it. She was nodding emphatically. Her cheeks were considerably brighter than they had been when I sat down, and it was not the sort of flush I associate with embarrassment. "You *bet* it is," she said, and I saw that furious look on her face again.

"Diane, why?" I hated the plaintive note I heard in my voice, a sound almost like a sheep's bleat, but there wasn't a goddamned thing I could do about it. *"Why?"*

"Oh Jesus," she said. "Are you telling me you really don't know?"

"Yes—"

Her cheeks were brighter than ever, the flush now rising almost to her temples. "No, probably you don't. Isn't that *typical*." She picked up her water and spilled the top two inches on the tablecloth because her hand was trembling. I flashed back at once—I mean *kapow*—to the day she'd left, remembering how I'd knocked the glass of orange juice onto the floor and how I'd cautioned myself not to try picking up the broken pieces of glass until my hands had settled down, and how I'd gone ahead anyway and cut myself for my pains.

"Stop it, this is counterproductive," Humboldt said. He sounded like a playground monitor trying to prevent a scuffle before it gets started, but his eyes were sweeping the rear part of the room, looking for our waiter, or any waiter whose eye he could catch. He was a lot less interested in us, at that particular moment, than he was in obtaining what the British like to call "the other half."

"I just want to know—" I began.

"What you want to *know* doesn't have anything to do with why we're *here*," Humboldt said, and for a moment he sounded as sharp and alert as he probably had been when he first strode out of law school with his diploma in his hand.

"Yes, right, *finally*," Diane said. She spoke in a brittle, urgent voice. "Finally it's not about what you *want*, what you *need*."

"I don't know what that means, but I'm willing to listen," I said. "We could try counselling, I'm not against it if maybe—"

She raised her hands to shoulder-level, palms out. "Oh God, Mr. Macho's gone New Age," she said, then dropped her hands back into her lap. "After all the days you rode off into the sunset, tall in the saddle. Say it ain't so, Joe."

"Stop it," Humboldt told her. He looked from his client to his client's soon-to-be ex-husband (it was going to happen, all right; even the slight unreality that comes with *not-smoking* couldn't conceal that self-evident truth from me by that point). "One more word from either of you and I'm going to declare this luncheon at an end." He gave us a small smile, one so obviously manufactured that I found it perversely endearing. "And we haven't even heard the specials yet."

That—the first mention of food since I'd joined them—was just before the bad things started to happen, and I remember smelling salmon from one of the nearby tables. In the two weeks since I'd quit smoking, my sense of smell had become incredibly sharp, but I do not count that as much of a blessing, especially when it comes to salmon. I used to like it, but now I can't abide the smell of it, let alone the taste. To me it smells of pain and fear and blood and death.

"He started it," Diane said sulkily.

You *started it,* you *were the one who walked out,* I thought, but I kept it to myself. Humboldt clearly meant what he said; he would take Diane by the hand and walk her out of the restaurant if we started that schoolyard *no-I-didn't, yes-you-did* shit. Not even the prospect of another drink would hold him here.

"Okay," I said mildly . . . and I had to work hard to achieve that mild tone, believe me. "I started it. What's next?" I knew, of course; papers, papers, papers. And probably the only satisfaction I was going to get out of this sorry situation was telling them that I wasn't going to sign any, or even look at any, on the advice of my lawyer. I glanced at Diane again, but she was looking down at her empty plate and her hair hid her face. I felt a strong urge to grab her by the shoulders and shake her inside her new blue dress like a pebble inside of a gourd. *Do you think you're in this alone?* I would shout at her. *Do you think you're in this alone? Well, the Marlboro Man has got news for you, sweetheart— you're a stubborn, self-indulgent little bi—*

"Mr. Davis?" Humboldt asked politely.

I looked around at him.

"There you are," he said. "I thought we'd lost you again."

"Not at all," I said.

"Good. Lovely."

He had several sheafs of paper in his hands. They were held together by those paperclips that come in different colors—red, blue, yellow, purple. They went well with the Impressionist drawings on the walls of the Gotham Café. It occurred to me that I had come abysmally unprepared for this meeting, and not just because my lawyer was on the twelve-thirty-three to Babylon, either. Diane had her new dress; Humboldt had his Brinks truck of a briefcase, plus documents held together by color-coded paperclips; all I had was a new umbrella on a sunny day. I looked down at where it lay beside my chair (it had never crossed my mind to check it) and saw there was still a price-tag dangling from the handle. All at once I felt like Minnie Pearl.

The room smelled wonderful, as most restaurants do since they banned smoking in them—of flowers and wine and fresh coffee and chocolate and pastry— but what I smelled most clearly was salmon. I remember thinking that it smelled very good, and that I would probably order some. I also remember thinking that if I could eat at a meeting like this, I could probably eat anywhere.

"I have here a number of forms which will allow both you and Ms. Davis to remain financially mobile while assuring that neither of you will have unfair access to the funds you've both worked so hard to accumulate," Humboldt said. "I also have preliminary court notifications which need to be signed by you, and forms that will allow us to put your bonds and T-bills in an escrow account until your current situation is settled by the court."

I opened my mouth to tell him I wasn't going to sign anything, and if that meant the meeting was over so be it, but I didn't get out so much as a single word. Before I could, I was interrupted by the maître d'. He was screaming as well as talking, and I've tried to indicate that, but a bunch of *e*'s strung together can't really convey the quality of that sound. It was as if he had a bellyful of steam and a teakettle whistle caught in his throat.

"That dog . . . Eeeeee! . . . I told you time and again about that dog . . . Eeeeee! . . . All that time I can't sleep . . . Eeeeee! . . . She says cut your face, that cunt . . . Eeeeee! . . . How you

*tease me! . . . Eeeeeee! . . . And now you bring that dog in here
. . . Eeeeeee!"*

The room fell silent at once, of course, diners looking up in astonishment from their meals or their conversations as the thin, pale, black-clad figure came
stalking across the room with its face outthrust and
its long, storklike legs scissoring. The maître d's bow-
tie had turned a full ninety degrees from its normal
position, so it now looked like the hands of a clock
indicating the hour of six. His hands were clasped
behind his back as he walked, and bent forward
slightly from the waist as he was, he made me think
of a drawing in my sixth-grade literature book, an
illustration of Washington Irving's unfortunate
schoolteacher, Ichabod Crane.

It was me he was looking at, me he was approaching. I stared at him, feeling almost hypnotized—it was
like one of those dreams where you discover that you
haven't studied for the exam you're supposed to take
or that you're attending a White House dinner in your
honor with no clothes on—and I might have stayed
that way if Humboldt hadn't moved.

I heard his chair scrape back and glanced at him. He
was standing up, his napkin held loosely in one hand.
He looked surprised, but he also looked furious. I suddenly realized two things: that he was drunk, quite
drunk, in fact, and that he saw this as a smirch on both
his hospitality and his competence. He had chosen the
restaurant, after all, and now look—the master of cer-
emonies had gone bonkers.

"Eeeeee! . . . I teach you! For the last time I teach you . . ."

"Oh my God, he's wet his pants," a woman at a

nearby table murmured. Her voice was low but perfectly audible in the silence as the maître d' drew in a fresh breath with which to scream, and I saw she was right. The crotch of the skinny man's dress pants was soaked.

"See here, you idiot," Humboldt said, turning to face him, and the maître d' brought his left hand out from behind his back. In it was the largest butcher-knife I have ever seen. It had to have been two feet long, with the top part of its cutting edge slightly belled, like a cutlass in an old pirate movie.

"*Look out!*" I yelled at Humboldt, and at one of the tables against the wall a skinny man in rimless spectacles screamed, ejecting a mouthful of chewed brown fragments of food onto the tablecloth in front of him.

Humboldt seemed to hear neither my yell nor the other man's scream. He was frowning thunderously at the maître d'. "You don't need to expect to see me in here again if this is the way—" Humboldt began.

"*Eeeeeee! EEEEEEEEE!*" the maître d' screamed, and swung the butcher-knife flat through the air. It made a kind of whickering sound, like a whispered sentence. The period was the sound of the blade burying itself in William Humboldt's right cheek. Blood exploded out of the wound in a furious spray of tiny droplets. They decorated the tablecloth in a fan-shaped stipplework, and I clearly saw (I will never forget it) one bright red drop fall into my waterglass and then dive for the bottom with a pinkish filament like a tail stretching out behind it. It looked like a bloody tadpole.

Humboldt's cheek snapped open, revealing his

teeth, and as he clapped his hand to the gouting wound, I saw something pinkish-white lying on the shoulder of his charcoal-gray suitcoat. It wasn't until the whole thing was over that I realized it must have been his earlobe.

"Tell this in your ears!" the maître d' screamed furiously at Diane's bleeding lawyer, who stood there with one hand clapped to his cheek. Except for the blood pouring over and between his fingers, Humboldt looked weirdly like Jack Benny doing one of his famous double-takes. *"Call this to your hateful tattle-tale friends of the street . . . you misery . . . Eeeeeee! . . . DOG-LOVER!"*

Now other people were screaming, mostly at the sight of the blood. Humboldt was a big man, and he was bleeding like a stuck pig. I could hear it pattering on the floor like water from a broken pipe, and the front of his white shirt was now red. His tie, which had been red to start with, was now black.

"Steve?" Diane said. *"Steven?"*

A man and a woman had been having lunch at the table behind her and slightly to her left. Now the man—about thirty and handsome in the way George Hamilton used to be—bolted to his feet and ran toward the front of the restaurant. *"Troy, don't go without me!"* his date screamed, but Troy never looked back. He'd forgotten all about a library book he was supposed to return, it seemed, or maybe about how he'd promised to wax the car.

If there had been a paralysis in the room—I can't actually say if there was or not, although I seem to have seen a great deal, and to remember it all—that broke it. There were more screams and other people got up. Several tables were overturned. Glasses and china shattered on the floor. I saw a man with his arm around the waist of his female companion hurry past behind the maître d'; her hand was clamped into his shoulder like a claw. For a moment her eyes met mine, and they were as empty as the eyes of a Greek bust. Her face was dead pale, haglike with horror.

All of this might have happened in ten seconds, or maybe twenty. I remember it like a series of photographs or filmstrips, but it has no timeline. Time ceased to exist for me at the moment Alfalfa the maître d' brought his left hand out from behind his back and I saw the butcher-knife. During that time, the man in the tuxedo continued to spew out a confusion of words in his special maître d's language, the one that old girl-friend of mine had called Snooti. Some of it really *was* in a foreign language, some of it was English but completely without sense, and some of it was striking . . . almost haunting. Have you ever read any of Dutch Schultz's long, confused deathbed statement? It was like that. Much of it I can't remember. What I can remember I suppose I'll never forget.

Humboldt staggered backward, still holding his lacerated cheek. The backs of his knees struck the seat of his chair and he sat down heavily on it. *He looks like someone who's just been told he's disinherited,* I thought. He started to turn toward Diane and me, his eyes wide and shocked. I had time to see there were tears spilling out of them, and then the maître d' wrapped both hands around the handle of the butcher-knife and buried it in the center of Humboldt's head. It made a sound like someone whacking a pile of towels with a cane.

"Boot!" Humboldt cried. I'm quite sure that's what his last word on planet Earth was—"boot." Then his weeping eyes rolled up to whites and he slumped forward onto his plate, sweeping his own glassware off the table and onto the floor with one outflung hand. As this happened, the maître d'—all his hair was sticking up in back, now, not just some of it—pried the long knife out of his head. Blood sprayed out of the head-wound in a kind of vertical curtain, and splashed the front of Diane's dress. She raised her hands to her shoulders with the palms turned out once again, but this time it was in horror rather than exasperation. She shrieked, and then clapped her bloodspattered hands to her face, over her eyes. The maître d' paid no attention to her. Instead, he turned to me.

"That dog of yours," he said, speaking in an almost conversational tone. He registered absolutely no interest in or even knowledge of the screaming, terrified people stampeding behind him toward the doors. His eyes were very large, very dark. They looked brown to me again, but there seemed to be black circles around the irises. "That dog of yours is so much rage. All the radios of Coney Island don't make up to dat dog, you motherfucker."

I had the umbrella in my hand, and the one thing I can't remember, no matter how hard I try, is when I grabbed it. I think it must have been while Humboldt was standing transfixed by the realization that his mouth had been expanded by eight inches or so, but I simply can't remember. I remember the man who looked like George Hamilton bolting for the door, and I know his name was Troy because that's what his companion called after him, but I can't remember picking up the umbrella I'd bought in the luggage store. It *was* in my hand, though, the price-tag sticking out of the bottom of my fist, and when the maître d' bent forward as if bowing and ran the knife through the air at me—meaning, I think, to bury it in my throat—I raised it and brought it down on his wrist, like an old-time teacher whacking an unruly pupil with his hickory stick.

"Ud!" the maître d' grunted as his hand was driven sharply down and the blade meant for my throat ploughed through the soggy pinkish tablecloth instead. He held on, though, and pulled it back. If I'd tried to hit his knife-hand again I'm sure I would have missed, but I didn't. I swung at his face, and fetched him an excellent lick—as excellent a lick as one can administer with an umbrella, anyway—up the side of his head. And as I did, the umbrella popped open like the visual punchline of a slapstick act.

I didn't think it was funny, though. The bloom of the umbrella hid him from me completely as he staggered backward with his free hand flying up to the place where I'd hit him, and I didn't like not being able to see him. In fact, it terrified me. Not that I wasn't terrified already.

I grabbed Diane's wrist and yanked her to her feet. She came without a word, took a step toward me, then stumbled on her high heels and fell clumsily into my arms. I was aware of her breasts pushing against me, and the wet, warm clamminess over them.

"Eeeee! You boinker!" the maître d' screamed, or perhaps it was a "boinger" he called me. It probably doesn't matter, I know that, and yet it quite often seems to me that it does. Late at night, the little questions haunt me as much as the big ones. *"You boinking bastard! All these radios! Hush-do-baba! Fuck Cousin Brucie! Fuck YOU!"*

He started around the table toward us (the area behind him was completely empty now, and looked like the aftermath of a brawl in a western movie saloon). My umbrella was still lying on the table with the opened top jutting off the far side, and the maître d' bumped it with his hip. It fell off in front of him, and while he kicked it aside, I set Diane back on her feet and pulled her toward the far side of the room. The front door was no good; it was probably too far away in any case, but even if we could get there, it was still jammed tight with frightened, screaming people. If he wanted me—or both of us—he would have no trouble catching us and carving us like a couple of turkeys.

"Bugs! You bugs! . . . Eeeeee! . . . So much for your dog, eh? So much for your barking dog!"

"Make him stop!" Diane screamed. *"Oh Jesus, he's going to kill us both, make him stop!"*

"I rot you, you abominations!" Closer, now. The umbrella hadn't held him up for long, that was for sure. *"I rot you and all your trulls!"*

I saw three doors, two of them facing each other in a small alcove where there was also a pay telephone. Men's and women's rooms. No good. Even if they were single toilets with locks on the doors, they were no good. A nut like this one behind us would have no trouble bashing a bathroom lock off its screws, and we would have nowhere to run.

I dragged her toward the third door and shoved through it into a world of clean green tiles, strong fluorescent light, gleaming chrome, and steamy odors of food. The smell of salmon dominated. Humboldt had never gotten a chance to ask about the specials, but I thought I knew what at least one of them had been.

A waiter was standing there with a loaded tray balanced on the flat of one hand, his mouth agape and his eyes wide. He looked like Gimpel the Fool in that Isaac Singer story. "What—" he said, and then I shoved him aside. The tray went flying, with plates and glassware shattering against the wall.

"Ay!" a man yelled. He was huge, wearing a white smock and a white chef's hat like a cloud. There was a red bandanna around his neck, and in one hand he held a ladle that was dripping some sort of brown sauce. "Ay, you can't come in here like-a dat!"

"We have to get out," I said. "He's crazy. He's—"

An idea struck me then, a way of explaining without explaining, and I put my hand over Diane's left breast for a moment, on the soaked cloth of her dress. It was the last time I ever touched her intimately, and I don't know if it felt good or not. I held my hand out to the chef, showing him a palm streaked with Humboldt's blood.

"Good Christ," he said. "Here. Inna da back."

At that instant, the door we'd come through burst open again and the maître d' rolled in, eyes wild, hair sticking out everywhere like fur on a hedgehog that's tucked itself into a ball. He looked around, saw the waiter, dismissed him, saw me, and rushed at me.

I bolted again, dragging Diane with me, shoving blindly at the softbellied bulk of the chef. We went past him, the front of Diane's dress leaving a smear of blood on the front of his tunic. I saw he wasn't coming with us, that he was turning toward the maître d' instead, and wanted to warn him, wanted to tell him that wouldn't work, that it was the worst idea in the world and likely to be the last idea he ever had, but there was no time.

"Ay!" the chef cried. "Ay, Guy, what's dis?" He said the maître d's name as the French do, so it rhymes with *free,* and then he didn't say anything at all. There was a heavy thud that made me think of the sound of the knife burying itself in Humboldt's skull, and then the cook screamed. It had a watery sound. It was followed by a thick wet splat that haunts my dreams. I don't know what it was, and I don't want to know.

I yanked Diane down a narrow aisle between two stoves that baked a furious dull heat out at us. There was a door at the end, locked shut by two heavy steel bolts. I reached for the top one and then heard Guy, The Maître d' from Hell, coming after us, babbling.

I wanted to keep at the bolt, wanted to believe I could open the door and get us outside before he could get within sticking distance, but part of me—the part that was determined to live—knew better. I pushed Diane against the door, stepped in front of her in a protective maneuver that must go all the way back to the Ice Age, and faced him.

He came running up the narrow aisle between the stoves with the knife gripped in his left hand and raised above his head. His mouth was open and pulled back from a set of dingy, eroded teeth. Any hope of help I might have had from Gimpel the Fool disappeared. He was cowering against the wall beside the door to the restaurant. His fingers were buried deep inside his mouth, making him look more like the village idiot than ever.

"*Forgetful of me you shouldn't have been!*" Guy screamed, sounding like Yoda in the *Star Wars* movies. "*Your hateful dog! . . . Your loud music, so disharmonious! . . . Eeeee! . . . How you ever—*"

There was a large pot on one of the front burners of the lefthand stove. I reached out for it and slapped it at him. It was over an hour before I realized how badly I'd burned my hand doing that; I had a palmful of blisters like little buns, and more blisters on my three middle fingers. The pot skidded off its burner and tipped over in midair, dousing Guy from the waist down with what looked like corn, rice, and maybe two gallons of boiling water.

He screamed, staggered backward, and put the hand that wasn't holding the knife down on the other stove, almost directly into the blue-yellow gasflame underneath a skillet where mushrooms which had been sautéing were now turning to charcoal. He screamed again, this time in a register so high it hurt my ears, and held his hand up before his eyes, as if not able to believe it was connected to him.

I looked to my right and saw a little nestle of cleaning equipment beside the door—Glass-X and Clorox and Janitor In A Drum on a shelf, a broom with a dustpan stuck on top of the handle like a hat, and a mop in a steel bucket with a squeegee on the side.

As Guy came toward me again, holding the knife in the hand that wasn't red and swelling up like an inner-tube, I grabbed the handle of the mop, used it to roll the bucket in front of me on its little casters, and then jabbed it out at him. Guy pulled back with his upper body but stood his ground. There was a peculiar, twitching little smile on his lips. He looked like a dog who has forgotten, temporarily, at least, how to snarl. He held the knife up in front of his face and made several mystic passes with it. The overhead fluorescents glimmered liquidly on the blade . . . where it wasn't caked with blood, that was. He didn't seem to feel any pain in his burned hand, or in his legs, although they had been doused with boiling water and his tuxedo pants were spackled with rice.

"Rotten bugger," Guy said, making his mystic passes. He was like a Crusader preparing to go into battle. If, that was, you could imagine a Crusader in a rice-caked tux. "Kill you like I did your nasty barking dog."

"I don't have a dog," I said. "I *can't* have a dog. It's in the lease."

I think it was the only thing I said to him during the whole nightmare, and I'm not entirely sure I *did* say it out loud. It might only have been a thought. Behind him, I could see the chef struggling to his feet. He had one hand wrapped around the handle of the kitchen's big refrigerator and the other clapped to his blood-stained tunic, which was torn open across the swelling of his stomach in a big purple grin. He was doing his best to hold his plumbing in, but it was a battle he was losing. One loop of intestines, shiny and bruise-colored, already hung out, resting against his left side like some awful watch-chain.

Guy feinted at me with his knife. I countered by shoving the mop-bucket at him, and he drew back. I pulled it to me again and stood there with my hands wrapped around the wooden mop-handle, ready to shove the bucket at him if he moved. My own hand was throbbing and I could feel sweat trickling down my cheeks like hot oil. Behind Guy, the cook had managed to get all the way up. Slowly, like an invalid in early recovery from a serious operation, he started working his way down the aisle toward Gimpel the Fool. I wished him well.

"Undo those bolts," I said to Diane.

"What?"

"The bolts on the *door*. Undo them."

"I can't move," she said. She was crying so hard I could barely understand her. "You're *crushing* me."

I moved forward a little to give her room. Guy bared his teeth at me. Mock-jabbed with the knife, then pulled it back, grinning his nervous, snarly little grin as I rolled the bucket at him again on its squeaky casters.

"Bug-infested stinkpot," he said. He sounded like a man discussing the Mets' chances in the forthcoming campaign. "Let's see you play your radio this loud now, stinkpot. It gives you a change in your thinking, doesn't it? *Boink!*"

He jabbed. I rolled. But this time he didn't pull back as far, and I realized he was nerving himself up. He meant to go for it, and soon. I could feel Diane's breasts brush against my back as she gasped for breath.

I'd given her room, but she hadn't turned around to work the bolts. She was just standing there.

"Open the door," I told her, speaking out of the side of my mouth like a prison con. "Pull the goddam bolts, Diane."

"I can't," she sobbed. "I can't, I don't have any strength in my hands. Make him stop, Steven, don't stand there *talking* with him, make him *stop*."

She was driving me insane. I really thought she was. "You turn around and pull those bolts, Diane, or I'll just stand aside and let—"

"*EEEEEEEE!*" he screamed, and charged, waving and stabbing with the knife.

I slammed the mop-bucket forward with all the force I could muster, and swept his legs out from under him. He howled and brought the knife down in a long, desperate stroke. Any closer and it would have torn off the tip of my nose. Then he landed spraddled awkwardly on wide-spread knees, with his face just above the mop-squeezing gadget hung on the side of the bucket. Perfect! I drove the mophead into the nape of his neck. The strings draggled down over the shoulders of his black jacket like a witch-wig. His face slammed into the squeegee. I bent, grabbed the handle with my free hand, and clamped it shut. Guy shrieked with pain, the sound muffled by the mop.

"*PULL THOSE BOLTS!*" I screamed at Diane. "*PULL THOSE BOLTS, YOU USELESS BITCH! PULL—*"

Thud! Something hard and pointed slammed into my left buttock. I staggered forward with a yell— more surprise than pain, I think, although it *did* hurt. I went to one knee and lost my hold on the squeegee handle. Guy pulled back, slipping out from under the stringy head of the mop at the same time, breathing so loudly he sounded almost as if he were barking. It hadn't slowed him down much, though; he lashed out at me with the knife as soon as he was clear of the bucket. I pulled back, feeling the breeze as the blade cut the air beside my cheek.

It was only as I scrambled up that I realized what had happened, what she had done. I snatched a quick glance over my shoulder at her. She stared back defiantly, her back pressed against the door. A crazy thought came to me: she *wanted* me to get killed. Had perhaps even planned it, the whole thing. Found herself a crazy maître d' and—

Her eyes widened. *"Look out!"*

I turned back just in time to see him lunging at me. The sides of his face were bright red, except for the big white spots made by the drain-holes in the squeegee. I rammed the mophead at him, aiming for the throat and getting his chest instead. I stopped his charge and actually knocked him backward a step. What happened then was only luck. He slipped in water from the overturned bucket and went down hard, slamming his head on the tiles. Not thinking and just vaguely aware that I was screaming, I snatched up the skillet of mushrooms from the stove and brought it down on his upturned face as hard as I could. There was a muffled thump, followed by a horrible (but mercifully brief) hissing sound as the skin of his cheeks and forehead boiled.

I turned, shoved Diane aside, and drew the bolts

holding the door shut. I opened the door and sunlight hit me like a hammer. And the smell of the air. I can't remember air ever smelling better, not even when I was a kid, and it was the first day of summer vacation.

I grabbed Diane's arm and pulled her out into a narrow alley lined with padlocked trash-bins. At the far end of this narrow stone slit, like a vision of heaven, was Fifty-third Street with traffic going heedlessly back and forth. I looked over my shoulder and through the open kitchen door. Guy lay on his back with carbonized mushrooms circling his head like an existential diadem. The skillet had slid off to one side, revealing a face that was red and swelling with blisters. One of his eyes was open, but it looked unseeingly up at the fluorescent lights. Behind him, the kitchen was empty. There was a pool of blood on the floor and bloody handprints on the white enamel front of the walk-in fridge, but both the chef and Gimpel the Fool were gone.

I slammed the door shut and pointed down the alley. "Go on."

She didn't move, only looked at me.

I shoved her lightly on her left shoulder. "Go!"

She raised a hand like a traffic-cop, shook her head, then pointed a finger at me. "Don't you touch me."

"What'll you do? Sic your lawyer on me? I think he's dead, sweetheart."

"Don't you patronize me like that. Don't you *dare*. And don't touch me, Steven, I'm warning you."

The kitchen door burst open. Moving, not thinking but just moving, I slammed it shut again. I heard a muffled cry—whether anger or pain I didn't know and didn't care—just before it clicked shut. I leaned my back against it and braced my feet. "Do you want to stand here and discuss it?" I asked her. "He's still pretty lively, by the sound." He hit the door again. I rocked with it, then slammed it shut. I waited for him to try again, but he didn't.

Diane gave me a long look, glarey and uncertain, and then started walking up the alleyway with her head down and her hair hanging at the sides of her neck. I stood with my back against the door until she got about three quarters of the way to the street, then stood away from it, watching it warily. No one came out, but I decided that wasn't going to guarantee any peace of mind. I dragged one of the trash-bins in front of the door, then set off after Diane, jogging.

When I got to the mouth of the alley, she wasn't there anymore. I looked right, toward Madison, and didn't see her. I looked left and there she was, wandering slowly across Fifty-third on a diagonal, her head still down and her hair still hanging like curtains at the sides of her face. No one paid any attention to her; the people in front of the Gotham Café were gawking through the plate-glass windows like people in front of the New England Aquarium shark-tank at feeding time. Sirens were approaching, a lot of them.

I went across the street, reached for her shoulder, thought better of it. I settled for calling her name, instead.

She turned around, her eyes dulled with horror and shock. The front of her dress had turned into a grisly purple bib. She stank of blood and spent adrenaline.

"Leave me alone," she said. "I never want to see you again, Steven."

"You kicked my ass in there," I said. "You kicked my ass and almost got me killed. Both of us. I can't believe you, Diane."

"I've wanted to kick your ass for the last fourteen months," she said. "When it comes to fulfilling our dreams, we can't always pick our times, can w—"

I slapped her across the face. I didn't think about it, I just did it, and few things in my adult life have given me so much pleasure. I'm ashamed of that, but I've come too far in this story to tell a lie, even one of omission.

Her head rocked back. Her eyes widened in shock and pain, losing that dull, traumatized look.

"You bastard!" she cried, her hand going to her cheek. Now tears were brimming in her eyes. "Oh, you *bastard!*"

"I saved your life," I said. "Don't you realize that? Doesn't that get through? *I saved your fucking life.*"

"You son of a bitch," she whispered. "You controlling, judgemental, small-minded, conceited, complacent son of a bitch. I hate you."

"Did you even hear me? If it wasn't for the conceited, small-minded son of a bitch, you'd be dead now."

"If it wasn't for you, I wouldn't have been there in the first place," she said as the first three police cars came screaming down Fifty-third Street and pulled up in front of the Gotham Café. Cops poured out of them like clowns in a circus act. "If you ever touch me again, I'll scratch your eyes out, Steve," she said. "Stay away from me."

I had to put my hands in my armpits. They wanted to kill her, to reach out and wrap themselves around her neck and just kill her.

She walked seven or eight steps, then turned back to me. She was smiling. It was a terrible smile, more awful than any expression I had seen on the face of Guy the Demon Waiter. "I had lovers," she said, smiling her terrible smile. She was lying. The lie was all over her face, but that didn't make it hurt any less. She *wished* it was true; that was all over her face, too. "Three of them over the last year or so. You weren't any good at it, so I found men who were."

She turned and walked down the street, like a woman who was sixty-five instead of twenty-seven. I stood and watched her. Just before she reached the corner I shouted it again. It was the one thing I couldn't get past; it was stuck in my throat like a chicken bone. "I saved your *life!* Your goddam *life!*"

She paused at the corner and turned back to me. The terrible smile was still on her face. "No," she said. "You didn't."

Then she went on around the corner. I haven't seen her since, although I suppose I will. I'll see her in court, as the saying goes.

I found a market on the next block and bought a package of Marlboros. When I got back to the corner of Madison and Fifty-third, Fifty-third had been blocked off with those blue sawhorses the cops use to protect crime-scenes and parade routes. I could see the restaurant, though. I could see it just fine. I sat down on the curb, lit a cigarette, and observed developments. Half a dozen rescue vehicles arrived—a scream of ambulances, I guess you could say. The chef went into the first one, unconscious but apparently still alive. His brief appearance before his fans on Fifty-third Street was followed by a body-bag on a stretcher—Humboldt. Next came Guy, strapped tightly to a stretcher and staring wildly around as he was loaded into the back of an ambulance. I thought that for just a moment his eyes met mine, but that was probably my imagination.

As Guy's ambulance pulled away, rolling through a hole in the sawhorse barricade provided by two uniformed cops, I tossed the cigarette I'd been smoking in the gutter. I hadn't gone through this day just to start killing myself with tobacco again, I decided.

I looked after the departing ambulance and tried to imagine the man inside it living wherever maître d's live—Queens or Brooklyn or maybe even Rye or Mamaroneck. I tried to imagine what his own dining room might look like, what pictures might be on the walls. I couldn't do that, but I found I could imagine his bedroom with relative ease, although not whether he shared it with a woman. I could see him lying awake but perfectly still, looking up at the ceiling in the small hours while the moon hung in the black firmament like the half-lidded eye of a corpse; I could imagine him lying there and listening to the neighbor's dog bark steadily and monotonously, going on and on until the sound was like a silver nail driving into his brain. I imagined him lying not far from a closet filled with tuxedos in plastic dry-cleaning bags. I could see them hanging there like executed felons. I wondered if he did have a wife. If so, had he killed her before coming to work? I thought of the blob on his shirt and decided it was a possibility. I also wondered about the neighbor's dog, the one that wouldn't shut up. And the neighbor's family.

But mostly it was Guy I thought about, lying sleepless through all the same nights I had lain sleepless, listening to the dog next door or down the street as I had listened to sirens and the rumble of trucks heading downtown. I thought of him lying there and looking up at the shadows the moon had tacked to the ceiling. Thought of that cry—*Eeeeeee!*—building up in his head like gas in a closed room.

"Eeeee," I said . . . just to see how it sounded. I dropped the package of Marlboros into the gutter and began stamping it methodically as I sat there on the curb. "Eeeee. Eeeee. Eeeeee."

One of the cops standing by the sawhorses looked over at me. "Hey, buddy, want to stop being a pain in the butt?" he called over. "We got us a situation here."

Of course you do, I thought. Don't we all.

I didn't say anything, though. I stopped stamping—the cigarette pack was pretty well dead by then, anyway—and stopped making the noise. I could still hear it in my head, though, and why not? It makes as much sense as anything else.

Eeeeeee.

Eeeeeee.

Eeeeeee.

That Feeling, You Can Only Say What It Is in French

Floyd, what's that over there? Oh shit.

The man's voice speaking these words was vaguely familiar, but the words themselves were just a disconnected snip of dialogue, the kind of thing you heard when you were channel-surfing with the remote. There was no one named Floyd in her life. Still, that was the start. Even before she saw the little girl in the red pinafore, there were those disconnected words.

But it was the little girl who brought it on strong. "Oh-oh, I'm getting that feeling," Carol said.

The girl in the pinafore was in front of a country market called Carson's—BEER, WINE, GROC, FRESH BAIT, LOTTERY—crouched down with her butt between her ankles and the bright-red apron-dress tucked between her thighs, playing with a doll. The doll was yellow-haired and dirty, the kind that's round and stuffed and boneless in the body.

"What feeling?" Bill asked.

"You know. The one you can only say what it is in French. Help me here."

"Déjà vu," he said.

"That's it," she said, and turned to look at the little girl one more time. *She'll have the doll by one leg,* Carol thought. *Holding it upside down by one leg with its grimy yellow hair hanging down.*

But the little girl had abandoned the doll on the store's splintery gray steps and had gone over to look at a dog caged up in the back of a station wagon. Then Bill and Carol Shelton went around a curve in the road and the store was out of sight.

"How much farther?" Carol asked.

Bill looked at her with one eyebrow raised and his mouth dimpled at one corner—left eyebrow, right dimple, always the same. The look that said, *You think I'm amused, but I'm really irritated. For the ninety trillionth or so time in the marriage, I'm really irritated. You don't know that, though, because you can only see about two inches into me and then your vision fails.*

But she had better vision than he realized; it was one of the secrets of the marriage. Probably he had a few secrets of his own. And there were, of course, the ones they kept together.

"I don't know," he said. "I've never been here."

"But you're sure we're on the right road."

"Once you get over the causeway and onto Sanibel Island, there's only one," he said. "It goes across to Captiva, and there it ends. But before it does we'll come to Palm House. That I promise you."

The arch in his eyebrow began to flatten. The dimple began to fill in. He was returning to what she thought of as the Great Level. She had come to dislike the Great Level, too, but not as much as the eyebrow and the dimple, or his sarcastic way of saying "Excuse me?" when you said something he considered stupid, or his habit of pooching out his lower lip when he wanted to appear thoughtful and deliberative.

"Bill?"

"Mmm?"

"Do you know anyone named Floyd?"

"There was Floyd Denning. He and I ran the downstairs snack bar at Christ the Redeemer in our senior year. I told you about him, didn't I? He stole the Coke money one Friday and spent the weekend in New York with his girlfriend. They suspended him and expelled her. What made you think of him?"

"I don't know," she said. Easier than telling him that the Floyd with whom Bill had gone to high school wasn't the Floyd the voice in her head was speaking to. At least, she didn't think it was.

Second honeymoon, that's what you call this, she thought, looking at the palms that lined Highway 867, a white bird that stalked along the shoulder like an angry preacher, and a sign that read SEMINOLE WILDLIFE PARK, BRING A CARFUL FOR $10. *Florida the Sunshine State. Florida the Hospitality State. Not to mention Florida the Second-Honeymoon State. Florida, where Bill Shelton and Carol Shelton, the former Carol O'Neill, of Lynn, Massachusetts, came on their first honeymoon twenty-five years before. Only that was on the other side, the Atlantic side, at a little cabin colony, and there were cockroaches in the bureau drawers. He couldn't stop touching me. That was all right, though, in those days I wanted to be touched. Hell, I wanted to be torched like Atlanta in* Gone With the Wind, *and he torched me, rebuilt me, torched me again. Now it's silver. Twenty-five is silver. And sometimes I get that feeling.*

They were approaching a curve, and she thought, *Three crosses on the right side of the road. Two small ones flanking a bigger one. The small ones are clapped-together wood. The one in the middle is white birch with a picture on it, a tiny photograph of the seventeen-year-old boy who lost control of his car on this curve one drunk night that was his last drunk night, and this is where his girlfriend and her girlfriends marked the spot—*

Bill drove around the curve. A pair of black crows, plump and shiny, lifted off from something pasted to the macadam in a splat of blood. The birds had eaten so well that Carol wasn't sure they were going to get out of the way until they did. There were no crosses, not on the left, not on the right. Just roadkill in the middle, a woodchuck or something, now passing beneath a luxury car that had never been north of the Mason-Dixon Line.

Floyd, what's that over there?

"What's wrong?"

"Huh?" She looked at him, bewildered, feeling a little wild.

"You're sitting bolt-upright. Got a cramp in your back?"

"Just a slight one." She settled back by degrees. "I had that feeling again. The déjà vu."

"Is it gone?"

"Yes," she said, but she was lying. It had retreated a little, but that was all. She'd had this before, but never so *continuously.* It came up and went down, but it didn't go away. She'd been aware of it ever since that thing about Floyd started knocking around in her head—and then the little girl in the red pinafore.

But, really, hadn't she felt something before either of those things? Hadn't it actually started when they came down the steps of the Lear 35 into the hammering heat of the Fort Myers sunshine? Or even before? En route from Boston?

They were coming to an intersection. Overhead was a flashing yellow light, and she thought, *To the right is a used-car lot and a sign for the Sanibel Community Theater.*

Then she thought, *No, it'll be like the crosses that weren't there. It's a strong feeling but a false feeling.*

Here was the intersection. On the right there *was* a used-car lot—Palmdale Motors. Carol felt a real jump at that, a stab of something sharper than disquiet. She told herself to quit being stupid. There had to be car lots all over Florida and if you predicted one at every intersection sooner or later the law of averages made you a prophet. It was a trick mediums had been using for hundreds of years.

Besides, there's no theater sign.

But there was another sign. It was Mary the Mother of God, the ghost of all her childhood days, holding out her hands the way she did on the medallion Carol's grandmother had given her for her tenth birthday. Her grandmother had pressed it into her hand and looped the chain around her fingers, saying, "Wear her always as you grow, because all the hard days are coming." She had worn it, all right. At Our Lady of Angels grammar and middle school she had worn it, then at St. Vincent de Paul high. She wore the medal until breasts grew around it like ordinary miracles, and then someplace, probably on the class trip to Hampton Beach, she had lost it. Coming home on the bus she had tongue-kissed for the first time. Butch Soucy had been the boy, and she had been able to taste the cotton candy he'd eaten.

Mary on that long-gone medallion and Mary on this billboard had exactly the same look, the one that made you feel guilty of thinking impure thoughts even when all you were thinking about was a peanut-butter sandwich. Beneath Mary, the sign said MOTHER OF MERCY CHARITIES HELP THE FLORIDA HOMELESS—WON'T *YOU* HELP *US?*

Hey there, Mary, what's the story—

More than one voice this time; many voices, girls' voices, chanting ghost voices. These were ordinary miracles; there were also ordinary ghosts. You found these things out as you got older.

"What's wrong with you?" She knew that voice as well as she did the eyebrow-and-dimple look. Bill's I'm-only-pretending-to-be-pissed tone of voice, the one that meant he really *was* pissed, at least a little.

"Nothing." She gave him the best smile she could manage.

"You really don't seem like yourself. Maybe you shouldn't have slept on the plane."

"You're probably right," she said, and not just to be agreeable, either. After all, how many women got a second honeymoon on Captiva Island for their twenty-fifth anniversary? Round trip on a chartered Learjet? Ten days at one of those places where your money was no good (at least until MasterCard coughed up the bill at the end of the month) and if you wanted a massage a big Swedish babe would come and pummel you in your six-room beach house?

Things had been different at the start. Bill, whom she'd first met at a crosstown high-school dance and then met again at college three years later (another ordinary miracle), had begun their married life working as a janitor, because there were no openings in the computer industry. It was 1973, and computers were essentially going nowhere and they were living in a grotty place in Revere, not on the beach but close to it, and all night people kept going up the stairs to buy drugs from the two sallow creatures who lived in the apartment above them and listened endlessly to dopey records from the sixties. Carol used to lie awake waiting for the shouting to start, thinking, *We won't ever get out of here, we'll grow old and die within earshot of Cream and Blue Cheer and the Dodgem cars down on the beach.*

Bill, exhausted at the end of his shift, would sleep through the noise, lying on his side, sometimes with one hand on her hip. And when it wasn't there she often put it there, especially if the creatures upstairs were arguing with their customers. Bill was all she had. Her parents had practically disowned her when she married him. He was a Catholic, but the wrong sort of Catholic. Gram had asked why she wanted to go with that boy when anyone could tell he was shanty, how could she fall for all his foolish talk, why did she want to break her father's heart. And what could she say?

It was a long distance from that place in Revere to a private jet soaring at forty-one thousand feet; a long way to this rental car, which was a Crown Victoria—what the goodfellas in the gangster movies invariably called a Crown Vic—heading for ten days in a place where the tab would probably be . . . well, she didn't even want to think about it.

Floyd? . . . Oh shit.

"Carol? What is it now?"

"Nothing," she said. Up ahead by the road was a little pink bungalow, the porch flanked by palms—seeing those trees with their fringy heads lifted against the blue sky made her think of Japanese Zeros coming in low, their underwing machine guns firing, such an association clearly the result of a youth misspent in front of the TV—and as they passed a black woman would come out. She would be drying her hands on a piece of pink towelling and would watch them expressionlessly as they passed, rich folks in a Crown Vic headed for Captiva, and she'd have no idea that Carol Shelton once lay awake in a ninety-dollar-a-month apartment, listening to the records and the drug deals upstairs, feeling something alive inside her, something that made her think of a cigarette that had fallen down behind the drapes at a party, small and unseen but smoldering away next to the fabric.

"Hon?"

"Nothing, I said." They passed the house. There was no woman. An old man—white, not black—sat in a rocking chair, watching them pass. There were rimless glasses on his nose and a piece of ragged pink towelling, the same shade as the house, across his lap. "I'm fine now. Just anxious to get there and change into some shorts."

His hand touched her hip—where he had so often touched her during those first days—and then crept a little farther inland. She thought about stopping him (Roman hands and Russian fingers, they used to say) and didn't. They were, after all, on their second honeymoon. Also, it would make that expression go away.

"Maybe," he said, "we could take a pause. You know, after the dress comes off and before the shorts go on."

"I think that's a lovely idea," she said, and put her hand over his, pressed both more tightly against her. Ahead was a sign that would read PALM HOUSE 3 MI. ON LEFT when they got close enough to see it.

The sign actually read PALM HOUSE 2 MI. ON LEFT. Beyond it was another sign, Mother Mary again, with her hands outstretched and that little electric shimmy that wasn't quite a halo around her head. This version read MOTHER OF MERCY CHARITIES HELP THE FLORIDA SICK—WON'T *YOU* HELP *US*?

Bill said, "The next one ought to say 'Burma Shave.'"

She didn't understand what he meant, but it was clearly a joke and so she smiled. The next one would say "Mother of Mercy Charities Help the Florida Hungry," but she couldn't tell him that. Dear Bill. Dear in spite of his sometimes stupid expressions and his sometimes unclear allusions. *He'll most likely leave you, and you know something? If you go through with it that's probably the best luck you can expect.* This according to her father. Dear Bill, who had proved that just once, just that one crucial time, her judgement had been far better than her father's. She was still married to the man her Gram had called "the big boaster." At a price, true, but what was that old axiom? God says take what you want . . . and pay for it.

Her head itched. She scratched at it absently, watching for the next Mother of Mercy billboard.

Horrible as it was to say, things had started turning around when she lost the baby. That was just before Bill got a job with Beach Computers, out on Route 128; that was when the first winds of change in the industry began to blow.

Lost the baby, had a miscarriage—they all believed that except maybe Bill. Certainly her family had believed it: Dad, Mom, Gram. "Miscarriage" was the story they told, miscarriage was a Catholic's story if ever there was one. *Hey, Mary, what's the story,* they had sometimes sung when they skipped rope, feeling daring, feeling sinful, the skirts of their uniforms flipping up and down over their scabby knees. That was at Our Lady of Angels, where Sister Annunciata would spank your knuckles with her ruler if she caught you gazing out the window during Sentence Time, where Sister Dormatilla would tell you that a million years was but the first tick of eternity's endless clock (and you could spend eternity in Hell, most people did, it was easy). In Hell you would live forever with your skin on fire and your bones roasting. Now she was in Florida, now she was in a Crown Vic sitting next to her husband, whose hand was still in her crotch; the dress would be wrinkled but who cared if it got that look off his face, and why wouldn't the feeling *stop?*

She thought of a mailbox with RAGLAN painted on the side and an American-flag decal on the front, and although the name turned out to be Reagan and the flag a Grateful Dead sticker, the box was there. She thought of a small black dog trotting briskly along the other side of the road, its head down, sniffling, and the small black dog was there. She thought again of the billboard and, yes, there it was: MOTHER OF MERCY CHARITIES HELP THE FLORIDA HUNGRY—WON'T *YOU* HELP *US?*

Bill was pointing. "There—see? I think that's Palm House. No, not where the billboard is, the other side. Why do they let people put those things up out here, anyway?"

"I don't know." Her head itched. She scratched, and black dandruff began falling past her eyes. She looked at her fingers and was horrified to see dark smutches on the tips; it was as if someone had just taken her fingerprints.

"Bill?" She raked her hand through her blond hair and this time the flakes were bigger. She saw they were not flakes of skin but flakes of paper. There was a face on one, peering out of the char like a face peering out of a botched negative.

"Bill?"

"What? Wh—" Then a total change in his voice, and that frightened her more than the way the car swerved. "Christ, honey, what's in your hair?"

The face appeared to be Mother Teresa's. Or was that just because she'd been thinking about Our Lady of Angels? Carol plucked it from her dress, meaning to show it to Bill, and it crumbled between her fingers before she could. She turned to him and saw that his glasses were melted to his cheeks. One of his eyes had popped from its socket and then split like a grape pumped full of blood.

And I knew it, she thought. *Even before I turned, I knew it. Because I had that feeling.*

A bird was crying in the trees. On the billboard, Mary held out her hands. Carol tried to scream. Tried to scream.

"Carol?"

It was Bill's voice, coming from a thousand miles away. Then his hand—not pressing the folds of her dress into her crotch, but on her shoulder.

"You okay, babe?"

She opened her eyes to brilliant sunlight and her ears to the steady hum of the Learjet's engines. And something else—pressure against her eardrums. She looked from Bill's mildly concerned face to the dial below the temperature gauge in the cabin and saw that it had wound down to twenty-eight thousand.

"Landing?" she said, sounding muzzy to herself. "Already?"

"It's fast, huh?" Sounding pleased, as if he had flown it himself instead of only paying for it. "Pilot says we'll be on the ground in Fort Myers in twenty minutes. You took a hell of a jump, girl."

"I had a nightmare."

He laughed—the plummy ain't-you-the-silly-billy laugh she had come really to detest. "No nightmares allowed on your second honeymoon, babe. What was it?"

"I don't remember," she said, and it was the truth. There were only fragments: Bill with his glasses melted all over his face, and one of the three or four forbidden skip rhymes they had sometimes chanted back in fifth and sixth grade. This one had gone *Hey there, Mary, what's the story . . .* and then something-something-something. She couldn't come up with the rest. She could remember *Jangle-tangle jingle-bingle, I saw daddy's great big dingle,* but she couldn't remember the one about Mary.

Mary helps the Florida sick, she thought, with no idea of what the thought meant, and just then there was a beep as the pilot turned the seat-belt light on. They had started their final descent. *Let the wild rumpus start,* she thought, and tightened her belt.

"You really don't remember?" he asked, tightening his own. The little jet ran through a cloud filled with bumps, one of the pilots in the cockpit made a minor adjustment, and the ride smoothed out again. "Because usually, just after you wake up, you can still remember. Even the bad ones."

"I remember Sister Annunciata, from Our Lady of Angels. Sentence Time."

"Now, *that's* a nightmare."

Ten minutes later the landing gear came down with a whine and a thump. Five minutes after that they landed.

"They were supposed to bring the car right out to the plane," Bill said, already starting up the Type A shit. This she didn't like, but at least she didn't detest it the way she detested the plummy laugh and his repertoire of patronizing looks. "I hope there hasn't been a hitch."

There hasn't been, she thought, and the feeling swept

over her full force. *I'm going to see it out the window on my side in just a second or two. It's your total Florida vacation car, a great big white goddam Cadillac, or maybe it's a Lincoln—*

And, yes, here it came, proving what? Well, she supposed, it proved that sometimes when you had déjà vu what you thought was going to happen next really did. It wasn't a Caddy or a Lincoln after all, but a Crown Victoria—what the gangsters in a Martin Scorsese film would doubtless call a Crown Vic.

"Whoo," she said as he helped her down the steps and off the plane. The hot sun made her feel dizzy.

"What's wrong?"

"Nothing, really. I've got déjà vu. Left over from my dream, I guess. We've been here before, that kind of thing."

"It's being in a strange place, that's all," he said, and kissed her cheek. "Come on, let the wild rumpus start."

They went to the car. Bill showed his driver's license to the young woman who had driven it out. Carol saw him check out the hem of her skirt, then sign the paper on her clipboard.

She's going to drop it, Carol thought. The feeling was now so strong it was like being on an amusement-park ride that goes just a little too fast; all at once you realize you're edging out of the Land of Fun and into the Kingdom of Nausea. *She'll drop it, and Bill will say "Whoopsy-daisy" and pick it up for her, get an even closer look at her legs.*

But the Hertz woman didn't drop her clipboard. A white courtesy van had appeared, to take her back to the Butler Aviation terminal. She gave Bill a final smile—Carol she had ignored completely—and opened the front passenger door. She stepped up, then slipped. "Whoopsy-daisy, don't be crazy," Bill said, and took her elbow, steadying her. She gave him a smile, he gave her well-turned legs a goodbye look, and Carol stood by the growing pile of their luggage and thought, *Hey there, Mary . . .*

"Mrs. Shelton?" It was the co-pilot. He had the last bag, the case with Bill's laptop inside it, and he looked concerned. "Are you all right? You're very pale."

Bill heard and turned away from the departing white van, his face worried. If her strongest feelings about Bill were her only feelings about Bill, now that they were twenty-five years on, she would have left him when she found out about the secretary, a Clairol blonde too young to remember the Clairol slogan that started "If I have only one life to live." But there were other feelings. There was love, for instance. Still love. A kind that girls in Catholic-school uniforms didn't suspect, a weedy, unlovely species too tough to die.

Besides, it wasn't just love that held people together. There were secrets, and the price you paid to keep them.

"Carol?" he asked her. "Babe? All right?"

She thought about telling him no, she wasn't all right, she was drowning, but then she managed to smile and said, "It's the heat, that's all. I feel a little groggy. Get me in the car and crank up the air-conditioning. I'll be fine."

Bill took her by the elbow (*Bet you're not checking out my legs, though,* Carol thought. *You know where they go, don't you?*) and led her toward the Crown Vic as if she were a very old lady. By the time the door was closed and cool air was pumping over her face, she actually had started to feel a little better.

If the feeling comes back, I'll tell him, Carol thought. *I'll have to. It's just too strong. Not normal.*

Well, déjà vu was never normal, she supposed—it was something that was part dream, part chemistry, and (she was sure she'd read this, maybe in a doctor's office somewhere while waiting for her gynecologist to go prospecting up her fifty-two-year-old twat) part the result of an electrical misfire in the brain, causing new experience to be identified as old data. A temporary hole in the pipes, hot water and cold water mingling. She closed her eyes and prayed for it to go away.

Oh, Mary, conceived without sin, pray for us who have recourse to thee.

Please ("Oh puh-lease," they used to say), not back to parochial school. This was supposed to be a vacation, not—

Floyd, what's that over there? Oh shit! Oh SHIT!

Who was Floyd? The only Floyd Bill knew was Floyd Dorning (or maybe it was Darling), the kid he'd run the snack bar with, the one who'd run off to New York with his girlfriend. Carol couldn't remember when Bill had told her about that kid, but she knew he had.

Just quit it, girl. There's nothing here for you. Slam the door on the whole train of thought.

And that worked. There was a final whisper—*what's the story*—and then she was just Carol Shelton, on her way to Captiva Island, on her way to Palm House with her husband the renowned software designer, on their way to the beaches and the rum drinks, and the sound of a steel band playing "Margaritaville."

They passed a Publix market. They passed an old black man minding a roadside fruit stand—he made her think of actors from the thirties and movies you saw on the American Movie Channel, an old yassuh-boss type of guy wearing bib overalls and a straw hat with a round crown. Bill made small talk, and she made it right back at him. She was faintly amazed that the little girl who had worn a Mary medallion every day from ten to sixteen had become this woman in the Donna Karan dress—that the desperate couple in that Revere apartment were these middle-aged rich folks rolling down a lush aisle of palms—but she was and they were. Once in those Revere days he had come home drunk and she had hit him and drawn blood from below his eye. Once she had been in fear of Hell, had lain half-drugged in steel stirrups, thinking, *I'm damned, I've come to damnation. A million years, and that's only the first tick of the clock.*

They stopped at the causeway toll-booth and Carol thought, *The toll-taker has a strawberry birthmark on the left side of his forehead, all mixed in with his eyebrow.*

There was no mark—the toll-taker was just an ordinary guy in his late forties or early fifties, iron-gray hair in a buzz cut, horn-rimmed specs, the kind of guy who says, "Y'all have a nahce tahm, okai?"—but the feeling began to come back, and Carol realized that now the things she thought she knew were things she really did know, at first not all of them, but then, by the time they neared the little market on the right side of Route 41, it was almost everything.

The market's called Corson's and there's a little girl out front, Carol thought. *She's wearing a red pinafore. She's got a doll, a dirty old yellow-haired thing, that she's left on the store steps so she can look at a dog in the back of a station wagon.*

The name of the market turned out to be Carson's, not Corson's, but everything else was the same. As the white Crown Vic passed, the little girl in the red dress turned her solemn face in Carol's direction, a country girl's face, although what a girl from the toolies could be doing here in rich folks' tourist country, her and her dirty yellow-headed doll, Carol didn't know.

Here's where I ask Bill how much farther, only I won't do it. Because I have to break out of this cycle, this groove. I have to.

"How much farther?" she asked him. *He says there's only one road, we can't get lost. He says he promises me we'll get to the Palm House with no problem. And, by the way, who's Floyd?*

Bill's eyebrow went up. The dimple beside his mouth appeared. "Once you get over the causeway and onto Sanibel Island, there's only one road," he said. Carol barely heard him. He was still talking about the road, her husband who had spent a dirty weekend in bed with his secretary two years ago, risking all they had done and all they had made, Bill doing that with his other face on, being the Bill Carol's mother had warned would break her heart. And later Bill trying to tell her he hadn't been able to help himself, her wanting to scream, *I once murdered a child for you, the potential of a child, anyway. How high is that price? And is this what I get in return? To reach my fifties and find out that my husband had to get into some Clairol girl's pants?*

Tell him! she shrieked. *Make him pull over and stop, make him do anything that will break you free—change one thing, change everything! You can do it—if you could put your feet up in those stirrups, you can do anything!*

But she could do nothing, and it all began to tick by faster. The two overfed crows lifted off from their splatter of lunch. Her husband asked why she was sitting that way, was it a cramp, her saying, Yes, yes, a cramp in her back but it was easing. Her mouth quacked on about déjà vu just as if she weren't drowning in it, and the Crown Vic moved forward like one of those sadistic Dodgem cars at Revere Beach. Here came Palmdale Motors on the right. And on the left? Some kind of sign for the local community theater, a production of *Naughty Marietta.*

No, it's Mary, not Marietta. Mary, mother of Jesus, Mary, mother of God, she's got her hands out . . .

Carol bent all her will toward telling her husband what was happening, because the right Bill was behind the wheel, the right Bill could still hear her. Being heard was what married love was all about.

Nothing came out. In her mind Gram said, "All the hard days are coming." In her mind a voice asked Floyd what was over there, then said, "Oh shit," then *screamed* "Oh shit!"

She looked at the speedometer and saw it was calibrated not in miles an hour but thousands of feet: they were at twenty-eight thousand and descending. Bill was telling her that she shouldn't have slept on the plane and she was agreeing.

There was a pink house coming up, little more than a bungalow, fringed with palm trees that looked like the ones you saw in the Second World War movies, fronds framing incoming Learjets with their machine guns blazing—

Blazing. Burning hot. All at once the magazine he's holding turns into a torch. Holy Mary, mother of God, hey there, Mary, what's the story—

They passed the house. The old man sat on the porch and watched them go by. The lenses of his rimless glasses glinted in the sun. Bill's hand established a beachhead on her hip. He said something about how they might pause to refresh themselves between the doffing of her dress and the donning of her shorts and she agreed, although they were never going to get to Palm House. They were going to go down this road and down this road, they were for the white Crown Vic and the white Crown Vic was for them, forever and ever amen.

The next billboard would say PALM HOUSE 2 MI. Beyond it was the one saying that Mother of Mercy Charities helped the Florida sick. Would they help her?

Now that it was too late she was beginning to understand. Beginning to see the light the way she could see the subtropical sun sparkling off the water on their left. Wondering how many wrongs she had done in her life, how many sins if you liked that word, God knew her parents and her Gram certainly had, sin this and sin that and wear the medallion between those growing things the boys look at. And years later she had lain in bed with her new husband on hot summer nights, knowing a decision had to be made, knowing

the clock was ticking, the cigarette butt was smoldering, and she remembered making the decision, not
telling him out loud because about some things you
could be silent.

Her head itched. She scratched it. Black flecks came
swirling down past her face. On the Crown Vic's
instrument panel the speedometer froze at sixteen
thousand feet and then blew out, but Bill appeared not
to notice.

Here came a mailbox with a Grateful Dead sticker
pasted on the front; here came a little black dog with
its head down, trotting busily, and God how her head
itched, black flakes drifting in the air like fallout and
Mother Teresa's face looking out of one of them.

MOTHER OF MERCY CHARITIES HELP THE FLORIDA HUN-
GRY—WON'T *YOU* HELP *US?*

Floyd. What's that over there? Oh shit.

She has time to see something big. And to read the
word DELTA.

"Bill? *Bill?*"

His reply, clear enough but nevertheless coming
from around the rim of the universe: "Christ, honey,
what's in your *hair?*"

She plucked the charred remnant of Mother Teresa's
face from her lap and held it out to him, the older version of the man she had married, the secretary-fucking
man she had married, the man who had nonetheless res-
cued her from people who thought that you could live
forever in paradise if you only lit enough candles and
wore the blue blazer and stuck to the approved skipping
rhymes. Lying there with this man one hot summer
night while the drug deals went on upstairs and Iron

Butterfly sang "In-A-Gadda-Da-Vida" for the nine billionth time, she had asked what he thought you got, you know, after. When your part in the show was over. He had taken her in his arms and held her, down the beach she had heard the jangle-jingle of the midway and the bang of the Dodgem cars and Bill—

Bill's glasses were melted to his face. One eye bulged out of its socket. His mouth was a bloodhole. In the trees a bird was crying, a bird was *screaming,* and Carol began to scream with it, holding out the charred fragment of paper with Mother Teresa's picture on it, screaming, watching as his cheeks turned black and his forehead swarmed and his neck split open like a poisoned goiter, screaming, she was screaming, somewhere Iron Butterfly was singing "In-A-Gadda-Da-Vida" and she was screaming.

"Carol?"

It was Bill's voice, from a thousand miles away. His hand was on her, but it was concern in his touch rather than lust.

She opened her eyes and looked around the sun-brilliant cabin of the Lear 35, and for a moment she understood everything—in the way one understands the tremendous import of a dream upon the first moment of waking. She remembered asking him what he believed you got, you know, *after,* and he had said you probably got what you'd always thought you *would* get, that if Jerry Lee Lewis thought he was going to Hell for playing boogie-woogie, that's exactly where he'd go. Heaven, Hell, or Grand Rapids, it was your choice—or the choice of those who had taught you what to believe. It was the human mind's final great parlor-trick: the perception of eternity in the place where you'd always expected to spend it.

"Carol? You okay, babe?" In one hand was the magazine he'd been reading, a *Newsweek* with Mother Teresa on the cover. SAINTHOOD NOW? it said in white.

Looking around wildly at the cabin, she was thinking, *It happens at sixteen thousand feet. I have to tell them, I have to warn them.*

But it was fading, all of it, the way those feelings always did. They went like dreams, or cotton candy turning into a sweet mist just above your tongue.

"Landing? Already?" She felt wide-awake, but her voice sounded thick and muzzy.

"It's fast, huh?" he said, sounding pleased, as if he'd flown it himself instead of paying for it. "Floyd says we'll be on the ground in——"

"Who?" she asked. The cabin of the little plane was warm but her fingers were cold. "Who?"

"Floyd. You know, the *pilot.*" He pointed his thumb toward the cockpit's lefthand seat. They were descending into a scrim of clouds. The plane began to shake. "He says we'll be on the ground in Fort Myers in twenty minutes. You took a hell of a jump, girl. And before that you were moaning."

Carol opened her mouth to say it was that feeling, the one you could only say what it was in French, something *vu* or *vous,* but it was fading and all she said was "I had a nightmare."

There was a beep as Floyd the pilot switched the seat-belt light on. Carol turned her head. Somewhere below, waiting for them now and forever, was a white car from Hertz, a gangster car, the kind the characters in a Martin Scorsese movie would probably call a Crown Vic. She looked at the cover of the news magazine, at the face of Mother Teresa, and all at once she remembered skipping rope behind Our Lady of Angels, skipping to one of the forbidden rhymes, skipping to the one that went *Hey there, Mary, what's the story, save my ass from Purgatory.*

All the hard days are coming, her Gram had said. She had pressed the medal into Carol's palm, wrapped the chain around her fingers. *The hard days are coming.*

I think this story is about Hell. A version of it where you are condemned to do the same thing over and over again. Existentialism, baby, what a concept; paging Albert Camus. There's an idea that Hell is other people. My idea is that it might be repetition.

1408

As well as the ever-popular premature burial, every writer of shock/suspense tales should write at least one story about the Ghostly Room At The Inn. This is my version of that story. The only unusual thing about it is that I never intended to finish it. I wrote the first three or four pages as part of an appendix for my On Writing *book, wanting to show readers how a story evolves from first draft to second. Most of all, I wanted to provide concrete examples of the principles I'd been blathering about in the text. But something nice happened: the story seduced me, and I ended up writing all of it. I think that what scares us varies widely from one individual to the next (I've never been able to understand why Peruvian boomslangs give some people the creeps, for example), but this story scared me while I was working on it. It originally appeared as part of an audio compilation called* Blood and Smoke, *and the audio scared me even more. Scared the hell out of me. But hotel rooms are just naturally creepy places, don't you think? I mean, how many people have slept in that bed before you? How many of them were sick? How many were losing their minds? How many were perhaps thinking about reading a few final verses*

from the Bible in the drawer of the nightstand beside
them and then hanging themselves in the closet beside
the TV? Brrrr. In any case, let's check in, shall we?
Here's your key . . . and you might take time to notice
what those four innocent numbers add up to.
     It's just down the hall.

I

Mike Enslin was still in the revolving door when he
saw Olin, the manager of the Hotel Dolphin, sitting in
one of the overstuffed lobby chairs. Mike's heart sank.
Maybe I should have brought the lawyer along again, after
all, he thought. Well, too late now. And even if Olin
had decided to throw up another roadblock or two
between Mike and room 1408, that wasn't all bad;
there were compensations.

Olin was crossing the room with one pudgy hand
held out as Mike left the revolving door. The Dolphin
was on Sixty-first Street, around the corner from Fifth
Avenue, small but smart. A man and a woman
dressed in evening clothes passed Mike as he reached
for Olin's hand, switching his small overnight case to
his left hand in order to do it. The woman was blond,
dressed in black, of course, and the light, flowery
smell of her perfume seemed to summarize New
York. On the mezzanine level, someone was playing
"Night and Day" in the bar, as if to underline the
summary.

     "Mr. Enslin. Good evening."
     "Mr. Olin. Is there a problem?"

Olin looked pained. For a moment he glanced around the small, smart lobby, as if for help. At the concierge's stand, a man was discussing theater tickets with his wife while the concierge himself watched them with a small, patient smile. At the front desk, a man with the rumpled look one only got after long hours in Business Class was discussing his reservation with a woman in a smart black suit that could itself have doubled for evening wear. It was business as usual at the Hotel Dolphin. There was help for everyone except poor Mr. Olin, who had fallen into the writer's clutches.

"Mr. Olin?" Mike repeated.

"Mr. Enslin . . . could I speak to you for a moment in my office?"

Well, and why not? It would help the section on room 1408, add to the ominous tone the readers of his books seemed to crave, and that wasn't all. Mike Enslin hadn't been sure until now, in spite of all the backing and filling; now he was. Olin was really afraid of room 1408, and of what might happen to Mike there tonight.

"Of course, Mr. Olin."

Olin, the good host, reached for Mike's bag. "Allow me."

"I'm fine with it," Mike said. "Nothing but a change of clothes and a toothbrush."

"Are you sure?"

"Yes," Mike said. "I'm already wearing my lucky Hawaiian shirt." He smiled. "It's the one with the ghost repellent."

Olin didn't smile back. He sighed instead, a little

round man in a dark cutaway coat and a neatly knotted tie. "Very good, Mr. Enslin. Follow me."

The hotel manager had seemed tentative in the lobby, almost beaten. In his oak-paneled office, with the pictures of the hotel on the walls (the Dolphin had opened in 1910—Mike might publish without the benefit of reviews in the journals or the big-city papers, but he did his research), Olin seemed to gain assurance again. There was a Persian carpet on the floor. Two standing lamps cast a mild yellow light. A desk-lamp with a green lozenge-shaped shade stood on the desk, next to a humidor. And next to the humidor were Mike Enslin's last three books. Paperback editions, of course; there had been no hardbacks. *Mine host has been doing a little research of his own,* Mike thought.

Mike sat down in front of the desk. He expected Olin to sit behind the desk, but Olin surprised him. He took the chair beside Mike's, crossed his legs, then leaned forward over his tidy little belly to touch the humidor.

"Cigar, Mr. Enslin?"

"No, thank you. I don't smoke."

Olin's eyes shifted to the cigarette behind Mike's right ear—parked on a jaunty jut the way an old-time wisecracking reporter might have parked his next smoke just below the PRESS tag stuck in the band of his fedora. The cigarette had become so much a part of him that for a moment Mike honestly didn't know what Olin was looking at. Then he laughed, took it down, looked at it himself, and looked back at Olin.

"Haven't had a one in nine years," he said. "Had an older brother who died of lung cancer. I quit after he died. The cigarette behind the ear . . ." He shrugged. "Part affectation, part superstition, I guess. Like the Hawaiian shirt. Or the cigarettes you sometimes see on people's desks or walls, mounted in a little box with a sign saying BREAK GLASS IN CASE OF EMERGENCY. Is 1408 a smoking room, Mr. Olin? Just in case nuclear war breaks out?"

"As a matter of fact, it is."

"Well," Mike said heartily, "that's one less worry in the watches of the night."

Mr. Olin sighed again, but this sigh didn't have the disconsolate quality of his lobby-sigh. Yes, it was the office, Mike reckoned. *Olin's* office, his special place. Even this afternoon, when Mike had come accompanied by Robertson, the lawyer, Olin had seemed less flustered once they were in here. And why not? Where else could you feel in charge, if not in your special place? Olin's office was a room with good pictures on the walls, a good rug on the floor, and good cigars in the humidor. A lot of managers had no doubt conducted a lot of business in here since 1910; in its own way it was as New York as the blond in her black off-the-shoulder dress, her smell of perfume, and her unarticulated promise of sleek New York sex in the small hours of the morning.

"You still don't think I can talk you out of this idea of yours, do you?" Olin asked.

"I know you can't," Mike said, replacing the cigarette behind his ear. He didn't slick his hair back with Vitalis or Wildroot Cream Oil, as those colorful fedora-wearing scribblers of yore had, but he still changed the cigarette every day, just as he changed his underwear. You sweat back there behind your ears; if he examined the cigarette at the end of the day before throwing its unsmoked deadly length into the toilet, Mike could see the faint yellow-orange residue of that sweat on the thin white paper. It did not increase the temptation to light up. How he had smoked for almost twenty years—thirty butts a day, sometimes forty—was now beyond him. *Why* he had done it was an even better question.

Olin picked up the little stack of paperbacks from the blotter. "I sincerely hope you're wrong."

Mike ran open the zipper on the side pocket of his overnight bag. He brought out a Sony minicorder. "Would you mind if I taped our conversation, Mr. Olin?"

Olin waved a hand. Mike pushed RECORD and the little red light came on. The reels began to turn.

Olin, meanwhile, was shuffling slowly through the stack of books, reading the titles. As always when he saw his books in someone else's hands, Mike Enslin felt the oddest mix of emotions: pride, unease, amusement, defiance, and shame. He had no business feeling ashamed of them, they had kept him nicely over these last five years, and he didn't have to share any of the profits with a packager ("book-whores" was what his agent called them, perhaps partly in envy), because he had come up with the concept himself. Although after the first book had sold so well, only a moron could have missed the concept. What was there to do after *Frankenstein* but *Bride of Frankenstein*?

Still, he had gone to Iowa. He had studied with Jane Smiley. He had once been on a panel with Stanley Elkin. He had once aspired (absolutely no one in his current circle of friends and acquaintances had any least inkling of this) to be published as a Yale Younger Poet. And, when the hotel manager began speaking the titles aloud, Mike found himself wishing he hadn't challenged Olin with the recorder. Later he would listen to Olin's measured tones and imagine he heard contempt in them. He touched the cigarette behind his ear without being aware of it.

"Ten Nights in Ten Haunted Houses," Olin read. *"Ten Nights in Ten Haunted Graveyards. Ten Nights in Ten Haunted Castles."* He looked up at Mike with a faint smile at the corners of his mouth. "Got to Scotland on that one. Not to mention the Vienna Woods. And all tax-deductible, correct? Hauntings are, after all, your business."

"Do you have a point?"

"You're sensitive about these, aren't you?" Olin asked.

"Sensitive, yes. Vulnerable, no. If you're hoping to persuade me out of your hotel by critiquing my books—"

"No, not at all. I was curious, that's all. I sent Marcel—he's the concierge on days—out to get them two days ago, when you first appeared with your . . . request."

"It was a demand, not a request. Still is. You heard Mr. Robertson; New York State law—not to mention two federal civil rights laws—forbids you to deny me a specific room, if I request that specific room and the room is vacant. And 1408 is vacant. 1408 is *always* vacant these days."

But Mr. Olin was not to be diverted from the subject of Mike's last three books—*New York Times* bestsellers, all—just yet. He simply shuffled through them a third time. The mellow lamplight reflected off their shiny covers. There was a lot of purple on the covers. Purple sold scary books better than any other color, Mike had been told.

"I didn't get a chance to dip into these until earlier this evening," Olin said. "I've been quite busy. I usually am. The Dolphin is small by New York standards, but we run at ninety per cent occupancy and usually a problem comes through the front door with every guest."

"Like me."

Olin smiled a little. "I'd say you're a bit of a special problem, Mr. Enslin. You and your Mr. Robertson and all your threats."

Mike felt nettled all over again. He had made no threats, unless Robertson himself was a threat. And he had been forced to use the lawyer, as a man might be forced to use a crowbar on a rusty lockbox which would no longer accept the key.

The lockbox isn't yours, a voice inside told him, but the laws of the state and the country said differently. The laws said that room 1408 in the Hotel Dolphin was his if he wanted it, and as long as no one else had it first.

He became aware that Olin was watching him, still with that faint smile. As if he had been following Mike's interior dialogue almost word for word. It was an uncomfortable feeling, and Mike was finding this an unexpectedly uncomfortable meeting. It felt as if he had been on the defensive ever since he'd taken out the minicorder (which was usually intimidating) and turned it on.

"If any of this has a point, Mr. Olin, I'm afraid I lost sight of it a turn or two back. And I've had a long day. If our wrangle over room 1408 is really over, I'd like to go on upstairs and—"

"I read one . . . uh, what would you call them? Essays? Tales?"

Bill-payers was what Mike called them, but he didn't intend to say that with the tape running. Not even though it was his tape.

"Story," Olin decided. "I read one story from each book. The one about the Rilsby house in Kansas from your *Haunted Houses* book—"

"Ah, yes. The axe murders." The fellow who had chopped up all six members of the Eugene Rilsby family had never been caught.

"Exactly so. And the one about the night you spent camped out on the graves of the lovers in Alaska who committed suicide—the ones people keep claiming to see around Sitka—and the account of your night in Gartsby Castle. That was actually quite amusing. I was surprised."

Mike's ear was carefully tuned to catch the undernotes of contempt in even the blandest comments about his *Ten Nights* books, and he had no doubt that he sometimes heard contempt that wasn't there—few creatures on earth are so paranoid as the writer who believes, deep in his heart, that he is slumming, Mike had discovered—but he didn't believe there was any contempt here.

"Thank you," he said. "I guess." He glanced down at his minicorder. Usually its little red eye seemed to be watching the other guy, daring him to say the wrong thing. This evening it seemed to be looking at Mike himself.

"Oh yes, I meant it as a compliment." Olin tapped the books. "I expect to finish these . . . but for the writing. It's the writing I like. I was surprised to find myself laughing at your quite unsupernatural adventures in Gartsby Castle, and I was surprised to find you as good as you are. As *subtle* as you are. I expected more hack and slash."

Mike steeled himself for what would almost certainly come next, Olin's variation of *What's a nice girl like you doing in a place like this*. Olin the urbane hotelier, host to blond women who wore black dresses out into the night, hirer of weedy, retiring men who wore tuxes and tinkled old standards like "Night and Day" in the hotel bar. Olin who probably read Proust on his nights off.

"But they are disturbing, too, these books. If I hadn't looked at them, I don't think I would have bothered waiting for you this evening. Once I saw that lawyer with his briefcase, I knew you meant to stay in that goddamned room, and that nothing I could say was apt to dissuade you. But the books . . ."

Mike reached out and snapped off the minicorder—that little red staring eye was starting to give him the willies. "Do you want to know why I'm bottom-feeding? Is that it?"

"I assume you do it for the money," Olin said mildly. "And you're feeding a long way from the bottom, at least in my estimation . . . although it's interesting that you would jump so nimbly to such a conclusion."

Mike felt warmth rising in his cheeks. No, this wasn't going the way he had expected at all; he had *never* snapped his recorder off in the middle of a conversation. But Olin wasn't what he had seemed. *I was led astray by his hands,* Mike thought. *Those pudgy little hotel manager's hands with their neat white crescents of manicured nail.*

"What concerned me—what *frightened* me—is that I found myself reading the work of an intelligent, talented man who doesn't believe *one single thing* he has written."

That wasn't exactly true, Mike thought. He'd written perhaps two dozen stories he believed in, had actually published a few. He'd written reams of poetry he believed in during his first eighteen months in New York, when he had starved on the payroll of *The Village Voice.* But did he believe that the headless ghost of Eugene Rilsby walked his deserted Kansas farmhouse by moonlight? No. He had spent the night in that farmhouse, camped out on the dirty linoleum hills of the kitchen floor, and had seen nothing scarier than two mice trundling along the baseboard. He had spent a hot summer night in the ruins of the Transylvanian castle where Vlad Tepes supposedly still held court; the only vampires to actually show up had been a fog of European mosquitoes. During the night camped out by the grave of serial killer Jeffrey Dahmer, a white, blood-streaked figure waving a knife *had* come at him out of the two o'clock darkness, but the giggles of the apparition's friends had given him away, and Mike Enslin hadn't been terribly impressed, anyway; he knew a teenage ghost waving a rubber knife when he saw one. But he had no intention of telling any of this to Olin. He couldn't afford—

Except he *could*. The minicorder (a mistake from the getgo, he now understood) was stowed away again, and this meeting was about as off-the-record as you could get. Also, he had come to admire Olin in a weird way. And when you admired a man, you wanted to tell him the truth.

"No," he said, "I don't believe in ghoulies and ghosties and long-leggety beasties. I think it's good there are no such things, because I don't believe there's any good Lord that can protect us from them, either. That's what I believe, but I've kept an open mind from the very start. I may never win the Pulitzer Prize for investigating The Barking Ghost in Mount Hope Cemetery, but I would have written fairly about him if he had shown up."

Olin said something, only a single word, but too low for Mike to make it out.

"I beg pardon?"

"I said no." Olin looked at him almost apologetically.

Mike sighed. Olin thought he was a liar. When you got to that point, the only choices were to put up your dukes or disengage totally from the discussion. "Why don't we leave this for another day, Mr. Olin? I'll just go on upstairs and brush my teeth. Perhaps I'll see Kevin O'Malley materialize behind me in the bathroom mirror."

Mike started to get out of his chair, and Olin put out one of his pudgy, carefully manicured hands to stop him. "I'm not calling you a liar," he said, "but, Mr. Enslin, *you don't believe*. Ghosts rarely appear to those who don't believe in them, and when they do, they are rarely seen. Why, Eugene Rilsby could have bowled his severed head all the way down the front hall of his home, and you wouldn't have heard a thing!"

Mike stood up, then bent to grab his overnight case. "If that's so, I won't have anything to worry about in room 1408, will I?"

"But you will," Olin said. "You will. Because there are no ghosts in room 1408 and never have been. There's *something* in there—I've felt it myself—but it's not a spirit presence. In an abandoned house or an old castle keep, your unbelief may serve you as protection. In room 1408, it will only render you more vulnerable. Don't do it, Mr. Enslin. That's why I waited for you tonight, to ask you, *beg* you, not to do it. Of all the people on earth who don't belong in that room, the man who wrote those cheerful, exploitative true-ghost books leads the list."

Mike heard this and didn't hear it at the same time. *And you turned off your tape recorder!* he was raving. *He embarrasses me into turning off my tape recorder and then he turns into Boris Karloff hosting The All-Star Spook Weekend! Fuck it. I'll quote him anyway. If he doesn't like it, let him sue me.*

All at once he was burning to get upstairs, not just so he could start getting his long night in a corner hotel room over with, but because he wanted to transcribe what Olin had just said while it was still fresh in his mind.

"Have a drink, Mr. Enslin."

"No, I really—"

Mr. Olin reached into his coat pocket and brought out a key on a long brass paddle. The brass looked old and scratched and tarnished. Embossed on it were the numbers 1408. "Please," Olin said. "Humor me. You give me ten more minutes of your time—long enough to consume a short Scotch—and I'll hand you this key. I would give almost anything to be able to change your mind, but I like to think I can recognize the inevitable when I see it."

"You still use actual keys here?" Mike asked. "That's sort of a nice touch. Antiquey."

"The Dolphin went to a MagCard system in 1979, Mr. Enslin, the year I took the job as manager. 1408 is the only room in the house that still opens with a key. There was no need to put a MagCard lock on its door, because there's never anyone inside; the room was last occupied by a paying guest in 1978."

"You're shitting me!" Mike sat down again, and unlimbered his minicorder again. He pushed the RECORD button and said, "House manager Olin claims 1408 not rented to a paying guest in over twenty years."

"It is just as well that 1408 has never needed a MagCard lock on its door, because I am completely positive the device wouldn't work. Digital wristwatches don't work in room 1408. Sometimes they run backward, sometimes they simply go out, but you can't tell time with one. Not in room 1408, you can't. The same is true of pocket calculators and cellphones. If you're wearing a beeper, Mr. Enslin, I advise you to turn it off, because once you're in room 1408, it will start beeping at will." He paused. "And turning it off isn't guaranteed to work, either; it may turn itself back on. The only sure cure is to pull the batteries." He pushed the STOP button on the minicorder without examining the buttons; Mike supposed he used a similar model for dictating memos. "Actually, Mr. Enslin, the only sure cure is to stay the hell out of that room."

"I can't do that," Mike said, taking his minicorder back and stowing it once more, "but I think I can take time for that drink."

While Olin poured from the fumed-oak bar beneath an oil painting of Fifth Avenue at the turn of the century, Mike asked him how, if the room had been continuously unoccupied since 1978, Olin knew that high-tech gadgets didn't work inside.

"I didn't intend to give you the impression that no one had set foot through the door since 1978," Olin replied. "For one thing, there are maids in once a month to give the place a light turn. That means—"

Mike, who had been working on *Ten Haunted Hotel Rooms* for about four months at that point, said: "I know what it means." A light turn in an unoccupied room would include opening the windows to change the air, dusting, enough Ty-D-Bowl in the can to turn the water briefly blue, a change of the towels. Probably not the bed-linen, not on a light turn. He wondered if he should have brought his sleeping-bag.

Crossing the Persian from the bar with their drinks in his hands, Olin seemed to read Mike's thought on his face. "The sheets were changed this very afternoon, Mr. Enslin."

"Why don't you drop that? Call me Mike."

"I don't think I'd be comfortable with that," Olin said, handing Mike his drink. "Here's to you."

"And you." Mike lifted his glass, meaning to clink it against Olin's, but Olin pulled his back.

"No, to you, Mr. Enslin. I insist. Tonight we should both drink to you. You'll need it."

Mike sighed, clinked the rim of his glass against the rim of Olin's, and said: "To me. You would have been right at home in a horror movie, Mr. Olin. You could have played the gloomy old butler who tries to warn the young married couple away from Castle Doom."

Olin sat down. "It's a part I haven't had to play often, thank God. Room 1408 isn't listed on any of the websites dealing with paranormal locations or psychic hotspots—"

That'll change after my book, Mike thought, sipping his drink.

"—and there are no ghost-tours with stops at the Hotel Dolphin, although they do tour through the Sherry-Netherland, the Plaza, and the Park Lane. We have kept 1408 as quiet as possible . . . although, of course, the history has always been there for a researcher who is both lucky and tenacious."

Mike allowed himself a small smile.

"Veronique changed the sheets," Olin said. "I accompanied her. You should feel flattered, Mr. Enslin; it's almost like having your night's linen put on by royalty. Veronique and her sister came to the Dolphin as chambermaids in 1971 or '72. Vee, as we call her, is the Hotel Dolphin's longest-running employee, with at least six years' seniority over me. She has since risen to head housekeeper. I'd guess she hadn't changed a sheet in six years before today, but she used to do all the turns in 1408—she and her sister—until about 1992. Veronique and Celeste were twins, and the bond between them seemed to make them . . . how shall I put it? Not *immune* to 1408, but its equal . . . at least for the short periods of time needed to give a room a light turn."

"You're not going to tell me this Veronique's sister died in the room, are you?"

"No, not at all," Olin said. "She left service here around 1988, suffering from ill health. But I don't rule out the idea that 1408 may have played a part in her worsening mental and physical condition."

"We seem to have built a rapport here, Mr. Olin. I hope I don't snap it by telling you I find that ridiculous."

Olin laughed. "So hardheaded for a student of the airy world."

"I owe it to my readers," Mike said blandly.

"I suppose I simply could have left 1408 as it is anyway during most of its days and nights," the hotel manager mused. "Door locked, lights off, shades drawn to keep the sun from fading the carpet, coverlet pulled up, doorknob breakfast menu on the bed . . . but I can't bear to think of the air getting stuffy and old, like the air in an attic. Can't bear to think of the dust piling up until it's thick and fluffy. What does that make me, persnickety or downright obsessive?"

"It makes you a hotel manager."

"I suppose. In any case, Vee and Cee turned that room—very quick, just in and out—until Cee retired and Vee got her first big promotion. After that, I got other maids to do it in pairs, always picking ones who got on well with each other—"

"Hoping for that bond to withstand the bogies?"

"Hoping for that bond, yes. And you can make fun of the room 1408 bogies as much as you want, Mr. Enslin, but you'll feel them almost at once, of that I'm confident. Whatever there is in that room, it's not shy.

"On many occasions—all that I could manage—I went with the maids, to supervise them." He paused, then added, almost reluctantly, "To pull them out, I suppose, if anything really awful started to happen. Nothing ever did. There were several who had weeping fits, one who had a laughing fit—I don't know why someone laughing out of control should be more frightening than someone sobbing, but it is—and a number who fainted. Nothing too terrible, however. I had time enough over the years to make a few primitive experiments—beepers and cell-phones and such—but nothing too terrible. Thank God." He paused again, then added in a queer, flat tone: "One of them went blind."

"What?"

"She went blind. Rommie Van Gelder, that was. She was dusting the top of the television, and all at once she began to scream. I asked her what was wrong. She dropped her dustrag and put her hands over her eyes and screamed that she was blind . . . but that she could see the most awful colors. They went away almost as soon as I got her out through the door, and by the time I got her down the hallway to the elevator, her sight had begun to come back."

"You're telling me all this just to scare me, Mr. Olin, aren't you? To scare me off."

"Indeed I am not. You know the history of the room, beginning with the suicide of its first occupant."

Mike did. Kevin O'Malley, a sewing machine salesman, had taken his life on October 13, 1910, a leaper who had left a wife and seven children behind.

"Five men and one woman have jumped from that room's single window, Mr. Enslin. Three women and one man have overdosed with pills in that room, two found in bed, two found in the bathroom, one in the tub and one sitting slumped on the toilet. A man hanged himself in the closet in 1970—"

"Henry Storkin," Mike said. "That one was probably accidental . . . erotic asphyxia."

"Perhaps. There was also Randolph Hyde, who slit his wrists, and then cut off his genitals for good measure while he was bleeding to death. *That* one wasn't erotic asphyxiation. The point is, Mr. Enslin, that if you can't be swayed from your intention by a record of twelve suicides in sixty-eight years, I doubt if the gasps and fibrillations of a few chambermaids will stop you."

Gasps and fibrillations, that's nice, Mike thought, and wondered if he could steal it for the book.

"Few of the pairs who have turned 1408 over the years care to go back more than a few times," Olin said, and finished his drink in a tidy little gulp.

"Except for the French twins."

"Vee and Cee, that's true." Olin nodded.

Mike didn't care much about the maids and their . . . what had Olin called them? Their gasps and fibrillations. He did feel mildly rankled by Olin's enumeration of the suicides . . . as if Mike was so thick he had missed, not the *fact* of them, but their *import*. Except, really, there *was* no import. Both Abraham Lincoln and John Kennedy had vice presidents named Johnson; the names Lincoln and Kennedy had seven letters; both Lincoln and Kennedy had been elected in years ending in 60. What did all of these coincidences prove? Not a damned thing.

"The suicides will make a wonderful segment for my book," Mike said, "but since the tape recorder is off, I can tell you they amount to what a statistician resource of mine calls 'the cluster effect.'"

"Charles Dickens called it 'the potato effect,'" Olin said.

"I beg your pardon?"

"When Jacob Marley's ghost first speaks to Scrooge, Scrooge tells him he could be nothing but a blob of mustard or a bit of underdone potato."

"Is that supposed to be funny?" Mike asked, a trifle coldly.

"Nothing about this strikes me as funny, Mr. Enslin. Nothing at all. Listen very closely, please. Vee's sister, Celeste, died of a heart attack. At that point, she was suffering mid-stage Alzheimer's, a disease which struck her very early in life."

"Yet her sister is fine and well, according to what you said earlier. An American success story, in fact. As you are yourself, Mr. Olin, from the look of you. Yet you've been in and out of room 1408 how many times? A hundred? Two hundred?"

"For very short periods of time," Olin said. "It's perhaps like entering a room filled with poison gas. If one holds one's breath, one may be all right. I see you don't like that comparison. You no doubt find it overwrought, perhaps ridiculous. Yet I believe it's a good one."

He steepled his fingers beneath his chin.

"It's also possible that some people react more quickly and more violently to whatever lives in that room, just as some people who go scuba-diving are more prone to the bends than others. Over the Dolphin's near-century of operation, the hotel staff has grown ever more aware that 1408 is a poisoned room. It has become part of the house history, Mr. Enslin. No one talks about it, just as no one mentions the fact that here, as in most hotels, the fourteenth floor is actually the thirteenth . . . but they know it. If all the facts and records pertaining to that room were available, they would tell an amazing story . . . one more uncomfortable than your readers might enjoy.

"I should guess, for example, that every hotel in New York has had its suicides, but I would be willing to wager my life that only in the Dolphin have there been a dozen of them *in a single room.* And leaving Celeste Romandeau aside, what about the natural deaths in 1408? The so-called natural deaths?"

"How many have there been?" The idea of so-called natural deaths in 1408 had never occurred to him.

"Thirty," Olin replied. "Thirty, at least. Thirty that I know of."

"You're lying!" The words were out of his mouth before he could call them back.

"No, Mr. Enslin, I assure you I'm not. Did you really think that we keep that room empty just out of some vapid old wives' superstition or ridiculous New York tradition . . . the idea, maybe, that every fine old hotel should have at least one unquiet spirit, clanking around in the Suite of Invisible Chains?"

Mike Enslin realized that just such an idea—not articulated but there, just the same—had indeed been hanging around his new *Ten Nights* book. To hear Olin scoff at it in the irritated tones of a scientist scoffing at a *bruja*-waving native did nothing to soothe his chagrin.

"We have our superstitions and traditions in the hotel trade, but we don't let them get in the way of our business, Mr. Enslin. There's an old saying in the Midwest, where I broke into the business: 'There are no drafty rooms when the cattlemen are in town.' If we have empties, we fill them. The only exception to that rule I have ever made—and the only talk like this I have ever had—is on account of room 1408, a room on the thirteenth floor whose very numerals add up to thirteen."

Olin looked levelly at Mike Enslin.

"It is a room not only of suicides but of strokes and heart attacks and epileptic seizures. One man who stayed in that room—this was in 1973—apparently drowned in a bowl of soup. You would undoubtedly call that ridiculous, but I spoke to the man who was head of hotel security at that time, and he saw the death certificate. The power of whatever inhabits the room seems to be less around midday, which is when the room-turns always occur, and yet I know of several maids who have turned that room who now suffer from heart problems, emphysema, diabetes. There was a heating problem on that floor three years ago, and Mr. Neal, the head maintenance engineer at that time, had to go into several of the rooms to check the heating units. 1408 was one of them. He seemed fine then— both in the room and later on—but he died the following afternoon of a massive cerebral hemorrhage."

"Coincidence," Mike said. Yet he could not deny that Olin was good. Had the man been a camp counselor, he would have scared ninety per cent of the kiddies back home after the first round of campfire ghost stories.

"Coincidence," Olin repeated softly, not quite contemptuously. He held out the old-fashioned key on its old-fashioned brass paddle. "How is your own heart, Mr. Enslin? Not to mention your blood-pressure and psychological condition?"

Mike found it took an actual, conscious effort to lift his hand . . . but once he got it moving, it was fine. It rose to the key without even the minutest trembling at the fingertips, so far as he could see.

"All fine," he said, grasping the worn brass paddle. "Besides, I'm wearing my lucky Hawaiian shirt."

Olin insisted on accompanying Mike to the fourteenth floor in the elevator, and Mike did not demur. He was interested to see that, once they were out of the manager's office and walking down the hall which led to the elevators, the man reverted to his less consequential self; he became once again poor Mr. Olin, the flunky who had fallen into the writer's clutches.

A man in a tux—Mike guessed he was either the restaurant manager or the maître d'—stopped them, offered Olin a thin sheaf of papers, and murmured to him in French. Olin murmured back, nodding, and quickly scribbled his signature on the sheets. The fellow in the bar was now playing "Autumn in New York." From this distance, it had an echoey sound, like music heard in a dream.

The man in the tuxedo said *"Merci bien"* and went on his way. Mike and the hotel manager went on theirs. Olin again asked if he could carry Mike's little valise, and Mike again refused. In the elevator, Mike found his eyes drawn to the neat triple row of buttons. Everything was where it should have been, there were no gaps . . . and yet, if you looked more closely, you saw that there was. The button marked 12 was followed by one marked 14. *As if,* Mike thought, *they could make the number nonexistent by omitting it from the control-panel of an elevator.* Foolishness . . . and yet Olin was right; it was done all over the world.

As the car rose, Mike said, "I'm curious about something. Why didn't you simply create a fictional resident for room 1408, if it scares you all as badly as you say it does? For that matter, Mr. Olin, why not declare it as your own residence?"

"I suppose I was afraid I would be accused of fraud, if not by the people responsible for enforcing state and federal civil rights statutes—hotel people feel about civil rights laws as many of your readers probably feel about clanking chains in the night—then by my bosses, if they got wind of it. If I couldn't persuade you to stay out of 1408, I doubt that I would have had much more luck in convincing the Stanley Corporation's board of directors that I took a perfectly good room off the market because I was afraid that spooks cause the occasional travelling salesman to jump out the window and splatter himself all over Sixty-first Street."

Mike found this the most disturbing thing Olin had said yet. *Because he's not trying to convince me anymore,* he thought. *Whatever salesmanship powers he had in his office—maybe it's some vibe that comes up from the Persian rug—he loses it out here. Competency, yes, you could see that when he was signing the maître d's chits, but not salesmanship. Not personal magnetism. Not out here. But he believes it. He believes it all.*

Above the door, the illuminated 12 went out and the 14 came on. The elevator stopped. The door slid open to reveal a perfectly ordinary hotel corridor with a red-and-gold carpet (most definitely not a Persian) and electric fixtures that looked like nineteenth-century gaslights.

"Here we are," Olin said. "Your floor. You'll pardon me if I leave you here. 1408 is to your left, at the end of the hall. Unless I absolutely have to, I don't go any closer than this."

Mike Enslin stepped out of the elevator on legs that seemed heavier than they should have. He turned back to Olin, a pudgy little man in a black coat and a carefully knotted wine-colored tie. Olin's manicured hands were clasped behind him now, and Mike saw that the little man's face was as pale as cream. On his high, lineless forehead, drops of perspiration stood out.

"There's a telephone in the room, of course," Olin said. "You could try it, if you find yourself in trouble . . . but I doubt that it will work. Not if the room doesn't want it to."

Mike thought of a light reply, something about how that would save him a room-service charge at least, but all at once his tongue seemed as heavy as his legs. It just lay there on the floor of his mouth.

Olin brought one hand out from behind his back, and Mike saw it was trembling. "Mr. Enslin," he said. "Mike. Don't do this. For God's sake—"

Before he could finish, the elevator door slid shut, cutting him off. Mike stood where he was for a moment, in the perfect New York hotel silence of what no one on the staff would admit was the thirteenth floor of the Hotel Dolphin, and thought of reaching out and pushing the elevator's call-button.

Except if he did that, Olin would win. And there would be a large, gaping hole where the best chapter of his new book should have been. The readers might not know that, his editor and his agent might not know it, Robertson the lawyer might not . . . but *he* would.

Instead of pushing the call-button, he reached up and touched the cigarette behind his ear—that old, distracted gesture he no longer knew he was making—and flicked the collar of his lucky shirt. Then he started down the hallway toward 1408, swinging his overnight case by his side.

II

The most interesting artifact left in the wake of Michael Enslin's brief stay (it lasted about seventy minutes) in room 1408 was the eleven minutes of recorded tape in his minicorder, which was charred a bit but not even close to destroyed. The fascinating thing about the narration was how *little* narration there was. And how odd it became.

The minicorder had been a present from his ex-wife, with whom he had remained friendly, five years before. On his first "case expedition" (the Rilsby farm in Kansas) he had taken it almost as an afterthought, along with five yellow legal pads and a leather case filled with sharpened pencils. By the time he reached the door of room 1408 in the Hotel Dolphin three books later, he came with a single pen and notebook, plus five fresh ninety-minute cassettes in addition to the one he had loaded into the machine before leaving his apartment.

He had discovered that narration served him better than note-taking; he was able to catch anecdotes, some of them pretty damned great, as they happened—the bats that had dive-bombed him in the supposedly haunted tower of Gartsby Castle, for instance. He had shrieked like a girl on her first trip through a carny haunted house. Friends hearing this were invariably amused.

The little tape recorder was more practical than written notes, too, especially when you were in a chilly New Brunswick graveyard and a squall of rain and wind collapsed your tent at three in the morning.

You couldn't take very successful notes in such circumstances, but you *could* talk . . . which was what Mike had done, gone on talking as he struggled out of the wet, flapping canvas of his tent, never losing sight of the minicorder's comforting red eye. Over the years and the "case expeditions," the Sony minicorder had become his friend. He had never recorded a first-hand account of a true supernatural event on the filament-thin ribbon of tape running between its reels, and that included the broken comments he made while in 1408, but it was probably not surprising that he had arrived at such feelings of affection for the gadget. Long-haul truckers come to love their Kenworths and Jimmy-Petes; writers treasure a certain pen or battered old typewriter; professional cleaning ladies are loath to give up the old Electrolux. Mike had never had to stand up to an actual ghost or psychokinetic event with only the minicorder—his version of a cross and a bunch of garlic—to protect him, but it had been there on plenty of cold, uncomfortable nights. He was hardheaded, but that didn't make him inhuman.

His problems with 1408 started even before he got into the room.

The door was crooked.

Not by a lot, but it was crooked, all right, canted just the tiniest bit to the left. It made him think first of scary movies where the director tried to indicate mental distress in one of the characters by tipping the camera on the point-of-view shots. This association was followed by another one—the way doors looked when you were on a boat and the weather was a little heavy.

Back and forth they went, right and left they went, tick and tock they went, until you started to feel a bit woozy in your head and stomach. Not that he felt that way himself, not at all, but—

Yes, I do. Just a little.

And he would say so, too, if only because of Olin's insinuation that his attitude made it impossible for him to be fair in the undoubtedly subjective field of spook journalism.

He bent over (aware that the slightly woozy feeling in his stomach left as soon as he was no longer looking at that subtly off-kilter door), unzipped the pocket on his overnighter, and took out his minicorder. He pushed RECORD as he straightened up, saw the little red eye go on, and opened his mouth to say, "The door of room 1408 offers its own unique greeting; it appears to have been set crooked, tipped slightly to the left."

He said *The door,* and that's all. If you listen to the tape, you can hear both words clearly, *The door* and then the click of the STOP button. Because the door *wasn't* crooked. It was perfectly straight. Mike turned, looked at the door of 1409 across the hall, then back at the door of 1408. Both doors were the same, white with gold number-plaques and gold doorknobs. Both perfectly straight.

Mike bent, picked up his overnight case with the hand holding the minicorder, moved the key in his other hand toward the lock, then stopped again.

The door was crooked again.

This time it tilted slightly to the right.

"This is ridiculous," Mike murmured, but that woozy feeling had already started in his stomach again.

It wasn't just *like* seasickness; it *was* seasickness. He had crossed to England on the *QE2* a couple of years ago, and one night had been extremely rough. What Mike remembered most clearly was lying on the bed in his stateroom, always on the verge of throwing up but never quite able to do it. And how the feeling of nauseated vertigo got worse if you looked at a doorway . . . or a table . . . or a chair . . . at how they would go back and forth . . . right and left . . . tick and tock . . .

This is Olin's fault, he thought. *Exactly what he wants. He built you up for it, buddy. He set you up for it. Man, how he'd laugh if he could see you. How——*

His thoughts broke off as he realized Olin very likely *could* see him. Mike looked back down the corridor toward the elevator, barely noticing that the slightly whoopsy feeling in his stomach left the moment he stopped staring at the door. Above and to the left of the elevators, he saw what he had expected: a closed-circuit camera. One of the house dicks might be looking at it this very moment, and Mike was willing to bet that Olin was right there with him, both of them grinning like apes. *Teach him to come in here and start throwing his weight and his lawyer around,* Olin says. *Lookit him!* the security man replies, grinning more widely than ever. *White as a ghost himself, and he hasn't even touched the key to the lock yet. You got him, boss! Got him hook, line, and sinker!*

Damned if you do, Mike thought. *I stayed in the Rilsby house, slept in the room where at least two of them were killed—and I did sleep, whether you believed it or not. I spent a night right next to Jeffrey Dahmer's grave and another two stones over from H. P. Lovecraft's; I brushed my teeth next to the tub where Sir David Smythe supposedly drowned both of his wives. I stopped being scared of campfire stories a long time ago. I'll be damned if you do!*

He looked back at the door and the door was straight. He grunted, pushed the key into the lock, and turned it. The door opened. Mike stepped in. The door did not swing slowly shut behind him as he felt for the light switch, leaving him in total darkness (besides, the lights of the apartment building next door shone through the window). He found the switch. When he flicked it, the overhead light, enclosed in a collection of dangling crystal ornaments, came on. So did the standing lamp by the desk on the far side of the room.

The window was above this desk, so someone sitting there writing could pause in his work and look out on Sixty-first Street . . . or *jump* out on Sixty-first, if the urge so took him. Except—

Mike set down his bag just inside the door, closed the door, and pushed RECORD again. The little red light went on.

"According to Olin, six people have jumped from the window I'm looking at," he said, "but I won't be taking any dives from the fourteenth—excuse me, the *thirteenth*—floor of the Hotel Dolphin tonight. There's an iron or steel mesh grille over the outside. Better safe than sorry. 1408 is what you'd call a junior suite, I guess. The room I'm in has two chairs, a sofa, a writing desk, a cabinet that probably contains the TV and maybe a minibar. Carpet on the floor is unremarkable—not a patch on Olin's, believe me. Wallpaper, ditto. It . . . wait . . ."

At this point the listener hears another click on the tape as Mike hits the STOP button again. All the scant narration on the tape has that same fragmentary quality, which is utterly unlike the other hundred and fifty or so tapes in his literary agent's possession. In addition, his voice grows steadily more distracted; it is not the voice of a man at work, but of a perplexed individual who has begun talking to himself without realizing it. The elliptical nature of the tapes and that growing verbal distraction combine to give most listeners a distinct feeling of unease. Many ask that the tape be turned off long before the end is reached. Mere words on a page cannot adequately convey a listener's growing conviction that he is hearing a man lose, if not his mind, then his hold on conventional reality, but even the flat words themselves suggest that *something* was happening.

What Mike had noticed at that point were the pictures on the walls. There were three of them: a lady in twenties-style evening dress standing on a staircase, a sailing ship done in the fashion of Currier & Ives, and a still life of fruit, the latter painted with an unpleasant yellow-orange cast to the apples as well as the oranges and bananas. All three pictures were in glass frames and all three were crooked. He had been about to mention the crookedness on tape, but what was so unusual, so worthy of comment, about three off-kilter pictures? That a *door* should be crooked . . . well, that had a little of that old *Cabinet of Dr. Caligari* charm. But the door *hadn't* been crooked; his eyes had tricked him for a moment, that was all.

The lady on the stairs tilted left. So did the sailing

ship, which showed bell-bottomed British tars lining the rail to watch a school of flying fish. The yellowish-orange fruit—to Mike it looked like a bowl of fruit painted by the light of a suffocating equatorial sun, a Paul Bowles desert sun—tilted to the right. Although he was not ordinarily a fussy man, he circled the room, setting them straight. Looking at them crooked like that was making him feel a touch nauseated again. He wasn't entirely surprised, either. One grew susceptible to the feeling; he had discovered that on the *QE 2*. He had been told that if one persevered through that period of increased susceptibility, one usually adapted . . . "got your sealegs," some of the old hands still said. Mike hadn't done enough sailing to get his sealegs, nor cared to. These days he stuck with his land legs, and if straightening the three pictures in the unremarkable sitting room of 1408 would settle his midsection, good for him.

There was dust on the glass covering the pictures. He trailed his fingers across the still life and left two parallel streaks. The dust had a greasy, slippery feel. *Like silk just before it rots* was what came into his mind, but he was damned if he was going to put that on tape, either. How was *he* supposed to know what silk felt like just before it rotted? It was a drunk's thought.

When the pictures were set to rights, he stepped back and surveyed them in turn: the evening-dressed lady by the door leading into the bedroom, the ship plying one of the seven seas to the left of the writing desk, and finally the nasty (and quite badly painted) fruit by the TV cabinet. Part of him expected that they would be crooked again, or fall crooked as he looked at them—that was the way things happened in movies like *House on Haunted Hill* and in old episodes of *The Twilight Zone*—but the pictures remained perfectly straight, as he had fixed them. Not, he told himself, that he would have found anything supernatural or paranormal in a return to their former crooked state; in his experience, reversion was the nature of things—people who had given up smoking (he touched the cigarette cocked behind his ear without being aware of it) wanted to go on smoking, and pictures that had been hanging crooked since Nixon was President wanted to go on hanging crooked. *And they've been here a long time, no doubt about that,* Mike thought. *If I lifted them away from the walls, I'd see lighter patches on the wallpaper. Or bugs squirming out, the way they do when you turn over a rock.*

There was something both shocking and nasty about this idea; it came with a vivid image of blind white bugs oozing out of the pale and formerly protected wallpaper like living pus.

Mike raised the minicorder, pushed RECORD, and said: "Olin has certainly started a train of thought in my head. Or a chain of thought, which is it? He set out to give me the heebie-jeebies, and he certainly succeeded. I don't mean . . ." Didn't mean what? To be racist? Was "heebie-jeebies" short for *Hebrew* jeebies? But that was ridiculous. That would be "Hebrew-jeebrews," a phrase which was meaningless. It—

On the tape at this point, flat and perfectly articulated, Mike Enslin says: "I've got to get hold of myself. Right now." This is followed by another click as he shuts the tape off again.

He closed his eyes and took four long, measured breaths, holding each one in to a five-count before letting it out again. Nothing like this had ever happened to him—not in the supposedly haunted houses, the supposedly haunted graveyards, or the supposedly haunted castles. This wasn't like being haunted, or what he imagined being haunted would be like; this was like being stoned on bad, cheap dope.

Olin did this. Olin hypnotized you, but you're going to break out of it. You're going to spend the goddamned night in this room, and not just because it's the best location you've ever been in—leave out Olin and you've got damned near enough for the ghost-story of the decade already—but because Olin doesn't get to win. Him and his bullshit story about how thirty people have died in here, they don't get to win. I'm the one in charge of bullshit around here, so just breathe in . . . and out. Breathe in . . . and out. In . . . and out . . .

He went on like that for nearly ninety seconds, and when he opened his eyes again, he felt normal. The pictures on the wall? Still straight. Fruit in the bowl? Still yellow-orange and uglier than ever. Desert fruit for sure. Eat one piece of that and you'd shit until it hurt.

He pushed RECORD. The red eye went on. "I had a little vertigo for a minute or two," he said, crossing the room to the writing desk and the window with its protective mesh outside. "It might have been a hangover from Olin's yarning, but I could believe I feel a genuine presence here." He felt no such thing, of course, but once that was on tape he could write almost anything he pleased. "The air is stale. Not musty or foul-smelling, Olin said the place gets aired every time it gets turned, but the turns are quick and . . . yeah . . . it's stale. Hey, look at this."

There was an ashtray on the writing desk, one of those little ones made of thick glass that you used to see in hotels everywhere, and in it was a book of matches. On the front was the Hotel Dolphin. In front of the hotel stood a smiling doorman in a very old-fashioned uniform, the kind with shoulder-boards, gold frogging, and a cap that looked as if it belonged in a gay bar, perched on the head of a motorcycle ramrod wearing nothing else but a few silver body-rings. Going back and forth on Fifth Avenue in front of the hotel were cars from another era—Packards and Hudsons, Studebakers and finny Chrysler New Yorkers.

"The matchbook in the ashtray looks like it comes from about 1955," Mike said, and slipped it into the pocket of his lucky Hawaiian shirt. "I'm keeping it as a souvenir. Now it's time for a little fresh air."

There is a clunk as he sets the minicorder down, presumably on the writing desk. There is a pause followed by vague sounds and a couple of effortful grunts. After these come a second pause and then a squeaking sound. "Success!" he says. This is a little off-mike, but the follow-up is closer.

"Success!" Mike repeated, picking the minicorder up off the desk. "The bottom half wouldn't budge . . . it's like it's nailed shut . . . but the top half came down all right. I can hear the traffic on Fifth Avenue, and all the beeping horns have a comforting quality. Someone is playing a saxophone, perhaps in front of the Plaza, which is across the street and two blocks down. It reminds me of my brother."

Mike stopped abruptly, looking at the little red eye. It seemed to accuse him. Brother? His brother was dead, another fallen soldier in the tobacco wars. Then he relaxed. What of it? These were the spook wars, where Michael Enslin had always come off the winner. As for Donald Enslin . . .

"My brother was actually eaten by wolves one winter on the Connecticut Turnpike," he said, then laughed and pushed STOP. There is more on the tape—a little more—but that is the final statement of any coherence . . . the final statement, that is, to which a clear meaning can be ascribed.

Mike turned on his heels and looked at the pictures. Still hanging perfectly straight, good little pictures that they were. That still life, though—what an ugly fucking thing that was!

He pushed RECORD and spoke two words—*fuming oranges*—into the minicorder. Then he turned it off again and walked across the room to the door leading into the bedroom. He paused by the evening-dressed lady and reached into the darkness, feeling for the light switch. He had just one moment to register

(*it feels like skin like old dead skin*)

something wrong with the wallpaper under his sliding palm, and then his fingers found the switch. The bedroom was flooded with yellow light from another of those ceiling fixtures buried in hanging glass baubles. The bed was a double hiding under a yellow-orange coverlet.

"Why say hiding?" Mike asked the minicorder, then

pushed the STOP button again. He stepped in, fascinated by the fuming desert of the coverlet, by the tumorous bulges of the pillows beneath it. Sleep there? Not at all, sir! It would be like sleeping inside that goddam still life, sleeping in that horrible hot Paul Bowles room you couldn't quite see, a room for lunatic expatriate Englishmen who were blind from syphilis caught while fucking their mothers, the film version starring either Laurence Harvey or Jeremy Irons, one of those actors you just naturally associated with unnatural acts—

Mike pushed RECORD, the little red eye came on, he said "Orpheus on the Orpheum Circuit!" into the mike, then pushed STOP again. He approached the bed. The coverlet gleamed yellow-orange. The wallpaper, perhaps cream-colored by daylight, had picked up the yellow-orange glow of the coverlet. There was a little night-table to either side of the bed. On one was a telephone—black and large and equipped with a dial. The finger-holes in the dial looked like surprised white eyes. On the other table was a dish with a plum on it. Mike pushed RECORD and said: "That isn't a real plum. That's a plastic plum." He pushed STOP again.

On the bed itself was a doorknob menu. Mike sidled up one side of the bed, being quite careful to touch neither the bed nor the wall, and picked the menu up. He tried not to touch the coverlet, either, but the tips of his fingers brushed it and he moaned. It was soft in some terrible wrong way. Nevertheless, he picked the menu up. It was in French, and although it had been years since he had taken the language, one of the breakfast items appeared to be birds roasted in shit. *That at least* sounds *like something the French might eat,* he thought, and uttered a wild, distracted laugh.

He closed his eyes and opened them.

The menu was in Russian.

He closed his eyes and opened them.

The menu was in Italian.

Closed his eyes, opened them.

There *was* no menu. There was a picture of a screaming little woodcut boy looking back over his shoulder at the woodcut wolf which had swallowed his left leg up to the knee. The wolf's ears were laid back and he looked like a terrier with its favorite toy.

I don't see that, Mike thought, and of course he didn't. Without closing his eyes he saw neat lines of English, each line listing a different breakfast temptation. Eggs, waffles, fresh berries; no birds roasted in shit. Still—

He turned around and very slowly edged himself out of the little space between the wall and the bed, a space that now felt as narrow as a grave. His heart was beating so hard that he could feel it in his neck and wrists as well as in his chest. His eyes were throbbing in their sockets. 1408 was wrong, yes indeed, 1408 was *very* wrong. Olin had said something about poison gas, and that was what Mike felt like: someone who has been gassed or forced to smoke strong hashish laced with insect poison. Olin had done this, of course, probably with the active laughing connivance of the security people. Pumped his special poison gas up through the vents. Just because he could *see* no vents didn't mean the vents weren't there.

Mike looked around the bedroom with wide, frightened eyes. There was no plum on the endtable to the left of the bed. No plate, either. The table was bare. He turned, started for the door leading back to the sitting room, and stopped. There was a picture on the wall. He couldn't be absolutely sure—in his present state he couldn't be absolutely sure of his own name—but he was *fairly* sure that there had been no picture there when he first came in. It was a still life. A single plum sat on a tin plate in the middle of an old plank table. The light falling across the plum and the plate was a feverish yellow-orange.

Tango-light, he thought. *The kind of light that makes the dead get up out of their graves and tango. The kind of light—*

"I have to get out of here," he whispered, and blundered back into the sitting room. He became aware that his shoes had begun to make odd smooching sounds, as if the floor beneath them were growing soft.

The pictures on the living room wall were crooked again, and there were other changes, as well. The lady on the stairs had pulled down the top of her gown, baring her breasts. She held one in each hand. A drop of blood hung from each nipple. She was staring directly into Mike's eyes and grinning ferociously. Her teeth were filed to cannibal points. At the rail of the sailing ship, the tars had been replaced by a line of pallid men and women. The man on the far left, nearest the ship's bow, wore a brown wool suit and held a derby hat in one hand. His hair was slicked to his brow and parted in the middle. His face was shocked and vacant. Mike knew his name: Kevin O'Malley, this room's first occupant, a sewing machine salesman who had jumped from this room in October of 1910. To O'Malley's left were the others who had died here, all with that same vacant, shocked expression. It made them look related, all members of the same inbred and cataclysmically retarded family.

In the picture where the fruit had been, there was now a severed human head. Yellow-orange light swam off the sunken cheeks, the sagging lips, the upturned, glazing eyes, the cigarette parked behind the right ear.

Mike blundered toward the door, his feet smooching and now actually seeming to stick a little at each step. The door wouldn't open, of course. The chain hung unengaged, the thumbbolt stood straight up like clock hands pointing to six o'clock, but the door wouldn't open.

Breathing rapidly, Mike turned from it and waded—that was what it felt like—across the room to the writing desk. He could see the curtains beside the window he had cracked open waving desultorily, but he could feel no fresh air against his face. It was as though the room were swallowing it. He could still hear horns on Fifth, but they were now very distant. Did he still hear the saxophone? If so, the room had stolen its sweetness and melody and left only an atonal reedy drone, like the wind blowing across a hole in a dead man's neck or a pop bottle filled with severed fingers or—

Stop it, he tried to say, but he could no longer speak. His heart was hammering at a terrible pace; if it went much faster, it would explode. His mini-

corder, faithful companion of many "case expeditions," was no longer in his hand. He had left it somewhere. In the bedroom? If it was in the bedroom, it
was probably gone by now, swallowed by the room;
when it was digested, it would be excreted into one of
the pictures.

Gasping for breath like a runner nearing the end of
a long race, Mike put a hand to his chest, as if to
soothe his heart. What he felt in the left breast pocket
of his gaudy shirt was the small square shape of the
minicorder. The feel of it, so solid and known, steadied
him a little—brought him back a little. He became
aware that he was humming . . . and that the room
seemed to be humming back at him, as if myriad
mouths were concealed beneath its smoothly nasty
wallpaper. He was aware that his stomach was now so
nauseated that it seemed to be swinging in its own
greasy hammock. He could feel the air crowding
against his ears in soft, coagulating clots, and it made
him think of how fudge was when it reached the soft-
ball stage.

But he was back a little, enough to be positive of
one thing: he had to call for help while there was still
time. The thought of Olin smirking (in his deferential
New York hotel manager way) and saying *I told you so*
didn't bother him, and the idea that Olin had somehow induced these strange perceptions and horrible
fear by chemical means had entirely left his mind. It
was the *room*. It was the goddamned *room*.

He meant to jab out a hand to the old-fashioned
telephone—the twin of the one in the bedroom—and
snatch it up. Instead he watched his arm descend to

the table in a kind of delirious slow motion, so like the arm of a diver he almost expected to see bubbles rising from it.

He closed his fingers around the handset and picked it up. His other hand dove, as deliberate as the first, and dialed 0. As he put the handset of the phone against his ear, he heard a series of clicks as the dial spun back to its original position. It sounded like the wheel on *Wheel of Fortune,* do you want to spin or do you want to solve the puzzle? Remember that if you try to solve the puzzle and fail, you will be put out into the snow beside the Connecticut Turnpike and the wolves will eat you.

There was no ring in his ear. Instead, a harsh voice simply began speaking. "This is *nine! Nine!* This is *nine! Nine!* This is *ten! Ten!* We have killed your friends! Every friend is now dead! This is *six! Six!*"

Mike listened with growing horror, not at what the voice was saying but at its rasping emptiness. It was not a machine-generated voice, but it wasn't a human voice, either. It was the voice of the room. The presence pouring out of the walls and the floor, the presence speaking to him from the telephone, had nothing in common with any haunting or paranormal event he had ever read about. There was something alien here.

No, not here yet . . . but coming. It's hungry, and you're dinner.

The phone fell from his relaxing fingers and he turned around. It swung at the end of its cord the way his stomach was swinging back and forth inside him, and he could still hear that voice rasping out of the black: "*Eighteen!* This is now *eighteen!* Take cover when the siren sounds! This is *four! Four!*"

He was not aware of taking the cigarette from behind his ear and putting it in his mouth, or of fumbling the book of matches with the old-fashioned gold-frogged doorman on it out of his bright shirt's right breast pocket, not aware that, after nine years, he had finally decided to have a smoke.

Before him, the room had begun to melt.

It was sagging out of its right angles and straight lines, not into curves but into strange Moorish arcs that hurt his eyes. The glass chandelier in the center of the ceiling began to sag like a thick glob of spit. The pictures began to bend, turning into shapes like the windshields of old cars. From behind the glass of the picture by the door leading into the bedroom, the twenties woman with the bleeding nipples and grinning cannibal-teeth whirled around and ran back up the stairs, going with the jerky delirious high knee-pistoning of a vamp in a silent movie. The telephone continued to grind and spit, the voice coming from it now the voice of an electric hair-clipper that has learned how to talk: "*Five!* This is *five!* Ignore the siren! Even if you leave this room, you can never leave this room! *Eight!* This is *eight!*"

The door to the bedroom and the door to the hall had begun to collapse downward, widening in the middle and becoming doorways for beings possessed of unhallowed shapes. The light began to grow bright and hot, filling the room with that yellow-orange glow. Now he could see rips in the wallpaper, black pores that quickly grew to become mouths. The floor sank into a concave arc and now he could hear it coming, the dweller in the room behind the room, the thing in the walls, the owner of the buzzing voice. *"Six!"* the phone screamed. *"Six,* this is *six,* this is *goddam fucking SIX!"*

He looked down at the matchbook in his hand, the one he had plucked out of the bedroom ashtray. Funny old doorman, funny old cars with their big chrome grilles . . . and words running across the bottom that he hadn't seen in a long time, because now the strip of abrasive stuff was always on the back.

CLOSE COVER BEFORE STRIKING.

Without thinking about it—he no longer *could* think—Mike Enslin tore out a single match, allowing the cigarette to drop out of his mouth at the same time. He struck the match and immediately touched it to the others in the book. There was a *ffffhut!* sound, a strong whiff of burning sulfur that went into his head like a whiff of smelling salts, and a bright flare of matchheads. And again, without so much as a single thought, Mike held the flaring bouquet of fire against the front of his shirt. It was a cheap thing made in Korea or Cambodia or Borneo, old now; it caught fire at once. Before the flames could blaze up in front of his eyes, rendering the room once more unstable, Mike saw it clearly, like a man who has awakened from a nightmare only to find the nightmare all around him.

His head was clear—the strong whiff of sulfur and the sudden rising heat from his shirt had done that much—but the room maintained its insanely Moorish aspect. *Moorish* was wrong, not even very close, but it was the only word that seemed even to reach toward what had happened here . . . what was still happening. He was in a melting, rotting cave full of swoops and mad tilts. The door to the bedroom had become the door to some sarcophagal inner chamber. And to his left, where the picture of the fruit had been, the wall was bulging outward toward him, splitting open in those long cracks that gaped like mouths, opening on a world from which *something* was now approaching. Mike Enslin could hear its slobbering, avid breath, and smell something alive and dangerous. It smelled a little like the lion-house in the—

Then flames scorched the undershelf of his chin, banishing thought. The heat rising from his blazing shirt put that waver back into the world, and as he began to smell the crispy aroma of his chest-hair starting to fry, Mike again bolted across the sagging rug to the hall door. An insectile buzzing sound had begun to sweat out of the walls. The yellow-orange light was steadily brightening, as if a hand were turning up an invisible rheostat. But this time when he reached the door and turned the knob, the door opened. It was as if the thing behind the bulging wall had no use for a burning man; did not, perhaps, relish cooked meat.

III

A popular song from the fifties suggests that love makes the world go 'round, but coincidence would probably be a better bet. Rufus Dearborn, who was staying that night in room 1414, up near the elevators, was a salesman for the Singer Sewing Machine Company, in town from Texas to talk about moving up to an executive position. And so it happened that, ninety or so years after room 1408's first occupant jumped to his death, another sewing machine salesman saved the life of the man who had come to write about the purportedly haunted room. Or perhaps that is an exaggeration; Mike Enslin might have lived even if no one—especially a fellow on his way back from a visit to the ice machine—had been in the hallway at that moment. Having your shirt catch fire is no joke, though, and he certainly would have been burned much more severely and extensively if not for Dearborn, who thought fast and moved even faster.

Not that Dearborn ever remembered exactly what happened. He constructed a coherent enough story for the newspapers and TV cameras (he liked the idea of being a hero very much, and it certainly did no harm to his executive aspirations), and he clearly remembered seeing the man on fire lunge out into the hall, but after that everything was a blur. Thinking about it was like trying to reconstruct the things you had done during the vilest, deepest drunk of your life.

One thing he was sure of but didn't tell any of the reporters, because it made no sense: the burning man's scream seemed to grow in volume, as if he were a stereo that was being turned up. He was right there in front of Dearborn, and the *pitch* of the scream never changed, but the volume most certainly did. It was as if the man were some incredibly loud object that was just arriving here.

Dearborn ran down the hall with the full ice-bucket

in his hand. The burning man—"It was just his shirt on fire, I saw that right away," he told the reporters—struck the door opposite the room he had come out of, rebounded, staggered, and fell to his knees. That was when Dearborn reached him. He put his foot on the burning shoulder of the screaming man's shirt and pushed him over onto the hall carpet. Then he dumped the contents of the ice-bucket onto him.

These things were blurred in his memory, but accessible. He was aware that the burning shirt seemed to be casting far too much light—a sweltering yellow-orange light that made him think of a trip he and his brother had made to Australia two years before. They had rented an all-wheel drive and had taken off across the Great Australian Desert (the few natives called it the Great Australian Bugger-All, the Dearborn brothers discovered), a hell of a trip, great, but spooky. Especially the big rock in the middle, Ayers Rock. They had reached it right around sunset and the light on its man faces was like this . . . hot and strange . . . not really what you thought of as earthlight at all . . .

He dropped beside the burning man who was now only the smoldering man, the covered-with-ice-cubes man, and rolled him over to stifle the flames reaching around to the back of the shirt. When he did, he saw the skin on the left side of the man's neck had gone a smoky, bubbly red, and the lobe of his ear on that side had melted a little, but otherwise . . . otherwise . . .

Dearborn looked up, and it seemed—this was crazy, but it seemed the door to the room the man had come out of was filled with the burning light of an Australian sundown, the hot light of an empty place where things no man had ever seen might live. It was terrible, that light (and the low buzzing, like an electric clipper that was trying desperately to speak), but it was fascinating, too. He wanted to go into it. He wanted to see what was behind it.

Perhaps Mike saved Dearborn's life, as well. He was certainly aware that Dearborn was getting up—as if Mike no longer held any interest for him—and that his face was filled with the blazing, pulsing light coming out of 1408. He remembered this better than Dearborn later did himself, but of course Rufe Dearborn had not been reduced to setting himself on fire in order to survive.

Mike grabbed the cuff of Dearborn's slacks. "Don't go in there," he said in a cracked, smoky voice. "You'll never come out."

Dearborn stopped, looking down at the reddening, blistering face of the man on the carpet.

"It's haunted," Mike said, and as if the words had been a talisman, the door of room 1408 slammed furiously shut, cutting off the light, cutting off the terrible buzz that was almost words.

Rufus Dearborn, one of Singer Sewing Machine's finest, ran down to the elevators and pulled the fire alarm.

IV

There's an interesting picture of Mike Enslin in *Treating the Burn Victim: A Diagnostic Approach,* the sixteenth edition of which appeared about sixteen months after Mike's short stay in room 1408 of the Hotel Dolphin. The photo shows just his torso, but it's Mike, all right. One can tell by the white square on the left side of his chest. The flesh all around it is an angry red, actually blistered into second-degree burns in some places. The white square marks the left breast pocket of the shirt he was wearing that night, the lucky shirt with his minicorder in the pocket.

The minicorder itself melted around the corners, but it still works, and the tape inside it was fine. It's the things on it which are not fine. After listening to it three or four times, Mike's agent, Sam Farrell, tossed it into his wall-safe, refusing to acknowledge the goose-flesh all over his tanned, scrawny arms. In that wall-safe the tape has stayed ever since. Farrell has no urge to take it out and play it again, not for himself, not for his curious friends, some of whom would cheerfully kill to hear it; New York publishing is a small community, and word gets around.

He doesn't like Mike's voice on the tape, he doesn't like the stuff that voice is saying (*My brother was actually eaten by wolves one winter on the Connecticut Turnpike* . . . what in God's name is *that* supposed to mean?), and most of all he doesn't like the background sounds on the tape, a kind of liquid smoosh-ing that sometimes sounds like clothes churning around in an oversudsed washer, sometimes like one of those old electric hair-clippers . . . and sometimes weirdly like a voice.

While Mike was still in the hospital, a man named Olin—the manager of the goddamned hotel, if you please—came and asked Sam Farrell if he could listen to that tape. Farrell said no, he couldn't; what Olin could do was take himself on out of the agent's office at a rapid hike and thank God all the way back to the fleabag where he worked that Mike Enslin had decided not to sue either the hotel or Olin for negligence.

"I tried to persuade him not to go in," Olin said quietly. A man who spent most of his working days listening to tired travellers and petulant guests bitch about everything from their rooms to the magazine selection in the newsstand, he wasn't much perturbed by Farrell's rancor. "I tried everything in my power. If anyone was negligent that night, Mr. Farrell, it was your client. He believed too much in nothing. Very unwise behavior. Very *unsafe* behavior. I would guess he has changed somewhat in that regard."

In spite of Farrell's distaste for the tape, he would like Mike to listen to it, acknowledge it, perhaps use it as a pad from which to launch a new book. There is a book in what happened to Mike, Farrell knows it—not just a chapter, a forty-page case history, but an entire book. One that might outsell all three of the *Ten Nights* books combined. And of course he doesn't believe Mike's assertion that he has finished not only with ghost-tales but with all writing. Writers say that from time to time, that's all. The occasional prima donna outburst is part of what makes writers in the first place.

As for Mike Enslin himself, he got off lucky, all things considered. And he knows it. He could have been burned much more badly than he actually was;

if not for Mr. Dearborn and his bucket of ice, he might have had twenty or even thirty different skin-graft procedures to suffer through instead of only four. His neck is scarred on the left side in spite of the grafts, but the doctors at the Boston Burn Institute tell him the scars will fade on their own. He also knows that the burns, painful as they were in the weeks and months after that night, were necessary. If not for the matches with CLOSE COVER BEFORE STRIK-ING written on the front, he would have died in 1408, and his end would have been unspeakable. To a coroner it might have looked like a stroke or a heart attack, but the actual cause of death would have been much nastier.

Much nastier.

He was also lucky in having produced three popular books on ghosts and hauntings before actually running afoul of a place that *is* haunted—this he also knows. Sam Farrell may not believe Mike's life as a writer is over, but Sam doesn't need to; Mike knows it for both of them. He cannot so much as write a postcard without feeling cold all over his skin and being nauseated deep in the pit of his belly. Sometimes just looking at a pen (or a tape recorder) will make him think: *The pictures were crooked. I tried to straighten the pictures.* He doesn't know what this means. He can't remember the pictures or anything else from room 1408, and he is glad. That is a mercy. His blood-pressure isn't so good these days (his doctor told him that burn victims often develop problems with their blood-pressure and put him on medication), his eyes trouble him (his ophthalmologist told him to start taking Ocuvites), he has consistent back problems, his prostate has gotten too large . . . but he can deal with these things. He knows he isn't the first person to escape 1408 without really escaping—Olin tried to tell him—but it isn't all bad. At least he doesn't remember. Sometimes he has nightmares, quite often, in fact (almost every goddam *night,* in fact), but he rarely remembers them when he wakes up. A sense that things are rounding off at the corners, mostly—melting the way the corners of his minicorder melted. He lives on Long Island these days, and when the weather is good he takes long walks on the beach. The closest he has ever come to articulating what he does remember about his seventy-odd (*very* odd) minutes in 1408 was on one of those walks. "It was never human," he told the incoming waves in a choked, halting voice. "Ghosts . . . at least ghosts were once human. The thing in the wall, though . . . that thing . . ."

Time may improve it, he can and does hope for that. Time may fade it, as it will fade the scars on his neck. In the meantime, though, he sleeps with the lights on in his bedroom, so he will know at once where he is when he wakes up from the bad dreams. He has had all the phones taken out of the house; at some point just below the place where his conscious mind seems able to go, he is afraid of picking the phone up and hearing a buzzing, inhuman voice spit, "This is *nine! Nine!* We have killed your friends! Every friend is now dead!"

And when the sun goes down on clear evenings, he pulls every shade and blind and drape in the house. He sits like a man in a darkroom until his watch tells him the light—even the last fading glow along the horizon—must be gone.

He can't stand the light that comes at sunset.

That yellow deepening to orange, like light in the Australian desert.

Riding the Bullet

I think I've said almost everything that needs to be said about this story in the Introduction. It's essentially my telling of a tale you can hear in almost any small town. And, like an earlier story of mine ("The Woman in the Room," in Night Shift*), it's an attempt to talk about how my own mother's approaching death made me feel. There comes a time in most lives when we must face the deaths of our loved ones as an actual reality . . . and, by proxy, the fact of our own approaching death. This is probably the single great subject of horror fiction: our need to cope with a mystery that can be understood only with the aid of a hopeful imagination.*

I've never told anyone this story, and never thought I would—not because I was afraid of being disbelieved, exactly, but because I was ashamed . . . and because it was *mine*. I've always felt that telling it would cheapen both me and the story itself, make it smaller and more mundane, no more than a camp counselor's ghost story told before lights-out. I think I was also afraid that if I told it, heard it with my own ears, I might start to disbelieve it myself. But since

my mother died I haven't been able to sleep very
well. I doze off and then snap back again, wide-
awake and shivering. Leaving the bedside lamp on
helps, but not as much as you might think. There are
so many more shadows at night, have you ever
noticed that? Even with a light on there are so many
shadows. The long ones could be the shadows of anything, you think.

Anything at all.

I was a junior at the University of Maine when Mrs.
McCurdy called about Ma. My father died when I was
too young to remember him and I was an only child, so
it was just Alan and Jean Parker against the world.
Mrs. McCurdy, who lived just up the road, called at the
apartment I shared with three other guys. She had gotten the number off the magnetic minder-board Ma
kept on her fridge.

"'Twas a stroke," she said in that long and drawling
Yankee accent of hers. "Happened at the restaurant.
But don't you go flyin off all half-cocked. Doctor says
it wa'ant too bad. She's awake and she's talkin."

"Yeah, but is she making sense?" I asked. I was trying to sound calm, even amused, but my heart was
beating fast and the living room suddenly felt too
warm. I had the apartment all to myself; it was
Wednesday, and both my roomies had classes all day.

"Oh, ayuh. First thing she said was for me to call you
but not to scare you. That's pretty sensible, wouldn't
you say?"

"Yeah." But of course I *was* scared. When someone
calls and tells you your mother's been taken from work

to the hospital in an ambulance, how else are you supposed to feel?

"She said for you to stay right there and mind your schoolin until the weekend. She said you could come then, if you didn't have too much studyin t'do."

Sure, I thought. Fat chance. I'd just stay here in this ratty, beer-smelling apartment while my mother lay in a hospital bed a hundred miles south, maybe dying.

"She's still a young woman, your Ma," Mrs. McCurdy said. "It's just that she's let herself get awful heavy these last few years, and she's got the hypertension. Plus the cigarettes. She's going to have to give up the smokes."

I doubted if she would, though, stroke or no stroke, and about that I was right—my mother loved her smokes. I thanked Mrs. McCurdy for calling.

"First thing I did when I got home," she said. "So when are you coming, Alan? Sad'dy?" There was a sly note in her voice that suggested she knew better.

I looked out the window into a perfect afternoon in October: bright blue New England sky over trees that were shaking down their yellow leaves onto Mill Street. Then I glanced at my watch. Twenty past three. I'd just been on my way out to my four o'clock philosophy seminar when the phone rang.

"You kidding?" I asked. "I'll be there tonight."

Her laughter was dry and a little cracked around the edges—Mrs. McCurdy was a great one to talk about giving up the cigarettes, her and her Winstons. "Good boy! You'll go straight to the hospital, won't you, then drive out to the house?"

"I guess so, yeah," I said. I saw no sense in telling

Mrs. McCurdy that there was something wrong with the transmission of my old car, and it wasn't going anywhere but the driveway for the foreseeable future. I'd hitchhike down to Lewiston, then out to our little house in Harlow if it wasn't too late. If it was, I'd snooze in one of the hospital lounges. It wouldn't be the first time I'd ridden my thumb home from school. Or slept sitting up with my head leaning against a Coke machine, for that matter.

"I'll make sure the key's under the red wheelbarrow," she said. "You know where I mean, don't you?"

"Sure." My mother kept an old red wheelbarrow by the door to the back shed; in the summer it foamed with flowers. Thinking of it for some reason brought Mrs. McCurdy's news home to me as a true fact: my mother was in the hospital, the little house in Harlow where I'd grown up was going to be dark tonight—there was no one there to turn on the lights after the sun went down. Mrs. McCurdy could say she was young, but when you're just twenty-one yourself, forty-eight seems ancient.

"Be careful, Alan. Don't speed."

My speed, of course, would be up to whoever I hooked a ride with, and I personally hoped that whoever it was would go like hell. As far as I was concerned, I couldn't get to Central Maine Medical Center fast enough. Still, there was no sense worrying Mrs. McCurdy.

"I won't. Thanks."

"Welcome," she said. "Your Ma's going to be just fine. And won't she be some happy to see you."

I hung up, then scribbled a note saying what had

happened and where I was going. I asked Hector Passmore, the more responsible of my roommates, to call my advisor and ask him to tell my instructors what was up so I wouldn't get whacked for cutting—two or three of my teachers were real bears about that. Then I stuffed a change of clothes into my backpack, added my dog-eared copy of *Introduction to Philosophy,* and headed out. I dropped the course the following week, although I had been doing quite well in it. The way I looked at the world changed that night, changed quite a lot, and nothing in my philosophy textbook seemed to fit the changes. I came to understand that there are things underneath, you see—*underneath*—and no book can explain what they are. I think that sometimes it's best to just forget those things are there. If you can, that is.

It's a hundred and twenty miles from the University of Maine in Orono to Lewiston in Androscoggin County, and the quickest way to get there is by I-95. The turnpike isn't such a good road to take if you're hitchhiking, though; the State Police are apt to boot anyone they see off—even if you're just standing on the ramp they give you the boot—and if the same cop catches you twice, he's apt to write you a ticket, as well. So I took Route 68, which winds southwest from Bangor. It's a pretty well-traveled road, and if you don't look like an out-and-out psycho, you can usually do quite well. The cops leave you alone, too, for the most part.

My first lift was with a morose insurance man and took me as far as Newport. I stood at the intersection of Route 68 and Route 2 for about twenty minutes, then got a ride with an elderly gentleman who was on his way to Bowdoinham. He kept grabbing at his crotch as he drove. It was as if he was trying to catch something that was running around in there.

"My wife allus told me I'd wind up in the ditch with a knife in my back if I kept on pickin up hitch-hikers," he said, "but when I see a young fella standin t'side of the rud, I allus remember my own younger days. Rode my thumb quite a bit, so I did. Rode the rods, too. And lookit this, her dead four year and me still a-goin, driving this same old Dodge. I miss her somethin turrible." He snatched at his crotch. "Where you headed, son?"

I told him I was going to Lewiston, and why.

"That's turrible," he said. "Your Ma! I'm so sorry!"

His sympathy was so strong and spontaneous that it made the corners of my eyes prickle. I blinked the tears back. The last thing in the world I wanted was to burst out crying in this old man's old car, which rattled and wallowed and smelled quite strongly of pee.

"Mrs. McCurdy—the lady who called me—said it isn't that serious. My mother's still young, only forty-eight."

"Still! A stroke!" He was genuinely dismayed. He snatched at the baggy crotch of his green pants again, yanking with an old man's oversized, clawlike hand. "A stroke's allus serious! Son, I'd take you to the CMMC myself—drive you right up to the front door—if I hadn't promised my brother Ralph I'd take him up to the nursin home in Gates. His wife's there, she has that forgettin disease, I can't think what in the world they call it, Anderson's or Alvarez or somethin like that—"

"Alzheimer's," I said.

"Ayuh, prob'ly I'm gettin it myself. Hell, I'm tempted to take you anyway."

"You don't need to do that," I said. "I can get a ride from Gates easy."

"Still," he said. "Your mother! A stroke! Only forty-eight!" He grabbed at the baggy crotch of his pants. "Fuckin truss!" he cried, then laughed—the sound was both desperate and amused. "Fuckin rupture! If you stick around, son, all your works start fallin apart. God kicks your ass in the end, let me tell you. But you're a good boy to just drop everythin and go to her like you're doin."

"She's a good Mom," I said, and once again I felt the tears bite. I never felt very homesick when I went away to school—a little bit the first week, that was all—but I felt homesick then. There was just me and her, no other close relatives. I couldn't image life without her. Wasn't too bad, Mrs. McCurdy had said; a stroke, but not too bad. Damn old lady better be telling the truth, I thought, she just better be.

We rode in silence for a little while. It wasn't the fast ride I'd hoped for—the old man maintained a steady forty-five miles an hour and sometimes wandered over the white line to sample the other lane—but it was a long ride, and that was really just as good. Highway 68 unrolled before us, turning its way through miles of woods and splitting the little towns that were there and gone in a slow blink, each one with its bar and its self-service gas station: New Sharon,

Ophelia, West Ophelia, Ganistan (which had once been *Af*ghanistan, strange but true), Mechanic Falls, Castle View, Castle Rock. The bright blue of the sky dimmed as the day drained out of it; the old man turned on first his parking lights and then his headlights. They were the high beams but he didn't seem to notice, not even when cars coming the other way flashed their own high beams at him.

"My sister'n-law don't even remember her own name," he said. "She don't know aye, yes, no, nor maybe. That's what that Anderson's Disease does to you, son. There's a look in her eyes . . . like she's sayin 'Let me *out* of here' . . . or *would* say it, if she could think of the words. Do you know what I mean?"

"Yes," I said. I took a deep breath and wondered if the pee I smelled was the old man's or if he maybe had a dog that rode with him sometimes. I wondered if he'd be offended if I rolled down my window a little. Finally I did. He didn't seem to notice, any more than he noticed the oncoming cars flashing their highs at him.

Around seven o'clock we breasted a hill in West Gates and my chauffeur cried, "Lookit, son! The moon! Ain't she a corker?"

She was indeed a corker—a huge orange ball hoisting itself over the horizon. I thought there was nevertheless something terrible about it. It looked both pregnant and infected. Looking at the rising moon, a sudden and awful thought came to me: what if I got to the hospital and my Ma didn't recognize me? What if her memory was gone, completely shot, and she didn't know aye, yes, no, nor maybe? What if the doctor told me she'd need someone to take care of her for the rest of her life? That someone would have to be me, of course; there was no one else. Goodbye college. What about that, friends and neighbors?

"Make a wish on it, boyo!" the old man cried. In his excitement his voice grew sharp and unpleasant—it was like having shards of glass stuffed into your ear. He gave his crotch a terrific tug. Something in there made a snapping sound. I didn't see how you could yank on your crotch like that and not rip your balls right off at the stem, truss or no truss. "Wish you make on the ha'vest moon allus comes true, that's what my father said!"

So I wished that my mother would know me when I walked into her room, that her eyes would light up at once and she would say my name. I made that wish and immediately wished I could have it back again; I thought that no wish made in that fevery orange light could come to any good.

"Ah, son!" the old man said. "I wish my wife was here! I'd beg forgiveness for every sha'ap and unkind word I ever said to her!"

Twenty minutes later, with the last light of the day still in the air and the moon still hanging low and bloated in the sky, we arrived in Gates Falls. There's a yellow blinker at the intersection of Route 68 and Pleasant Street. Just before he reached it, the old man swerved to the side of the road, bumping the Dodge's right front wheel up over the curb and then back down again. It rattled my teeth. The old man looked at me with a kind of wild, defiant excitement—everything about him was wild, although I hadn't seen that at first; everything about him had that broken-glass feeling. And everything that came out of his mouth seemed to be an exclamation.

"I'll take you up there! I will, yessir! Never mind Ralph! Hell with him! You just say the word!"

I wanted to get to my mother, but the thought of another twenty miles with the smell of piss in the air and cars flashing their brights at us wasn't very pleasant. Neither was the image of the old fellow wandering and weaving across four lanes of Lisbon Street. Mostly, though, it was him. I couldn't stand another twenty miles of crotch-snatching and that excited broken-glass voice.

"Hey, no," I said, "that's okay. You go on and take care of your brother." I opened the door and what I feared happened—he reached out and took hold of my arm with his twisted old man's hand. It was the hand with which he kept tearing at his crotch.

"You just say the word!" he told me. His voice was hoarse, confidential. His fingers were pressing deep into the flesh just below my armpit. "I'll take you right to the hospital door! Ayuh! Don't matter if I never saw you before in my life nor you me! Don't matter aye, yes, no, nor maybe! I'll take you right . . . *there!*"

"It's okay," I repeated, and all at once I was fighting an urge to bolt out of the car, leaving my shirt behind in his grip if that was what it took to get free. It was as if he were drowning. I thought that when I moved, his grip would tighten, that he might even go for the nape of my neck, but he didn't. His fingers loosened, then slipped away entirely as I put my leg out. And I wondered, as we always do when an irrational moment of panic passes, what I had been so afraid of in the first place. He was just an elderly carbon-based life-form in an elderly Dodge's pee-smelling ecosystem, looking disappointed that his offer had been refused. Just an old man who couldn't get comfortable in his truss. What in God's name had I been afraid of?

"I thank you for the ride and even more for the offer," I said. "But I can go out that way"—I pointed at Pleasant Street—"and I'll have a ride in no time."

He was quiet for a moment, then sighed and nodded. "Ayuh, that's the best way to go," he said. "Stay right out of town, nobody wants to give a fella a ride in town, no one wants to slow down and get honked at."

He was right about that; hitchhiking in town, even a small one like Gates Falls, was futile. I guess he *had* spent some time riding his thumb.

"But son, are you sure? You know what they say about a bird in the hand."

I hesitated again. He was right about a bird in the hand, too. Pleasant Street became Ridge Road a mile or so west of the blinker, and Ridge Road ran through fifteen miles of woods before arriving at Route 196 on the outskirts of Lewiston. It was almost dark, and it's always harder to get a ride at night—when headlights pick you out on a country road, you look like an escapee from Wyndham Boys' Correctional even with your hair combed and your shirt tucked in. But I didn't want to ride with the old man anymore. Even now, when I was safely out of his car, I thought there was something creepy about him—maybe it was just the way his voice seemed full of exclamation points. Besides, I've always been lucky getting rides.

"I'm sure," I said. "And thanks again. Really."

"Anytime, son. Anytime. My wife . . ." He stopped, and I saw there were tears leaking from the corners of his eyes. I thanked him again, then slammed the door shut before he could say anything else.

I hurried across the street, my shadow appearing and disappearing in the light of the blinker. On the far side I turned and looked back. The Dodge was still there, parked beside Frank's Fountain & Fruits. By the light of the blinker and the streetlight twenty feet or so beyond the car, I could see him sitting slumped over the wheel. The thought came to me that he was dead, that I had killed him with my refusal to let him help.

Then a car came around the corner and the driver flashed his high beams at the Dodge. This time the old man dipped his own lights, and that was how I knew he was still alive. A moment later he pulled back into the street and piloted the Dodge slowly around the corner. I watched until he was gone, then looked up at the moon. It was starting to lose its orange bloat, but there was still something sinister about it. It occurred to me that I had never heard of wishing on the moon before—the evening star, yes, but not the moon. I wished again I could take my own wish back; as the dark drew down and I stood there at the crossroads, it was too easy to think of that story about the monkey's paw.

* * *

I walked out Pleasant Street, waving my thumb at cars that went by without even slowing. At first there were shops and houses on both sides of the road, then the sidewalk ended and the trees closed in again, silently retaking the land. Each time the road flooded with light, pushing my shadow out ahead of me, I'd turn around, stick out my thumb, and put what I hoped was a reassuring smile on my face. And each time the oncoming car would swoosh by without slowing. Once someone shouted out, "Get a job, monkeymeat!" and there was laughter.

I'm not afraid of the dark—or wasn't then—but I began to be afraid I'd made a mistake by not taking the old man up on his offer to drive me straight to the hospital. I could have made a sign reading NEED A RIDE, MOTHER SICK before starting out, but I doubted if it would have helped. Any psycho can make a sign, after all.

I walked along, sneakers scuffing the gravelly dirt of the soft shoulder, listening to the sounds of the gathering night: a dog, far away; an owl, much closer; the sigh of a rising wind. The sky was bright with moonlight, but I couldn't see the moon itself just now—the trees were tall here, and had blotted it out for the time being.

As I left Gates Falls farther behind, fewer cars passed me. My decision not to take the old man up on his offer seemed more foolish with each passing minute. I began to imagine my mother in her hospital bed, mouth turned down in a frozen sneer, losing her grip on life but trying to hold onto that increasingly slippery bark for me, not knowing I wasn't going to make it simply because I hadn't liked an old man's shrill voice, or the pissy smell of his car.

I breasted a steep hill and stepped back into moonlight again at the top. The trees were gone on my right, replaced by a small country graveyard. The stones gleamed in the pale light. Something small and black was crouched beside one of them, watching me. I took a step closer, curious. The black thing moved and became a woodchuck. It spared me a single reproachful red-eyed glance and was gone into the high grass. All at once I became aware that I was very tired, in fact close to exhausted. I had been running on pure adrenaline since Mrs. McCurdy called five hours before, but now that was gone. That was the bad part. The good part was that useless sense of frantic urgency left me, at least for the time being. I had made my choice, decided on Ridge Road instead of Route 68, and there was no sense beating myself up over it—fun is fun and done is done, my mother sometimes said. She was full of stuff like that, little Zen aphorisms that almost made sense. Sense or nonsense, this one comforted me now. If she was dead when I got to the hospital, that was that. Probably she wouldn't be. Doctor said it wasn't too bad, according to Mrs. McCurdy; Mrs. McCurdy had also said she was still a young woman. A bit on the heavy side, true, and a heavy smoker in the bargain, but still young.

Meantime, I was out here in the williwags and I was suddenly tired out—my feet felt as if they had been dipped in cement.

There was a stone wall running along the road side of the cemetery, with a break in it where two ruts ran through. I sat on the wall with my feet planted in one of these ruts. From this position I could see a good length of Ridge Road in both directions. When I saw headlights coming west, in the direction of Lewiston, I could walk back to the edge of the road and put my thumb out. In the meantime I'd just sit here with my backpack in my lap and wait for some strength to come back into my legs.

A groundmist, fine and glowing, was rising out of the grass. The trees surrounding the cemetery on three sides rustled in the rising breeze. From beyond the graveyard came the sound of running water and the occasional plunk-plunk of a frog. The place was beautiful and oddly soothing, like a picture in a book of romantic poems.

I looked both ways along the road. Nothing coming, not so much as a glow on the horizon. Putting my pack down in the wheelrut where I'd been dangling my feet, I got up and walked into the cemetery. A lock of hair had fallen onto my brow; the wind blew it off. The mist roiled lazily around my shoes. The stones at the back were old; more than a few had fallen over. The ones at the front were much newer. I bent, hands planted on knees, to look at one which was surrounded by almost-fresh flowers. By moonlight the name was easy to read: GEORGE STAUB. Below it were the dates marking the brief span of George Staub's life: January 19, 1977, at one end, October 12, 1998, at the other. That explained the flowers which had only begun to wilt; October 12th was two days ago and 1998 was just two years ago. George's friends and relatives had stopped by to pay their respects. Below the name and dates was something else, a brief inscription. I leaned down further to read it—

—and stumbled back, terrified and all too aware that I was by myself, visiting a graveyard by moonlight.

Fun Is Fun and Done Is Done

was the inscription.

My mother was dead, had died perhaps at that very minute, and something had sent me a message. Something with a thoroughly unpleasant sense of humor.

I began to back slowly toward the road, listening to the wind in the trees, listening to the stream, listening to the frog, suddenly afraid I might hear another sound, the sound of rubbing earth and tearing roots as something not quite dead reached up, groping for one of my sneakers—

My feet tangled together and I fell down, thumping my elbow on a gravestone, barely missing another with the back of my head. I landed with a grassy thud, looking up at the moon which had just barely cleared the trees. It was white instead of orange now, and as bright as a polished bone.

Instead of panicking me further, the fall cleared my head. I didn't know what I'd seen, but it couldn't have been what I *thought* I'd seen; that kind of stuff might work in John Carpenter and Wes Craven movies, but it wasn't the stuff of real life.

Yes, okay, good, a voice whispered in my head. *And if you just walk out of here now, you can go on believing that. You can go on believing it for the rest of your life.*

"Fuck that," I said, and got up. The seat of my jeans was wet, and I plucked it away from my skin. It wasn't exactly easy to reapproach the stone marking George Staub's final resting-place, but it wasn't as hard as I'd expected, either. The wind sighed through the trees, still rising, signalling a change in the weather. Shadows danced unsteadily around me. Branches rubbed together, a creaky sound off in the woods. I bent over the tombstone and read:

GEORGE STAUB
JANUARY 19, 1977–OCTOBER 12, 1998
Well Begun, Too Soon Done

I stood there, leaning down with my hands planted just above my knees, not aware of how fast my heart had been beating until it started to slow down. A nasty little coincidence, that was all, and was it any wonder that I'd misread what was beneath the name and dates? Even without being tired and under stress, I might have read it wrong—moonlight was a notorious misleader. Case closed.

Except I *knew* what I'd read: *Fun Is Fun and Done Is Done.*

My Ma was dead.

"Fuck that," I repeated, and turned away. As I did, I realized the mist curling through the grass and around my ankles had begun to brighten. I could hear the mutter of an approaching motor. A car was coming.

I hurried back through the opening in the rock wall,

snagging my pack on the way by. The lights of the approaching car were halfway up the hill. I stuck out my thumb just as they struck me, momentarily blinding me. I knew the guy was going to stop even before he started slowing down. It's funny how you can just know sometimes, but anyone who's spent a lot of time hitchhiking will tell you that it happens.

The car passed me, brakelights flaring, and swerved onto the soft shoulder near the end of the rock wall dividing the graveyard from Ridge Road. I ran to it with my backpack banging against the side of my knee. The car was a Mustang, one of the cool ones from the late sixties or early seventies. The motor rumbled loudly, the fat sound of it coming through a muffler that maybe wouldn't pass inspection the next time the sticker came due . . . but that wasn't my problem.

I swung the door open and slid inside. As I put my backpack between my feet an odor struck me, something almost familiar and a trifle unpleasant. "Thank you," I said. "Thanks a lot."

The guy behind the wheel was wearing faded jeans and a black tee-shirt with the arms cut off. His skin was tanned, the muscles heavy, and his right bicep was ringed with a blue barbwire tattoo. He was wearing a green John Deere cap turned around backward. There was a button pinned near the round collar of his tee-shirt, but I couldn't read it from my angle. "Not a problem," he said. "You headed up the city?"

"Yes," I said. In this part of the world "up the city" meant Lewiston, the only city of any size north of Portland. As I closed the door, I saw one of those pine-tree air fresheners hanging from the rearview mirror. That was what I'd smelled. It sure wasn't my night as far as odors went; first pee and now artificial pine. Still, it was a ride. I should have been relieved. And as the guy accelerated back onto Ridge Road, the big engine of his vintage Mustang growling, I tried to tell myself I *was* relieved.

"What's going on for you in the city?" the driver asked. I put him at about my age, some townie who maybe went to vocational-technical school in Auburn or maybe worked in one of the few remaining textile mills in the area. He'd probably fixed up this Mustang in his spare time, because that was what townie kids did: drank beer, smoked a little rope, fixed up their cars. Or their motorcycles.

"My brother's getting married. I'm going to be his best man." I told this lie with absolutely no premeditation. I didn't want him to know about my mother, although I didn't know why. Something was wrong here. I didn't know what it was or why I should think such a thing in the first place, but I knew. I was positive. "The rehearsal's tomorrow. Plus a stag party tomorrow night."

"Yeah? That right?" He turned to look at me, wide-set eyes and handsome face, full lips smiling slightly, the eyes unbelieving.

"Yeah," I said.

I was afraid. Just like that I was afraid again. Something was wrong, had maybe started being wrong when the old geezer in the Dodge had invited me to wish on the infected moon instead of on a star. Or maybe from the moment I'd picked up the telephone and listened to Mrs. McCurdy saying she had some bad news for me, but 'twasn't s'bad as it could've been.

"Well that's good," said the young man in the turned-around cap. "A brother getting married, man, that's good. What's your name?"

I wasn't just afraid, I was terrified. Everything was wrong, *everything,* and I didn't know why or how it could possibly have happened so fast. I did know one thing, however: I wanted the driver of the Mustang to know my name no more than I wanted him to know my business in Lewiston. Not that I'd be getting to Lewiston. I was suddenly sure that I would never see Lewiston again. It was like knowing the car was going to stop. And there was the smell, I knew something about that, as well. It wasn't the air freshener; it was something *beneath* the air freshener.

"Hector," I said, giving him my roommate's name. "Hector Passmore, that's me." It came out of my dry mouth smooth and calm, and that was good. Something inside me insisted that I must not let the driver of the Mustang know that I sensed something wrong. It was my only chance.

He turned toward me a little, and I could read his button: I RODE THE BULLET AT THRILL VILLAGE, LACONIA. I knew the place; had been there, although not for a long time.

I could also see a heavy black line which circled his throat just as the barbwire tattoo circled his upper arm, only the line around the driver's throat wasn't a tattoo. Dozens of black marks crossed it vertically. They were the stitches put in by whoever had put his head back on his body.

"Nice to meet you, Hector," he said. "I'm George Staub."

My hand seemed to float out like a hand in a dream. I wish that it had been a dream, but it wasn't; it had all the sharp edges of reality. The smell on top was pine. The smell underneath was some chemical, probably formaldehyde. I was riding with a dead man.

The Mustang rushed along Ridge Road at sixty miles an hour, chasing its high beams under the light of a polished button moon. To either side the trees crowding the road danced and writhed in the wind. George Staub smiled at me with his empty eyes, then let go of my hand and returned his attention to the road. In high school I'd read *Dracula,* and now a line from it recurred, clanging in my head like a cracked bell: The dead drive fast.

Can't let him know I know. This also clanged in my head. It wasn't much, but it was all I had. *Can't let him know, can't let him, can't.* I wondered where the old man was now. Safe at his brother's? Or had the old man been in on it all along? Was he maybe right behind us, driving along in his old Dodge, hunched over the wheel and snapping at his truss? Was he dead, too? Probably not. The dead drive fast, according to Bram Stoker, and the old man had never gone a tick over forty-five. I felt demented laughter bubbling in the back of my throat and held it down. If I laughed he'd know. And he mustn't know, because that was my only hope.

"There's nothing like a wedding," he said.

"Yeah," I said, "everyone should do it at least twice."

My hands had settled on each other and were squeezing. I could feel the nails digging into the backs of them just above the knuckles, but the sensation was distant. I couldn't let him know, that was the thing. The woods were all around us, the only light was the heartless bone-glow of the moon, and I couldn't let him know that I knew he was dead. Because he wasn't a ghost, nothing so harmless. You might *see* a ghost, but what sort of thing stopped to give you a ride? What kind of creature was that? Zombie? Ghoul? Vampire? None of the above?

George Staub laughed. "Do it twice! Yeah, man, that's my whole family!"

"Mine, too," I said. My voice sounded calm, just the voice of a hitchhiker passing the time of day——night, in this case——making agreeable conversation as some small payment for his ride. "There's really nothing like a funeral."

"Wedding," he said mildly. In the light from the dashboard his face was waxy, the face of a corpse before the makeup went on. That turned-around cap was particularly horrible. It made you wonder how much was left beneath it. I had read somewhere that morticians sawed off the top of the skull and took out the brains and put in some sort of chemically treated cotton. To keep the face from falling in, maybe.

"Wedding," I said through numb lips, and even laughed a little——a light little chuckle. "Wedding's what I meant to say."

"We always say what we mean to say, that's what I think," the driver said. He was still smiling.

Yes, Freud had believed that, too, I'd read it in

Psych 101. I doubted if this fellow knew much about Freud, I didn't think many Freudian scholars wore sleeveless tee-shirts and baseball caps turned around backward, but he knew enough. Funeral, I'd said. Dear Christ, I'd said funeral. It came to me then that he was playing me. I didn't want to let him know I knew he was dead. *He* didn't want to let me know that he knew I knew he was dead. And so I couldn't let him know that I knew that he knew that . . .

The world began to swing in front of me. In a moment it would begin to spin, then to whirl, and I'd lose it. I closed my eyes for a moment. In the darkness the afterimage of the moon hung, turning green.

"You feeling all right, man?" he asked. The concern in his voice was gruesome.

"Yes," I said, opening my eyes. Things had steadied again. The pain in the backs of my hands where my nails were digging into the skin was strong and real. And the smell. Not just pine air freshener, not just chemicals. There was a smell of earth, as well.

"You sure?" he asked.

"Just a little tired. Been hitchhiking a long time. And sometimes I get a little carsick." Inspiration suddenly struck. "You know what, I think you better let me out. If I get a little fresh air, my stomach will settle. Someone else will come along and—"

"I couldn't do that," he said. "Leave you out here? No way. It could be an hour before someone came along, and they might not pick you up when they did. I got to take care of you. What's that song? Get me to the church on time, right? No way I'm letting you out. Crack your window a little, that'll help. I know it doesn't smell exactly great in here. I hung up that air freshener, but those things don't work worth a shit. Of course, some smells are harder to get rid of than others."

I wanted to reach out for the window-crank and turn it, let in the fresh air, but the muscles in my arm wouldn't seem to tighten. All I could do was sit there with my hands locked together, nails biting into the backs of them. One set of muscles wouldn't work; another wouldn't stop working. What a joke.

"It's like that story," he said. "The one about the kid who buys the almost new Cadillac for seven hundred and fifty dollars. You know that story, don't you?"

"Yeah," I said through my numb lips. I didn't know the story, but I knew perfectly well that I didn't want to hear it, didn't want to hear any story this man might have to tell. "That one's famous." Ahead of us the road leaped forward like a road in an old black-and-white movie.

"Yeah, it is, fucking famous. So the kid's looking for a car and he sees an almost brand-new Cadillac on this guy's lawn."

"I said I—"

"Yeah, and there's a sign that says FOR SALE BY OWNER in the window."

There was a cigarette parked behind his ear. He reached for it, and when he did his shirt pulled up in the front. I could see another puckered black line there, more stitches. Then he leaned forward to punch in the cigarette lighter and his shirt dropped back into place.

"Kid knows he can't afford no Cadillac-car, can't

get within a *shout* of a Caddy, but he's curious, you know? So he goes over to the guy and says, 'How much does something like that go for?' And the guy, he turns off the hose he's got—cause he's washin the car, you know—and he says, 'Kid, this is your lucky day. Seven hundred and fifty bucks and you drive it away.'"

The cigarette lighter popped out. Staub pulled it free and pressed the coil to the end of his cigarette. He drew in smoke and I saw little tendrils come seeping out between the stitches holding the incision on his neck closed.

"The kid, he looks in through the driver's-side window and sees there's only seventeen thou on the odometer. He says to the guy, 'Yeah, sure, that's as funny as a screen door in a submarine.' The guy says, 'No joke, kid, pony up the cash and it's yours. Hell, I'll even take a check, you got a honest face.' And the kid says . . ."

I looked out the window. I *had* heard the story before, years ago, probably while I was still in junior high. In the version I'd been told the car was a Thunderbird instead of a Caddy, but otherwise everything was the same. The kid says *I may only be seventeen but I'm not an idiot, no one sells a car like this, especially one with low mileage, for only seven hundred and fifty bucks.* And the guy tells him he's doing it because the car smells, you can't get the smell out, he's tried and tried and nothing will take it out. You see he was on a business trip, a fairly long one, gone for at least . . .

". . . a coupla weeks," the driver was saying. He was smiling the way people do when they're telling a joke that really slays them. "And when he comes back, he finds the car in the garage and his wife in the car, she's been dead practically the whole time he's been gone. I don't know if it was suicide or a heart attack or what, but she's all bloated up and the car, it's full of that smell and all he wants to do is sell it, you know." He laughed. "That's quite a story, huh?"

"Why wouldn't he call home?" It was my mouth, talking all by itself. My brain was frozen. "He's gone for two weeks on a business trip and he never calls home once to see how his wife's doing?"

"Well," the driver said, "that's sorta beside the point, wouldn't you say? I mean hey, what a bargain— *that's* the point. Who wouldn't be tempted? After all, you could always drive the car with the fuckin windows open, right? And it's basically just a story. Fiction. I thought of it because of the smell in *this* car. Which is fact."

Silence. And I thought: *He's waiting for me to say something, waiting for me to end this.* And I wanted to. I did. Except . . . what then? What would he do then?

He rubbed the ball of his thumb over the button on his shirt, the one reading I RODE THE BULLET AT THRILL VILLAGE, LACONIA. I saw there was dirt under his fingernails. "That's where I was today," he said. "Thrill Village. I did some work for a guy and he gave me an all-day pass. My girlfriend was gonna go with me, but she called and said she was sick, she gets these periods that really hurt sometimes, they make her sick as a dog. It's too bad, but I always think, hey, what's the alternative? No rag at all, right, and then I'm in trouble, we both are." He yapped, a humorless bark of sound. "So I went by myself. No sense wasting an all-day pass. You ever been to Thrill Village?"

"Yes," I said. Once. When I was twelve.

"Who'd you go with?" he asked. "You didn't go alone, did you? Not if you were only twelve."

I hadn't told him that part, had I? No. He was playing with me, that was all, swatting me idly back and forth. I thought about opening the door and just rolling out into the night, trying to tuck my head into my arms before I hit, only I knew he'd reach over and pull me back before I could get away. And I couldn't raise my arms, anyway. The best I could do was clutch my hands together.

"No," I said. "I went with my dad. My Dad took me."

"Did you ride the Bullet? I rode that fucker four times. Man! It goes right upside down!" He looked at me and uttered another empty bark of laughter. The moonlight swam in his eyes, turning them into white circles, making them into the eyes of a statue. And I understood he was more than dead; he was crazy. "Did you ride that, Alan?"

I thought of telling him he had the wrong name, my name was Hector, but what was the use? We were coming to the end of it now.

"Yeah," I whispered. Not a single light out there except for the moon. The trees rushed by, writhing like spontaneous dancers at a tentshow revival. The road rushed under us. I looked at the speedometer and saw he was up to eighty miles an hour. We were riding the bullet right now, he and I; the dead drive fast. "Yeah, the Bullet. I rode it."

"Nah," he said. He drew on his cigarette, and once again I watched the little trickles of smoke escape from the stitched incision on his neck. "You never. Especially not with your father. You got into the line, all right, but you were with your Ma. The line was long, the line for the Bullet always is, and she didn't want to stand out there in the hot sun. She was fat even then, and the heat bothered her. But you pestered her all day, pestered pestered pestered, and here's the joke of it, man—when you finally got to the head of the line, you chickened. Didn't you?"

I said nothing. My tongue was stuck to the roof of my mouth.

His hand stole out, the skin yellow in the light of the Mustang's dashboard lights, the nails filthy, and gripped my locked hands. The strength went out of them when he did and they fell apart like a knot that magically unties itself at the touch of the magician's wand. His skin was cold and somehow snaky.

"*Didn't* you?"

"Yes," I said. I couldn't get my voice much above a whisper. "When we got close and I saw how high it was . . . how it turned over at the top and how they screamed inside when it did . . . I chickened out. She swatted me, and she wouldn't talk to me all the way home. I never rode the Bullet." Until now, at least.

"You should have, man. That's the best one. That's the one to ride. Nothin else is as good, at least not there. I stopped on the way home and got some beers at that store by the state line. I was gonna stop over my girlfriend's house, give her the button as a joke." He tapped the button on his chest, then unrolled his window and flicked his cigarette out into the windy night. "Only you probably know what happened."

Of course I knew. It was every ghost story you'd ever heard, wasn't it? He crashed his Mustang and when the cops got there he'd been sitting dead in the crumpled remains with his body behind the wheel and his head in the backseat, his cap turned around backward and his dead eyes staring up at the roof and ever since you see him on Ridge Road when the moon is full and the wind is high, *wheee-oooo,* we will return after this brief word from our sponsor. I know something now that I didn't before—the worst stories are the ones you've heard your whole life. Those are the real nightmares.

"Nothing like a funeral," he said, and laughed. "Isn't that what you said? You slipped there, Al. No doubt about it. Slipped, tripped, and fell."

"Let me out," I whispered. "Please."

"Well," he said, turning toward me, "we have to talk about that, don't we? Do you know who I am, Alan?"

"You're a ghost," I said.

He gave an impatient little snort, and in the glow of the speedometer the corners of his mouth turned down. "Come on, man, you can do better than that. Fuckin *Casper*'s a ghost. Do I float in the air? Can you see through me?" He held up one of his hands, opened and closed it in front of me. I could hear the dry, unlubricated sound of his tendons creaking.

I tried to say something. I don't know what, and it doesn't really matter, because nothing came out.

"I'm a kind of messenger," Staub said. "Fuckin

FedEx from beyond the grave, you like that? Guys like me actually come out pretty often—whenever the circumstances are just right. You know what I think? I think that whoever runs things—God or whatever—must like to be entertained. He always wants to see if you'll keep what you already got or if he can talk you into goin for what's behind the curtain. Things have to be just right, though. Tonight they were. You out all by yourself . . . mother sick . . . needin a ride . . ."

"If I'd stayed with the old man, none of this would have happened," I said. "Would it?" I could smell Staub clearly now, the needle-sharp smell of the chemicals and the duller, blunter stink of decaying meat, and wondered how I ever could have missed it, or mistaken it for something else.

"Hard to say," Staub replied. "Maybe this old man you're talking about was dead, too."

I thought of the old man's shrill handful-of-glass voice, the snap of his truss. No, he hadn't been dead, and I had traded the smell of piss in his old Dodge for something a lot worse.

"Anyway, man, we don't have time to talk about all that. Five more miles and we'll start seeing houses again. Seven more and we're at the Lewiston city line. Which means you have to decide now."

"Decide what?" Only I thought I knew.

"Who rides the Bullet and who stays on the ground. You or your mother." He turned and looked at me with his drowning moonlight eyes. He smiled more fully and I saw most of his teeth were gone, knocked out in the crash. He patted the steering wheel. "I'm taking one of you with me, man. And since you're here, you get to choose. What do you say?"

You can't be serious rose to my lips, but what would be the point of saying that, or anything like it? Of course he was serious. Dead serious.

I thought of all the years she and I had spent together, Alan and Jean Parker against the world. A lot of good times and more than a few really bad ones. Patches on my pants and casserole suppers. Most of the other kids took a quarter a week to buy the hot lunch; I always got a peanut-butter sandwich or a piece of bologna rolled up in day-old bread, like a kid in one of those dopey rags-to-riches stories. Her working in God knew how many different restaurants and cocktail lounges to support us. The time she took the day off work to talk to the ADC man, her dressed in her best pants suit, him sitting in our kitchen rocker in a suit of his own, one even a nine-year-old kid like me could tell was a lot better than hers, with a clipboard in his lap and a fat, shiny pen in his fingers. Her answering the insulting, embarrassing questions he asked with a fixed smile on her mouth, even offering him more coffee, because if he turned in the right report she'd get an extra fifty dollars a month, a lousy fifty bucks. Lying on her bed after he'd gone, crying, and when I came in to sit beside her she had tried to smile and said ADC didn't stand for Aid to Dependent Children but Awful Damn Crapheads. I had laughed and then she laughed, too, because you had to laugh, we'd found that out. When it was just you and your fat chain-smoking Ma against the world, laughing was quite often the only way you could get through without going insane and beating your fists on the walls. But there was more to it than that, you know. For people like us, little people who went scurrying through the world like mice in a cartoon, sometimes laughing at the assholes was the only revenge you could ever get. Her working all those jobs and taking the overtime and taping her ankles when they swelled and putting her tips away in a jar marked ALAN'S COLLEGE FUND—just like one of those dopey rags-to-riches stories, yeah, yeah—and telling me again and again that I had to work hard, other kids could maybe afford to play Freddy Fuckaround at school but I couldn't because she could put away her tips until doomsday cracked and there still wouldn't be enough; in the end it was going to come down to scholarships and loans if I was going to go to college and I *had* to go to college because it was the only way out for me . . . and for her. So I had worked hard, you want to believe I did, because I wasn't blind—I saw how heavy she was, I saw how much she smoked (it was her only private pleasure . . . her only vice, if you're one of those who must take that view), and I knew that someday our positions would reverse and I'd be the one taking care of her. With a college education and a good job, maybe I could do that. I *wanted* to do that. I loved her. She had a fierce temper and an ugly mouth on her—that day we waited for the Bullet and then I chickened out wasn't the only time she ever yelled at me and then swatted me—but I loved her in spite of it. Partly even *because* of it. I loved her when she hit me as much as when she kissed me. Do you understand that? Me either. And that's all right. I don't think you can sum up lives or explain families, and we *were* a family, she and I, the smallest family there is, a shared secret. If you had asked, I would have said I'd do anything for her. And now that was exactly what I was being asked to do. I was being asked to die for her, to die in her place, even though she had lived half her life, probably a lot more. I had hardly begun mine.

"What say, Al?" George Staub asked. "Time's wasting."

"I can't decide something like that," I said hoarsely. The moon sailed above the road, swift and brilliant. "It's not fair to ask me."

"I know, and believe me, that's what they all say." Then he lowered his voice. "But I gotta tell you something—if you don't decide by the time we get back to the first house-lights, I'll have to take you both." He frowned, then brightened again, as if remembering there was good news as well as bad. "You could ride together in the backseat if I took you both, talk over old times, there's that."

"Ride to where?"

He didn't reply. Perhaps he didn't know.

The trees blurred by like black ink. The headlights rushed and the road rolled. I was twenty-one. I wasn't a virgin but I'd only been with a girl once and I'd been drunk and couldn't remember much of what it had been like. There were a thousand places I wanted to go—Los Angeles, Tahiti, maybe Luckenbach, Texas—and a thousand things I wanted to do. My mother was forty-eight and that was *old,* goddammit. Mrs. McCurdy wouldn't say so but Mrs.

McCurdy was old herself. My mother had done right by me, worked all those long hours and taken care of me, but had I chosen her life for her? Asked to be born and then demanded that she live for me? She was forty-eight. I was twenty-one. I had, as they said, my whole life before me. But was that the way you judged? How did you decide a thing like this? How *could* you decide a thing like this?

The woods bolting by. The moon looking down like a bright and deadly eye.

"Better hurry up, man," George Staub said. "We're running out of wilderness."

I opened my mouth and tried to speak. Nothing came out but an arid sigh.

"Here, got just the thing," he said, and reached behind him. His shirt pulled up again and I got another look (I could have done without it) at the stitched black line on his belly. Were there still guts behind that line or just packing soaked in chemicals? When he brought his hand back, he had a can of beer in it—one of those he'd bought at the state line store on his last ride, presumably.

"I know how it is," he said. "Stress gets you dry in the mouth. Here."

He handed me the can. I took it, pulled the ringtab, and drank deeply. The taste of the beer going down was cold and bitter. I've never had a beer since. I just can't drink it. I can barely stand to watch the commercials on TV.

Ahead of us in the blowing dark, a yellow light glimmered.

"Hurry up, Al—got to speed it up. That's the first

house, right up at the top of this hill. If you got something to say to me, you better say it now."

The light disappeared, then came back again, only now it was several lights. They were windows. Behind them were ordinary people doing ordinary things—watching TV, feeding the cat, maybe beating off in the bathroom.

I thought of us standing in line at Thrill Village, Jean and Alan Parker, a big woman with dark patches of sweat around the armpits of her sundress, and her little boy. She hadn't wanted to stand in that line, Staub was right about that . . . but I had pestered pestered pestered. He had been right about that, too. She had swatted me, but she had stood in line with me, too. She had stood with me in a lot of lines, and I could go over all of it again, all the arguments pro and con, but there was no time.

"Take her," I said as the lights of the first house swept toward the Mustang. My voice was hoarse and raw and loud. "Take her, take my Ma, don't take me."

I threw the can of beer down on the floor of the car and put my hands up to my face. He touched me then, touched the front of my shirt, his fingers fumbling, and I thought—with sudden brilliant clarity—that it had all been a test. I had failed and now he was going to rip my beating heart right out of my chest, like an evil *djinn* in one of those cruel Arabian fairytales. I screamed. Then his fingers let go—it was as if he'd changed his mind at the last second—and he reached past me. For one moment my nose and lungs were so full of his deathly smell that I felt positive I was dead myself. Then there was the click of the door opening and cold fresh air came streaming in, washing the death-smell away.

"Pleasant dreams, Al," he grunted in my ear and then pushed. I went rolling out into the windy October darkness with my eyes closed and my hands raised and my body tensed for the bone-breaking smashdown. I might have been screaming, I don't remember for sure.

The smashdown didn't come and after an endless moment I realized I was already down—I could feel the ground under me. I opened my eyes, then squeezed them shut almost at once. The glare of the moon was blinding. It sent a bolt of pain through my head, one that settled not behind my eyes, where you usually feel pain after staring into an unexpectedly bright light, but in the back, way down low just above the nape of my neck. I became aware that my legs and bottom were cold and wet. I didn't care. I was on the ground, and that was all I cared about.

I pushed up on my elbows and opened my eyes again, more cautiously this time. I think I already knew where I was, and one look around was enough to confirm it: lying on my back in the little graveyard at the top of the hill on Ridge Road. The moon was almost directly overhead now, fiercely bright but much smaller than it had been only a few moments before. The mist was deeper as well, lying over the cemetery like a blanket. A few markers poked up through it like stone islands. I tried getting to my feet and another bolt of pain went through the back of my head. I put my hand there and felt a lump. There was sticky wetness, as well. I looked at my hand. In the moonlight, the blood streaked across my palm looked black.

On my second try I succeeded in getting up, and stood there swaying among the tombstones, knee-deep in mist. I turned around, saw the break in the rock wall and Ridge Road beyond it. I couldn't see my pack because the mist had overlaid it, but I knew it was there. If I walked out to the road in the lefthand wheelrut of the lane, I'd find it. Hell, would likely stumble over it.

So here was my story, all neatly packaged and tied up with a bow: I had stopped for a rest at the top of this hill, had gone inside the cemetery to have a little look around, and while backing away from the grave of one George Staub had tripped over my own large and stupid feet. Fell down, banged my head on a marker. How long had I been unconscious? I wasn't savvy enough to tell time by the changing position of the moon with to-the-minute accuracy, but it had to be at least an hour. Long enough to have a dream that I'd gotten a ride with a dead man. What dead man? George Staub, of course, the name I'd read on a grave-marker just before the lights went out. It was the classic ending, wasn't it? Gosh-What-An-Awful-Dream-I-Had. And when I got to Lewiston and found my mother had died? Just a little touch of pre-cognition in the night, put it down to that. It was the sort of story you might tell years later, near the end of a party, and people would nod their heads thought-fully and look solemn and some dinkleberry with leather patches on the elbows of his tweed jacket would say there were more things in Heaven and earth than were dreamed of in our philosophy and then—

"Then shit," I croaked. The top of the mist was moving slowly, like mist on a clouded mirror. "I'm never talking about this. Never, not in my whole life, not even on my deathbed."

But it had all happened just the way I remembered it, of that I was sure. George Staub had come along and picked me up in his Mustang, Ichabod Crane's old pal with his head stitched on instead of under his arm, demanding that I choose. And I *had* chosen—faced with the oncoming lights of the first house, I had bartered away my mother's life with hardly a pause. It might be understandable, but that didn't make the guilt of it any less. No one had to know, however; that was the good part. Her death would look natural— hell, would *be* natural—and that's the way I intended to leave it.

I walked out of the graveyard in the lefthand rut, and when my foot struck my pack, I picked it up and slung it back over my shoulders. Lights appeared at the bottom of the hill as if someone had given them the cue. I stuck out my thumb, oddly sure it was the old man in the Dodge—he'd come back this way looking for me, of course he had, it gave the story that final finishing roundness.

Only it wasn't the old guy. It was a tobacco-chewing farmer in a Ford pickup truck filled with apple-baskets, a perfectly ordinary fellow: not old and not dead.

"Where you goin, son?" he asked, and when I told him he said, "That works for both of us." Less than forty minutes later, at twenty minutes after nine, he pulled up in front of the Central Maine Medical Center. "Good luck. Hope your Ma's on the mend."

"Thank you," I said, and opened the door.

"I see you been pretty nervous about it, but she'll most likely be fine. Ought to get some disinfectant on those, though." He pointed at my hands.

I looked down at them and saw the deep, purpling crescents on the backs. I remembered clutching them together, digging in with my nails, feeling it but unable to stop. And I remembered Staub's eyes, filled up with moonlight like radiant water. *Did you ride the Bullet?* he'd asked me. *I rode that fucker four times.*

"Son?" the man driving the pickup asked. "You all right?"

"Huh?"

"You come over all shivery."

"I'm okay," I said. "Thanks again." I slammed the door of the pickup and went up the wide walk past the line of parked wheelchairs gleaming in the moonlight.

I walked to the information desk, reminding myself that I had to look surprised when they told me she was dead, had to look surprised, they'd think it was funny if I didn't . . . or maybe they'd just think I was in shock . . . or that we didn't get along . . . or . . .

I was so deep in these thoughts that I didn't at first grasp what the woman behind the desk had told me. I had to ask her to repeat it.

"I said that she's in room 487, but you can't go up just now. Visiting hours end at nine."

"But . . ." I felt suddenly woozy. I gripped the edge of the desk. The lobby was lit by fluorescents, and in that bright even glare the cuts on the backs of my hands stood out boldly—eight small purple crescents like grins, just above the knuckles. The man in the pickup was right. I ought to get some disinfectant on those.

The woman behind the desk was looking at me patiently. The plaque in front of her said she was YVONNE EDERLE.

"But is she all right?"

She looked at her computer. "What I have here is S. Stands for satisfactory. And four is a general-population floor. If your mother had taken a turn for the worse, she'd be in ICU. That's on three. I'm sure if you come back tomorrow, you'll find her just fine. Visiting hours begin at—"

"She's my Ma," I said. "I hitchhiked all the way down from the University of Maine to see her. Don't you think I could go up, just for a few minutes?"

"Exceptions are sometimes made for immediate family," she said, and gave me a smile. "You just hang on a second. Let me see what I can do." She picked up the phone and punched a couple of buttons, no doubt calling the nurses' station on the fourth floor, and I could see the course of the next two minutes as if I really *did* have second sight. Yvonne the Information Lady would ask if the son of Jean Parker in 487 could come up for a minute or two—just long enough to give his mother a kiss and an encouraging word—and the nurse would say oh God, Mrs. Parker died not fifteen minutes ago, we just sent her down to the morgue, we haven't had a chance to update the computer, this is so terrible.

The woman at the desk said, "Muriel? It's Yvonne. I have a young man down here at the desk, his name is"—she looked at me, eyebrows raised, and I gave her my name—"Alan Parker. His mother is Jean Parker, in 487? He wonders if he could just . . ."

She stopped. Listened. On the other end the nurse on the fourth floor was no doubt telling her that Jean Parker was dead.

"All right," Yvonne said. "Yes, I understand." She sat quietly for a moment, looking off into space, then put the mouthpiece of the telephone against her shoulder and said, "She's sending Anne Corrigan down to peek in on her. It will only be a second."

"It never ends," I said.

Yvonne frowned. "I beg pardon?"

"Nothing," I said. "It's been a long night and—"

"—and you're worried about your mom. Of course. I think you're a very good son to drop everything the way you did and come on the run."

I suspected Yvonne Ederle's opinion of me would have taken a drastic drop if she'd heard my conversation with the young man behind the wheel of the Mustang, but of course she hadn't. That was a little secret, just between George and me.

It seemed that hours passed as I stood there under the bright fluorescents, waiting for the nurse on the fourth floor to come back on the line. Yvonne had some papers in front of her. She trailed her pen down one of them, putting neat little checkmarks beside some of the names, and it occurred to me that if there really was an Angel of Death, he or she was probably just like this woman, a slightly overworked functionary with a desk, a computer, and too much paperwork. Yvonne kept the phone pinched between her ear and one raised shoulder. The loudspeaker said that Dr. Farquhar was wanted in radiology, Dr. Farquhar. On the fourth floor a nurse named Anne Corrigan would now be looking at my mother, lying dead in her bed with her eyes open, the stroke-induced sneer of her mouth finally relaxing.

Yvonne straightened as a voice came back on the line. She listened, then said: "All right, yes, I understand. I will. Of course I will. Thank you, Muriel." She hung up the telephone and looked at me solemnly. "Muriel says you can come up, but you can only visit for five minutes. Your mother's had her evening meds, and she's very soupy."

I stood there, gaping at her.

Her smile faded a little bit. "Are you sure you're all right, Mr. Parker?"

"Yes," I said. "I guess I just thought—"

Her smile came back. It was sympathetic this time. "Lots of people think that," she said. "It's understandable. You get a call out of the blue, you rush to get here . . . it's understandable to think the worst. But Muriel wouldn't let you up on her floor if your mother wasn't fine. Trust me on that."

"Thanks," I said. "Thank you so much."

As I started to turn away, she said: "Mr. Parker? If you came from the University of Maine up north, may I ask why you're wearing that button? Thrill Village is in New Hampshire, isn't it?"

I looked down at the front of my shirt and saw the button pinned to the breast pocket: I RODE THE BULLET

AT THRILL VILLAGE, LACONIA. I remembered thinking he intended to rip my heart out. Now I understood: he had pinned his button on my shirt just before pushing me into the night. It was his way of marking me, of making our encounter impossible not to believe. The cuts on the backs of my hands said so; the button on my shirt said so, too. He had asked me to choose and I had chosen.

So how could my mother still be alive?

"This?" I touched it with the ball of my thumb, even polished it a little. "It's my good-luck charm." The lie was so horrible that it had a kind of splendor. "I got it when I was there with my mother, a long time ago. She took me on the Bullet."

Yvonne the Information Lady smiled as if this were the sweetest thing she had ever heard. "Give her a nice hug and kiss," she said. "Seeing you will send her off to sleep better than any of the pills the doctors have." She pointed. "The elevators are over there, around the corner."

With visiting hours over, I was the only one waiting for a car. There was a litter-basket off to the left, by the door to the newsstand, which was closed and dark. I tore the button off my shirt and threw it in the basket. Then I rubbed my hand on my pants. I was still rubbing it when one of the elevator doors opened. I got in and pushed for four. The car began to rise. Above the floor-buttons was a poster announcing a blood drive for the following week. As I read it, an idea came to me . . . except it wasn't so much an idea as a certainty. My mother was dying now, at this very second, while I rode up to her floor in this slow industrial elevator. I had made the choice; it therefore fell to me to find her. It made perfect sense.

The elevator door opened on another poster. This one showed a cartoon finger pressed to big red cartoon lips. Beneath it was a line reading OUR PATIENTS APPRECIATE YOUR QUIET! Beyond the elevator lobby was a corridor going right and left. The odd-numbered rooms were to the left. I walked down that way, my sneakers seeming to gain weight with every step. I slowed in the four-seventies, then stopped entirely between 481 and 483. I couldn't do this. Sweat as cold and sticky as half-frozen syrup crept out of my hair in little trickles. My stomach was knotted up like a fist inside a slick glove. No, I couldn't do it. Best to turn around and skedaddle like the cowardly chickenshit I was. I'd hitchhike out to Harlow and call Mrs. McCurdy in the morning. Things would be easier to face in the morning.

I started to turn, and then a nurse poked her head out of the room two doors up . . . my mother's room. "Mr. Parker?" she asked in a low voice.

For a wild moment I almost denied it. Then I nodded.

"Come in. Hurry. She's going."

They were the words I'd expected, but they still sent a cramp of terror through me and buckled my knees.

The nurse saw this and came hurrying toward me, her skirt rustling, her face alarmed. The little gold pin on her breast read ANNE CORRIGAN. "No, no, I just meant the *sedative* . . . she's going to sleep. Oh my God, I'm so stupid. She's fine, Mr. Parker, I gave her her Ambien and she's going to sleep, that's all I meant.

You aren't going to faint, are you?" She took my arm.

"No," I said, not knowing if I was going to faint or not. The world was swooping and there was a buzzing in my ears. I thought of how the road had leaped toward the car, a black-and-white movie road in all that silver moonlight. *Did you ride the Bullet? Man, I rode that fucker four times.*

Anne Corrigan led me into the room and I saw my mother. She had always been a big woman, and the hospital bed was small and narrow, but she still looked almost lost in it. Her hair, now more gray than black, was spilled across the pillow. Her hands lay on top of the sheet like a child's hands, or even a doll's. There was no frozen stroke-sneer such as the one I'd imagined on her face, but her complexion was yellow. Her eyes were closed, but when the nurse beside me murmured her name, they opened. They were a deep and iridescent blue, the youngest part of her, and perfectly alive. For a moment they looked nowhere, and then they found me. She smiled and tried to hold out her arms. One of them came up. The other trembled, rose a little bit, then fell back. "Al," she whispered.

I went to her, starting to cry. There was a chair by the wall, but I didn't bother with it. I knelt on the floor and put my arms around her. She smelled warm and clean. I kissed her temple, her cheek, the corner of her mouth. She raised her good hand and patted her fingers under one of my eyes.

"Don't cry," she whispered. "No need of that."

"I came as soon as I heard," I said. "Betsy McCurdy called."

"Told her . . . weekend," she said. "Said the weekend would be fine."

"Yeah, and to hell with that," I said, and hugged her. "Car . . . fixed?"

"No," I said. "I hitchhiked."

"Oh gorry," she said. Each word was clearly an effort for her, but they weren't slurred, and I sensed no bewilderment or disorientation. She knew who she was, who I was, where we were, why we were here. The only sign of anything wrong was her weak left arm. I felt an enormous sense of relief. It had all been a cruel practical joke on Staub's part . . . or perhaps there had been no Staub, perhaps it had all been a dream after all, corny as that might be. Now that I was here, kneeling by her bed with my arms around her, smelling a faint remnant of her Lanvin perfume, the dream idea seemed a lot more plausible.

"Al? There's blood on your collar." Her eyes rolled closed, then came slowly open again. I imagined her lids must feel as heavy to her as my sneakers had to me, out in the hall.

"I bumped my head, Ma, it's nothing."

"Good. Have to . . . take care of yourself." The lids came down again; rose even more slowly.

"Mr. Parker, I think we'd better let her sleep now," the nurse said from behind me. "She's had an extremely difficult day."

"I know." I kissed her on the corner of the mouth again. "I'm going, Ma, but I'll be back tomorrow."

"Don't . . . hitchhike . . . dangerous."

"I won't. I'll catch a ride in with Mrs. McCurdy. You get some sleep."

"Sleep . . . all I do," she said. "I was at work, unloading the dishwasher. I came over all headachy. Fell down. Woke up . . . here." She looked up at me. "Was a stroke. Doctor says . . . not too bad."

"You're fine," I said. I got up, then took her hand. The skin was fine, as smooth as watered silk. An old person's hand.

"I dreamed we were at that amusement park in New Hampshire," she said.

I looked down at her, feeling my skin go cold all over. "Did you?"

"Ayuh. Waiting in line for the one that goes . . . way up high. Do you remember that one?"

"The Bullet," I said. "I remember it, Ma."

"You were afraid and I shouted. Shouted at you."

"No, Ma, you—"

Her hand squeezed down on mine and the corners of her mouth deepened into near-dimples. It was a ghost of her old impatient expression.

"Yes," she said. "Shouted and swatted you. Back . . . of the neck, wasn't it?"

"Probably, yeah," I said, giving up. "That's mostly where you gave it to me."

"Shouldn't have," she said. "It was hot and I was tired, but still . . . shouldn't have. Wanted to tell you I was sorry."

My eyes started leaking again. "It's all right, Ma. That was a long time ago."

"You never got your ride," she whispered.

"I did, though," I said. "In the end I did."

She smiled up at me. She looked small and weak, miles from the angry, sweaty, muscular woman who had yelled at me when we finally got to the head of the line, yelled and then whacked me across the nape of the neck. She must have seen something on someone's face—one of the other people waiting to ride the Bullet—because I remember her saying *What are you looking at, beautiful?* as she led me away by the hand, me snivelling under the hot summer sun, rubbing the back of my neck . . . only it didn't really hurt, she hadn't swatted me *that* hard; mostly what I remember was being grateful to get away from that high, twirling construction with the capsules at either end, that revolving scream machine.

"Mr. Parker, it really is time to go," the nurse said.

I raised my mother's hand and kissed the knuckles. "I'll see you tomorrow," I said. "I love you, Ma."

"Love you, too. Alan . . . sorry for all the times I swatted you. That was no way to be."

But it had been; it had been *her* way to be. I didn't know how to tell her I knew that, accepted it. It was part of our family secret, something whispered along the nerve-endings.

"I'll see you tomorrow, Ma. Okay?"

She didn't answer. Her eyes had rolled shut again, and this time the lids didn't come back up. Her chest rose and fell slowly and regularly. I backed away from the bed, never taking my eyes off her.

In the hall I said to the nurse, "Is she going to be all right? Really all right?"

"No one can say that for sure, Mr. Parker. She's Dr. Nunnally's patient. He's very good. He'll be on the floor tomorrow afternoon and you can ask him——"

"Tell me what *you* think."

"I think she's going to be fine," the nurse said, leading me back down the hall toward the elevator lobby. "Her vital signs are strong, and all the residual effects suggest a very light stroke." She frowned a little. "She's going to have to make some changes, of course. In her diet . . . her lifestyle . . ."

"Her smoking, you mean."

"Oh yes. That has to go." She said it as if my mother quitting her lifetime habit would be no more difficult than moving a vase from a table in the living room to one in the hall. I pushed the button for the elevators, and the door of the car I'd ridden up in opened at once. Things clearly slowed down a lot at CMMC once visiting hours were over.

"Thanks for everything," I said.

"Not at all. I'm sorry I scared you. What I said was incredibly stupid."

"Not at all," I said, although I agreed with her. "Don't mention it."

I got into the elevator and pushed for the lobby. The nurse raised her hand and twiddled her fingers. I twiddled my own in return, and then the door slid between us. The car started down. I looked at the fingernail marks on the backs of my hands and thought that I was an awful creature, the lowest of the low. Even if it had only been a dream, I was the lowest of the goddam low. *Take her,* I'd said. She was my mother but I had said it just the same: *Take my Ma, don't take me.* She had raised me, worked overtime for me, waited in line with me under the hot summer sun in a dusty little New Hampshire amusement park, and in the end I had hardly hesitated. *Take her, don't take me.*

Chickenshit, chickenshit, you fucking chickenshit.

When the elevator door opened I stepped out, took the lid off the litter-basket, and there it was, lying in someone's almost-empty paper coffee cup: I RODE THE BULLET AT THRILL VILLAGE, LACONIA.

I bent, plucked the button out of the cold puddle of coffee it was lying in, wiped it on my jeans, put it in my pocket. Throwing it away had been the wrong idea. It was my button now—good-luck charm or bad-luck charm, it was mine. I left the hospital, giving Yvonne a little wave on my way by. Outside, the moon rode the roof of the sky, flooding the world with its strange and perfectly dreamy light. I had never felt so tired or so dispirited in my whole life. I wished I had the choice to make again. I would have made a different one. Which was funny—if I'd found her dead, as I'd expected to, I think I could have lived with it. After all, wasn't that the way stories like this one were supposed to end?

Nobody wants to give a fella a ride in town, the old man with the truss had said, and how true that was. I walked all the way across Lewiston—three dozen blocks of Lisbon Street and nine blocks of Canal Street, past all the bottle clubs with the jukeboxes playing old songs by Foreigner and Led Zeppelin and AC/DC in French—without putting my thumb out a single time. It would have done no good. It was well past eleven before I reached the DeMuth Bridge. Once I was on the Harlow side, the first car I raised my thumb to stopped. Forty minutes later I was fishing the key out from under the red wheelbarrow by the door to the back shed, and ten minutes after that I was in bed. It occurred to me as I dropped off that it was the first time in my life I'd slept in that house all by myself.

It was the phone that woke me up at quarter past noon. I thought it would be the hospital, someone from the hospital saying my mother had taken a sudden turn for the worse and had passed away only a few minutes ago, so sorry. But it was only Mrs. McCurdy, wanting to be sure I'd gotten home all right, wanting to know all the details of my visit the night before (she took me through it three times, and by the end of the third recitation I had begun to feel like a criminal being interrogated on a murder charge), also wanting to know if I'd like to ride up to the hospital with her that afternoon. I told her that would be great.

When I hung up, I crossed the room to the bedroom door. Here was a full-length mirror. In it was a tall, unshaven young man with a small potbelly, dressed only in baggy undershorts. "You have to get it together, big boy," I told my reflection. "Can't go through the rest of your life thinking that every time the phone rings it's someone calling to tell you your mother's dead."

Not that I would. Time would dull the memory, time always did . . . but it was amazing how real and immediate the night before still seemed. Every edge and corner was sharp and clear. I could still see Staub's good-looking young face beneath his turned-around cap, and the cigarette behind his ear, and the way the smoke had seeped out of the incision on his neck when he inhaled. I could still hear him telling the story of the Cadillac that was selling cheap. Time would blunt the edges and round the corners, but not for awhile. After all, I had the button, it was on the dresser by the bathroom door. The button was my souvenir. Didn't the hero of every ghost-story come away with a souvenir, something that proved it had all really happened?

There was an ancient stereo system in the corner of the room, and I shuffled through my old tapes, hunting for something to listen to while I shaved. I found one marked FOLK MIX and put it in the tape player. I'd made it in high school and could barely remember what was on it. Bob Dylan sang about the lonesome death of Hattie Carroll, Tom Paxton sang about his own ramblin' pal, and then Dave Van Ronk started to sing about the cocaine blues. Halfway through the third verse I paused with my razor by my cheek. *Got a headful of whiskey and a bellyful of gin,* Dave sang in his rasping voice. *Doctor say it kill me but he don't say when.* And that was the answer, of course. A guilty conscience had led me to assume that my mother would die *immediately,* and Staub had never corrected that assumption—how could he, when I had never even asked?—but it clearly wasn't true.

Doctor say it kill me but he don't say when.

What in God's name was I beating myself up about? Didn't my choice amount to no more than the natural order of things? Didn't children usually outlive their parents? The son of a bitch had tried to scare me—to guilt-trip me—but I didn't have to buy what he was selling, did I? Didn't we all ride the Bullet in the end?

You're just trying to let yourself off. Trying to find a way to make it okay. Maybe what you're thinking is true . . . but when he asked you to choose, you chose her. There's no way to think your way around that, buddy—you chose her.

I opened my eyes and looked at my face in the mirror. "I did what I had to," I said. I didn't quite believe it, but in time I supposed I would.

Mrs. McCurdy and I went up to see my mother and my mother was a little better. I asked her if she remembered her dream about Thrill Village, in Laconia. She shook her head. "I barely remember you coming in last night," she said. "I was awful sleepy. Does it matter?"

"Nope," I said, and kissed her temple. "Not a bit."

My Ma got out of the hospital five days later. She walked with a limp for a little while, but that went away and a month later she was back at work again—only half shifts at first but then full-time, just as if nothing had happened. I returned to school and got a job at Pat's Pizza in downtown Orono. The money wasn't great, but it was enough to get my car fixed. That was good; I'd lost what little taste for hitchhiking I'd ever had.

My mother tried to quit smoking and for a little while she did. Then I came back from school for April vacation a day early, and the kitchen was just as smoky as it had ever been. She looked at me with eyes that were both ashamed and defiant. "I can't," she said. "I'm sorry, Al—I know you want me to and I know I should, but there's such a hole in my life without it.

Nothing fills it. The best I can do is wish I'd never started in the first place."

Two weeks after I graduated from college, my Ma had another stroke—just a little one. She tried to quit smoking again when the doctor scolded her, then put on fifty pounds and went back to the tobacco. "As a dog returneth to its vomit," the Bible says; I've always liked that one. I got a pretty good job in Portland on my first try—lucky, I guess—and started the work of convincing her to quit her own job. It was a tough sled at first. I might have given up in disgust, but I had a certain memory that kept me digging away at her Yankee defenses.

"You ought to be saving for your own life, not taking care of me," she said. "You'll want to get married someday, Al, and what you spend on me you won't have for that. For your real life."

"*You're* my real life," I said, and kissed her. "You can like it or lump it, but that's just the way it is."

And finally she threw in the towel.

We had some pretty good years after that—seven of them in all. I didn't live with her, but I visited her almost every day. We played a lot of gin rummy and watched a lot of movies on the video recorder I bought her. Had a bucketload of laughs, as she liked to say. I don't know if I owe those years to George Staub or not, but they were good years. And my memory of the night I met Staub never faded and grew dreamlike, as I always expected it would; every incident, from the old man telling me to wish on the harvest moon to the fingers fumbling at my shirt as Staub passed his button on to me, remained perfectly clear. And there came a day when I could no longer find that button. I knew I'd had it when I'd moved into my little apartment in Falmouth—I kept it in the top drawer of my bedside table, along with a couple of combs, my two sets of cufflinks, and an old political button that said BILL CLINTON, THE SAFE SAX PRESIDENT—but then it came up missing. And when the telephone rang a day or two later, I knew why Mrs. McCurdy was crying. It was the bad news I'd never quite stopped expecting; fun is fun and done is done.

When the funeral was over, and the wake, and the seemingly endless line of mourners had finally come to its end, I went back to the little house in Harlow where my mother had spent her final few years, smoking and eating powdered doughnuts. It had been Jean and Alan Parker against the world; now it was just me.

I went through her personal effects, putting aside the few papers that would have to be dealt with later, boxing up the things I'd want to keep on one side of the room and the things I'd want to give away to the Goodwill on the other. Near the end of the job I got down on my knees and looked under her bed and there it was, what I'd been looking for all along without quite admitting it to myself: a dusty button reading I RODE THE BULLET AT THRILL VILLAGE, LACONIA. I curled my fist tight around it. The pin dug into my flesh and I squeezed my hand even tighter, taking a bitter pleasure in the pain. When I rolled my fingers open again, my eyes had filled with tears and the words on the button had doubled, overlaying each other in a shimmer.

It was like looking at a 3-D movie without the glasses.

"Are you satisfied?" I asked the silent room. "Is it enough?" There was no answer, of course. "Why did you even bother? What was the goddam point?"

Still no answer, and why would there be? You wait in line, that's all. You wait in line beneath the moon and make your wishes by its infected light. You wait in line and listen to them screaming—they pay to be terrified, and on the Bullet they always get their money's worth. Maybe when it's your turn you ride; maybe you run. Either way it comes to the same, I think. There ought to be more to it, but there's really not—fun is fun and done is done.

Take your button and get out of here.

Luckey Quarter

In the fall of 1996, I crossed the United States from Maine to California on my Harley-Davidson motorcycle, stopping at independent bookstores to promote a novel called Insomnia. *It was a great trip. The high point was probably sitting on the stoop of an abandoned general store in Kansas, watching the sun go down in the west as the full moon rose in the east. I thought of a scene in Pat Conroy's* The Prince of Tides *where the same thing happens, and an enraptured child cries out, "Oh, Mama, do it again!" Later, in Nevada, I stayed in a ramshackle hotel where the turn-down maids left two-dollar slots chips on the pillow. Beside each chip was a little card that said something like, "Hi, I'm Marie, Good Luck!" This story came to mind. I wrote it longhand, on hotel stationery.*

"Oh you cheap son of a bitch!" she cried in the empty hotel room, more in surprise than in anger.

Then—it was the way she was built—Darlene Pullen started to laugh. She sat down in the chair beside the rumpled, abandoned bed with the quarter in one hand and the envelope it had fallen out of in the other, looking back and forth between them and laughing until tears spilled from her eyes and rolled down her cheeks. Patsy, her older kid, needed braces. Darlene had absolutely no idea how she was going to pay for them, she had been worried about it all week, and if this wasn't the final straw, what was? And if you couldn't laugh, what *could* you do? Find a gun and shoot yourself?

Different girls had different places to leave the all-important envelope, which they called "the honeypot." Gerda, the Swede who'd been a downtown corner-girl before finding Jesus the previous summer at a revival meeting in Tahoe, propped hers up against one of the bathroom glasses; Melissa put hers under the TV controller. Darlene always leaned hers against the telephone, and when she came in this morning and found 322's on the pillow instead, she had known he'd left something for her.

Yes, he certainly had. A little copper sandwich, one quarter-dollar, In God We Trust.

Her laughter, which had been tapering off to giggles, broke out in full spate again.

There was printed matter on the front of the honeypot, plus the hotel's logo: the silhouettes of a horse and rider on top of a bluff, enclosed in a diamond shape.

Welcome to Carson City, the friendliest town in Nevada! [said the words below the logo]. *And welcome to The Rancher's Hotel, the friendliest lodging in Carson City! Your room was made up by* Darlene. *If anything's wrong, please dial 0 and we'll put it right "pronto." This envelope is provided should you find*

*everything right and care to leave a little "extra some-
thing" for this chambermaid.*

    *Once again, welcome to Carson, and welcome to the
Rancher's.*

*William Avery
Trail-Boss*

Quite often the honeypot was empty—she had
found envelopes torn up in the wastebasket, crumpled
up in the corner (as if the idea of tipping the chambermaid actually infuriated some guests), floating in the
toilet bowl—but sometimes there was a nice little surprise in there, especially if the slot machines or the
gaming tables had been kind to a guest. And 322 had
certainly used his; he'd left her a quarter, by God! That
would take care of Patsy's braces *and* get that Sega
game system Paul wanted with all his heart. He
wouldn't even have to wait until Christmas, he could
have it as a . . . a . . .

"A Thanksgiving present," she said. "Sure, why not?
And I'll pay off the cable people, so we won't have to
give it up after all, we'll even add the Disney Channel,
and I can finally go see a doctor about my back . . .
shit, I'm rich. If I could find you, mister, I'd drop down
on my knees and kiss your fucking feet."

No chance of that; 322 was long gone. The
Rancher's probably *was* the best lodging in Carson
City, but the trade was still almost entirely transient.
When Darlene came in the back door at seven A.M.,
they were getting up, shaving, taking their showers, in
some cases medicating their hangovers; while she was
in Housekeeping with Gerda, Melissa, and Jane (the

head housekeeper, she of the formidable gunshell tits and set, red-painted mouth), first drinking coffee, then filling her cart and getting ready for the day, the truckers and cowboys and salesmen were checking out, their honeypot envelopes either filled or unfilled.

322, that gent, had dropped a quarter in his. And probably left her a little something on his sheets as well, not to mention a souvenir or two in the unflushed toilet. Because some people couldn't seem to stop giving. It was just their nature.

Darlene sighed, wiped her wet cheeks with the hem of her apron, and squeezed open the envelope— 322 had actually gone to the trouble of sealing it, and she'd ripped off the end in her eagerness to see what was inside. She meant to drop the quarter back into it, then saw there was something inside: a scrawled note written on a sheet from the desk-pad. She fished it out.

Below the horse-and-rider logo and the words JUST A NOTE FROM THE RANCH, 322 had printed nine words, working with a blunt-tipped pencil:

This is a luckey quarter! Its true! Luckey you!

"Good deal!" Darlene said. "I got a couple of kids and a husband five years late home from work and I could use a little luck. Honest to God I could." Then she laughed again—a short snort—and dropped the quarter into the envelope. She went into the bathroom and peeped into the toilet. Nothing there but clean water, and that was something.

* * *

She went about her chores, and they didn't take long. The quarter was a nasty dig, she supposed, but otherwise, 322 had been polite enough. No streaks or spots on the sheets, no unpleasant little surprises (on at least four occasions in her five years as a chambermaid, the five years since Deke had left her, she had found drying streaks of what could only have been semen on the TV screen and once a reeking puddle of piss in a bureau drawer), nothing stolen. There was really only the bed to make, the sink and shower to rinse out, and the towels to replace. As she did these things, she speculated about what 322 might have looked like, and what kind of a man left a woman who was trying to raise two kids on her own a twenty-five-cent tip. One who could laugh and be mean at the same time, she guessed; one who probably had tattoos on his arms and looked like the character Woody Harrelson had played in that movie *Natural Born Killers*.

He doesn't know anything about me, she thought as she stepped into the hall and pulled the door closed behind her. *Probably he was drunk and it seemed funny, that's all. And it was funny, in a way; why else did you laugh?*

Right. Why else had she laughed?

Pushing her cart across to 323, she thought she would give the quarter to Paul. Of the two kids, Paul was the one who usually came up holding the short end of the stick. He was seven, silent, and afflicted with what seemed to be a perpetual case of the sniffles. Darlene also thought he might be the only seven-year-old in the clean air of this high-desert town who was an incipient asthmatic.

She sighed and used her passkey on 323, thinking

that maybe she'd find a fifty—or even a hundred—in this room's honeypot. It was almost always her first thought on entering a room. The envelope was just where she had left it, however, propped against the telephone, and although she checked it just to be sure, she knew it would be empty, and it was.

323 *had* left a little something for her in the toilet, though.

"Look at this, the luck's starting to flow already," Darlene said, and began to laugh as she flushed the john—it was just the way she was built.

There was a one-armed bandit—just that single one—in the lobby of the Rancher's, and although Darlene had never used it during her five years of work here, she dropped her hand into her pocket on her way to lunch that day, felt the envelope with the torn-off end, and swerved toward the chrome-plated foolcatcher. She hadn't forgotten her intention to give the quarter to Paul, but a quarter meant nothing to kids these days, and why should it? You couldn't even get a lousy bottle of Coke for a quarter. And suddenly she just wanted to be rid of the damned thing. Her back hurt, she had unaccustomed acid indigestion from her ten o'clock cup of coffee, and she felt savagely depressed. Suddenly the shine was off the world, and it all seemed the fault of that lousy quarter . . . as if it were sitting there in her pocket and sending out little batches of rotten vibes.

Gerda came out of the elevator just in time to see Darlene plant herself in front of the slot machine and dump the quarter out of the envelope and into her palm.

"You?" Gerda said. "*You?* No, never—I don't believe it."

"Just watch me," Darlene said, and dropped the coin into the slot which read USE 1 2 OR 3 COINS. "That baby is gone."

She started to walk off, then, almost as an after-thought, turned back long enough to yank the bandit's lever. She turned away again, not bothering to watch the drums spin, and so did not see the bells slot into place in the windows—one, two, and three. She paused only when she heard quarters begin to shower into the tray at the bottom of the machine. Her eyes widened, then narrowed suspiciously, as if this was another joke . . . or maybe the punchline of the first one.

"You vin!" Gerda cried, her Swedish accent coming out more strongly in her excitement. "Darlene, you vin!"

She darted past Darlene, who simply stood where she was, listening to the coins cascade into the tray. The sound seemed to go on forever. *Luckey me,* she thought. *Luckey, luckey me.*

At last the quarters stopped falling.

"Oh, goodness!" Gerda said. "Goodness me! And to think this cheap machine never paid me anything, after all the quarters I'm stuffing it with! Vut luck is here! There must be fifteen dollars, Darl! Imagine if you'd put in *tree* quarters!"

"That would have been more luck than I could have stood," Darlene said. She felt like crying. She didn't know why that should be, but it was; she could feel the tears burning the backs of her eyeballs like weak acid. Gerda helped her scoop the quarters out of the tray, and when they were all in Darlene's uniform pocket, that side of her dress sagged comically. The only thought to cross her mind was to think that she ought to get Paul something nice, some toy. Fifteen dollars wasn't enough for the Sega system he wanted, not by a long shot, but it might buy one of the electronic things he was always looking at in the window of Radio Shack at the mall, not asking, he knew better, he was sickly but that didn't make him stupid, just staring with eyes that always seemed to be inflamed and watering.

The hell you will, she told herself. *You'll put it toward a pair of shoes, is what you'll do . . . or Patsy's goddam braces. Paul wouldn't mind that, and you know it.*

No, Paul wouldn't mind, and that was the hell of it, she thought, sifting her fingers through the weight of quarters in her pocket and listening to them jingle. You minded things *for* them. Paul knew the radio-controlled boats and cars and planes in the store window were as out of reach as the Sega system and all the games you could play on it; to him that stuff existed to be appreciated in the imagination only, like pictures in a gallery or sculptures in a museum. To her, however . . .

Well, maybe she *would* get him something silly with her windfall. Something silly and nice. Surprise him.

Surprise herself.

She surprised herself, all right.

Plenty.

That night she decided to walk home instead of taking the bus. Halfway down North Street, she turned into the Silver City Casino, where she had never been before in her life. She had changed the quarters—there had been eighteen dollars' worth in all—into bills at the hotel desk, and now, feeling like a visitor inside her own body, she approached the roulette wheel and held these bills out to the croupier with a hand entirely void of feeling. Nor was it just her hand; every nerve below the surface of her skin seemed to have gone dead, as if this sudden, aberrant behavior had blown them out like overloaded fuses.

It doesn't matter, she told herself as she put all eighteen of the unmarked pink dollar chips on the space marked ODD. *It's just a quarter, that's really all it is no matter what it looks like on that runner of felt, it's only someone's bad joke on a chambermaid he'd never actually have to look in the eye. It's only a quarter and you're still just trying to get rid of it, because it's multiplied and changed its shape, but it's still sending out bad vibes.*

"No more bets, no more bets," the wheel's minder chanted as the ball revolved counterclockwise to the spinning wheel. The ball dropped, bounced, caught, and Darlene closed her eyes for a moment. When she opened them, she saw the ball riding around in the slot marked 15.

The croupier pushed eighteen more pink chips—to Darlene they looked like squashed Canada Mints—over to her. Darlene picked them up and put them all back down on the red. The croupier looked at her, eyebrows raised, asking without saying a word if she was sure. She nodded that she was, and he spun. When red came up, she shifted her growing pile of chips to the black.

Then the odd.

Then the even.

She had five hundred and seventy-six dollars in front of her after that last one, and her head had gone to some other planet. It was not black and green and pink chips she saw in front of her, not precisely; it was braces and a radio-controlled submarine.

Luckey me, Darlene Pullen thought. *Oh luckey, luckey me.*

She put the chips down again, all of them, and the crowd that always forms behind and around sudden hot-streak winners in gambling towns, even at five o'clock in the afternoon, groaned.

"Ma'am, I can't allow that bet without the pit-boss's okay," the roulette wheel's minder said. He looked considerably more awake now than he had when Darlene walked up in her blue-and-white-striped rayon uniform. She had put her money down on the second triple—the numbers from 13 to 24.

"Better get him over here then, hon," Darlene said, and waited, calm, her feet on Mother Earth here in Carson City, Nevada, seven miles from where the first big silver mine opened up in 1878, her head somewhere deep in the deluminum mines of the Planet Chumpadiddle, as the pit-boss and the minder conferred and the crowd around her murmured. At last the pit-boss came over to her and asked her to write down her name and address and telephone number on a piece of pink memo paper. Darlene did it, interested to see that her handwriting hardly looked like her own. She felt calm, as calm as the calmest deluminum miner who had ever lived, but her hands were shaking badly.

The pit-boss turned to Mr. Roulette Minder and twirled his finger in the air—spin it, son.

This time the rattle of the little white ball was clearly audible in the area around the roulette table; the crowd had fallen entirely silent, and Darlene's was the only bet on the felt. This was Carson City, not Monte Carlo, and for Carson, this was a monster bet. The ball rattled, fell into a slot, jumped, fell into another, then jumped again. Darlene closed her eyes.

Luckey, she thought, she prayed. *Luckey me, luckey mom, luckey girl.*

The crowd moaned, either in horror or ecstasy. That was how she knew the wheel had slowed enough to read. Darlene opened her eyes, knowing that her quarter was finally gone.

Except it wasn't.

The little white ball was resting in the slot marked 13 Black.

"Oh my God, honey," a woman behind her said. "Give me your hand, I want to rub your hand." Darlene gave it, and felt the other one gently taken as well—taken and fondled. From some distance far, far away from the deluminum mines where she was having this fantasy, she could feel first two people, then four, then six, then eight, gently rubbing her hands, trying to catch her luck like a cold-germ.

Mr. Roulette was pushing piles and piles of chips over to her.

"How much?" she asked faintly. "How much is that?"

"Seventeen hundred and twenty-eight dollars," he said. "Congratulations, ma'am. If I were you—"

"But you're not," Darlene said. "I want to put it all down on one number. That one." She pointed. "25." Behind her, someone screamed softly, as if in sexual rapture. "Every cent of it."

"No," the pit-boss said.

"But—"

"No," he said again, and she had been working for men most of her life, enough of it to know when one of them meant exactly what he was saying. "House policy, Mrs. Pullen."

"All right," she said. "All right, you chickenshit." She pulled the chips back toward her, spilling some of the piles. "How much *will* you let me put down?"

"Excuse me," the pit-boss said.

He was gone for almost five minutes. During that time the wheel stood silent. No one spoke to Darlene, but her hands were touched repeatedly, and sometimes chafed as if she were a fainting victim. When the pit-boss came back, he had a tall bald man with him. The tall bald man was wearing a tuxedo and gold-rimmed glasses. He did not look at Darlene so much as through her.

"Eight hundred dollars," he said, "but I advise against it." His eyes dropped down the front of her uniform, then back up at her face. "I think you should cash in your winnings, madam."

"I don't think you know jack shit in a backyard out-house," Darlene said, and the tall bald man's mouth tightened in distaste. She shifted her gaze to Mr. Roulette. "Do it," she said.

* * *

Mr. Roulette put down a plaque with $800 written on it, positioning it fussily so it covered the number 25. Then he spun the wheel and dropped the ball. The entire casino had gone silent now, even the persistent ratchet-and-ding of the slot machines. Darlene looked up, across the room, and wasn't surprised to see that the bank of TVs which had previously been showing horse races and boxing matches were now showing the spinning roulette wheel . . . and her.

I'm even a TV star. Luckey me. Luckey me. Oh so luckey me.

The ball spun. The ball bounced. It almost caught, then spun again, a little white dervish racing around the polished wood circumference of the wheel.

"Odds!" she suddenly cried. "What are the odds?"

"Thirty to one," the tall bald man said. "Twenty-four thousand dollars should you win, madam."

Darlene closed her eyes . . .

. . . and opened them in 322. She was still sitting in the chair, with the envelope in one hand and the quarter that had fallen out of it in the other. Her tears of laughter were still wet on her cheeks.

"Luckey me," she said, and squeezed the envelope so she could look into it.

No note. Just another part of the fantasy, misspellings and all.

Sighing, Darlene slipped the quarter into her uniform pocket and began to clean up 322.

* * *

Instead of taking Paul home as she normally did after school, Patsy brought him to the hotel. "He's snotting all over the place," she explained to her mother, her voice dripping with disdain which only a thirteen-year-old could muster in such quantities. "He's, like, *choking* on it. I thought maybe you'd want to take him to the Doc in the Box."

Paul looked at her silently from his watering, patient eyes. His nose was as red as the stripe on a candy cane. They were in the lobby; there were no guests checking in currently, and Mr. Avery (Tex to the maids, who unanimously hated the little prick) was away from the desk. Probably back in the office, choking his chicken. If he could find it.

Darlene put her palm on Paul's forehead, felt the warmth simmering there, and sighed. "Suppose you're right," she said. "How are you feeling, Paul?"

"Ogay," Paul said in a distant, foghorning voice.

Even Patsy looked depressed. "He'll probably be dead by the time he's sixteen," she said. "The only case of, like, spontaneous AIDS in the history of the world."

"You shut your dirty little mouth!" Darlene said, much more sharply than she had intended, but Paul was the one who looked wounded—he winced and looked away from her.

"He's a baby, too," Patsy said hopelessly. "I mean, really."

"No, he's not. He's sensitive, that's all. And his resistance is low." She fished in her uniform pocket. "Paul? Want this?"

He looked back at her, saw the quarter, and smiled a little.

"What are you going to do with it, Paul?" Patsy asked him as he took it. "Take Deirdre McCausland out on a date?" She snickered.

"I'll thing of subething," Paul said.

"Leave him alone," Darlene said. "Don't bug him for a little while, could you do that?"

"Yeah, but what do I get?" Patsy asked her. "I walked him over here safe, I *always* walk him safe, so what do I get?"

Braces, Darlene thought, *if I can ever afford them.* And she was suddenly overwhelmed by unhappiness, by a sense of life as some vast cold junkpile—deluminum slag, if you liked—that was always looming over you, always waiting to fall, cutting you to screaming ribbons even before it crushed the life out of you. Luck was a joke. Even good luck was just bad luck with its hair combed.

"Mom? Mommy?" Patsy sounded suddenly concerned. "I don't want anything, I was just kidding around, you know."

"I've got a *Sassy* for you, if you want," Darlene said. "I found it in one of my rooms and put it in my locker."

"This month's?" Patsy sounded suspicious.

"Actually this month's. Come on."

They were halfway across the room when they heard the drop of the coin and the unmistakable ratchet of the handle and whir of the drums as Paul pulled the handle of the slot machine beside the desk and then let it go.

"Oh you dumb hoser, you're in trouble now!" Patsy cried. She did not sound exactly unhappy about it. "How many times has Mom told you not to throw your money away on stuff like that? Slots're for the tourists!"

But Darlene didn't even turn around. She stood looking at the door that led back to the maid's country, where the cheap cloth coats from Ames and Wal-Mart hung in a row like dreams that have grown seedy and been discarded, where the time-clock ticked, where the air always smelled of Melissa's perfume and Jane's Ben-Gay. She stood listening to the drums whir, she stood waiting for the rattle of coins into the tray, and by the time they began to fall she was already thinking about how she could ask Melissa to watch the kids while she went down to the casino. It wouldn't take long.

Luckey me, she thought, and closed her eyes. In the darkness behind her lids, the sound of the falling coins seemed very loud. It sounded like metal slag falling on top of a coffin.

It was all going to happen just the way she had imagined, she was somehow sure that it was, and yet that image of life as a huge slagheap, a pile of alien metal, remained. It was like an indelible stain that you know will never come out of some favorite piece of clothing.

Yet Patsy needed braces, Paul needed to see a doctor about his constantly running nose and constantly watering eyes, he needed a Sega system the way Patsy needed some colorful underwear that would make her feel funny and sexy, and she needed . . . what? What did she need? Deke back?

Sure, Deke back, she thought, almost laughing. *I need him back like I need puberty back, or labor pains. I need . . . well . . .*

(nothing)

Yes, that was right. Nothing at all, zero, empty, *adiós*. Black days, empty nights, and laughing all the way.

I don't need anything because I'm luckey, she thought, her eyes still closed. Tears, squeezing out from beneath her closed lids, while behind her Patsy was screaming at the top of her lungs. "Oh shit! Oh shit-a-booger, you hit the jackpot, Paulie! You hit the damned jackpot!"

Luckey, Darlene thought. *So luckey, oh luckey me.*

RELUCTANT DAD

CARLA CASSIDY

Published by Silhouette Books

America's Publisher of Contemporary Romance

SILHOUETTE BOOKS

ISBN 0-373-07856-0

RELUCTANT DAD

Copyright © 1998 by Carla Bracale

Printed in U.S.A.

Chapter 1

Dead. Her husband was dead. Melissa Newman stumbled backward and bumped into the dresser as a scream tried to release itself. She heard the sound of whimpering and realized with a start that the noise came from her.

Swallowing hard, she fought for control, fought to keep out of the clutches of hysteria. She knew she needed to do something, call someone, but her mind refused to work. What had happened? *How* had this happened?

She staggered out of the bedroom and into the kitchen. Leaning weakly against the wall, she picked up the telephone. Without conscious thought, she punched in the number for her sister's office. Samantha would know what to do.

"Justice Inc." A deep male voice she didn't recognize answered the phone at the law firm.

"Samantha—I need to talk to Samantha," Melissa said. Sobs welled up inside her as horror began to penetrate the fog of shock.

"She's not here right now. Can I take a message?"

Melissa moaned. "Where is she? This is her sister. I—I need her."

"Melissa, this is Dominic Marcola. Samantha and Tyler drove into Kansas City for dinner and a movie. I don't expect them to be back for several hours." There was a moment of hesitation. "Is there something I can do to help?"

Although Melissa didn't know Dominic well, her need was too great to wait for her sister and brother-in-law's return. "He's dead," she blurted. "Please, you've got to help me…do something. He's dead."

"Who? Who's dead?"

"Bill. Bill's dead. He took a nap and when I went in to wake him, he was dead…stabbed. My husband's been murdered." The sobs she'd been holding back, swallowing against, overcame her.

"Melissa, don't touch anything. I'll be right there."

Before she could reply, Dominic hung up. She replaced the receiver, horror once again seeping through her as she saw the bloodstains her fingers left on the phone.

She swiped her hand down the front of her dress, her mind struggling to comprehend everything. Bill was dead. Someone had snuck into the house while she'd been at the store, or while she'd been lying down in the living room.

Melissa went to the sink and washed her hands. Over and over again she lathered and rinsed, lathered and rinsed. Dead. He was dead. A knife protruded from his chest and blood pooled on the front of his shirt.

Who could have killed him? How had they gotten in? Questions began to penetrate her numbness. Why? Oh, God, perhaps this was a dream. Maybe she was still napping on the sofa and this was all just a ghastly nightmare.

She touched her swollen stomach when the baby suddenly twisted and turned as if to confirm this wasn't a dream. She wouldn't suddenly wake up and find herself next to Bill in bed, his snores filling the silence of the room.

Although she should be afraid, she wasn't. She'd been asleep on the sofa for almost an hour. If someone had wanted to harm her, he would have had a perfect opportunity.

But Bill was dead. *Dead.* The word reverberated in her head as waves of horror washed over her. And the worst horror of all was the sudden recognition that in some deep part of herself, what she felt was pure relief—a relief bordering on joy.

Dominic Marcola had a bad feeling in his gut. He drove down Main Street of the small town of Wilford, Kansas, toward the northern outskirts where Samantha's sister and her husband lived. He'd gotten the exact address from Samantha's Rolodex.

Melissa had been crying hysterically when he'd hung up on her, but from her disjointed statements, he'd managed to get the gist of the situation.

Bill Newman was dead. Murdered. Dominic clenched his hands on the steering wheel. He'd hoped he could manage to work for Samantha and Tyler and the Justice Inc. law firm as a private investigator without getting involved in a *murder* case.

Murder. He still suffered nightmares, still felt the mental and emotional wounds from having been on trial six months ago...for the murder of his ex-girlfriend.

The last place he wanted to be was driving to the scene of another homicide. But he knew Samantha would want him to respond to her sister's hysterical call. And he would do anything for Samantha and Tyler Sinclair. They'd taken his own case pro bono and cracked it wide open, exposing the real killer and giving Dominic back his life.

He frowned as he turned down the tree-lined county road that led to the Newman house. He'd only been out in this area once before. At that time he'd been a cop, summoned to respond to a break-in call. Then, as now, he noticed how isolated the houses were, how dark the night could be with no streetlights and little traffic.

He turned into the Newman driveway, unsurprised to see light shining from every window and Melissa silhouetted in the open doorway.

She stepped onto the front porch as he got out of his car. As always, and despite the dire circumstances, Dominic was instantly struck by her beauty. The porch light turned her pale hair into a golden halo and emphasized her delicate features. Though in an advanced stage of pregnancy, she remained thin, radiating fragility and vulnerability.

It wasn't until he drew closer that he saw the sickly pallor of her skin, the dark navy of her shadowed eyes, and the bright blood that stained the front of her dress.

"Thank God you're here," she said as he reached the porch. She gripped his arm, her eyes fevered with emotion. "I...I didn't know who to call...what to do."

"Where is he?" Dominic asked, gently disentangling her hand from his forearm.

"In the master bedroom." She shivered and wrapped her arms around her shoulders.

Dominic led her into the house and motioned for her to sit on the sofa. "Stay here. I'll be right back."

He walked down the hallway toward the bedroom at the end, the one he assumed to be the master bedroom. Immediately his cop instincts took over, sweeping aside any emotional baggage that might interfere.

He stepped into the room, instantly seeing the body on the bed. There was no denying that Bill was dead. Dominic touched nothing and backed out of the room so he wouldn't compromise the crime scene.

"Have you called the police?" he asked as he returned to the living room. Melissa shook her head. He'd assumed she'd know to call them. Dominic picked up the phone and dialed the number, knowing the police should have been called the instant she found the body.

As he made the call, she got up from the sofa and walked to the window. With her back to him, she remained still, her gaze apparently transfixed on something in the darkness outside.

He'd intentionally kept his distance from her whenever she'd come into the office to see her sister, knowing there was something about her that attracted him. A forbidden attraction. After all, she was married and carrying her husband's child.

After he summoned the police, he hung up the phone. He would do what needed to be done until Samantha and Tyler arrived, then he would put Melissa Dark Newman back where she belonged—out of his mind.

She turned to look at him, her face still pale, her eyes huge. A trembling hand tucked a strand of her shining blond hair behind her ear. "I can't believe this is happening. It all feels so unreal, like a nightmare. But I'm not dreaming, am I?" Her eyes searched his, as if begging him to tell her everything would be all right.

But Dominic couldn't tell her that. He knew this was just the beginning for her. Eventually her shock would pass and she would mourn her tragic loss. Eventually she would realize she'd lost the man she loved and would now be a single mother with a baby who would never know his father.

But first there would be questions and suspicions. Dominic frowned, remembering the night he'd been arrested for Abigail's murder. Hopefully Melissa wouldn't have to go through the hell he'd endured. "Come sit down and tell me what happened," he said as he motioned her back to the sofa.

Like a zombie, she moved to the couch and sank down, looking small and vulnerable against the oversize cushions. "What happened? I don't know what happened."

Dominic sat in the chair across from her. "Did Bill go to work today? Did he come home at the usual time?"

She nodded. "He came home when he always does, at about four forty-five. He took a quick shower and changed his clothes, then stretched out on the bed for a nap. He always sleeps from five to six."

"Did he seem agitated, upset about anything?"

"No." The answer came after a moment's hesitation and in the depths of her eyes he thought he saw the inkling of secrets. He looked away. He didn't want to know her secrets. He didn't want to know anything about her; he just wanted to know what had happened here.

"No, he was fine," she continued. "After he'd fallen asleep, I realized we were out of his favorite soda, so I made a quick trip to the store."

She closed her eyes and once again wrapped her arms around herself, as if cold to the bone. "I—I thought he was still sleeping when I got home. I sat down here to wait for him to wake up, but I fell asleep, too." She opened her haunted eyes. "When I woke up I went in to wake him up for supper." She shivered. "And that's when I found him."

Dominic raked a hand through his hair. "You didn't hear anything? No sound came from the bedroom at all?"

"No. Nothing." Her eyes held the yawning darkness of a survivor, one who didn't quite understand why she was still alive while a loved one was dead.

Dominic knew there was nothing he could say to erase that look from her eyes, no platitudes he could offer her. He knew, as an ex-cop, that the finger of suspicion would point first to her. Statistics proved that in the case of a homicide, the prime suspect was almost always the spouse.

He knew from painful personal experience that Melissa's life with Bill would be prodded and picked apart, explored and examined from every possible angle. Her privacy would be destroyed, her love for her husband exploited by the media and political glory-seekers.

Dominic's thoughts were interrupted by the wail of sirens approaching the house.

He fought the impulse to touch her, comfort her, to pull her into his arms. Melissa's ride through hell was only just beginning.

Within two hours, Bill's body had been removed and the police had cordoned off the house with the familiar yellow tape that proclaimed to the world that a tragedy had occurred within.

Melissa sat on the sofa as she'd been instructed by Detective Mawlins, one of the officers responding to the call. She still felt as if she was functioning in a fog. The only thing that stabbed through her daze was the relentless pain that had started in her lower back and upper thighs.

"You don't have to answer any questions," Dominic said. "Maybe you should wait for Samantha and Tyler to get here before you speak with the officers."

She looked at him in surprise. "I don't mind speaking with them. I want to do whatever I can to help them catch whoever did this."

They both turned as Detective Mawlins walked into the room. He nodded to Dominic, then sank onto the sofa next to Melissa. His eyes flickered to her swollen stomach. "You doing okay?" he asked, his deep voice curt.

She nodded. She just wanted to get through this. Later she would cry for Bill—not because she loved him, not because she would miss him, but because no human being deserved what had happened to him.

"I just need to ask you a few questions for now." Detective Mawlins opened up a notepad and pulled a pen from the breast pocket of his suit. "Okay, let's start at the beginning."

As Melissa explained what had happened, she was vaguely aware of Dominic pacing back and forth in silent disapproval. He'd made it clear that he thought she shouldn't talk to the police without an attorney present, but Melissa wanted to do what she could to help.

"What time did you go to the store?" Detective Mawlins asked when she'd finished her monologue of events.

"I left here at about twenty after five and got back home at five forty-five."

"Did you see anyone at the store?"

Melissa looked at the detective in surprise. "The cashier who checked me out. It was a young woman."

"Do you know her name?"

"No. She was thin and...blond."

He nodded and scribbled something down on his pad. "Did you lock the door when you left here?"

The question shot an arrow of guilt straight through her. "No," she whispered. Was it her fault Bill was dead? Had she unwittingly allowed the killer access to Bill? "You think whoever did this came through the door?" Tears splashed her cheeks. "But the bedroom window was open—Bill never opened windows. I thought…''

Detective Mawlins's features softened slightly. ''We aren't sure yet exactly how the killer entered. I know this is difficult for you,'' he said, his voice filled with sympathy.

Melissa swiped the tears from her face, indicating that she was ready for him to continue his questions.

''Did your husband mention anyone who might have been angry at him? Perhaps somebody from work?''

''No, but we rarely talked about his work.''

''He owned a heating-and-cooling business, right?''

''Yes, Newman's Climate Control.'' Melissa frowned, thinking of the men who worked for Bill. She didn't know them well, had only seen them a few times. Bill had made it a point to keep her fairly isolated. She shifted positions, trying to accommodate the dull ache in her back.

''Look, isn't this enough for tonight?'' Dominic asked. ''It's almost midnight, and Mrs. Newman has had a terrible shock.''

Melissa flashed him a grateful look. All she wanted was to lie down and stop the pain in her back, which was beginning to make it difficult for her to think.

''Just a few more questions,'' Detective Mawlins replied, then focused on Melissa. ''How was your marriage?''

The question caught her off guard. For the first time she realized she was the most obvious suspect, and she saw the cutting edge of suspicion in the officer's eyes. His concern, the sympathy he'd emanated, had apparently been a ruse to lull her. "I—we— Our marriage was fine. We had some problems, like all married couples, but we were working on them."

She bit back hysteria, hoping he didn't see through the lie. How could she tell him she'd intended to leave Bill, that she had an escape fund hiding in the cookie jar? She'd only been waiting for the birth of the baby, then she'd intended to disappear from her husband's life.

She suddenly realized the ugly truth. Her abusive marriage provided a strong motive for her to kill Bill. Tears once again welled up in her eyes and spilled down her face. Tears for herself and her unborn child... Tears for Bill and the mess they'd made of their lives together.

"That's enough for tonight," Dominic exclaimed. "If you want to ask her more questions, please do it tomorrow when she's rested." He held Detective Mawlins's gaze for a long moment, then the detective slapped his notebook closed.

"I'm afraid you'll have to stay someplace else for a couple of days. This house is a crime scene and will be in the custody of the Wilford Police Department until all the forensic evidence has been gathered." He stood. "I'll go with you while you pack a bag of clothing and whatever else you need for a couple of days."

"And then I'll drive you to Samantha's place," Dominic offered.

Melissa nodded and followed Detective Mawlins into the bedroom. She forced herself not to look at the bed where she'd found Bill's lifeless body. Still in a state of shock, with ambivalent feelings roaring through her, she quickly pulled together enough clothes and toiletries for a couple of days away from home.

"You'll be at your sister's house?" the detective asked when they returned to the living room. "That's Samantha Sinclair?"

"Yes." A sickness roiled in her stomach, a combination of the pain in her back and the mistrust in the detective's eyes.

"Come on. Let's get you to Samantha's." Dominic took her by the elbow and pulled her closer, into his protective arms.

"Oh, God, they think I did it, don't they?" she said as they reached Dominic's car in the driveway.

"It's only natural they'd suspect you. Right now you're all they have." He helped her into the car.

She watched as he walked around the front to the driver's side. He was a handsome man, with strongly chiseled features and thick, dark hair. Although she'd noticed him several times in Samantha and Tyler's law offices, she couldn't remember ever seeing him smile.

Of course, the woman he'd loved had been brutally murdered, and he'd spent time in jail, charged with the crime. That kind of life experience could steal away smiles. Melissa knew all about losing the energy, the will, the reasons to smile.

As he got into the car, she focused her gaze out the passenger window, felt the sting of tears burning at her eyes. She knew she was experiencing some sort of emotional shock, and that sooner or later she would grieve.

Eventually she would mourn Bill's death, even

though she'd fallen out of love with him long ago. She would also mourn the death of her dreams, which had occurred the first time Bill— She shook her head to ward off the thoughts. At the moment she found it difficult to concentrate on anything except the deep, rolling pains throbbing in her back.

"You all right?" Dominic asked, casting her a quick glance before returning his gaze to the road.

"I just can't believe this is happening." She shifted position, in an effort to accommodate the cramping sensation, which seemed far more intense than it had moments before.

She looked back at Dominic, trying to keep her mind off the pain. "I didn't kill him." She wanted to tell him the truth—how she'd grown to hate Bill, fear him, but that she wasn't capable of an act like murder. Her secrets were her own, though, and she knew to share them would muddy the waters of any investigation into Bill's death. She would have to keep her secrets locked inside.

"I'm not the one you have to convince," he replied, his expression not changing from one of cool detachment.

"Why would I kill my husband? The father of my child? It makes no sense." She heard the hysterical rise of her voice, knew she was on the verge of losing all control.

"I'm sure the police will do what they can to find out who killed Bill. Right now, what you need more than anything is some rest. This will all sort itself out in the next day or two."

Although he said the right words, his voice lacked conviction. He turned into the driveway of the im-

pressive Dark family home. Bleakly Melissa stared at
the mansion, from whose windows no lights shone.

She'd run from this house six years ago, run to Bill,
believing that he would fulfill her fantasies of love
forever more. God, she'd been such a young, naive
fool.

"Samantha and Tyler must not be home yet,"
Dominic said as he shut off the car's engine. "Do
you have a key?"

She nodded and dug through her purse to produce
it. She handed it to him, then got out of the car as he
did the same. He grabbed her overnight bag from the
back seat, and together they walked to the front door.

"I'm sure Tyler and Samantha will be home any
minute," he said as he unlocked the door. He opened
it and reached inside to turn on the entry-hall light.
He dropped her bag just inside the door, then spun
around to help her inside. "I'm sure everything is
going to be fine, Melissa. Get a good night's sleep
and everything will be better in the morning."

Melissa stared at him, suddenly realizing what her
body had been trying to tell her for the past several
hours. "Dominic, I'm going to have a baby."

"Yeah, I know," he replied, obviously misunderstanding what she was trying to tell him.

She grabbed his hands, squeezing tight as an overwhelming need to bear down crashed upon her. "You
don't understand," she gasped, as a contraction
gripped her stomach. "This baby is coming right
now." And at those words, her water broke.

Chapter 2

Melissa released Dominic's hands and moaned as she sank down to the entry-hall floor. He stared at her in horror. Surely *this* wasn't happening. This *couldn't* be happening. Oh, God, she was going to have the baby right now. There was no time to get her to the hospital, no time to wait around for help. Dominic swallowed around the lump of panic that lodged in his throat.

He hadn't wanted to get involved with her in any way, had only come to her aid as a favor to her sister, and now it appeared he was going to deliver her baby. Life seemed to be hurling a series of fastballs at him, and he definitely didn't have a mitt.

Another low moan escaped her and jolted him from his momentary inertia. He leaned down and scooped her up in his arms. There was no way he was going to let her deliver her baby on the entryway floor.

"Don't leave me. Please don't leave me." She wrapped her arms around his neck and held tight as he carried her into the living room.

"I'm not going anywhere," he said, trying to re-assure her despite the dread pounding in his heart. "I promise I'll stay right here."

He placed her on the sofa, then spied a phone on the nearby table. Grabbing the receiver, he punched in the emergency number. When the operator an-swered, he quickly explained the situation, indicating they needed an ambulance dispatched to the house immediately.

He didn't stay on the line, knew the dispatcher could tell him nothing he didn't know from the police training he'd gone through. When he hung up, he rushed into a nearby bathroom and grabbed a stack of towels.

Before he returned, Melissa had pulled up her dress and kicked off her underpants, readying herself to give birth to her baby.

Although she didn't make a sound, he could tell the contractions were coming one after another. Her efforts reddened her face as she gasped and panted, and her hands clutched the towels convulsively.

He stood next to the sofa, trying to maintain his distance, not only physically, but emotionally as well. He knew this was her first child, and he'd always heard that first babies took a long time to be born. Surely help would get here before she actually gave birth.

Melissa reached for him. Awkwardly, he stepped closer, allowing her to grasp his hands as she rode another wave of pain.

"That's it…breathe through it," he said. "Breathe, don't push," he instructed. "For God's sake, whatever you do, don't push."

"Easy for you to say," she retorted between pants.

"Isn't it too early? Maybe it's just false labor," Dominic said, although he knew he was wrong. Water didn't break with false labor.

"There's nothing false about this," she exclaimed. "And it's not that early. My due date is in two weeks," She groaned. "I'm trying not to push…but—"

"An ambulance should be here soon. Once they get here you can push all you want."

She nodded and bit her bottom lip.

He wanted to pull his hands away, but her grip was almost painfully strong. It should be Bill here, Dominic thought. Her husband should be here sharing this moment. But Melissa's husband was dead. Suddenly Dominic's need for emotional distance faded away as he realized that he was all she had.

With one hand he swept a strand of her damp, pale hair away from her forehead, unsurprised to find it soft as silk. "Help is on the way."

Her gaze held his, and in the blue depths of her eyes, he saw gratefulness and strength. As another pain racked her body, she bore it stoically, silently, and he wondered why he'd ever gotten the impression that this woman was weak, fragile.

Her eyes rolled back in her head and she emitted shallow, rapid breaths. When she looked at him again, he saw the pain and fear that darkened the blue of her eyes. "Dominic, if I die, you have to tell Samantha and Tyler to raise the baby." The words came between pants, through clenched teeth. "And you have to tell them...tell them I *didn't* kill Bill."

"Shh, you aren't going to die." Where in the hell was the ambulance? Why didn't somebody come to help them? "It's all right, you're doing just fine." His voice held nothing but cool confidence.

"I'm glad you're here. I'm so glad you're here." Her hands clutched again, grabbing the towels so tightly her knuckles turned white.

Again Dominic was struck by the fact that she didn't scream, didn't cry out despite the contractions that tore through her. With a washcloth he dabbed her forehead, murmuring words of encouragement, reminding her to breathe, and praying for help to arrive.

"Help isn't going to get here in time," she gasped. "We've got to do it. We've got to do it right now." Her face reddened as she bore down. Dominic set the washcloth aside and moved to her feet.

After losing Abigail and being charged with her murder, Dominic had believed that nothing could ever touch him again. But when he saw the head of the baby crowning as he moved into position to aid the baby's arrival into the world, the utter wonder of birth filled him.

"I can see the head," he cried, a euphoria sweeping through him as he placed his hands beneath it. "Push, Melissa. Come on, you can do it. Push."

She closed her eyes and strained, and Dominic found himself caught up in the moment, his heart pounding frantically as he gently guided the baby's head and shoulders.

"It's a boy," Dominic exclaimed as he held the

precious baby in his hands. The infant gave a little cough, then cried lustily.

Dominic laughed in exhilaration as he counted fingers and toes. "He's perfect...absolutely perfect." Pale hair decorated the top of the baby's head and his face was reddened from his cries. A miracle.

Dominic felt a lump of emotion in the back of his throat. As he held the warm, wiggly bundle, the infant seemed to look at him, newborn blue eyes appearing to study him as the crying momentarily ceased.

For a brief moment, Dominic wished this child was his, wished that he could be there for every step of life this little boy would take.

He placed the baby on Melissa's stomach and as her gaze captured his, he knew a bond had been established not only between mother and child, but between him and Melissa, as well. It didn't matter that he hardly knew her; he'd just shared with her one of the most intimate, thrilling experiences two people could share.

From this moment on he would have a special place in her life, no matter what happened afterward.

Sirens wailed in the distance, then sounded closer and closer. "That must be the paramedics. I'll go let them in," Dominic said.

Suddenly, more than anything, he wanted to be away from this woman and the child whose first sight of the world had been his face. He *needed* to be away from this woman, whom tragedy had touched just before giving her ultimate joy.

"Dominic?"

He hesitated at the doorway and looked back at her. Even with her hair in damp ringlets around her face, and wearing the strain of exhaustion, she was beautiful.

"Thank you." Her eyes grew luminous with the press of tears, and he knew that reality, when it struck, would hit her hard.

The reality was that a life had been stolen from her, and another given to her. A bittersweet exchange of souls, one to mourn, one to celebrate. He nodded, turned and went to let the paramedics into the house.

Within fifteen minutes, a stretcher bore Melissa and baby to the ambulance. Dominic had promised her he would remain behind and explain the night's events to Samantha and Tyler.

He stood watching as the ambulance pulled out of the driveway, its lights shooting scarlet beams into the night. When the vehicle disappeared from sight, he closed the door and went back into the living room to await Samantha and Tyler's return.

Sinking down onto the sofa, he leaned his head back and drew a deep breath. Now that the adrenaline euphoria of the birth had waned, exhaustion seeped through him. What a night.

He dreaded having to be the one to release the barrage of news to Samantha. As of tonight, not only did Samantha have a new nephew, but her brother-in-law had been murdered and the prime suspect was her younger sister, Melissa.

Dominic swiped a hand down his face and frowned thoughtfully. He believed Melissa when she said she hadn't killed Bill, but there were questions that nagged at him, that undermined her fierce denial of guilt. And one of the biggest questions he entertained at the moment was how Melissa had gotten the bruises on her legs.

As he'd delivered the baby, he'd noticed fading, yellowish marks on her thighs and calves, along with several livid purple areas that indicated more recent injury.

How would a young woman get such bruises? A fall? It would have to have been more than a single fall to explain the different ages of the bruises.

He shook his head, telling himself that surely there was a logical explanation. In any case, it was none of his business. *She* was none of his business.

Melissa awoke to early-morning sunlight streaking through the window of her hospital room. Her first conscious thought after a night of dreamless sleep was of the baby. *Her* baby. *Her son.* Her heart swelled, and she felt as if she'd accomplished something better than any woman had ever done before or would ever do after. She'd birthed a perfect, beautiful baby boy.

She turned her head to look at the baby sleeping in the infant bed next to her. Wrapped in a blue blanket, with a little blue hat covering his pale hair, he was snuggled into a ball. Joy mingled with love and flooded through her.

After the doctor had checked over the infant and pronounced him in perfect health, she'd examined him in minute detail. She'd marveled at the tiny hands with perfect little fingernails, had been awed by the blue eyes that peered at her so solemnly. Everything seemed a miracle, from the sweetness of his silky skin to the lusty cries he made when hungry.

As if aware of her scrutiny, now his little face wrinkled in a frown, and he emitted an awakening bleat for attention. Although she was sore, Melissa eased herself out of bed and to his side. She picked him up and cuddled him against her, then got back into her bed.

As she removed his cap, her heart pounded with a love she'd never felt before—a protective, maternal love that had only been hinted at during her pregnancy. She caressed the top of his head, felt the silky strands of his pale blond hair.

"You're a sweet baby boy," she whispered. His eyes gazed into hers with complete acceptance, abiding innocence and total trust. It was as if he knew she would never do anything to harm him.

Tears blurred Melissa's vision as she thought of Bill. Even though she'd grown to hate him, she hadn't wished this kind of death for him—although if she searched her heart, she knew she would find a dark corner where she'd sometimes fantasized his death. But not by brutal murder. Never in such violence.

Bill didn't have any family, so there was nobody to contact, there were no relatives to grieve. Only her. And her grief was superficial, forced by the fact that she felt she *should* grieve.

"The one night my husband decides to take me out for dinner and a movie, all hell breaks loose." Samantha Dark Sinclair stalked into the room like a comet broken free from its projected path. "Oh, Missy, what in the hell happened last night?"

As Samantha pulled a chair up to the side of the bed and grabbed Melissa's hand, Melissa burst into tears. The strain and utter horror of Bill's death, combined with the unexpected birth, was simply too much.

"Oh, honey, I'm so sorry about Bill." Samantha's eyes sparkled with tears of sympathy. "I can't imagine the grief you must be feeling."

The fact that her sister thought her tears were all for her husband only made Melissa cry harder. The baby added his wails, and it was his cries that made Melissa cease sobbing, regain control.

"Let me see that big boy," Samantha said as she reached to pick him up. "He's beautiful," she exclaimed. "I couldn't believe it when Dominic told me he'd helped you give birth to this little munchkin."

"Thank goodness Dominic was there. I don't know what would have happened if he hadn't been," Melissa replied, thinking of the way Dominic had encouraged her, comforted her through her fear and pain.

Even though she felt grateful to Dominic, she also felt a twinge of embarrassment as she thought of the unexpected intimacy the birth had created between them.

"Yeah, Dominic is a good guy." Samantha handed the baby back to Melissa who began to breastfeed him. "Now, let's talk about last night." She scooted her chair closer to Melissa's bed.

Melissa stroked the top of her little boy's head. "I'm going to name him Jamison, after Dad," she said.

"That's nice. Dad would have liked that."

Melissa looked at her sister. "No, he probably would have hated it. He hated Bill."

Samantha looked at her in surprise. "He did?"

Of course Samantha didn't know; couldn't know how vehemently Jamison Jackson Dark had opposed Melissa's marriage to Bill. Samantha had left Wilford when Melissa was eighteen, leaving Melissa behind to cope with their cold, autocratic father. Samantha had only been back in town six months, and it was only recently that the two sisters had managed to recapture the closeness they'd once shared.

Two months after Samantha had left Wilford, Bill had moved to town. Bill, with his sweet little smile and his laughing blue eyes. Bill, who had made Melissa feel beautiful and desired. He'd been a panacea for the cold indifference she'd suffered from her father, an escape from the mansion that held no warmth, no love.

"Dad thought Bill was too old for me," she explained to her sister. "He was thirty when we met, but I didn't care what Dad said. I wanted a life with Bill. Dad didn't even come to our wedding and never accepted Bill as a son-in-law."

"Did that cause problems between you and Bill?" Samantha asked.

Melissa shook her head. "Not really. Bill didn't seem to care. Dad wasn't one who was into family gatherings."

"No kidding," Samantha replied dryly.

For a moment the two sisters were silent, and Melissa knew Samantha was thinking about their father. It was only after his death almost a year ago that Melissa was finally able to forgive him for being incapable of filling his daughters' emotional needs.

"Melissa, we need to talk about last night...about Bill's murder."

"I know." Once again Melissa stroked her son's head. He'd fallen asleep. Melissa didn't want to think about Bill—his life or his death. She wanted it all to just go away. All her emotions were too close to the surface, too mixed-up to sort out.

"I tried to get some information from the police before I came here, but they aren't releasing anything yet," Samantha said. "Tell me what happened, Melissa."

For the third time, Melissa explained the events that had led up to her discovering Bill murdered. Samantha listened silently, asking only an occasional question. Melissa could tell by Samantha's questions that she was assessing the situation not as her sister, but as an attorney.

"It looks bad, doesn't it?" Melissa finally asked.

"Right now, perhaps," Samantha agreed. "But I'm sure when the police finish their investigation, they'll find forensic evidence of an intruder...somebody else's presence in the house." She patted Melissa's hand reassuringly.

"Detective Mawlins thinks I did it. He thinks I killed Bill. I saw it in his eyes last night when he questioned me."

Samantha snorted. "Detective Mawlins is a disgrace to the department. He's lazy, so he'll look to solve this as quickly and easily as possible."

Melissa sighed. "I keep thinking I should know something—somebody who was angry enough with Bill to do this. But I can't think of anyone." Except me, she added to herself.

"Melissa, it's possible this was just a random act of violence. A robbery gone bad."

Melissa frowned. Samantha's suggestion didn't feel right. Bill's business van had been parked in the driveway. She'd had stew warming on the stove. Surely a burglar would be more discerning in choosing a house to rob. She sighed once again and rubbed her forehead.

"You're tired. I'll get out of here." Samantha stood, leaned down and kissed Melissa's cheek, then the baby's head. "Don't you worry about a thing. I'm going to put Dominic and Tyler to work on this case. You just get your strength back and take care of this precious little boy."

Melissa nodded, suddenly exhausted. Bill's death still felt oddly distant, almost surreal to her. She knew she hadn't yet felt its full impact.

"Melissa?" Samantha paused in the doorway and looked back at her. "You and Bill... Things were okay between the two of you, right?"

Oh, how she wanted to tell Samantha the truth, that things had been horrible; that in marrying Bill she had exchanged one kind of prison for a far worse one. But shame kept her silent; the folly of her stupidity was too painful.

"Everything was great with me and Bill," she finally answered.

As Samantha left the hospital room, a cold wind of despair blew through Melissa. She was tangling herself up in a web of lies. Hopefully nobody would be able to see through the gossamer strands to learn the truth. Because Melissa knew that in that truth was the perfect motive for murder.

Chapter 3

Dominic gripped the floral bouquet more tightly, feeling silly as he walked down the hospital corridor toward the maternity unit. It had been two days since the birth. Despite his intentions to stay uninvolved, in spite of the fact that he had no desire to form any sort of emotional attachment to either Melissa Newman or her baby, he'd been unable to stop himself from this visit.

He wanted to see the infant who had entered this world in Dominic's hands. And he felt pity for the woman who'd lost her loved one. There would be no flowers from a beaming husband, no blue-banded cigars passed around, no daddy to boast with pride about his new addition to the family.

A tragedy. That was what it was. And Dominic knew all about tragedy.

He hesitated just outside Melissa's hospital room,

fighting the impulse to run. *What the hell are you trying to do?* an inner voice mocked.

He just wanted to see the baby, that was all. He wanted to see those big, blue innocent eyes that had gazed so trustingly into his. Those eyes that had not judged, not censured, only accepted. It had been a long time since Dominic had seen that in anyone's eyes.

Besides, he wanted to assure himself that the infant was well and healthy, that there were no ill effects from the crazy circumstances of the birth.

Drawing a deep breath, he stepped into the room and stopped short at the sight that greeted him. Melissa was asleep, the baby in her arms.

The room smelled of baby powder and a faint floral perfume. The afternoon sunshine streamed through the window, outlining the bed and Melissa with its golden beams.

Dominic felt an emotional pull deep in his gut as one tiny hand came free from the blue blanket and waved in the air, as if beckoning him closer.

He stood still, uncertain whether to leave the flowers and back out, or wait for her to wake up. Before he could make up his mind, her eyes opened.

"Dominic." She offered him a sweet, sleepy smile as she moved to a sitting position. "Please...come in." She motioned him toward the chair next to the bed.

"I brought these for you," he said, gesturing to the flowers he held. "I'll just put them here." He walked over to a small table, where another arrangement sat in colorful glory. He recognized Samantha's handwriting on the card that poked out of the flowers.

"Thank you. They're beautiful," Melissa replied.

"I just thought I'd stop by and see how you and the baby were getting along." He shifted from one foot to the other. He'd always hated hospitals.

"We're doing fine." She beckoned him closer, smiling down at the baby boy in her arms. "Even though you've already met him, allow me to officially introduce you to Jamison Jackson Newman."

"Pretty big name for such a little boy," Dominic said as he peered down at the infant.

"He'll grow into it." She picked up the baby and held him out to Dominic. "Here, hold him. You helped bring this little bundle of joy into the world."

"Oh, no, I—" Dominic's protests were cut short as she placed the baby in his arms. He sank into the chair, afraid to remain standing while holding the precious child. The scent of baby powder and the snuggly warmth against his chest momentarily took away his capacity to speak.

He'd once wanted children. A houseful. He'd fantasized about marrying Abigail and starting a family of healthy, beloved children. But Abigail had married another man, then had been murdered, and Dominic's dreams had died at the same time. There would be no children for him; no love, no marriage.

Still, his heart went out to this little fatherless child, born amid chaos, forced into a premature entrance into the world by his mother's emotional stress.

"Dominic, I'd like for you to be his godfather."

He looked at Melissa in surprise. "Oh, no... No, I couldn't." He stood and handed the baby back to her, trying to ignore the hurt that momentarily darkened her eyes. "Look, I'm honored by the thought, but I just really don't think it's right."

She fussed with the baby's blanket, her gaze averted from his. "You're probably right. It was just a crazy impulse."

There was a moment of uncomfortable silence and Dominic wished he'd handled the situation with more diplomacy. Once again he shifted from foot to foot, seeking a graceful way to escape.

"Tell me what's going on with the investigation," she said, breaking the awkward silence. "I've been so isolated I don't know what's been happening. I need to know what progress has been made in finding Bill's killer."

Dominic hesitated before answering. How could he tell her that according to the newspapers, according to the scuttlebutt he'd heard, the police believed they had the murderer—and the murderer was her?

"The investigation is ongoing," he hedged.

She sighed impatiently. "I know that, but surely by now they have some sort of leads, some clues they're pursuing."

Dominic sank back down in the chair. "There's not a lot of official information coming from the police yet," he explained. "But from what little I've been able to glean, the authorities have pretty well ruled out a 'stranger' homicide or a burglary gone awry."

She frowned and Dominic noticed the color of her eyes exactly matched the aquamarine flowers that dotted her hospital gown. "I don't understand. What would make the police come to that conclusion?"

"They believe Bill's death was a rage killing. And rage usually means somebody close to the victim."

He hoped she wouldn't pursue it further; he wasn't comfortable sharing the grim details with her.

"A rage killing?" She studied him thoughtfully, her hand absently stroking the baby's little arm. "How many times was he stabbed?"

He was surprised by her acumen, her instant grasp of the situation. "Twenty-two."

She closed her eyes with a swift intake of breath. Dominic felt an empathetic swirl of sadness inside his chest. The details of a death were never pretty, but somehow always more palatable when devoid of such obvious overkill.

She looked at him once again. "What about fingerprints on the knife?"

"They haven't gotten results back from the lab."

She nodded and took a moment to rearrange the blanket around the baby. "I'm surprised nobody from the police department has been in to ask me more questions."

Dominic smiled. "You can thank your sister for that. She told the hospital personnel that she'd personally sue them all if any police got in to see you, and she told Detective Mawlins he could interview you once you were out of here."

"She also talked them into keeping me a day longer than usual. I'm going home tomorrow morning," she said. "Samantha told me the police have released the house."

"And I've been trying to tell her she shouldn't go back there. She should stay with me and Tyler," Samantha said as she walked into the room. Tyler followed behind her and both nodded a greeting to Dominic.

"Samantha, I explained to you yesterday, I need to go home…to my home. Staying with you and Tyler will only postpone the inevitable." Melissa plumped the pillow behind her head and sat up straighter. "Besides, the baby's room is all set up there. It just makes sense for me to go home."

She looked down at the baby. "Bill is gone, and I can't do anything to change that, but I won't let them take my home from me as well." Her voice was deep, full of emotion.

Again Dominic marveled at the strength, the fortitude that would allow her to return to the house where her husband had been murdered. At the same time, he understood her need to be there, to take her son back to the place where she and her husband had lived, had loved.

"I'll just get out of here and let you all talk," Dominic said as he stood.

"No, please, stay," Samantha protested. "We have some things to discuss that include you." Samantha walked over to the bed and swept a caressing finger over the baby's cheek. "Why don't we put this little guy in his own bed?" She took the baby and placed him in the crib across the room, then returned to Tyler's side.

Samantha leaned against Tyler, and Dominic noticed the way Tyler's hand went to her waist in a completely unconscious gesture of married intimacy.

Dominic had a feeling that whatever news they'd brought was not good, and he watched Melissa as she squared her shoulders, as if preparing herself for it.

"It seems Detective Mawlins has you in his crosshairs," Samantha said.

The words caused Melissa to frown worriedly. "Has some new information come to light?" she asked.

"There was no sign of forced entry, and the murder weapon was from your kitchen drawer." Samantha hesitated for a moment and Tyler's hand moved from her waist to her shoulder, as if silently offering strength. "Apparently the only prints on the knife were yours."

Melissa gasped. "But...but that's impossible!"

"Not really," Dominic replied. "You probably touched your knives a thousand times—using them, washing them, then putting them away. If the killer wore gloves, then your prints would be the only ones that showed up."

"Then that's got to be what happened," Melissa exclaimed.

"Yes, well, Mawlins thinks you did it, and the official investigation seems to be focused solely on proving your guilt," Samantha said. "You had access to the weapon, you don't have a substantiated alibi for the three-hour period when the murder occurred. The only thing the police are lacking at this moment is a logical motive."

Melissa winced ruefully. Her sister never sugarcoated her words.

"Harvey Mawlins hated your father, which gives him a personal reason to go after you," Tyler added. "Your father regularly discredited Mawlins on the witness stand in a variety of cases. Harvey's hatred runs deep."

"You need a lawyer, Melissa. Tyler and I both

think it best if you get a lawyer right away," Samantha said.

"Okay...you're hired," Melissa retorted.

Samantha shook her head. "It's never a good idea to represent family members. Jurors don't believe lawyers whose clients are family."

Melissa closed her eyes, a wave of despair twisting her features. Dominic could guess the thoughts that scurried through her head. The word "jurors" implied a trial with her as the defendant.

He remembered how frightened, how utterly helpless he'd felt when he'd realized he was the only suspect in Abigail's murder; that the police had already tried and convicted him without pursuing any other leads.

"We've contacted Richard Wallace. He's a criminal trial attorney in Kansas City. He's agreed to represent you. He's a good lawyer, Melissa," Samantha said. "He's coming to town tomorrow to speak with you."

Melissa nodded wearily.

"I know this is all a little overwhelming at the moment," Tyler added. "But we'd rather err on the side of caution."

"If you insist on going back to your house tomorrow, then I'd like Dominic to go with you, to stay with you for the next couple of days," Samantha said.

Dominic didn't know whose face registered more surprise, his own or Melissa's.

"Hear me out." Samantha raised a hand to stifle any protests from her sister. She moved to the side of the bed. "You don't just have yourself to think about anymore." She glanced at the baby sleeping in the nearby crib. "Melissa, you told me the other day that you couldn't remember the last time you'd gone to the store while Bill was taking his early-evening nap. You said it was your normal routine to be in the house cooking dinner at that hour."

Dominic instantly realized where Samantha was going, what she was speculating. As he looked at the young woman on the bed, a shiver of apprehension for her rippled through him.

"I don't understand. Why would that make it necessary for Dominic to stay with me?" Melissa asked.

"Because if it was not your normal routine to leave the house, then perhaps the killer was not just after Bill, but after you, as well," Dominic said softly. He watched as Melissa's blue eyes darkened with sudden comprehension and fear.

"But why would anyone want to kill me?" she whispered.

Nobody answered, but Dominic knew it was a question they would have to address in the next couple of days, or else Melissa would find herself charged with a murder he knew in his heart she couldn't, wouldn't commit.

Melissa stood at the window of her hospital room, awaiting Dominic's arrival to take her home. She wasn't particularly pleased with the idea of having Dominic in the house, but she was more fearful of the idea of being alone in the house with a killer possibly after her.

She rubbed the back of her neck. A tension headache had taken hold from the moment Samantha had delivered her bombshell yesterday.

Why? Why would somebody want to hurt her? Why had somebody killed Bill? She was the only one who'd had a motive for murder. Who else might have wanted Bill dead? Who else had harbored the kind of rage that it took to stab him twenty-two times? And how could the police believe her capable of such a crime?

"Melissa?"

She jumped at the sound of the familiar male voice and turned to see Dominic standing in the doorway. He looked as uncomfortable as she felt, and she realized he probably wasn't any more thrilled at the idea of staying in the house with her and her newborn than she was.

"You ready to go home?" he asked. He held himself aloof, not venturing into the room.

She nodded. "I'm supposed to wait for a nurse to bring a wheelchair. Hospital policy." She busied herself gathering the last of her things into an overnight tote.

She'd been secretly somewhat hurt when he'd declined her offer to be Jamison's godfather. She now realized it had been a ridiculous idea. Despite the fact that he'd shared the intimacy of birth with her, he was a stranger. And now, a stranger who would be living in her house.

"Dominic?" She zipped the overnight bag, then looked at him. "I know you can't be thrilled to be assigned the task of baby-sitting me and Jamison."

His lips curved up, but she could hardly consider the gesture a smile. No light brightened his eyes, no warmth emanated from him. "Samantha and Tyler think it's necessary. They want you to be safe." He shrugged his broad shoulders. "I don't mind." Just then a nurse appeared at the doorway, pushing a wheelchair, and Dominic moved out of her way.

"Here we are," the young nurse stated cheerfully. "Transportation to the front door for mother and baby."

Melissa sat down in the chair, and the nurse handed her Jamison.

"I'll get the bag," Dominic offered. He picked up the tote, then the group left the room.

It took them only minutes to reach the curb outside the front entrance. Dominic left them waiting there while he went to get his car.

"Is that your husband?" the nurse asked, her gaze admiring Dominic as he walked away from them. The sun sparkled in his dark hair, and his jeans fit tight against his long legs and slender hips.

"No. Just a friend." Melissa was surprised the woman hadn't heard about the murder. She'd seen the curious looks, heard the muted whispers the few times she'd left her room. She knew she'd been the topic of conversation among the hospital staff—and half the town.

At least in the privacy of her own home she wouldn't be subjected to the stares, the whispers. Home. Thoughts of returning to the house filled her with anxiety.

"Some hunk of a friend," the young woman observed with admiration.

Dominic pulled his car up and quickly jumped out of the driver's seat. The nurse took the baby from Melissa, and Dominic helped her out of the chair. As she stood, Dominic's hand rested on the small of her back, gently guiding her.

The touch, so small, so natural, most women would scarcely notice it, filled Melissa with a rush of warmth. She couldn't remember the last time she'd been touched with such tenderness, such caring.

She watched as the nurse buckled the baby into the infant seat in the back, then Melissa slid into the passenger seat. "Good luck," the nurse said and waved as she closed Melissa's car door.

As Dominic walked around the front of the car, she watched him. Some hunk of a friend. Yes, Dominic would be considered a "hunk." Tall, with broad shoulders and slender hips, he radiated a quiet confidence that was instantly appealing.

His face was a study in contrasts. A sharp, angular jawline, soft full lips. A strong, straight nose and sinfully long eyelashes.

She averted her gaze as he slid behind the wheel, immediately filling the interior of the car with the scent of minty soap and woodsy cologne.

"Feel good to be out of there?" he asked as he pulled out onto the street.

"Yes and no." She smiled when he looked at her curiously. "The food was horrible, I didn't sleep well, but thanks to Samantha, I was isolated from everything that has happened."

"Unfortunately, that isolation will end now."

"I know." She turned and checked on Jamison, whose bright eyes seemed to be focused on the back of her seat. She leaned her head back and released a sigh. "It still feels so unreal. The murder, the police suspicions." She once again looked back at Jamison, who'd fallen asleep. "Even his birth seems like it happened in a dense fog."

Dominic flashed her a tight smile. "Not to me. I can tell you honestly it was the most terrifying moment of my life."

She smiled warmly, remembering the gentle touch of his hand on her forehead, the encouraging words he'd whispered as she'd been engulfed in pain. "I didn't know you were terrified. You were wonderful."

A deep blush stained his cheeks. "I'm just glad you and the baby are all right."

Melissa's smile faded, and she studied him thoughtfully. It felt awkward to be with him. She didn't know him at all, knew the only reason he was here with her now was because of his allegiance to Samantha and Tyler. "I didn't kill Bill, Dominic. I need you to believe that."

"If I didn't believe you, I wouldn't be here," he answered, not taking his eyes from the road.

"Why do you believe me?" She wasn't sure why his answer seemed so important to her, why she cared what this man thought of her. But she did.

He looked at her, his gaze momentarily connecting with hers." "I believe you for several reasons." He returned his gaze to the front window. "First of all, women rarely resort to stabbing as a method for murder—it's too up close and personal. Second, at the moment there's no motive. You and Bill were expecting a child, which implies a commitment to each other. And, if the rumor is true, you have a trust fund you'll collect in a couple of months. That discounts a money motive."

She nodded.

"Besides—" He looked at her again, and in the depths of his dark eyes she saw a whisper of warmth. "Call it intuition, gut instinct or whatever...I just believe you couldn't possibly be capable of such a thing."

Melissa was overcome with emotion, and her eyes filled with grateful tears. She swallowed against them. "Too bad you aren't the officer in charge of this case." She shifted position. "Speaking of that, why didn't you go back to the police force when the charges against you were dismissed?"

He frowned and his hands tightened on the steering wheel. "I knew there was no point. For all intents and purposes, my career as a cop was over."

"But why? You were innocent of the charges."

"There are a lot of people in this town who don't remember that. They remember the headlines that were splashed across the papers, the juicy details of a cop arrested for killing his ex-lover. I would have been a public-relations nightmare for the department." He relaxed somewhat, his knuckles regaining color. "Anyway, it's all in the past now. I like working for Samantha and Tyler. It suits me for now."

Melissa nodded and turned her gaze out the passenger window. She had a feeling Dominic's words covered a deep well of suffering. She wondered how many friends had abandoned him, how many colleagues had turned their backs on him. She also wondered if he'd meant his words to be a warning of what she might expect.

He didn't have to worry about her suffering that particular fate. Bill had kept her so well secluded that she had no friends, no colleagues. Even when Samantha had returned to town after a six-year absence, Bill had made it difficult for the two sisters to maintain a close relationship.

Dominic pulled up in front of her home where yellow crime-scene tape still clung to the front door. Melissa stared at the house. It was difficult to believe Bill wouldn't be there, would never again walk through the garage door and into the kitchen after a day at work. He would never again bellow at her, rage at her, hurt her.

Still, the house would never be the peaceful sanctuary she'd dreamed of when they'd bought it, now that somebody had snuck into it and brutally killed her husband. She shivered.

"You okay?" Dominic asked as he parked the car and shut off the engine.

"No...yes...I don't know." She raked a trembling hand through her hair. "Maybe I shouldn't have come back here, maybe this was a mistake."

"You want me to take you to Samantha and Tyler's?"

She thought of the gaily decorated nursery inside. Bill had indulged her need to prepare it, but he hadn't been a part of it. In fact, Melissa couldn't remember her husband ever setting foot into the smallest of the three bedrooms.

This was her home. She couldn't allow anyone or anything to keep her away. "No, it will be fine. I need to be here. Jamison's room is ready for him. I'll be fine. I have to be," she said, looking back at her precious son.

He hesitated for a moment, as if to make sure she

was certain, then he got out of the car and went around to her side.

He opened her door, and she got out, then flipped the front seat forward and unbuckled Jamison. She held the baby out for him to take so she could grab the tote bag from the back seat.

He hesitated, then took the baby, who stirred and yawned, his little arms stretching from the blanket. A grin filled Dominic's face, warming the dark brown of his eyes and lighting his features attractively.

A tug of emotion pulled at Melissa as she watched Dominic cradle her son as if the little boy was the cutest, most amazing infant he'd ever seen. It was like viewing a scene from her heart's fantasy.

Her mind flashed a warning. Oh, she would have to be careful or this man might crawl into her heart. And that would be the absolute worst mistake she could ever make.

She was a grieving widow with a fatherless newborn. It was a role she had to embrace, with no space left in it for Dominic.

She could just imagine what the police would think of her if she followed through on any sort of attraction to Dominic. Bill wasn't even buried yet and she felt a magnetic pull toward the handsome stranger holding her son. If Detective Mawlins sensed any interest for Dominic on her part, it would add fuel to his suspicions of her.

A tangled web seemed to be closing around her, a web of her own secrets and fears. Allowing Dominic into her heart in any way, sharing with him any of those secrets could have grave consequences, ones that just might land her in prison for the rest of her life.

With a shiver of fear clawing at her insides, she reached for her son, needing to hold him close, afraid of what the future held.

Chapter 4

Dominic pulled the pieces of yellow tape from the front door and added them to the trash bag he carried. As he worked, the late-May sun warmed his back.

He and Melissa had been inside the house only a few minutes when he'd decided to come out here, remove the tape and inspect the premises. He intended to take the job of bodyguard seriously. And from his police background, he knew the first thing he needed to do was learn the territory around the house.

When they'd first gone inside, Melissa had directed him to carry her bag into the nursery. On one side of the room was a wooden crib, on the other side a single bed, where he supposed she intended to sleep. He wasn't surprised that she'd steered clear of the master bedroom.

She offered him the use of the second bedroom, a

nondescript spare room with a double bed and dresser. He'd retrieved his bag from the car, placed it on the bed, then gone outside to give her some privacy and himself the chance to look around.

He now sat beneath a large oak tree in the front yard, observing the house with a critical eye. It was so isolated, with the trees and brush providing hundreds of hiding places. A perfect place for a murder. It was easy to imagine somebody sneaking into the house, killing Bill, then sneaking back out and fading into the brush amid the dusky shadows.

He frowned and rubbed his forehead thoughtfully. He hadn't lied when he'd told Melissa he believed in her innocence. Or at least, he wanted to believe in it. Suddenly the bruises on her legs flashed into his mind, leaving a niggling, disturbing doubt. How had those injuries occurred? Again he told himself there was probably a perfectly logical, perfectly innocent explanation.

It made no sense for Melissa to kill Bill. She'd been carrying the man's baby. Dominic's frown deepened. It had made no sense for him to kill Abigail, either, but that hadn't stopped the police from arresting him, or the district attorney from pressing charges.

Thoughts of Abigail always gave him a bad taste in his mouth. It was partially the taste of grief, a grief that had begun on the day she'd told him she intended to marry Morgan Monroe, the town's wealthy banker.

The taste was also the bitterness of failure, the acrid flavor of self-hatred. He should have been able to save Abigail. He'd been a cop, sworn to serve and protect, but in the end, she'd been killed while he'd lain unconscious next to her.

He stood, irritated by his walk down memory lane—a lane that led straight to hell. The past was gone. What mattered now was seeing that Melissa and her child were kept safe, and that Bill's real killer was caught.

Dominic made a mental note to talk to Samantha about installing a security system. The house had too many doors and windows for any one man to watch.

The lawn was well kept, Dominic noted as he walked around the side of the house toward the back. He stopped in his tracks, instantly spying Melissa at the very edge of the backyard.

The area where she stood appeared more wildlife refuge than yard. A half-dozen bird feeders hung on poles of various heights. Rosebushes not yet in bloom surrounded a concrete birdbath, and the baby carrier sat on a stone bench in front of a flower bed bursting with late-spring blossoms.

Still, it wasn't the beauty of nature that captured Dominic's attention, rather it was the beauty of the woman who stood at its center.

She'd changed from the slacks and blouse she'd worn home from the hospital and instead wore a long, gauzy, pale pink dress that billowed in the warm breeze. Her hair sparkled as if infused with gold glitter. Had Dominic not known better, it would have been impossible for him to believe this slender woman had given birth only three days before.

As she filled one of the bird feeders with seed, he could hear the melodic whisper of her voice talking to the baby. She rehung the feeder, then spun around and saw him.

He walked toward her, not wanting her to think

he'd been standing there staring at her. "Shouldn't you be in bed or something?" he asked, reminding himself that she had just given birth.

She smiled. "Dominic, I had a baby, not some dread disease. I feel fine. He was small but perfectly healthy, and as you know, the delivery was without complications."

"You shouldn't have come out here alone without telling me," he chided.

The smile on her face faded, and the pink of her cheeks paled. "You're right. That was thoughtless of me."

"I can see why you'd want to come out here. It's nice," he observed as he stopped beside the birdbath. He could smell the scent of the sweet flowers, which was much like the perfume he'd noticed her wearing earlier.

"Yes. This is my sanctuary."

She bent down and pinched off several dead blossoms. He watched her curiously. "Sanctuary" implied "escape," a "haven" or "refuge." What would she need refuge from?

"The moment I saw this area, I knew this was the house I wanted to buy," she said as she smiled up at him. "The bench and the birdbath were already here. I—we added the feeders and the flowers." Her smile faded, and she looked back down at the flower bed.

A stab of pity flowed through him. Was she remembering the happy day she and her husband had planted the flowers? Hung the bird feeders? Had they planned to watch the flowers grow, spend their years together nurturing this place as they nurtured their marriage?

As far as he knew, she had yet to grieve properly for all she'd lost. He imagined her grief had been postponed by the horror of discovering herself a prime suspect in her husband's murder case. But sooner or later it would come, and by that time Dominic would be long gone from her life.

A birdsong broke the silence between them, the cheerful tune a contrast to his thoughts. He cleared his throat and sat down on the bench next to the sleeping baby. "I think you should have a security system installed."

She stood and brushed her hands together to dislodge any dirt. "Okay," she agreed readily. "Do you know a good company?"

He nodded. "If it's okay with you, I'll make the arrangements tomorrow."

"I appreciate it."

She sank down beside him, so close he could smell the sweet scent that emanated from her, feel the warmth of her body radiating toward him. He tensed against the sensory assault.

"This is the calm before the storm, isn't it?" she asked softly.

He didn't pretend not to know what she was talking about. "Probably. By this afternoon the police will know you've been released from the hospital, as will every reporter in town."

"Bill's funeral is going to be day after tomorrow." She raised her face toward the sun, as if to gather inner strength. The sunshine emphasized her delicate features, bathing them in warm gold tones.

Dominic fought the impulse to reach out and touch her cheek, feel her soft skin beneath his fingertips. A

flush of warmth swept through him at the thought.
What was it about her that affected him on such a
primal level? Stirred a longing inside him?

"You hungry?" she asked suddenly. She turned
and looked at him. "It's almost noon."

He nodded. "I could eat."

She stood. "What would you like? Ham sandwiches? Hamburgers? Or maybe you prefer something more substantial? I think I have some steak in
the freezer. I could thaw it in the microwave, or
maybe..." A frantic energy radiated from her, as if
the most important element in her life at the moment
was to please him with lunch.

He held up a hand to stop her. "I don't get that
many choices at the local diner," he said, watching
a small stain of blush sweep over her cheeks. "Melissa, I might be here for several days. I don't expect
you to wait on me. We're kind of like partners in this
mess."

"Partners?" She looked at him for a long moment.
"Okay, but what I could really use right now is a
friend." She held her hand out to him. "Would you
be my friend, Dominic?"

He saw her need shining in her eyes. The need for
a companion to guide her through the hell that was
sure to come, a friend to support her through the grief
and horror. Surely it wouldn't hurt to offer her his
friendship.

Maybe his attraction to her was nothing more than
his own need for a friend. His friends had fallen away
like leaves from a tree in autumn when he'd been
arrested, and he'd never had the inclination or the
desire to rake them up after he'd been released.

He enclosed her hand with his, the strength of her grip surprising him. "Friends," he agreed.

She smiled. A full, wonderful smile with enough warmth to rival the sun. Desire for her hit Dominic square in the gut. He quickly released her hand, shamed by his inappropriate need.

"Let's go eat," she said. She picked up the baby and started toward the house.

Dominic followed more slowly, knowing this promised to be the most difficult assignment he would ever undertake.

They had just finished ham-and-cheese sandwiches and were sharing the cleanup when the doorbell rang. Melissa froze, knowing a visitor could only be the precursor of something terrible.

"Stay here. I'll answer it," Dominic said. As he left the kitchen, Melissa moved closer to Jamison, who slept in his carrier in the center of the table. So far he'd been an exceptionally good baby, crying only when hungry and sleeping the rest of the time. It was as if the chaos of his unexpected birth had been more than enough for him, and he was content now just to sleep.

"It was a reporter," Dominic said as he reentered the kitchen. "I sent him away."

"Good. Thank you." She sank into a chair at the table, her gaze fixed on her son. She could see both Bill and herself in his tiny features—Bill's strong jaw, the very round shape of her own eyes.

"Melissa?" Dominic's voice was soft, inquiring.

She looked up at him in despair. "What if they charge me with Bill's murder? What if I end up being convicted? Who is going to love Jamison like I do?" Her voice thickened with emotion. "I'll miss everything—his first steps, his first words...."

"We aren't going to let that happen." Dominic joined her at the table. "Melissa, if the police aren't going to find the real killer, then we'll have to."

"But how?" Melissa felt a bubble of hysteria rise into the back of her throat. Damn Bill. Even in death he had the last word, continued the abuse. She could almost hear his laughter taunting her.

"We're going to have to pick apart Bill's life, find out everything we can about him. We need to go through his work records, his personal papers, whatever we can find that might yield a clue."

"But aren't the police already doing all that?" she asked.

"Not if what Samantha and Tyler said is true. If the police have narrowed their focus to you alone, then they aren't looking for other suspects, aren't following any other avenues. The only reason they haven't grilled you yet is because you've been in the hospital."

Melissa sighed. She'd only been home a couple of hours and already she was tired—far too tired for a twenty-five-year-old. "So, where do we begin?"

Before he could answer, the doorbell rang again. Dominic immediately stood. "I'll be right back."

She assumed it was probably another reporter, looking for an exclusive interview with the murder suspect. Melissa knew this would be a juicy story, especially given the social status of her maiden name.

The fact that her father had been a wealthy, highly respected attorney before his death, would only add fuel to the fires of gossip. There was nothing people loved more than a prominent person's fall from grace.

She rose in surprise when Dominic returned to the kitchen, this time in the company of an older, portly gentleman with a shock of silver hair.

"Richard Wallace," the man said, holding out a hand toward her. "I spoke with your sister yesterday."

"Oh, yes. Thank you for coming." Melissa shook his hand, realizing he was the lawyer Samantha had contacted about representing Melissa. "Please, sit down. Let me just take the baby to his room." She knew it was silly, but she didn't want Jamison in the center of the table while they spoke of the heinous crime and her supposed part in his father's death.

It took her only moments to put the baby to bed in the room where teddy bears danced on the wallpaper border. Then Melissa stood in the center of the floor, breathing in the scent of her son, capturing it in her lungs to give her strength.

Richard Wallace's appearance suddenly made everything frighteningly real. Bill was dead, and the police believed she was responsible.

If they didn't find the real killer, then she would go to prison, possibly for the rest of her life. Her son would grow up motherless, fatherless....

She turned and left the room. In the hallway, she looked toward the master bedroom. The door was closed and she had yet to go into the room where Bill had died, even though Samantha had told her she'd thoroughly cleaned it the day before. Too bad Samantha couldn't cleanse Melissa's memory as effectively.

When she returned to the kitchen, Dominic was making coffee, and Richard had opened a briefcase and was pulling paperwork out across the table.

It took them only a few minutes to discuss the business end of Richard's representation. "I knew your father," Richard said when she'd signed the contract that retained him as her counsel. "A fine man. An exceptional lawyer."

And a rotten father, Melissa mentally added. But, since her father's death seven months earlier, Melissa had found a healing peace where Jamison Jackson Dark's inadequacies as a father were concerned. In fact, she wished he were here now, to help her out of this mess. Jamison hadn't been a compassionate, loving father, but he had been a brilliant lawyer.

Now she had to depend on Richard Wallace to carry her through the legal entanglements. Just as she had to depend on Dominic to be a friend. A *friend.* The word sounded wonderful.

"I understand you were separated from Bill for a period of time," Richard said, a legal pad opened before him.

"Only a couple of months," Melissa answered.

"Did you want the separation or did Bill?"

Melissa wrapped her fingers around her coffee cup. "We mutually agreed we needed some time apart." It was a tiny white lie—one she couldn't imagine would hurt anyone. Bill had never wanted a separation, had been surprised by her uncharacteristic resolve and determination to break free of him. In an equally uncharacteristic display of indulgence, he'd agreed to give her some space, then had set in motion a campaign to win her back.

Melissa tightened her grip on her coffee cup, wishing she hadn't given in to him, wishing she could go back and be strong enough, smart enough to realize he would never change, and his promises of reformation had been nothing more than empty lies.

"Bill was pleased by your pregnancy?"

"That's what made us decide to put the marriage back together again." At least she wasn't lying about that. Initially Bill had seemed ecstatic at the news of her pregnancy. He'd told her how important it was for them to be a family once again, how desperately he wanted to be a good father. Then, when she'd agreed to get back together and after they'd moved into this house, he hadn't mentioned her pregnancy again.

Richard continued his questions, asking her about the reconciliation, her movements and activities on the night of the murder, their financial situation at the time of Bill's death. She answered each question as truthfully as possible, guarding only the secret that would cast doubt on her innocence.

Richard Wallace exuded a calm confidence, an innate intelligence that helped ease Melissa's worries. His questions were sharp and to the point, and he seemed to believe in her innocence, although he never asked her directly if she was responsible for Bill's death.

Dominic sat so close to her she could smell his attractive, masculine scent. His nearness also helped chase away some of her apprehension. Surely with two such strong, intelligent men on her side, she couldn't help but get through this all right.

"You know the name of the store clerk who

checked you out on the evening of the murder?'' Richard asked.

"Sandy. Sandy Mason.''

The phone rang, interrupting them. Dominic answered. ''She's not available for comment,'' he said, then hung up. Immediately the phone rang again.

"I suggest you get an answering machine or turn off your phone,'' Richard advised. ''I absolutely don't want you saying anything to any reporter. In fact, I don't want you discussing this case with anyone without my presence. I'll release whatever information we want to go out to the press.''

"That's fine with me,'' Melissa agreed. She had no desire to speak with any reporters and feed the gossipmongers.

"Samantha told me yesterday that there are some concerns about your safety,'' Richard continued. ''After hearing all the facts, I think you're right to be concerned.''

"That's why I'm here,'' Dominic said.

Richard nodded. ''Melissa, I don't want you leaving this house without Dominic. I don't want you going to your mailbox, answering the door or wandering around the yard without him by your side.''

"That's like being a prisoner in my own home,'' she said softly.

Richard offered her a grim smile. ''No, my dear. It's nothing like being a prisoner. Keeping you out of prison is what we're going to try to do.''

Melissa felt a shiver whisper up her spine at his words. Prison. Surely the police case against her wouldn't go so far. Surely they would discover who had really murdered Bill long before she was actually charged. "What can I do to help you learn the identity of the real killer?" she asked.

Richard looked at her, his silver eyebrows dancing upward in surprise. "My dear, it's not my job to find the real killer. It's my job simply to prove that *you aren't* the killer. Leave the investigation to the police, and I'll take care of the legal work."

He placed his papers back in his briefcase and stood. "That's really all we can do for now. Detective Mawlins wants to question you tomorrow. He wanted you at the station, but I insisted he question you here. He's to meet with us at two."

"Thank you. I much prefer not having to go to the station."

"Then I'll see you here tomorrow about one-thirty," Richard said as he, Melissa and Dominic walked out of the kitchen and toward the front door. "Don't worry, everything is going to be just fine."

Melissa forced a smile, even though she had a feeling nothing was ever going to be fine again. She opened the door and Richard took a step out, then turned back to her.

"Oh, one more thing," he said. "There's a simple way to get yourself pretty clear of any suspicions."

"What's that?" Melissa asked hopefully.

"Take a lie-detector test."

The words hung in the air. Melissa felt the weight of not only Richard's gaze on her, but Dominic's, as well. She wanted to say she would, but she was afraid.

"Although they aren't admitted into evidence in a court case, it would alleviate some of the police suspicion," Richard explained.

What if they asked her about her relationship with

Bill? What if they asked her if she'd ever wanted him dead? It was too risky. Contrary to what Richard thought, a lie-detector test would not eliminate her as a suspect; it would only strengthen a case against her.

"I...I can't do that," she finally answered.

Richard nodded, seeming unfazed by her reply. "Okay, then, I'll see you tomorrow."

As she watched Richard go down the sidewalk to his car, she felt Dominic's gaze on her, studying her with surprise, in confusion.

"I'm going to go check on the baby," she said, refusing to address the unspoken questions in his eyes.

As she walked down the hallway, she could still feel Dominic watching her, and she knew he was wondering if he'd been wrong about her innocence, and if she really had killed Bill.

She wasn't sure why, but she wanted Dominic to believe her without reservation. She needed him to believe in her.

Suddenly the confidence she'd felt earlier ebbed away, leaving her in the cold, clammy grip of despair.

Chapter 5

The house was silent, dark except for the single light Dominic had burning in the living room. Melissa had stayed in the baby's room for most of the afternoon and evening, coming out only to tell Dominic to help himself to anything he wanted to eat for dinner.

He'd made himself a couple of sandwiches, eaten alone in the kitchen and had cleaned up his mess. Then, after checking to make certain all of the doors and windows were locked tight for the night, he'd flopped down on the sofa, his thoughts his only company.

He had to admit, Melissa's refusal to take a lie-detector test had thrown him for a loop. Although he understood why Richard hadn't pressed the issue. Richard didn't care if Melissa was guilty or not, and as a lawyer, he wouldn't want a test that indicated deception. His job was to defend her...period.

However, if she was innocent, why would she deny herself an opportunity to prove it by taking a lie-detector test? It made no sense.

Had she killed Bill? And if she had...why? Or was it possible she knew who might have committed the crime? Was she protecting someone? And if so, whom? And why?

Or was it simpler than that? Did she realize how easily the questions on a lie-detector test could be twisted to imply guilt when no guilt was present?

She'd left the front door unlocked, which had allowed the killer access to the house. It was possible that fact alone was enough to make her feel partially responsible for Bill's murder.

Dominic leaned back against the cushions of the sofa and looked around the room curiously. Melissa was obviously a spotless housekeeper. No clutter marred the room, no magazines splayed across the coffee table. A place for everything and everything in its place.

This area of the house radiated little warmth, as if this room hadn't seen much entertainment, much living. And yet, the easy chair in front of the television bore the depression of a man's weight.

A coaster on the table nearby implied nights of Bill sitting in the chair, perhaps drinking a cold beer or soda as he relaxed after a hard day's work. The room seemed more male than female, spartan and without feminine touches.

It seemed odd to him. In the short time he'd spent with Melissa, she'd struck him as a woman who would have the need to feather her nest in her own distinctive style. He could easily put her in a home filled with cut wildflower arrangements, fragile knick-knacks that each had special meaning, wind chimes tinkling to welcome in a morning breeze.

He thought of her as he'd seen her that afternoon, standing amid the flowers, whispering sweet nothings to her infant as she filled the bird feeders.

It was difficult to imagine her being able to commit a murder. There was a gentleness about her that would seem to make such an act practically impossible.

A gentleness in her soul and a hint of dark secrets in her eyes. He frowned and rubbed a hand across his jaw. Maybe it wasn't secrets at all, but merely the shadows of grief not yet explored.

He sat up as he heard the distant cry of the baby. A moment later the sounds grew closer and Melissa walked into the living room, carrying the crying infant in her arms. She jumped in surprise at the sight of Dominic, as if she'd forgotten his presence in the house or was afraid of disturbing him in any way.

"Hi. I didn't realize you were still up. It's time for his nine o'clock feeding," she explained. "I need to make him a bottle."

He followed her out to the kitchen, where she shifted the baby from one arm to the other as she pulled a can of formula from the cabinet.

"You want me to hold him while you do that?" he asked after a moment of hesitation.

She smiled gratefully. "Thanks. I appreciate it." She handed Jamison to him, the baby's displeasure obvious at having to wait for his meal.

"He's got healthy lungs," Dominic said teasingly. Jamison's face was red, his forehead wrinkled with his cries. Dominic touched a finger to Jamison's cheek. Soft. Like nothing he'd touched before. He laughed as the baby stopped crying and turned his head toward Dominic's finger. "You're a demanding little fellow," he said. Jamison quieted, as if intrigued by the sound of Dominic's voice.

Again Dominic was struck with awe by the miracle of such a tiny human being. Eventually the baby would grow to have wants and dreams, to love and be loved. But he would live his life without a father's guidance, without a father's love.

Melissa heated the bottle in a contraption obviously designed for such a thing. "He wouldn't have to wait so long if I'd been able to breast-feed him," she said, a stain of embarrassment coloring her cheeks. "Unfortunately my milk didn't come in well enough. The doctor said it was probably because of stress."

"I doubt very much that this little guy cares," Dominic said.

"You're right," she said. "Besides, this will be better if...if things go wrong."

She retrieved the bottle, then took Jamison from Dominic. "Let's go back in the living room," she suggested.

She settled into the cushions of the sofa, and Dominic sat down in the easy chair and watched as she began to feed her son. Jamison ate greedily, the bottle nipple hissing as he tugged at it. Melissa's features softened with love as she gazed down at the infant in her arms.

Dominic allowed himself to get caught up in the moment as he watched mother and child bond in silent communication with each other. It was a beautiful scene, and suddenly he felt like an intruder peeking in through curtains at an intimacy he shouldn't be sharing.

He stood and walked to the front window, focusing his gaze into the darkness of the night, trying not to think of how Melissa's navy robe made her eyes appear a darker blue than normal, how it emphasized the paleness of her golden hair.

"Richard Wallace seems like a pretty good man," he said, reaching for a subject that reminded him of why he was here.

"Yes, let's just hope he's a good lawyer," she replied. "Was it like this for you?"

He turned and looked at her curiously. "What do you mean?"

"Did you feel like you were in the middle of a train trestle and running as fast as you could to escape a locomotive bearing down on you?"

Dominic relaxed in the chair as she placed the baby over her shoulder and rubbed his back. "Not exactly. In my particular case, I never got the opportunity to run. The train was on top of me before I knew it. I was arrested minutes after Abigail was murdered."

The memory of that night—coming to on Abigail's bed to discover her dead beside him, the police bursting into the room—filled him with sorrow...with anger...with grief.

"You'd been drugged, hadn't you?" Melissa asked curiously.

Dominic nodded. "Seems the first Mrs. Morgan wasn't pleased with the second Mrs. Morgan. She paid big money to have Abigail killed. I just happened to be in the wrong place at the wrong time."

"I can definitely relate to that." Melissa frowned. "I keep thinking if I hadn't gone to the store, if I hadn't left the door unlocked…would he be dead now?" The baby burped, and Melissa cradled him back in her arms, rocking him in the ageless rhythm of motherhood.

"Those kinds of thoughts will make you crazy," Dominic warned. He knew all too well how dangerous it was to be alone with your thoughts.

He wondered if he'd not gone to Abigail's house that night, if he'd talked her into meeting him someplace else, would she still be alive?

Dominic leaned toward Melissa. "The one thing we can't do is wait to see what the police intend to do. We need to approach this thing aggressively." He didn't want to talk about his particular case anymore. He didn't want to give to Melissa the pieces of himself he kept hidden away—the regret…the pain…the guilt. They belonged locked away in his heart where only he could pull them forth and examine them.

She nodded her agreement. "Richard Wallace can only work for me if I get arrested. I don't want it to go that far." She paused, her eyes holding Dominic's gaze for a long moment. She looked as if she wanted to say something—something important—then she gazed back down at the baby, breaking the momentary connection with Dominic. A curious relief flooded through him. He didn't want those pieces of her soul, either.

"I just can't imagine who would do something like this to Bill. He had no enemies that I was aware of— he spent all his spare time with me." She broke off, obviously frustrated.

"Tell me about the men who worked for Bill," he said.

She frowned, a small wrinkle puckering in the center of her forehead. "I didn't know them very well. There's Sam Jacobson. He's the oldest of the three. He's been with the company since Bill first started it a little over six years ago. Mike Withers is in his early twenties. He's worked for Bill for about two years, and Neal Cook is middle-aged and has been with the company for five or six months."

"You know anything about their backgrounds? How they got along with Bill?"

She shook her head. "No. I've met them all several times, occasionally when I'd go to the shop or when one of them would come here to pick something up. But Bill didn't talk about work much. When he got home in the evenings, he just relaxed."

Dominic nodded, imagining quiet evenings, shared meals, the sweet companionship of love. "In the next couple of days you're probably going to have to decide what you want to do with Bill's business," he said, breaking the silence that had grown between them.

"Yes...I know." She sighed and looked down at the sleeping baby in her arms. "I don't know anything about running a business, but I hate to put the other men out of their jobs."

"Maybe you could promote one of them to manager. Or maybe one of them will be interested in purchasing the business from you."

"Maybe." She flashed him a bittersweet smile. "Life goes on even after murder, doesn't it? Decisions have to be made, problems faced." She leaned her head back against the sofa and released another deep sigh. "It just all seems overwhelming at the moment."

Dominic steeled himself against the soft vulnerability she radiated. He'd always been a sucker for women in need. He would have to remember that the only thing Melissa needed was for the real killer to be found. He tried to ignore the fact that he was no longer convinced that the killer wasn't her.

"It shouldn't be too hard to check into the alibis of the men who worked with Bill, find out where they were at the time of his death," he said thoughtfully. "At least it will be a start."

"We don't have much else to go on, do we?" she replied, her voice soft. She studied him, her eyes contemplative and achingly blue. "Maybe the police are wrong. Maybe it really was a stranger who came in to rob us and panicked when he saw Bill was here."

A tinge of hope colored her tone. Dominic knew it was always easier to believe that a loved one had been killed by some crazed madman, not someone familiar. If she wasn't responsible for Bill's death, then the idea of somebody sneaking into her home and killing him so brutally had to be terrifying.

"Maybe," he agreed, although he knew his voice lacked any real conviction. "But if that's true, it just makes finding the perpetrator more difficult for us."

Despair swept across her features, and Dominic fought the desire to move from his chair to sit beside her on the sofa, take her in his arms and tell her everything would be all right. The impulse irritated him. *She* suddenly irritated him, with her gorgeous eyes and beautiful hair and soulful expressions that made a man want to be a hero for her.

"You'd better get some sleep," he said more brusquely than he'd intended. "Tomorrow is going to be a long day."

"Of course. You're right." She stood and shifted the baby in her arms. She started to turn to walk away, but froze, her gaze captured by the window. "Dominic…there's somebody out there." Although she kept her voice low, he heard the fear that trembled in it "Somebody is outside…. He was looking in the window."

Dominic slowly stood. "Stay here. Act natural. I'm going to check it out, and I don't want your actions to tip off whoever might be out there watching us." He spoke calmly despite the adrenaline that shot through him. "When I go out the door, lock it behind me."

She nodded her understanding and Dominic walked in studied casualness across the room and into the entryway. Once past the view of the window, he burst into action. He twisted the lock and threw open the door, then stepped out into the night.

Without pause he moved stealthily across the front of the house, allowing his eyes to adjust to the dim moonlight. His feet made no sound on the lush, newly green grass as he approached the corner. The living room not only had a large window at the front of the house, but also a smaller window in the west side.

Not breathing, not making a single sound, he leaned forward and peeked around the side of the house, immediately spying the dark silhouette of a man at the living-room window.

Dominic didn't wait to ask questions. He hadn't been able to protect Abigail, but he wasn't about to allow anyone to harm Melissa or her son. He launched himself around the corner and toward the intruder.

The man turned, his mouth opening in protest. Whatever he'd been about to say exploded in an "Umph" as Dominic dived and hit him just below the knees, buckling them and bringing both men to the ground.

Dominic scrambled for dominance as the man beneath him flailed wildly with his arms and legs. "Marcola...stop! It's me, Gary," a familiar voice sputtered.

Dominic cursed roundly and stood, offering a hand to the man on the ground. "Gary, what in the hell are you doing out here peeping through windows?"

Gary Watters pulled himself off the ground, a sheepish expression on his moon-shaped face. "What do you think I was doing? Trying to get a story." The thin reporter dusted off his jeans and grabbed a small notepad that had fallen to the ground in the brief scuffle.

"You're lucky I didn't pull my gun on you. Otherwise you might have collected a bullet instead of a story," Dominic snarled. He drew a deep breath, trying to control the adrenaline rush that still raged inside him. He raked a hand through his hair and eyed the reporter irritably. "Since when does the Wilford *Sun* employ their reporters to peek into windows?"

Gary didn't quite meet Dominic's gaze. "Since nobody is talking, and this is the hottest story around these parts since you were arrested." His gaze lowered slyly to Dominic's face. "So, what are you doing here? Are you and the lovely widow close friends?"

Dominic laughed dryly. "Ah, Gary. You're a piece of work. I should beat the hell out of you and have you arrested for trespassing."

"But you won't because I was one of the few reporters who tried to be fair about your case," Gary reminded him with a confident smile.

It was true. Gary's feature articles following Dominic's arrest had been among the few that hadn't proclaimed Dominic's guilt, hadn't jumped to conclusions but instead had remained unbiased and objective. "But that doesn't mean I intend to give you any information, either," Dominic replied. "However, I can tell you the name of Melissa's lawyer. It's Richard Wallace. If you want an official statement, you can contact him."

"From what I've heard, she's going to need a good lawyer," Gary observed.

"So, what exactly have you heard?" Dominic asked, knowing Gary's sources were always the best.

"Oh, no." Gary laughed. "Quid pro quo. You scratch my back, I'll scratch yours."

Dominic thought for a moment. "All right," he relented. "I'm here because I've been hired by Samantha and Tyler Sinclair to protect Melissa."

"Protect her from what?" Gary countered. "According to my police sources, her prints were all over the murder weapon, and there was no signs of forced entry. When the police arrived, she had blood all over her dress. And just between you and me, they're livid because the dress was destroyed by the hospital on the night she had the kid."

Dominic frowned. He remembered the blood smears on her dress when he'd arrived at the scene on the night of the murder. The bloodstains had been minimal, and he assumed she'd been checking her husband for signs of life.

But he knew the police would make the missing dress part of their case. He could just hear old Chester Sparks, the district attorney, transforming that dress into damning evidence.

"Melissa is a victim, just like her husband was," Dominic replied, as much to convince himself as Gary. "While the cops spin their wheels, trying to make her the criminal, the real killer is running loose, laughing at them."

"Can I quote you on that?" Gary asked.

"No. What you'd better do is get out of here before I forget I like you and have you arrested for playing Peeping Tom on an innocent woman."

"Innocent or not, I've got it on good authority that she'll be arrested within the next week or two," Gary said as he and Dominic walked around to the front of the house. "Mawlins is planning on running for chief of police, and he figures on riding this high-profile case right into the position. He's just getting all his ducks in a row." Gary flashed a quick grin. "They want to make sure their case is airtight before an arrest is made. The sting of your arrest still tastes bad in their mouths."

"Yeah, well, I hope they choke on that taste for a long time to come," Dominic replied dryly. "Now get out of here."

With a wave, Gary took off down the driveway and disappeared into the darkness.

Dominic watched him go, then stifled a groan. Whenever politics were involved, things definitely were more complicated. Mawlins wouldn't want the good people of Wilford to believe a crazed killer was on the loose, wreaking havoc on the small town. Much cleaner, much easier to arrest Melissa and assure the public that the killing was nothing more than a domestic squabble turned deadly.

A domestic squabble. The bruises on her thighs. The subtle need to please. He shook his head, afraid of jumping to conclusions. In any case, things were definitely not looking good for Melissa. How long would it take before the evidence mounted and she was arrested?

Dominic turned and walked back to the front door. "Melissa. It's all right, open the door," he said as he knocked. He heard the dead bolt shoot free, then the door opened and Melissa looked out, her eyes huge and dark with fear.

"Who was it?" she asked when he stepped inside and once again locked the door.

"Nobody... Just a snooping reporter."

Melissa sagged against the wall near him. "Thank God...just a reporter." She shook her head, her gaze remaining on Dominic. "I was so scared. When you didn't come back right away, I thought... I just got scared." She swiped trembling fingers through her hair.

Instantly, remorse swept through Dominic, along with a burst of confusion. He hadn't thought of her waiting for him in here, wondering what was happening, fearing the worst. If she'd killed Bill, then she wouldn't be afraid that there was a murderer on the loose. But if she'd gone to the grocery store for a six-pack of soda and had returned home to find her husband murdered, then of course she would be scared.

"I'm sorry. I should have come back in immediately and told you what was going on."

"Don't apologize. It's all right now." She reached out and touched his arm lightly, a touch that seared right through him, directly to his heart. "I was just so frightened for you."

Her words stunned Dominic. He'd assumed her fear had been for herself, the fear of a woman who might be a target. He hadn't considered that she might be frightened for his safety.

She dropped her hand immediately. "I...I think I'll go on to bed." He watched as she picked up the baby from the sofa and started down the hallway toward the nursery.

He remained standing after she'd disappeared, the lingering scent of her floral perfume swirling in the air around him. Innocent victim or cold-blooded murderess? Innocent victim or calculating actress hiding her guilt? There was another possibility. Had she killed Bill in an act of self-defense and then, in guilt and fear, was attempting to lead him and the police in another direction?

He had no answers. In any case, it was a very long time before he could no longer feel the warm imprint of her hand on his arm.

Melissa sank into the mattress on the single-size bed in the nursery. The room smelled of baby powder and innocence, but she could still smell the scent of Dominic—provocative and masculine...and dangerous. Dangerous in that something about him, something in the look in his eyes, reminded her that she was a young, vibrant woman who'd been without love for too long.

What Bill had given to her throughout their marriage had nothing to do with love. She'd realized that for some time now. Bill had believed it was love, but it had been obsession, possession—something ugly and cruel.

She longed for the kind of love she'd once dreamed existed—a love both passionate and tender. She rolled over on her back and stared up at the play of moonlight on the ceiling.

Perhaps that kind of love didn't exist. Maybe those wistful dreams of hers had simply been the fantasies of a lonely girl raised in a cold, uncaring home.

Still, it would be all too easy to find herself falling for Dominic, with his dark eyes and air of tragedy. She knew he'd suffered horribly, not only from the death of the woman he loved, but also from having been charged for her murder. That was the darkness that lingered in his eyes, drawing from her the desire to fill him with light.

With a sigh of irritation, she turned over and stared at the baby crib silhouetted in the moonlight that drifted through the nearby window. She must be out of her mind, thinking such crazy thoughts. Fill him with light, indeed!

She'd been trapped for too long with a man she no longer loved in a cruel marriage. Was it any wonder she was drawn to the first decent man she'd come in contact with?

Two survivors—that's what she and Dominic were.

They'd both been dealt a bad hand from fate. That was probably why she felt so drawn to him. The camaraderie of survivors. She frowned as she realized the fallacy of this thought; Dominic had survived his ordeal, but hers was only just beginning.

Chapter 6

Melissa stood by the grave site, flanked by Samantha and Tyler, who looked like two somber guards as the minister spoke about Bill.

Dominic stood across from them, slightly away from the small crowd that had turned out for Bill's funeral. It was a beautiful spring day. The scent of fresh grass and newly budded flowers rode the warm breeze, and birds chirped merrily in the nearby trees. But Dominic didn't pay much attention to the beauty of the day. He concentrated on watching the people in attendance.

Detective Mawlins stood off to one side, his gaze focused intently on Melissa. A wave of dislike swelled up inside Dominic. The detective had spent three hours the previous afternoon grilling Melissa. He'd asked about her actions the night of the murder, and about the status of the Newman marriage. He'd implied guilt; had badgered and bullied her until her lawyer had protested and ended the interview.

Within minutes of returning to the house, the security company had arrived, and the evenings hours were eaten up by the installation of the house alarm system.

They'd begun this morning with a trip to the office of Bill's heating-and-cooling business, where they'd retrieved any files they thought might yield some clue as to who had killed him.

Thankfully, Bill had been meticulous about keeping records. They'd found detailed reports of work performed and people interviewed for jobs. So far, Dominic had only managed to find time to give them a cursory look. He was hoping to examine them more thoroughly this afternoon.

"Hi, son."

Dominic turned at the familiar male voice and smiled at his father. He'd known Jeb would be around somewhere. As cemetery caretaker of the Chapelwoods Cemetery, he was rarely anywhere else.

"Dad."

"Looks like you've gotten yourself caught in another tough case," Jeb observed.

Dominic nodded. He took his dad's arm and moved several paces back from where the minister still spoke, obviously loving the sound of his own booming voice. "Does she look like a killer?" Dominic asked his father as he gestured with his head toward Melissa.

Samantha held Jamison, leaving Melissa's hands free to clutch the skirt of her navy dress. Her face was unnaturally pale, her eyes unusually large as she stared straight ahead.

There was an air of bewilderment about her, as if she'd awakened to find herself in a group of strangers, at a solemn ceremony being conducted in a foreign language.

"Hell, I know Melissa would never do anything like this," Jeb said. "Now, if it were Samantha..." The old man grinned and looked at Samantha fondly.

Dominic remembered when he'd been young how Samantha would run away from home, run away from her father's strict rules and always find her way to Jeb here. Jeb had been her surrogate father, like a beloved uncle who never judged, only accepted.

"Now that one is full of spit and vinegar," Jeb exclaimed, then frowned. "But Melissa?" He shook his head. "She always struck me as a timid, captured bird. She always did exactly what was expected of her, never rocked any boat in any way. She'd never do anything like this—not in a million years."

Even though Dominic felt the same way on an emotional level, intellectually he was confused and didn't know what to think. Still, it felt good to have his dad proclaim his belief in Melissa's innocence. He put an arm around Jeb's thin shoulders. "You doing okay, Dad?"

Jeb smiled. "I'm doing fine, son. It's you I worry about. You be careful, hear? Somebody murdered that poor man while he slept. I hear you're staying in the house with Melissa. I don't want you getting hurt."

"Don't worry about me, Dad. I'll be fine."

"I can't help but worry about you, that's what fathers do." The old man flashed Dominic a grin, then he scanned the crowd. "You think the man who killed Bill might be here?"

"It's possible." Dominic followed his father's gaze. He recognized some of the people, but there were several men he didn't know. He assumed the band of three men who stood together were the men who worked for Bill. They appeared to be the approximate ages of the employees Melissa had told him about.

Gary Watters stood off by himself, also observing Melissa and the crowd. As he and Dominic locked gazes, Gary grinned and acknowledged Dominic with a nod of his head.

Dominic had been pleased to open the paper that morning and find no article written about his and Gary's scuffle the night before. The paper had contained a small follow-up, simply stating that nobody had been arrested yet in connection with the crime.

"I'd better get going," Jeb said, and Dominic realized the minister had finally finished the service and people were dispersing.

"I'll see you later, Dad." He gave Jeb a quick hug, smelled the familiar scent of cinnamon chewing gum, spice aftershave and menthol muscle rub. It was a fatherly scent that always evoked feelings of warmth, of security...of love.

Dominic watched as his father walked across the lush grass, his crippled leg making him cast heavily to one side. Love swelled in his heart for the man who'd raised him, the man who had given him a sense of strength, of values.

Dominic looked back to where Melissa now held her baby, a little boy who would never know the joy

of a loving father. Jamison was the real victim in all
this. He would never know the utter commitment of
a father's love. And if Detective Mawlins had his
way, the child would never know his mother's love,
either.

Dominic couldn't let that happen. Somehow, some
way, he had to make sure Melissa didn't go to prison.
If she wasn't the murderer, then they had to find out
who had killed Bill Newman. And if she was…he
refused to take the possibility further. He pulled himself from his thoughts as Melissa, Samantha and Tyler
approached him.

"It was a nice ceremony, but I'm surprised the
crowd wasn't bigger," Samantha said as they joined
Dominic.

Melissa shrugged. "Bill and I weren't particularly
social. We didn't have a lot of friends. Besides, it's
a weekday. Lots of people are at work."

Samantha nodded. "Still, you'd better expect a big
group at the house. Those who couldn't make it here
will want to stop by and pay their respects."

"You mean gawk at the murder suspect." Two
spots of high color dotted Melissa's cheeks.

"That, too," Samantha agreed, not contradicting
Melissa's assessment. She leaned over and kissed Melissa on the cheek. "We'll see you at the house." The
couples parted ways; Samantha and Tyler headed for
their car, while Melissa and Dominic walked toward
his.

"Everyone is going to be talking about the fact that
I didn't cry," Melissa said when they were on their
way back to the house. "I tried. I knew I should, but
I couldn't."

"Everyone reacts differently at funerals," Dominic said. "I've heard of some people who burst into hysterical giggles."

Melissa smiled faintly. "At least I didn't do that. That would have had people talking for years."

"Melissa, you're under a lot of scrutiny right now, but it will eventually pass. People will find another scandal to occupy their minds, new dirt to talk about."

"How did you handle it? All the sly looks, the questioning stares?"

"For the most part, I ignored it. Although my case was a little different. I was arrested so quickly, I didn't have a chance to feel the town judging me until after I was released."

She turned her head and stared out the window. "I'm going to get through this. I'll do whatever it takes to find the real killer." She looked back at Dominic and for the first time he saw a steely strength radiating from her eyes. "If Detective Mawlins thinks he's going to railroad me for a crime I didn't commit, then he'd better think again."

A touch of anger deepened her voice and the blush of her cheeks intensified with the emotion. "This evening, after everyone leaves, we'll go through Bill's files. If Bill was killed by somebody he knew, then we'll find out."

Dominic nodded, again confused by her and the situation. If she was guilty, would she go to such lengths to pretend to look for another guilty party? And if she had killed Bill, how far would she carry the pretense of innocence before something inside her snapped?

One thing was certain. She didn't look so vulnerable anymore; she didn't look like a victim. She looked like a fighter, readying herself for the fight of her life.

Melissa carried Jamison into his bedroom and pulled the shade against the late-afternoon sunshine. Drifting down the hallway from the living room came the sounds of people talking, the clink of silverware and an occasional burst of laughter.

Samantha had been right. The afternoon hours had brought an influx of people to the Newman home. Bearing casseroles and cold cuts, macaroni salads and baked ham, they came on the pretense of paying their last respects to the widow and her newborn son.

Melissa supposed some of them had come as friends, offering emotional support, but most of them were there to see how she was doing, to speculate on what had really happened within the walls of her house on the night of the murder.

Jamison was unusually fussy, flailing his hands and bleating cries of irritation. She suspected he'd been cooed over and held by too many strangers, stroked by too many hands. She paced the close confines of the nursery, gently rocking Jamison in her arms.

It was odd, but somehow the funeral had evoked a renewed strength in her. It was as if the pall of Bill's shadow over her had finally been dispersed. Along with the strength had come the first blossom of anger—anger at herself for remaining for so long under his control, and anger that his killer had placed her in the position of needing to defend herself.

She put Jamison in his crib and covered him with

a soft blue receiving blanket. Staring down at her son, she felt strength flowing through her, filling her. She'd been her father's victim for years, then had become Bill's victim. No more. As of this moment, she intended to put the past behind her and rediscover who exactly Melissa Dark Newman was. She owed it to herself. She leaned down and gently patted her son's little bottom. "I owe it to you," she whispered to the sleeping infant.

She straightened as the door to the nursery opened and Dominic peered in. "I thought this might be where you sneaked off to," he said. "Everything all right?"

She nodded and joined him at the door. "He was getting fussy." She stepped out into the hallway and pulled the nursery door closed behind her. "I asked the guys who worked for Bill to stay for a few minutes after everyone else leaves," she explained. "I'm sure they're worried about their jobs and I want to assure them I don't intend to do anything rash."

"Good. Perhaps we can get some useful information from them at the same time." His expression seemed to hold a hint of speculation as he looked at her.

She wasn't sure what had caused it, what he was fishing for, and so she said nothing. *Useful information.* None seemed to be forthcoming so far, Melissa thought as she followed Dominic back to the living room, where the crowd appeared to have thinned out somewhat. Samantha walked over to her. "Jamison all right?" she asked.

Melissa nodded. "He's sleeping."

"You've got enough food in the kitchen to last you

for the next month," Samantha said. "At least people have been generous."

"A ham or a casserole is a small price to pay to get a glimpse of a husband-killer," Melissa replied sarcastically, then grimaced. "Sorry."

"Don't be. You have a right to be angry. I'd say it's a healthy emotion under the circumstances," Samantha said. "Damn Mawlins and his ineptitude."

"Dominic told me he's looking to make chief."

Samantha raised her gaze upward in an exaggerated gesture. "If that happens, heaven help the good people of Wilford."

At the cemetery, Melissa had felt the detective's gaze focused on her for the duration of the service. Dark, full of suspicion, his eyes had played on her with an enmity that had sent a chill up her spine. God help her if Mawlins learned that Bill had been an abusive spouse. He would have his motive and she would be sent to prison.

She remembered what Tyler had said, about Mawlins hating her father. It would somehow be easier to accept his suspicions if she didn't believe that his personal feelings were coloring that suspicion.

"Uh-oh, don't look now but Mabel Harrison is coming our way," Samantha whispered.

Mabel Harrison was the seventy-year-old president of the Wilford Ladies' Club, a group that gathered once a month to discuss civic projects and raise money for charity. Melissa's father had always accused the female group of being a pack of hens, squawking gossip and pecking up trouble. Melissa braced herself as the slender gray-haired woman descended on them.

"Darling girl," she oozed as she hugged Melissa to her bony body. The scent of lavender that wafted from her nearly suffocated Melissa. Mabel finally released her. "Your daddy must be spinning in his grave with all that's happened."

"Yes...I..." Melissa struggled to find a reply, but was cut short by Mabel.

"Now you know, my dear, I'd never criticize you in your time of grief," Mabel continued. "But do you really think it wise to have a man like Dominic Marcola staying here with you so soon after your husband's death?" Mabel's eyes glittered with the hunger for gossip. "I mean, it's rather scandalous."

"A man like Dominic?" Melissa gazed coolly at the woman. "You mean because he's single, or because he was an innocent man falsely charged in Abigail Monroe's death?"

"Well, you must admit, Melissa. It isn't exactly proper for a young widow to have a single man staying in her home."

"Perhaps you'd find it more acceptable if Melissa stayed here alone and left herself as a target for Bill's real killer," Samantha said in clipped tones. "Dominic Marcola works for me. I hired him to stay here for Melissa's and Jamison's protection."

"Oh, my, we never considered that Melissa might be in danger," Mabel replied, her gaze shifting from Melissa to Samantha, then back again. "Well, then, I guess that explains the situation." She pursed her thin lips together and nodded, as if satisfied that the morals of the town weren't being corrupted. "You let me know if there's anything the ladies' club can do for you." Without waiting for a reply, she turned and hurried back to a group of women standing by the front windows.

Melissa shook her head and cast a small smile at her sister. "Amazing. What did she think was going on here? That Dominic and I were carrying on a torrid affair, making love in the middle of the bed where Bill was murdered?"

"As far as that bunch of women is concerned, that would be more of a moral outrage than you killing your husband. Killing a man might be understandable, cheating on your marriage vows is something else."

Melissa looked over to where Dominic stood near the television, talking to Roger Canon. Roger owned a small Italian restaurant where Melissa and Bill had occasionally eaten.

Dominic was clad in charcoal dress slacks. He'd taken off the matching jacket as soon as they'd come back from the funeral. He looked handsome and virile, with his shirtsleeves shoved up, exposing strong forearms. His face was animated as he spoke with Roger. He turned his head suddenly, as if made aware of her gaze on him.

For a moment their eyes locked and he smiled. It was an unguarded, easy smile that stole her breath away.

A torrid affair. It sounded sinful, ugly, and yet as she gazed at Dominic, she couldn't imagine anything ugly or wrong about being held in his arms, kissed by his sensual lips.

"Melissa, Tyler and I have to go," Samantha said, forcing Melissa's attention away from Dominic. "I've got a deposition to be at in half an hour. It shouldn't take long. You want us to come back later and help with the cleanup?''

Melissa shook her head. "That's not necessary. Dominic and I can handle it.''

Samantha looked at Melissa for a long moment. "This working out okay? I mean, with Dominic staying here?''

"Sure. He's easy to be with.'' It was true. In the three days they'd been sharing the house, Dominic had demanded nothing from her, had accepted both her company and the time she spent isolated in the baby's room.

"Yes, he's a good man. I hope someday he'll find some woman who will chase the shadows from his eyes.'' She hugged Melissa. "In the meantime, I feel better knowing he's here for your protection.''

Melissa nodded, although she was beginning to wonder if perhaps they'd overreacted to the implied threat to her. It had been six days since Bill's death, and she'd not been threatened in any way.

The next hour flew by in a haze for Melissa. Finally, the only people left in the house besides herself and Dominic were the three men who worked for Bill's company.

Sam Jacobson sat on the sofa, his face looking more lined and creased than Melissa remembered. Next to him was Neal Cook, a fair-haired man who appeared to be in his early forties. Mike Withers paced the living-room floor. The youngest of the three, in his early twenties, he looked both bored and impatient at the same time.

"Thank you for staying,'' Melissa said to the three. She sat in the easy chair across the room. Jamison, who'd awakened a few minutes before, was in his baby carrier at her feet. The little boy waved his hands in the air, as if trying to capture the waning sunbeams that danced through the window.

Dominic stood just behind her, his presence silently supportive. She was grateful he was here as she faced the three men who'd been an integral part of Bill's life, but not of hers.

"Mrs. Newman, we're all real sorry about what happened to Bill, but I'd be lying if I told you we weren't worried about our jobs," Sam Jacobson said.

"Yeah, we've got bills to pay and no money coming in at the moment," Mike said, his darkly handsome features twisted in frustration. "So what happens now?" He looked at Melissa, as if she were personally responsible for his finances. "Should we start looking for new jobs?"

"What I propose is for the next couple of weeks we keep things running as usual." Melissa looked at Sam. "You've been with Bill since he opened the business. I'd like you to take over the position of manager."

Sam nodded, the wrinkles in his face easing somewhat as he realized they weren't being handed their walking papers.

"So, we show up for work tomorrow morning just like usual?" Neal asked.

"Just like usual," Melissa agreed. "And I'll see that you all are paid for the work missed in the last couple of days."

"Great." Mike looked at his wristwatch. "Now I gotta go," he said as he flashed her a cocky smile. "I've got a hot date, and the lady hates it when I'm late." Without waiting for a reply, the young man left.

Neal Cook stood and raked a hand through his gray-laced sandy hair. "I'm mighty sorry for your loss, Mrs. Newman," he said, his blue eyes exuding sympathy. "I hadn't worked for Mr. Newman very long, but he seemed like a fine man."

Melissa nodded, suddenly weary. She just wanted this day done. "Thank you," she replied softly.

"If we're finished here...?" Neal looked at her hesitantly.

"Yes, we're through for now."

Neal nodded, mumbled a goodbye, then hurried toward the door, as if he, too, just wanted this finished.

Sam pulled himself up off the sofa. "If there's anything I can do, just let me know."

"Sam, could I ask you just a few more questions?" Melissa asked, looking at the man who'd probably been as close to Bill as anyone.

"Sure." He sank back down and looked at her curiously.

"You probably knew Bill better than anyone, knew what went on with the business, too. Was there anyone angry with Bill? A disgruntled customer...anyone you can think of who might have wanted to hurt him?"

Sam frowned thoughtfully and Melissa was aware of Dominic leaving the spot behind her chair and moving to sit beside the older man. "Anything you can think of might help," Dominic urged. "No matter how small or insignificant it seemed at the time. Is it possible Bill might have owed money to somebody?"

Sam shook his head vehemently at the last question. "No way. We're the only heating-and-cooling business in town. We've got more work than we know what to do with. The business is financially solid." He hesitated a moment, then raked a hand across his jaw. "I *can* tell you this—Bill intended to fire Mike."

Dominic sat up straighter, and Melissa felt a stir of excitement flutter in her stomach. "Was Mike aware of Bill's intention?" she asked.

"I don't know how he couldn't have been. Bill put him on probation a month ago, but the kid still continued to show up late, doing shoddy work that customers complained about."

"I don't suppose you'd know where Mike was on the evening of Bill's murder?" Dominic asked.

"Sorry, I don't have any idea," Sam replied.

"Could you look around the office to see if Bill documented the customer complaints over the last four to six weeks?" Dominic asked.

"Sure, I can look," Sam agreed.

"Thank you, Sam, for all your help," Melissa added. "I'm depending on you to help me make decisions concerning the business."

He nodded solemnly and stood. "I'll do whatever I can to help."

After Sam had left, Melissa turned to Dominic and asked, "You think it's possible Mike killed Bill?"

"At this point anything is possible," Dominic said. He opened a trash bag and deposited several used paper cups and plates inside. "But he's somebody we definitely need to check out." He paused and looked at Melissa curiously. "I noticed nobody from Bill's family showed up today."

"There's no family to show up," Melissa told him. She picked up several foam coffee cups and tossed them into the garbage bag. "Bill's parents died when he was young. He was raised by an elderly aunt who died just before we married. It was his inheritance from her that he used to open the heating-and-cooling business in Wilford."

"And where did he live before Wilford?"

Melissa frowned. "A small town in western Kansas—I can't think of the name of it right now. Bill didn't talk much about his life before Wilford." She picked up the baby who had begun to fuss. "Let me fix him a bottle, and I'll be right back to help finish cleaning up."

Dominic nodded, and she went into the kitchen. As she waited for the bottle to heat, she thought of Dominic's question about Bill's past.

One of the things that had first attracted Melissa to Bill had been his capacity to listen. In the early weeks of their courtship, he'd encouraged her to talk about herself, her hopes, her dreams, her unhappy childhood, her ambiguous feelings about her father. Melissa had found his interest a heady thing. Never before had anyone cared what she had to say, but Bill had cared, and he'd listened.

It was only now that she realized how reticent he'd been about his own past. She sat down at the table and began to feed Jamison, racking her brain for the name of the small town that had been Bill's home before Wilford.

By the time the baby had finished eating and had fallen back to sleep, she realized she would never remember the name of the little town that had been mentioned only once or twice.

She put the baby to bed, then returned to the living room, where Dominic had finished cleaning. "We'll tidy up the kitchen, then everything will be back in order," he said.

She smiled. "I didn't know garbage detail was part of your job description."

"That's what's special about this kind of work—there is no job description," he replied.

In the kitchen, with the ceiling light turned on against the approach of dark, they worked silently, putting away leftover food and disposing of trash.

Melissa found herself casting surreptitious glances at Dominic, remembering Samantha's words that she wished he would find a nice woman to chase the shadows from his eyes.

"Your mother died when you were young, didn't she?" Melissa asked as she covered the last casserole dish and placed it in the refrigerator.

Dominic looked up from where he'd been tying closed the trash bag, his eyes registering surprise at the question. "Yeah, she died in the car accident that crippled my father. Why?"

"My mother died when I was young, too." She leaned against the cool surface of the refrigerator. "I was just thinking that you and I have a lot in common."

He flashed her a quick grin. "Yeah, we're the two most notorious people in Wilford."

She laughed, surprised by how good it felt. She couldn't remember the last time she'd felt like laughing. The laughter stopped abruptly as she realized how inappropriate it was.

She sank down at the table. "I buried my husband this morning and everyone in town thinks I killed him. I shouldn't be laughing." Despite her words, a small smile tugged at the corners of her lips as she thought of Mabel Harrison's outrage—not that she might have killed Bill, but that she might dishonor Bill's memory by falling into bed with Dominic.

"Why don't I make us a pot of coffee?" he suggested.

She nodded and watched as he got the coffee from the cabinet and prepared a pot. Up until this moment in time, she'd viewed Dominic as the man here to protect her, the man who'd delivered her son, the man with whom she had in common the horrible experience of being wrongly accused of a heinous crime.

Now she found herself studying him simply as a man. The overhead artificial lights picked up auburn glints in his rich dark hair. Her fingers tingled as she thought of curling them into that thick darkness, pulling his face close enough to hers that she could taste the heat of his mouth.

"Maybe we should go over those files from Bill's office while we have coffee," she suggested, uncomfortable with the flush of heat, the sudden jolt of desire that accompanied her thoughts.

"Good idea." Dominic pulled the file folders from the kitchen drawer where they had placed them the day before. He set them down in the center of the table, then poured them each a cup of coffee. He pulled his chair around to her side of the table—far too close for Melissa's comfort in her present state of mind.

It wasn't only that she found herself vastly attracted to him in a physical sense; she genuinely liked him, appreciated what seemed to be a gentle nature. She liked the way his eyes lit up in unguarded moments, the quiet strength that flowed from him when she needed it most.

She wished she could tell him the truth about her marriage, that she could confess the hell she'd endured at Bill's hands. But she couldn't. She couldn't reveal her own weaknesses to him, and she couldn't hand him the motive that the police sought. She knew he had doubts about her innocence, saw them in his eyes at unguarded moments. She couldn't bear it if that doubt became certainty.

"Why don't you look over the personnel files, and I'll check over the work invoices," he suggested. As he pushed one of the folders in front of her, she noticed his hand. Long, artistic fingers, they implied not only strength, but gentleness. She'd seen them stroke Jamison's cheek and wondered what they would feel like caressing her shoulders, sliding down her back.

She slapped open the folder, irritated by the inappropriate direction of her thoughts. What was wrong with her? She'd buried her husband that morning. *A husband she hadn't loved,* a little voice reminded her.

She stared down at the paperwork in front of her, trying to concentrate on the words, but all she was conscious of was the press of Dominic's thigh against her own, while the heat and scent of him wafted over her.

The words on the paper wavered as her mind filled

with images, and her body imagined the sensation of being held in strong male arms—touched with tenderness, caressed with love. Not just any arms, but Dominic's arms.

"Sam wasn't kidding when he said the company wasn't having any money problems," Dominic said, breaking into her thoughts. "Here, take a look at these figures." He pushed a ledger in front of her, then scooted his chair even closer, placing an arm around her back as he leaned toward her.

"This is the average monthly income," he said as he pointed to a figure.

His cheek was so close to hers she imagined she could feel the soft brush of whiskers. "And this is what goes out each month in rent, salaries and miscellaneous." He pointed to another figure. "I'd say the business is on sound financial ground."

The hand that had been on the back of her chair suddenly moved up to her shoulder. Melissa's breath caught in her chest. She felt as if all the molecules in the air around them had been displaced. Dominic must have felt it too, for the finger that pointed at the page trembled slightly.

She turned her head, surprised to find him looking at her. No, *looking* was too passive a word to describe the way his eyes played on her. Shadows gone, hunger shone, desire gleamed. She parted her lips—wanting, needing him to kiss her, knowing he wanted to kiss her.

He leaned toward her, and she closed her eyes, a shiver racing through her as she anticipated the velvet touch of his lips against hers.

A shrill alarm rang through the air. Melissa's eyes

flew open in time to see Dominic dart toward the
security panel on the wall. She knew the system dis-
played a code for the area of the house that had been
breached. Any desire she might have felt vanished as
fear took its place.

"It's the nursery," he said as he raced out of the
room.

"Jamison!" Melissa cried. She stood, her chair
crashing to the floor as she ran down the hall toward
her son's room.

Chapter 7

Dominic's heart raced as he ran down the hallway toward the baby's room. He was vaguely aware of Melissa behind him, her breaths coming in quick gasps of panic. The alarm had changed from warning beeps to a full siren that blared discordantly throughout the house.

He expelled a sigh of relief as he entered the room and saw Jamison, safe and sound in his crib. The curtains bedecked with pink and blue dancing bears were drawn across the window. Dominic pulled the material back and grimaced. The screen hung half off the frame although the window remained tightly closed and locked.

"Whoever it was...the alarm must have frightened them away," he said to Melissa, who had picked up the crying baby and held him close to her chest. "I'll go shut off the alarm."

Dominic took a detour into his room just long enough to get his gun, then returned to the kitchen with Melissa trailing behind. He punched in the code to stop the alarm. Almost immediately the phone rang. "That will be the security company." He answered, gave the password to indicate all was well, then hung up.

"We need to call the police, make a report," he said to Melissa.

Her eyes darkened. "Detective Mawlins will probably say I slipped outside and pulled off the screen to cast doubts on his suspicions about me."

"But we know that isn't true." He picked up the receiver and punched in the number for the Wilford Police Station. It took him only moments to explain to the dispatcher that they'd had a possible break-in attempt.

"At least we know the alarm system works," Melissa said when Dominic hung up the phone.

Dominic nodded, pleased that, indeed, the home alarm system had worked, but irritated that his own internal alarm system had been disappointingly mute.

In those seconds, that long stretch of eternity when his eyes had locked with Melissa's and desire had momentarily been reflected in her eyes, his inner alarm should have been screaming like a siren.

"I'm going to go out and wait for the officers. Lock the door behind me." He didn't wait for her reply, but instead stalked out of the kitchen, through the living room and out the front door.

Warm, fragrant air embraced him as he stood on the porch and stared into the darkness surrounding the house. How long was he going to be able to survive staying here with Melissa without losing his mind? He'd been here less than a week and already his sleep was filled with dreams of her—of kissing her... touching her....

He looked up and stared at the half-crescent moon overhead. Why was it that he seemed to desire most the women who were unattainable to him?

He supposed some psychiatrist would believe it had something to do with his mother's absence while he was growing up—her unintentional abandonment through death. Perhaps that early-childhood tragedy had set him up to always fall for women he couldn't have...shouldn't have.

Irritated by his thoughts, he stepped off the porch and flipped off the safety on his gun. Even though he knew the potential intruder had probably been scared off by the alarm, he didn't intend to take any chances.

He walked around the perimeter of the house, noting the crushed grass beneath the nursery window. Apparently someone had stood there for several minutes—watching...waiting.

Gary? Was it possible the reporter had come back and in his never-ending quest for a story had stood at the window, peeked inside, then accidentally fallen against the window screen?

But the screen didn't look as if anyone had fallen into it. It looked as though somebody had tried to remove it. He stepped closer to the window, grateful for the spill of moonlight that filtered down from the half-moon.

Careful not to step on the area of grass where the perpetrator had stood, he peered carefully at the screen. Along the edge, where wood met metal, it looked as if some instrument had been used to pry the screen loose.

Dominic frowned, realizing this definitely wasn't Gary's style. Gary might peek into windows and listen to private conversations in an effort to gain a headline, but he wouldn't take it so far as to try to break into a house.

Dominic walked back to the front of the house just as a patrol car pulled up, its flashing lights reflecting off the nearby trees and thickets. He felt himself relax somewhat as a tall, lanky officer got out of the driver's seat.

Matt Hampstead. Melissa would be pleased it wasn't Detective Mawlins responding to their call. Matt was a good man, a good cop, and one of the few who hadn't turned their backs on Dominic when he'd gotten arrested. In fact, there had been a time when Dominic had considered Matt a good friend.

"Matt." Dominic stuck his hand out as the tall, blond man approached.

"Hey, Dominic." Matt shook Dominic's hand. "I heard you were staying out here, keeping an eye on things. Want to tell me what happened?"

"We were sitting in the kitchen, going over some paperwork, and the alarm went off, indicating a breach of security in the back bedroom. Whoever it was must have been scared off by the alarm."

Matt clicked on a flashlight. "Let's have a look."

The two men went back around the house, Matt's flashlight cutting a wide swath through the darkness. "It looks like somebody tried to get in," Matt observed as he studied the screen frame and the ground beneath the window. "Got any ideas who it might have been?"

"None. Although I caught Gary Watters skulking around the house a couple of nights ago. Still, this doesn't seem his style," Dominic replied.

"Why don't we go inside, and I'll write up a report."

Dominic nodded and together they went back to the front door, where Dominic knocked for Melissa to let them in.

In the time that he'd been outside, she'd placed Jamison in his infant carrier on the floor by the sofa and he now slept peacefully, as if the blaring siren had only been a forgotten nightmare.

Dominic introduced Matt to Melissa, then stood nearby as the two sat down on the sofa so Matt could fill out his report.

As Melissa and Matt spoke, Dominic found himself watching her, remembering the sweet fragrance of her perfume as they'd looked over the files. Over the past several days, he'd come to identify the floral scent as a distinctive signature that was hers alone.

Since the funeral that morning, Dominic had noticed subtle changes in her. She seemed stronger, more substantial than she had before. It was as if she had suddenly realized Bill was gone, she was alone, and she was gearing herself to rise to the challenge of being a single parent, a strong widow.

She was a woman in transition, making the shift from being part of a couple to being alone. The last thing she wanted or needed in her life was to be the recipient of this ex-cop's lust. And yet, in those moments before the alarm rang, he'd seen the secrets disappear from her eyes, to be replaced by stark desire.

Need. That was what he'd seen. The misplaced need of a frightened woman facing too many unknowns. At that moment she'd needed an anchor. She'd needed strong arms to hold her and tell her everything would be all right. He'd been the only strong arms in the room. It was only natural she would look to him with desire in her eyes. Not desire for Dominic the man, but a simple basic need to connect with someone…anyone.

Dominic had to be careful not to fall into the delusion that there could be anything between them. Apparently they were both at a needy place in their lives; the biggest mistake they could make would be to find temporary relief in each other's arms.

"I think I've got everything I need to file a report," Matt said as he stood from the sofa. "But you realize probably nothing will come from this. Unless whoever it was confesses, we probably won't find out who tried to break in and why."

Melissa nodded and stood as well. "Still, I appreciate you coming here so quickly."

"I'll walk you out," Dominic said to Matt. Melissa and Matt exchanged goodbyes as Dominic led him outside.

"Thank God you had a security system," Matt said as they stood on the front porch. He scanned the area. "Pretty isolated out here. The attempted break-in might be nothing more than an attempted robbery."

"Knowing a man was stabbed to death here a week ago, don't you find that a pretty big coincidence?" Dominic asked.

"Yeah, but you know that's what Mawlins will chalk it up to." Matt leaned against the passenger door of his patrol car. "I know you're here because Samantha and Tyler Sinclair think Melissa might be in danger from the same person who killed Bill. But, as far as Mawlins is concerned, there is no danger to Melissa. No threats have been made against her, nothing has happened to indicate she might be in jeopardy."

"Except we don't know who tried to break in tonight, or why," Dominic reminded Matt, although he'd had the same thoughts himself. He wanted to believe in Melissa's innocence, but he couldn't forget those bruises, and the secrets he sensed she guarded.

"Right."

"You know anything about the alibis of the men who worked for Bill?" Dominic asked.

Matt frowned thoughtfully. "I know they were questioned. Seems to me like Sam Jacobson was having dinner with his wife…and I can't remember about the other two." Matt looked off in the distance. "I could check out the reports, let you know."

Dominic looked at him in surprise. "I wouldn't want you to do anything to get your butt in a sling."

Matt grinned and looked back at Dominic. "I'm a master at covering my butt." His smile faded. "Why didn't you come back to the department, Dominic? You were a good cop—one of the best."

This time it was Dominic who looked off into the distance, afraid Matt would see the gratitude shining in his eyes. Matt's words were balm for a wounded spirit, succor for a damaged soul. "Because even though Abigail's killer was caught, even though my name was cleared, I know there are still guys on the force who believe I had to have had something to do with her death. I couldn't go back and see that in my fellow officers' eyes.''

''Most of us believed in your innocence from the very beginning,'' Matt said. ''And no matter how bad the evidence looked, we continued to believe in your innocence.''

Dominic nodded, this time meeting Matt's gaze. ''Thanks. That's nice to hear.''

Matt went around the car to the driver's door. ''I'll be in touch concerning those alibi statements.''

''I appreciate it.''

With a quick wave, Matt got into his car and a moment later drove down the driveway. Dominic watched until the car lights disappeared, as if swallowed by the shadows of night, then turned and walked back up the porch.

It surprised him, how good it felt to know that there had been fellow officers who'd believed in him despite the incriminating circumstances of Abigail's murder.

And even though he knew he was innocent of all culpability where Abigail's death was concerned, he couldn't rid himself of the weight of guilt that remained—the guilt of a man who'd loved a woman he shouldn't have, who'd known all along that loving her was futile, but who'd been unable to stop.

Even though Abigail and Melissa were two very different kinds of women, Dominic realized something about Melissa was drawing him into those same old feelings. Once again he was beginning to care about a woman who was inappropriate for him, and if he allowed his feelings to continue, it could only lead to heartache.

He started for the front door, then hesitated, reluctant to go back into the house where he would see Melissa, smell the sweet scent of her.

Instead, he sat down on the porch. He closed his eyes, remembering that moment earlier when Melissa had looked up at him, her lips parting as if eagerly anticipating the touch of his. Thank God the alarm had gone off before he had managed to do something incredibly stupid. And kissing Melissa would definitely have been stupid.

If Melissa was innocent, then somehow, some way, he had to find out who had killed Bill as soon as possible. He had to discover who was responsible and see them arrested so that Melissa would be out of danger and he could get the hell out of her house...and out of her life.

"Mike Withers was supposedly with his girlfriend on the night of Bill's murder, but when Tyler leaned on her, she wasn't sure if they were actually together around six o'clock or if it was somewhat later." Samantha paced back and forth across the kitchen floor.

It had been ten days since the attempted break-in, and two days since Dominic's friend at the police department had called him to inform him about the alibis of the men who worked for Bill. For the last two days, Samantha and Tyler had been chasing around confirming those alibis.

"What about Neal Cook?"

"Neal Cook says he was in the diner eating supper at the time of the murder," Tyler said. "I spoke with

Wanda down at the diner and she says Neal eats there most evenings, but she can't be sure he was there that particular evening.''

"And Sam Jacobson's alibi is that he was home with his wife." Dominic frowned. "Three alibis, but none of them ironclad."

Samantha began moving back and forth, her footsteps short and staccato against the tiled kitchen floor. "You didn't find anything at all in Bill's files that sent up a red flag?"

"No. Nothing," Melissa replied. "And could you please stop pacing? You're making me dizzy." Samantha halted, obviously surprised by the sharpness of Melissa's tone. "Sorry, I didn't mean to snap at you," Melissa apologized as Samantha joined them at the table.

"It's okay." Samantha smiled reassuringly and touched Melissa's hand. "You have a right to be a bit churlish."

"I just feel as if an ax is hanging over my head. If I'm going to be charged with Bill's murder, I just wish they'd go ahead and do it. At least then I'd have a better idea of what I'm up against." Melissa sighed in frustration.

"Not what *you're* up against—what *we're* up against," Samantha replied. "You aren't in this alone, Melissa."

Melissa nodded and shot a quick glance at Dominic, who stared out the window as if detached from the conversation. Detached. He'd been that way ever since the night of the attempted break-in, the night of their almost-kiss.

Even now, the memory of the look in his eyes, the

warmth of his hand on her shoulder caused a responding warmth throughout her body. She should be grateful the alarm had rung, stopping the moment before a mistake was made. What would Dominic have thought of her if she'd followed through on her desire, encouraged a kiss, a caress with her husband barely cold in his grave?

And if in a moment of weakness she allowed the secret of Bill's abuse to spill from her, he would never understand. Nobody would.

She also knew Dominic continued to have some doubts concerning her innocence in Bill's death—doubts that showed in his eyes at unguarded moments, in the occasional questions he asked. She could do nothing to convince him of her innocence; she could do nothing to take those doubts from his eyes.

"So, what do we do now?" she asked in an attempt to dispel thoughts of Dominic—thoughts of being held in warm, safe arms, making love—from her mind.

"Keep doing what we've been doing," Tyler answered. "Keep turning over rocks, digging for dirt, hoping we get a break. Somebody wanted Bill dead, and I'm certainly convinced it wasn't just a random act of violence. The killer was smart enough to leave nothing behind."

Samantha nodded. "There was a reason for this murder, and if we can just discover that, we'll be closer to discovering who the hell did it. You still haven't remembered where Bill came from? Where he lived before coming to Wilford?

"No." A cold wind of despair blew through Melissa. "I keep hoping it will come to me, or we'll run across some paperwork that will tell us."

"Keep looking," Samantha replied as she stood. "Now we've got to run. We've got to be in court by three."

Melissa stood as well to walk her sister and brother-in-law to the door. As they passed through the living room, Samantha paused to smile down at the baby who slept peacefully on a blanket on the floor. "When he wakes up, you give him a great big kiss from his Aunt Samantha."

Melissa smiled. The one spot of joy in all the madness that was her life, was little Jamison. He transformed her despair into hope, eased her pain with his unconditional love. He kept her strong, willing to fight, whatever came her way. "You've got it," she replied.

"You must have missed Samantha when she was gone from Wilford," Dominic commented moments later when he and Melissa were alone in the kitchen.

Melissa leaned against the refrigerator, thinking back to that time almost seven years before when Samantha had left Wilford. "I did miss her, and I hated her for leaving Wilford, leaving me behind."

She looked at Dominic who still sat at the table. "You and your father are close, aren't you?" He nodded. "You're lucky. My father wasn't close to either Samantha or me. At the best of times, he was merely distant, uninvolved. At the worst of times he could be cold and cruel."

She wrapped her arms around herself, remembering those days after Samantha had left—days when she'd felt so alone in the big house that had never been a real home. "I hated Samantha for being strong enough to escape, hated her for being able to leave and never look back." She shrugged, not wanting to dwell on her childhood, on things that couldn't be changed. "Then I met Bill and we got married, and I didn't have time to be angry at Samantha anymore. I was too busy changing from the role of perfect daughter into that of perfect wife." To her horror, tears blurred her vision.

"I'm sorry. I didn't mean to upset you." Dominic's voice—so deep, so gentle—caused her tears to flow faster. He took a step toward her, obviously wanting to comfort her but unsure how.

Melissa knew exactly how she wanted him to comfort her. Without hesitation, she moved to where he stood. His arms opened, as if with an unconscious will, and she leaned into him, wanting to be held, needing to be held.

For a moment his arms remained opened, as if he was afraid to embrace. It wasn't until she wound her arms around his back that he enfolded her. She buried her face in the dark recess of his neck where a strong, solid pulse beat. She smelled the heady masculine scent of him as her tears continued to fall.

She wasn't even sure why she was crying; she knew only that emotion pressed thick and heavy in her chest.

"Shh, it's all right," he whispered softly as he pulled her closer against him.

The solid wall of his chest comforted her. It had been so very long since she'd been held in masculine arms, unafraid that the embrace would be followed by a sly pinch or a sudden slap.

Her tears ebbed and she curled her fingers into the hair at the nape of his neck, kept her face burrowed against the warm skin of his throat. Where before, sadness mingling with a touch of bitterness had swelled inside her, forcing the tears, now a different emotion flooded through her.

Desire. It filled her, sweeping away all other thoughts, distilling every other sentiment, leaving no room for anything else in her head...in her heart. As she leaned into Dominic, pressing her body intimately against his, she realized he felt it, too. She realized it in his swift intake of breath, in the swell of his body against hers.

She tilted her head to look up at him. Only his eyes expressed his desire. Dark and heated, they gazed at her, and in them she saw not only desire but a flare of surprise, as well.

She had no idea whose head moved first, whose action initiated the kiss. She only knew that their lips touched—softly at first, then hungrily. She closed her eyes and gave in to the moment.

He plied her lips with heat, and she responded by opening her mouth to him, wanting to deepen the kiss. She could feel the beating of his heart against hers, mirroring the rapid, out-of-control rhythm of her own.

Someplace in the back of her mind, she knew this was wrong—dangerous not only to her peace of mind but to the facade she'd carefully presented to the world concerning her marriage to Bill.

For the first time in her life she didn't care what was proper, what was right. At this moment, being in Dominic's arms, tasting the heat of his kiss felt good, felt right.

She felt his withdrawal first when he dropped his arms from around her, then as he framed her face with his hands. Slowly, as if reluctantly, his kiss ended, and she opened her eyes to see him looking at her. His eyes sparked like the embers of a banked fire, but they also held a wealth of regret. "Melissa..." He dropped his hands from her face and took a step backward. "I...I don't know what to say...."

The doorbell rang, preempting any reply Melissa might have made.

Dominic sighed in obvious relief and hurried to answer. As he left the room, Melissa sank into a chair at the table, wondering how long it would take for the heat to leave her body, the imprint of his lips to stop burning on her own.

She shouldn't have kissed him. She'd known instinctively that kissing him would be pleasant. Now she realized it wasn't enough. She wanted more from Dominic Marcola, and in that wanting was a certain shame—a little over two weeks a widow and already desiring another man.

She sat up straighter, shoving the shame aside. Wasn't she allowed to seek happiness? Wasn't she allowed to feel desire without the dreadful anticipation of humiliation or abuse? Bill hadn't made love to her since the night they'd conceived Jamison, and even then she didn't classify it as "making love." For her, it had simply been a wifely duty, void of tenderness, empty of love.

She stood as Dominic reentered the kitchen, this time with Neal Cook trailing behind. "I'm sorry to bother you, Mrs. Newman," Neal said in greeting.

"No problem. What can I do for you, Neal?" she

asked. She studiously kept her gaze away from Dominic, afraid her husband's co-worker would see some spark, some remnant of the desire that had flared so quickly between her and Dominic.

"Sam sent me over. We need some extra ductwork for a job we're doing on a furnace, and Sam said Bill kept some spare parts here in your basement."

Melissa nodded and motioned for him to follow her down the stairs that led to the unfinished basement of the house. "I'm not sure what all is down here," she explained. "Bill was always bringing home furnace and air-conditioning parts to store here because there was so little storage space at the office."

When she reached the concrete basement floor, she pointed to where ductwork, vent covers, an assortment of wiring and various other parts were spread across the floor in neat piles.

As Neal poked around, seeking the proper size and shape of vent he needed, Melissa looked around the basement with a touch of sadness. When they'd first moved into the house, she'd envisioned this area as a playroom for the children she would have. Bill had agreed, eagerly telling her his plans for refinishing the room, feeding her fantasies with his lies.

"Ah, here it is," Neal said as he held up an elbow-shaped piece of vent. "Thanks," he said to Melissa.

"I'll walk you out, Neal," Dominic said and together the two men disappeared up the stairs.

Melissa remained behind, her thoughts still on the dreams she'd once had; dreams she'd lost but which now flirted at the edge of her consciousness.

Bill was gone. He was never coming back. Her wish to be free of him had come true, albeit through tragedy. She would get through whatever charges might be leveled against her and live to fulfill those distant dreams.

A surge of optimism filled her. It was as if she'd been Sleeping Beauty, trapped in a curse of her own making, and Dominic's kiss had awakened her to all the possibilities.

She could still turn this basement into a playroom. She would need to find another place to store all the parts, but that could be accomplished by renting storage space or erecting a small shed in the backyard.

As she contemplated this idea, she walked amid the bits and pieces of Bill's business. In the meantime, the items could be stacked more compactly to take up less space.

She began to move pieces of vent pipe into one corner of the basement. She paused as she heard Dominic's footsteps coming back down the stairs. He appeared at the bottom and for a moment they simply looked at each other. She knew by the expression on his face he was thinking of the kiss they'd shared before Neal had interrupted them. She could see that Dominic was not only thinking about it, but was regretting it.

"Melissa," he began.

She picked up a piece of pipe, not looking at him. "I was just thinking that this would make a perfect playroom for Jamison when he gets a little older." She carried the pipe to the corner with the others, then returned to pick up several more pieces.

"A little Sheetrock, a drop ceiling, some carpeting and it would be a cozy space for children to play." She knew she was babbling, but she didn't want to give him an opportunity to apologize for the kiss, to somehow try to take it back. "I think I'll call somebody in the next week or two to give me an estimate on what it would cost. I figure if I stack all this stuff in the corner, whoever comes out will be able to get a better idea of what I want."

There was a long moment of silence. "I can help you stack," he finally said.

She breathed a sigh of relief, grateful he didn't intend to follow up on the subject of their kiss. "That would be great."

They worked silently, shifting items to the corner. Melissa desperately tried to keep her thoughts schooled away from the heat of his lips, the warm comfort of his arms surrounding her. She knew she would be a fool to follow through on any desire she might feel for Dominic.

It was only natural that she would feel a certain kinship with him. He'd delivered her child, had stood beside her as she'd buried the man she'd been married to. Surely it was only the circumstances of their forced cohabitation, and her own vulnerability, which made him so appealing.

Besides, she would be a fool to believe that he could feel anything for her except the natural sympathy of a man for a recent widow. And if she confessed what her relationship with Bill had really been like, his sympathy would turn to pity. And in his pity, she would find shame. The shame that had made her keep her secret for so long, the shame of what she'd been willing to sacrifice in the name of love.

"Melissa, there's something here."

Dominic's voice pulled her from her thoughts. She

looked over to where he pointed, to a manila envelope shoved between two pieces of pipe. "What is it?" she asked as she set down the last of the items they'd moved.

He picked it up and opened it. He withdrew what appeared to be a photograph. Studying it for a moment, his forehead wrinkled into a frown. "It's a wedding picture," he said. He looked at her, his eyes filled with questions—and concern.

"What's one of our wedding pictures doing down here?" she asked rhetorically as she moved toward him. His eyes darkened and a shiver of apprehension climbed up her spine. She reached out and took the picture. She gazed down at it in confusion, bewilderment.

Dominic was right. It was definitely a wedding photograph. The bride and groom stood before a stained-glass window, their hands clasped to show the sparkling wedding rings each wore. Clad in a white tuxedo, Bill smiled as he looked into the eyes of his bride—a woman Melissa had never seen before.

Chapter 8

"**B**ill never mentioned anything about being married before?" Dominic asked a few minutes later as they sat at the kitchen table. Melissa sat across from him, her face still reflecting utter bewilderment as she stared at the wedding picture.

"No, he… Maybe it's a hoax." She looked at Dominic, her eyes wide and dark blue with confusion. "You know, one of those pictures where you dress up and pretend?" For a moment hope lightened the color of her eyes and her features relaxed slightly. "Bill and I once had a picture taken of us as pioneers. It was at a carnival that came to town. I wore a saloon dress, and the photographer put Bill in buckskins."

She bit her bottom lip and stared at the photograph once more. "But this isn't like that, is it? It's not a Polaroid and it was obviously taken by a professional."

Gently Dominic took the picture from her. The bride looked young, with soft blond hair cascading to her shoulders. Her brown eyes were set a little too close together, and a faint scar marred one cheek. Still, she was a pretty young woman whose eyes sparkled with love, with hope for the future.

He flipped the photo over and spied small print at the bottom. "Do you have a magnifying glass?" he asked.

Melissa nodded, got up and rummaged in a kitchen drawer. A moment later she returned and handed him a small magnifying glass. He studied the small print. "Dano's Photography Studio. There's a date, too." He put the glass down and looked at Melissa. "The picture was taken eight years ago."

"Two years before Bill came to Wilford," Melissa replied. She frowned thoughtfully. "There's no address?"

"None. Just the name of the studio and the date." Dominic set the picture down and gazed at Melissa. He tried not to focus on her mouth, which had opened so eagerly beneath his.

He didn't want to think about the kiss they'd shared—a kiss that had stirred depths in him he'd forgotten he possessed. It had been a mistake, one he didn't intend to repeat.

If he really cared about Melissa, he would help her escape the pending charges of murder. If what she said was true, she'd lost her husband to a violent crime.

"We have to assume that eight years ago Bill married this woman," he said. Her eyes darkened once again, but Dominic steeled himself against the visible

sign of her pain. They couldn't afford to get caught
up in emotions. "There's only one reason I can think
of that Bill wouldn't tell you he'd been married before."

"Because he had something to hide," Melissa answered softly. She scooted her chair back and stood,
as if finding immobility abhorrent. "Why didn't he
tell me he'd been married before? What could he possibly have been hiding?"

She paced back and forth, her brow wrinkled in
thought. "Maybe it was just an unhappy marriage,
something he didn't want to dredge up. Bill wasn't a
man who talked about himself much." Her features
softened. "Initially that's what charmed me about
him, the fact that he seemed so interested in me—my
thoughts, my dreams, my world." Instantly, all soft-
ness faded, swept away by a hard glint in her eyes.
"I was too young and naive to realize his feigned
interest in me might have been manipulation to keep
the focus off him."

It was the first time Dominic had seen a crack in
the facade, a hint that all had not been well in the
Newman marriage. "Don't be so hard on yourself.
Sometimes when you're in love, you only see what
you want to believe."

She looked at him in surprise. "You sound like you
speak from experience." She sank back down at the
table. "Tell me about Abigail."

Dominic didn't want to dredge up all the old baggage, all the emotional trauma he'd tried to get beyond. And yet he knew Melissa wanted something,
anything to momentarily ease her own fears, delay the
dissection of her own life with a man who'd obvi-

ously had secrets—secrets that might have led to his death and her own possible peril.

He leaned back in his chair, aware of the ticking of the kitchen clock, the expectant gaze on Melissa's face, the soft cooing of Jamison in his infant carrier on the floor nearby. Everything seemed to fade as he thought back to Abigail—her life, and her death.

"Although Abigail and I both grew up here in Wilford, she was four years younger than me, so we were never in school together. We didn't really officially meet until one night about three years ago when her apartment was broken into and I was the officer who responded."

His chest tightened with emotion as he dived into the past. "Abigail was smart, funny, and ambitious. She'd been poor all her life and was determined to change that." He smiled as a rush of memories swept over him. "She was always reading the society pages, magazines that focused on the wealthy. She studied the way the women dressed, the way they carried themselves, then emulated them."

"You two started dating," Melissa said, more a comment than a question.

Dominic nodded. "Yeah." He raked a hand through his hair and leaned forward. "Abigail told me I was her transitional guy, that she was only dating me until she found Mr. Wealthy. But I didn't believe that. I thought if I was patient, her obsession with money would eventually wane."

"You must have loved her very much." Melissa's words were filled with a bittersweet wistfulness.

Dominic looked at her for a long moment. "I did, and I thought at the time that love would be enough for her. But I was wrong. It wasn't enough. She married old man Monroe, along with all his banking money.''

As always, his stomach rolled as he thought of the last time he'd seen Abigail...lying dead beside him. ''She called me the evening of her murder, begged me to meet her at her apartment. Against my better judgment, I went. She told me she was going to leave Monroe. She encouraged me to celebrate with her, pouring glasses of champagne from a bottle we didn't know had been drugged.''

He got up from the table, irritated that Melissa had dragged him back to the night that had changed everything in his life. ''None of this matters anymore. The past is gone.''

''But the past is never really gone, is it?'' Melissa said. She picked up the picture of Bill and the bride. ''I mean, this is proof that history can come back to haunt you.''

Dominic nodded, although he had no intention of ever allowing his past to haunt him. He just wanted to forget it. Learn from his mistakes and go on.

He sat back down at the table, shoving any lingering thoughts of Abigail and the night of her murder aside. ''That picture probably has nothing to do with Bill's death, but it does speak of secrets in his past—secrets we need to explore. Maybe the answer to whoever killed him lies in that past.''

''But we know by the date on the back that we're talking eight years ago. I don't even remember where Bill lived before Wilford. How on earth are we going to explore any of it?''

Dominic frowned, a headache scouting for a place

to pound at the back of his head. "We've got the name of the photographer. We'll start by trying to find him. I've got a few friends left in the police department who can make some inquiries, see if we can't hunt down some information on Bill. You said you thought he was from a small town in western Kansas?" Melissa nodded. "Then we'll start in the state of Kansas and see what we can find on Bill Newman."

"I just have this terrible feeling that time is running out, and we're no closer to finding out who killed Bill than we were the day it happened," she said.

Innocent victim or cool, calculating killer? Again Dominic was filled with confusion. No matter what the truth, he found himself fighting the impulse to take Melissa into his arms and kiss away the worry lines that furrowed her forehead.

This kind of caring was new to him. It went deeper than anything he'd ever felt for anyone else before. And it scared the hell out of him.

"We'll figure it out, Melissa." He stood, realizing the headache had gained a foothold and now thudded with dull intensity at the base of his skull. "In the meantime, I'm going to go back downstairs and see if I can find anything else that we might have missed."

"And I'll search up here." She straightened her back, her eyes shining with steely resolve. "I—I haven't been in the bedroom since…that evening, but I'll check all the drawers, the closet, and see if I can't find something, anything that the police might have missed."

Dominic knew that entering that bedroom would

be traumatic for her, guilty or innocent. He admired the determination that tightened her features. She might look vulnerable and fragile on the outside, but she obviously had a well of inner strength to draw from when needed. "You want me to go in there with you?" he asked.

She shook her head. "We can cover more territory if we search different areas. I should have scoured this entire house the moment I had the opportunity to see if there was anything here that might point to Bill's killer."

Again Dominic fought the irrational impulse to gather her close to him, enfold her against his chest. Instead, he turned and headed for the stairs leading down.

Once in the basement again, he leaned his forehead against the concrete wall, hoping its coolness would ease the throb of his headache. He knew his head hurt because a battle waged inside his brain—good sense fighting bad, logic contesting illogic. And he knew it was all a result of kissing Melissa and the simple knowledge that he wanted to kiss her again and again.

It shouldn't have happened, and he wished with all his heart he could take it back, forget the sweet heat of her mouth, the way her body had leaned into his so intimately.

He had to forget his desire for her. The worst thing he could do would be to allow the close proximity of their living arrangements, the trauma that she was experiencing to mask itself as some sort of developing love between them.

At best, Dominic would be a rebound man in her life, a temporary solution to loneliness. He couldn't go through that again. He refused to allow his heart to bear that kind of pain.

Besides, although he saw the way Melissa occasionally looked at him—the shy, sweet glances of a woman attracted to a man—he couldn't forget the secrets that shadowed her eyes; secrets she wasn't sharing.

He had been a cop, and in his soul ran the blood of a man who believed in justice done, justice served. So where was justice in this case? Was Melissa guilty of Bill's death? Should he go to Detective Mawlins with his suspicions that she was abused by her husband?

His heart rebelled. He had doubts as to her innocence, but he had doubts as to her guilt, too. If Bill had been responsible for those marks on her legs, then the man had been an animal. He frowned. There were still so many unanswered questions. He would wait, see what happened. Follow his heart instead of his head.

He pushed away from the wall, reminding himself that his job was to protect Melissa from any potential attacker and help her find evidence of who the real killer might be. Nothing more. If he found proof that she'd killed Bill, *then* he would decide what to do. But until then, he would do what he was hired to do.

He couldn't afford to care for her and little Jamison on any deeper level. His heart had suffered enough bruises for one lifetime.

Melissa set Jamison's carrier on the floor in the hallway just outside the master bedroom. Even though she knew it was ridiculous, she didn't want the baby in the room where his father had been killed.

She stared at the closed bedroom door for a long moment, dread walking up her spine with heavy fingers.

The first night she and Bill had stayed in the house had been some months ago, on the night before the movers arrived with their furniture. They'd slept in sleeping bags on the floor of the bedroom, and her mind had been filled with all of Bill's false promises.

Bill had been in an unusually good mood, a mood she now identified as one of triumph. He'd managed to talk her into a reconciliation. She was pregnant with his child and afraid to be alone. He'd won. And in his triumph he'd been magnanimous. It had been one of the few happy moments she'd known in this house.

Why had she stayed? Like so many women in these circumstances, she didn't have an easy answer. She'd believed she loved Bill. She'd wanted to prove to her father that she could make her marriage work; she'd believed if she loved Bill enough, he would change. Her reasons for staying were all tied up in her own emotional needs, in fulfilling distant dreams, in a fantasy she tried desperately to create.

Shoving these thoughts aside, she gripped the doorknob and opened the door. She breathed a sigh of relief as she realized Samantha had done a thorough job of cleaning up after the police.

The room looked as it always had except a bedspread she'd never seen before covered the bed. Of course, the old one would have been taken in for evidence. For a few moments she simply wandered around the room, touching items here and there, allowing her initial dread to slowly dissipate.

Regret ached in her heart as she picked up Bill's comb from the top of the dresser. If she hadn't reconciled with him, would he still be alive? Even though there had been times in the past several months when she'd truly hated him, hated the things he said to her, the meanness that sparked inside him, she'd never really wanted him dead—not this way.

But God help her, she was glad he was gone—glad she would no longer wake up with the metallic taste of fear in her mouth and fall asleep drowning in salty tears.

Shoving aside these thoughts, she started her search first in the closet. After she went through each pair of pants, every suit jacket, she methodically folded them and made a pile on the bed. Bill's clothes would not go back in the closet. She would box them up and give them to charity.

It didn't take her long to go through the clothing. Her hunt yielded several matchbooks, a few scraps of paper with customers' names and phone numbers written on them, some loose change and several pens. Nothing suspicious, nothing out of the ordinary.

Next, she tackled the boxes that lined the shelf in the top of the closet. One box held the paperwork for the house, another contained photos that had been taken during their marriage. She pawed through the pictures and picked out one that had been taken on her wedding day.

Sinking down on the bed, she studied the photo, consciously comparing it to the one Dominic had found downstairs. There were lots of similarities. Bill wore a white tuxedo in this photo, and he gazed at Melissa with the same adoring look he'd given the other woman.

Although Melissa and Bill had had no pictures taken in front of a stained-glass window, the one Melissa held depicted them before the church altar, with glowing candles on either side.

Melissa stared at the image of herself, so young, so filled with hope, with dreams of a future full of love. And the first year of their marriage had pretty much lived up to her expectations. It was in the second year that tiny cracks began to mar the happiness; insidious incidents, seemingly small and isolated, but ones that set up a pattern that eventually became Melissa's imprisonment.

"Find anything?" Dominic asked from the doorway.

She looked up at him, her vision surprisingly blurred by tears. Self-consciously she swiped at her eyes, then shook her head.

Dominic came over to her and gently took the wedding photo from her fingers. He gazed at it momentarily, then dropped it into the box. "It does get better. Grief never really goes away, but it does become more manageable."

Melissa bit her bottom lip, afraid she might laugh out loud at his words. She knew he thought her tears were for Bill. He had no idea that what she really grieved for was her own stupidity, the years lost to fear.

How she wished she could tell him what was really in her heart, unburden herself of the secret of spousal abuse. But she couldn't.

"I haven't found anything that might help," she said as she stood from the bed. "What about you? Did you find anything else downstairs?"

"No. Nothing."

She heard the tinge of discouragement in his tone. "Why don't we stop and have some dinner, then we can go through the drawers in here and search the rest of the house later?"

"Sounds good to me," he agreed.

Together they left the room, Melissa stopping only long enough to pick up Jamison. In the kitchen, she placed the baby in his carrier on the table, then turned on the lights to ward off the shadows of dusk that crept into the room.

Dominic went to the refrigerator, at ease with the routine they'd fallen into when it came to preparing meals. "How about I fix us a couple of hamburgers?" he asked.

"That sounds fine," she agreed. "And I'll make some macaroni salad to go with them."

For a few minutes they worked silently but it was a comfortable silence, broken only by the sounds of pots and pans, sizzling hamburger and Jamison's coos—domestic sounds that, oddly, filled Melissa with a sense of contentment, of rightness.

While the macaroni boiled, she sat down at the table and fed Jamison a bottle, her gaze lingering on Dominic, who busied himself cutting up tomatoes to garnish the burgers.

"You seem very much at ease in a kitchen," Melissa observed.

He flashed her a quick grin, one that created a coil of heat in the pit of her stomach. "Self-defense.

Growing up, my dad wasn't exactly a terrific cook. By the time I was twelve, I had taken charge of the kitchen.''

She tried to imagine him as a boy, but found it nearly impossible to consider him as anything but the wide-shouldered, handsome man he was at this moment. ''Tell me about your childhood. What did you like to do, what kind of a little boy were you?''

Dominic flipped the hamburgers. ''If you asked my father, he'd probably tell you I was too somber as a kid.'' He leaned against the stove, his gaze reflective. ''When my mom died and my dad's leg was hurt, I knew the life we'd had was over. For a long time Dad couldn't work, so we ended up losing our house and practically everything else. Then Dad was offered the job as caretaker out at the cemetery and we moved into the little house there.'' He flashed her a wry grin. ''Growing up in a cemetery tends to make one rather somber.''

''I'll bet you were teased a lot.''

''Mercilessly.'' He carried the macaroni from the stove to the colander in the sink. He rinsed it with cold water, then turned back to her. ''There were a couple of older guys who were real vicious with their taunts and teasing. That's when I started to fantasize about becoming a policeman and one day arresting their butts.''

''Did you get a chance to do that? Arrest them?''

''One of them. He was a two-bit punk who bungled a gas-station robbery here in town. The other guy moved away. Last I heard, he was mayor of a small town in Colorado.''

''Funny how things turn out, isn't it?'' She burped

Jamison, then placed him back in his carrier. "I mean, strange that the winds of fate blew us together."

"And when this case is over, those same winds will blow us apart." Although he said the words lightly, she sensed them to be a subtle warning. A warning to her not to depend on him, not to grow to care for him; a warning prompted by the impulsive kiss they'd shared.

"What are plans your when this is all over?" she asked as she busied herself preparing the macaroni salad.

"I'm not sure. There are days the idea of leaving Wilford and all my bad memories behind sounds real appealing."

She looked at him in surprise. "Where would you go?"

"I don't know. Right now the idea of leaving is just a vague one." He removed the hamburgers from the skillet. "I pretty much just take things day to day right now." He turned and looked at her and again she sensed his words were specifically directed at her. "I just know I've got no real place here where I feel like I belong. My future isn't here."

The doorbell pealed, interrupting the conversation. As Dominic went to answer, Melissa picked up Jamison and trailed after him. He punched off the security, then opened the front door. Melissa's heart dropped as she saw Detective Mawlins, flanked by two uniformed police officers.

"Melissa Newman," he spoke around Dominic, directly to her. "You are under arrest for the murder of Bill Newman. Would you step out here, please?"

Melissa grabbed Dominic's arm, suddenly realizing that the feeling she'd had earlier of time running out had been true. Time had indeed run out.

Chapter 9

Melissa stared at Detective Mawlins in horror, hoping she'd misunderstood him. She tightened her grip on Dominic's arm, and held Jamison against her chest, wanting to hold him so tightly that nobody could take her away.

"You have a warrant?" Dominic demanded, his voice filled with suppressed anger.

Mawlins withdrew a piece of paper from his pocket and handed it to Dominic. "You'll see it's all nice and proper."

Dominic scanned the warrant, then looked at Melissa. "You'll have to go with them, Melissa," he said gently. He looked at Mawlins, his eyes shooting daggers. "This could have been done another way. You could have contacted Richard Wallace and made arrangements for him to bring her in."

Mawlins mouth sneered. "I don't need to make any

arrangements with a big-city lawyer. This is my town, and I do things my way.'' He motioned Melissa out of the house with a gesture of impatience.

She released her hold on Dominic and handed him the baby, her heart aching with despair. She stepped out onto the porch, chilled despite the warmth of the evening air. She stood still, silent, as Mawlins read her her rights. It wasn't until one of the uniformed officers pulled her hands behind her back and she felt the cold bite of handcuffs that the reality of what was happening struck her.

''Wait...'' She struggled to get free of the hand restraints. ''What about my baby? What about Jamison?'' Tears splashed her cheeks—hot, frightened tears.

''Melissa, don't fight the cuffs, you'll only wind up hurting yourself.'' Dominic stepped close to her and touched her chin. ''And don't worry about Jamison.'' He looked down at the baby in his arms. ''I'll take care of him until we can get you back home.''

''You'll call Richard? Tell him what's happened?'' Melissa fought to contain her tears. ''And Samantha. Call Samantha,'' she cried as the officers pulled her off the porch and toward the waiting patrol car.

''I will,'' Dominic replied.

They placed her in the back seat with one of the officers. Mawlins got into the passenger side while the other cop got behind the wheel.

As they pulled out of the driveway, Melissa twisted in her seat and looked back. Dominic stood on the porch, Jamison in his arms, both of them brushed by the golden twilight. How long would it be before she saw them again? How long would it be before she held her son in her arms?

She turned back around, unable to bear looking at them until they were no longer visible. She closed her eyes, seeking the inner strength that had gotten her through the last painful days, and through the years of her marriage. The only thing she found inside was fear. A ripping, clawing terror.

What would happen now? Would Richard be able to get her out on bail, or would she spend the next months languishing in a jail cell awaiting trial?

She stared at the back of Mawlins's head, wondering what had made him finally decide for certain that she was a murderer. "Why now? What's different today from yesterday or last week? Why did you decide to arrest me now?"

Mawlins turned and eyed her, his gaze unfriendly and damning. "Motive," he answered succinctly. "We finally figured out what yours was."

Melissa felt the blood drain from her face, and she drew a deep breath to alleviate a burst of light-headedness. How had they found out about the abuse? Bill had always been careful not to harm her anyplace visible, and he had never done the kind of damage that required hospitalization or emergency-room treatment. How on earth had they found out?

Mawlins laughed, a distinctly unpleasant sound. "Yeah, I'll bet you figured we'd never find out about your husband's little fling with Grace Harrison."

"What?" Melissa stared at the detective in bewilderment. "What are you talking about?"

Mawlins snorted. "Ah, so we're playing the innocent act. Okay, I'll play it your way. We figure you found out about your hubby's afternoon trysts with Grace. There you were, pregnant with his child, and the man is playing footsie with another woman.''

Melissa stared at him in horror, unable to make sense of his words. Grace Harrison and Bill? Grace was the twenty-year-old granddaughter of Mabel Harrison. Mabel was the wealthy, outspoken president of the Wilford Ladies' Club. Mabel's daughter—Grace's mother, Claudia—was equally overbearing. Melissa's impression of Grace had always been of a young woman painfully shy, lost in the shadows of her strong mother and grandmother.

"The way we speculate it happened," Mawlins continued, "is that you finally confronted Bill about his little affair. Maybe you demanded he give her up, and maybe he told you he had no intention of giving her up. In any case, you argued. Maybe he turned over to take a nap, telling you he wasn't going to talk about it anymore. Now that filled you with rage—the fact that he could just calmly take a nap while you were so hurt, so angry."

Melissa listened to his scenario, appalled that he could make a set of falsehoods sound so reasonable.

"So you went into the kitchen, got a big old butcher knife and stabbed him."

"That's not what happened," Melissa said faintly. "I didn't kill Bill!"

Mawlins snorted again. "You can tell it to the judge," he said as he turned back around to face forward in his seat.

The next forty-five minutes passed in a haze of unreality for Melissa. Once they arrived at the Wilford County Jail, she was fingerprinted and photographed. Her personal items were taken from her, then she was led to a jail cell.

"You're in luck," the jailer said as he locked her inside the small six-by-eight cell. "Looks like you won't have to share these deluxe accommodations with anyone else."

When he left, the utter silence rang in Melissa's ears. She looked around, wondering how anyone managed to live years of their lives in such surroundings. How long would she be here? Surely Richard could get her out on bail. Surely she wouldn't have to spend an entire night here.

She walked over to the iron bunkbeds and sat down on the lower bunk. Her head ached. She rubbed her brow with two fingers, her head spinning with the new information she'd gained.

Bill and Grace? A week ago Melissa would never have believed it possible. Bill didn't have affairs. But a week ago she hadn't found a wedding picture with Bill as the groom and another woman as the bride.

She'd thought she'd known her husband. Or at least, she'd never dreamed he was capable of such deceit. Surely the police were wrong about Grace. Bill had been many things, but not an adulterer.

Still, as she thought of that damning photo Dominic had found, all confidence in her husband's fidelity seeped away.

Had Bill somehow known that Melissa intended to leave him when the baby was born? Had he started seeing Grace to hedge his bets? Bill was a man who'd never liked to be alone.

If it was true that he had been seeing Grace, perhaps he intended to fill the void Melissa would leave behind by installing Grace as the next Mrs. Newman. If that was the case, the killer had not only saved Melissa from further abuse, he'd probably saved Grace, as well.

She stretched out on the bunk, her thoughts drifting to Dominic and Jamison and that moment when she'd seen them standing on the porch as she'd been taken away.

Her heart constricted painfully as she thought of her son. Her arms ached with emptiness. When would she see him again...hold him again? And how would she ever tell her son about his father, a man she now realized she knew nothing about?

She could only hope that Richard Wallace would be able to defend her against these charges, that eventually she would be able to get out of here, live a normal life with her son, maybe even find a healthy, happy relationship with a man—a man like Dominic.

For those moments in the kitchen earlier while they'd prepared the evening meal, she'd been able to imagine what her life would be like with him. She'd been able to imagine that after they'd eaten dinner and cleared away the dishes, he would take her in his arms, carry her into the bedroom and they would make beautiful, tender love to each other.

For the first time since her arrest, tears filled her eyes. Tears for Bill, who even though he'd been a cold, mean man, hadn't deserved to die. Tears for her son, who would never know his biological father and might know his mother only through visits to prison. She cried for herself, for all the lost years she'd given to Bill, all the dreams that had been destroyed. Finally, she cried because she might never get an op-

portunity to know a good, wonderful kind of love—
the kind she thought Dominic had to offer to the right
woman. She sobbed because she knew she would
never be that woman.

"Mawlins did this on purpose," Dominic said to
Samantha and Tyler, who had arrived only minutes
after Melissa had been taken away. "By arresting her
this late in the day he knew she would have to spend
at least one night in jail, that no arraignment can take
place until tomorrow."

Dominic's heart squeezed tight as he thought of
Melissa's face—so stark, so frightened, looking out
the back window of the patrol car.

"You called Richard?" Samantha asked.

Dominic nodded. "Before I called you. He's on his
way, said he'd meet you down at the jail, and you
could put your heads together about bail."

"The D.A. will probably request no bail or an ex-
orbitant amount," Tyler said. "Melissa's trust fund is
tied up until she's twenty-six. That's still six months
away." He looked at his wife. "We can always use
the law firm to obtain a bond."

Samantha moved to Tyler and they embraced. Seeing their love, their utter commitment to each other,
intensified a lonely ache inside Dominic, an ache he
hadn't been aware of until this moment. And it scared
him when he realized that somehow the ache was tied
to Melissa's absence.

How had it happened that in the space of a little
over three weeks he had become so accustomed to
having her around? That he anticipated the scent of
her that wafted through the house? That he looked

forward to the gift of her smile on the rare occasions when she bestowed him with one?

"Mawlins is going to be sorry. He's made a big mistake in thinking Melissa is the murderer," Samantha said as she moved away from Tyler.

"What does he have against the Dark family?" Dominic asked curiously. He looked at Tyler. "You mentioned that Harvey Mawlins hated Jamison Dark, that they'd battled in the courtroom on various occasions, but surely this vendetta has to do with something other than a couple of tough cross-examinations."

Tyler smiled wryly. "Actually, it was a little more than tough cross-examinations. About twelve years ago Harvey decided he was tired of law enforcement and wanted to dabble in local politics. He threw his hat into the ring in the mayoral race and most people assumed he'd win. About two weeks before the election, Harvey was called to the witness stand in a case. Jamison was the defending attorney, and Jamison tore him apart."

Tyler paused for a moment to draw Samantha close against him. "Jamison made Mawlins look stupid, ineffectual and lazy. He raised questions about the man's honesty and integrity. By the time Jamison was finished with him, Mawlins withdrew his name from the ballot and crawled into a hole to lick his wounds."

"So Mawlins definitely has a reason to want to see Melissa behind bars." Dominic felt his heart ache for the woman caught in an old war of resentment and grudges that had nothing to do with her.

"Dominic." Samantha stepped toward him and

placed her hand on his arm. "I know baby-sitting wasn't exactly what you had in mind when you came to work for us, but—"

"Don't worry about little Jamison. I'll stay right here with him." Dominic patted her hand in reassurance. "The important thing is for you and Tyler to meet up with Richard and figure out a way to get Melissa back home as soon as possible."

Samantha nodded, squeezed his hand, then walked with Tyler to the front door. "We'll be in touch," she said, then she and Tyler left.

The silence of the house immediately pressed in on Dominic. He hated not being able to do something to help, being left behind to baby-sit. And yet, he knew his job was as important as any other to Melissa. The safety and welfare of her son would be utmost in her mind.

Dominic left the living room and went to the nursery. Inside the small room, he turned on the lamp on the dresser and peered into the crib. Jamison Dark Newman slept the peaceful slumber of the innocent, unaware that his father had been murdered, or that his mother was in jail.

As Dominic stared down at the tiny boy, Jamison's hands opened and closed, and a smile lifted the corners of his mouth, as if happy dreams were just within his reach. If only Dominic could see to it that Jamison always got his dreams.

Strange, how a baby he'd known nothing about four weeks before had managed to crawl so deep into his heart. Was it because his hands had been the first to hold Jamison? His face the first the infant had gazed at? Was that what made Dominic feel so...so paternal?

He covered the baby with a lightweight blanket, then left the nursery. In the living room, he picked up the phone and punched in the numbers for the police station. When his call was answered, he asked for Officer Matt Hampstead. Matt was not only a good cop, he was something of a computer nut.

Several moments later, Matt answered. "Matt, Dominic Marcola."

"Dominic, you just caught me. I was about to head home," Matt said.

"Would it be too much trouble for you to stop at Melissa Newman's place on your way home?"

"Another break-in?"

"No, nothing like that," Dominic said hurriedly.

"Sure, I'll stop by." Matt's voice was filled with curiosity. "I'll be there in about fifteen, twenty minutes."

After hanging up, Dominic went into the kitchen and made a pot of coffee, then sat at the table to await Matt's arrival. He picked up the wedding photo that had been left on the table earlier.

Who was the woman in the wedding dress? And why hadn't Bill told his wife he'd been married before? Certainly they hadn't been able to find any answers for the motive to his murder in his time in Wilford. Was it possible his past had come to haunt him, bearing a deadly weapon?

Was it possible Melissa was telling the truth? If she was completely innocent of the murder, then was it possible someone from his past had returned with a score to settle?

He frowned. Bill had lived in Wilford for over six years. It seemed impossible to imagine that something that had happened before that time could prompt his murder so recently.

He traced a finger over the face of the woman in the photograph. Had Melissa's face possessed that glow on her wedding day? He closed his eyes, his mind filling with a vision of her clad in a long, sweeping dress. The white silk would emphasize the blue of her eyes and the peach hue of her skin.

He felt a stir deep within him as he remembered the kiss they'd shared. He'd not been surprised that her lips were velvet soft and sweet as honey. What had surprised him was the hunger—no, the apparent starvation he'd sensed as she'd clung to him.

Melissa struck Dominic as a woman who deserved to be kissed deeply and often. He also had a feeling her husband hadn't kissed her deeply or often enough.

He tossed the wedding picture aside, irritated by the fanciful flight of his thoughts. He had to keep his distance from Melissa, not only for her sake, but for his, as well. He couldn't handle another go-around with a woman who needed him only to get through a rough patch in her life.

The doorbell rang, tugging him from his thoughts, and with a sigh of relief, he went to admit Matt. Dominic waited until they were both settled at the table, coffee mugs in front of them, before he explained to Matt what he wanted.

"As I remember, you used to do a little computer work," Dominic said.

Matt nodded and flashed him a grin. "Yeah, I'm a hacker of sorts. Why?"

Dominic didn't immediately answer Matt's question, but instead replied with one of his own. "Do you know if Mawlins has checked into Bill Newman's past at all?"

Matt shrugged. "I think he talked to a few of Bill's customers, but I don't think he dug too deep. Mawlins truly believes it was a domestic spat gone too far. Especially since he found out about Bill's affair with Grace Harrison."

"What?" Dominic listened as Matt told him the latest that Mawlins had learned. "Are you sure Bill's affair is fact and not just idle speculation or ugly gossip?"

"The way I heard it, Grace herself came in and talked to Mawlins. According to her, Bill was supposed to leave Melissa and marry Grace as soon as the baby was born. Mawlins figured that provided the motive that had previously eluded them where Melissa's guilt was concerned."

So that was why Melissa was arrested, Dominic thought. The missing piece of the puzzle for Mawlins had been provided.

And now he had proof that the Newman marriage apparently hadn't been a happy one. He wondered if Melissa had known about the affair. Somehow he didn't think so. He remembered the look on her face when Dominic had shown her the wedding photo. Shock. It hadn't been manufactured. She'd been utterly shocked. If she'd been aware of Bill's affair, surely the old photo wouldn't have been such a stunning surprise.

"So, as far as you know, Mawlins didn't check into

Bill's life before Bill came to Wilford six years ago?''
Dominic asked.

"Naw, Mawlins wouldn't take the time or the trouble on a case he figured was already closed." Matt sipped his coffee, studying Dominic thoughtfully. "So, is that what you want from me? A check into Newman's background?"

Dominic nodded. "That, and one other thing." He picked up the wedding photo and showed Matt the printing on the back. "We know this photo was taken eight years ago. We know it was taken by a place called Dano's Photography Studio, but we don't know where this business is located or if it's still in existence."

"Whew!" Matt whistled beneath his breath. "That's a pretty tall order. Checking into Newman's background should be a piece of cake, but tracking down a photography studio without a location might be a little more difficult."

"I'd appreciate anything you can do to help us out," Dominic told him.

Matt leaned back in the chair, his gaze still focused on Dominic. "You're getting pretty involved personally in this, Dominic." He paused for a moment, then added softly, "Is she worth it?"

Dominic felt a flush heat his face, but he didn't break eye contact with Matt. "I get personally involved when I think an innocent person is being railroaded for a crime."

Matt nodded. "You had a tough break, Dominic. You should never have been arrested for Abigail's murder. But don't let your experience give you tunnel vision about this case."

"I'm not."

"You thought you had a handle on Abigail before she up and married Morgan Monroe," Matt reminded him.

"There's an important difference here," Dominic countered. "I was in love with Abigail and I'm not in love with Melissa."

Matt stood and clapped Dominic on the back. "I just know you've had a rough time of it." Dominic relaxed, realizing Matt's words had come from friendship, not censure.

"I appreciate you stopping by," Dominic said as he walked with Matt to the front door. "And you'll let me know as soon as you have anything."

"Definitely, although it might take a couple of days. I can only work on this in my spare time."

Dominic nodded, fighting an edge of frustration. Melissa had already been arrested. He wanted the information from Matt yesterday. Still, he fought the impulse to put additional pressure on Matt. "Thanks for coming by. I'll be anxious to hear from you."

Nodding goodbye, Matt left, leaving Dominic alone in the silence of the house. Only his thoughts rattled discordantly in what should have been total tranquillity.

Looking at his watch, he realized it was almost ten o'clock. He'd heard nothing from Tyler and Samantha and assumed no news meant exactly no news. From that, he could also assume that Melissa wouldn't be coming home tonight. It was still up in the air whether she would be coming home at all.

A sudden, mewling cry from the nursery pulled

Dominic down the hallway. Jamison always had his last bottle of the night at about this time.

"Hey, little guy," Dominic greeted the crying baby. "Shh, no need to work yourself up. I'm here, and I'm going to take care of you." Jamison quieted, as he always did at the sound of Dominic's voice.

"We'll get you a bottle, but first I think a change of diaper is in order." While Dominic unsnapped the blue sleeper Jamison wore and removed a soggy diaper, the baby chewed on a tiny fist and his blue eyes gazed unblinking at Dominic. And in those bright blue depths, Dominic saw Melissa.

He saw the sleepy blue of her eyes first thing in the morning...and the sapphire glow of love each time she gazed at her son. Those eyes of hers, reflecting a thousand different emotions. They'd been smoky blue when he'd kissed her, and he had a feeling that blue would deepen to midnight when she made love.

He finished diapering Jamison and picked him up in his arms. The baby smelled of talc and innocence and the floral fragrance of his mother. In that moment Dominic knew he'd lied to Matt. He *was* personally involved in this case; in fact he was precariously close to falling in love with Melissa Newman.

Chapter 10

Melissa got out of Tyler and Samantha's car, then watched as they drove off. They'd wanted to come in, talk trial strategy, but after a night and almost a full day in a tiny jail cell, all Melissa wanted was an evening of holding her son and spending time with Dominic.

Before she could get to the door, it opened and Dominic stepped out on the porch, the late-afternoon sun casting shadows on his features. He held Jamison in his arms, as if he knew how much she would need to see him and hold him, the moment she got home.

She ran toward him, and he immediately held the baby out to her. She hugged Jamison tightly, his wiggly warmth a soothing balm that banished momentarily the horrible night in the jail.

She smiled at Dominic. "I'm home."

"Thank God they gave you bail," he replied.

She nodded. "We got lucky. The judge was an old crony of my father's. He didn't think I was a flight risk and took into consideration I had a baby here." She leaned against the porch railing and breathed in Jamison's sweet baby scent. "Samantha and Tyler used the law firm to make my bail."

"Are you all right?" he asked softly.

"Yes. Oh, I'm exhausted. I didn't sleep very well, and I can't wait to take a bath. I feel dirty, like all the grime and despair and hopelessness in that jail cell somehow rubbed off on me." She looked at him curiously. "Was it that way for you?"

"Yeah." He frowned, as if remembering his days and weeks in a jail cell, incarcerated for a murder he hadn't committed.

She placed a hand on his arm. She felt his muscles tense beneath her touch. "I'm sorry. All this must be bringing back horrible memories for you."

"I can live with my memories, I'm just sorry you had to go through it." He stepped back from her. "Come on, let's go inside."

"Dominic, I can't thank you enough for being here for my baby, for taking care of him," she said, once they were in the house.

He shook his head as if to dismiss her grateful words. "Ah, Jamie and I got along just fine. It was no big deal."

"Jamie?"

Dominic's smile widened as his gaze lingered on the baby in her arms. "Jamison is far too big a name for such a little guy. He told me he much prefers Jamie to Jamison."

Melissa smiled. Jamie. Yes, it felt right, much

warmer and more informal than Jamison. "He learned to talk while I was gone?" she teased.

"Only in tiny whispers that nobody except me can hear."

Melissa laughed, her laughter ending with a sudden sob as the stress of the past twenty-four hours spilled out. She drew a deep breath and swallowed hard against the emotion, refusing to give in to it. "Anyway, I'm set for trial in two months."

"Who's prosecuting?"

"Chester Sparks."

Dominic frowned. "The same man who prosecuted my case. He's good, but I'm sure Richard Wallace is better."

Melissa flashed him a quick smile. "Thanks for the vote of confidence. I need all I can get." She sank into the overstuffed chair where Bill had sat every night to watch television. "Have you heard the latest?"

"You mean about Grace Harrison?"

She nodded and ran a finger over the slightly worn arm of the chair. "It's funny, I was married to Bill for six years, and I'm finding out that I didn't know him at all."

"You had no idea that he was having an affair?"

"None." Melissa bit back a burst of bitter laughter. If only she'd known. She'd worked so hard to make her marriage succeed, wanting to believe the vows of love forever. She'd endured Bill's temper, overlooked his cruelty, believing that if she was a good enough wife, he would change and become the man she'd believed she'd married.

She stood, not wanting to talk anymore, afraid she

would spill the secret that would let Dominic know how stupid she really was. She didn't want anyone to know about Bill's abuse, but she especially didn't want Dominic to know. "I'm going to put this little fellow down for a nap, then take a shower."

She left the room and went down the hallway to the nursery. She placed Jamison in his crib, smiling at him as he kicked his feet and waved his hands, his gaze seeming to focus on the mobile above his head. She reached out and smoothed a strand of his fine blond hair, her heart filling with love.

Jamison had been the reason she'd decided to reconcile with Bill. He'd also been the reason she'd decided to leave Bill. The baby had given her the strength to make the final break from her husband and all the dreams she'd once possessed.

Jamison was her strength, and her weakness. She had two months to spend with him before her trial. If she was convicted, she would miss all the important firsts in his life, would be only a peripheral part of his growing up.

She fought the impulse to pick him up, hug him to her heart and never let him go. He was the one thing good that had come out of her marriage to Bill. She pressed a kiss to her fingertips, then laid it on his cheek.

Moments later she entered the bathroom, instantly smelling the scent of Dominic. He'd apparently taken a shower earlier, and the fragrance of his soap and cologne still filled the small interior.

Melissa stepped into the hot spray of the shower, her mind filled with thoughts of Dominic. He'd been on her mind the entire night. And each moment of those thoughts had been filled with regret. Regret that he'd entered her life at the wrong time. Regret that she might never get an opportunity to taste his lips again.

But she had to be realistic. She was a young widow with a baby, and she was facing murder charges. This wasn't exactly the right time to be thinking of an intimate relationship.

Besides, she knew her meandering thoughts of Dominic and love were moot. Dominic was a good man who'd suffered enough heartache for a lifetime. He deserved a woman without baggage, a woman who could give him his own babies, not another man's child. He deserved a strong woman, not a weak fool like herself, who'd remained with an abusive man for as long as she had because she was more afraid of being alone.

She stood in the shower for a long time, letting the warm water cascade over her, allowing relaxation to replace stress. Other than the faint stretch marks that crossed her lower abdomen, her body had returned to normal, as if the birth had been years ago instead of just a month.

Finally, hair squeaky clean and skin flushed, she turned off the water. She dried quickly, ran a brush through her hair, then pulled on a robe and went back into the nursery.

She peeked into the crib and froze. Jamison was gone, his blanket tossed to one side of the empty bed. A flash of panic burst in her mind.

But after checking the window, she saw nothing amiss. No alarm had rung. She swallowed against her fear and left the nursery. Before she reached the kitchen, she knew Jamison was safe in Dominic's arms. As she walked down the hall, she heard Dominic talking to the baby.

She paused, peeking into the kitchen. Her breath caught. Jamison was there, cradled against Dominic's bare chest. Dominic paced back and forth, rocking the baby in his arms. Dominic's deep voice cooed and whispered sweet words to comfort the fussy baby.

Melissa leaned against the wall in the hallway, listening for a long moment. Her heart swelled. It was as if one of her dreams had popped out of her head and right into her kitchen. Of course, in her dreams, her son had been held in the loving arms of his father.

Closing her eyes, she drew a deep breath as she realized she was on the verge of falling desperately in love with Dominic Marcola.

Dominic turned as Melissa entered the kitchen. "He started crying while you were in the shower," he explained. Warmth swept through him as he realized her gaze lingered on his bare chest. "He—uh—spit up all over me when I picked him up. I might have fed him too much right before you got home."

She smiled, the warmth of the gesture curling Dominic's toes. "Here, I'll take him." As she took the baby from his arms, her fingers brushed his chest. He fought a flinch, wondering if she had any idea how she affected him.

She walked back and forth across the expanse of the kitchen, sweet-talking her son, kissing his forehead and gazing at him as if she might gobble him up. With each step she took, her robe flipped open, exposing her long, shapely legs.

Dominic turned away, feeling as if the walls of the kitchen had closed in and the temperature had risen several degrees. He wasn't sure exactly what was causing his pulse to race and his thoughts to turn carnal. Maybe it was because she looked so damned sexy in her peach silk robe. Or perhaps it was simply because he'd missed her presence and now was supersensitive to her closeness.

"You hungry?" he asked as he opened the refrigerator door and peered inside.

"No, but help yourself."

He closed the door. "Naw, I'm really not very hungry, either." At least, not for anything that the refrigerator might contain.

"You want to talk?" He needed something, anything to keep his mind off her fresh, clean scent and those sexy legs.

"Not about the case. I'm sick to death of talking about it. For the rest of today, I'm taking a vacation from rational thought." She sank down at the table and once again kissed the top of Jamison's head.

"It feels so good to be home. Did you miss me, sweetie? Did you miss your mama?" she asked the baby. "Oh, Dominic, look…he's smiling." Joy exploded in her voice, and Dominic came closer in time to see the little guy grin. "Did you see?" she asked, her eyes the neon blue of a late-summer sky. "It's probably gas," she finally said.

"It looked like a real smile to me," Dominic assured her.

She gazed at him warmly, then looked back down at Jamison. "I want it to be a real smile. It kind of renews my faith, that in all the madness that's been my life lately, this little guy can smile.''

"All he knows is he's warm and secure and loved," Dominic said.

Melissa looked at him again with a wistful, haunted expression. "That's what we all want, isn't it?"

"I guess so," Dominic replied, discomfited by the soft vulnerability she radiated.

She stroked Jamison's fuzzy blond hair. "This little guy will need a godfather. Are you sure you won't change your mind about it?"

"Melissa, I'm just a temporary man in your life…in Jamison's life. It wouldn't be fair to him for me to be his godfather." Dominic knew his words were rather harsh, but he felt he needed a shot of harsh reality to douse the fire she stirred in him.

"I suppose you're right." Her gaze didn't quite meet his, and he knew she was disappointed by his answer.

He realized he needed to get some distance from her. Something about her sitting there holding her baby, talking about the desire to be loved, touched him on a visceral level. "You've got some sacks of seed out in the garage. Is that what you use to fill the bird feeders out back?"

"Yes…why?"

"I noticed this morning the feeders were empty. I think I'll go fill them." He walked to the door that led to the garage. "I'll lock you in as I go out," he said.

He breathed a sigh of relief as he stepped out into the garage and closed the door behind him. He picked up one of the ten-pound sacks of seed and punched the code that would open the garage door, closed it, then reset the security system.

He walked outside, drawing in a deep breath of the warm spring air. He had to get a handle on his feelings where Melissa was concerned. From the moment she'd stepped out of Tyler and Samantha's car, Dominic had felt off-balance and out of control.

Walking around the side of the house toward the backyard, he tried to figure out exactly why he'd lost his equilibrium where she was concerned.

Maybe it had to do with the fact that he'd spent nearly twenty-four hours caring for her son. Maybe in holding, feeding, and cuddling Jamie he'd somehow cultivated a strange affinity with Jamie's mother.

Or perhaps his heightened awareness of her came from the fact that he'd slept in her bed in the nursery last night. The sheets had smelled of her and he'd imagined the heat of her body lingering amid the bedding.

Godfather. There was a part of him that had longed to tell her yes, to bind himself to the child he'd helped birth. But there was another, stronger part that didn't want to be tied, a part that knew that in tying himself to the child, he bound himself to the mother.

He frowned, irritated with himself and his wayward, dangerous thoughts. He focused on the bird feeders, removing the lids and filling them with the seed.

"I decided to join you."

He jumped, startled by her voice, and spilled the seed on the ground. He looked up to see her standing nearby. She'd changed from her robe to a sleeveless floral shift that skimmed her breasts, then fell gracefully to the ground. "Where's the baby?"

"Asleep."

"I hope you brought a key, otherwise we're locked out."

She reached into a pocket and pulled out a key ring. "Taken care of." She smiled and sank onto the concrete bench. "It's a beautiful day. Summer is right around the corner. I just hope I'm here to enjoy it," she added softly.

"You will be." Dominic's voice was gruff as he focused on filling the last of the feeders. He'd come out here to get some distance from her and there she sat, alluring and smelling as sweet as the flowers that surrounded them.

She stretched out her legs, her bare toes curling into the lush grass. She sighed, as if finding the action sensually pleasing.

A coil of heat unfurled inside Dominic, filling the pit of his stomach and rushing throughout his body. He slapped the lid back on the feeder and hung it on the pole, then carefully folded the top of the bag.

"Sit down for a minute, Dominic," she urged him, patting the space next to her on the bench. Her gaze was guileless, innocent. She had no awareness of what she was doing to him. With a helpless sense of resignation, he sat next to her.

"I've got a pair of redbirds that stay here all year long," she said, searching the trees as if looking for them. "They're so beautiful. The male stands guard while the female eats, and they always come and go together."

"Do they mate for life?"

"No. If something happens to one of them, the survivor finds a new mate. It's like fate gives them more than one chance to be happy." She shot him a sideways glance. "Do you believe in second chances, Dominic?"

"For some people. Not for everyone," he replied. Not for me, he silently added.

She turned and looked at him, her eyes shining with fervor. "I have to believe in second chances. I have to believe that I'll get a chance to be happy...after all I—" She broke off and bit her bottom lip.

"After all what?" Dominic urged.

"Oh, you know...after all this, Bill's murder and the trial and everything." She averted her gaze from Dominic, but not before he saw the dark shadows of secrets. Again he had the feeling that she was hiding something, protecting someone. But who? And why?

"Melissa, have you told me everything you can think of about that night...the night of Bill's murder?" He held his breath, wanting her to tell him what darkened her eyes.

"Of course I have."

Dominic felt an odd disappointment. Why didn't she trust him? A silence grew between them, a silence charged with tension.

"So, have you always been a bird lover?" he asked to change the subject.

She nodded. "Always." Some of the tension seemed to leave her. "When I was ten, a friend gave me a parakeet for my birthday. I set his cage on a table right in front of my bedroom window." She leaned her head back and stared at the trees. "I loved that bird, but it bothered me that he was in a cage instead of outside flying free.''

She smiled at Dominic. ''After about a week, I decided to give him his freedom. I opened my window, opened his cage door and watched him fly outside. He perched on the limb of a nearby tree, and for the first time he chirped happily.'' Her smile faded. ''Of course, my father told me how stupid I'd been, that the bird would probably not live more than a couple of days. But I didn't care. I knew he was happy being free. Nothing except criminals should be caged up, either with real bars or imaginary ones. There were days when I was growing up when I wished I could just flap my wings and fly away.''

She stood suddenly, as if sorry she'd said as much as she had. ''We'd better go in. It's cooling off as the sun goes down and you don't even have a shirt on.'' Her gaze lingered on the width of his chest, and Dominic didn't feel the cool evening air. He felt far too warm beneath the heat of her gaze.

Together they walked around the house to the front. ''Why don't you go on inside the front door and open the garage door for me?'' Dominic said.

She nodded. It took her only a moment to disappear inside the house, and a few minutes later the garage door lifted.

Dominic placed the bag of seed back where he'd gotten it, then closed the garage door and entered the house. Melissa stood in the kitchen, as if waiting for him. He tensed as she walked toward him, stopping only when she stood mere inches from him.

''The whole time I was in that jail cell last night I was scared to death that I would never get out. That

I'd never get to hold Jamison again, that I'd never sit in this kitchen and watch the birds outside the window.'' Tentatively she reached a hand out and placed it on his chest. "And I was afraid I'd never be held again, never again be kissed by you.''

"Melissa.'' Her name released from him in a half groan. He knew he should step back, move away from her touch, but his brain wasn't communicating with his body.

"Just hold me, Dominic. Even if it's only for a little while." She didn't give him an opportunity to deny her, but instead moved into his arms and pressed herself firmly against his length.

A myriad of reactions swept through him. A protest rose to his lips even as his arms enfolded her close. "Melissa." He'd meant it to be an admonishment, but her name spilled out of him sounding like a prayer. The protest he'd meant to voice got lost amid the physical sensations that ripped through him as she leaned against him, molding her body tightly to his.

She raised her head and looked at him, her eyes the midnight blue he'd imagined they would be when lit with desire. The hunger that Dominic had been fighting from the moment she'd arrived home exploded inside him. He took her lips and possessed them, forcing rational thought and any remaining protests to fall away.

His mouth demanded and devoured hers, and she took and gave it back to him, her tongue darting to deepen the kiss while her hands stroked magic on the planes of his back.

He was intensely aware of her breasts against his chest. He guessed she wore no bra, as he could feel the pebble-like hardness of her nipples through the thin cotton of her dress. Blood surged through him at the thrilling sensation.

He broke the kiss and gazed down at her. She trembled in his arms, but he knew it wasn't fear that made her quiver. "Melissa, I won't lie to you. I want you." He hesitated, giving her the chance to stop this now, to break away from his embrace and call a halt before things progressed further.

"I want you, too." She spoke softly, but her words thundered in Dominic's head. "Oh, Dominic, I don't want to think about yesterdays or tomorrows. I just want you to hold me, touch me. I want to get lost in you."

Her words snapped any lingering control Dominic might have possessed. He swept her up in his arms and carried her into the bedroom where he'd been staying. He stopped at the edge of the bed and released her.

Lost. Yes, that was exactly what he was. Lost to her allure. Lost to her desire and to his own. And heaven help him, he wanted to be lost. Once again he wrapped her in his arms and claimed her lips, finding the scent of her breathtaking, the taste of her addictive.

She broke the kiss long enough to step back from him. She turned around and indicated for him to unzip the zipper that ran from her neckline to the top of her buttocks. He unzipped slowly, his mouth tasting each inch of her skin as it was exposed.

He heard the quickening of her breath with each touch of his lips, and his own pulse raced in mirrored rhythm. When the zipper was finally undone, she turned back to face him, her features obscured by shadows of the advancing night.

She shrugged, allowing the shoulders of the dress to drop down. For a moment, she held the bodice against her breasts in shy modesty; then, with a smile that stoked the flames of his desire, she allowed the dress to slide down her body and pool at her feet.

Just as he'd suspected, she wore no bra. Her breasts were high and full. Dominic had never realized before how sexy simple white cotton panties could be, but on Melissa they stole his breath away.

He picked her up in his arms and gently deposited her on the bed. He took off his jeans, then joined her, reveling in the feel of her flesh against his own.

Someplace in the back of his mind, he knew they were making a mistake. But as her mouth clung to his, and his hands found the soft fullness of her breasts, he told himself it was all right. She understood the rules; they both knew he was a temporary fix. He gave himself to the pleasure of getting lost in her, and she did the same with him.

He drank of her mouth, then moved his lips to taste the sweet skin of her neck, her shoulder, and finally her breast. She moaned beneath him, tangling her hands in his hair. Again, Dominic had the impression of a woman starved for human touch, aching with the need to be kissed and caressed.

Each flick of his tongue evoked a tiny cry of delight from her. And with each small cry, Dominic wanted to give her more, fill her with pleasure.

Her skin was soft, supple, inviting stroke after stroke of his hands, kiss after kiss from his lips. She was not merely a willing recipient, but an active participant. Her fingers danced across his naked flesh, exploring, evoking flames of desire each place they touched.

It wasn't until he slid his fingers beneath the waistband of her panties and felt the tiny ridges of stretch marks that he remembered she'd given birth about three weeks ago. There was no way he could turn her pleasure into pain by attempting actual lovemaking. Her mind might be willing, but her body wasn't ready.

Still, he intended to give her all the pleasure that was in his power. He touched the marks again and she quieted beneath him, tensed. "The doctor said they'd eventually go away," she said in embarrassment.

Dominic lowered his head and kissed one of the red marks. "It doesn't matter if they do or not. They're a small price to pay for Jamie."

She relaxed, as if his words had stilled some inner fear. Dominic gently removed her panties, then touched her intimately. She gasped and arched up to meet him, her cries of pleasure pulling Dominic deeper into a vortex of swirling desire where no further thought was possible and there was only Melissa.

Some time later, Dominic lay on his back. Melissa slept next to him, one of her arms across his chest and her breathing a soft warm breeze against his neck.

They'd pleasured each other with hands and mouths, and Dominic felt that what they'd shared had been more intimate than actual lovemaking.

He was grateful she'd fallen asleep almost immediately. He didn't want to talk, was too confused to discuss what they'd just shared. There was no longer any doubt in his mind. He loved Melissa. And he hated himself for loving her, didn't want to be in love with her.

Melissa needed somebody in her life and Dominic was handy. She needed somebody to cling to, and Dominic had allowed himself to be her lifeline.

He was such a fool, so easily manipulated. However, there was one difference this time. Abigail Monroe had consciously manipulated him, used him when it suited her. But Dominic truly believed that Melissa wasn't purposely trying to manipulate him. She was frightened, alone, and reeling from the secrets exposed about her husband.

Still, what bothered Dominic more than anything were those dark shadows that sometimes filled Melissa's eyes. The shadows of secrets.

He turned his head and gazed at her. Her blond hair created a halo around her head and her features were achingly soft with sleep.

How could he love somebody he didn't completely trust? She was holding something back, refusing to reveal something important.

He stared back up at the ceiling, a wave of desolation sweeping through him. He needed to make certain that what they'd just shared didn't happen again. It only complicated things. She was facing a murder charge. And he had to figure out what he intended to do with the rest of his life. He knew his job with Samantha and Tyler was a temporary arrangement—his attempt to pay back his debt to them for defending him in Abigail's murder. Both he and Melissa were in transitional stages of their lives. They would be fools to seek love amid such chaos.

Chapter 11

"**Y**our husband lived in Canon Creek, Kansas, before coming to Wilford," Matt said to Melissa.

"That's right!" she exclaimed. "I couldn't remember the name before, but the minute you said it, I knew it was right." A week before, she would have grabbed Dominic's hand in excitement, but ever since the night they'd made love, he'd withdrawn from her both emotionally and physically.

It had been a trying week, filled with meetings with Richard Wallace, discussions and debates about trial strategy. As distressing as the trial preparation was, the distance Melissa felt from Dominic since their night of lovemaking was as upsetting.

"I tracked him with his social-security number," Matt continued. "Found out he worked at a gas station two years before coming here."

"At a gas station?" Melissa frowned. "He never

mentioned anything about working at a gas station.''
She looked from Matt to Dominic, then back again.

''There's a two-year window after that where I
couldn't find any place of employment, no records to
indicate he was working at all during that time.
There's something else, too.'' Matt frowned. ''He
changed his name legally six years ago.''

''What?'' Melissa stared at Matt in surprise.

''His name used to be William Newsom.'' Matt
shrugged. ''I couldn't find a reason for the change.
There are no arrests or outstanding warrants under
either name.''

''When did he start using the name of Bill Newman?'' Dominic asked.

''When he moved here,'' Matt replied.

''What about the photography business? Have you
been able to find anything there?'' Dominic asked.

Matt shook his head. ''Nothing. Dano's Photography Studio might have been in business eight years
ago, but it isn't in business now, and I can't find any
reference to it anywhere.'' Matt pushed away from
the table and stood. ''I've got to get to the station.
I'm supposed to be in a meeting in twenty minutes.''

Both Dominic and Melissa walked the officer to
the front door. ''I appreciate all your work,'' Dominic
said.

''I'm just sorry it took so long. I had to do most
of the search on the computers down at the station
and that meant sneaking time when nobody was
watching.'' He looked at Melissa, then back to Dominic. ''I'm not sure anything I found out is useful, but
I did what I could.''

''Thank you, Matt,'' Melissa added. As the two

men walked out on the porch, Melissa went back to
the kitchen. She stood at the window, staring out into
the backyard, trying to make sense of the little that
Matt had been able to learn.

Bill Newman hadn't even been his real name. The
man she'd married, the man who'd bound her to him
through fear and intimidation, had been a figment of
fiction. A man changed his name only because he was
trying to hide from something—or someone. What
had Bill been hiding? Something had happened after
he left Canon Creek and before he moved to Wilford
that had made him construct a new identity. What was
it?

She turned as Dominic came back into the room.
"We have to go to Canon Creek. The answers are
there. They have to be," she said.

"Whoa, slow down," Dominic exclaimed. "We
don't know there are any answers there. We don't
even know for sure if Bill lived someplace else between Canon Creek and Wilford. You heard what
Matt said, there's a two-year window where we don't
know where he was or what he was doing."

"But at least Canon Creek is a place to start."
Melissa felt as if she would explode from the frustration that simmered inside her. "I can't afford to leave
anything to chance. In seven weeks I go on trial for
murder. If we don't get some answers, I'll spend the
rest of my life in prison."

Dominic raked a hand through his hair and sank
down at the table. "You've got to trust that Samantha
and Tyler and Richard will see to it that you don't
spend the rest of your life in prison."

"Trust?" She stared at him incredulously. All the

frustrations, all the uncertainty of the past weeks seemed to pull together into a tight knot of anger in her chest. "I trusted my father when I was young, and he returned that trust by being cold and distant, reminding me over and over again that Samantha was the smart one and I'd better marry quickly because I wasn't smart enough for much else."

Tears spilled from her eyes, but they weren't tears of grief or sadness. They were tears of unadulterated anger burning down her cheeks. "I trusted Bill, and what a laugh that was. He lied and cheated and he—" She stopped and bit her lip to still the passage of heated words.

"And he what?" Dominic stared at her intently.

"And...and he betrayed our vows with Grace." She flushed and averted her gaze from his.

"Okay, your father and Bill were bastards. But you trust Samantha and Tyler, don't you?"

She drew a deep breath, willing the burst of anger away. She couldn't afford to lose control, to let slip things she wanted nobody to know. "Of course I trust them," she replied.

"What about me? Do you trust me, Melissa?" His gaze seemed to penetrate her skin, right through to her soul.

She thought of their lovemaking the week before, the utter giving that she'd received from him. Her mind flashed with visions of him holding Jamie, helping with dinner preparation, the little things that happened all day that proved him a man of integrity.

"Of course I trust you," she finally answered.

Dominic leaned forward, his gaze still holding her intently. "Then tell me what you haven't told me."

"I don't know what you're talking about." She felt the blood leave her face as the lie fell from her lips.

"Yes, you do," he countered. "You're hiding something. If you can't trust me enough to tell me, then how can I help you?"

"There's nothing to tell." Melissa's voice was flat, her momentary burst of anger gone, leaving behind only a bone-weariness. She averted her gaze from his and sank down at the table across from him. "I'm so confused, Dominic. I was married to a man who apparently had affairs and changed his name, a man whose past seems to be made up of smoke and mirrors." She sighed and leaned back in the chair. "I don't know. Maybe my father was right. Maybe I am stupid. I mean, I didn't see any signs that Bill was having an affair. I didn't suspect anything."

"You aren't a stupid woman, Melissa," Dominic told her. "Bill was just very good at hiding things." He frowned and shook his head slightly, as if she'd stirred something inside him that was unpleasant. "Maybe I could take a trip to Canon Creek. It's only an hour-and-a-half drive. I could check things out, see if there's anything there that might help."

"Oh, Dominic, would you?" She grabbed his hand and pulled it close to her heart. "It would mean so much to me. I'd feel so much better knowing we'd left nothing to chance."

"I'll talk to Samantha and Tyler and make the necessary arrangements." He pulled his hand away from her grip. "In fact, I've been meaning to talk to them anyway. I think it's time we let you have your house back to yourself."

Melissa looked at him in surprise. "What?" She

was shocked by the anguish that ripped through her at the thought. She couldn't imagine this place without him, couldn't imagine not seeing him first thing in the morning and last thing before she went to sleep. "But...but why?"

He stood, his features unreadable. He leaned against the refrigerator, looking so handsome, so virile, that Melissa felt a recurrent stir of desire deep within her. "Melissa, I've been here over a month and nothing has happened to indicate that your life is in danger."

"But what about the night the alarm went off? Somebody tried to break into the nursery," she protested.

"That might have been a reporter who stumbled against the window screen, a nosy neighbor trying to see into the house—it could have been anything." He raked a hand through his hair and walked across the room to stand by the window. He stared outside, his posture rigid. "I can't remain here indefinitely." He turned and looked at her once again. "This is your home. I don't belong here. Sooner or later you're going to have to deal with getting on with your life."

"I know." Just not yet, she wanted to say, but didn't. She knew he was right. There had been no threats, no reason to believe she was in any danger. It was time for her to let him go back to his life...time to reclaim her own.

"Look, I'm not going to do anything until I talk with Samantha and Tyler." His tone was gentle, as if he knew the thought of him leaving would unsettle her. "Now, in the meantime, didn't you say something about needing to get some groceries?"

She nodded and stood. "I have a list of things I need to pick up."

Dominic looked at his watch. "It's almost noon. Why don't we go on into town and grab some lunch at the diner, then do the shopping."

"Okay. I'll just get Jamison ready."

It took her only minutes to change Jamison's diaper and dress him in a two-piece outfit with matching little socks.

As she dressed the baby, she tried to imagine the house, her life without Dominic. It was nearly impossible. He'd become such a part of her daily existence. But she knew he was right. He was here with her because he'd been hired to do a job. He believed his job was done, so there was no reason for him to remain.

Except she wanted him to. She wanted him to take her in his arms once again, she wanted to feel his body against her own, taste the passion on his lips. But that wasn't fair, either. She'd told him on the night they'd made love that for that moment there was no yesterday, no tomorrow. It wasn't fair for her to try to claim his tomorrows now—not when she wasn't sure how many she had left.

Even if she did manage to beat the murder charges, she knew she would be a fool to pursue a relationship with Dominic. She had a feeling he was a man who would brook no secrets in a relationship, and she absolutely refused to part with the secret that burned in her soul, the secret that filled her with humiliation.

She picked up the baby along with his infant carrier and left the room.

Moments later they were on their way into the heart

of Wilford. It was another gorgeous late-spring day and Melissa rolled her window partway down to enjoy the warm summerlike breeze. It was almost sinful to think of murder on such a beautiful day, but murder filled Melissa's head.

"Maybe Grace killed Bill because he told her he wouldn't leave me and the baby." Even as she said the words, she knew it was a ridiculous supposition. Grace Harrison was no more capable of committing such an act than Melissa herself. "Never mind, that was stupid."

Dominic smiled. "It's not stupid to speculate. Right now, speculation is about all we have. But if I had to guess, I'd guess that the killer was male, not female."

"Why?" Melissa looked at him curiously, trying to ignore how the wind ruffled his hair into charming disarray.

He frowned, as if the idea was forming in his head as the words left his mouth. "The method of killing, the rage involved." He shrugged. "It just feels male to me."

"Will you still go to Canon Creek?"

He gazed at her quickly and offered a smile. "Melissa, I'm moving out of your house, not off the case. I plan on doing whatever I can to help your defense."

"Thank you. I'm grateful for all you've done already." Somehow the words sounded incredibly inadequate after what they'd shared.

His brow wrinkled. "I know."

They fell silent for the remainder of the drive to the diner. Always, before, their silences had been comfortable ones. This one felt tense, full of regrets and words unspoken. Melissa knew it was just her mood coloring the moment.

She felt guilty for lying to him earlier, when he'd asked her about what she was holding back. Even a lie of omission was a lie. But in revealing Bill's abuse, she would add nothing to the case except complications. Nothing positive could be gained by it.

"You hungry?" Dominic asked as he parked the car in the diner lot.

"Yes, I am." She smiled, deciding to push thoughts of the murder, of all the uncertainties of her life, aside for the moment. This was the first time she and Dominic had ventured out of the house for a meal, and she intended to enjoy both the food and the company.

They took a booth near the front of the diner. Melissa placed the infant seat next to her as Dominic slid in across from her. The diner was a popular place for local business people to grab quick lunches and shoppers to seek sustenance between stores.

"Must be a little early for the lunch crowd," Dominic observed as he looked at all the empty tables and booths.

Melissa looked at her watch and nodded. "It's only a few minutes after eleven. The crowd should start coming in within the next half hour." Actually, Melissa was glad there were few diners. She hadn't been out in public much since Bill's funeral, and she couldn't forget the morbid curiosity and the hint of accusation of those in attendance.

Still, Wilford was her home and the people here were her neighbors. She needed to look them in the eye, show she wasn't embarrassed to go out in public, that she had nothing to hide or feel guilty about.

She opened a menu and studied it, once again trying to cast off her gloomy melancholy and simply enjoy the outing. "Hmm, I must be hungrier than I thought because everything sounds wonderful," she exclaimed. "I think I'm going to have the chicken-fried steak."

"Hmm, sounds good." Dominic closed his menu and looked at Jamie, who chewed on his fist as if it were a gourmet meal. "It won't be long before that little guy will be big enough to sit in a high chair and demand his own food."

"Don't remind me." She looked at her son, her heart swelling with protective love. "Children grow up so fast. In a heartbeat they go from baby to toddler, from toddler to teenager."

"Whoa, I've barely got him sitting up, and you've already got him driving a car."

Melissa laughed. "Believe me, I'm in no hurry for him to grow up. I want him to have a wonderful, carefree childhood."

The conversation was interrupted by the arrival of the waitress. She took their orders, cooed to Jamie, then departed. Melissa took a sip of her water, studying Dominic.

As always, he looked handsome and utterly masculine in a navy T-shirt and his worn, tight-fitting jeans. His hair was still slightly mussed by the breeze that had blown through the car, but it only added to his appeal. Just remembering the heat of his kisses, the gentle touch of his hands, created a swirl of warmth inside her.

Soon he would be walking out of her life and she had a feeling that despite what they'd shared, he would never look back.

"You have regrets, Dominic?" she asked.

His dark brows rose in surprise. "Regrets?"

She nodded. "You know…about things that have happened in your life, people who have passed through—" She broke off, a blush warming her cheeks.

Dominic's eyes darkened and he leaned back in the booth, his brow furrowed in thought. "Sure, I've got regrets. Doesn't everyone?"

"Tell me about them." Melissa leaned forward as well, wondering if it was possible to regret things that hadn't yet been. Because as she looked into Dominic's dark eyes, she felt a million regrets for what would never be.

"What's the point of talking about them?" he countered, his eyes glazed with shutters that kept her out. "Dwelling on regrets is a useless waste of energy. Thinking about things that can't be changed, actions that can't be called back." A touch of anger had filled his voice, as if by the question alone she'd delved too deeply into his personal space and he resented it.

Melissa suddenly realized that although she and Dominic had shared the same home for the past month, had even shared physical intimacy, there were still spaces he hadn't allowed her into, just as she had guarded pieces of herself.

"I'm sorry, I didn't mean to pry," she said.

He shook his head. "No, I'm sorry. I didn't mean to snap at you."

The waitress appeared with their orders, her presence dispelling any lingering tension. While they ate, their conversation was light and easy. They chose mundane topics—the weather, the town, the food—to talk about, carefully steering clear of more unpleasant subjects.

For the duration of the meal, Melissa was almost able to forget that she was a murder suspect, and that her husband had been the victim of an unexplained homicide. For the first time in months—no years—she felt like a normal young woman enjoying a meal with an attractive male.

They lingered over coffee until Jamie got fussy. "We'd better get on to the grocery store and then get him home for a nap," Melissa finally said as she finished her second cup of coffee.

Twenty minutes later, Melissa situated Jamie and his infant seat in a grocery cart and started down the first aisle of the store. Dominic walked beside her and for a moment it was tempting for Melissa to fantasize that they were a married couple out on their weekly shopping trip.

It was a fantasy she had to resist, knowing that to fall under its spell would only sharpen the ache of her regret later on.

As she filled the basket, by placing the items around Jamie's infant carrier, she noticed that Dominic added nothing to the food supplies, offered no advice on what she should buy. She knew it was because in his mind he'd already left her, had no intention of remaining in the house, eating this food.

The knowledge pierced her heart, as if he were already gone from her, and she realized then the depth of her feelings where Dominic was concerned. She loved him. She nearly dropped a loaf of bread as she recognized the emotion that filled her heart, with both joy and bittersweet pain.

Wrong time, wrong place—right man. It was as if fate held out a shining gold coin to a pauper, dangled it tantalizingly close, only to snatch it away before the poor man could grasp it.

She carefully kept her gaze averted from Dominic's, not wanting him to see what was in her heart. It would only complicate things. Love had no place in her life—not now, and perhaps not ever.

"I'm going to pick up a few personal items," Dominic said. "I'll meet you by the cashier."

She nodded, relieved as he walked ahead down the aisle and disappeared around the corner. When he'd gone, she leaned against the cart, a deep sorrow invading her soul.

Love had been elusive throughout her life. She'd loved her father, who'd been incapable of returning that love. She'd loved Bill, and that love had been used against her, wielded with power and abuse.

And now, she was in love with a good man, a man she knew didn't have the capacity for cruelty, a man who deserved loving and being loved by a good woman. It broke her heart to know she wasn't that woman, and never would be.

She leaned down and touched Jamie's cheek. Dominic didn't even want to be godfather to her son. Why on earth would he want to be a stepfather? Straightening her shoulders, she pushed the cart down the aisle and into the next one, almost colliding with Grace Harrison.

For a moment the two women faced each other in silent shock. Melissa knew that most women, when faced with their husband's lover, would feel resentment; but as she gazed at the wan, achingly thin young woman, the only thing she felt was sympathy.

She knew Grace had been just another of Bill's victims, caught in a web of his lies and manipulation. Grace's face blossomed with the fire of a blush. She mumbled something and turned as if to leave.

"Grace." Melissa's mouth was dry. She had no idea what she intended to say, but felt the need to say something. Grace turned back to her, her body still poised as if to flee, her eyes widened as if expecting a physical blow.

"I didn't kill him," Melissa said.

"Then who did?" Grace's eyes filled with tears.

"I don't know. I can only tell you it wasn't me."

Grace shrugged and swiped at her tears. "I never really thought you did it." She averted her gaze. "I know you probably hate me. I—I never meant to fall in love with him." Her tears came faster, and she stopped wiping at them, as if realizing the futility of the gesture. "He—he was going to take me away from here. He made me feel so important. He made me feel beautiful and funny and so smart."

Melissa listened to her with a growing sense of horror and fascination. She shouldn't be standing here, listening to this, but a perverse interest kept her in place. It was as if Grace had been a witness to Melissa's budding relationship with Bill when she'd first met him.

"He listened to me...really listened to me like nobody else ever had in my life."

Melissa's blood chilled as she heard the words she'd said to Dominic explaining Bill's initial attraction now echoed by Grace.

"I've got to go. I—I—" Grace turned and ran, whatever she'd been about to say lost amid choking sobs.

Melissa fought the impulse to run after her. What more could be said? They were both victims, casualties of Bill's lies. And Melissa had a feeling there was another victim, a blond woman in a wedding dress. What had happened to her? Maybe Dominic could find that answer, along with others, on his trip to Canon Creek.

She pushed her cart toward the produce section, eager to finish the shopping and get Jamie home for his nap. He was fussy, emitting little cries of displeasure. She knew he wanted his own bed in his own room. She also knew Dominic was probably waiting for her at the checkout.

She picked up her pace, adding a head of lettuce and a bag of radishes to her cart. She muttered irritably as she picked up a bag of oranges and three of them slipped through a hole in the bag and tumbled across the floor. Racing after them, she wondered what else could possibly go wrong.

She picked up the first two and leaned down for the third, which had gone under one of the vegetable bins. She was vaguely aware of the sound of footsteps. Suddenly she was shoved, hard enough to knock her down to the floor. Her head crashed into the front of the bin and her knee hit the floor with a painful jolt. For a moment she saw stars.

Errant orange forgotten, she pulled herself up off

the floor, her knee throbbing in tune with her forehead. Wobbly, unsure exactly what had happened, she turned for her shopping cart. Gone. The cart was gone. Hysteria bubbled up in her throat. Where was Jamie? Dear God, where was her baby?

Chapter 12

The scream ripped through the relative silence of the store and raised the hairs on the nape of Dominic's neck. *Melissa!* Her name exploded in his mind as he threw down the magazine he'd been thumbing through and raced toward the front of the store.

He nearly bumped into her, her eyes wide, face pale. "He's got Jamie!" she screamed and pointed out the store window, where Dominic saw a man running with a cart across the asphalt parking lot.

Dominic ran out the door and after the man. Jamie's cries mingled with the sound of the cart rolling and the slap of the man's footsteps against the pavement. He had a big head start, but his speed was hampered by the cart. Dominic gained on him, his heart pounding as fast as his feet, Jamie's frightened cries spurring him on.

The man glanced back only once, so quickly Dominic couldn't get a good look at his features. The hood of his black sweatshirt covered his hair, making identification impossible.

As he reached the edge of the parking lot, he lifted Jamie's infant carrier from the cart and continued to run. He crossed Main Street, while Dominic's heart jumped into his throat as the man dodged several cars before continuing on down the sidewalk. Dominic followed, aware of the screech of tires and an angry curse from a driver as he flew across the street.

Dominic drew closer—so close he could smell the man, the scent of sweat and fear. He could have dived for him, probably cut him at the knees, but he feared that in doing so he would hurt Jamie.

They continued for a block when the man apparently made a decision. He dropped the infant carrier, which skidded on the pavement but thankfully remained upright, then continued on, gaining distance as Dominic pulled up.

Dominic's pulse pounded at his temples as he crouched down next to the baby to catch his breath. Jamison's cries had reddened his face and his little breaths came in gasps amid sobs. Dominic unbuckled him from the carrier and picked him up, then cradled him tightly against his chest.

Dear God. Dominic's heart ached as he realized what a close call it had been. He kissed Jamie's forehead, breathing in the sweet scent. All of Dominic's insides shook as he thought of losing this child.

Within moments the baby's cries had ebbed, but fear and anger still ripped through Dominic. What in the hell had happened here? Why would somebody want to snatch Jamie?

A shudder swept through him as he realized how lucky they'd been that the man had opted to drop Jamie. He might have gotten away with the child.

Dominic stood, Jamie still cradled in his arms. He turned to see Melissa running toward them, tears streaking down her cheeks. "Oh, thank God he's all right." She reached them and kissed first the baby's head, then Dominic's cheek. "Thank God you're both all right."

He handed her the baby. It was then he noticed the goose egg in the center of her forehead. He touched it gently, rage rising in him once again. "Are you all right?" He lowered his hand from the lump and instead pulled her close, careful not to crush the baby in her arms. Who had dared to do this? What could be the motivation behind it?

She shivered in his embrace and he knew it was the release of emotion, dissipating fear coupled with overwhelming relief. He released her and picked up the baby carrier. "Tell me what happened."

She hugged the baby tighter and whispered a kiss on his forehead. "It all happened so fast. I dropped some oranges, and when I stooped down to pick one up, somebody knocked me to the floor. When I got up, my cart was gone."

"Come on. Let's go back to the store and call the police."

"Dominic, why is this happening? Why would that man want Jamie?"

"I wish I knew." Dominic's stomach knotted as he realized again just how close they'd come to losing Jamie.

By the time they got back to the store, it was obvious somebody had already called the police. Two patrol cars were there, their lights whirling as the officers stood out front talking to the cashier.

"Oh, no, it's Mawlins," Melissa groaned as they drew close enough to recognize the police officers who had responded.

"It will be all right," Dominic tried to reassure her. "There's no question who the victim is here. He can't do anything more to hurt you."

"Yeah, he's already arrested me for murder. What else can he do?" she replied dryly.

Dominic fought the impulse to shelter her and the baby in his arms. He cursed himself for letting down his guard, believing because there had been no real threats in the last month, there was no danger. He'd been a fool to grow complacent.

It took nearly an hour for Mawlins to sort out the events of what had happened and write up a report. Dominic could offer little as a description of the kidnapper. He'd not been able to see facial features or hair color, only knew the man had been tall and slender and could run like the wind, even carrying a baby.

"I think if I spent enough time with that man, I would be capable of murder," Melissa said as she and Dominic drove home. He smiled, knowing exactly what man she referred to. "I can't believe he honestly thinks whoever took Jamison was probably just a nutcase who didn't want a suspected murderer raising a child."

Dominic let her vent for a few more minutes. Her anger was a good thing to see. It was healthy. She deserved to be angry about the curves life had thrown her in the past month.

For the first time, Dominic had no doubts as to her innocence. He didn't know what demons she'd faced in her marriage, nor did he know what secrets she held on to so tightly. What he did know was that there were too many questions, too many things going on, for Bill's death to have been a domestic situation gone awry.

As he drove toward her house, he realized something else. There was no way he could bow out of her life now, not while her safety—and Jamie's safety—was at risk.

He remembered the night the alarm had rung and they'd discovered the screen displaced from the nursery window. That incident by itself was concerning, but now it was absolutely chilling. Without the security on the house, it was possible that on that night Melissa would have found the crib empty. Whoever was doing this was trying to lull them into a false sense of security—and it had almost worked.

"You have to go to Canon Creek as soon as possible," Melissa said, interrupting his thoughts.

He frowned. "I don't know, Melissa. I don't think it's a good idea for me to go anywhere right now."

She leaned over and grabbed his arm, her gaze intense. "But don't you see, Dominic? It's more important now than ever that we find out about Bill's past." She leaned back in her seat. "Whatever happened today with Jamie and that man, you can't tell me it isn't somehow tied into Bill's murder. It's all connected, and everything seems to point to the secrets of Bill's past."

She looked into the back seat, where Jamie had finally fallen asleep. "Whoever that man was today…he'll be back.'' Dominic chilled at the certainty of her words. "You know he'll come back. He wanted Jamie, and he didn't succeed in getting him. If you go to Canon Creek, maybe we'll get some answers. Please, Dominic. Go soon. Go tomorrow.''

He pulled into the driveway without giving her a reply. He had to think, decide what was best. His head told him she made sense, but his heart rebelled at the thought of leaving her and Jamie without knowing who might be a threat to them. And what he would really like to know was when his heart had managed to get so damned involved?

"Dominic, even if all this isn't somehow tied to Bill's past, I have to have some answers. I need to know about the man I was married to. Not just for my own sake, but for Jamie's as well.'' Her eyes appealed to him. "I have to know what happened to that woman in the photograph.''

They entered the house, and Melissa immediately went to the kitchen to fix a bottle for Jamie. As she sat there, feeding Jamie, Dominic used the living-room phone to call Samantha and tell her what had happened at the store.

"I want to go to Canon Creek,'' he told her. "Melissa and I both believe I'll find some answers there.''

"When?''

"As soon as possible. I'd like to go tomorrow morning.'' Dominic had decided to follow his head and ignore his heart, which urged him to remain, not leave Melissa and the baby.

"What about Melissa and Jamison?'' Samantha asked, as if reading his mind. "I'm not sure it's a good idea for them to be there in the house all alone.''

"Maybe she and Jamie could stay at your place for the day. Nobody would know they were there."

"Why don't you put her on the phone and let me talk to her? We'll work out the details, but I think you're right. It's important that somebody go to Canon Creek and find out whatever they can about Bill."

"Hang on, she's in the kitchen with Jamie." Dominic called out to Melissa to pick up the kitchen extension. When he heard her voice on the line, he hung up.

He moved to the sofa and sank down, his thoughts on the woman in the next room and the baby in her arms. He'd sworn to himself when he'd been cleared of Abigail's murder that he would never again allow himself to fall in love. Loving Abigail had been such a mixture of pleasure and pain. He'd never wanted to experience that again.

Yet he couldn't help the way his heart quickened as Melissa stepped out of the kitchen and into the living room, with Jamie asleep in her arms. "I'm going to put him to bed," she said softly. She walked down the hall, leaving a trail of her floral fragrance behind.

Dominic closed his eyes, wishing it were as easy to close his heart. But in that moment when Jamie had been in danger, he'd realized just how far his heart had opened to embrace both the little boy and his lovely mother.

He didn't hear Melissa come back into the room, didn't realize she was near until he felt the sofa cushion next to him sag beneath her weight, smelled the sweet fresh scent he knew somehow he would never forget. He prayed she wouldn't touch him, felt suddenly incredibly vulnerable to her.

Opening his eyes, he gazed at her. Before he knew his own intentions, he pulled her into his arms. She came willingly, nestling her head against his chest with a deep sigh.

They stayed that way for a long time, the beating of their hearts the only communication necessary. Dominic stroked her hair, the strands like fine silk beneath his fingers. He moved his hand to touch the smooth, sweet skin of her cheek, trace the outline of her jaw.

She was such an incredible mixture of strength and fragility. His fingers touched the lump on her forehead. It had gone down a little, but she flinched from his touch and stirred in his arms.

"You're going tomorrow?" she asked, her blue eyes solemn as she gazed at him.

He nodded.

"You won't be coming back here, will you?"

He looked at her in surprise. "Of course I'll be coming back, hopefully with some answers."

"That's not what I mean." She bit her bottom lip in the gesture that had become so familiar, so dear to him. "Things will be different...between us...won't they?"

"They have to be," he answered, not bothering to pretend he didn't understand what she was talking about. She nodded, her eyes reflecting a sadness that ached in his heart.

She laid her head back on his chest. "We're both at bad places in our lives," he continued, feeling the need to explain. "We've grown too close because of the circumstances. We'd be fools to allow it to continue.'' Whatever he'd wanted to say next caught in his throat as her fingers moved beneath his T-shirt, skimming the muscles of his stomach and dancing heatedly against his skin.

She looked up at him once again. ''But that's tomorrow, right?'' she whispered, her moist full lips parting in invitation. ''That means we still have tonight.''

His body instantly responded to her words, tensing as blood raced hot and thick through his veins. ''No regrets?''

''No regrets.''

He lowered his head down to taste her lips, so sweet beneath his. She wound her arms around his neck, pressing her body against the length of his.

He fought against the ravenous hunger that swept through him, knowing if he allowed it to take control, everything would happen too fast. And he didn't want it fast. He wanted it slow—agonizingly, breathtakingly slow. He wanted to savor each kiss, linger in every caress.

They undressed each other slowly, the act of preparing for lovemaking as sensual as the very act itself. Late-afternoon sunshine streamed in through the windows, coloring their nakedness a warm golden hue.

As she stretched out on the sofa, Dominic went to the windows and pulled the shades, remembering Gary Watters's penchant for window peeking. He didn't want anyone to see her, wanted no one to intrude on their intimacy. For this moment in time, she was his, and he was hers.

He joined her on the sofa, keeping the bulk of his

weight on elbows and knees so as not to hurt her. His mouth found hers again, tasting the hungry need and heated passion. Her body was hot, as if fevered when she moved her hips beneath him, teasing… enticing…inviting. With a groan of sheer pleasure, Dominic allowed himself to be drawn into the vortex of desire, where rational thought was impossible, where there was only Melissa.

As Dominic's mouth moved down to capture the tip of one of her breasts, a low moan escaped Melissa. His lips felt like fire, his fingers flames that burned imprints upon her body she knew she would never forget.

She'd told him no regrets, but she already regretted. Regretted loving him, being in love with him, and knowing there would be no "happily ever after."

She was a woman facing murder charges, a young widow with a newborn baby. Dominic had made it clear he wanted no future part in her life. But even these thoughts could not stop her from wanting him to keep kissing her, keep touching her, could not prevent her from urging him to possess her utterly and completely.

His hands were so gentle that tears misted her eyes. He healed her as he caressed her, sweeping away any memory of Bill's rough touch, banishing the remembrances of unhappy times.

She gave herself completely to the man and the moment, reveling in each kiss, losing herself in every tender touch. When she could bear it no longer, when the tension inside her nearly exploded, she gripped Dominic's forearms and gazed at him. "Please, I want you inside me," she said.

"We can't," he replied, his voice deep and full of desire. "It's too soon.... I don't want to hurt you."

"You won't. Please, Dominic, I need to feel you inside me, as part of me." She reached down and circled him with one hand, felt the power that pulsated there. "Love me," she whispered.

His eyes flashed his response. Gently he entered her. She held her breath, tears once again springing to her eyes as he eased into her a little at a time. She knew all she had to do was grunt or moan and he would instantly withdraw, sacrifice his pleasure for her pain.

But there was no pain, only pleasure. Sweet, warm fires of pleasure as he buried himself inside her. Where before, their lovemaking had been tentative, that of two people exploring new territory, this time they loved as if they'd been lovers for a lifetime and knew each and every secret place to touch to heighten pleasure.

Melissa wanted this moment to last forever. She wanted to keep him with her always, but knew that even after they'd finished making love, long after he'd moved on in life and left her behind, she would always have a piece of him wrapped in her soul.

As he moved inside her, his mouth locking on to hers, thought became impossible and she let herself be swept away by the passion spinning out of control.

Some time later, Melissa went to the bathroom and got her robe. When she returned to the living room, Dominic was sitting on the edge of the sofa, wearing his jeans and shirt. "Melissa, I..."

She held up a hand to stop whatever he intended

to say. She didn't want to hear apologies or excuses for what they had just done. She didn't want him to explain to her that he wanted her, but didn't love her; that he desired her, but couldn't offer her anything else. She knew all that.

"Dominic, please, don't ruin what we just shared by talking about it. We're both adults. We acted on physical desire and no explanations are necessary." She belted her robe at her waist, momentarily averting her gaze from his. "I don't expect anything from you." She'd learned from experience not to count on anything from the men in her life.

She looked back at him again. "My life has been a complicated mess for the past month. I needed somebody to hold me, to make love to me, and I'll always be grateful that you were here for that."

She was surprised to see his eyes flash darkly. "I was more than happy to accommodate you," he said, a touch of anger in his voice.

She frowned, realizing that she'd made him angry. "I'm handling this poorly." She sighed and raked a hand through her tousled hair. All she'd wanted to do was ease any guilt he might have about sleeping with her, but she seemed to be making a muddle of things. "I—I guess I just wanted to say thank-you for all you've done for me."

He nodded, his eyes still dark with an emotion she couldn't discern.

"I think I'll go check on the baby," she finally said, afraid that pursuing the discussion would only aggravate him more. She started to leave but hesitated when he called her name. She turned back to him.

"Before I leave for Canon Creek in the morning,

is there anything you need to tell me? Anything at all you haven't told me about Bill?''

"I—no—of course not." She stumbled over the words. What would happen if she finally confessed to him that Bill had been an abusive husband? What would he think if she finally bared the secret that had burned in her soul for so long?

She stood there, staring at him. The words begged to be released, the secret laid open, but still she held it inside. Because for her, the real source of shame wasn't that Bill had abused her...but that somehow she'd deserved it. "There's nothing," she finally said.

"Okay," he replied, disappointment drawing his eyebrows closer together. "Okay, then that's that."

There was such a note of finality in his words, Melissa knew that something had broken between them—something she hadn't even been fully aware existed. "Dominic, I..."

This time he held up his hand to quiet her. "Tomorrow I go to Canon Creek, and hopefully I'll gain some answers that will give you back your life. Then I can get back to my own."

Melissa nodded, her heart heavier than she could ever remember it having been. She turned and walked down the hallway toward the nursery, somehow knowing that she'd lost Dominic before she'd ever had him.

Chapter 13

Dominic rolled down his car window, allowing in the scent of the green fields and farmlands he passed as he drove toward Canon Creek. The wedding picture of Bill and the mysterious woman was in his breast pocket, along with a more recent photo of Bill. But his thoughts were far distant from the farms he passed, far away from Bill and the mystery bride. Dominic's every thought was filled with Melissa.

Melissa. He'd known the first time he'd seen her in Samantha's office that she was a woman who could make his heart ache, weaken his knees and muddle his mind. That was why he'd steered clear of her for so long. She'd been married, and there was no place in her life for Dominic. Then Bill had died and Dominic had been swept into her life at the whim of fate.

The problem was he had fallen in love with Melissa and what she gave him in return felt like manipulation. After they'd made love, she had seemed to assure him so easily that that was all she expected from him. Like Abigail. No emotional entanglements, just a warm body to cling to, a male to have dinner with and make love to.

Melissa was lost, her world destroyed by an unknown assailant. Dominic was convenient to hang on to, offering momentary respites from pain in exchange for long moments of passion.

He realized he wanted to be more to her than a temporary respite, an impermanent safe haven against a world gone mad. But he would be a fool to offer himself up, expose his heart to her as he'd done with Abigail.

He'd been down this road before, and knew it led to heartache. There was only one thing he wanted to do: find out who had killed Bill, clear Melissa of all the charges against her, give her back her life. He would let her keep whatever secrets darkened her eyes, those things she refused to reveal. Then he would walk away, his heart bruised but not broken.

The drive to Canon Creek was a pleasant one. The day was another sunny presummer show of warmth and sunshine. The rural landscape soothed him, filled him with a peace he hadn't felt for a long time.

He was healing. Finally, the horror of being arrested, of being charged with Abigail's murder and seeing friends fall away, had ebbed. He had begun to realize that much of the isolation he'd felt through the ordeal had been of his own making.

He'd pulled inside himself, haunted by shame, tormented by thoughts of his weakness where Abigail was concerned. His guilt had been over loving blindly—a mistake he wouldn't make again. Abigail had had secrets in her eyes, and he'd dismissed them, ignored them until it was too late. He would never again fully trust himself to a woman with secrets.

He sat up straighter in the seat as the speed limit lowered and a sign announced the town of Canon Creek. Even smaller than Wilford, the business district of Canon Creek consisted of a few stores lined up along a short block on Main Street.

He drove slowly, unsure exactly where to begin his search for answers. He decided to start at the Canon Creek Café, an establishment that looked as if it had been in the center of town since the dawn of time.

The scents of frying bacon and eggs, biscuits and strong coffee greeted him as he walked in. The place was already busy, men in overalls sitting at the counter and several older couples in the red booths. Friendly voices rumbled, the sounds of people at ease with each other.

Dominic scooted onto a stool at the counter and nodded to the waitress, a plump older woman. She returned the smile and handed him a worn menu, then poured him a cup of coffee.

"What can I get for you, handsome?" she asked, her eyes twinkling with merriment as if life were one big joke.

"Just the coffee is fine," Dominic replied. "And maybe you'd answer a question or two for me." He withdrew the wedding photograph from his breast pocket. "You know these people?"

She took the picture from him, looked at it for a moment, then shook her head. "Never seen them before."

Dominic tucked the photo back in his pocket. He hadn't expected this to be easy. "Have you lived in Canon Creek long?"

"For five long, miserable years." She flashed him a flirtatious grin. "Now you wouldn't want to sweep me off my feet and take me away from all this, would you? It would just take me an hour or two to pack up my six kids and be ready to go."

Dominic grinned. "I'd have to get a bigger car."

She threw up her hands in mock despair. "Ah, it's always one excuse or another with you men." She gestured to his pocket. "So, who are they? Missing relatives? Long-lost friends?"

Dominic shrugged. "A long story. You ever heard of a place called Dano's Photography Studio?"

She shook her head. "Afraid not. We want to get our pictures took around here, we go to the local discount store. About twice a year they have a photographer come in."

"This place would have been around eight years ago."

"'Fraid I can't help you, then." She looked down the counter. "Hey, George." An old man looked up from his plate. "You ever remember there being a place called Dano's Photography Studio here in Canon Creek?"

He frowned for a moment, shook his head, then resumed eating.

"I don't know…. You might try Betty Wardman over at the post office. She's been around for a hundred years. Always seems to know everyone else's business."

Bingo, Dominic thought.

It was exactly the kind of information that usually proved vital. Every town had a busybody, and he hoped this Betty Wardman proved that most busy-bodies loved to talk about other people's business. "Thanks, I'll do that."

He drank two cups of coffee, left a generous tip, then headed to the post office, hoping Betty Wardman would live up to her reputation.

Samantha lay on a blanket on the living-room floor next to Jamie. Melissa grinned as she listened to her sister talk gibberish to the baby, who stared at her as if she were a fascinating alien.

Samantha had shown up as Dominic left for his trip to Canon Creek. Despite Melissa's protests that she would be fine in the house alone while Dominic was gone, Samantha had insisted she would at least spend the morning with her.

Samantha had court in the afternoon and although she'd offered to try to get out of it, Melissa had insisted that would be silly. After all, the house was equipped with a state-of-the-art alarm system and Melissa felt perfectly safe within the walls of her home.

Samantha rolled over and sat up, a frown furrowing her brow. "I don't think your son is appreciating all my efforts to entertain him."

"He might not be appreciating them, but I am."

Samantha stuck her tongue out, then joined Melissa on the sofa. For a long moment the two sisters looked at each other.

There had been a time when Melissa had thought she'd never be close to her sister again. When their father had died and Samantha had returned to town eight months ago, there had been a lot of baggage between the two sisters—old resentments that their father had fostered throughout their teenage years, and Melissa's anger that her sister had managed to escape their father's tyrannical rule but had left her behind. There had been a hundred issues that had to be muddled through before they could reaffirm the intense bonds of sisterly love they felt for each other.

Samantha smiled and shook her head. "You amaze me," she said.

Melissa looked at her in surprise. "Why?"

"You've handled everything that's happened remarkably well." Samantha took Melissa's hand in hers. "I could never be as strong as you've been. You've always been so much stronger than me."

Again, surprise winged through Melissa. "What are you talking about? You were the one who was strong enough to break away, courageous enough to build a life away from Father and Wilford."

Samantha shook her head. "I ran, Melissa. It doesn't take strength or courage to run. But you...you stayed, worked out the problems with Father and built something special with your husband."

Emotion rose inside Melissa and she pulled her hand from Samantha's and stood. What she wanted to tell Samantha was that she'd sold out, bargained her soul to Bill in order to escape their father. She'd sacrificed years of her life to a man who'd been cold and cruel because she'd been too afraid to make changes, afraid to be alone.

But she couldn't, wouldn't tell Samantha, who would never understand the choices Melissa had made. She couldn't expose herself to her sister's ridicule, the scorn she so feared she would receive.

She walked over to Jamie and picked him up, cradling him close to her as she fought to get her emotions under control. She turned back to her sister. "I'm not strong, Samantha, and there have been days in the past month when I wasn't sure how I was going to go on. And then I remember him—my baby—and I know I have to go on. I have to fight the charges against me, I have to put the past behind and go on."

"Oh, Melissa, don't you see? That is strength. Even when we were younger, I always admired the fact that you could move on. No matter what mean things Father said to you, you were able to take it, grow from it. You..."

Melissa held up a hand to silence her sister. "Samantha, please. I don't want to talk about this anymore."

"I'm sorry," Samantha immediately replied. "I don't mean to open old wounds. I just want you to know how much I love you and how much I admire you."

Tears misted Melissa's eyes. She nodded, then went into the kitchen to get Jamie a bottle. Melissa wished she could take comfort in Samantha's loving words, but her regard for Melissa was built on lies. Just as Melissa's entire marriage had been.

As she waited for the bottle to warm, she moved to the kitchen window and stared out into the backyard. Her redbird was there, his bright scarlet feathers vivid against the green leaves of the branch where he sat. His mate ate from the feeder, daintily picking out the oiled sunflower seeds they loved.

Melissa remembered the conversation she'd had with Dominic, about birds and second chances and love. Had she known then that she loved him? Not consciously. And she would have preferred her love for him to remain unrealized, unacknowledged to herself. It would have been so much less painful.

Melissa retrieved the bottle and began to feed Jamie. She looked up as Samantha came in and sat down across from her at the table. "You know, the night you told me you were pregnant and you and Bill were getting back together, I thought you were the luckiest woman in the world," Samantha said.

Melissa looked down at the baby, remembering the fragile hope that had flowed through her at that time—the hope that things would be different with Bill, that finally she would find the happiness and love that had been so elusive for all her life.

Now she'd found the kind of love she knew would make her happy—with Dominic. But even that was all wrong. Dominic had made it clear he had no intention of remaining in her life in any way. "So, when are you and Tyler going to give this little guy a cousin?" she asked, forcing a light tone to hide behind.

Samantha grinned. "We're working on it." Her smile fell away and she looked at her watch. "I wonder when we'll hear from Dominic."

"Hopefully as soon as he learns anything," Melissa replied, wondering how it was that the mere sound of his name could cause her heart to quicken, her pain to deepen. She brushed Jamie's forehead with her lips, her eyes filling as she thought of the sweetness of Dominic's touch, the pleasure she'd found in his arms.

"Missy? You okay?" Samantha asked softly.

Melissa nodded and drew a deep breath. "Sometimes life really delivers a kick in the pants, doesn't it?"

Samantha touched her arm. "I know it doesn't seem possible right now, but you will get through this. The charges against you will be dropped. Eventually the pain of Bill's death will ebb and your heart will heal."

Melissa nodded. "Samantha, I've gone and done something incredibly foolish." Melissa wouldn't, couldn't confess Bill's sins, but she could confess her own. "I've somehow managed to fall in love with Dominic."

Samantha dropped her hand and stared at Melissa. "What are you talking about?"

Melissa forced a small laugh. "I assumed my statement was pretty self-explanatory."

Samantha stood and ran a hand through her hair, her eyes radiating her bewilderment. She began to pace, her bewilderment turning to irritation. "I should have seen this coming," she finally said.

Melissa looked at her in surprise. "What do you mean?"

Samantha stopped pacing and shrugged. "Dominic is an attractive man, and you're particularly vulnerable now." Her eyes flashed darkly. "If he took advantage of you…"

"No, he didn't. He wouldn't." Melissa's cheeks flamed warm. There was no way she would share with her sister the fact that they had made love, had shared an intimacy like no other Melissa had ever experienced.

"But what about Bill?" Samantha's expression held confusion. "How could you just fall in love with Dominic so easily after being married to Bill for six years?" Samantha once again sat down across from Melissa.

Melissa stared back down at Jamie, wondering what she could say to her sister, how to explain the circumstances with Bill without revealing her hateful, horrid secret. "You know Bill and I were having problems, that we'd separated right before you came back to Wilford."

Samantha nodded. "But when you found out you were pregnant, I thought you worked through whatever problems you had."

"Oh, Samantha. I wanted my marriage to work more than anything. I wanted to prove that Father was wrong about Bill, that I'd been smart to marry him. But a year into the marriage, I knew I'd made the biggest mistake of my life."

"What do you mean?" Samantha stared at her intently, as if willing her to spill her secrets, probing into her soul to see what resided there.

Melissa shifted Jamie to her shoulder and rubbed his back while her mind worked to answer Samantha as clearly as possible without giving away the final piece of the puzzle. "At first, things were wonderful. But as time went by Bill started acting just like Father, always telling me how stupid I was, belittling everything I did, making me feel inadequate and ugly." She averted her gaze from Samantha, unable to look at her, and gave Jamison his bottle once again.

"Oh, Missy." Samantha grabbed her forearm and squeezed tightly. "Why did you stay with him?"

"I don't know." Melissa had asked herself that same question millions of times. Why had she stayed? "It felt normal...became comfortable." She forced a smile and shook her head ruefully. "I know it sounds crazy, but I knew what to expect from Bill and the thought of leaving him and trying to survive on my own terrified me."

"But you did finally leave him," Samantha said.

Melissa nodded. "Yeah, I realized I couldn't stay in the marriage just to prove something to Father. Then I discovered I was pregnant, and Bill made so many promises that, fool that I was, I believed him. He seemed so happy about the baby, I thought everything would change, but it didn't." She smiled down at her son. "I was going to leave Bill when I had Jamison. When I went to the hospital to give birth, I'd never intended to go back home with Bill. I was never going to give him the chance to treat the baby the way he treated me."

"Oh, Melissa, why didn't you ever tell me this before? Maybe I could have stopped you from going back to him when you found out you were pregnant."

Melissa smiled. God, she loved her sister. "Honey, as I recall, in those first few weeks of your return to Wilford, your life was pretty much a mess. You threw yourself into defending Dominic, you were trying to force Tyler out of the law firm, and you had a burning anger for Father that had you half blind to everything else."

Samantha laughed. "Yeah, funny how things work out. The case was dropped against Dominic, I married

Tyler and forgave Father for being less than what I needed while I was growing up.''

''And now it's my turn to get my life together. I've got a murder charge against me to beat, a son to raise and some time to heal.''

''We're going to be all right, aren't we?'' Samantha smiled, then looked at her watch. ''And I've got to get out of here.'' She stood reluctantly. ''Are you sure you're going to be okay here all alone?''

''Fine. I've got the security system and nobody knows Dominic isn't here. Trust me, if I was worried, I'd make you take me someplace else.'' She stood and walked with Samantha to the front door.

''Bye-bye, Jamie,'' Samantha said, chucking him beneath his chin, her reward a wide, happy grin. ''I'll call you the minute I get out of court,'' she told Melissa.

''I'll be here.''

Samantha started out the door, then turned back to Melissa. ''Bill… It was all verbal, right? I mean, he never hurt you physically?''

Melissa stared at her sister, saw the torment that darkened her eyes and the slight curl of her upper lip, as if the entire subject was rather distasteful. ''How could you even think such a thing?'' she hedged, unsurprised to see the obvious relief that swept across Samantha's face. ''Now, get out of here. You don't want to be late for court.''

When Samantha had gone, Melissa closed the door and reactivated the alarm system. She put Jamie down for a nap and thought about the lie she'd told. A lie of evasion, but a lie nevertheless.

Bill had been so good at hiding his physical abuse.

A shove or a slap instead of fists, which might have left marks. And if there were marks or bruises, they were always in areas not visible unless she was practically naked.

What was the point of revealing the horrible details of her marriage now? Bill was dead. There would be no more pain.

Except the pain when Dominic left.

Her heart ached as if he'd already packed his bags and disappeared from her life. When he'd left that morning, she'd somehow known it wasn't just physical distance separating them; he'd already begun to isolate himself from her emotionally.

And she was helpless to do anything but let him go. She loved him, but couldn't make him love her enough to want to bind himself to her. She was a bad bet, a tarnished penny, a widow with baggage. He deserved so much more.

If he could find the answers that would give her back her life, it would be enough. It had to be.

Chapter 14

Dominic's heart raced with the anticipation of answers. Betty Wardman, the postmistress, had been a veritable font of mostly useless information. He'd learned that Walter Craig, the old widower who lived on Main Street, had eyes for Gladys Canfield, the town librarian. He heard that Barbara Alden's son had written his name in the freshly poured concrete in front of the grocery store, and that Betty's daughter-in-law was nothing but a floozy who'd trapped her poor son into a loveless marriage.

Dominic had listened patiently as she'd rambled on about the town gossip until finally she'd returned to the original question he'd asked.

She'd told him Dano's Photography Studio had been run by Stewart Dano. He lived alone in a rented room over the drugstore.

Thankfully, Dano was a man who seemed to remember every name of every customer he'd ever photographed in the three years he'd been in business. A short talk with the photographer had produced some of the elusive answers Dominic had sought.

The woman in the old wedding photo was Susan Newsom. Stewart had no idea where Susan was, but her mother lived alone in a small house on the north side of town.

It was early afternoon when Dominic pulled up in front of the neat, white-painted house and checked the address against the one Stewart had given him. They were the same.

Getting out of the car, he pulled the old photograph from his pocket. He had no idea what to expect here, hoped to discover that the woman in the picture was happily married with a half-dozen kids. He knew that was what Melissa wanted to hear—among other things.

A petite, white-haired woman answered his knock. "Yes?" Faded blue eyes met his.

"I'm sorry to bother you, but I wonder if I could ask you a few questions."

She frowned with suspicion. "You aren't going to try and sell me anything, are you?"

"No, ma'am. Can you tell me, is the woman in this photo your daughter?" He held out the picture.

She took it from him, her hand trembling slightly. She looked at it, emitted a soft gasp, then closed her eyes. When she opened them, they were no longer soft blue, but rather flashing with fire. "Yes. Yes, that's my daughter…and the devil himself. Where did you get that picture?"

"We found it in a basement in Wilford. A…uh…a

friend of mine married this man. He was going by the name of Bill Newman. I'm doing a little checking into his background for my friend.''

Her forehead furrowed in a frown. ''You'd better come in, Mr...?''

''Dominic. Dominic Marcola.''

''And I'm MaryAnne Cook.'' She stepped aside to allow him entry. The living room was neat and tidy, although the furniture showed signs of age and wear. She directed him toward the sofa. ''Please, sit down. If I'm going to talk about that devil, I'd better be sitting.''

She eased herself into a chair across from him. ''I knew one day we'd hear about William Newsom again. Like a bad penny, I knew he'd turn up. What did you say he's calling himself nowadays?''

''Bill Newman. What can you tell me about him?''

Shaking her head, she seemed to grow smaller, her eyes once again fading with sadness. ''He destroyed us.'' The words, so stark, so simple, rang with an undeniable truth. ''He met my Susie just after she'd been involved in a car wreck and had received a big insurance settlement. She was only eighteen, so young and foolish.'' She clasped her trembling hands together in her lap. ''You see, the car accident left her with a scar on her face. She was so self-conscious about it, but she told me William made her forget all about it. He made her feel so important, so beautiful. Within weeks of meeting him they were talking about getting married.''

She shook her head. ''I told her to wait, to give it some time, but she wouldn't listen. She thought she was in love.''

Dominic realized this story was just like Melissa's. After years of living with an emotionally cold father, she'd been ripe to fall for a charismatic charmer. And apparently Susie, reeling from the scarring of a car accident, had been just as vulnerable.

"When did Susie and William divorce?" Dominic asked.

"Far as I know, they didn't." She looked at him curiously as he started in surprise. "I'd recommend that friend of yours check, 'cause I suspect she married a bigamist. And if she has any money at all to call her own, she'd better hide it because he'll take it all, just like he did Susie's."

"He took her insurance money?"

MaryAnne nodded. "Every last dime. And the last thing he did before he left here was take her mind."

Dominic frowned, wondering if he'd understood correctly. "'Took her mind'?"

MaryAnne shifted in the chair, one shaky hand reaching up to stroke across her brow. For a moment she was silent, her expression letting him know she was gathering unpleasant memories. "Almost immediately after the wedding, Susie became pregnant. I knew things weren't right between them, but Susie insisted everything was fine." MaryAnne's hand moved from her brow to her heart. "But a mother knows. A mother knows when things aren't right with her children."

Dominic could feel her pain. It shone from her tired eyes, radiated from her petite body. For a moment, it seemed to consume all the air in the room. He wasn't sure what to say, whether it was possible for him to say anything that would help ease some of her pain. He opted for silence.

She drew a deep breath and reclasped her hands in her lap. "When Susie was seven months pregnant, she and I were supposed to meet for lunch one day. I went to the restaurant and waited and waited. When an hour passed, I got worried. I went to William and Susie's house and found her at the foot of the basement stairs, bleeding and half-conscious. When she came to in the hospital, she insisted she'd slipped and fallen on her own." MaryAnne's eyes narrowed. "But I think he pushed her."

Dominic sat forward. "What makes you think so?"

"She always had red marks and bruises all over her. Oh, she tried to hide them, wore long sleeves and slacks. But he was beating her, I know he was."

Dominic thought of the bruises he'd seen on Melissa and a cold knot of certainty materialized in his chest. She'd been abused by her husband. The man who had promised to love and cherish her had hit her, hurt her.

As he thought of Melissa's silky flesh, the sweetness of her skin, then thought of Bill hitting her, slapping her, rage engulfed him. If Bill Newman hadn't already been dead, Dominic would have made him wish he was.

"Did you ask Bill, uh, William about the fall?" Dominic asked.

She shook her head. "We never saw him again. He'd taken all the money and disappeared. Susie lost the baby and the will to live. She crawled inside herself where nobody can reach her, where nobody will ever be able to hurt her again." For a long moment

MaryAnne stared off into space, as if lost to her surroundings.

"Where is she now?"

MaryAnne jerked her gaze back to him, as if surprised by his presence. "She's in a nursing home in Rainerville."

Dominic had passed through the small town of Rainerville on his way here to Canon Creek. Rainerville was about halfway between Canon Creek and Wilford. "What is her prognosis?"

MaryAnne shrugged, looking far older than she had when Dominic had first arrived. "Nobody seems to know. She has good days and bad ones. He broke her spirit, and if you're smart, you'll get your friend away from him before he breaks hers, too."

"William Newsom isn't going to hurt anyone anymore. He's dead."

MaryAnne stared at him for a long moment. "I may go to hell for this, but I'm glad. He destroyed my family. Susie's in a hospital, and her brother has been in mourning for her for years."

"Her brother?" Before she answered, Dominic knew. He hadn't made the connection until this moment. Dammit, he should have known. Signals should have gone off in his head the moment the old woman introduced herself. Neal Cook. Neal, who had taken a job with Bill six months ago. Neal, a man who must have hated Bill for devastating his family, breaking his sister.

"Neal and Susie were always close. But even he hasn't been able to pull her out of her deep depression."

An urgency filled Dominic. It pressed against his

chest, suffocating him as he realized it was quite possible that Neal Cook had killed Bill. And as he thought of the tall, lanky man he'd chased—the man who'd grabbed Jamison from the grocery cart—he realized that had also probably been Neal.

"Could I use your phone?" he asked. He had to let Melissa know. He had to tell her that Neal Cook was dangerous. He didn't know what on earth Neal would want with little Jamie, but he had to let Melissa know the man was a threat, to both her and her son.

Melissa stood at the back window, watching the birds eating at the feeders. She leaned closer as she saw the flash of red amid the green leaves. The male cardinal. He perched on a branch and Melissa knew if she opened her window, she would hear his distinctive song.

Where was the female? Melissa watched the trees carefully, seeking the less colorful mate of the scarlet male. Where was she? She had to be there...she had to be.

Pressing her forehead against the window, Melissa felt a kind of wild despair she knew in the back of her mind was inappropriate for the situation. But it was important to her that the redbirds be together, be a couple.

There. Melissa's heart fluttered as the female appeared and together the two birds alighted on the feeder. Melissa relaxed, soothed by the very rightness of the scene.

If only there was a like scene for her. She watched for a moment longer, then turned away from the window, her heart heavy as her thoughts turned to Dominic.

Dominic, who would walk out of her life when he got home. He would take her heart with him, and she would do nothing to stop him from leaving. He deserved more than her, better than her.

Feeling the press of tears close to the surface of her eyes, she shook her head to dispel them, then went to the oven to check on the cake she had baking.

After Samantha had left and Jamison had gone down for his nap, she'd decided to bake a chocolate cake. Bill had hated chocolate. Looking into the oven, Melissa decided another three or four minutes and it would be done.

She'd just set the timer when the doorbell rang. She opened one of the kitchen drawers and took out the pistol Dominic had insisted she keep with her while he was gone. It was surprisingly lightweight and warm to her touch.

She tucked it into the pocket of the apron she wore and wondered if she would be able to actually use it. Could she shoot someone? As she thought of her baby soundly sleeping in his crib, she knew she could. If it came to protecting him—or herself—she could pull the trigger.

She hurried to the front door and peered out the peephole, instantly recognizing Neal Cook. She frowned, trying to decide what to do. He was probably here for another piece of vent pipe or some other spare part in the basement. She had the gun. Surely that would keep her safe from harm if Neal intended any.

She punched off the security and opened the door. "Hi, Neal, what can we do for you?"

"I'm sorry to bother, you, Mrs. Newman. Sam sent me over for some more vent. We're doing a job over at the Wellsleys', and we're short a twelve-inch length."

She nodded and opened the door to allow him inside. She pointed toward the basement door, then slid her hand into the apron, touching the gun reassuringly. "You can go on down and get what you need," she said.

As he walked to the basement door, she relaxed somewhat. He disappeared down the stairs just as the oven timer dinged. Returning to the kitchen, Melissa told herself to relax. She couldn't afford to give way to paranoia.

She pulled the cake out of the oven, pleased with the chocolate scent that wafted into the air. She inverted the cake onto a cooling rack, then went back to the top of the basement stairs.

"Neal? Did you find what you need?"

No answer. Not a sound floated up the stairs. She stood for another moment, listening. Still no indication that Neal was in the basement. She turned and saw the front door standing partway open. Apparently Neal had found what he'd come for and left. She closed the door and reset the alarm system, then went back into the kitchen.

After replacing the gun to the drawer, she went to the window. She stood looking out, thinking of her years with Bill, thinking of her nights with Dominic. In the space of two nights, of five weeks of sharing days, Dominic had managed to touch places in her heart she'd never offered to Bill.

What she'd believed to be love at eighteen years of age with Bill had been nothing more than infatuation for the first man who'd treated her with something other than the usual coldness and censure she'd received from her father. Bill had first offered her escape, then had trapped her in his prison, chipping away at her self-esteem, making her afraid of everything and everyone, making her feel utterly incompetent.

Dominic was different. And what she felt for him was like nothing she'd ever felt before. It was a love deep enough to let him go.

Like the parakeet she'd released, she knew she had to let Dominic walk out of her life, had to allow him the opportunity to find love with another woman, a better woman. One who didn't face murder charges, one who didn't have a baby from another man, a woman who had no scars on her soul.

She jumped as the phone rang. She answered, then closed her eyes as Dominic's voice filled the line. "Everything okay there?" he asked.

"Fine. What about with you? Have you found out anything?"

"Plenty." The single word was filled with an urgency that instantly set Melissa's nerves on alert.

"What?" She gripped the phone cord tightly.

"I can't go into it all right now, but I think I know who killed Bill."

"Who?" Melissa held her breath.

"Neal Cook."

The name shot through Melissa like an arrow, leav-

ing an open wound of fear. "But—but he was just
here. He came to get some vent pipe."

"Where's Jamie?"

The wound of fear bled terror. Melissa dropped the
phone receiver and raced down the hallway toward
the nursery. Please. Let him be there. Let him be
sleeping.... Safe...let him be safe.

She tore into the room and over to the crib. Empty.
"Oh, God, no!" The protest ripped her throat raw as
she grabbed up the blanket that had covered Jamie
when she'd put him down for his nap.

She stumbled from the nursery, suffocating, gasping for air as she fought against hysteria. Her stomach
ached, deep inside. Emptiness. Fear. Light-
headedness. Nausea. She felt as if she were swimming
against the tide when she staggered toward the
kitchen where the phone dangled from the wall.

She grabbed up the receiver. "He's gone, Dominic.
God help me. He's gone!" She broke into sobs.

Chapter 15

Dominic was playing a hunch. As he sped toward Rainerville, he prayed he was right, for a little boy's life hung in the balance. If he'd had any doubts before about how he felt about Jamie, the thundering of his heart answered those questions now.

He loved the child. He loved Jamie as if he were his own. Dominic had delivered Jamie into the world. For the past five weeks he'd held the baby, fed him and whispered to him of dreams. He'd watched Jamie gain weight, smile, had felt the baby's little fingers close around his thumb.

And in Dominic's heart was where his fear thundered. Fear that he might play the wrong hunch, that he might be wrong in trying to anticipate what Neal intended to do with Jamie, and the end result would be precious time lost. At this thought, fear rose up in his throat, bringing with it a bad taste.

What if he'd guessed wrong? What if Neal intended to exact his final revenge on Bill by hurting his child? Dominic tightened his grip on the steering wheel, refusing to entertain such a scenario.

He pressed on the accelerator, unmindful of the fifty-five-mile-an-hour speed limit. According to Melissa, Neal only had a short head start. If, indeed, as Dominic suspected, he was going to the Rainerville Nursing Home, then Dominic intended to be there when Neal arrived.

He'd instructed Melissa to call Detective Mawlins and have him meet Dominic at the nursing home. Although Rainerville was out of Mawlins's jurisdiction, Dominic wanted the detective there when Dominic confronted Neal about Bill's death.

Melissa. Her name echoed in every chamber of his heart. What she must be going through. She'd sounded as if she'd shattered into a million pieces when she'd cried into the phone that her baby was gone.

It had taken Dominic several precious moments to calm her down enough to instruct her what to do. She'd seemed to sense that now was not the time to break down. She'd swallowed her sobs and become almost frighteningly calm. The core of strength Dominic had always known she possessed had surfaced.

He loved her. He couldn't deny what was in his heart. But he would not take a chance again on love. Abigail had taught him well. The fact that Melissa had held secret Bill's abuse, that she'd refused to trust Dominic with that secret, only made him that much more determined to steer clear of thinking of any future with her. Never again would he contemplate a future with a woman who kept secrets. He wouldn't...couldn't put himself through it again.

He slowed as he passed a sign that indicated Rainerville was three miles ahead. He didn't have directions to the nursing home, but hoped there would be a sign or something to direct him there.

Sure enough, another mile ahead he spied a small sign for the nursing home that pointed down a narrow asphalt road. He turned and sped up again, his heart resuming a thudding rhythm of fear.

He now had the information that would exonerate Melissa of the murder charges. He could give her back her life, but what kind of a life would that be without her son?

He hoped he wasn't wrong about this. He prayed that in second-guessing Neal he'd made the right guess. If he was wrong... He shook his head, refusing to finish the thought.

As he drove over a small rise in the landscape, the nursing home came into view. The long, sprawling one-story building nestled into the green valley like a jewel set amid velvet. The late-afternoon sun played on the beige building, making it appear as if it had been sprinkled with gold dust.

He slowed once again to turn into the gates. Instantly he spied a blue pickup he recognized as Neal's. "Damn!" He slammed his palm against the steering wheel. He'd hoped to get here before Neal, head the man off before he could get inside.

He parked his car on the opposite side of the lot, where he could see Neal's truck but didn't think Neal would notice him if he came out of the nursing home.

Shutting off the engine, Dominic frowned. He

didn't know what to do, but as an ex-cop, he knew the danger of confronting a killer alone. And although he had no absolute proof, he knew Neal was a killer. He knew with a cop's instincts, with a man's common sense, that it had been Neal who had sneaked into Melissa's home and viciously stabbed Bill to death.

He thought of all those agonizing times when he'd believed Melissa responsible. The strange thing was, he would have been able to understand if she had been guilty. After hearing about the kind of man Bill Newman had been, Dominic ached as he thought of what Melissa must have endured over the years of her marriage.

A squeal of tires interrupted his thoughts. He turned to see Melissa's car roaring through the parking lot. She must have driven as fast or faster than he had to arrive here so quickly, he thought. With another squeal, she brought the car to a halt and jumped out of the driver's seat.

Dominic tore out of his car and grabbed Melissa's arm before she could dash through the nursing-home front door. "Where is he? Where's Jamie?" Her eyes were wide, nearly black, and her face was devoid of all color.

"Come to my car." Dominic took her arm and tried to gently guide her away from the building.

She jerked her arm from his grasp. "Just tell me where he is. I've got to get him."

He grabbed her by the shoulders, felt her uncontrollable trembling, knew she was on the verge of losing all rational thought. "Melissa, you can't just barge in there. We don't know what room Neal is in, and we don't know what his state of mind is." He spoke firmly, trying to penetrate her raging maternal instinct to protect her child and make her understand how careful they had to be. "Now, come back to my car and let's figure out what we need to do."

She looked at him, her eyes begging him to do something, to save her son. Some of the wildness dissipated from her gaze and the energy that had vibrated through her faded away. She allowed him to lead her to his car.

"Did you call Mawlins?" he asked once they were seated in the car.

She nodded. "I'm not sure how much sense I made, but he agreed to meet us here." Once again she gazed at Dominic, a wealth of pain in her eyes. "We have to do something!" she cried as she looked at the building. "We can't just sit here."

"We have to stay here," Dominic told her. "Melissa, we've got to wait for Mawlins. At this point anything we might do could make a bad situation worse. If you go in there, there's no way I can guarantee your safety. For all we know, Neal wanted you dead along with Bill."

Her eyes widened and a shuddery sigh escaped from her. "Did you see Jamie? Was he all right?"

How Dominic wished he could set her fears to rest. He considered lying, telling her he'd seen Neal go into the building and Jamie had been safe. But they'd come too far in their relationship to opt for anything except the absolute truth. "I got here too late to see Neal go in. But his truck is here and I know he's inside with Jamie."

She drew a deep breath, a hint of color faintly

brushing her cheeks. "What's he doing here? Why did he take Jamie?"

"His sister, Susan, was the woman in the wedding photograph we found in your basement. She lives here."

"What?" She looked at him in surprise. "Why? What's wrong with her?"

Dominic took Melissa's trembling hand in his and explained to her what he had learned from Susan's mother. He told her about the suspicions of Bill's abuse and the fall down the stairs that had resulted in Susan's miscarriage.

Melissa's eyes filled with tears as he spoke—tears he knew were not for herself, but for the woman who'd been destroyed by Bill. Her tears for Susan only made Dominic love her more.

"So, you think it's possible Neal took Jamie in some strange desire to replace the baby Susan lost?" Melissa asked when Dominic was finished.

Dominic shrugged. "It makes a crazy kind of sense, doesn't it?"

"I suppose. As much as any of this makes sense." Anxiously she looked toward the building once again. "You—you don't think he'll hurt Jamie?"

Dominic hesitated before answering. "I don't think he will." He frowned thoughtfully, then added, "But, Melissa, the man is obviously unstable. We can't take anything for granted."

She nodded, tears sparkling on the tips of her lashes. Dominic recognized the tight rein she held on her control—so tight it threatened to snap at any moment. He pulled her into his arms. "Melissa, you've been so strong through all of this. Just hang on a little while longer.''

She trembled in his arms and he wished he'd met her years ago, before Abigail, before Bill, when they'd both been young and innocent and untainted by their life experiences. But there was no way to go back. They could only go forward, and Dominic prayed that Neal wouldn't snap and harm the baby that both he and Melissa loved.

Seconds passed—long, agonizing seconds that turned into minutes. And with each minute that passed, Melissa's despair increased.

Although the inactivity threatened to steal her sanity, she knew the foolishness of rushing into an unknown situation where her son's life might be jeopardized. Unable to do anything else, she clung to Dominic, needing his strength, drawing from it to get herself through this.

''There are so many things about all this I don't understand,'' Melissa said, swallowing the hysteria that was only a heartbeat away. ''If Neal was Bill's brother-in-law, then why did Bill hire him? And why didn't Neal kill him sooner?''

''I don't know. Hopefully we'll get those answers before it's all over.''

''What if Mawlins doesn't come?'' she asked, finally moving out of Dominic's embrace.

''He'll come.'' Dominic's voice was strong with assurance. ''He'll come because he'll be afraid he'll miss out on something if he doesn't.''

As if summoned by Dominic's words, Mawlins drove through the gates and into the parking area.

Both Dominic and Melissa stepped out of Dominic's car and waved to the detective, who pulled up next to where they stood.

"This better not be some damned wild-goose chase," he said as he got out of his car. "If it is, we waste time finding the baby."

"It's not," Dominic replied. As he filled Mawlins in on what he'd discovered about Neal and Susan Cook and Bill, Melissa stood off to one side. She didn't want to hear it all again—how Bill had destroyed not just one person, but apparently an entire family with his lies and deceit, his abuse and brutality.

At that moment one of the double glass doors swung open and a woman in a nurse's uniform emerged. The thin, distant wail of a child drifted out along with her. Not any child. Jamie. The sound caused Melissa's womb to ache and a rush of adrenaline to sweep through her.

She didn't care what the consequences were to herself, she had to get to her child. Maternal instinct propelled her forward.

She entered the building, vaguely aware of Dominic shouting her name, but she didn't stop, didn't even hesitate. Her baby was crying, frightened, and she had to get to him.

She found herself in a large lobby with two hallways veering off in opposite directions. She paused only a moment, listening for the sound that would lead her. A faint cry came from the hallway on the right. Like a sea siren's song, it pulled her down the corridor with no other thought than to reach it, reach him.

Passing several rooms, she remained focused on the

cry, only vaguely aware of the murmur of voices drifting from the rooms she passed.

At least he's alive, she thought. He's alive and well enough to cry. She came to a closed door and knew that beyond it was her son—and the man who'd taken him.

For the first time since she'd heard Jamie's sobs, she hesitated. Surely Neal wasn't a monster. Surely nothing she could do would provoke him to hurt the baby. A vision of Bill lying on the bed filled her mind. Over twenty stab wounds. Raw fear shimmied up her spine. It had been the work of a monster.

She leaned against the wall just outside the closed door, drawing in deep breaths, trying to think, trying to decide what to do.

For six long years Bill had abused her. She'd taken the slaps, the pinches, the punches. And she'd felt her self-esteem being chipped away with each hateful, hurtful word he said. She'd taken it because she hadn't known she had choices, that she had power over her own life.

It had been Jamie who had given her the strength to decide to leave Bill. It had been her son who'd given her the courage to carry on despite facing murder charges. There was no way she could allow her baby to be used as a pawn in Neal's revenge against Bill. If he wanted his revenge, she would offer herself.

Her decision made, she turned the doorknob and slowly opened the door. The first thing she saw was a drawn, pale young woman in a hospital bed. She instantly recognized her as the woman in the wedding photograph.

Susan. Her eyes were closed, her face as pale as the bedsheets. Someone had obviously tried to fix her up, as her long blond hair looked freshly washed and brushed and a blue barrette held back one side.

Melissa swung the door wider. Neal saw her at the same time she saw him. He sat on a chair, with Jamie tucked into the crook of one of his arms. Neal's eyes widened in surprise and he showed her the gun he held in his other hand...a gun pointed at her baby's head.

"What are you doing here?" he asked, his voice rising unevenly.

"I've come for my baby." Melissa didn't move, was afraid to move while he had the gun, which was now at Jamie's head.

"No. He's for Susie. He's going to make Susie better."

Melissa took a step closer, then froze as Neal pressed the tip of the barrel against her son's head. "Don't come any closer. I don't want to have to hurt him," Neal warned.

"Neal, please." She studied his face, then noted the trembling of the hand that held the gun. Surely there was still some semblance of a rational human being beneath his rage. He obviously cared deeply about his sister and Melissa knew it was vital she touch whatever core of goodness in him that had not been destroyed by Bill.

"He's crying, Neal. He wants me. He wants his mother," Melissa said softly.

"No. Susie is going to be his mother!" Neal exclaimed. "He's going to make her well. He's *got* to make her well!'' Neal's voice trembled with emotion, but the gun didn't waver.

Holding her breath, hoping his tenuous grip on reality would hold, Melissa stepped up to the side of Susan's bed. She touched a strand of Susan's shiny blond hair. ''You must love her very much.''

''Don't touch her!'' Neal yelled, the gun swerving away from Jamie and pointing at Melissa. Melissa nearly sagged to her knees in relief. She would rather be the target than have the gun aimed at Jamie.

Melissa withdrew her hand from Susan's hair. ''I wouldn't hurt her, Neal.''

''But *he* did. He shattered her. He made her love him, then he stole her money and ruined her life.'' Tears filled Neal's eyes as he stared at his sister.

''And so you killed him, didn't you? You killed Bill.''

Neal nodded, the tears dissipating as his eyes took on an icy hardness. ''He needed to die for what he did. It took me a long time to hunt him down. He thought he was so smart, changing his name. But that didn't stop me from finding him. Just took me a little longer, that's all.''

''Why didn't you just kill him and leave town? Why work for him?'' Melissa demanded, wanting answers—and wanting to keep him talking until Dominic and Detective Mawlins could figure out a way to get both her and Jamie out of here safely.

''Initially, that was my plan.'' His gaze flickered to Jamie, who'd stopped crying, but squirmed in the cradle of his arm. ''Then I heard you were pregnant with his baby, and I knew maybe it would help Susie.'' He frowned, his gaze lingering for a moment on his sister, who had not moved or opened her eyes since Melissa had entered the room. "I told Bill I wanted a job, that if he didn't give me one I'd tell you and the authorities that he was a bigamist. Then I waited for the right time to kill him."

He looked at Melissa again. "You should thank me. I got rid of him before he could break you. He intended to stay with you until you got your inheritance, then he was going to take your money and run. He had a new victim in his sights."

"Grace Harrison."

He nodded and once again his gaze drifted to his sister. "I was her big brother. I promised her I'd always take care of her." His eyes teared and his voice shook with feeling. "When we were young, she was always tagging along with me, telling me I was her protector. But I couldn't protect her from him." Jamie began to cry, as if sensitive to the emotional tension in the room.

"Neal, just give me my baby. Let me have my son," she pleaded and took several steps forward, then paused. "He needs me. Susan can't take care of him."

"No, I told you he's going to make her well." Neal sobbed, his voice rising to be heard above Jamie's cries.

"That's too big a burden to place on a baby," Melissa protested, tears running down her cheeks. "He can't help anybody. He's so little he can't even help himself."

She took another step forward, so close to him now, she could smell his fear and the grief that clung to him. "It's over, Neal. Put down your gun and let me have my son."

"No!" The gun trembled in his hand, but remained pointed at her. "Don't come any closer. I...I don't want to hurt you. I never wanted to hurt anyone but William."

Jamie's wails rose in intensity, his little face puckered up and red. This is truly hell, Melissa thought. Seeing your child in need...afraid... Hearing his cries and being unable to hold him, soothe him.

Neal's shoulders shook with sobs as tears tracked down his cheeks, adding to the clamor of Jamie's cries. "I just wanted to help her," Neal said, the words torn from his throat with anguish.

"This isn't the way," Melissa replied. She licked her lips, tasting the salt of her own tears, unsure whom she cried for—the squalling baby, the tormented man, or the silent woman in the bed. And the man who'd caused it all was probably laughing in hell.

At that moment, above the noise, the sound of sirens broke through. Neal half rose, his gaze focusing out the window. Dominic burst through the doorway, past Melissa and toward Neal.

The gun exploded. Melissa screamed.

Chapter 16

The gunshot shattered the window and for a moment deafened Melissa. She watched in horror as Dominic knocked the gun from Neal's grasp and it went spinning across the tiled floor and disappeared beneath the bed.

For a moment the two men stared at each other, Dominic obviously afraid of harming Jamie, and Neal using the baby as a shield.

As the last echo of the gunshot blast left her ears, Jamie's cries took its place. Beneath the baby's sobs, she could hear the sound of Dominic's uneven breathing...or was it her own?

"It's over, Neal," Dominic said, his voice calm. "The police are waiting for you outside. Why don't you give me the baby and let's call it a day."

Neal seemed to fold into himself, grow small and confused. He looked at his sister, then down at the crying baby in his arms. "I never meant to hurt him," he said softly. "I just...I just had to do something to try to help."

"We know that," Dominic said, his voice holding no judgment, no censure.

Melissa held her breath as Neal once again looked at Susan. As Neal held Jamie out to Dominic, a wrenching sob escaped her. The moment Neal no longer held the baby, Detective Mawlins and two other uniformed officers rushed into the room. As they handcuffed Neal, Dominic placed Jamie in Melissa's arms.

She hugged him to her heart, breathing in the sweet baby scent of him as tears of relief flowed down her cheeks. He nestled against her, his cries changing to soft whimpers, then ceasing as if the only thing he'd wanted in the world was his mother's arms.

As she continued to hug Jamie, Neal was led away. "Come on, let's get out of here," Dominic said to her.

She shook her head. "Give me just a minute, okay?" With Jamie in her arms, she moved to the side of Susan's bed.

Susan's eyes were shut, but Melissa sensed a tension in her, an awareness belied by her closed eyes. An abiding sadness swept through Melissa as she gazed at the pretty young woman. Bill's abuse of her had been horrid, but the true tragedy was that instead of becoming a survivor, Susan had totally succumbed to being a victim.

Melissa looked at Susan's hand atop the sheet, recognizing the plain gold band that adorned her ring finger. It was an exact replica of the one in Melissa's drawer at home. Melissa had stopped wearing hers during her pregnancy because her fingers had often swelled, and hadn't put it back on after Bill's death.

She took Susan's hand in hers, wishing she could pass on some of her strength to the broken woman, wanting to somehow connect on the basis of the sisterhood they had shared, both as wives of Bill, and as women who'd known abusive love.

"I'm sorry," she whispered. "I'm sorry you've been hurt. Hopefully some day you'll be able to live again and not be afraid." There were so many things Melissa wanted to say. She wanted to tell Susan that if she continued to surrender, Bill would have won. She wanted to tell Susan that there was hope—hope for the future, hope for happiness. But, she was aware of Dominic waiting for her and in any case, wasn't sure Susan would—or could—hear.

She started to pull her hand away, then gasped softly as Susan's hand squeezed hers. Brief, but distinctive and firm, the connection lasted only a moment, then her hand was once again lax in Melissa's.

As Melissa left the room, a burst of optimism soared through her. Susan's spirit was not completely gone. It was merely hidden, healing. Hopefully, after time and with therapy, she would go on to lead a happy, fulfilled life.

Dominic was silent as he led her out of the building and into the bright sunshine of the late afternoon. The optimism that had filled Melissa only moments before seeped away.

It was over. The police had the man who'd murdered Bill. She and Jamie were safe, and she was glad for that. Now there was no reason for Dominic to stay in her house, remain in her life, and this thought filled her with a renewed despair.

He knows, she thought. He knows the kind of man Bill was, the kind of marriage we had. Dominic couldn't help but know that she'd been abused, and she wondered if that knowledge was what caused the shadows of distance in his eyes.

"The infant seat is in my car," Dominic told her. "Why don't you and Jamie drive home with me, and Mawlins can get an officer to follow with your car?"

Before she could reply, Detective Mawlins came over to where they stood. Melissa tensed, making Jamie squirm in protest at her tight hold on him. Dominic moved closer to her, as if to protect her from whatever the detective might have to say.

The big man plunged his hands into his pockets and looked decidedly uncomfortable. "I owe you an apology," he said without preamble. He withdrew his hands from his pockets and shifted his weight from one foot to the other. "I've got no excuses except my own bullheadedness. Every lead I had pointed to you. I'll call the D.A., make arrangements for the charges to be dropped."

Melissa nodded and Mawlins looked at Dominic. "Nice work, Marcola." He held his hand out to Dominic, who, after a moment of hesitation, shook it.

As Dominic made arrangements with Mawlins for an officer to drive Melissa's car back home, she strapped Jamie into the infant seat in the back of Dominic's car, then got into the passenger seat.

Her gaze automatically went to Dominic, her heart tearing in half. She'd known he would leave. But somehow she wished he'd never learned of Bill's abuse. She hadn't wanted him to go with the knowledge of her weakness, her stupidity—the character flaws she believed had kept her in the relationship with Bill.

She wished he was leaving with the memory of a passionate, strong woman instead of a woman who'd compromised herself because she was too much a coward to break free.

It wasn't until they were on their way back to Wilford that Melissa realized she *wanted* to tell Dominic about her life with Bill, *wanted* somehow to explain the choices she'd made.

"He didn't hit me the first year we were married."

"You don't have to do this. You don't owe me any explanations," Dominic replied, his gaze fixed on the road ahead.

"But I want to," she protested. She needed to talk about it with somebody, purge herself of the memories. She looked out the window, unable to gaze at him while she dredged up the past.

She closed her eyes, remembering those first months of her marriage. "The first couple of months with Bill were good ones. He fulfilled the fantasies I'd had about love, but at the same time he subtly began to chip away at what little self-esteem growing up with my father had left me."

She squeezed her eyes more tightly closed, fighting the tears that threatened as she remembered how desperate she'd been to please Bill, how innocently vulnerable she'd been to his machinations for power and control. "I was desperate to make the marriage work, terrified that Bill would leave me because I wasn't good enough at cleaning or cooking. God, he played me like a fiddle. He knew which buttons to push, what fears to exploit, what weaknesses to manipulate in order to keep me constantly on guard and afraid. By the time he actually hit me, I'd lost the ability to think, to believe that I could get away.''

''I don't want to hear any more,'' Dominic interrupted her, his voice filled with tension.

She looked at him, saw the rigid set of his jaw and the way his hands gripped the steering wheel. Disgust. That had to be what he was feeling. She disgusted him in having been so weak, and so willing a participant in such a dysfunctional relationship.

Once again she stared out the window, a hollow ache filling her heart. She should have known better than to try to explain, than to try to justify things to a man like Dominic. People who were well-adjusted, who had never had their self-esteem attacked, couldn't understand. In truth, Melissa wasn't sure she would ever understand all the forces at work that had kept her helpless to escape Bill.

She closed her eyes, again trying to contain the tears that burned hot behind her eyelids. She'd been a fool to try to explain it. Dominic's reaction was exactly the reason why she'd kept her secret for as long as she had—because in her heart she'd always known that somehow she was as much at fault as Bill had been.

Silence filled the car for the duration of the drive home. Dominic didn't attempt to breach the tension, and Melissa saw his silence as an indication of his final withdrawal from her.

She didn't know why it hurt so much. She'd expected it. Despite their lovemaking, she'd had no il-

lusions about a future with him. He'd never pretended
there was any hope; he'd made it clear he didn't even
want to be Jamie's godfather. And yet, her heart had
hoped. And the penalty for unrealized hope was pain.

She was almost grateful to get home. She wanted
him packed and gone quickly; didn't want the pain to
linger any longer than necessary.

"I'll just get my things together," he said as she
unlocked the door and they entered the house. She
nodded, and carried Jamie to the nursery.

There, she changed his diaper and began to put him
into a fresh outfit. He cooed and smiled, earlier tears
dried, previous fears forgotten. Oh, how she wished
she had the ability to forget the sensation of being
held in Dominic's arms, the hot taste of his lips
against hers. How she wished she could forget the
deep, husky sound of his laughter, the gentleness he'd
shown in caring for her son.

As she changed Jamie's clothes, she was aware of
the sounds of Dominic packing in the next room.
Each scrape of a hanger against the closet rod re-
sounded in the empty chambers of her heart.

When Jamie was dressed, she picked him up and
grabbed his infant seat. The house felt claustrophobic.
She didn't want to sit in here and listen to the sounds
of her heart breaking.

Carrying Jamie in his seat, she went out the back
door, seeking refuge where she'd often run to escape
Bill's scathing remarks and hurtful words.

Sitting down amid the profusion of flowers, she
placed Jamie next to her on the concrete bench. The
sun was setting, bathing the area in the warm golden

hues of twilight. The stillness of the air made the flowers' bouquet especially sweet and strong.

Birds sang their sweet, final lullabies before night claimed what was left of the day. Melissa closed her eyes, seeking the peace this place had always brought to her. But peace remained elusive.

She should be happy. At least she'd been cleared of the murder charges. There would be no prison term for her, no time away from her precious son. She was enjoying a renewed close relationship with her sister, and Bill could never hurt her again. She should be delirious. Her future stretched out before her, calm and peaceful— And achingly lonely.

Her thoughts suddenly turned to Susan. Susan had curled into isolation, choosing to be alone rather than risk being hurt again. She'd lost her will to live, abandoned all hope for a future.

Melissa couldn't do that. To give in to a despair so profound it obliterated the possibility of a happy future, would be the ultimate win for Bill.

She tilted her head as she heard the sweet redbird's song. She saw the flash of scarlet darting from tree to tree, the male followed by his mate. She remembered her conversation with Dominic about second chances, and her utter belief in them.

Footsteps sounded behind her and she turned to see Dominic approaching, his suitcase in hand. The sight of the suitcase created a renewed twist of pain in her heart.

He dropped the case and sat down next to her. She closed her eyes against the assault of his physical nearness, trying to ignore the spicy scent of him, the warmth of his body close to hers.

"I thought I'd find you back here," he said.

She looked at him, forced a smile, and tried to ignore the way slanted rays of the setting sun sharpened the handsome lines of his face, highlighted the rich color of his hair "So, what are your plans now that you're finished here?" I love you, her heart cried. I love you and you're walking out of my life.

For a moment, as he gazed at her consideringly, she wondered if her thoughts had somehow escaped from her lips. "I'm not sure," he answered. "I'm thinking about trying to get my job back on the police force."

"Oh, Dominic, that's wonderful. They'll be lucky to have you back on the force." Her heart was so full of her love for him, she suddenly knew that she had to tell him.

It didn't matter if he didn't love her back. It didn't matter if there would never be a future for them. For her to keep her feelings inside, for her to be afraid to voice them, made her like Susan, made Bill win once again.

"Dominic." She waited until he was looking at her. "I love you." The words escaped from her with a sigh of release. His eyes widened, his jaw dropped as if she'd shocked him. "I'm not telling you this because I expect anything from you. I just couldn't let you leave here without telling you."

"Melissa..." He averted his gaze from her and raked a hand through his hair. "Maybe you think what you feel is love. You've gone through a tough time, and you've had to face some terrible things since Bill's death. You were alone and I was around. It's probably gratitude."

Melissa stared at him. Anger began as a small burning in her stomach, a fire that swiftly ignited out of control. She stood, her body trembling from the force of her anger. "How dare you," she said, her voice low and husky with emotion. "How dare you tell me what I feel."

She walked several feet away, then turned back to face him. "For the first eighteen years of my life, my father told me how I felt and what to think. Then I married Bill and he became the keeper of my thoughts and feelings." Tears pressed at her eyes, tears not because she knew he didn't love her, but because he'd so frivolously discounted the validity of what she felt. "I'll never allow that again. I won't allow you to diminish what I feel for you, to somehow turn it into a case of insignificant gratitude."

He still had a stunned look on his face, as if she were somehow speaking a foreign language he didn't quite understand. "I love you," she repeated. "And nothing you say will change that. I understand that you can't return those feelings for me, that you can't get past the disgust you feel about me and my relationship with Bill. I felt your disappointment, your revulsion in the car while I was talking to you about my marriage. I just—I just had to tell you how I felt about you before you left. It's a gift, no strings attached. You made me hope again. You made me dream again. And for that, I am grateful."

She turned away, unable to stop the tears, and unwilling to share them with him. She didn't want his pity, didn't want him to feel in any way responsible for her.

* * *

Dominic stared at her back, so many emotions flooding him it was difficult to sort through them all. The confusing emotions had begun in the car, while he'd listened to her talk about her marriage to Bill. The confusion had continued while he'd packed, his thoughts jumping from Melissa to Abigail and back again.

But as he heard Melissa talk about him feeling disgust for her, that confusion cleared. He stood, went over to her and placed his hands on her shoulders. "Melissa." He turned her around to face him. "What you thought was my revulsion was anger. Anger at the man who hurt you, who owned you as if you were a possession instead of a wife. And I was angry because you didn't trust me enough to tell me the truth about your relationship with Bill. That despite everything we'd shared, you had kept this a secret."

"I was afraid to tell. Afraid people would think it was my fault, that I was stupid, that I was weak."

"Oh, Melissa." He framed her face with his hands, his thumbs caressing the silky skin of her cheeks. "You were a victim, Melissa. You have no reason to feel ashamed. And as far as being weak—you are the strongest woman I know. When you ran into that hospital room and faced Neal, I thought my heart had stopped." He fought a residual shudder of fear as he thought of her rushing into that room, braving Neal and his gun.

"I couldn't let him hurt Jamie. No matter what, I couldn't let that happen," she replied.

Dominic nodded and dropped his hands from her face. "Come, sit back down. I need to tell you something."

She looked at him curiously, but did as he asked. When they were once again seated beside Jamie on the concrete bench, Dominic drew a deep breath for courage; he was delving into uncharted waters, into facts he'd denied to himself for too long.

"I led you to believe that I loved Abigail. And I thought I did until I heard you talking about your relationship with Bill. Then I suddenly realized it wasn't love, it was a sick kind of dysfunctional co-dependency."

Melissa looked at him in shocked surprise. "What do you mean?"

For a moment the words stuck inside him, and he knew what he felt was the same sort of sick dread in confessing weakness that had kept Melissa silent about her abuse for so long. He knew that in telling her what he was about to reveal, he would be diminished in her eyes. But if nothing else, perhaps his confession would help heal the scars she carried on her heart.

He stared at the rosebushes, unable to talk about his relationship with Abigail while looking at Melissa. "In the very beginning, I thought Abigail's ambition was cute, and the fact that I knew she had secrets from me was intriguing. I knew she was seeing other men, seeking one who had enough money to keep her in the way she wanted to become accustomed. But I thought if I loved her enough...that love alone would be enough."

He paused for a moment, pressure tight in his chest as he remembered how manipulated he'd been, how willing he'd been to settle for any little piece Abigail would give of herself to him. "She'd tell me she loved me, but that she'd never live on a policeman's pay. She ridiculed my work as a cop, made me wonder if maybe something was wrong with me. She pushed me away, then pulled me back, and like a puppet, I danced to her tune.''

He finally turned and looked at Melissa. ''How can I feel disgust for you because you lost yourself to Bill when I did the same thing with Abigail? I settled for less than I wanted, less than I was worth, because the alternative was to be alone.''

She smiled—a sad, bittersweet smile that ripped at his heart. ''We're quite a pair, aren't we? We've both had terrific experience in the wrong kind of loving. Love isn't supposed to hurt. It's not supposed to steal your power. There's no shame in being a victim. The shame comes in when you begin to believe you deserve the abuse.''

She stood and picked up Jamie from his seat. ''This little guy still needs a godfather. I want him to have somebody in his life who is strong and good, who will teach him about love and ethics, about dignity and charity. Dominic, no matter what you feel for me, I'm going to ask you one last time. Will you be a godfather to my son?''

Emotion, intense and thick, once again pressed against his chest. She looked so beautiful, standing before him with the waning sunlight dancing on her. Jamie's blue eyes gazed at him solemnly, then a smile lifted the corners of his lips—a beguiling smile that shot straight to Dominic's heart.

When had it happened? When had this lovely, passionate, giving woman and her baby managed to banish all the shadows from his heart? When had she given him back the possibility of his dreams?

As he looked at the woman and child before him, he realized the dreams he'd believed had died with Abigail hadn't died at all. They'd just been buried, waiting for a special woman to free them.

Those dreams exploded now in his head. A little boy, holding his hand as the child learned to walk. A woman, sharing his life, his hopes and his passion. Not just any little boy, but Jamie. And not just any woman, but Melissa.

"Dominic?"

He stood and faced her. "No, I don't want to be Jamie's godfather," he said. Her eyes lost some of their shine and he hurried on. "I want to be his father." He heard the intake of her breath and he pulled her and the baby into his arms. "And I want to go to sleep each night with you in my arms, wake every morning with you by my side."

She trembled, tears once again filling her eyes and clinging to the tips of her lashes. "Are you sure?" she asked, her voice breathless.

"I've never been more sure of anything in my life." He dipped his head and captured her mouth with his. She smelled of sweet flowers and sunshine, and tasted of hopes and dreams. "Marry me, Melissa," he said when the kiss ended. "Marry me and let me love you forever. Let me be Jamie's father."

"Yes...oh, yes," she replied. "Oh, Dominic, I want a life with you. Yes, I'll marry you."

Again their lips met in a kiss of fiery passion and promise. Dominic's heart was so filled with her, there was no room for doubt, no room for anything but the love he'd tried for too long to deny.

"It's right this time," she said when his lips finally left hers. She gazed at him, her eyes the clear blue of summer skies. "Don't you feel how right it is?"

He nodded. Yes, as he looked at her beloved face, saw the love shining from her eyes, he knew the utter rightness of loving her.

He touched Jamie's cheek. The little boy grinned, a string of drool lacing his chin. Dominic laughed, for in that drooling baby smile and in the eyes of the woman who held him, he saw a future of love.

Epilogue

"Melissa, you look absolutely beautiful!" Samantha exclaimed as she smoothed the skirt on the bridal gown one last time.

"I can't believe this is happening." Melissa hugged her sister, then turned back to the mirror to look at her reflection. The long white silk dress was simple and elegant, but the shine of its pearl buttons could not compete with the glow of happiness in her eyes.

In five minutes she would say the vows that would make her Dominic's wife. It had been three months since they'd arrested Neal, three months since she and Dominic had confessed their love for each other. It had taken that long to disentangle Bill's lies from the truths, learn that she wasn't a widow. She and Bill had never been legally married—he'd never divorced Susan.

In the past three months she'd found the true meaning of love, the give-and-take that occurs, the exchange of hopes and dreams, of passion and of tenderness. Rather than taking away her power, loving Dominic had filled her with power.

She turned away from the mirror and looked at her sister. "Oh, Samantha, I never knew happiness could feel this way."

Samantha took Melissa's hands in hers. "I just wish you had been able to tell me everything sooner. I wish I had known so I could have helped you."

Melissa squeezed her sister's hands. "I couldn't tell you. I couldn't tell anyone." She frowned thoughtfully. "That's what's so insidious about abuse...the shame that keeps it secret." She shook her head, not wanting to look back, but instead only wanting to focus on the glorious future ahead of her. She leaned forward and kissed Samantha on the cheek. "It's over now, and there're only tranquil waters in my future."

"Are you nervous?"

Melissa shook her head. "Not a bit. There's nothing to be nervous about." She thought of Dominic and the time they'd spent together. Each day had only made their love grow stronger and Melissa knew that, unlike her redbirds, she and Dominic were mates for life.

The faint sound of organ music drifted up the stairs and into the bedroom where the two women stood. "I think that's your cue," Samantha said. "Come on. It's time."

Time. Time to walk down the stairs and into the living room where Dominic and the minister awaited her. Time to legalize what was already legal and right in her heart.

As the strains of the wedding march filled the Dark family home, Melissa slowly descended the stairs, her heart thudding the rhythm of joy. There were no doubts, no uncertainty, only her love, a bright and shining force, propelling her eagerly forward.

She stepped off the last stair and turned into the living room. She paused, her breath catching in her chest. Dominic stood at the opposite end of the room, looking handsome and proud. In his arms, he held the best man. In the past three months Jamie had transformed from a tiny, half-bald baby into a chubby, laughing delight with a full head of blond curls.

Dominic smiled at her, a smile so filled with love, so filled with promise, her heart quickened and she moved forward, eager to officially begin their life together. She smiled at the two men who held her heart: the groom, clad in a black tuxedo this time around, and the best man—in diapers. These were her heroes.

* * * * *

PAULA DETMER RIGGS

**Continues the
twelve-book series—
36 Hours—in May 1998
with Book Eleven**

THE PARENT PLAN

Cassidy and Karen Sloane's marriage was on the rocks—and had been since their little girl spent one lonely, stormy night trapped in a cave. And it would take their daughter's wisdom and love to convince the stubborn rancher and the proud doctor that they had better things to do than clash over their careers, because their most important job was being Mom and Dad—and husband and wife.

For Cassidy and Karen and *all* the residents of Grand Springs, Colorado, the storm-induced blackout was just the beginning of 36 Hours that changed *everything!* You won't want to miss a single book.

Available at your favorite retail outlet.

The World's Most Eligible Bachelors are about
to be named! And Silhouette Books brings
them to you in an all-new, original series....

World's Most Eligible Bachelors

Twelve of the sexiest, most sought-after men share
every intimate detail of their lives in twelve never-
before-published novels by the genre's top authors.

Don't miss these unforgettable stories by:

Dixie Browning

Marie Ferrarella

Jackie Merritt

Tracy Sinclair

BJ James

Rachel Lee   Suzanne Carey

Gina Wilkins

VICTORIA PADE

Maggie Shayne   *Anne McAllister*

Susan Mallery

Look for one new book each month in the
World's Most Eligible Bachelors series beginning
September 1998 from Silhouette Books.

Silhouette®

Available at your favorite retail outlet.

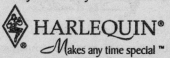